More Praise for the Novels of E

The Blue Bist

"A perfectly enjoyable beach book."

"This brand-new book is sure to become a summer favorite."
—ReadersDigest.com (chosen as their #1 Unforgettable Beach Read)

"A wonderfully poignant behind-the-scenes journey into the world of high-end restaurants, island life, and the inner workings of the human heart. A great summer story." —Lolly Winston, author of *Good Grief*

The Love Season

"Summer fare that's a cut above the usual . . . Hilderbrand serves up a mouthwatering menu, keeps the Veuve Clicquot flowing, and tops it all with a dollop of mystery that will have even drowsy sunbathers turning pages until the very satisfying end." —*People* (four stars)

"Hilderbrand's fifth book is a fulfilling tale of familial excavation and self-exploration. . . . It's a refreshing, resonant summertime treat."
—*Publishers Weekly*

"Hilderbrand's sensitive portrayal of a young motherless woman on a journey of self-discovery, and her guilt-ridden godmother's attempt to find the courage to confront the past, is very moving." —*Booklist*

"A good page-turner." —*Library Journal*

Summer People

"Striking not only for the ingenuity of its riveting plot, but also for the acute sense of character and the finely tuned craftsmanship with which Hilderbrand brings its every nuance to life."
—Madison Smartt Bell, author of *The Stone that the Builder Refused*

"Entertaining beach reading." —*Booklist*

"Reading *Summer People* makes you feel like you've taken a long weekend in Nantucket. . . . Simply a great read."
—Kathleen Hughes, author of *Dear Mrs. Lindbergh*

Nantucket Nights

"What a perfect summer pleasure Elin Hilderbrand provides . . . mixing the complexities of family life and friendship with suspense, romance, and moonlit Nantucket nights." —Nancy Thayer, *New York Times* bestselling author of *The Hot Flash Club*

"Things get more twisted at every turn, with enough lies and betrayals to fuel a whole season of soap operas. . . . Readers will be hooked."
—*Publishers Weekly*

"Efficiently juxtaposes the surface calm of the season with the turbulence of the characters' lives. More entertaining beach reading from [Elin Hilderbrand]." —*Booklist*

The Beach Club

"Surprisingly touching . . . A work of fiction you're likely to think about long after you've put it down." —*People*

"A strong emotional pull . . . Readers will remain absorbed until the surprising denouement." —*Publishers Weekly*

"A feisty novel . . . Lively enough to keep a sunbather awake."
—*Kirkus Reviews*

THE BLUE BISTRO
&
THE LOVE SEASON

Also by Elin Hilderbrand

Here's to Us

Winter Stroll

The Rumor

Winter Street

The Matchmaker

Beautiful Day

Summerland

Silver Girl

The Island

The Castaways

A Summer Affair

Barefoot

Summer People

Nantucket Nights

The Beach Club

Elin Hilderbrand

THE BLUE BISTRO & THE LOVE SEASON

St. Martin's Griffin New York

These are works of fiction. All of the characters, organizations, and events portrayed in these novels are either products of the author's imagination or are used fictitiously.

Printed in the United States of America. For information, address St. Martin's Press, 175 Fifth Avenue, New York, N.Y. 10010.

www.stmartins.com

Designed by Kathryn Parise

The Library of Congress Cataloging-in-Publication Data
is available upon request.

ISBN 978-1-250-14062-3 (trade paperback)

Our books may be purchased in bulk for promotional, educational, or business use. Please contact your local bookseller or the Macmillan Corporate and Premium Sales Department at 1-800-221-7945, extension 5442, or by email at MacmillanSpecialMarkets@macmillan.com.

First Edition: June 2017

10 9 8 7 6 5 4 3 2 1

Special Introduction

by Elin Hilderbrand

In the summer of 2000, when my first novel, *The Beach Club,* was published, I went out to dinner with friends at a glamorous restaurant on Nantucket. During our meal, the owner of the establishment came over to me and said, "We all loved your book . . . but we decided you could never write a novel about a restaurant because it would be too scandalous."

With that one line, *The Blue Bistro* was born.

I am a rarity in that I, alone, it seems, among my friends and acquaintances, have never worked at a restaurant (unless you count one four-hour shift at Pizza Hut where the tight brown polyester pants and the task of cleaning the "sneeze guard" caused me to quit). I was strictly a diner, a customer, a guest—I had never seen a commercial kitchen, I had never presented a bottle of wine for tasting, I had never taken a reservation.

That's still true to this day. However, once I decided I was going to write a novel about a restaurant on Nantucket, I started interviewing—both formally and casually—every person I came across about their work experience in restaurants. I met with nearly a dozen restaurant professionals on Nantucket—owners, servers, bartenders, pastry chefs. I even "worked" one fateful night at the legendary restaurant 21 Federal. The manager at 21, a friend of mine named Robert, invited me to come in over Nantucket's Christmas Stroll, telling me he would allow me to pour water. When I arrived, however, he'd had a change of heart. Pouring water was hazardous for the uninitiated, and so he set me to work hanging up coats. What I remember most about that night was how hard it was to spend six hours on my feet. For in the restaurant business, there is no sitting down.

I garnered great and funny stories from my interviews that year. One restaurant owner, who had also been a server at several Nantucket restaurants, told a story about a man who came in and ripped the page out of her all-important reservation book—a story which is now, in the digital age, charmingly outdated. At the time, however, without her diagram for the evening, chaos ensued. I heard about naughty diners under the age of four, and credit card wars, and two diners who were found in a compromising position in a back room after the restaurant had closed for the night.

In addition to learning about the restaurant life, I also gained a wealth of knowledge about food and wine. As anyone who has read one or more of my books can tell, I am a gourmet at heart. I live to eat, and I love to cook. Perhaps the most fun I had during the writing of *The Blue Bistro* was creating the menu. (And no, I have never made savory doughnuts, but maybe someday, when I'm retired.) In *The Love Season,* I adored creating the dinner that Marguerite cooks for her goddaughter, Renata. This meal I have made for my own guests many times over.

Indeed, I had so much material after researching *The Blue Bistro* that there was enough left over for a second novel—and in this way, *The Love Season* came to be. When I ask a hundred Elin Hilderbrand fans what their favorite novel is, ninety-nine will say *The Blue Bistro.* Only half that number will even have read *The Love Season.* Of all my novels, it is, perhaps, the most underappreciated. However, it is a jewel box of a novel waiting to be discovered.

The Love Season takes place over the course of one day—it is a sort of emotional descendant of Virginia Woolf's *Mrs Dalloway,* if Woolf had cared at all about food. It tells the story of Marguerite Beale, who receives a phone call from her goddaughter, Renata, whom she hasn't seen in years. Renata all but invites herself over for dinner. And hence, for the first time in sixteen years, Marguerite, once a famous chef, prepares a meal. The inspiration for this novel came from the now closed but once famous Nantucket restaurant, The Opera House. For a span of years, everyone who was anyone could be found at The Opera House. For someone as interested in the long brown hair that spilled over his shoulders and down his back. He wore a blue blazer over a white T-shirt, jeans, and sandals. Between the lapels of his jacket, Adrienne could only read a single word printed on the front of his shirt: CASTRO.

"It's nice to meet you, Luke," Adrienne said. "Let me show you to your table."

As she walked the Parrishes out to the awning, Rex launched into "Hello, Dolly!" Adrienne heard Darla behind her. "Isn't she just lovely? Isn't she exquisite? She used to live in Aspen. And Hawaii. Adrienne's a real adventure girl, aren't you, Adrienne?"

Adrienne pulled out a chair for Darla. She handed Luke and Grayson their menus. "Just to let you know, there aren't any desserts tonight. Our pastry chef is on vacation."

"On vacation in the middle of July?" Grayson said. He leaned closer to Luke. "That must mean they fired him."

"So I'll get your drinks, then," Adrienne said. "Stoli tonic and Southern Comfort old-fashioned. Luke, what can I bring you?"

"A beer, please," he said.

"We have Cisco Summer Brew on tap. Is that okay?"

"Perfect," he said. "And a shot of tequila, please."

"A beer and a shot of tequila," Adrienne said. "I'll be right back."

She put in the drink order with Duncan and went back to the kitchen to give Paco the VIP order. Antonio was expediting.

"Where's Fiona?" Adrienne asked Paco.

"Lying down," he said. "She's upset."

"About Mario?"

"No," Paco said. "Something about JZ. Eddie got the story."

"Have you heard from Mario?" Adrienne asked.

Paco scoffed. "He's out getting drunk somewhere. Getting drunk and looking for ladies."

"You think?" Adrienne said. She seemed to be the only one who was worried about him. She couldn't bear to peek around the corner and see the abandoned pastry station.

Back in the dining room, she sat tables: the local author was in; Mr. Kennedy; a real jackass named Doyle Chambers; and one of the local contractors with a party of twelve. Adrienne opened a bottle of champagne for Kennedy—his wife, Mitzi, was now a devotee of the Laurent-Perrier—and then she swung back into the kitchen to pick up the chips for Parrish and put in two more VIP orders. She headed for the Parrishes' table. From behind, Luke looked like a girl in men's clothing. But that wasn't quite right; his hair wasn't feminine so much as biblical. He looked like the original Luke, the one who wrote the Gospel. But this Luke had inherited the Parrish demeanor. Adrienne found the three of them sitting in silence, sipping their drinks. The shot of tequila had been drained and pushed to the edge of the table. Adrienne scooped it up as she set down the chips and dip.

"Another?" she asked Luke.

"Please," he said.

This seemed to startle Darla from her reverie. "Oh, Adrienne, honey, won't you please stay and chat with us for a second?"

"I'd love to."

"I told Darla that arranged marriages have been out of fashion for over a hundred years," Grayson said. "She refuses to believe me."

Darla laughed and threw her hand in the air. "I just thought they might have something in common. Luke loves to travel. After Amherst, he spent a year in Egypt."

"Egypt?" Adrienne said. "I've always wanted to see that part of the world. I had a boyfriend once who offered to take me to Morocco, and at times I regret not going."

Luke tented his fingers. He was looking at Adrienne longingly, she thought, but then she realized that he was eyeing the empty shot glass in her hands. He wanted his tequila.

"How old are you, Adrienne?" Darla asked.

"Twenty-eight."

"And Luke is twenty-nine!" Darla said. "He's our youngest."

"And our nuttiest," Grayson piped in. "It was a hard lesson but I finally learned that our three boys were not mined from the same quarry. This guy"—and here he pounded Luke on the shoulder—"is a free spirit."

"Josh and Timmy are more traditional," Darla said.

"They're into wearing suits and paying alimony," Luke said.

"Okay, well," Adrienne said. "I'll get you another tequila. Darla, Grayson, can I bring you anything else right now?"

caught her eye and waved. Adrienne went to the bar and reclaimed her second glass of champagne.

Charlie, Duncan's friend, owner of the gold marijuana leaf necklace, was seated at the bar drinking a Whale's Tale Ale. He gave Adrienne the up-down, as he did every time he came in. It was one of a dozen things about the man that made Adrienne shiver with dislike. He smelled like very strong soap.

"This is her roommate?" Charlie asked Duncan.

"Yes," Duncan said. He smirked at Adrienne. "I was just telling Charlie about the stunt Caren pulled."

"It's not a *stunt,*" Adrienne said. "She went to a concert."

"With another guy," Charlie said.

"A friend of hers," Adrienne said. She glanced back over her shoulder at her father. He waved. Scene where Adrienne defends her roommate's decision to share a hotel room with another man. "You have women in here every night throwing themselves at you. You hardly have a right to get angry."

"I'm not angry," Duncan said. "But I'm onto her."

"What's the guy's name again?" Charlie asked.

"Tate something," Duncan said.

"Tate," Charlie said. "Goddamned prep school name if I ever heard one."

"What I don't understand," Duncan said, "is why they're sharing a room. If he's so *rich* and well-connected, he should be able to afford two rooms."

"He didn't want two rooms," Charlie said. "He wants to be in the same room with your bitch."

Adrienne glanced at Duncan to see how he would react to Caren's being so designated, and Duncan looked at her, possibly for the same reason. Adrienne shrugged.

"You eating tonight?" she asked Charlie.

"I need a menu."

"Do you want something other than the steak?"

"Maybe," he said. "Why don't you bring me a menu."

Duncan pulled a menu out from behind the bar. Charlie pretended to study it, his brow wrinkled and threatening.

Joe set a highball glass on the bar. "The woman who ordered this asked for Finlandia on the rocks."

"That is Finlandia," Duncan said.

"She swore it was Grey Goose," Joe said.

"It is Grey Goose," Duncan admitted. His neck started to redden around the collar of his shirt. "We're out of Finlandia. I can't believe she could tell the difference."

"She could tell the difference," Joe said. "She's a serious vodka drinker."

"Tell her we're out of Finlandia," Duncan said. "We have the Grey Goose or Triple 8."

"You're making me look bad," Joe said.

Duncan threw his hands in the air. "What is this? Beat-up-the-bartender night?"

"Yeah," Charlie said to Joe. "Lay off my friend here. His woman skipped town."

Thatcher came up behind Adrienne. "The VIP order is up for your dad. Would you let Paco know we need three more?"

"Sure," Adrienne said. She turned to Charlie and eyed his necklace. It was the dog tag of his stupidity. "Do you know what you'd like?" she asked. "I'm headed for the kitchen. I could put your order in."

"I'll have the steak," he said. "Well-done. If there's even a little bit of pink, I'll be sick. I swear."

"Well, we don't want that," Adrienne said. She checked, one more time, on her father. He waved.

The kitchen was ridiculously hot. Fiona was drenched in sweat. "We're short our dishwasher," she said. "Jojo went to see the Rolling Stones last night in the big city and hasn't managed to find his way home. I don't know why one of these clowns didn't go with him, but they'll pay. Paco, when you're done with the chips, you're dish bitch. And Eddie, I don't want to hear one word about the weeds from you."

Paco and Eddie groaned.

"Save the whining for your cousin," Fiona said. "Maybe next time you'll clue him in on how to find the bus station." She glanced over at Adrienne, who was scribbling out a ticket for the bar: one steak, killed. "How are you doing?"

"I'm okay," Adrienne lied. She held up three fingers for Paco, who

Jack Nicklaus, Tom Watson, Greg Norman, Payne Stewart, Seve Ballesteros.

"Everyone you named is either dead or on the seniors tour," he said.

Still, he asked her out and they went to the Chatham Squire for drinks after her shift one night. Adrienne found him easy to be with. On days when she was free, he let his tee times go; he cancelled lessons so that he could take Adrienne out to lunch, and eventually, he arranged to have the same day off as she did each week. He told her he loved her after only three weeks—and he had all the symptoms: he lost weight, he lost sleep, and he shunned his friends. He wasn't sure what was happening, he told her one evening as they walked Lighthouse Beach at sunset, but he thought this was "it."

The summer as Sully's girlfriend flew by—days at work, nights eating ice cream at Candy Manor and strolling down to Yellow Umbrella Books where they bought novels they never found time to read, partying on the beach with people from work. Bonfires, fireworks, summer league baseball games, days off cruising around in the Boston Whaler, strolling in Provincetown, whale watching. Adrienne loved the flowers that arrived at the desk, she loved waking up in the middle of the night to find him staring at her, she loved it every time he picked up the phone to cancel a golf lesson. She loved his dark hair, his freckles, the way his strong back twisted in the follow-through of his golf swing. The e-mails to her father that summer were full of exclamation points. "I've met a guy! A guy who treats me the way you are always telling me I DESERVE to be treated! I am having the time of my LIFE in this town!"

At the beginning of August, Sully drove Adrienne to Quincy to meet his parents. His father was a neurosurgeon at Brigham and Women's Hospital and his mother had spent many years working as a nurse before she quit to stay home and raise six boys. His parents had both grown up in south Boston and they had stayed there. They lived in a huge Victorian house that was filled with photographs and crucifixes and needlepointed Irish blessings. Sully's mother, Irene, was a lady of about sixty with red hair and a huge bosom. She hugged Adrienne tightly to her chest the moment Adrienne stepped out of the car and, in essence, never let her go. (Adrienne still sent Irene Sullivan a postcard every few months.) They sat on the sunporch and drank iced tea and ate shortbread and Irene filled Adrienne in on the business of her six sons. "God didn't bless me with a daughter," she said, "but I'm thankful for the boys. They're good boys." Kevin, the oldest, was a priest; Jimmy and Brendan were married with sons of their own; Matthew lived in New York City. "Matthew's a homosexual," Irene said, breaking her shortbread into little pieces. "Not what his father and I wanted, but he has a friend who comes for the holidays. I figure I already have six boys, what's one more?" Then there was Michael, then Felix, the youngest, who was a freshman at Holy Cross. Irene brought out pictures of all the boys at their first communion, then in their Boston Latin football uniforms. She brought out pictures of the grandsons, and a picture of Matthew and his boyfriend in Greenwich Village with their arms wrapped around each other. "And here are some of Mikey." All of the pictures showed Sully golfing—in Scotland, in British Columbia, at Pebble Beach. "He has a gift, no question," Irene said, sighing. "But we wish he would settle down."

Adrienne left the Sullivan house feeling like she could move in and become part of the family. When they got in the car to leave there was waving and blown kisses; Adrienne had Irene's shortbread recipe in her purse.

"What did you think?" Sully asked.

"I wish she was mine," Adrienne said.

As autumn approached, Sully began to talk about "the next round." He received a job offer in Vero Beach, and then, a coup: a job offer in Morocco at a course built for the king. Sully wanted Adrienne to come with him to Morocco, and he wanted to get engaged.

"Engaged?" Adrienne said. They were lying in bed, watching Sunday night football on ESPN. How had "the next round," which Adrienne tolerated as yet another innocuous golf term, become *engaged*?

"I want to marry you," Sully said.

"You do?" Adrienne said. This was the moment every girl waited for—wasn't it?—the perfect guy proposing marriage. And yet, what struck Adrienne most forcefully was her shock followed by her ambivalence. She thought of life married to Michael Sullivan—and she had to admit, she could think of worse lives. They could travel, he could golf, she could work hotels until they had a child. Adrienne could call Irene Mom, and the two of them could enjoy a lifetime of chats at the kitchen table.

■

Thatcher and Adrienne dropped Dr. Don off at the Beach Club and headed back to the restaurant. Adrienne tried to explain the train wreck that was her morning, but Thatcher seemed distracted.

"What's wrong?" she said. "Did my father say something inappropriate? He's famous for that."

Thatcher took her hand. "He wants your blessing. With Mavis."

"He has my blessing. I sent him and Mavis a bottle of Cristal at the Pearl tonight."

"That's my girl," Thatcher said.

"What else did you talk about?" Adrienne asked.

"Baseball. Football. Notre Dame. My family's business. I think your dad wanted to get a sense of me. I tried to give it to him."

"Did my name come up?"

"From time to time. Like I said, he wants you to feel okay about Mavis."

"Did you talk about . . . us? You and me?"

"A little."

Adrienne banged her head against the window. *What a morning!* "I need you to tell me word for word what was said."

Thatcher smiled. "That's not my style and you know it." He grabbed her knee. "Hey, it's fine. I had a really nice time. Your father is a quality person."

They pulled up in front of the restaurant. Fiona was sitting on the edge of the dory, crying into her hands. Thatcher hopped out and went to her. Adrienne stayed in the truck, wishing she could vaporize. Should she walk into the Bistro as though nothing were wrong, or approach them and make herself the most egregious of intruders? Sitting in the car, gaping, wasn't an option. She got out.

"Harry brought down the purchase and sale agreement," Fiona wailed. "And I *signed* it."

Thatcher sat next to her. "That's what you were supposed to do."

"So we're really going to sell?"

"It was your idea."

"Yes, but . . ." She let out a staccato breath. "Mario was right. They're going to tear it down. Next year it will be a fat mansion."

"It's better that way," Thatcher said. "Think how awful it would be if it were still a restaurant but not *our* restaurant."

Fiona nodded with her lips pressed together in an ugly line. She raised her eyes and noticed Adrienne standing there.

"What do you think?" Fiona asked. "Are we making a mistake?"

"That's not for me to say."

"If it were your restaurant, would you sell it?"

"If you had asked me a few hours ago . . ." But now Adrienne regarded the Bistro: the dory filled with geraniums; the menu hanging in a glass box; the smells of the kitchen wafting through the front door; the way the guests' faces glowed when they walked in and saw candlelit tables and heard piano music; the sound of a champagne flute sliding across the blue granite; the crackers—God, the crackers.

"No," she said. "I wouldn't."

"Thatcher is one great guy."

"So you've said."

Adrienne and her father were sitting under a canary yellow umbrella at the Beach Club eating sandwiches from Something Natural. Mavis was having a massage in the room.

"Your mother would have loved him."

"She loved everybody."

"True." Dr. Don popped open a bottle of Nantucket Nectars and studied the label. "These things are just filled with sugar." He took a long swill.

"So what did you and Thatcher talk about on the boat?"

Dr. Don leaned back in his beach chair. "Oh, you know. The Fighting Irish. His father's business. His decision to sell to his brothers. And the restaurant. It sounds like he has quite a friendship with this Fiona person."

There was an understatement. "He does," Adrienne said.

"She's sick?"

"He told you that?"

Dr. Don took a bite of his smoked turkey and cheddar.

"So that's why they're closing the restaurant," Adrienne said. "She's on the list for a transplant."

social history of Nantucket as I am, the story of a spot that was the beating heart of the nightlife of the island held irresistible appeal. I re-created the sparkling evenings that I imagined took place in real life on Water Street in Nantucket in the 1970s, and made my character, Marguerite Beale, the culinary goddess in charge. The novel tells a gripping present-day story, but it also harkens back to the glitter of decades before.

I hope you savor both of these novels. I am a firm believer that choosing fine ingredients and taking care in preparing meals and savoring the things we eat and the people we eat them with is one of the joys we are given in life. Especially in the summer. As Thatcher Smith tells Adrienne Dealey at the beginning of *The Blue Bistro*, "Imagine it's a balmy night, you've spent all day at the beach, you've napped, you've showered, you've indulged in a cocktail or two. Then you're led to a table in the sand for the best all-you-can-eat fried shrimp in the world while sitting under the stars. It's one of those life-is-good moments."

Bon appétit!

THE BLUE BISTRO

Finally, one for the kids.
To my sons, Maxwell and Dawson,
and to my goddaughter, Chloe.
Love, love, love.

Menu, Summer 2005

Starters

Corn chowder with red peppers and smoked Gouda	$8
Shrimp bisque, classic Chinatown shrimp toast	$9
Blue Bistro Caesar	$6
Warm chevre over baby mixed greens with candy-striped beets	$8
Blue Bistro crab cake, Dijon cream sauce	$14
Seared foie gras, roasted figs, brioche	$16

Entrées

Steak frites	$27
Half duck with Bing cherry sauce, Boursin potato gratin, pearls of zucchini and summer squash	$32
Grilled herbed swordfish, avocado silk, Mrs. Peeke's corn spoon bread, roasted cherry tomatoes	$32
Lamb "lollipops," goat cheese bread pudding	$35

MENU, SUMMER 2005

Lobster club sandwich, green apple horseradish, coleslaw $29

Grilled portobello and Camembert ravioli with cilantro pesto sauce $21

Sushi plate: Seared rare tuna, wasabi aioli, sesame sticky rice, cucumber salad with pickled ginger and sake vinaigrette $28

**Second Seating (9:00 P.M.) only*

Shellfish fondue

Endless platter of shrimp, scallops, clams. Hot oil for frying. Selection of four sauces: classic cocktail, curry, horseradish, green goddess $130 (4 people)

Desserts—All desserts $8

Butterscotch crème brûlée

Mr. Smith's individual blueberry pie à la mode

Fudge brownie, peanut butter ice cream

Lemon drop parfait: lemon vodka mousse layered with whipped cream and vodka-macerated red berries

Coconut cream and roasted pineapple tart, macadamia crust

Homemade candy plate: vanilla marshmallows, brown sugar fudge, peanut brittle, chocolate peppermints

Executive Chef, Fiona Kemp
Pastry Chef, Mario Subiaco

Proprietor, Thatcher Smith

1

Breakfast

Adrienne needed a job.

She arrived on Nantucket Island with two maxed-out credit cards, forty borrowed dollars, and three rules scribbled on an Amtrak cocktail napkin. She spent seven of the dollars on a dorm bed at the hostel in Surfside and slept with the cocktail napkin under her pillow. When she awoke the next morning in a room full of slumbering college students, she read the rules again. *Rule One: Become self-sufficient. Rule Two: Do not lie about past. Rule Three: Exercise good judgment about men.* The last thing Adrienne had done before leaving Aspen was to turn her boyfriend, Doug, in to the authorities. Doug had been living with Adrienne in the basement of the Little Nell, where Adrienne worked as a concierge; he had been stealing money from the hotel rooms to buy cocaine, and he had stolen more than two thousand dollars from Adrienne.

Adrienne quietly slipped into clothes and stashed her belongings in a locker, which was free until noon. She set out into the bright but chilly May morning with her money and the napkin, repeating a tip that a man had given her on the ferry the night before. A tip about a job.

The Blue Bistro, 27 North Beach Extension. The man who suggested this place was a freelance writer who had been coming to Nantucket for over twenty years. He came across as a normal guy, despite his square wire-rimmed glasses, thirty years out of style, and the way he licked his lips every five seconds, as though Adrienne were a T-bone steak. They had started chatting casually over the ketchup dispenser at the snack bar. He asked her if she was coming to Nantucket for a vacation. And Adrienne had laughed and said, *Hardly. I need a job. I need money.*

If it's money you want, the man had said, *the Blue Bistro is where you should go.*

I don't work in restaurants, Adrienne had said. *I work in hotels. At the front desk. I'm a hotel person.*

There's a hotel down the street from the bistro, the man had said. He paused, wet his lips. *But, like I said, if it's money you want . . .*

Adrienne walked to the North Beach Extension, stopping twice for directions. The road was quiet. There were a few houses along the way but most of them were still boarded up; one had a crew of painters working. Then, to the right, Adrienne saw a parking lot and a one-story cedar-shingled building with a green slate roof, all by itself on a stretch of windswept beach. Adrienne stopped in the road. This was the restaurant. The hotel, as the man on the ferry had described it, was down the street on the left. She should go to the hotel. But then she caught a scent of roasting meat and she thought about money. She decided it couldn't hurt to check the place out.

A sign taped to the front door read: THE BLUE BISTRO, OPENING FOR ITS FINAL SEASON JUNE 1ST. Adrienne perused the menu. The food was expensive, it sounded delicious, and her stomach complained. She'd trekked halfway across the island without any breakfast.

She peered in the dark window, wondering what she might say. She had never worked in a restaurant before; she knew nothing about the business except that it was, prostitution aside, the quickest way to make money. She supposed she could lie and say that she'd waited tables in college. She could pick up the skills once she started. Kyra, her desk manager at the Little Nell, had told her that waiting tables was a piece of cake. Nantucket had been Kyra's idea. After the whole disaster with Doug, Kyra suggested that Adrienne get as far away from the Rocky Mountains as possible. *If it's money you want, Nantucket is where you should go.*

Adrienne tried the door. Locked. She tapped on a windowpane. *Hello?*

She felt like the Little Match Girl, hungry and tired, bereft and friendless. *Can you save me?*

She thought of her father, at that minute probably elbow deep in a root canal. Since Adrienne's mother died, his concern for Adrienne's well-being seemed so heavy as to actually pull the corners of his mouth into a frown. He worried about her all the time. He worried that she was too adventurous, working in all these exotic locales where the men weren't necessarily principled. And he was right to worry. He was so right that Adrienne hadn't been able to tell him how guests of the Little Nell had been complaining about cash missing from their rooms and about how Kyra had interrogated the battalion of Mexican chambermaids. When the chambermaids proved a dead end, Kyra had come to Adrienne and asked if she had any idea who might be taking the money. Adrienne was confused about why Kyra was asking *her* but then, somehow, she realized that Kyra meant Doug. Doug, who had lost his job in February and whose behavior was becoming increasingly erratic. Doug, who traveled down-valley several times a week to visit a "friend" in Carbondale. Adrienne had snuck down to their basement apartment while she was supposed to be at work. She found her hotel master key card in the pocket of Doug's ski jacket. And then, on a second dreadful hunch, she checked the tampon box where she saved her tips, the money for her Future, which she had always thought of with a capital "F"—money for something bigger and better down the road, a house, a wedding, a business. The box was empty. He had stolen her Future; he had snorted it. Instead of killing Doug herself, Adrienne followed Kyra's advice and called the Pitkin County police. They caught him robbing the Alpine Suite in the middle of the day. He was arrested for larceny and possession, and Adrienne left town in the midst of his court proceedings, flat broke.

She had only asked her father for a small loan—two hundred dollars—enough to get her back east on the train and set up someplace else. But he must have sensed something in her voice, because he sent her three hundred, no questions asked.

Adrienne heard someone shout, "Hey!" She whipped around. A man was striding toward her from a silver pickup truck in the parking lot. She smiled at him, squinting in a way that she hoped conveyed her innocence. *I'm not trying to rob you. I just want . . . a job?* When he got closer, she saw he had red-gold hair and freckles—he was a man who looked like a twelve-year-old boy. His hand shot out as though he'd been expecting her.

"Thatcher Smith," he said. "Thatch."

"Oh. Uh." Adrienne was so nervous, she couldn't remember her name. The man raised his pale eyebrows expectantly, waiting for her to identify herself. "Adrienne."

"Adrienne?"

"Dealey."

"Adrienne Dealey." His tone of voice said, *Of course, Adrienne Dealey*, like they had an appointment. "Can I help you, Adrienne?"

Adrienne opened her mouth but no sound came out. So much for knocking them dead with her confidence and charm.

Thatcher Smith laughed. A short, one-syllable "ha!" Loud and spontaneous, as if she had karate-chopped his funny bone. "Cat got your tongue?"

"I guess," she said. "Sorry. I came for a job. Is there an application or something I can fill out?"

"Application?" He looked at her in a strange but pleasant way, as though he'd never heard the word before.

"Don't you work here?" Adrienne asked.

"I own here."

"Oh." The *owner*? Adrienne took another look at this guy. He was about six feet tall with sloping shoulders, strawberry blond hair, green eyes, freckles. He wore jeans, running shoes, a red fleece jacket that was almost too bright to look at in the morning sun. She couldn't tell if he resembled Huckleberry Finn or if it was just the name, Thatcher—like Becky Thatcher—that summoned the image. He had a clean, friendly Midwestern vibe about him. He wasn't handsome so much as wholesome looking. Adrienne corrected her posture and cleared her throat. She was so destitute it was hard to feel impressive. "Would it be okay if I filled out an application, then?"

"We don't have any applications. It's not that kind of place. I do all the hiring face-to-face. What kind of job are you after? Front of the house? Back of the house? Because I can tell you right now, we're not hiring any back of the house."

Adrienne had no idea what he was talking about. She was after money, a thick wad of twenties she could roll out like a Mafia boss.

"I thought maybe I could wait tables?"

"Do you have any experience?" Thatcher asked.

I waited tables in college, she thought. But she couldn't make herself say it.

"None," she said. "But I'm willing to learn. Someone told me it's a piece of cake."

Thatcher laughed again—"ha!" He moved past her to the door of the restaurant and took a giant ring of keys from his jacket pocket. Adrienne noticed a wooden dory by the front of the restaurant filled with fresh soil. They probably grew flowers in the dory all summer. That was a nice touch. This was a nice restaurant. Too nice for Adrienne. If she wanted to be self-sufficient, she would have to sell her laptop.

"Never mind," Adrienne said. "Thanks for your time."

She turned to leave, making an alternate plan of attack. Back to the road, down the street to the hotel. After she filled out an application there, she would have to surrender some of her money for breakfast.

"You understand?" Thatcher said. "I can't exactly hire you to wait tables when you've had no experience."

"I understand," Adrienne said. "I was just checking. Someone I met on the boat told me how great your restaurant was. He also said there's a hotel down here?"

"The Nantucket Beach Club and Hotel," Thatcher said. "But Mack won't hire you without experience either."

"I have hotel experience," Adrienne said. "I just came from Aspen. I worked at the Little Nell."

Thatcher's pale eyebrows shot up. "The Little Nell?"

She nodded. "You've heard of it?"

"Of course, yeah. What did you do there?"

"Front desk," she said. "Concierge."

Thatcher pointed his head at the open door. "Are you hungry?" The door of the restaurant swung open. "I was going to have an omelet. Would you like to join me?"

Adrienne glanced back at the sandy road. She should go. An omelet, though, sounded tempting. "I don't know," she said.

"Oh, come on," Thatcher said. "I hate to eat alone." He ushered Adrienne in. The roasting meat and garlic smell was so overpowering that Adrienne nearly fell to her knees in hunger. What had she had for dinner last night on the ferry? A hotdog that had spent seven hours spinning on a rack and a cup of gluey clam chowder.

"Someone's cooking?" she said.

"My partner," Thatcher said. "She never sleeps. Follow me. I'll give you the grand tour."

When they stepped inside the front door, Adrienne was overcome with anxiety. She checked her watch, a jogging watch with an altimeter. It was just after ten o'clock; she was three feet above sea level. What was she doing? She had to find a job today. Still, she trailed Thatcher, trying to seem polite and interested. *Free food,* she thought. *Omelet.*

Thatcher stopped at an oak podium. "This is the host station, where we greet guests and make reservations. We have two public phone lines and a private line. The private line is very private, but sometimes guests get ahold of it. Don't ask me how."

He led her past a bar topped with a shiny slab of blue-gray stone. "Now here," he said proudly, "is our blue granite bar. We found the stone in a quarry in northern Vermont." The wall behind the bar was stocked with bottles on oak shelves. "We only sell call and top shelf. I don't ever want to drink Popov and I don't want my guests drinking it. Not in here," Thatcher said. There were two small tables in the bar area and a black baby grand piano. "We have live music six nights a week. My guy knows everything from Rogers and Hart to Nirvana." Down two steps was the dining room, maybe twenty tables, all with views of the ocean. The restaurant had no walls—it was open from the waist up. In winter, Adrienne could see, they hung plastic sheeting to keep the wind and sand out. There was an awning skeleton off the back. They placed six tables under the awning on a deck, Thatcher said, and four four-tops out in the sand under the stars.

"Those are the fondue tables," he said. "It makes a royal mess."

They returned to the bar, where the tables were set with white tablecloths, china, silver, wineglasses. Thatcher indicated Adrienne should sit.

"Let me take your jacket," he said.

"I'll keep it on," Adrienne said.

"You're going to eat with your *jacket* on?" he said.

She handed him her purple Patagonia Gore-tex that she'd bought with an employee discount from the ski shop at the Little Nell, and lowered herself daintily into a white wicker chair, as though she were accustomed to having breakfast in glamorous bistros like this all the time. Thatcher hung up her jacket then disappeared into the back, leaving Adrienne alone.

"The Blue Bistro," she said to herself. This was the kind of place that Doug would have called, disparagingly, "gourmet"; if it wasn't deep-fried or residing between two pieces of bread, Doug didn't want to eat it. Prison food would suit him fine.

Adrienne took a white napkin off her plate and unfolded it on her lap. She lifted the fork; it was heavy, beautiful silver. And the charger—she flipped it over. Limoges. She replaced the plate quickly—this was the restaurant equivalent of checking someone's medicine cabinet. Before she could inspect the pedigree of the stemware, Thatcher was back with two glasses of juice.

"Fresh-squeezed," he said. "The last of the blood oranges." He set the glasses down then disappeared again.

Adrienne eyed her glass. "The last of the blood oranges," she whispered. The juice was the fiery pink of some rare jewel. Was it okay to take a sip before he got back? Adrienne listened for noises from the kitchen. It was silent. She took a deep breath. The air smelled like something else now: toast. *Hunger and thirst,* she thought. *They'd get you every time.* Thatcher hurried out of the kitchen with two plates and set one in front of Adrienne with a flourish, as though she were someone very important.

It was the best omelet Adrienne had ever eaten. Perfectly cooked so that the eggs were soft and buttery. Filled with sautéed onions and mushrooms and melted Camembert cheese. There were three roasted cherry tomatoes on the plate, skins splitting, oozing juice. Nutty wheat toast. Thatch had brought butter and jam to the table. The butter was served like a tiny cheesecake on a small pedestal under a glass dome. The jam was apricot, homemade, served from a Ball jar.

Adrienne dug in, wondering where to start in the way of conversation. She decided the only safe thing was to talk about the food.

"This jam reminds me of when I was little," Adrienne said, spreading a thick layer on her toast. "My mother made jam."

"Is she a good cook?" Thatcher said.

"Who?"

"Your mother."

Adrienne paused. *Rule Two: Do not lie about past!* But it was hard when someone hurled a question at her like a pitch she couldn't hit.

"Yes."

For Adrienne, the silence that followed was studded with guilt. She should have just said, "She was," but then, by necessity, there would be tedious personal explanations about ovarian cancer and a motherless twelve-year-old that she was never in the mood for. She would rather talk about her felonious ex-boyfriend and her empty Future. *It's okay,* she thought. She would never see this guy again after today and she vowed she would tell the truth to the next person she met. Her mother was dead.

"Well," Adrienne said. "This is the most delicious breakfast I've ever had in my life."

"I'll tell Fee," he said. "She likes to feed people."

Adrienne ate every bite of her eggs and mopped up the tomato juices with her bread crust and drained her juice glass, thinking to herself—*Manners, manners! Turn the fork upside down on the plate when you're finished, very European.* If nothing else, this would make a great e-mail to her father. Her first morning on Nantucket she ends up eating a breakfast of champions in a restaurant that wasn't even *open.*

She collapsed in her chair, drunk with food, in love with this restaurant. If she ever caught up enough to pay off her credit cards and refund her father with interest, she'd come here for dinner and order the foie gras. "Why is it your last season?" she asked.

"Ahhh," Thatcher said. He pushed away his plate—half his omelet remained and Adrienne stared at it, wondering how audacious it would be to ask if she might finish it. Thatcher propped his elbows on the table and tented his fingers. Even his fingers, Adrienne noticed, were freckled. "The time has come."

The time has come? That was a noncommittal answer, an art form Adrienne wished she could perfect. So she, too, had asked a tricky question. In the interest of changing the subject, Adrienne offered up something else.

"I just got here last night."

"You've never been to the island before?"

"Never."

"You came straight from Aspen?"

"I did."

"I'm intrigued by the Little Nell. They say it's the best."

"One of. Relais and Chateaux and all that. They gave me housing."

"In the hotel?"

"Yes."

"That must have been sweet."

"It was okay," Adrienne said. She and Doug had lived in a studio apartment with his retriever, Jax, even though pets weren't allowed. No pets, no drugs, no stealing from the rooms!

"Did you go out at night?" Thatcher asked.

"Sometimes."

"My bartender here, Duncan, works at the Board Room in Aspen all winter. You ever go there?"

"Sometimes."

"So you know Duncan?"

Adrienne tried not to smile. She knew Duncan. Every single woman between the ages of twenty-one and thirty-nine who had been in Aspen for more than five minutes knew Duncan from the Board Room. There had actually been a picture of him in *Aspen* magazine making an espresso martini. Kyra had been *dying* to sleep with him, and so she dragged Adrienne to the Board Room during the week when she guessed the bar would be less crowded—but it was three deep from après ski until close. It drove Doug crazy. He not only disliked gourmet, he disliked *popular.* Still, Adrienne and Kyra went so often that Duncan began to remember their drinks—a cosmo for Kyra and a glass of champagne for Adrienne. He knew everyone's drinks.

"He works *here*?"

"He's the best bartender on the island," Thatcher said. "Maybe in the whole country. All the men want to get him for golf and all the women want to get him into bed."

"That sounds right," said Adrienne.

"Where else have you worked?" Thatcher asked.

"All over," she said. "The Princeville in Kauai, the Mar-a-Lago in

Palm Beach. The Chatham Bars Inn. And I spent a year in Thailand."

"Thailand?"

"Koh Samui," she said, thinking of Kip Turnbull, another one of her poor companionship choices. "Chaweng Beach. Have you ever been there?"

"I haven't been anywhere," he said. "But that will change. As soon as we close this place, I'm taking Fee to the Galápagos. She wants to see the funny birds."

"Is she your wife?"

Thatcher drained his juice glass then spun it absentmindedly on the table. Maybe he hadn't heard her. Maybe it was another trick question. Or maybe it was like when her father's patients asked Adrienne if Mavis, the hygienist, was her *mother.* Not worth answering. Adrienne noticed Thatcher wasn't wearing a wedding ring.

"So you came here for a job," he said. "But you have no restaurant experience. None? Not even Pizza Hut?"

"Not even Pizza Hut," she said. She envisioned herself with a tray piled high with dishes and food, glasses and drinks. She would drop it. "I don't know what I was thinking." She had been thinking of money, of Rule One: *Become self-sufficient.* But she didn't belong here; she belonged down the street, at the hotel. The hotel front desk was the right place for Adrienne. The pay wasn't great, but housing was almost always included. It wasn't loud or messy or hot. And the transience of a hotel suited her. All through high school she had worked as a receptionist in her father's dental offices (three offices in ten years and now he was somewhere new again—the eastern shore of Maryland). She had attended two high schools and three colleges. Since her mother died, Adrienne's life had been like a hotel. She checked in, she stayed for a while, she checked out. "I mean, don't get me wrong. This place is lovely and the food is amazing. I'll come back for dinner once I have some . . ."

"Money?" Thatcher said.

"Friends," she said.

Thatcher poked the uneaten portion of his omelet with his fork. "We open next week," he said. "We'll be booked solid for two seatings every night in July and August. Maybe, *maybe,* on a Monday night in June you can get a table without a reservation. By eleven o'clock every night the bar is full and I have to put someone at the door. I have to hire a bouncer, *here,* at a high-end *bistro* because there is always a line out into the parking lot. People get in fistfights over cutting in line, like they're in fifth grade. I try to tell the people, 'It's just a cocktail.' Ditto for dinner reservations. 'It's just a dinner. Just one night in the landscape of your *whole life.*' But what I have grown to realize is that it's more than just a cocktail and more than just dinner. They want to be a part of the scene. And how can I deny them that? This place . . ." He swept his arm in a circle. "Has magic."

Adrienne might have laughed. She might have thought Thatcher Smith was full of himself, but she had been here for thirty minutes. She had eaten the best breakfast of her life and now she couldn't even sit up, much less bring herself to leave.

"You must be good at what you do," Adrienne said.

"Fee is good at what she does," Thatcher said. "She's the best. The best, best, best. And we got lucky." He pressed his eyes closed for a long second, like he was praying. Then he collected their plates. "Fee will want these."

"I should go," Adrienne said. She grabbed the armrests of the wicker chair; she was positively slouching. "I have to find something today."

Thatcher held up a palm. "Wait, please. Please wait . . . thirty seconds. I have an idea. Will you wait?"

She didn't have to move just yet. She would wait.

"Back in thirty seconds." He gathered every dirty dish and utensil from the table, as well as the cake of butter and the jam that had caused Adrienne to break Rule Two, and balanced them on an outstretched arm. He vanished into the kitchen. Adrienne listened. If he was talking to this Fee person, she wanted to know what he was saying. It was silent, except for the sound of the ocean. She closed her eyes. She could hear the ocean. And then Thatcher's voice.

"This is the most popular restaurant on Nantucket. It has been for ten years. The food is delicious, the food is fun. It's a fun place to eat. It is see and be seen. It is laugh and talk and sing in here every night of the summer. The Blue Bistro is what a summer night on this island is all about, okay?" He was standing in front of the table.

"I can tell it's a special place," Adrienne said. "Really, I can."

"It just so happens, I got a phone call this morning from my assistant manager who spent the winter in Manhattan. He told me he's not coming back," Thatcher said. "And so now I have a gaping hole in the front of the house. I need someone to answer the phone, work the book, arrange a seating chart, learn the guests, make everyone feel not just welcome, you know, but *loved.* Keep track of the waitstaff, the wine, the requests for the piano player. Stroke the VIP tables—birthdays, anniversaries, the whole shebang. I need someone to be me. I need . . . another . . . me." He laughed again—"ha!" Like he knew what he'd just said was ludicrous. "And when you first asked, I thought, *Who in their right mind would give a* manager's *position to someone without a day of restaurant experience?* That would be foolish. Bad business! But now I'm thinking that what I need is someone with concierge skills. I need someone who understands old-fashioned service."

"I do understand old-fashioned service," Adrienne said. Hadn't she warmed towels in the dryer for guests with a newborn baby at the Princeville? Hadn't she finagled a veterinarian appointment for a couple with a sick parrot at the Mar-a-Lago? Hadn't she arranged for private lighthouse tours while at the Chatham Bars Inn?

"Most of my staff has been here since we opened twelve years ago. They love it here. They love it because Fee puts out the best family meal on the island and at midnight she sends out homemade crackers. Ninety-nine percent of the world think that crackers only come out of a box, and then here's Fee sending out baskets of hot, crisp cheese crackers and after eight hours of busting their asses and raking in three, four hundred bucks, the staff gets first dibs—and that's why they want to work here. Because of the crackers. And the money, of course." He grinned at Adrienne. "This is our last hurrah. The end of an era. I need someone *good.* I've never hired a woman for this position before. I've never hired someone without any restaurant background. But I'm not afraid to try. Well, to be honest, I am a little afraid."

"Wait a second," Adrienne said. She was confused. What was happening here? Was he offering her a job?

She glanced around the restaurant. Even through the plastic sheeting the ocean was brilliant blue. It made her head spin. That and the food smells and this man who was like nobody she'd ever met before. He was as honest and as nutty as the toast.

"Your second is up," Thatcher said. "Do you want the job?"

Did she want the job? It would be a huge risk, but something about that appealed to her. Not a single decision she had made in the past six years had worked out all that well, and she had promised herself on the train east that Nantucket would be different. Working here would be really different. She was so busy thinking, *Should I say yes, should I say no,* that she never actually gave Thatcher Smith an answer, but he didn't seem to notice.

"Good," he said. His face came alive; it looked like his freckles were dancing. "You're hired."

TO: DrDon@toothache.com
FROM: Ade12177@hotmail.com
DATE: May 24, 2005, 3:54 P.M.
SUBJECT: The Blue Bistro

Found a job. You're going to freak out so close the door to your office and sit down, okay? I took a job in a restaurant. Not waiting tables! Not cooking (obviously)! I am going to be the assistant manager at a place called the Blue Bistro. It's a French-American menu, four dollar signs, right on the beach. Owned by a very nice guy named Thatcher Smith. His partner, Fiona, is the chef and she's famous, but she's a recluse. Never comes out of the kitchen. I haven't even met her—though I will, I guess, soon enough.

I'm making twenty-five an hour—can you believe *that*? But I don't start for another week and I need to buy some clothes and pay my first month's rent. Is there any chance you might wire me a thousand dollars, please, sweet Dad? I am trying to put some structure in my life, and this time I will pay you back with interest, I promise!

I rented a room in a cottage from one of the women who waits tables at the restaurant. Her name is Caren. She's waited tables since the place opened and she makes so much money in the summer that after Christmas she goes down to St. Bart's for the winter and she doesn't have to work. She said the job I have is harder to get than a seat on the space shuttle.

How do you like the eastern shore? Eaten any crab cakes? Love.

TO: Ade12177@hotmail.com
FROM: DrDon@toothache.com
DATE: May 24, 2005, 5:09 P.M.
SUBJECT: You Blue Me Away

No crab cakes yet. We're still getting settled in. The schmo in here before me made a mess of his records and the bookkeeper said she can't untangle his billing. But we'll figure it out. We always do.

About your new job. Mavis says restaurants are dangerous places to work. Sexual harassment and the like. Foul language in the kitchen. Alcohol. Drugs. Everybody suffering from too much cash money. These are not people who floss, honey. (And that's a joke, but you know what I mean.) Be careful! You're an adult and I know you like the way you live but I am growing older by the day fretting about the situations you get yourself into. Which brings me to the question of money. I won't go on about how you're twenty-eight years old or about how I'm not your personal bank. I will just wire you the thousand dollars as long as you promise me that one of these days you'll pick a place and settle down. Love, love.

TO: DrDon@toothache.com
FROM: Ade12177@hotmail.com
DATE: May 24, 2005, 7:22 P.M.
SUBJECT: none

You're one to talk!!!

TO: Ade12177@hotmail.com
FROM: DrDon@toothache.com
DATE: May 25, 2005, 8:15 A.M.
SUBJECT: I'm Blue without you

Just please, please be careful. Love, love, love.

Adrienne felt like one of the born-again Christians on early Sunday morning TV. She had been saved! New job, decent, affordable housing, complete with Internet and a used ten-speed bike. The first morning in her new bed she lay with her eyes closed and banished Doug Riedel from her mind once and for all. In the six months of their dating, he had lied to her about his drug use and stolen all her money. But it hadn't been all bad. At the bottom of her trunk rested a lovely pair of shearling gloves that Doug had given her when they first started dating, and there had been some nice walks, the two of them throwing Jax sticks along the snowy banks of the Frying Pan River. Adrienne felt some white noise coming from her heart, but she sensed it was because she missed Jax. She loved that dog.

So it was good-bye and good riddance to another man, another town, another phase of her life. Nantucket would be the start of sound decision-making, a healthy lifestyle, the straight and narrow. Adrienne loved the island already—the historic downtown homes with their lilac bushes and their snapping flags; the wild, pristine beaches. It was so easy to breathe here.

Adrienne's new housemate, Caren Friar, had been a waiter at the Blue Bistro since the beginning. (When they first met, Adrienne made the mistake of calling her a waitress and Caren curtly corrected her—*Waitresses worked at diners in the 1950s, okay? This is fine dining and I bust my ass as hard as any man out there. . . .*) Caren was tall and extremely thin. She had been with a ballet company in New York City for three years before she accepted that she was never going to make a living at it. That's when she got sucked into what she called the life of hash and cash. Caren had a long, graceful neck, regal posture, a way of floating from place to place rather than walking. She wore her dark auburn hair in a bun so tight it made Adrienne's head ache just to look at it. Caren knew the ropes at the bistro—she knew the dirt on every person who ate there and every person who worked there—and although Adrienne was dying to mine the woman for information, most pressingly about the chef, Fiona, she intuited that she should proceed with caution.

Adrienne had already done a little bit of research on her own. The day she was hired, she dug up three articles about the Blue Bistro from the magazine archives of the public library: one in *Cape Cod Life* (August 1997), one in *Bon Appétit* (June 2000), and one in *Travel & Leisure* (May 2003). The articles offered variations on the same information: The Blue Bistro was wildly popular because it was the only restaurant on the beach on Nantucket and because of the food. *T & L* called the food "consistently delightful . . . Fiona Kemp is one of the most talented chefs in New England today." *Cape Cod Life* said, "Fiona Kemp never does interviews but her plates speak volumes. . . . She is a master at giving every diner an unforgettable taste experience." Each article referred to Thatcher and Fiona as partners and *Bon Appétit* mentioned that they had grown up together in South Bend, Indiana. Fiona attended the Culinary Institute of America in Hyde Park, New York, and she landed her first job as a line cook at the Wauwinet Inn on Nantucket. Thatcher was quoted as saying, "She convinced me to come out to the island for a visit in 1992. She had found a great spot for a restaurant. Once I saw it, I decided to leave the family business in South Bend behind. We were up and running the following year." Thatcher went on to explain how, the first two summers, they struggled to get the menu right. "We were trying to make the food really grand. It took us a while to figure out that fancy French food wasn't the answer. The answer was simple, fresh, fun. Food you'd want to eat on the beach." A photograph of Thatcher appeared in each article—Thatcher holding up a bowl of coral-colored soup, Thatcher in a white wicker chair grinning in a Notre Dame baseball cap. And the most surprising was a photo of Thatcher in a navy blazer and red paisley tie standing behind the oak podium. It was Huck Finn, all gussied up. There were no pictures of Fiona.

Caren had rented the same two-bedroom cottage on Hooper Farm Road for as many years as she'd worked at the restaurant and she took a roommate every year. Thatcher had asked Caren—as a favor to him—to rent the spare bedroom to Adrienne. Adrienne had been forced upon her, basically, because nobody turned Thatcher down and certainly not in the final year, when there might be a farewell bonus for loyal employees to consider. Adrienne was just happy for housing, and not only housing, but company. In the morning, Adrienne and Caren sat at the kitchen table drinking espresso. The following night was the first night of work, the soft opening. Adrienne was unsure of what to wear. She had two trunks of clothes from her days on the front desk, but somehow looking nice-at-a-day-job clothing didn't seem suitable for representing the front of the house at the hottest restaurant on Nantucket. She asked Caren.

"The other assistant managers have all been men," Caren said. "They dressed like Thatch."

"He wears a coat and tie?" Adrienne said.

"A tie if there's somebody big on the books. Otherwise he wears blazers and shirts from Thomas Pink. And Gucci loafers, a new pair every year. At first, he couldn't stand the idea of spending three hundred bucks on shoes, coming from Indiana and all, but he grew into it, and now his loafers are a part of the whole show. They're as much of an institution as the blue granite and the crackers."

"I heard about the crackers," Adrienne said.

"Let's look in your closet," Caren said. "Another espresso?"

"No, thanks," Adrienne said. The espresso machine was Caren's. She hauled it between Nantucket and St. Bart's the same way Adrienne schlepped her laptop. Caren even owned a set of demitasse cups and saucers. It was a very sophisticated setup except Adrienne discovered she didn't like espresso. It tasted like a cross between gasoline and tree bark, but she'd accepted a cup to be polite and now that the caffeine was coursing through her blood, she was ready to leap out of her skin. Soft opening tomorrow night! She needed to find something to wear!

As she feared, Caren deemed every item of clothing Adrienne owned too frumpy, too corporate, too Banana Republic. "You've worked in resorts for six years," Caren said, "and you haven't learned how to *shop*?"

Caren took her to Gypsy on Main Street where Adrienne's pulse reached an unsafe speed. The clothes were so gorgeous, and so expensive, that Adrienne thought she was going to pass out.

"We have to go someplace else," Adrienne said. "I can't afford any of this."

"Oh, come on," Caren said. "You're going to be making more money than you know what to do with."

"I doubt that," Adrienne said. Still, she mustered enough courage to browse the sale rack, and there she found two pairs of silk pants and a stunning Chloe dress that was marked down 70 percent. Adrienne put the dress back but bought both pairs of pants; then, at the last minute, she decided to try the dress on.

Caren whistled. "You can't pass that one up."

Adrienne scowled at herself in the mirror. Becoming self-sufficient did not mean spending exorbitant amounts of money on last year's designer clothing. She would probably get fired her first week and end up living in the back of a junkyard car . . . but no, she couldn't pass the dress up.

Adrienne bought the dress, her hand trembling as she signed the credit card slip, a combination of the price and the espresso. Once she had enough clothes to get her through the weekend, she felt better about starting this new life. This, after all, was what she had needed. A clean slate. A chance to get it just right.

2

Menu Meeting

"Let's pretend for twenty minutes of every day that the restaurant business is about food," Thatcher said.

Adrienne wrote on a yellow legal pad: "Restaurant = food." She sat at one end of a very long table, a twelve-top, in the dining room with the rest of the staff—five waiters; three bussers; the bartender, Duncan; and a young female bar back. Thatcher was the professor. Adrienne was the nerdy kid who took too many notes—but Thatcher had asked her to *Please absorb every word I say,* so that this, the soft opening, might go as smoothly as possible.

The dining room had been completely transformed since the morning of her breakfast. The wood floors had been polished, the wicker chairs had been cleaned, the plastic sheeting was rolled up so that every table had an unimpeded view of the gold sand beach and Nantucket Sound. Landscapers had planted red and pink geraniums in the window boxes that lined the outer walls of the restaurant and in the wooden dory out front. All of the tables were set for service and the waiters (three veterans, two newcomers) had arrived early to polish the glasses. The waiters wore black pants, crisp white shirts, and long white aprons. The busboys and the bar back wore black pants and white oxfords. Duncan wore khakis, a blue silk shirt, a sailboat-print tie, and black soccer sneakers. Adrienne had decided on her new pink silk pants with a gauzy white top and a pair of Kate Spade slides that she bought off the sale rack at Neiman's in Denver. Her black hair was short enough that she only had to blow it dry and fluff it. She would have looked okay except that morning had been so sunny and warm that she had headed off to the beach. She came home sunburned, and when she applied her fuchsia lipstick it matched not only her toenail polish and her new pants, but the stripe across her cheeks and the bridge of her nose. Ten minutes ago, when she'd arrived, Thatcher had narrowed his eyes at her (just the way her father would if he could see her). She was certain she was going to get a word about sunscreen.

"Diaphanous top on the first night," he said. "Gutsy. I like it. What size are you?"

Was this any of his business? "A six."

He nodded. "The shoes won't work, though." He checked his watch—she thought it was a Patek Philippe. "But you don't have time to go home and change. Sorry. Menu meeting at table nine, right now." He handed her the yellow legal pad. "Please absorb every word I say. You're trailing me tonight. Soft opening. That means friends of the house. Nobody gets a bill for anything but alcohol, and everything has to be as close to perfect as possible. Then, tomorrow night, close isn't going to cut it."

Now he was lecturing. The professor in his Gucci loafers and twenty-thousand-dollar watch. Everyone around the table sat in rapt attention. This was the big time. The Harvard Business School of resort dining.

"I thought Fee might come out and tell you about the food, but she's in the weeds back there. No additions tonight. There are a lot of our standards on this year's menu but there's some new stuff, too, and since we have two new waitpeople, two new bussers, and a new assistant manager, and since the rest of you spent all winter skiing bumps or sizzling in the equatorial sun, I'm going to run through the menu with you now. Everyone's met Adrienne Dealey, right?" Thatcher held out his arm to introduce Adrienne and the staff turned to look at her. She blushed on top of her sunburn. "On the floor, Adrienne is going to be my second in command, taking over for Kevin who conned his way into the maître d' job at Craft in New York. As some of you know, Fee and I might be gone more often this summer than we've been in years past. And Adrienne is going to run the floor in my stead and alongside of me. But let's give her a week or two to learn what it is we do here. She has never worked in a restaurant before. Not even Pizza Hut."

Adrienne was sure she heard groans. But then one of the waiters, shiny-bald, black square glasses, said, "Let's welcome, Adrienne."

"Welcome, Adrienne," the rest of the staff echoed.

Adrienne smiled at her yellow legal pad. She heard someone say, "You drink champagne." She looked up. Duncan was pointing at her.

She nodded, overcome with a bizarre shyness. He remembered her. Hopefully, he didn't remember her as the woman whose boyfriend had been ripping off the esteemed patrons of the Little Nell.

"You drink champagne?" Thatcher said. "That gives me an idea. Make a note to ask me about champagne. Now, let's pretend for *eighteen* minutes that the restaurant business is about food."

Adrienne never worked in restaurants, but she loved to eat in them. Until her mother died of ovarian cancer when Adrienne was twelve, her family had lived in Valley Forge, Pennsylvania, and her father ran a successful dental practice in King of Prussia. They used to eat out all the time—at the original Bookbinders in downtown Philadelphia, the City Tavern, and her mother was a sucker for all of the new, funky cafés on South Street. What was it Adrienne loved about restaurants? The napkins folded like flowers, the Shirley Temples with maraschino cherries speared on a plastic sword, seeing her endless reflection in the mirrors of the ladies' room. The pastel mints in a bowl by the front door.

After her mother died and Adrienne and her father took up with wanderlust, Adrienne became exposed to new foods. For two years they lived in Maine, where in the summertime they ate lobster and white corn and small wild blueberries. They moved to Iowa for Adrienne's senior year of high school and they ate pork tenderloin fixed seventeen different ways. Adrienne did her first two years of college at Indiana University in Bloomington, where she lived above a Mexican cantina, which inspired a love of tamales and anything doused with habanero sauce. Then she transferred to Vanderbilt in Nashville, where she ate the best fried chicken she'd ever had in her life. And so on, and so on. Pad thai in Bangkok, stone crabs in Palm Beach, buffalo meat in Aspen. As she sat listening to Thatcher, she realized that though she knew nothing about restaurants, at least she knew something about food.

"This year, as every year, the first thing that hits the table—after the cocktails—is the bread basket." There was an appreciative moan, and Caren arched her eyebrows at Adrienne from across the table. "The bread basket is one of two things. Bruno! Go into the kitchen and get me two baskets, one of each, please." The bald waiter zipped into the kitchen. *Bruno.* Adrienne mentally pinned the name to him. Bald Bruno, who had welcomed her earlier. His voice had a little bit of a sashay to it, like he was from the south or was gay. She would ask Caren later.

Bruno reappeared with two baskets swathed in white linen napkins and a ramekin of something bright yellow.

Thatcher unveiled one basket. "Pretzel bread," he said. He held up a thick braid of what looked to be soft pretzel, nicely tanned, sprinkled with coarse salt. "This is served with Fee's homemade mustard. So right away the guest knows this isn't a run-of-the-mill restaurant. They're not getting half a cold baguette, here, folks, with butter in the gold foil wrapper. This is warm pretzel bread made on the premises, and the mustard ditto. Nine out of ten tables are licking the ramekin clean." He handed the bread basket to a waiter with a blond ponytail (male—everyone at the table was male except for Adrienne, Caren, and the young bar back who was hanging on to Duncan's arm). The ponytailed waiter—name?—tore off a hunk of bread and dipped it in the mustard. He rolled his eyes like he was having an orgasm. *The appropriate response,* Adrienne thought. But remembering her breakfast she guessed he wasn't faking it.

"The other basket contains our world-famous savory doughnuts," Thatcher said. He whipped the cloth off like a magician, revealing six golden-brown doughnuts. Doughnuts? Adrienne had been too nervous to think about eating all day, but now her appetite was roused. After the menu meeting, they were going to have family meal.

The doughnuts were deep-fried rings of a light, yeasty, herb-flecked dough. Chive, basil, rosemary. Crisp on the outside, soft on the inside. Savory doughnuts. Who wouldn't stand in line for these? Who wouldn't beg or steal to access the private phone line so that they could make a date with these doughnuts?

"If someone wants bread and butter—and it happens every night—we also offer warm Portuguese rolls. But the guest has to ask for it. Most people will be eating out of your hand after these goodies."

Thatcher disappeared into the kitchen. Seconds later, he was out, carrying another plate. "All VIPs get the same canapé," he said. "Years ago, Fee knocked herself out dreaming up precious little *amuses-bouches,* but then we came up with the winner. Chips and dip." He set the plate on the table next to Adrienne and she nearly wept with gratitude. He was standing beside her now, so she could study his watch. Her suspicions were confirmed: It was a Patek Philippe, silver, rectangular face, black leather band. The watch matched Thatcher's shoes, the Gucci loafers, black with sleek silver buckles. Adrienne had to admit, when he was dressed up, the man had a certain elegance. "You're getting the idea, now, right? We have pretzels and mustard. We have doughnuts. And if we really, really like you, we have chips and dip. This is fun food. It isn't stuffy. It isn't going to make anyone nervous. The days of the waiter as a snob, the days of the menu as an *exam* the guest has to *pass* are over. But at the same time, we're not talking about cellophane bags here, are we? These are hand-cut potato chips with crème fraîche and a dollop of beluga caviar. This is the gift we send out. It's better than Christmas."

He offered the plate to Adrienne and she helped herself to a long, golden chip. She scooped up a tiny amount of the glistening black caviar. Just tasting it made her feel like a person of distinction.

Adrienne hoped the menu meeting might continue in this vein—with the staff tasting each ambrosial dish. But there wasn't time; service started in thirty minutes. Thatcher wanted to get through the menu.

"The corn chowder and the shrimp bisque are cream soups, but neither of these soups is heavy. The Caesar is served with pumpernickel croutons and white anchovies. The chevre salad is your basic mixed baby greens with a round of breaded goat cheese, and the candy-striped beets are grown locally at Bartlett Farm. Ditto the rest of the vegetables, except for the portobello mushrooms that go into the ravioli—those are flown in from Kennett Square, Pennsylvania. So when you're talking about vegetables, you're talking about produce that's grown in Nantucket soil, okay? It's not sitting for thirty-six hours on the back of a truck. Fee selects them herself before any of you people are even *awake* in the morning. It's all very Alice Waters, what we do here with our vegetables." Thatcher clapped his hands. He was revving up, getting ready for the big game. In the article in *Bon Appétit,* Thatcher had mentioned that the only thing he loved more than his restaurant was college football.

"Okay, okay!" he shouted. It wasn't a menu meeting; it was a pep rally! "The most popular item on the menu is the steak frites. It is twelve ounces of aged New York strip grilled to order—and please note you need a *temperature* on that—served with a mound of garlic fries. The duck, the sword, the lamb lollipops—see, we're having *fun* here—are all served at the chef's temperature. If you have a guest who wants the lamb killed—by which I mean *well done*—you're going to have to take it up with Fiona. The sushi plate is all spelled out for you—it's bluefin tuna caught forty miles off the shore, and the sword *is* harpooned in case you get a guest who has just seen a *Nova* special about how the Canadian coast is being overfished."

Just then the door to the kitchen opened and a short, olive-skinned man carried out a stack of plates, followed by his identical twin, who carried a hotel pan filled with grilled steaks. The smell was unbelievable.

"That's your dinner," Thatcher said. "I just have a few more things."

A third guy, taller, with longer hair, but the same look of Gibraltar as the other two men, emerged with a hotel pan of French fries, and two bottles of ketchup dangling from his fingers. The staff shifted in their chairs. Adrienne wiggled her feet in her slides. *What,* she wondered, *is wrong with my shoes?*

"The last thing I want to talk about is the fondue. Second seating only, four-tops only, otherwise it's a logistical nightmare. You all know what fondue is, I assume, remembering it from your parents' dinner parties when you were kids? We put out a fondue pot with hot peanut oil and we keep it hot with Sterno. So already, servers, visualize moving through the crowded dining room holding a pot of boiling oil. Visualize lighting the Sterno without setting the tablecloth on fire. Adding this to the menu tacked *thousands* of dollars to our insurance policy. But it's our signature dish. The table gets a huge platter of shrimp, scallops, and clams dredged in seasoned flour. They get nifty fondue forks. What they're doing, basically, is deep-frying their own shellfish. Then we provide sauces for dipping. So imagine it's a balmy night, you've spent all day on the beach, you've napped, you've showered, you've indulged in a cocktail or two. Then you're led to a table in the sand for the best all-you-can-eat fried shrimp in the world while sitting under the stars. It's one of those life-is-good moments." Thatcher smiled at the staff. "This is our last year. Everything we do this year is going to reflect our generosity of spirit. You will notice I never use the word 'customer' or 'client.' The people who eat at this restaurant are our *guests.* And like good hosts, we want to make our guests happy. Now go eat. And for those of you who are new—all wine questions go to me—and familiarize yourself with the dessert menu while you chow."

Everyone charged for the food. A few more cooks in spiffy white coats materialized from the kitchen. They were all lean and muscular with skin like gold leaf and dark hair. Latino? They looked alike to Adrienne—maybe they were brothers?—but this, surely, was just an example of her ignorance. The most handsome of the bunch stood in front of Adrienne in line. He looked her up and down—checking her out? Her diaphanous top? Then he grinned.

"Man," he said. "Everyone's in the shit back there. Except for me, of course, but I have the easy job."

Adrienne peered over his shoulder at the hotel pan filled with steaks. And a vat of béarnaise—how had she missed that? "What's the easy job?" she asked.

"I'm the pastry chef," he said. "You're new?"

"Adrienne." She offered him her hand.

"Mario. How're you doing? I heard about you. Fiona's been making a big deal all week because you're a woman."

Adrienne studied him. Although he looked like he hailed from the Mediterranean, his accent said Chicago. He was several inches taller than she was, his hair was buzzed down to his scalp, and he had very round black eyes. Beautiful eyes, really. His skin was shiny with sweat and inside the collar of his chef 's jacket at the base of his neck she saw a scar, a raised purple welt.

"I'm sorry? Fiona's making a big deal about *me*?" Adrienne said. "I don't even know her. I've never met her."

"I know," he said cheerfully. He helped himself to a steak, gave it a generous ladle of béarnaise, plopped a handful of golden fries right on top.

Adrienne followed suit. There was salad, too, a gorgeous crisp-looking salad that had already been lightly dressed with something. Adrienne mounded her crowded plate with salad, thinking about what Thatcher had said about the vegetables. Fiona picked them out before the sun was up.

Fiona! Fiona, whom Adrienne could not pick out of a crowd of two, was making a *big deal* about her. Adrienne needed to question this Mario person further to find out what was being said. Fiona Kemp, the reclusive genius chef, had been making a big deal all week because Adrienne was a woman. What had Thatcher said? He'd never hired a woman for the job before.

Adrienne poured herself a tall glass of water then sat down next to the waiter with the blond ponytail. Mario took his dinner back to the kitchen. Adrienne felt weak, like her legs were made of baby greens. Before she got here she had been nervous to meet Fiona; now she was afraid.

No one was talking. The only sounds were knives and forks on plates, the occasional palm tapping the bottom of the ketchup bottle. Two waiters were studying the menus. The new guys. One pale and thin with a bushy head of loose curls and a weak chin, and one handsome dark-haired guy wearing two gold hoop earrings. The guy with the earrings was reading the menu so intently that he shot food off his plate when he cut his steak. Adrienne concentrated on eating carefully—one drop of ketchup on the diaphanous white blouse and . . . well, there was no time to go home and change and nothing at home to change into. Adrienne ate her steak, the béarnaise, the garlicky fries—did she even need to say it? It was steak frites from a rainy-day-in-Paris dream. The steak was perfectly seasoned, perfectly cooked, pink in the middle, juicy, tender. The salad was tossed in a lemony vinaigrette but it tasted so green, so young and fresh, that Adrienne began to worry. This person Fiona had a *way.* If the staff meal tasted this good then the woman was possessed, and Adrienne didn't want a possessed woman on her case.

The whole thing had been too easy, she saw now. She shouldn't be here, she didn't belong here, but she had been swept along by her own greed and by Thatcher, who had been described in a major food magazine as "charismatic, compelling . . . he could talk a teetotaler into a bottle of Chateau Lafite." He had convinced her, somehow, to take this leap. Adrienne thought it was weird that she hadn't even *met* Fiona, but she'd chalked it up to the fact that Fiona was a recluse. A culinary Greta Garbo, or J. D. Salinger. Were Thatcher and Fiona married, engaged, committed, together, dating—or, worst of all, *exes*? She had to ask Caren. Caren who was three seats down eating a plate of only salad. Drinking, yes, espresso. Caren had advised Adrienne to keep a toothbrush and toothpaste at the restaurant. Caren knew everything.

There was soft female laughter, as jarring to Adrienne as a tray of stemware crashing to the floor. She looked around to see Duncan and the bar back engaged in quiet conversation. They looked so familiar, so at ease—the girl grabbed Duncan's forearm when she talked. Adrienne wondered if something was going on between them. The girl was young—in college still, Adrienne guessed—she had curly light brown hair and big brown eyes. Big boobs, too, and her oxford was unbuttoned one too far.

Adrienne was one to talk. *Diaphanous top . . . gutsy . . . I like it.* "Diaphanous" didn't mean transparent. You certainly couldn't see anything. Besides, she was wearing a very sturdy, very modest beige bra. And her shoes—what, exactly, was wrong with her shoes?

Adrienne did *not* like the idea that while she was getting moved into the cottage, setting up her bank account, and strictly adhering to all three of her rules, someone she'd never laid eyes on was down here talking about her. News of the diaphanous top and the inappropriate shoes had probably already made it back into the kitchen. What would Fiona say to *that*?

Thatcher appeared, holding a flute of pink champagne. "You're all done."

It wasn't a question, though Adrienne still had food on her plate, and she didn't want to be separated from it. He nodded toward the front door. "Service starts in ten minutes. Mr. and Mrs. Parrish will be here *at* six. There are some other things I have to explain."

Adrienne cleared her plate into three bins the way she'd seen others doing, though it killed her to throw food away. She followed Thatcher, who was holding the champagne out in front of him. "You liked dinner?" he asked.

"It was delicious." This felt like a gross understatement and she wondered what words might convey the physical pain she felt at scraping her plate. "Did you eat?"

He laughed, the old karate-chop "ha!" It was a noise he made not when something was funny, she realized, but when something was preposterous. "No. I eat with Fee after service."

Is she your wife? Girlfriend? Can someone please turn on the lights so I can see? Is this the restaurant's last year because you've split up? Is the fact that I'm a woman going to be a bigger problem than you initially anticipated? Adrienne followed him silently, but not silently at all. Her shoes were making a tremendous racket against the wooden floors.

"I'm clomping," she said.

Thatcher turned to her. "Yes. The shoes. I told you. You have to watch the way you walk. Tomorrow night, different shoes. A soft sole. Slippers or something, but elegant, okay?"

Adrienne deducted another hundred dollars from her rapidly diminishing savings for elegant slipper shoes. Fine for pants, but the dress she'd bought would look funny without heels.

"Taking this job was a mistake," she said. "Behind the front desk of a hotel, no one could even see my shoes."

They reached the oak podium, home to the phone, the reservation book, a Tiffany vase with a couple dozen blue irises. A shallow bowl of Blue Bistro matches. A leather cup containing three sharpened pencils and a funny-looking wine key. Thatcher held up the champagne flute.

"This is a glass of Laurent-Perrier rosé," he said. "We sell it at the bar for sixteen dollars a glass, ninety-five dollars a bottle. This is what you're going to drink on the floor."

"I *said,* taking this job was a mistake."

"We both took a gamble," he said. "Please give it one night. I promise you will love it so much you will be counting the minutes until you can come back. If you don't feel that way, then we'll talk. But we can't talk now. Right now, I'm going to talk and you're going to listen, okay?"

His okays were purely rhetorical.

"I want to brush my teeth," she said.

Before she knew what was happening, Thatcher leaned over and kissed her. Very quickly, very softly. "You're fine," he said. "I detect a trace of vinaigrette, but it's really very pleasant." He held the flute out to her, and as it gave her something to do other than fall over backward, she accepted it.

"My father is a dentist," she said. If her father had seen what just happened—well, she could hear him now. *These are not people who floss, honey.* Adrienne looked at Huck Finn, the professor, resplendent in his watch and shoes, a yellow linen shirt and navy blazer. He did not seem at all fazed by what had just happened. *The professor kissed me! It was really very pleasant, the kiss. This champagne is what I drink on the floor. I wear diaphanous tops and clompy shoes. He kissed me! No wonder they talk about me back in the kitchen!*

"Pretend you're hosting a cocktail party," he said. "You greet people at the door holding your glass of Laurent-Perrier rosé. The first thing they'll notice is your pretty face, then your clothes. Then what you've got in your hand. They will want to drink pink champagne just like the beautiful hostess. Sixteen dollars a glass, you see? When you're working the room, you should always have your flute of pink champagne. Right away, it gives you an identity, it gives you style. Your champagne is an accessory. You don't have to get tanked. In fact, I'd appreciate it if you didn't. But a glass or two—three on a busy night, sure. Duncan will fill you up." He watched her while she took a sip. "This is great," he said. "Kevin drank bourbon—nothing sexy about that—and occasionally he deigned to walk around with a glass of merlot, but he didn't enjoy it and the guests could tell."

"Do you drink while you work?" Adrienne asked.

"I'm an alcoholic," he said. He gazed at her so intently she thought he might kiss her again. What was going *on* here? It felt like she was breaking one of her rules, though she was so flustered she couldn't remember what her rules were. Was there a rule about not kissing her boss?

"Oh."

"There's something else you have to know," Thatcher said. "Something I should have mentioned when I hired you."

Adrienne's dinner shifted in her stomach. Something else?

He lowered his voice. "There's no press allowed in the kitchen."

"Okay."

"I don't care if it's the *New York Times Magazine.* I don't care if it's the *Christian Science Monitor.*"

"Okay."

"I don't care if they tell you they have an appointment. They don't. There is no press allowed in the kitchen. And no guests, of course. I mention the press because they come here all the time trying to get a story about Fiona. Word has gotten out that it's our last year, therefore it's crucial you understand."

"No press in the kitchen," Adrienne said.

"Very good. I'm sorry to be so strict."

"You don't have to be sorry."

"Tonight, it's friends of the house," Thatcher said. "I want you to shadow me around the dining room so you learn the faces. I want you to man the host station if I'm back in the kitchen."

"Am I allowed in the kitchen?" Adrienne asked.

Thatcher looked at her strangely.

"Thatcher!" Bruno was calling from the dining room. Both Thatcher and Adrienne spun around to find the dining room transformed. All of the candles had been lit and the waiters stood in a line, hands behind their backs, military-style, among the impeccably dressed tables with their starched tablecloths, the sparkling stemware, a single blue iris in a silver bud vase. Behind the restaurant, the sun was dropping in the sky. Just then a few notes came from the piano, like peals of a glass bell. A tall mop-haired man in a black turtleneck had started to play.

"It's beautiful," Adrienne whispered. It was like a theater set before the opening performance and she found herself wanting it to stay like this. She didn't want anything to ruin it, but no sooner did Adrienne wish for this than a white Mercedes pulled into the parking lot.

"This is it," Thatcher said. "The beginning of the end."

At the Blue Bistro, the service wasn't the only thing that was old-fashioned. There was no computer. Tickets were written by hand and delivered to the kitchen by the server, a system that was as outdated as the pony express. Reservations were made in pencil, in a big old book with a tattered binding. Most tables were marked with the party's last name; VIP tables had the first and last name.

"Some restaurants actually write 'VIP' next to a name," Thatcher said. "Or, if they're trying to be tricky, they'll use other initials, like 'PPX.' But too many people today are tuned into that kind of thing. It causes problems."

"What makes someone a VIP?" Adrienne asked. "Does it have to do with money?"

"Money?" Thatcher said. "No. It has to do with how often someone dines with us. The Parrishes, for example. The ultimate VIPs." Thatcher checked his watch. "You see, it's the stroke of six."

At that second, a couple Adrienne took to be the Parrishes stepped in the door. They were an older couple who exuded an air of gracious retirement: golf, grandchildren, travel on European ships. Mr. Parrish wore kelly green pants and a green-and-white striped shirt, a navy blazer. He had silver hair, he was sunburned and he shook ever so slightly when he leaned over to kiss Adrienne. Another kiss—this time from a complete stranger.

Adrienne stole a glance at Thatcher. Was kissing a part of the job description that she had missed? Mrs. Parrish gave Thatcher a hug. On her right hand, which rested on the front of Thatcher's butter-yellow shirt, she wore one enormous emerald-cut diamond ring and a platinum band with sapphires and diamonds. She had dark hair styled like Jackie Onassis, and clear blue eyes that took Adrienne in and immediately understood that she was motherless. Adrienne had met other women with this power—mothers of friends and boyfriends who wanted to adopt Adrienne, like a nine-year-old with a stray kitten, and Adrienne had never been able to resist their kind words or fluttering of attention (except in the case of Mavis—Mavis was not her mother!). Mrs. Parrish released her hold on Thatcher and reached out to Adrienne with both hands. Adrienne set her champagne down on the podium.

"Thatcher," Mrs. Parrish said. "Where did you find such a lovely girl?"

"Darla, Grayson, may I introduce Adrienne Dealey," Thatcher said. "She's never worked in a restaurant before."

"Good for you," Mrs. Parrish whispered. She leaned over and kissed Adrienne: Adrienne felt the lipstick, a cool spot of paint on her cheek. Was that *good for you* for never working in a restaurant? Or *good for you* for landing a job here, alongside the world's most charismatic restaurateur? Since Adrienne didn't know how to respond, she smiled. Her sunburn made her face feel funny, like her skin was too tight. She hoped there wasn't anything stuck in her teeth.

Thatcher led the Parrishes into the dining room and although he said Adrienne should shadow him, she felt foolish doing so. She popped into the ladies' room, a mere four feet from the oak podium, to wipe the lipstick from her face and check her teeth. Regrettably, no time to brush. She could hear Thatcher's voice asking about someone named Wolf; she could hear Mr. Parrish offer up a round of golf at Sankaty. And then she heard the phone.

She rushed back to the hostess station. It was, of all things, the private line. Thatcher hadn't said anything about how he wanted her to answer the phone and especially not the private line. But hey—six years of resorts, five front desks including one in which she had to answer in Thai. One thing she could do correctly in this restaurant was answer the phone.

"Good evening," she said. "The Blue Bistro."

"Yeah." There was a telltale crackle. Cell phone, bad signal. "We're running late. Ten minutes. Make that twenty to be safe."

"No problem, sir," Adrienne said, though she had no idea if this were a problem or not. She tried to catch Thatcher's eye. He was across the room, seating the Parrishes at table twenty, which Adrienne knew to be the best table. The dining room was shaped like a triangle, and table twenty was the top, the focus of everybody else in the restaurant. Thatcher was up to his neck in schmooze; he was unreachable. "We'll see you when you get here," Adrienne said into the phone. "Thank you for calling." But the man had already hung up. And then Adrienne realized she hadn't gotten his name.

She tried to explain this enormous gaffe to Thatcher when he returned—the first task she tackled on her own a complete failure—but he didn't seem interested. "If the call came in on the private line, it was probably Ernie Otemeyer," he said, making a note by the name "Ernie Otemeyer" in the book, table sixteen for two people at six fifteen. "He's our plumber. He comes twice a year—soft opening and his birthday in August. He's always late because he has to stop on the way and buy his own beer. He drinks Bud Light."

Adrienne wondered about her legal pad—what had she done with it? Here was the kind of thing she needed to write down. *Plumber Ernie comes twice a year and brings his own Bud Light.*

"I don't know what I did with my legal pad," Adrienne confessed. Through the open door, she saw more cars pulling in. The piano man was playing "What I Did for Love."

"I have good news," Thatcher said.

"What?"

"The Parrishes want you to bring them their bread."

"Why is that good news?"

"It means they like you. They want to see you at their table. Please wait until Bruno gets their cocktails. You have to be watching. And don't think you have plenty of time because Duncan knows their drinks—heck, the whole staff knows their drinks—Stoli tonic with lime for Grayson and a Southern Comfort old-fashioned for Darla. See that? The drinks are up. Now, as soon as Bruno delivers them, you get the bread. They like bread and butter—always."

"Where do I get the bread?" Adrienne asked.

"In the kitchen."

"So it's okay if I . . ."

A party of six stepped in the door—four men, rugby-playing types, and two teenaged boys who looked like Abercrombie & Fitch models with mussed hair and striped ties loose at the neck. "Thatcher!" one of the men boomed like he was yelling across a playing field.

"Get the bread," Thatcher whispered, nudging Adrienne toward the kitchen. He moved to the front of the podium and started slapping backs.

Adrienne eyeballed the kitchen door. Well, she worked here now. And for some reason the Parrishes wanted her to deliver their bread. She felt singled out. Special. The Parrishes wanted her. They were not offended by her diaphanous top. They weren't put off because she was a *woman.*

Adrienne pushed open the door.

The kitchen was brightly lit. And very, very hot. And quiet except for the sounds of knives—*rat-tat-tat-scrape*—against cutting boards and the hiss of the deep fryers. Adrienne saw a line of bodies in white coats, but nobody's face. There were two six-burner ranges side by side, there was a grill shooting flames, and up above, blocking everyone's face, was a shelf stacked with what must have been fifty blackened sauté pans. Adrienne watched a pair of hands preparing the doughnuts. She watched another pair of hands filling ramekins with mustard. She noticed a cappuccino machine, big brother to the one that Caren owned, and next to it, a huge refrigerator, a cold stainless-steel wall. Where, exactly, was the bread? The kitchen was filled with people, yet there was no one to ask.

"Yes?"

A woman's voice. Adrienne's eyes adjusted to this alternate universe that was the restaurant kitchen and she saw Fiona Kemp. She knew it was Fiona Kemp because it said so in cobalt blue script on her white chef's jacket. Fiona Kemp who, contrary to every vision Adrienne held in her mind's eye, was only five feet tall and may have weighed a hundred pounds with a pocket full of change. She was small. And adorable. She had long honey-blond hair in a braid and huge blue eyes. She wore diamond stud earrings. Adrienne had expected a hunchback, a hermit; she had expected the old woman who lived in a shoe.

"You're Fiona?"

"Yes."

"I'm Adrienne."

"I know."

Should they shake hands? Fiona made no move to do so and Adrienne was too intimidated. She had never been clear on when women should shake hands, anyway.

"I came for the bread."

"For whom?"

Adrienne watched a batch of doughnuts descend into the deep fryer. Her brain was deep-frying. "The Parrishes."

"Thatcher takes them their bread."

"Okay," Adrienne said. "Is there a special place the bread is kept?"

"Yes."

"Where is that?"

Fiona nodded at the stainless-steel counter to Adrienne's left. "The Parrishes' bread is right there. You're running for Thatcher?"

Adrienne stared at the basket of rolls and the cake of butter covered by a glass dome. "He told me I'm supposed to take the Parrishes their bread."

"Thatcher takes the Parrishes their bread," Fiona said. "That's the way it works around here. Especially on the first night."

"He said they asked for me."

Fiona stared at Adrienne as though she was trying to figure out what had prompted Thatcher to offer her a job. Adrienne didn't look like Heidi Klum, and she didn't have enormous breasts. So why else would he cajole her into taking a job that she wasn't qualified to do? *I have no idea!* Adrienne wanted to shout.

"Thatcher was right about you, then," Fiona said.

"Right about me how?" Adrienne asked. "What did he say?"

Fiona pinched her lips together. She had freckles across her nose, like someone had sprinkled it with cinnamon.

"You're not going to tell me?"

"No."

"Is my working here going to be a problem?" Adrienne asked. She felt like in the bright lights her top was positively sheer.

"Since it's only the first hour of the first night, that remains to be seen," Fiona said. "But I can tell you one thing."

"What's that?"

"The Parrishes are very important to us. They shouldn't have to wait for their bread." She pointed at the door. "Go."

Adrienne was shaking when she reached the Parrishes' table. Normally when she felt uncomfortable, she sent a mental e-mail to her father. But now Adrienne was facing a blank screen. What had happened in there? No time to wonder because the Parrishes wanted to chat about Aspen. They had vacationed in Aspen long ago, before it was fashionable, and they stayed at the Hotel Jerome. Adrienne learned that Grayson's business was importing custom tile and stone from Italy, a business his sons now ran that was doing better than ever due to the home-improvement boom. The Parrishes had three sons, the oldest was thirty-six, and none of the sons was currently married. They had one grandchild, a little boy named Wolf who "lived with his mother." Adrienne managed to keep up the conversation until she felt Bruno breathing on the back of her neck, and she excused herself.

She returned to the hostess station and drank down her pink bubbly. The exchange with Fiona nagged at her. She had to talk to Caren. There wasn't time now, of course. No sooner had Adrienne set her empty glass on the blue granite for Duncan to refill than the front door became inundated with three six-thirty reservations and the late arriving Ernie Otemeyer carrying a paper bag. The place was hopping. Busboys presented baskets of pretzel bread and doughnuts. The piano man launched into "Some Enchanted Evening." Caren floated by, taking Adrienne by the elbow.

"I have apps up on table seven. Can you run some food for me?"

Adrienne glanced at the clot of people by the front door. Thatcher was in the thick of it.

"Run some food?" This sounded suspiciously out of bounds. "I'm not trained for that. And what about Thatcher? Can he seat all those tables by himself?"

"It'll take two seconds," Caren said. She vanished into the kitchen and came back balancing a tray of plates on the palm of one hand and carrying a stand in the other. Adrienne followed her out into the dining room. Caren snapped open the stand and lowered the tray. Adrienne felt a bloom of optimism from the champagne. Fiona was an ogre trapped in a doll's body, like some screwed-up fairy tale, but just look at the food: two salads with the red-and-white striped beets, a foie gras, a crab cake, and two corn chowders. Absolutely beautiful.

"The salads go to the two ladies closest to you," Caren whispered. "Serve from their right."

Adrienne watched Caren's graceful movements. She tried to imitate her. She slid the salads in for a landing on top of the Limoges chargers. Caren served the last two plates, then asked if anyone cared for freshly ground pepper. A burst of laughter came from the rugby players' table. The piano man segued into "The Entertainer." It jangled in Adrienne's head. She had served the two plates without incident. Piece of cake! And now . . . what? Thatcher was leading the plumber to his table, two down from the Parrishes. He held out the paper bag.

"Would you ask Duncan to put this on ice?" Thatcher said. "And get a cold one in a pilsner for Ernie and a glass of the merlot for his wife, Isadora, please." Under his breath, he said, "Champagne, champagne."

"It's at the bar," Adrienne said. "I'll get it right now." There were still people waiting at the podium. She had to hurry! She carried the paper bag through the dining room to the bar. Even over the conversation, the clink of glasses and silver and china, and the piano, Adrienne could hear her shoes. She sounded like a Clydesdale.

"Adrienne!"

Thatcher was at her back. "The Parrishes want you to serve their wine."

"I don't know how to do that," she said. She pictured snapping the cork in half, or spilling cabernet down the front of her diaphanous blouse. "Don't make me do that."

"I told them you haven't been trained with the wine key yet," he said. "I told them you would do it next time. But you can deliver their chips and dip. They just want your face at their table. Where's your champagne?"

"I told you, I'm getting it." She wanted to give the beer to Duncan and order the merlot before she forgot. Thatcher set off to deal with the people at the podium.

Adrienne paid close attention to where she placed her feet. It forced her to slow down. Confrontation with Fiona aside, the first hour wasn't going badly. She had answered the phone, she had conducted a pleasant conversation with two VIPs, she had served two plates of salad without dumping them in the guests' laps. Now, at the bar, she delivered the plumber's beer and ordered the merlot, and without even having to ask, Duncan slid a flute of champagne across the blue bar. She took a sip, then put it down. She had to go back into the kitchen for the chips and dip. The piano man played "Somewhere, Beyond the Sea." This had been Adrienne's parents' favorite song; she was never able to listen to it without getting weepy. But what was nice about the restaurant business, Adrienne realized, was that there was no time to reflect on the way her parents used to dance together at weddings. There wasn't time to worry if her father was now dancing with Mavis. There wasn't time to muse over Doug or Kip or Sully or any of the men she'd sat at a table for two with over the last six years and question her own good sense. There wasn't even time to wonder about the kiss from Thatcher. The restaurant business was doing her a favor. It locked her into the moment: her glass of pink champagne, the trip back into Fiona's lair. Locating her yellow legal pad. Learning the table numbers and the wine key. Getting a look—just a look—at all the beautiful food. History in the making. The last soft opening of the Blue Bistro.

By the end of the first seating, Adrienne's legs ached. And her lower back. In three hours of work she had walked at least five miles. So that was it, absolutely, for the fucking slides. She would never wear them again.

There were seventy reservations on the books and forty-two of those were sitting at nine o'clock.

"First seating was *nothing*," Thatcher said. "It was a *warm-up.*"

At eighty thirty there was a nice lull—most of the tables had finished their dinners and were lingering over dessert. Thatcher snatched a piece of the brown sugar fudge from one of the candy plates headed back into the kitchen and handed it to Adrienne.

"I always wondered if you ate off the plates," she said.

"Taste it," he said.

The fudge was an explosion of vanilla and caramel, and it gave her a much-needed sugar kick. She checked in on the Parrishes. They were one of those couples who didn't speak to each other during dinner; only when Adrienne approached did they brighten. When she had delivered their caviar, they chatted with her about their home on Cliff Road. Between courses, at Thatcher's prompting, Adrienne checked in with them again. They were both staring out at the water, each seemingly lost in thought. But when Adrienne appeared, Darla raved about the crab cake, and Grayson swirled his white burgundy in his glass. They asked Adrienne if she cooked at home and the expression on her face—which was horror and quite genuine—gave them all a good laugh. At a little after eight, Adrienne delivered a cup of decaf cappuccino to Darla and a glass of tawny port to Grayson. She placed the check (which consisted only of the bar tab and the two-hundred-dollar bottle of wine) on the table in what she hoped was a discreet way, and informed them that they were welcome to stay and enjoy the sea air for as long as they wished. This was not, of course, true—the entire restaurant was being reseated at nine. When Darla and Grayson made their move to stand, Adrienne floated—this was her goal, to float like Caren—to their table and held Grayson's arm all the way to the front door. Before they left, Darla kissed Adrienne again—more lipstick—and Grayson pressed money into her hand, which took her so by surprise that she nearly dropped it. The Parrishes then lavished Thatcher with attention and sent their love "to darling Fiona. Tell her everything was superb. We'll see you Friday at six." And they set off into the night. Thatcher winked at Adrienne; she felt sorry to see them go. It was like visiting with her grandparents when she was young, complete with the gift of money. Adrienne checked her palm. Grayson had given her a hundred dollars.

She showed the bill to Thatcher. "What should I do with it?"

"Keep it."

"What about Bruno?" she asked. "What about Tyler?" Tyler was a busboy who was a senior at Nantucket High School. In the thirty seconds Adrienne had conversed with him, she could tell he was precocious. He had, he informed her, twelve days until graduation when he planned to get shit-faced at a bonfire on the beach just down the way from the restaurant. The only reason he got this job in the first place, he said, was because his father was the island's health inspector.

"There was a tip added to the bill for them," Thatcher said. "If anybody puts money in your hand—unless he tells you it's for someone else—then it's yours to keep."

An electric thrill ran up Adrienne's spine, the singular pleasure of windfall. The start of her new Future! She tucked the money into her pocket.

"The Parrishes didn't speak to one another during dinner," she said.

"They never do," Thatcher said. "That's why they like to have someone visit their table, three, four times a night. It peps things up."

The rest of the tables were slowly rising and moving around. Some people headed for the door, some walked to the edge of the restaurant to peer at the water. The busboys worked like crazy to strip the tables. The piano man took a break and the CD player kicked in with Billie Holiday. Adrienne's sunburn throbbed like a red alarm; she was tired. She could easily go home and sleep with the hundred dollar bill under her pillow until morning.

"Now," said Thatcher. "Now you're going to earn your money."

Adrienne wanted to tell Thatcher about her exchange with Fiona. She wanted to ask what he'd said about her but there wasn't time. Between seatings, Thatcher reviewed the book with Adrienne.

"You're going to have to learn our guest list night by night," he said. "Some of our favorite guests only stay on Nantucket for one week of the summer, but they eat here three times during that week. They've been doing so for twelve years."

Adrienne had found her yellow notepad. It was handed to her by the young bar back whose name was Delilah. Delilah was not Duncan's paramour, but rather, his kid sister. She had just finished her junior year at Bennington, she said, and all her life she'd been waiting for her parents to give her the okay to work with Duncan.

"I have two other brothers," she said. "David and Dennis. And they are such sticks-in-the-mud. They have kids." As if that explained it. "Duncan is the only person in our family who leads an exciting life, and so I said to the parents, 'As soon as I turn twenty-one, I go where he goes.' " She gave Adrienne a toothy smile with her eyes all scrunched, and headed, butt-first, into the kitchen, bracing a crate of dirty bar glasses against her midsection.

Adrienne was glad for the return of her notepad. She studied the diagram of circles and squares and rectangles that was the seating chart—it might have seemed as easy as nursery school but it was more like plane geometry. She looked expectantly at Thatcher. Nerdy student a hundred dollars richer at the ready!

While some of the guests of the soft opening were summer people who had arrived early, most were year-round Nantucketers. Mack Peterson, the manager of the Nantucket Beach Club and Hotel, was coming with Cecily Elliott, the hotel owners' daughter.

"Great guy," Thatcher said. "He sends us *tons* of business. Good business, too—people who show up on time, drink a lot of expensive wine, et cetera."

Adrienne wrote down their names. "Are they married?" she asked. "Mack and Cecily?"

"No," Thatcher said. He furrowed his brow. It was funny, Adrienne thought, how Thatcher's hair was red but his eyebrows were the palest blond. "What is your obsession with whether people are married?"

Adrienne wanted to inform him that asking if one couple was married could hardly be classified as an *obsession,* but then she remembered that she had also asked about him and Fiona. "I'm sorry," she said, with as much poison in her voice as she could muster in her state of weariness.

Thatcher held up his pen. "Never mind."

She recalled Fiona's words. *Thatcher was right about you, then.* "You don't know the first thing about me," Adrienne said.

"Well, I know that your father is a dentist," he said. "Your mother is a good cook. You worked in Aspen at the Little Nell, and in Thailand, Palm Beach, Hawaii, and on the Cape. You have black hair and green eyes. You're a size six. You go to the beach without sun protection. You don't know how to walk in slides. And"—he pointed his pen at her—"tonight is your first night of restaurant work." He smiled. "How'd I do?"

Adrienne stared at the faint blue lines of her legal pad. She desperately wanted to set the record straight about her mother—although her mother *had been* a good cook, she had also been dead for sixteen years. But Adrienne didn't have the energy. She was tired. And he was right that she went to the beach without lotion and didn't know how to walk in these shoes. Her legs hurt, her face hurt. She wanted to sit down.

"Let's just do this," she said.

"We have a lot of Realtors coming in tonight," he said. "Hopefully one of them will help me sell this place. The president of the bank is coming. The electrician is coming with her husband, her sister and brother-in-law. I don't need to tell you how important the contractors are, right? Ernie the plumber and Cat the electrician. They are the *most* important. Because if one of the toilets overflows or an oven quits in the middle of service on a

Saturday night, we need to be able to call that person's cell phone and have them show up in *minutes.* Let's see . . . we have a famous CEO coming with a party of ten—I'll let you be surprised. No other celebrities, really—a couple of local painters and writers. They drink a lot. Where is your champagne? We didn't sell a single glass of Laurent-Perrier first seating."

"Sorry," Adrienne said. She felt oddly culpable, like maybe she wasn't enticing enough, or worthy of emulation. She headed over to the bar and when Duncan saw her he whipped a clean flute off the shelf.

"This is your third glass," Duncan said. "How many did Thatch say you could have?"

"Three, if it's busy."

"It's going to be busy in a few minutes," he said. He poured a glass and slid it across the bar. "You'd better nurse this, though. I'll pour you however much you want after service."

"Thanks," Adrienne said. "But after service, I'm going home to bed."

"Maybe you should have an espresso," Duncan said. "Do you want me to order you an espresso?"

"No, thanks." But since it was nice of him to offer, she said, "I met your sister. She's cute."

Duncan rolled his eyes, wiped down the blue granite with a rag, and checked the level of his cranberry juice. "She doesn't know what the fuck she's doing."

Adrienne twirled her flute by the stem. "That makes two of us."

Caren appeared with two espressos. "Let's do a shot," she said to Duncan. They both threw back the coffee. Caren pointed at Adrienne's champagne. "Better watch it. That stuff will kill you."

Adrienne wandered back toward the front door as headlights started to pull into the parking lot. The piano player returned, smelling like cigarettes. The two new waiters had also been out on the beach smoking. The guy with the hoop earrings—name?—offered bushy hair—name?—an Altoid. The piano player—name?—glissando-ed into "We've Only Just Begun."

Somehow Adrienne caught a second wind. The people who arrived for second seating were younger and better looking. In fact, they all looked like models. Cat, the electrician, was a six-foot blonde in a pair of Manolo Blahniks. She was one of the most attractive women Adrienne had ever seen and she was the electrician. Welcome to Nantucket! When Thatcher introduced Adrienne, Cat's eyes went first to Adrienne's shoes, then to her glass.

"You're drinking pink champagne," she said. "That's what I want. Pink champagne. Let's get a bottle. No, a magnum."

Adrienne smirked at Thatcher. Redeemed! Thatcher led Cat's party to table twenty while Adrienne sat a husband and wife Realtor team with a party of six. When she returned to the podium, Holt Millman—a CEO who was famous for being not only obscenely rich but legitimately so—was heading up a party of ten.

In her mind, Adrienne dashed a one-line e-mail to her father. *Holt Millman looks just like his picture on the cover of* Fortune*!* Thatcher sat the Millman party and left Adrienne to handle a party of six women, wives of the owners of other restaurants in town. Thatcher had told Adrienne that this table was super-VIP. "Because we want them to return the favor when we go out on the town."

One of these women—again, gorgeous, red hair, fabulous shoes—said, "You're new."

"I'm Adrienne Dealey."

The redhead shook Adrienne's hand and squeezed it. "I've been telling Thatcher for years that he should have a woman up front. Don't let Fiona give you a hard time."

This caught Adrienne off-guard. *How did you know Fiona would give me a hard time?* she wanted to ask. *What does everybody on this island know about Fiona that I don't?*

"I won't," Adrienne assured her. She felt not only redeemed, but validated. Fiona was famous for giving people a hard time. So there. Adrienne handed out menus to the women and summoned enough courage to say, "I've been drinking Laurent-Perrier rosé champagne. Can I interest you ladies in a bottle?"

"Sure," the redhead said. "Sounds great."

Adrienne was afraid that if she stopped moving, she would keel over. She led the good citizens of Nantucket to their tables, handed out menus, and delivered drinks for Caren and Bruno who she could see were getting slammed. A local author came in with a party of eight. They had been barhopping in town and as soon as the author stepped in the door, she started singing along with the piano. Another party of four stepped in, among them a woman with a luscious pink pashmina who pointed at Adrienne's shoes.

"Great shoes!" she cried.

You can have them, Adrienne thought.

Thatcher approached the podium. "I don't want you to look right now," he said. "But in a second, casually, study the man to Holt Millman's left. He is Public Enemy Number One."

Instinctively, Adrienne turned.

"Don't look," Thatcher said. "Because he's watching us."

"Who is it?" Adrienne said.

"Drew Amman-Keller. Freelance journalist. He's basically on Holt's payroll writing pieces for *Town & Country* and *Forbes* about Holt and Holt's friends. He's been so aggressive in pursuing a story about Fiona that we had to ban him from the restaurant. But he's not stupid. He comes with Holt."

"Can I look now?"

"In a second. Let me walk away. I see table seven is drinking Laurent-Perrier."

"I suggested it."

"I want you to deliver the VIP order to Holt's table," Thatcher said. "In fact, I want you to deliver the VIP orders from now on. All summer. That will be your job."

"But . . ."

"Go to the kitchen right now," Thatcher said. "Don't turn around."

Adrienne learned that the person making the chips and dip was a kid named Paco, the assistant to the garde-manger. Paco was gangly, pimply, wearing a Chicago White Sox hat. Adrienne went right to him for pickup, sidestepping the frenetic scene that was going on between the waitstaff and Fiona and the line cooks and Fiona.

The kitchen, which had been so peaceful when Adrienne had first entered it, was now a house on fire. Fiona wasn't actually cooking; she was standing in front of what Paco referred to as the pass, yelling out orders from the tickets.

"Ordering table eight: one crab cake, two beets, one Caesar."

From the other side of the stoves, a cook called out, "Ordering one crab cake, chef."

The garde-manger, whose name was Eddie, called out, "Two beets and one Caesar, chef." Adrienne watched Eddie reach into two giant bowls of greens to plate the salads. She was entranced by the speed and the grace of this kind of cooking. It was as amazing as watching someone blow glass or weave on a loom, and it was all the more impressive because these men were barely men. Eddie might have been legal to drink, but Paco looked about nineteen. Adrienne watched him slice potatoes on a mandolin—*pfft, pfft, pfft*—until he had a pile of potatoes in perfect coins.

"Ordering table seven: one crab cake, one chowder, one bisque, two beets, one foie gras," Fiona said. For such a small individual, her voice was very forceful. "And where is table twenty's chowder? That's Cat, people, *vamos*!"

"You know," Adrienne said to Paco, "this is going to a party of ten. Maybe we should give them extra?"

"Party of ten?" Paco said. He, too, had a Chicago accent. "Why the fuck didn't you tell me?" He dropped another batch of sliced potatoes into the oil. It hissed like a snake.

"Ordering table twenty-five: two foie gras, two bisque, two crab cake, one SOS," Fiona said. A crab cake appeared in front of her and she studied it, tasted the sauce with a spoon, then wiped the edge of the plates with a towel. She tasted a bowl of shrimp bisque and sprinkled it with chives. "Where is Spillman?" she said. "Table thirty is up." She glanced over at Adrienne, who shifted her eyes to the slabs of foie gras sizzling in the sauté pans. "Are you running for Spillman?"

"Who's Spillman?" Adrienne asked.

Fiona huffed in a way that meant nothing good. Adrienne wanted to ride her second wind right out of the kitchen. As soon as Paco supplemented her chip plate for Holt Millman's table, she bolted. The dining room, with its open walls, was much cooler than the kitchen. It was sparkling with candlelight and was alive with music and conversation.

"Compliments of the chef," Adrienne said to the table at large, though her eyes landed, light as a butterfly, on the man to Holt Millman's left.

"Ooohrrg," she said. "Hi." The man whom Thatcher had identified as

Public Enemy Number One, Drew Amman-Keller, was the same man Adrienne had met on the ferry, the man who was responsible for her being here in the first place. He was staring at her over the top of his Bordeaux glass, but he said nothing. Maybe he didn't recognize her. Was that too much to hope for?

Adrienne set the plate down in front of Mr. Millman. "Hand-cut russet potato chips with crème fraîche and beluga caviar." Holt Millman beamed. A woman in a gray toile pillbox hat clapped her hands. Thatcher was right; even if you had all the money in the world, it was better than Christmas.

The night kept going and going. People ordered wine—and five tables ordered champagne—and Thatcher made Adrienne follow him into the wine cave, which was a room next to the bathroom that was cool and dry and filled with wine.

"This used to be a utility closet," he said. "We had it totally reoutfitted." The red wine rested on redwood racks and the white wine and champagne were kept in a refrigerated unit that took up a whole wall. Thatcher showed Adrienne how to identify a wine by its bin number from the wine list.

"We're selling a lot of the Laurent-Perrier," he said. "Get yourself another glass."

Adrienne's head was so loose that she was afraid it was going to unscrew completely and go flying through the dining room.

"I don't need another glass," she said.

"Get another glass," he said.

She informed Duncan that this was an order from Thatcher and she was given another glass. Duncan was moving fluidly behind the bar. Everyone wanted cocktails replenished; everybody wanted wine by the glass. A handful of men had actually left their tables to talk to Duncan at the bar, so the whole time he was wiping and pouring and shooting mixers out of the gun, he was talking about his winter in Aspen and the people who were regulars at the Board Room. Elle McPherson, Ed Bradley, Kofi Annan.

Adrienne scoffed. "Kofi Annan was a regular at the Board Room?"

A bead of sweat threatened to drop into Duncan's eye. "He drinks Cutty Sark."

"Okay," Adrienne said. She had no interest in busting Duncan's rap;

she'd had so much to drink that she should really keep her mouth shut. She picked up her fourth glass of champagne and was about to walk away when he said, "Listen, I'm out of limes. Can you find my sister and ask her to get me more limes, pronto?"

"Sure." Adrienne feared Delilah was in the kitchen, but then she saw her pop out of the ladies' room. "Your brother needs limes," Adrienne said to her. "Right away, I guess."

Delilah flashed her a toothy smile. Her eyes were bright. "Okay!" she said. "I love this job, don't you?"

"Hot oil!" someone called. The weak-chinned waiter. Adrienne still didn't know anyone's name. "Out of the way!" He had a fondue pot by the handle and the heating rack and the sterno in the other hand. A second waiter who had definitely not been at the menu meeting or family meal, a tall, heavyset black man, followed with a huge platter of seafood. He caught Adrienne's eye. "My name is Joe," he said. "This is going to table twenty. Would you mind running the sauces for me? They're on the counter."

Since he had so politely identified himself, Adrienne could hardly say no, even though his request put her back in the kitchen. She pushed through the door, narrowly missing Bruno with another fondue pot. Adrienne shrieked—to have splattered Bruno with hot oil on her first night! Fiona shot Adrienne a look of blue fire, then called out, "Ordering table fourteen: one sword, three frites—rare, medium rare, medium well, two clubs, one duck SOS, two sushi, and a lamb killed for Mr. Amman-Keller. It appears he didn't learn anything about food over the winter. Can I help you, *Adrienne*?"

The use of her name threw her. "Sauces?" she squeaked.

"Who has time to get the girl some sauces?" Fiona said. "Eddie?"

A wicked laugh came from the garde-manger station. The rest of the cooks didn't even deign to answer. There were six sauté pans on the range and Adrienne watched a piece of marinated swordfish hit the grill. One of the cooks pulled a pan of steaks from the oven. Paco lowered a batch of fries into the oil.

Fiona checked the tickets hanging like they were pieces of laundry she wanted to dry. "I don't have time for this," she said.

"Joe said they'd be out on the counter," Adrienne said.

"Someone else took those."

"Can you tell me where to look?"

Fiona stormed away. Adrienne watched Eddie construct the lobster club sandwich; she was hungry again. Someone spoke up from behind the pass. "You'd better go with her, girlfriend."

Adrienne hurried after Fiona's braid, her slides clomping even worse in here with the cement floor. Fiona, Adrienne noticed, was wearing black clogs. They stepped into a huge refrigerator. "This is the walk-in," Fiona said. She used the overly patient, patronizing voice of a teacher speaking to a very stupid pupil. "The sauces are parceled out and kept in here." She handed Adrienne four bowls that comprised a lazy Susan that went around the fondue pot. "Cocktail, goddess, curry, horseradish. Please identify the sauces when you put them on the table."

"Yes, chef," Adrienne said. Then wondered if that sounded snide. She took the bowls from Fiona. "Thank you for your help." She wanted to say something to save herself. "Your cooking is the best I've ever tasted. You probably hear that all the time."

Fiona shook her head, said nothing.

On the way back to the hot line, Adrienne spied Mario standing at a marble-topped table in a back enclave of the kitchen. He wore surgical gloves and was blasting the top of a crème brûlée with a blowtorch. He was listening to something on a Walkman that was making him dance. When Adrienne and Fiona walked by, he whistled.

"That's enough, Romeo," Fiona called out. "I know you're not whistling at me."

"You got that right, chef," he said.

Adrienne was too embarrassed to breathe.

Back at the pass, the tickets had multiplied in the thirty seconds that they'd been gone. Adrienne had belly flopped with Fiona, and now she had to worry about how to lift the fondue pot to get the sauces in place.

Someone from the line called out, "Eighty-six the sword."

"Damn it!" Fiona shouted, so loudly and angrily that Adrienne nearly dropped the sauces. "How did that happen?"

"We're out of ripe avocados," the cook said. "I thought there was a whole other crate, but I just checked them and they're hard as rocks. You want to put a different sauce on the fish?"

"No," Fiona said. She yanked a ticket down and studied it. "Hey, Adrienne! You want to fly to California and get us some ripe avocados? If you need an escort, Mario will happily join you."

The guys on the hot line hooted. Adrienne smiled weakly. She was being teased. Adrienne took it as a possible sign of improvement.

She ran the sauces to Cat at table twenty, she fetched a bottle of Laurent-Perrier from the wine cave for Bruno, she checked in with the table of women—all enjoying their appetizers. The local author's table was on their third round of cocktails; they'd decimated two baskets of pretzel bread and one of the doughnuts, but hadn't ordered a thing. Caren was growing frustrated. "They're not getting their fucking chips until they order," she growled in Adrienne's ear. "And if the kitchen runs out of beluga, it will serve them right."

As Adrienne walked by Holt Millman's table, Drew Amman-Keller flagged her down. She stopped, confused. He indicated that she should bow to him.

"Can I help you?" she asked.

"I'm glad everything worked out," he said.

"Excuse me?"

"For you. With the job."

Drew Amman-Keller's voice was melodious, like a radio announcer's. She didn't remember that from the ferry ride.

"Yes," she said. "Thank you for suggesting it. It's only my first night, but . . ." Okay, wait. She wasn't supposed to be talking to this guy. If Thatcher found out she already knew him, he might fire her. Before Adrienne could escape, Drew Amman-Keller pressed some money into her hand.

"One is for you," he said. "And one is for Rex."

"Rex?"

"The piano player. Would you ask him to play 'The Girl from Ipanema'?"

Adrienne nodded and turned away. She hid behind a pillar and checked the bills. Two hundreds. Adrienne stared at the money for a few silly seconds. What to do? She clomped over to Rex.

" 'The Girl from Ipanema,' please," she said. "For Holt Millman's table."

"As ever," he said wearily.

Since he didn't have a cup out, Adrienne left one of the hundreds on the ledge above the piano keys. Rex eyed her quizzically. Was there another place she was supposed to put it? It did look crass, a hundred dollar bill laid out on the piano. She picked it back up. "I'll give it to you on your break?" she said. He nodded. She put the two bills from Public Enemy Number One in her pocket. Rex played "The Girl from Ipanema."

By the time desserts went out, coffee, and after-dinner drinks, it was midnight. Adrienne went to the ladies' room and nearly fell asleep on the toilet. How would she keep this up all summer? It felt like she'd been here seven days, not seven hours. And even worse—she was starving! The steak frites at family meal was another lifetime ago. Back when she was young, naïve, and . . . poor. She had two hundred dollars in tips now and eight hours of work would bring two hundred more. It was all going right into the bank. At this rate, she could pay her father back by the end of the week.

She emerged from the ladies' room as some tables were leaving. Thatcher bid everyone good-bye and Adrienne took her place next to him at the podium, the two of them waving like Captain Stubing and Julie McCoy from *The Love Boat.*

"We're lucky tonight because there isn't any bar business," Thatcher said. "Tomorrow night the bar will be mobbed."

"Great," Adrienne said.

"I'm going to do a sweep," Thatcher said. "See if I can get table eighteen to move things along." That was the author's table. They had only now received their entrées. "You stay here."

The author's table were just cutting into steaks and two tables out in the sand were still eating fondue. If these tables ordered dessert, they had a good forty minutes left. Everybody else was paying the bill or close to it.

Holt Millman's party stood up to leave. Adrienne kept her eyes on Drew Amman-Keller. Thatcher had made it sound like he might try to sneak into the kitchen, but he simply slid on his blazer and meandered toward the door with the rest of Holt's contingency. Adrienne murmured good-byes. Drew Amman-Keller ushered everybody out the door ahead of him in a way that seemed very polite. Then he turned to Adrienne and handed her a business card.

"Good to see you again," he said. "Call me if you ever want to talk."

Adrienne was so startled that she laughed—"ha!"—sounding just like Thatcher.

Drew Amman-Keller disappeared out the door.

Adrienne checked out his card, but then the husband–wife Realtor team was on top of her, and so Adrienne slipped the card into her pocket with her tips. Cat and her husband followed on the Realtors' heels.

"The fondue was phenomenal," Cat said. "Is Fiona coming out to take a bow?"

Adrienne laughed, like this was a joke. "I'll tell her you said hello."

A second later, Thatcher reappeared. "Where's your champagne?"

"You're kidding, right?"

"Go to the bar," he said. "Right now. That's an order."

Huck Finn, fascist dictator, she thought as she limped toward the bar. She wanted a blue granite gravestone. The entire waitstaff was crowded around the bar and she could barely wedge her way in. They were eating from two baskets. The crackers. They were eating the crackers. Adrienne had no hope of getting even a crumb; she was the runt at the trough. But then Joe, whom she barely remembered in the blur of new faces, turned around and gave her a handful.

"Thanks for running those sauces."

Adrienne accepted the crackers like a hungry beggar. She gobbled the first cracker and it was so delicious that she let the second one sit on her tongue until it melted in a burst of flavor. It tasted like the crisped cheese on top of onion soup that she used to devour after a day of skiing. But better, of course, because everything that came out of this kitchen was better.

Two more baskets of crackers were delivered to the bar and Adrienne was able to procure another handful. Thatcher waved at her from the podium. More tables were leaving. Rex played "If." Adrienne put her crackers on a napkin, and went to help Thatcher send the guests on their way. The bank president palmed Adrienne some money. The redhead from the all-women table touched the sleeve of Adrienne's blouse.

"I own a women's clothing store in town called Dessert," she said. "If you come in, I'd love to dress you, free of charge."

Mack Peterson, manager of the Beach Club, who was another sandy-haired Midwesterner, shook Adrienne's hand and assured her he would only send her his best clients.

"You know, Mack," Thatcher said. "This girl used to work at the Little Nell in Aspen. She's a hotel person."

"Well, if you ever want to come back from the dark side," Mack said, "we'd love to have you."

"I'll keep that in mind," Adrienne said, though she had to admit, after only one night she was hooked on the restaurant business. Yes, she was in pain and she was exhausted. But she wasn't trading in this job. She loved it and it wasn't just because of the money—it was because of the crackers.

Hunger and thirst, she thought. *They'd get you every time.*

3

See and Be Scene

Andrew Amman-Keller
Journalist

P.O. Box 383
Providence, RI 05271

P.O. Box 3777
Nantucket, MA 02584

Cell: 917-555-5172
aakack@metronet.net

When Caren emerged from her bedroom the next morning, her hair was down. It was a good look for her, Adrienne thought. She looked softer, sexier, more approachable, which was handy since Adrienne wanted to approach her, first thing, on the subject of Fiona. Caren was wearing a white T-shirt that had the words LE TOINY stitched in red on the left breast. The T-shirt was just long enough to cover Caren's ass in what looked to be thong underwear. She beelined for her espresso machine.

"You want?" she asked Adrienne.

"No, thanks. I have tea." Ginger-lemon herbal tea that Adrienne drank for a hangover, which she was nursing right now. There had been six glasses of champagne before the night was over because after the last guests left (as it happened, the author's table) Duncan poured a drink for everyone on the staff and he had poured two glasses for Adrienne in the interest of finishing off the bottle of Laurent-Perrier. So that was a whole bottle over the course of one evening, probably four glasses too many. Adrienne had taken three Advil and chugged a glass of ice water when she got home, but she still felt dull and flannel-mouthed this morning. It was such a gorgeous day—so sunny and crystalline—that Adrienne had entertained thoughts of going for a jog. But her legs ached too much. She was excited to have the whole day to herself—well, until five o'clock—and she wished she could just shrug off the pain and enjoy it.

So the tea. And three more Advil. She wanted to go to the beach again, with sunscreen. She wanted to buy a pair of quiet shoes and send the first installment of payback to her father. But mostly she wanted to figure out what was going on at that restaurant. The place had mystique that seemed to come from a flurry of secrets, some of them just below the surface and some of them deeper-seated. And Adrienne had her own secret, which now that she wasn't working, she had the luxury of thinking about: Thatcher had kissed her.

Last night after service, Duncan poured every member of the staff a drink except for Thatcher and Fiona. They were back in the kitchen counting money and eating dinner. Eating dinner at one o'clock in the morning! This information was served up by Bruno. Fiona and Thatcher ate in the small office that had a back door that opened to the beach. Adrienne had had enough to drink to accept this tidbit from Bruno then ask for more. "So what's the deal with those two, anyway? Are they an item?" And Bruno, who was drinking a vodka martini, laughed so shrilly that there was no room for speculation: The man was gay. When Adrienne asked why he was laughing, Bruno only laughed harder. He was turning heads; Duncan popped him in the eye with a lime wedge. Adrienne judged that the moment had come to either leave or make an ass of herself. She called a cab from the podium and waited for the cab outside, hoping Bruno didn't share the nature of their conversation with anyone.

The espresso machine geared up; it was as loud as an airplane ready for takeoff. Adrienne tried to select the least intrusive and obvious words to broach the subject of Fiona. When the espresso was done, Caren poured herself a tiny cup, threw it back like a dose of cough medicine, and poured herself another. Adrienne shuddered. At least she hadn't vomited; those crackers at the bar had saved her life.

"So what did you think of last night?" Adrienne asked.

Caren shrugged. "What did *you* think?"

"It was fun," Adrienne said. In retrospect, the night seemed like a manic blur, as if she had been backstage at a rock concert, blinded by the lights, deafened by the music—and yes, pursued by journalists. "My feet hurt. It was a lot of standing up. My shoes were all wrong."

Caren tossed back the second espresso. "Well, yeah."

"I'm going to buy some new shoes today."

"Go to David Chase," Caren said. "Main Street."

"Okay."

Caren smiled in a knowing way. "Did you make money last night?"

"Yeah. A lot."

"Me, too. As a rule, though, never tell how much you bring in. Everyone is so damn greedy. And something else you might not know is that if you have someone helping you out in the kitchen, you should slide him money every once in a while."

"Like Mario?" Adrienne said.

"Mario?" Caren said. A mischievous smile spread across her face. "Mario might help you out, but it's nothing you should pay him for. Did he come on to you *already*?"

"No," Adrienne said. Why had she said Mario? She hadn't meant Mario, she'd meant Paco, the chip kid.

"Don't be surprised if he does," Caren said. "He's a ladies' man. As charming as they come and a great dancer, but *truh-bull.* Anyway, I was talking about one of the guys on the line. Hector, Louis, Henry . . ."

"Paco?"

"Exactly," Caren said. "Some time this weekend, give Paco fifty bucks. He'll be on your team for the rest of the summer. I always tip out the guys in the kitchen and they time my food perfectly. They slide me snacks. And Fiona likes it. She thinks the money we make on the floor is a cardinal sin."

Fiona's name was as bright as an open door. All Adrienne had to do was step through.

"I wanted to ask you about Fiona," Adrienne said.

Caren turned away. She opened a cabinet and brought down another espresso cup, which she filled. Adrienne was confused, and worried that the espresso was meant for her. Then she became even more confused because she heard the toilet flush in the hall bathroom. Was there someone else in the house? A few seconds later, a half-naked man sauntered into their kitchen. Adrienne tried to keep her composure. Never mind that her vague but very important overture was floating away like a released balloon. Never mind that because the shirtless man in their kitchen was Duncan. He was wearing his khaki pants from the night before. Adrienne could see one inch of the top of his boxers—they were white with black martini glasses. His brown hair was mussed and Adrienne was temporarily mesmerized by his bare torso. His beautiful chest and arms, a black cord choker around his neck with a silver key on it. He must have noticed her staring because the first thing he did was hold the key out to show it to her. "This opens my ski locker at the Aspen Club Lodge," he said. "Where did you work?"

Adrienne was reminded of her ex-boyfriend Michael Sullivan. Sully was a golfer and he loved golf lingo. In this instance, he would have suggested Adrienne *play through.*

"The Little Nell."

"And your friend? She worked there, too?"

"Kyra. Yep."

"You got a pass with the job?"

"Of course."

"How many days did you ski?"

"I didn't keep track."

Duncan nodded thoughtfully, and Adrienne could tell he was swallowing the urge to brag about how many days he'd skied. Men were like that—Doug, for example, had marked the days on his calendar when he got six runs in. Duncan accepted the espresso from Caren. He threw it back and Caren poured him another.

The kitchen, like the rest of the rental cottage, was unremarkable. The appliances were all about fifteen years old and barely functional. There was a white Formica counter, three ceramic canisters decorated with sunflowers, two magnets hanging on the fridge from a liquor store on Main Street called Murray's. Adrienne sat drinking her tea at a round wooden table that had been sawed in half so it would sit flush against the wall. And yet, in this humdrum room, a drama unfolded—well, maybe not a drama, but a situation that Adrienne never would have guessed on her own.

Duncan and Caren were sleeping together. Or had slept together last night.

The sight of Caren's hair down and the knowledge of her thong underwear and the smooth, tan skin of Duncan's chest and the flushing toilet—had he even *closed the door*?—only served to make Adrienne hot and uncomfortable. So, too, the way they stood at the counter with their tiny cups of poison like two strangers at a bar in Milan.

Adrienne moved to the microwave and heated her tea, which had grown cold. Thirty seconds—with her back to them, they felt free to touch. Adrienne heard the sucking noises of kisses. The microwave beeped and Adrienne took her tea, retreated down the hall.

"You don't have to leave," Caren said.

"Oh, I know," Adrienne said quickly, though there was no way she was going to be part of their postcoital espresso ritual. "I have to send some e-mail."

She would write to her father with the news of Holt Millman, the six hundred dollars in tips and a basic celebration that she had survived an entire night in the restaurant business. The e-mail to Kyra in Carmel would detail the first scoop of the summer—Adrienne working at the same restaurant as Duncan and Duncan sleeping with Adrienne's roommate. But before Adrienne turned on her computer, she studied the business card from Drew Amman-Keller. Something was going on at the restaurant that he wanted to know about, and Adrienne intended to find out what it was. She would not stand by, blissfully unaware, while the person closest to her robbed her blind. Not this time.

Adrienne's second night at the restaurant was called "first night of bar," and the place had a different feel. The nervous anticipation of soft opening had vanished and in its place was "we mean business." Everyone was paying tonight.

We mean business. When Adrienne arrived, Thatcher inspected her outfit: tonight, the sensational Chloe dress and a new pair of shoes.

"I know you suggested slippers," Adrienne said. "But a dress needs heels."

"It's okay," Thatcher said. "I like the shoes."

"Do you?" Adrienne said. They were Dolce & Gabbana thong sandals with a modest heel, in pink leather with black whipstitching. The pink of the leather matched the trim of the Chloe dress as well as her pink pants, and the salesperson at David Chase assured her that a thong sandal would be more comfortable, not to mention quieter, than a slide. They had cost Adrienne more than half of her cash earnings of the night before, but as soon as she tried the shoes on, she'd been hooked. She never imagined owning such gorgeous shoes, especially since she was in such dire straits. However, she felt that after the rigors of her first night, she deserved a treat.

"I like the dress, too," Thatcher said. "It suits you better than the pants did. But I don't know—we have to work on defining a look for you."

"I don't want a look," Adrienne said.

"You will when we find the right one."

Thatcher was both charming and annoying her. Or annoying her because he was charming. She wanted to whipstitch his mouth shut. Thatcher had his own look: the Patek Philippe, the Gucci loafers, and tonight a gorgeous blue shirt with pink pinstripes and pants that were halfway between khaki and white. The navy blazer. He looked wonderful but that, too, irritated her. She liked him better as she had first seen him—in jeans and sneakers. The dress-up clothes and the watch made it seem like he was trying too hard. But she was being mean. He smiled at her in a warm, genuine way then offered his arm and escorted her to the twelve-top for menu meeting.

After menu meeting came a delicious family meal: fried chicken with honey pecan butter, mashed potatoes, coleslaw. As Adrienne slathered her fried chicken with butter she thought happily of all the money she would save on food this summer. She ate without looking left, right, or toward the water. She would not be cheated out of one bite of this meal! When all that remained on her plate were chicken bones and a film of gravy, she raised her eyes to the rest of the staff. Caren sat across from her with her hair back in its usual tight bun. Duncan ate at the other end of the table with his sister.

That morning, after Duncan had driven off in his black Jeep Wrangler, Caren tapped on Adrienne's door. Adrienne was standing in front of her mirror diligently applying sunscreen to her face and chest. Caren was still in just the T-shirt, but now that Duncan had left, her face had changed; instead of glowing, she looked tired, artificially revved up on jet fuel.

"I'm sorry if Duncan freaked you out," Caren said.

"He didn't freak me out."

"I wasn't planning on bringing him back here. It just sort of happened."

"Believe me, I understand," Adrienne said.

"I've known him a long time," Caren said. "I guess with this being the last year and all, we both felt a little funny. Like it's now or never."

"You don't have to explain," Adrienne said. "I don't care who sleeps over."

"Nobody else knows about this," Caren said.

"I'm not going to tell," Adrienne said. "I don't even know anyone's name."

Adrienne cleared her plate and silverware into the bins and collected her yellow pad from the podium. Thatcher gnawed on a pencil as he went over the reservations.

"Are you ready for a briefing?" he asked.

She held up her pad. "I'm supposed to be managing these people," she said. "And I don't even know who they are." She headed back to the table.

Adrienne assured each member of the staff that this reconnaissance mission was for names only—she wasn't a cub reporter for the tabloids and she didn't work for the IRS. Still, she found that no one was content to state only his name, and so she learned other things as well. The new waiter with the bushy hair and weak chin was named Elliott Gray. He was getting his doctorate in Eastern religions at Tufts. The good-looking waiter with the gold earrings was Christo. He had been a waiter at the Club Car for seven years, the whole time waiting for a job to open up at the Bistro. The blond ponytail was Spillman—this was actually his last name, his first name was John. Spillman, along with Caren and Bruno, had worked at the bistro since the beginning. Spillman was married to a woman named Red Mare who was part Native American; she worked as a hostess at the Pearl. Then there was Joe, the black waiter, who in addition to being a waiter, worked in the kitchen. He wanted to be a chef, but he earned too much money waiting tables to make the switch. Fiona paid him to do prep work in the morning. That morning, he told Adrienne, he had been in charge of making the "pearls" of zucchini and summer squash that accompanied the duck. He made the pearls with a parisienne scoop, something the French invented to make lives like his miserable. "Now that," Joe said, "was hard work."

The busboys were Tyler, son of the health inspector, whom Adrienne had already met, and Roy and Gage. Roy had just finished his junior year at Notre Dame. He called Thatcher for a job after reading about the restaurant in *Notre Dame* magazine, an article Adrienne had missed at the public library. She made a mental note to go back and read it. Gage was older, with long hair in a ponytail and a face that looked like it had been stamped by too much loud music, too many cigarettes, and too little sleep. He said he'd met Thatcher at an AA meeting.

It was a lot of names but Adrienne was good with names. And although she was mostly worried about the front of the house, she decided to ask Joe about the kitchen staff.

"Eight guys work back there," he said. "They're all cousins. Last name Subiaco, they're from Chicago, they're Cuban-Italian and proud of it. Most importantly, they're White Sox fans. Mario brought the whole gang here in 'ninety-three when the place opened. He knew Fee from culinary school."

"Mario, the pastry chef?"

"He's a lady slayer," Joe said. "He calls himself King of the Sweet Ending and he doesn't mean desserts."

Adrienne blushed. "Well, I'm not writing that down."

"You asked," Joe said.

It was ten minutes before service, and Adrienne returned to the podium. Her notebook had some actual information in it now.

"Champagne," Thatcher said.

Adrienne sighed. Duncan was wiping down the bar. She felt strange knowing that under his seersucker shirt and Liberty of London tie was the black cord and the key. She walked over. He saw her, and with a quick flourish of his wrist, Adrienne heard the new sound of *we mean business*: a cork popping.

We mean business. The tablecloths were white and crisp, the irises fresh, the glasses polished, the candles lit. The waiters lined up for inspection, a band of angels. Rex played "Someone to Watch Over Me." Cars pulled into the parking lot. The well-dressed, sweet-smelling guests cooed at Thatcher and some of them at Adrienne. She received four compliments on her shoes. Cocktails were ordered and two glasses of Laurent-Perrier and then a bottle. The pretzel bread went out. The doughnuts. The sun began its descent toward the water, and the guests watched it with the anticipation of the ball dropping in Times Square. It was New Year's Eve here every night.

A man at table twelve beckoned Adrienne over with an impatient finger wagging in the air, and immediately the spell was broken. Didn't he notice her dress, her shoes, her champagne? She was the hostess here, not his bitch.

"Yes, sir, can I help you?"

He held up the basket of doughnuts. "What are *these*? If I'd wanted to eat at Krispy Kreme, I would have stayed in New York."

Adrienne stepped back. The man had very close cut ginger-colored hair and so many freckles that they gave him patches of disconcertingly brown skin. He wore strange yellow-lensed glasses.

Adrienne glanced at the basket but did not take it from the man. Table twelve: she tried to remember if he was a VIP.

"Have you tasted the doughnuts?" she asked. "They're not sweet—they're onion and herb doughnuts. If I do say so, they're delicious."

The woman to the man's left had very short black hair and the same funny glasses with lavender lenses. "I'll try one, Dana."

The man named Dana thrust the basket at Adrienne's nose. "We don't want doughnuts."

"But you haven't tried them. I assure you, if . . ."

"We don't want doughnuts."

Adrienne took the basket, but the man, Dana, was holding on tighter than she expected so the exchange took on the appearance of a struggle. The basket zinged into Adrienne's chest. There was a smattering of applause and both Adrienne and the man named Dana pivoted to face the rest of the room. The applause was for the sun, which had just set.

"Would you like bread and butter, sir?" Adrienne asked. "Or we have pretzel bread. That's served with the chef's homemade mustard."

"You have *got* to be kidding me."

"I'll get you bread and butter, then."

"Yes," Dana said. "Do that."

Adrienne walked away thinking *Asshole, asshole, asshole!* What could she do to get back at him? Order the chips and dip for all the tables surrounding his? Run her tongue across the top of his perfect cake of sweet butter?

She searched for a busboy, but they were all humping—pouring water, delivering doughnuts—so that now the worst thing about the ugly freckled man who looked at the world through urine-colored glasses was that he was forcing Adrienne into the kitchen.

She pushed through the door. Hot, bright, quiet. Eddie wolf-whistled and Adrienne felt all eyes on her. Including Fiona's.

"Did you get those avocados?" Fiona asked.

Adrienne had spent a good part of her day at the beach wondering how to get Fiona to like her. But now, thanks to a man named *Dana,* she was in no mood to be joked to or about. "No, chef."

"What are you doing in here, then? It will be at least another six minutes for the chips. Right, Paco?"

Pfft, pfft, pfft. "Right, chef."

Adrienne put the doughnuts on the counter in a way that indicated slamming without actually slamming.

"If table twelve wanted to eat at Krispy Kreme, he would have stayed in New York."

"The salient phrase there is 'stayed in New York,' " Fiona said. "And people wonder why I don't come out of the kitchen."

"Is there bread, chef?"

"Of course."

"Where?"

"We went over this last night, did we not? The bread is where the bread is kept."

"I don't know where that is," Adrienne said. "You never told me. So, please. Chef."

Fiona eyeballed her for a long time, long enough to indicate a showdown. *Fire me,* Adrienne thought. Fire me for asking for bread for a man who looks like one of the villains in a Batman comic. But instead of yelling, Fiona smiled and she became someone else completely. She went from being a little fucking Napoleon to a china doll. She reminded Adrienne of her favorite friend from Camp Hideaway, where she had been shipped the summer her mother was dying. In the second that Adrienne was thinking of this other girl—her name was Pammy Ipp; she was the only girl at camp that Adrienne had told the truth—Fiona left and reappeared with a basket of rolls and the butter. So Adrienne still had not learned where the bread was kept.

"I told him how good the doughnuts were," Adrienne said.

Fiona rolled her blue eyes. "Get out of here," she said.

Table twelve was turning out to be a real problem. Adrienne delivered the bread and butter with a smile, but a few minutes later she saw Spillman engaged in a heated conversation with the man named Dana over what appeared to be his bottle of wine. Spillman tasted the wine himself then carried the bottle, gingerly, like it was an infant, over to Thatcher at the podium. Adrienne was chatting with an older couple at table five—neighbors of the Parrishes as it turned out—but when she saw this happening, she excused herself. She wanted to know what was going on.

"What's going on?" she asked Spillman.

"The guy's a menace," Spillman whispered. "He ordered a 1983 Chevalier-Montrachet at four hundred dollars a bottle and he claims it's bad. I tasted it and it tastes like fucking heaven in a glass. But Menace says he has a cellar full of this wine at home and he knows how it's supposed to taste, which is not like this. I asked him if he wanted me to decant it because the wine's been in that bottle for over twenty years, it could probably do with a little elbow room, and he just said, 'Take it away.' He said they're going to stick with cocktails. He orders the most expensive bottle on the list and now suddenly he wants vodka. Plus, he harassed me about the apps. He insisted he wanted the foie gras *cooked through.* Fiona said it would taste like a rubber tire. I hope it does."

Adrienne looked at Thatcher. He seemed on the verge of a smile.

"It's not funny," she said. "The guy gave me a hard time about the doughnuts. He said if he wanted to eat at Krispy Kreme he would have stayed in New York."

"That's an old one," Spillman said. "I hear that one every year."

Thatcher checked the reservation book. "The reservation was made four weeks ago by his secretary." He scribbled a note in the book then pointed the eraser end of his pencil at Adrienne. "Okay, that's the last time we take a reservation from a secretary. Except for Holt Millman. His secretary is a great lady named Dottie Shore. Not only did I give her the private number, I gave her my home number. But nobody else makes a reservation through a secretary. If they want to eat here, they have to call us themselves. It's a little late in the game to be making up new rules. However"—Thatcher turned to Spillman—"we'll offer the wine by the glass as a special. Twenty dollars a glass, only six glasses available and that's a bargain. We'll take a hit on the bottle. Adrienne, I want you to offer table twelve a round of cocktails on the house."

Adrienne gasped. "Why?"

"The guy obviously had an unhappy childhood. He's angry for whatever reason, he wants something from us. We could send him out the caviar, but we don't like him. So we'll give him drinks. And I'm going to let you be the hero."

"I'd rather not go over there again," Adrienne said. "Spillman can do it."

Spillman had already walked away; Adrienne watched him present the bottle to Duncan at the bar.

Thatcher took Adrienne's shoulder and wheeled her toward the dining room. "I'm going to let you be the hero," he said. "Old-fashioned service. You said you knew all about it."

Adrienne straightened the seams of her dress and tried to straighten out her frame of mind as she headed to table twelve. She put her hand on the back of Dana's wicker chair; she couldn't bring herself to touch him and she wasn't sure she was supposed to. "We're sorry about the bottle of wine," she said. "We'd like to buy you a round of drinks on the house."

"Lovely," the woman in lavender glasses murmured. For the first time, Adrienne noticed the other couple at the table. They were in their fifties, distinguished-looking, Asian.

"Thank you," the Asian man said, dipping his head at Adrienne.

But Adrienne was waiting to hear from the man named Dana. She was the hero and she wanted him to acknowledge as much. He said nothing, and after a second Adrienne realized that he was one of those people who didn't have anything to offer unless he was angry or upset. He deserved an old-fashioned kick in the balls.

In two seatings, only one person ate at the bar—a man in his midthirties who wore a red sailcloth shirt over a white T-shirt. He smiled at Adrienne every time she passed by. Red Shirt chatted with Duncan and drank a glass of Whale's Tale Pale Ale. Then a huge portion of chips and dip came out. So the guy was a VIP. He was wearing jeans and driving moccasins. He had brown hair receding a very little bit and nice brown eyes. He looked kind and responsible, no flashy good looks, no whiff of creepy lying bastard. *Rule Three: Exercise good judgment about men!*

Red Shirt's appetizer was the beet salad. Adrienne liked men who weren't afraid to order a salad. When she wandered up to the bar to have her champagne glass refilled she actually bent her leg at the knee to show off her new shoes. Rex played "Waltzing Matilda," and Adrienne said, to no one in particular, "Oh, I love this song." Duncan introduced Red Shirt to Delilah, but Adrienne didn't catch his name. *Introduce me!* she thought.

Adrienne ran appetizers for Joe, she retrieved three bottles of wine from the wine cave, she replaced the toilet paper in the ladies' room, she delivered two checks and got a lesson on the credit card machine from Thatcher. When she found a second to float by the bar again, Red Shirt was eating the lobster club, the entrée Adrienne herself most wanted to try. She approached Thatcher at the podium.

"Nine bottles of Laurent-Perrier tonight," he said. "Our experiment is really working. I still have to teach you how to use the wine key. When you can open wine, that will free me up. And champagne. There's a nice quiet way to open champagne. I'll show you."

"Who's that sitting at the bar?" she asked.

Thatcher didn't even look up. "Jasper Zodl."

"Jasper Zodl?"

"JZ. He drives the delivery truck. He comes every morning at ten."

"Will you introduce me?"

"No."

"Why not?"

Conveniently, the phone rang.

The phone had been ringing all night. Half were reservation calls, half were inquiries about the bar. Was tonight, as rumor had it, first night of bar? This call was about the bar.

"The bar is open tonight until one," Thatcher said.

When he hung up, Adrienne said, "I heard about this huge bar scene, I heard about you hiring a bouncer and a line out into the parking lot, and yet, the only person at the bar is the delivery driver who is so undesirable you won't even introduce me."

"He's not undesirable," Thatcher said. "He's a very nice guy. As for the bar, you just wait. Wait and see."

Adrienne would have been just as happy if nobody had shown up. At the end of second seating, there was a problem with one of the guest's credit cards. She ran it and ran it and each time the machine informed her that the card was unacceptable but Adrienne wasn't about to tell the guest this when she had only learned the credit card machine that night and it could just as easily have been she who was unacceptable. So she kept Joe waiting, as well as the guests, who had told Adrienne that they wanted to get home and pay the babysitter. She didn't take the problem to Thatcher primarily because she thought it was time she worked through a crisis by herself but also because he had refused to introduce her to JZ.

Joe, whom Adrienne had initially characterized as heavyset now just seemed big and soft and rather handsome—his skin a chocolaty brown, distinct from the deep-fried russet color of the Subiacos. But even Joe, so polite and gentlemanly, had his limits. He glared at her as she ran the card again, punching the numbers in one by one.

"What the fuck is taking so long?" he said.

Adrienne brandished the card. "It's no good. I've run the card six times, three times manually, and I can't get a bite. You're going to have to tell them."

"And jeopardize my tip? No way, sister. You tell them."

Adrienne peered over Joe's shoulder at the table. The lovely dark-haired wife was sitting sideways in her chair; she was all wrapped up in her pashmina like a present, her Louis Vuitton clutch purse in her lap. The husband had his pen poised. There would be no lengthy calculations with the tip, forty, fifty, a nice round number on the generous side, a dashed off signature, and these people were *out the door.*

"Okay, I'll tell them," she said.

Joe studied the card, "Tell them it's expired," he said. "This card expired in May. Today is the second of June. Didn't Thatch tell you to check the expiration first thing?"

Of course he had. Adrienne hurried the card back over to the couple, explained the problem, and the man, with apologies, offered her an identical card with a different expiration, and Adrienne ran it without incident. Sixty seconds later the couple was breezing past her with a happy, rushed wave.

Thatcher in the meantime had asked Joe what the problem was—he had seen Joe and Adrienne conferring by the credit card machine as he chatted with one of the fondue tables out in the sand—and Joe had tattled.

Thatcher handed Adrienne another leather folder. "Run this. And always remember to check the expiration. I'm surprised you didn't learn that on your five front desks."

She wanted to tell him to go to hell, but she would be satisfied if nobody showed up for first night of bar, if the place didn't turn out to be as "wildly popular" as Thatcher and Duncan and *Bon Appétit* thought it was. Plus, she was tired again tonight. She'd had two glasses of champagne, two glasses of water, and a regular coffee loaded with cream and sugar. As the guests from second seating finished up and wandered toward the door, Adrienne stood at the podium and bid them good-bye, hoping nobody could tell that the podium was holding her up.

JZ rose from the bar—he had finished his meal with Mario's ethereal candy plate—and Adrienne thought he, too, was leaving. But he walked wide of the podium like he was headed for the men's room. Except he bypassed the men's room and pushed open the door of the kitchen.

The kitchen. Adrienne stared at the swinging door with dread. What had Thatcher said? *No guests allowed in the kitchen.* Adrienne waited a second to see if JZ would come flying out on his butt. She stopped Caren.

"That guy who was sitting at the bar—did you see him?—he went into the kitchen. He just . . . I didn't realize that's where . . . is that okay?"

"Who, JZ?" Caren said.

"Yeah."

"Well, you know who he is, right?"

"The delivery driver?" Adrienne said.

Caren laughed and pushed into the kitchen behind him.

And then, just when the restaurant was beginning to take on a sense of calm—Tyler, Roy, and Gage the only flurry of activity as they cleared tables and stripped them—the headlights started pulling into the parking lot. The first people to reach the door were four large college boys wearing oxford shirts over tie-dye and loafers from L.L. Bean. One of them had a black cord at the neck like Duncan's only this cord had a purplish bead on it. From Connecticut, Adrienne thought. Listened to Phish.

"Bar open?" the one with the necklace asked, and Adrienne surveyed the bar. Its four bar stools were deserted and Duncan was checking over his bottles while Delilah worked around him, replacing glasses. Adrienne held up a finger. Boys like this—boys like the ones she used to date at the three colleges she attended (Perry Russell, junior year at Vanderbilt, from Connecticut, listened to Phish)—now made her feel old and prim. Like a librarian.

She went over to check with Duncan; Thatcher was MIA. "Is the bar open?"

This was possibly the dumbest question of all time—why would tonight be called first night of bar if the bar wasn't open? But Duncan simply straightened his tie, squared his shoulders, punched a button on the CD player—R.E.M.'s "I Am Superman"—and said, "I'm as ready as I'll never be."

It was nearing eleven o'clock. The four boys shook hands with Duncan, claimed the bar stools with a whoop, and ordered Triple 8 and tonics. Adrienne returned to the podium. A couple on a date came in followed by a group of six women who called themselves the Winers, followed by two older men who informed Adrienne of her loveliness and told her they'd just finished an exquisite meal at Company of the Cauldron and wanted a nightcap. More women—a bachelorette party. The return of the local author and her entourage. By ten after eleven, Adrienne couldn't even see Duncan through the throng of people. He'd turned up the stereo and the floorboards vibrated under Adrienne's shoes. Headlights continued to pull into the parking lot.

Where, exactly, was Thatcher?

Caren and Spillman still had tables out in the sand finishing dessert, but the other waiters would be cashing out. Adrienne found Thatcher doling out tips from the cash box at a small deuce in the far corner of the restaurant.

"People keep pulling in," Adrienne said. "Where's the bouncer?"

"I was kidding about the bouncer," Thatcher said. "Go back up front. When Duncan gives you the 'cutthroat' sign, start your line. And then it's one for one. One person goes out, one person comes in."

"Is the line moving?"

"No."

"No," he said. "It never does."

"So some people stay in this line until closing?"

"Oh, sure," he said. He smiled at the adorable couple on their date and Adrienne could tell he recognized them but didn't remember their names.

"Eat," she said. She felt wonderful saying this. She knew better than to count on him!

It was midnight; only one hour left of this madness. As Thatcher walked into the kitchen, JZ emerged. They exchanged a few quiet words. Adrienne was so keenly interested in what they were saying that it took her a moment to notice the author and her entourage on their way out.

"We're going to the Chicken Box," the author said. "Want me to count off eight heads for you?"

"Please," Adrienne said.

So her line was less by eight—Adrienne was happy to see the young couple make it in—but there were still a dozen people in her line and now the person at the front was the wet-haired "friend" of Duncan. He glared at Adrienne in such an overtly malicious way that she considered asking him why he was wearing a marijuana leaf around his neck. Did he want people to know he smoked pot? Did he think it would encourage interest from the right kind of women? Her thoughts were interrupted when JZ handed her a basket of crackers.

"Thank you," Adrienne said. "Thank you, thank you."

"I'm JZ," he said.

Adrienne held out her hand. "Adrienne Dealey. The new assistant manager."

"I know. Fiona told me."

Adrienne tasted a cracker. They were a different kind tonight—cheddar with sesame seeds. Scrumptious. Wet Hair watched her eat the cracker with envy and Adrienne hoped he was hungry. She hoped that all he'd had for dinner were fries from Stubby's on the strip by Steamship Wharf.

"What did Fiona say?" Adrienne asked JZ.

"That the gorgeous brunette by the front door was Adrienne Dealey, the new assistant manager."

At this point, Wet Hair, who had been eavesdropping, felt entitled to join the conversation. "I had a feeling you were new," he said. "Otherwise you would have let me in."

Adrienne ignored him. "Did Fiona actually call me a gorgeous brunette?"

"No," JZ said. "I did." He pointed to the basket of crackers. "Please, help yourself. I have to make the rounds with these, then get out of here. I have a buddy at the airport waiting to fly me home."

"Fly you home?"

"I live on the Cape. Normally I take the boat back and forth every day."

"That's quite a commute."

"Lots of people do it," he said. "I sleep on the boat. And it pays the bills. Listen, it was nice meeting you."

Adrienne was so crestfallen he was leaving that even the pile of crackers didn't cheer her. She stacked them on the podium like so many gold coins. She watched JZ pass the basket to Delilah, the busboys, and Joe, who was left with a single cracker. Then JZ said good-bye to a bunch of people at the bar and headed for the door.

He waved to Adrienne on his way out.

"Bye," she said.

Wet Hair roused Adrienne from her reverie by tapping her arm. "He left, right? So I can go in?"

"No," she said.

Somehow, she got drunk. To avoid further conversation with Wet Hair, Adrienne concentrated on her crackers and her crackers made her thirsty so she drank her champagne. Someone in the bachelorette party decided to buy every woman in the restaurant a shot called prairie fire, which was a lethal combination of tequila and Tabasco. This same woman convinced Duncan to play "It's Raining Men" at top decibel and further convinced him to allow the bride-to-be to dance on the blue granite in her bare feet. Adrienne watched all this from the safety of the podium, thinking about how much more she would enjoy these shenanigans if she didn't have Wet Hair breathing into the side of her face. Then Caren appeared, wearing a black halter top that showed off her perfectly flat, perfectly tanned stomach, and a pair of low-slung white jeans. She was dressed like a twenty-year-old but she looked better than any twenty-year-old could ever hope to. Adrienne suddenly felt dowdy; here she was in Chloe and Dolce & Gabbana in an attempt to get away from the kid stuff.

Caren held out a shot glass, Adrienne's prairie fire, because she did, after all, qualify as a woman in the restaurant.

"Come on," Caren said. "Let's do them together."

Adrienne accepted the shot glass. Well, it was better than espresso.

They did the shots and Caren offered Adrienne a swig from her beer as a chaser. Adrienne's throat burned, her eyes watered. The bride-to-be was doing the twist on the bar, every man in the place looking up her Lilly Pulitzer skirt.

Then Caren screamed, "Charlie!"

She hugged the man with the wet hair. He threw Adrienne a look of enormous satisfaction and contempt over Caren's shoulder. Adrienne felt no remorse, only distaste that Caren should actually know this person.

"This is Charlie," Caren explained. "A friend of Duncan's. He doesn't have to wait."

Adrienne was just as happy to have Wet Hair leave her proximity. "Go," she said. The tequila and Tabasco had warmed her mood. "Enjoy."

The new head of the line was a kid who looked about twelve. He was short and had acne around his nose. *Do I have to card?* Adrienne wondered. She wasn't going to card. Her job was pure mathematics—one out, one in. She heard a deep, metallic thrum; it sounded like a gong. Adrienne looked to the bar to see Duncan holding an enormous hand bell, the kind used in church choirs. "Last call!" he shouted. Last call, music to her ears. Paco wandered past the podium still in his chef's whites, and Adrienne yelled out to him. She pulled a fifty-dollar bill out of her change purse, which was stashed inside the podium.

"You've been a big help," she said. "Thank you." She pressed the bill into Paco's hand.

"Thank *you*!" Paco said. "You want me to get you a drink?"

"Yes," Adrienne said, surveying the dancing, pulsing crowd. "Two."

She should have gone home when the restaurant closed—it was very late—but Caren told her about a party at the Subiaco house in Surfside. Practically the whole staff was going and Caren felt that Adrienne should go, too.

"To prove you're one of the gang," she said.

Adrienne agreed to go with Caren and Duncan in Caren's Jetta. She would stay for one drink then call a cab and be home in bed by three o'clock at the very latest. It wasn't until Adrienne was already ensconced in the backseat of the car that she realized Wet Hair Charlie was coming with them. The opposite door opened and he climbed in. Adrienne's enthusiasm flagged.

"I don't know about this," Adrienne said. "It's getting late."

"I figured you for a stick-in-the-mud," Charlie said.

"Come on," Caren said. "It'll be fun."

During the ride, Charlie pulled out a joint, lit up, and passed it around. Adrienne refused, then cracked her window. This was what she'd always thought the restaurant life would be like: two o'clock in the morning doing drugs on her way to a party where she would proceed to drink even more than she had drunk during her eight-hour shift. She laughed and then Charlie laughed, though he had no idea what was funny.

The Subiaco house was huge and funky. It had curved steps that led up to a grand front porch with a swing. The house had diamond-shaped windows, some panes of stained glass, and a turret. Inside, though, it was a bad marriage of down-at-the-heels beach cottage and urban bachelor pad. In the first living room Adrienne entered, the furniture was upholstered in faded, demure prints, there was a rocking chair and a few dinged tables. There was a second living room with a cracked leather sofa and a state-of-the-art entertainment system: flat-screen TV on the wall, surround sound, stereo thumping with ten-year-old rap. Adrienne couldn't stand the noise. She headed out to the sun porch, where there was wicker furniture and an old piano. She took a seat on the piano bench. Caren appeared, bearing two bright red drinks, and she handed one to Adrienne.

"What's this?" Adrienne asked.

"I don't know," Caren admitted.

Adrienne took a sip. It tasted like a mixture of Kool-Aid and lighter fluid. She put the drink down on the piano.

"Duncan didn't make this?"

"No," Caren said. "It was in a punch bowl on the kitchen table."

"They're trying to poison us so they can take our money," Adrienne said. She had left her change purse, with three hundred dollars in it, in Caren's car.

Duncan came onto the sun porch and he and Caren settled down on the wicker sofa. Then Charlie walked in and after looking around the room—no doubt hoping for better company—he plopped down on the piano bench next to Adrienne. That was all she needed.

"I'm getting out of here," she said.

"Stay," Caren said. "It's fun."

"Stick-in-the-mud," Charlie said.

Adrienne peeked into the next room. Elliott, Christo, and a few of the unidentified Subiacos were smoking cigarettes watching *Apocalypse Now* to a soundtrack of Dr. Dre. Fun? In the kitchen, Tyler and Roy, the most definitely underage busboys, were doing shots of Jägermeister. Adrienne thought she might get sick just watching them.

"Phone?" she said.

They pointed down the hall. She located a wobbly pie crust table where the last rotary phone in America rested on a crocheted doily.

Adrienne called A-1 Taxi but was unable to give them her exact location. "Out by the airport?" she said. "Surfside? It's a big house at the end of a dirt road? The Subiaco house?"

"Subiaco?" the cab driver said. "I'll be there in twenty minutes."

"Okay," Adrienne said. She went outside to retrieve her change purse from Caren's car and decided to wait for the cab on the bottom step of the porch. Then she heard someone whisper her name. She turned around. Mario was lying on the porch swing, drinking a beer. "What are you doing here?" he asked.

"I came to the party," she said, wondering if because she was a manager this would sound weird. She climbed the steps to the porch and leaned back against the railing, checking it first to make sure it wouldn't give way, dumping her into the bushes. "But I have to go home. I'm tired."

"You can sleep upstairs with me," he said.

"No, thanks," she said. "I've been warned about you."

"Oh, really?"

"The King of the Sweet Ending?"

Mario laughed. "Please," he said. "Just call me King." He drained his beer then sat up. He wore jeans and a black T-shirt. *There was something about him,* Adrienne thought. He emanated heat. Smoldered, like all the other womanizers she had ever known.

"How'd you get that scar on your neck?" Adrienne asked.

"Pulling a cookie sheet out of a high oven," he said. "A million years ago, in culinary school."

"You went to school with Fiona?"

"Met her in Skills One," he said. "It was a very tough class. We bonded." He laughed. "She's a big hotshot now but when I first met her she couldn't even carry a tray of veal bones, okay? We had to roast fifty pounds a day for stock and that's more than half Fee's body weight. Our instructor did a double-take when he saw her. He was like, 'How did a fourth grader get into our classroom?'"

Adrienne turned around to search the darkness for the lights of her cab. It felt dangerous to be talking about Fiona like this, though of course Adrienne was enthralled. "Was cooking school tough?"

"A killer," he said. He patted the spot next to him on the swing. "Sit here, I'll tell you all about it."

"I'm fine," Adrienne said.

"You got that right," Mario said. "If you're wondering how an inner city Cuban schlub like me got into the CIA, the answer is, I'm a minority." He laughed again. "And a fucking genius, of course."

Adrienne tried to smile but she was too tired. She checked behind her. Nothing.

"I'm only kid-ding," Mario sang out. "My whole family works in kitchens. My old man and his three brothers worked the line at the Palmer House in Chicago, and all the brothers had sons. There are eleven of us altogether and we all work in kitchens. My brother Louis was a prep cook at Charlie Trotter, Hector worked at Mango, Eddie flipped eggs at the North Side. I worked at so many places I can't even remember them all, but after high school I got tired of making five bucks an hour. I wanted to learn technique. So off I go to the best cooking school in the country and it kicked my ass. I nearly quit."

"Really?"

"I hated the hot line. Hated it. Now Fiona, she loved the hot line. The hotter and the busier it was, the more she liked it. The other guys worshipped her. Tiny little thing like that couldn't even get the veal bones from the oven to the counter and here she is doing eighty plates an hour, swearing like a sailor. She was the one who told me I belonged in pastry, but you know what I thought? Pastry is for chicks. So I got a big, brawny externship at the Pump Room back home and that made school look like *Sesame Street.* When I went back to the CIA and tried pastry, I realized there's worse things in life than being in a room full of chicks."

"I guess so."

"You like dessert?"

"Of course I like dessert."

"Everybody likes dessert," Mario said. "And pastry is cool, okay? It's quiet. It's solitary. It's a place where you have the time and space to lavish the ingredients with love. I'm all about the love."

He made the word "love" sound like a big soft bed she could fall into. Adrienne gripped the railing. *Rule Three!* She took a big drink of night air. It was absurdly late. She checked the gravel driveway and the dirt road again. She couldn't tell if the glow in the distance were headlights or lights from the airport.

"So you brought everybody here?" Adrienne said. "All your cousins."

"Three stayed back home," Mario said. "My brother Mikey is a lawyer. And Hector's twin brothers, Phil and Petey, didn't want to leave Chicago. They work together at the hottest sushi place in the city and have season tickets to the Bulls. So."

"So," Adrienne said. "What will you do next year, when the restaurant is closed?"

"Cry my eyes out," Mario said. "But it's far from over. We have a long summer ahead."

"Yeah," Adrienne said. It was going to be a very long summer if she didn't get any sleep. Her head felt like it was filled with dried beans. But then she saw headlights, actual true headlights and even better, the bright top hat of a taxi. The cab stopped in front of the house and the door popped open.

"Hey, everybody!" a voice called out. It was Delilah. She was, inexplicably, wearing a belly dancer costume—a red satin bra and transparent harem pants. She ran up the steps, dinging finger cymbals. Adrienne hurried past her, before the cab drove off. As she pulled away, Adrienne gazed back at the house in time to see Mario, ever the gentleman, leading Delilah inside.

TO: DrDon@toothache.com
FROM: Ade12177@hotmail.com
DATE: June 7, 2005, 8:37 A.M.
SUBJECT: See and be scene

At first I thought the Bistro was all about the food but after a week of work I can tell you, it's all about the drinks. It's a huge scene. Some nights it's like a fraternity party and some nights it's something else entirely (think of a dozen women in for a fiftieth birthday party belting out "New York, New York" while doing chorus line kicks). Last night, I let a man into the bar and he tipped me five hundred dollars. I told him I couldn't possibly accept it and he said, 'You want me to give it to the bartender instead?' So I put it in an envelope and mailed it off to you this morning. Only five hundred to go!

I never considered myself a night owl but since I started work I haven't gotten to bed before two. I sleep until at least eight then take a nap on the beach. I haven't gone jogging even once! But I am brushing and flossing and doing my best to stay away from the candy plate. How are the smiles in Maryland? Love.

TO: Ade12177@hotmail.com
FROM: DrDon@toothache.com
DATE: June 7, 2005, 8:45 A.M.
SUBJECT: Nobody knows the troubles I've scene

I'm not sure how I'm supposed to handle being the father of the doyenne of Nantucket nightlife. Should I be worried or proud? Or both? Mavis says she wants to visit Nantucket—I know I always promise and never come, but this time I think we might. Can you research some B & Bs? And book us a night at your restaurant, of course. I'd love to see my little girl in action. Love, love.

TO: DrDon@toothache.com
FROM: Ade12177@hotmail.com
DATE: June 7 2005, 8:52 A.M.
SUBJECT: Don't book 'em yet, Don-o

Let me get my sea legs before you show up, okay? Promise me you won't book anything without double-triple-checking with me first?

TO: Ade12177@hotmail.com
FROM: DrDon@toothache.com
DATE: June 7, 2005, 8:59 A.M.
SUBJECT: I promise

Love, love, love.

TO: kyracrenshaw@mindspring.com
FROM: Ade12177@hotmail.com
DATE: June 7, 2005, 9:04 A.M.
SUBJECT: sex, drugs, and lobster roll

Duncan has spent every night here for the past nine nights. They always look so tuckered out in the morning—thank God the walls are thick! Caren thinks it's this big secret, but one of the other waiters at work said he was pretty sure the only reason Duncan shacked up here was because he doesn't want to sleep in the same apartment with his sister. I, of course, pretended like I didn't know what he was talking about.

Aspen seems like a million years ago. I haven't thought about Doug in weeks. I miss you, though. How's Carmel? Seen Clint Eastwood?

4

Reservations

Adrienne wasn't sure how long her father's affair with Mavis had been going on. When he set up his dental practice in 1984, the office had three employees: Adrienne's father, whom everyone called Dr. Don, Adrienne's mother, Rosalie, who worked the reception desk, booked appointments, and did all the billing, and Mavis, the hygienist. Five years later, when Adrienne's mother got sick, Adrienne was old enough to fill in for her mother after school and on Saturdays—and to work during the week they had hired a retired woman named Mrs. Leech.

But there had always been Mavis with her blond Dorothy Hamill haircut, her smell of antiseptic soap, and the Juicy Fruit gum that she chewed to freshen her breath after lunch (despite Dr. Don's fatwa on chewing gum of any kind). When she was first hired, Mavis was a single mother with three-year-old twin boys named Coleman and Graham, who was deaf. Mavis's husband had left her and Mavis's family lived in the French part of Louisiana, which she described as a "stinking swamp." She had no desire to return. Adrienne's parents took pity on Mavis, especially Adrienne's mother, who was prone to fits of do-gooding. As a happy coincidence, it turned out that Mavis was a talented hygienist. She had a light touch, a Southern accent, and because she dealt on a daily basis with her deaf son, she took great pains to make her communications with children gentle and clear. How many times had Adrienne heard her go through the brushing spiel? *Now I'm just gonna put a little bit of paste on the brush—see, it tastes like bubble gum. Don't tell the doctor! The brush is gonna move in really fast circles so it might tickle a bit. You're laughing already, I can't bee-leeve it!*

It was impossible to think of Mavis without thinking of Rosalie, not only because Rosalie and Mavis were best friends, but also because as Rosalie's presence in Adrienne's life waned, Mavis's increased. Rosalie's illness came on very strong and suddenly. There might have been a clue in the fact that Rosalie had lost her first child in a hard labor, and after Adrienne, Dr. Don and Rosalie had not been able to conceive another child. But Rosalie's outlook was that some people were blessed with many children and some with only one, and she reveled in the fact that her one child was as well-adjusted and delightful as Adrienne. Then when Adrienne was eleven going on twelve (and was, at that age, neither well-adjusted nor delightful) Rosalie started having pains. She went to her gynecologist and came home looking like she had seen a ghost. A biopsy a week later at the Hospital of the University of Pennsylvania had diagnosed her with inoperable ovarian cancer and four to six months to live.

Adrienne knew these details now, as an adult, but at the time she had not been well-informed. Her father, a graduate of the dental school at Penn, was friends with the head of internal medicine at HUP and Adrienne was aware of her father's conversations with him and other doctors at the hospital. Initially, she thought it was Dr. Don who was sick because it was he who looked like he might die. Eventually both her parents sat her down and told her that Rosalie had cancer.

It was Mavis's idea to send Adrienne to Camp Hideaway in the Pocono Mountains. Adrienne didn't want to go. She claimed she wanted to help take care of her mother, but really she didn't want to leave her friends and she was addicted to *General Hospital* and she knew from reading the brochure that Camp Hideaway didn't have a single TV. She begged her father to let her stay home and when begging didn't work, she threatened him. She would run away. She would hitchhike. She would accept a ride with any stranger, even if it was a man with yellow teeth. Finally, Adrienne appealed to her mother. Adrienne knew her mother loved her to the point of distraction. Once she had snooped through Rosalie's desk, where she found a tablet on which Rosalie had written Adrienne's name a hundred times, and in the middle of the page, it said, "Unconditional love." When Adrienne spoke to Rosalie about camp, Rosalie said, "Please do as your father says. He and Mavis think it's for the best." Rosalie's tone of voice was distant; it was as if she were already gone.

Adrienne went to Camp Hideaway for six weeks, and when Adrienne looked back on her life, she could say that she went to Camp Hideaway as one kind of person and left as another. Her first day at camp was up and down. The cabin was musty, her top bunk stared right into the cobwebby rafters, her cabin mates were all scrawny and knew nothing about puberty, the bathhouse smelled like a chemical toilet, the water at the fountain tasted like rust, and the dining hall served stale potato chips. However, things improved during taps, the flag lowering, and the campfire where one very cute male counselor played the guitar. There was the promise of swimming the next day, and canoeing and a scavenger hunt. After lights out, in the dark musty cabin, where some of her cabin mates were actually *crying*, Adrienne started telling lies. She told the twelve girls she had just met that she had been sent to camp because her brother was dying. Maybe she had meant to say "mother," but she didn't. She said, very distinctly, "brother," and the girls were hooked. Adrienne felt bad almost immediately and wished that she could retract the claim or amend it, but there was no way to do so without being labeled a fake, a liar, a person to be gossiped about for the next six weeks. She told herself it wasn't a complete lie because Adrienne had had a brother once upon a time—her mother had delivered a stillborn baby three years before Adrienne, a baby named Jonathan. Adrienne had wondered for years about Jonathan and what he had looked like and whether or not he was technically her brother if he had died before she was even born. She wondered why Jonathan's name hadn't been on her mother's tablet with the words "Unconditional love." When the girls in her cabin asked her what her dying brother's name was, she told them, and saying it out loud had made him seem real.

On the last night of camp, Adrienne confessed the truth to Pammy Ipp. By this time, Adrienne and Pammy were such good friends that Adrienne wanted to set the record straight: It wasn't her brother who was dying, in fact, she had no brother. It was her mother who was dying.

Pammy Ipp had looked nonplussed. "Why didn't you just tell us that in the first place?" she said.

■

When Adrienne walked into her mother's hospital room upon her return home, she gagged. All of Rosalie's hair was gone; she looked like a health class skeleton, a space alien. The worst thing was that Rosalie seemed to know how hideous she looked and she told Adrienne that she didn't have to visit the hospital again if she didn't want to. Didn't have to visit her own sick mother!

Adrienne went home and cried. She was plagued by confusion and guilt. Why had she lied to her camp friends? Why had she bothered telling Pammy Ipp the truth at the last minute? Pammy hadn't said a proper good-bye that final morning and Adrienne had seen her whispering with the other girls. Telling them, probably. Adrienne had lied and her mother was getting worse, not better, and Adrienne felt responsible.

She begged her father to take her to the hospital every day. Rosalie wore head scarves or an old Phillies baseball cap. She and Adrienne drank Pepsi and watched *General Hospital* and they talked about Adrienne's friends at school. They did not talk about death, or even love, until the very end. Rosalie made it clear that the worst thing about dying would be leaving Adrienne behind without a mother. Adrienne wanted to ask her mother about the tablet she had found, she wanted to ask about Jonathan, and most of all, she wanted to confess to the insidious lies of the summer, but she didn't want to upset her mother or make her sicker. And then, the night before Adrienne was supposed to start seventh grade, Rosalie fell into a coma and died.

It was at the reception following the funeral that Adrienne decided to hate Mavis. Mavis called the school to say Adrienne wouldn't be starting for two weeks. Mavis made the tea sandwiches and her mother's favorite asparagus roll-ups; Mavis kept her arm around Adrienne's shoulders and steered her toward this person and that person who wanted to express their condolences. In the days following, Mavis prodded Adrienne to write thank-you notes for flowers and food. Despite these things, or perhaps because of these things, Mavis became the enemy. Adrienne was relieved—happy, even—when, a few weeks later, her father told her they were moving to Maine. Adrienne wanted to leave. The town where she lived had become a minefield—here was the road where Rosalie once got a speeding ticket, here was the expressway that led to the hospital, here was the cemetery where Rosalie was now buried. Adrienne wanted to leave her friends who barely understood what had happened and her teachers who fully understood and treated Adrienne so gingerly it was as though she was the one with the disease. But most of all, Adrienne wanted to leave Mavis.

They sold their house and moved to Maine at the beginning of November. By Christmas, Adrienne's father still hadn't hired a hygienist. He was doing every single cleaning himself and it was too much. Finally, he hired a young girl named Curry Jones who had just finished her hygiene courses. Because she was brand-new, Dr. Don figured he could train her to work just like Mavis. Curry Jones was a pretty girl with a permanent scowl. During every cleaning, she dug the probe into the patient's soft pink gums until blood sprang to the surface. Don fired her after two weeks.

He called Mavis in Philadelphia, he helped her find a school that would take Graham, and she relocated. The first thing she said to Adrienne upon arriving in the new office was, "I couldn't stand to think of your father working with that *sadist.*" That, Adrienne later realized, was probably when the affair started, less than six months after Rosalie's death. Adrienne was thirteen and the twins were eight. Adrienne was called on time and time again to babysit for them while her father and Mavis worked late. Adrienne had actually learned the alphabet in sign language.

Mavis followed them three years later to Iowa and eighteen months after that to Louisville, Kentucky. Dr. Don was a good dentist and he was respected and well-loved in each of his practices, but he didn't have staying power. Before this last move, to the eastern shore, he tried to explain it to Adrienne over the phone. He couldn't bear to have any place become his home.

"My home was with Rosalie," he said. One thing Adrienne felt glad about was that even though Don and Mavis had now been together longer than Don and Rosalie, Don did not refer to Mavis as his home. He still loved Adrienne's mother; he would always love her.

Adrienne didn't fault her father for his peripatetic nature; since graduating from high school, Adrienne hadn't stayed anywhere for more than two years. She couldn't count the number of times she had been asked, "Where's your home?" And when she couldn't provide an answer, the well-intentioned soul might ask, "Where does your mother live?" Even at twenty-eight years old, home was where her mother lived. Everywhere. Nowhere.

Adrienne was still in her pajamas, reading and rereading the e-mail from her father and worrying prematurely about a visit from him and Mavis, when the phone rang. Adrienne had heard the growl of the espresso machine a few minutes earlier, and so she knew Caren—and probably Duncan—were awake. The ringing stopped and Caren tapped on the door with her fingernails. She cracked the door and handed in the phone. "It's for you," she said. "It's Thatch."

Adrienne stared at the phone. She had yet to tell Thatcher the truth about her mother. She wanted to tell him but with all that was happening at the restaurant, there was never a good time. He was going to think she was a mental case.

"Hello?" she said.

"Can you come in?" Thatcher asked. "I know it's short notice, but I have reconfirmation calls from ten to noon and I forgot I'm supposed to meet with my priest."

Adrienne might have laughed, but a few nights earlier, a busy Saturday night, Thatcher and Fiona had both been an hour late because they attended five o'clock mass at St. Mary's. His meeting with a priest seemed to follow in this vein.

"I was there until two last night," she said. "And I was hoping to go to the beach today."

"I'll pay you," Thatcher said.

"Obviously."

"I'll have Fee make you lunch."

Adrienne smiled into the phone, thinking: teeth, clothes, her ten-speed bike. "I can be there in fifteen minutes."

According to her sports watch, it only took her twelve minutes to make it to the fork in the road, but that wasn't fast enough. She saw Thatcher driving toward her in his silver pickup on his way into town.

"Good, you're here," he said, though she was still three hundred yards from the restaurant. "I left the book open for you with a list of people to call to reconfirm. It's easy. Just remind them of their time and the number in their party and note any changes, any special requests. Birthdays, that kind of thing. Okay?"

Adrienne was dying to ask him why he was going to see a priest. "What if someone calls for a reservation?"

"Write down the name and number and I'll call back after twelve."

Adrienne saluted and Thatcher drove away.

Adrienne pedaled toward the Bistro. It was another glorious day—bright sunshine, crisp, clean sea air. She had worn her bikini under her clothes; after Thatcher returned, she was going to lie on the beach in front of the restaurant.

Adrienne had expected the restaurant to be deserted but there were five cars and a big Sid Wainer truck in the parking lot. The delivery truck. Adrienne's heart trilled at the thought of JZ, whom she hadn't seen since the first night of bar. A second later she caught a glimpse of him from the back, in uniform, engaged in a heated conversation. Adrienne stopped her bike behind the car she knew to be Fiona's—a navy blue Range Rover with tinted windows. Though she heard JZ's voice, she couldn't make out what he was saying. The back of his delivery truck was open, and in its dim interior she spied crates of lemons and limes, long braids of garlic, cartons of eggs, and a wooden box stamped HAAS AVOCADO—CALIFORNIA. Adrienne dismounted her bike and walked it closer to the front door. As she did, she heard one sentence very clearly. "I love you so much it's making me weak."

And then she heard someone answer. "It's not *enough,* JZ. It will never be enough."

Adrienne knew it was Fiona—of course, it was Fiona—but she had to get a visual. She peeked around the next closest car, Mario's red Durango. From there, she could see them: JZ in his olive drab pants and white uniform shirt, and Fiona in cut-off jean shorts, a pale pink tank top, and pink leather clogs. Both of them looked anguished, close to tears. And then Fiona started to cough, a deep wracking cough that sounded like she was trying to dislodge a piece of concrete from her lungs. It caused her to bend at the waist, one hand bracing her knee, one hand covering her mouth. JZ picked her up under her arms and pressed her tiny body against his. Fiona's clogs dropped from her feet. Adrienne couldn't tear her eyes away—she could sense Fiona's lightness and JZ's strength, their mutual sadness and rage—God, how long had it been since she felt that way about someone? Ever? Fiona continued to cough, her face hidden in JZ's shirt.

Adrienne leaned her bike against the geranium-filled dory and proceeded inside. It was, quite possibly, the most heartbreaking embrace she had ever seen.

The Bistro looked different during the day. It seemed tired and exposed, like a lady of the evening roused from sleep the next morning without her makeup. The tables were bare and the white wicker chairs had been flipped upside down on top of them so that the cleaning crew could do the floors. But the cleaning crew hadn't arrived yet, and the floor was covered with dropped food and sticky puddles.

Since she knew Fiona wasn't in the kitchen, Adrienne poked her head in. Half the crew was at work prepping. Joe was making the mustard in a twelve-quart stockpot. Adrienne watched him for a minute, in awe of the sheer volume of ingredients: a pound of dry mustard, five cups of vinegar, eight cups of sugar, a whole pound of butter, and a dozen eggs. Joe added sixteen grinds of white pepper from a pepper mill that was longer than his arm. Adrienne blew Joe a kiss, then she poked her head around the corner into pastry.

Mario was rolling out dough. She watched him flour the marble counter and work a huge mass of dough with his Walkman on.

When he saw her, he removed his headphones. "What are you doing here?"

"Working," she said. "What are you making?"

"Pies," he said. He checked his watch and wiped his brow on his shoulder. "And I have two kinds of ice cream to make. And a batch of marshmallows. And lemon curd. And I have pineapple to roast. And the rolls, but I save those for last."

"You're in the weeds, then?" she asked.

"Never me, baby," he said.

Adrienne wanted to ask him about Fiona and JZ, but she was afraid that either he wouldn't tell her what she wanted to know or else he would tell Fiona that she'd asked. So instead, Adrienne said, "How's Delilah?" (It came as no surprise to find out that, after the night of the harem pants and finger cymbals, Mario and Delilah were having a fling.)

"Oh, honey," he said. He cut twenty perfect rounds out of the dough and draped them into doll-sized pie pans.

"What?" Adrienne said.

"You want me to tell you about the sex?"

"No," Adrienne said.

"Then what did you ask about Delilah for?"

She was just making conversation. Anything so she could stay and watch Mario work. He moved the pie dough into the freezer and set a timer. Then he began the ice cream. He took a carton of sixty eggs from the walk-in and proceeded to separate the yolks from the whites by sifting the whites through his fingers.

"Some people think sugar is the key to desserts," Mario said. "But I am here to tell you that if you want a good dessert, you have to start with a fresh egg." He held out his palm, displaying a whole, perfect, bright orange yolk, which he slipped into his Hobart mixer.

"What do you do with the whites?" Adrienne asked. "Throw them away?"

"I use them in the marshmallows," he said. "Have you ever tasted one of my marshmallows?"

She shook her head.

"Lighter than air," he said. "I make the best marshmallows in the country, maybe the world."

"Okay, Marshmallow King," she said. "I have to get to work."

Mario replaced his headphones and separated another egg while doing the samba.

Back in the kitchen, Hector was peeling and deveining shrimp with a tool that looked like a plastic dentist's probe. He had a mountain of shrimp on his left and a mountain on his right—uncleaned and cleaned. He tossed the shells into a stockpot.

"That's a lot of shrimp," Adrienne said.

"Shrimp bisque," Hector said without looking up. "Shrimp toast, shrimp for fondue."

The oldest Subiaco, Antonio, a man with a mustache and gray hair around his ears, trimmed lamb. He worked so fast Adrienne feared he would cut himself, especially as he seemed intent on listening to what sounded like a baseball game being broadcast in Spanish on the Bose radio.

The baseball game broke for commercial and Antonio called out, "Where's the steak?"

"It's still on the truck," somebody answered.

"Well, go get it, Louis."

"No fucking way," Louis said. "They're out there fighting."

They're out there fighting. Adrienne hung around for a beat to see if anyone would respond to this, but no one did, and Adrienne took this as her cue to leave. As she stepped into the dining room, she bumped into Fiona. Fiona alone, her eyes pink and watery. She stopped when she saw Adrienne and brushed an imaginary hair from her face.

"Thank you for covering the phones," Fiona said. "I know I'm supposed to make you lunch, but I can't today. I have to get out of here for a while. I'll ask Antonio to do it. You know Antonio? He's my sous."

Adrienne smiled. "Sure. Whatever."

"What would you like?"

"Anything," Adrienne said. "I don't mean to complicate your day."

Fiona coughed—briefly, dryly—into her hand. "Fine," she said. "One anything. I'll have him bring it out to you in an hour or so."

Thatcher had left a list of fifty names and numbers. Eighteen reservations for first seating, thirty-two for second. About half the reservations were people staying at hotels and inns—three reservations from the Beach Club, two from the White Elephant, two from the Pineapple Inn. Next came a bunch of names that Adrienne, after a week of work, recognized: Parrish (six o'clock, of course, it was Tuesday,) Egan, Montero, Kennedy (no relation, though Mr. Kennedy was one of the investors, and Adrienne saw the word "comp" next to his name in the book), Jamieson, Walker, and Lefroy. This last name was underlined and followed by three exclamation points, and Adrienne realized that it was Tyler the busboy's parents—his father the health inspector. That's right, she remembered now: The cleaning crew was coming in late today so that everything had a better chance of staying spic-and-span. The staff was eating family meal out on the beach, picnic-style—sloppy joes, potato salad, and root beer handmade by Henry Subiaco, the sauté cook. If the root beer tasted good, Henry was going to try to market it next year when the restaurant was closed. Next year, when the restaurant was closed, Adrienne might have finally figured out what was going on while the restaurant was open. She glanced up to see Fiona rush out the front door. Through the window, Adrienne watched her climb, climb, climb (Pammy Ipp up the sycamore tree) into the cab of JZ's truck. They were in love. Adrienne felt victorious about this knowledge, despite the fact that she would now have to erase JZ from her shortlist of possible men to date.

The work Thatcher left seemed very straightforward. Taking reservations was another story; that involved the calculus of who fit where and what time and—most crucially—at which table. Apparently some guests got their feelings hurt over where in the restaurant they sat, so this was Thatcher's department. Adrienne called the first name on the list: Devlin. Next to the name Devlin, it said "birthday/dessert-candle/no chocolate."

A woman picked up on the first ring.

"Hello?"

"Good morning," Adrienne said. "Is this Mrs. Devlin?"

"Why, yes it is." The woman sounded both wary and hopeful, like maybe Adrienne was calling from Publishers Clearing House and maybe she'd won something.

"This is Adrienne calling from the Blue Bistro."

"Yes?" More hopeful now than wary.

"Just calling to confirm your reservation tonight for a party of six at six. It's somebody's birthday?"

"It's my birthday," she said. "But I didn't know we had reservations at the bistro. For six at six, you say? I hope we're not bringing the kids. Maybe you'd better talk to my husband, Brian. He's right here."

During the switch of the phone, Adrienne checked the notes after the Devlins' name: "birthday/dessert-candle/no chocolate." Nowhere, *nowhere*, did it say "surprise," and yet that was clearly what it was. Adrienne had single-handedly ruined the woman's birthday surprise.

Mr. Devlin was appropriately gruff. "Thanks a lot," he said.

The next three phone calls were easy—Adrienne left clear, concise messages on voice mail for the guests who were out swimming or golfing or shopping from the Bartlett Farm truck on Main Street. Adrienne called the White Elephant and confirmed for those guests. She called Mack Peterson at the Beach Club, who was also on her shortlist of potential dates, but he showed no special interest in the fact that it was Adrienne calling rather than Thatcher. He was all business. "We have a guest who thinks she may have left her sunglasses there last night," he said. "I guess they're Chanel sunglasses and *très cher.* Last name Cerruci."

Adrienne checked the shelf inside the podium. "I . . . don't . . . see them here," she said. She scanned the book from the night before to see if Thatcher had written a note about sunglasses. "Well," she said, "the Cerrucis sat down last night at nine fifteen. What are the chances that Mrs. Cerruci was wearing her sunglasses at nine fifteen?"

"Oh, Adrienne," Mack said wearily. "You just don't understand the people I deal with all day."

Adrienne glanced at the disheveled dining room. "The cleaning crew hasn't been here yet," she said. "I'll call you if we find them."

"Thank you," Mack said, and he hung up.

Adrienne wrote herself a note—"Sunglasses"—while she dialed the Parrishes' number. Darla picked up.

"Hello?"

"Good morning, Darla. It's Adrienne from the Blue Bistro."

"Oh, you sweetheart!"

"Just calling to confirm two people at six tonight," Adrienne said.

There was a long pause on the other end. *Oh, God,* Adrienne thought. *What now?*

"We have Wolfie," Darla said.

"I'm sorry?"

"We have Wolfie, our grandson, for the next two weeks. I told Thatcher this! To change the next two weeks of reservations to include Wolfie. I told him! Oh, wait, maybe I didn't. Maybe I'm thinking of that darling Mateo at the Boarding House. We eat there every Wednesday. Sorry, sorry. The next four reservations we'll be a party of three because of Wolfie. He's six years old. And here's the thing: He's a picky eater."

"Okay," Adrienne said. Next to the Parrishes' name, she erased "2" and penciled in "3" with an asterisk next to the three that said, "Wolfie—picky eater."

"A very picky eater."

Adrienne remembered babysitting for Mavis's twins. Graham would eat anything she put in front of him, but Coleman, the one who could hear, would eat only mayonnaise sandwiches.

"What does he eat?" Adrienne asked. "I can make a note for the kitchen."

"He likes Froot Loops," Darla said. "And a certain kind of yogurt that is bright pink and has a dinosaur on the package."

"Is that it?" Adrienne asked. She was pretty sure cereal and children's yogurt weren't going to come out of the kitchen, even for the Parrishes. "Does he eat French fries?"

Darla laughed. "Of course! I'm almost certain. Let's just get him French fries, then. Will you write it down?"

"I'm writing it down," Adrienne said.

"It's just . . . well, he lives with his mother."

"Say no more," Adrienne said, as if she understood what that was supposed to mean. Though really, she didn't want to hear it. She liked Darla and wanted to keep it that way. "We'll see you at six."

At eleven thirty Antonio, the sous chef, brought Adrienne her lunch. She was on the phone with Mrs. Lefroy, otherwise she would have kissed the man. The plate looked gorgeous. As soon as Adrienne hung up, she poked her head into the kitchen to say "Thank you, gracias, thank you." Antonio waved. Adrienne sat at a table in the bar and dug in. This was Antonio's interpretation of "anything": succulent black olives, sun-dried tomatoes and marinated artichokes, three kinds of salami, tiny balls of fresh mozzarella, roasted cherry tomatoes, some kind of creamy eggplant dip that made her swoon, and a basket of warm focaccia. Miraculously, the phone stayed quiet while she ate. She had two calls remaining and she was done.

She finished her lunch, took her plate into the kitchen, and returned to the podium to make the phone calls. One to the Wauwinet Inn, one to the message machine of a beauty salon; the woman who cut Thatcher's hair was coming in at nine. Then, just as Adrienne took her first longing look at the beach, Thatcher's truck pulled into the parking lot.

Adrienne greeted him smiling widely. It had been a good morning.

"You have something in your teeth," he said.

She bolted for the ladies' room. Sure enough, tomato skin.

"My worst nightmare," she said when she emerged. "With my father and all."

"How did the calls go?"

"Fine," she said. "I ruined Jennifer Devlin's birthday. You didn't tell me it was a surprise."

"Oops," he said.

"The Parrishes are bringing their grandson."

He winced. "Is it that time of year already?" he said. "What does he eat these days?"

"French fries. Darla said French fries."

Thatcher shook his head. "We served him French fries last year. He fed them to the seagulls. She's forgotten."

"There's a list of people for you to call back. A man named Leon Cross called on the private line to say it was urgent and top secret."

"It's always urgent and top secret with Leon," Thatcher said. "Anything else?"

"I had a delicious lunch."

"Good. Fiona made it for you?"

"Uh, Antonio, I think."

"Okay," Thatcher said. Adrienne thought he looked pale and a little distracted but she was not going to ask him about the priest.

"Can I go?" she asked.

"Wait," he said. "I have something for you." He held up a white shopping bag. "Here."

Now Adrienne was nervous. She peeked in the bag. Clothes? She pulled out a blue dress made of washed silk that was so soft it felt like skin. Size six. There was another dress in a champagne color—the same cut, very simple, a slip dress to just above the knee. There was a third outfit—a tank and skirt in the same silk, bottle green.

"These are for me?"

"Let's see how they look."

She took the bag into the ladies' room and slipped the blue dress on over her bikini. It fell over Adrienne's body like a dress in a dream—and it would look even better when she had the right underwear. So here was her look. She checked the side of the shopping bag. The clothes had come from a store called Dessert, on India Street, and Adrienne recognized the name of the store as the one owned by the chef's wife, the redhead who had been so kind during soft opening. *If you come in, I'd love to dress you, free of charge.* So maybe Thatch didn't pay for these clothes. Still, it was weird. Weird that Thatcher had told her she needed a look, weird that he (or the redhead) had perfectly identified it, and weird that she now had to model it for him, proving him right. She stepped out into the dining room.

He gazed at her. And then he gave a long, low whistle. That did it: Her face heated up, the skin on her arms tingled. She had never felt so desirable in all her life.

"Tomorrow's your night off?" he said.

She nodded. Wednesday was her night off. Last Wednesday, because everyone she knew on the island worked at the restaurant, she stayed home, ate frozen ravioli, and watched a rerun of the *West Wing.*

"I scheduled myself off, too," he said. "I want to take you out for dinner."

This stunned her so much she may have actually gasped. "Who's going to work?" she asked.

"Caren," he said. "She loves to do it. And we only have seventy on the book."

Adrienne ran her hands down the sides of her new dress. The silk was irresistible.

"Will you go out with me?" he asked.

Rule Three: Exercise good judgment about men! Dating her boss did not seem wise. It seemed dangerous, more dangerous than getting entangled with Mario. And yet, she wanted to go. Rules, after all, were made to be . . .

"Sure," she said.

When Adrienne saw Thatcher at work that night, she thought things would be different between them. But Thatcher was preoccupied by the Lefroys' reservation. It wasn't a health inspector *visit,* but he wanted the restaurant to be clean. He wanted it to sparkle. And so, when Adrienne arrived, expecting compliments on the new champagne-colored dress, he set her to work polishing glasses and buffing the silver with the servers. At the menu meeting, he demonstrated the way he wanted the busboys to use the crumbers (and they were short a busboy since Tyler would be eating tonight with his parents). The staff ate family meal on the beach and Thatcher made them brush every grain of sand from their person and wash their feet in a bucket before they were allowed back in the restaurant.

As if that wasn't bad enough, Thatcher assigned Adrienne to the Parrishes during first seating.

"I want you to really watch them," he said. "Anticipate their needs. Especially Wolf's."

"It sounds like you're asking me to babysit," Adrienne said.

"We're going to do what it takes to give Darla and Grayson some peace," Thatcher said. "We want them to enjoy their meal, yes or no?"

The Parrishes arrived fifteen minutes late, which was unheard-of, and what this meant was that instead of getting them squared away early on, they were smushed at the entrance with three other parties who needed to be seated, and two gorgeous blond women who showed up without a reservation. Adrienne directed the Swedish bikini duo to the bar, sat the Devlins at table twenty-five, and led a deuce staying at the White Elephant under the awning. Then she returned to the podium to properly greet the Parrishes.

"Sorry," Adrienne said.

Grayson held up a palm. "It's our fault," he said. "We had a little trouble getting out of the house."

Darla was holding a little boy's hand. "This is Wolfie," Darla said.

Wolf had white-blond hair and eyes that were mottled and puffy. His breathing was hiccupy. Adrienne crouched down. Despite her years of babysitting the twins, she did not consider herself someone who was good with children and yet now she wanted to succeed, if only to impress Thatcher.

"Hi, Wolf," she said. "My name is Adrienne."

He harrumphed and locked his arms over his chest.

Darla smiled at him with all the love in the world, then whispered to Adrienne, "He's not having a good night."

Adrienne led the Parrishes to table twenty, and Bruno appeared seconds later with their drinks.

Adrienne pulled Bruno off to the side. "Order of frites, pronto," she said. "Wolfie's not having a good night and Thatcher wants Mr. and Mrs. P to be able to eat in their accustomed silence."

"Bitchy!" Bruno said. He paused. "Is that a new dress?"

"Yes," Adrienne said. "Thank you for noticing."

Caren approached Adrienne with a stone face. "I'm going to kill you."

"Why?"

"You put those girls at the bar."

"What girls?" Adrienne checked the bar. Ah, yes, the girls. They were laughing, and flashing Duncan with their remarkable cleavage. Adrienne instantly understood the problem, but come on! She was busy and they were all adults here. Well, everyone except for Wolfie.

"They didn't have a reservation," Adrienne said.

"You could have put them at three."

"I guess I could have, but . . ."

"They're all *over* him," Caren said. "And he's just eating it up. Oh, and look. They ordered apple martinis. What an insipid drink."

"Okay, well, I'm sorry. I have to put a . . ."

Thatcher passed by, touching Adrienne's arm. He raised one pale eyebrow.

"I have to put a VIP order in," Adrienne said to Caren.

"Champagne?" Thatcher said.

"I'll get your champagne," Caren said. "Let me get it." She strode toward the bar.

Bruno breezed by with a huge plate of fries. "These are for Dennis the Menace," he said. "You want to deliver?"

"I have to put their VIP order in," Adrienne said.

"Already done," Bruno said. He handed Adrienne the plate of fries. "You go, girl."

The Parrishes were sitting in silence, the elder two focused on their drinks while Wolf lay splayed across the wicker chair, his face sullen.

"Fries!" Adrienne said brightly. She took the seat next to Wolfie, but he couldn't be convinced to eat even one. She tried to lead by example, eating one fry, then another, then another. "You don't know what you're missing," she said.

"Please, Wolfie," Darla said. "Just try one. Just one for Gam. Please."

"I want yogurt," he said.

Grayson finished his Stoli tonic and flagged Bruno for another. "Why don't you take Wolf down to the water, Adrienne?"

"To the water?" Adrienne said. She considered informing Grayson Parrish that she had work to do. The restaurant was buzzing around her. Thatcher sat tables, Elliott and Joe recited specials, Gage and Roy poured water and delivered doughnuts. Rex played "Happy Birthday" as Spillman popped a bottle of champagne for the Devlins. Adrienne wanted to get up and join the adult activity.

Bruno came to her rescue. He eased up alongside Adrienne as he served apps to the adjoining table and whispered, "You're needed at the bar."

"I'm needed at the bar," Adrienne told the Parrishes. "I'll be right back."

At the bar, the blondes were splitting a VIP order, and at the far end, by the cherries and the citrus, Adrienne's champagne beckoned. She took a long swill, appraising the situation. Duncan was MIA. It was much commented upon that Duncan had the world's sturdiest bladder—he never used the restroom during service. Christo swaggered up to Adrienne and said, "I need a vodka grapefruit and a glass of zin."

"Who do I look like?"

"The assistant manager," he said.

"Where's Duncan?" Adrienne asked.

Christo shrugged. "I just work here, lady. You gonna get my drinks?"

One of the blondes whipped around. She was one of the most attractive women Adrienne had ever seen, if judged by the standards that certain American men tended to use. Lots of natural blond, lots of natural tan, lots of natural breast.

"I think his girlfriend's pissed at him," she said. "She snatched him away."

The other blonde, who was wearing a blue sequined halter top, sipped her apple martini. "We were just *talking* to him."

"So he's gone?" Adrienne said. "And where's Delilah?"

"Night off," Christo said. He grinned at the blondes.

"Okay, fine," Adrienne said. She was thinking many things at once: She was the assistant manager, this was—if looked at from a very warped and immature point of view—partially her fault, and it had always seemed like fun to be a bartender. Not to mention it gave her an excuse to blow off the Parrishes. Adrienne slipped behind the bar. She felt like she was about to drive an expensive race car. Look at all the stuff—the sink, the fridge, the rows of mixers, the gun, the fruit, the bottles in the well, the bottles of wine. She picked up a bottle of red and scrutinized the label.

"Zin, you said?"

"Zin."

"Well, this is a Syrah," Adrienne said. She eyed the podium. It was clear. "I wonder where the zin is."

"I'd like it this century," Christo said, then he checked to see if either of the blondes had laughed. No such luck. "Ah, fuck it, I'll be back."

"Adrienne!"

Thatcher's hand smacked the blue granite. She felt like, well, she felt like she'd just been caught in her parents' liquor cabinet. One of her heels snagged on the rubber hex mat and she stumbled backward. Her ass hit the rack of bottles behind her.

"I'm trying to help," she said.

"Table twenty," he hissed. "Take Wolf to the water."

Wolf threw the fries, one by one, to the seagulls. Adrienne found herself surrounded by big rats with wings, cawing and pecking. She glanced longingly back at the restaurant, at Grayson eating his chips and dip, at Duncan, returned to his post, wooing his new lady friends. When the fries were gone, Wolf threw rocks in the water.

"Don't you want to go back up?" Adrienne asked. He didn't answer. She tried another tack. "Where do you live?" He didn't answer. "Cat got your tongue?" she asked. He looked at her quizzically, and she could see his mind working: Was she talking about a real cat? But he wasn't curious enough to ask. He sat in the wet sand, shed his dock shoes, rolled up the pant legs of his khakis, and waded into the water. Adrienne wished she had the words to reel him back in. She was afraid to turn around to face Grayson and Darla. What if Wolf went under? She couldn't very well return him to his grandparents soaking wet. She wandered down the beach, saying, "I hope the sharks aren't out there tonight, Wolf. Or the stinging jellyfish." That got him out, though his pant legs were wrinkled and his seat was damp and sandy.

"Do you want to go back up?" Adrienne asked.

"No."

"Why not?"

"I just don't."

"Don't you want to be with your grandparents?"

"No."

"Why not?"

"I miss my mom."

"I miss my mom, too," Adrienne said.

Wolf tossed another rock. "Where is she?"

"She's dead," Adrienne said. It was easy to tell the truth to a child. Wolf said nothing, but he let her take his hand and lead him back to the restaurant. The footbath they had used after family meal came in handy. Adrienne rinsed Wolf's feet and squidged them back into his dock shoes. Then, with her sitting next to him, he choked down a roll smothered with butter.

Darla was elated. "I've never seen him eat like this before," she said. "Can we bring you home with us?"

At the end of first seating, Grayson tipped Adrienne two hundred dollars. She tucked the bills into her change purse.

"That," she said to Thatcher, "was above and beyond the call of duty."

"Nothing is above and beyond the call of duty," he said. "Not here."

No sooner had the Parrishes walked out the door than Caren yanked Adrienne into the wine cave.

"They're still here," Caren said.

"Who?"

"Those girls. They finished dinner twenty minutes ago and they're still here."

"You need to calm down," Adrienne said.

"I can't handle this," Caren said. She plopped down on an untapped keg of beer. "I cannot handle being the bartender's girlfriend."

"He's not doing anything wrong," Adrienne said.

"He's flirting," Caren said. "You notice he put in a VIP order? When I saw that, I flipped. Two nobodies, never been here before, and he VIPs them? I let him have it."

"What did he say?"

"He admitted he was flirting. He said it was part of his job."

"Well, it is, sort of, isn't it?"

"You're not helping!" Caren said. "You put them at the bar in the first place! You should have put them on three. I would have waited on them myself and they'd be at the Rose and Crown by now."

"Okay," Adrienne said. "Next time there are beautiful unescorted women without a reservation, I will put them at three."

"Do you promise?" Caren said. "Promise me."

"I promise," Adrienne said.

Second seating brought the Lefroys—Mr. and Mrs.—along with Tyler and his younger sister, a girl of about thirteen who had the worst case of adolescence Adrienne had ever seen. She was a chubby girl stuffed into a pink satin dress that would have looked awful on anyone; she wore braces and glasses and had greasy hair of no determinate color forced back in an unforgiving ponytail. Tyler looked mortified to be seen with her, not to mention his parents: Mrs. Lefroy had dyed blond hair and the defined biceps of a woman who spent all her free time at the gym, and Mr. Lefroy was easily six foot five, balding, bespectacled, lurching.

Thatcher slapped Tyler on the back and made some perfunctory (and much exaggerated) comment about what a stellar employee he was. Then he handed four menus to Adrienne and said, "Seat them. Table twenty."

"I never eat out," Mr. Lefroy said on his way through the dining room.

"No?" Adrienne said. "And why is that?"

"Well, when you've seen what I've seen . . ."

"On the job, you mean?"

"The cross-contamination dangers alone," he said.

"Dad," Tyler said. "Please shut up. People are trying to eat."

Adrienne let the family settle, then she handed out menus. "Enjoy your meal," she said.

The Lefroys' table was assigned to Spillman, but within minutes he found Adrienne at the bar, where she was drinking her champagne and trying to eavesdrop on Duncan and the two bombshells.

"Lefroy wants you," Spillman said.

"You're kidding."

"He wants your opinion on the menu," Spillman said. "My opinion apparently doesn't matter."

Adrienne returned to table twenty with her champagne. She complimented the sister, Rochelle, on a rhinestone bracelet she was wearing and she asked Tyler about his finals. He made a flicking motion with his hand. "Aced them."

Mr. Lefroy pointed to Adrienne's glass. "Now, what's that you're drinking?"

"A glass of the Laurent-Perrier brut rosé."

Mr. Lefroy looked to his wife. "You want one of those?"

"Sure," Mrs. Lefroy said. "It's my lucky day."

"One of those," Mr. Lefroy said. "And what is fresh on this menu?"

"It's all fresh," Adrienne said. "The fish is delivered every afternoon, the vegetables are hand-selected by our . . ."

"That's nice," Mr. Lefroy said. "But what is *really* fresh?"

When Adrienne returned to the podium, Thatcher was grinning.

"What?" she said.

"Lefroy can't keep his eyes off you."

"Shut up."

"It's because you're so damn fetching in that dress."

For the first time all night, Adrienne felt the electricity that had buzzed up her spine that morning when Thatcher whistled. She was beginning to think she'd imagined it.

The Lefroy family had a wonderful meal. In the end, they all ordered the steak, which was not fresh, but aged, though Adrienne did not point this out. Adrienne asked Thatcher if he wanted to comp the meal, as it was Tyler's family.

"I can't," Thatcher said. "The man is the health inspector."

The two blondes unstuck themselves from the bar at ten o'clock. Off to the Boarding House, they said.

"Cute bartender," the girl in the blue halter said. "He needs to lose the uptight girlfriend."

"Okay, bye-bye," Adrienne said. She was relieved to see them go. It had been another very, very long night, and it wasn't over yet. At eleven, Thatcher helped her bounce, and this was something new. Adrienne relayed the saga of Caren and Duncan as they watched the headlights pull in.

"The bar is popular for two reasons," he said. "Duncan and our indifference."

"Our indifference?"

"Well, Fiona's indifference. She hates the bar. She think it's all about money."

"Isn't it all about money?"

"Oh, yes," he said. "Yes, it is."

At midnight, the crackers came out of the kitchen: parmesan rosemary. Adrienne took a handful and offered the basket to Thatch. He nodded at the kitchen door. "I'm going to eat," he said. "I'll pick you up tomorrow night at seven."

"Where are we going?" Adrienne asked.

"Where aren't we going?" he said.

5

Night Off

Notre Dame magazine,
Volume LXVII,
September 2004
"GREEN AND GOLD GOES BLUE"

Thatcher Smith (B.A. 1991) believes there are two kinds of people in the world: those who eat to live and those who live to eat. Until he was twenty-two years old, Smith, owner of the Blue Bistro, a highly successful restaurant on Nantucket Island in Massachusetts, categorized himself as the former.

"I grew up in South Bend, a town that is virtually devoid of cuisine. My mother left the family when I was young and my father and brothers and I subsisted on shredded wheat, bologna sandwiches, and pizza. And Burger King, of course. But nothing you would ever call cuisine."

So how did this native of South Bend, and Notre Dame graduate, end up in the restaurant business? He gives credit to the girl next door.

Fiona Kemp (daughter of Hobson Kemp, a professor of

electrical engineering at Notre Dame since 1966) lived four houses down from Smith growing up.

"There's a picture of Fiona and I on our first day of kindergarten," Smith says. "I can't remember not knowing her."

Because of a childhood illness, Ms. Kemp could not participate in sports. So she turned her energies to an indoor activity: cooking.

"She was always making something. I remember when we were about twelve she made a chocolate swirl cheesecake sitting in a puddle of raspberry sauce. She invited some of the boys from the neighborhood over to eat it, but it was so elegant, none of us had the heart."

After graduating from John Adams High School together in 1987, Smith and Kemp went their separate ways. Smith enrolled at Notre Dame, where he majored in economics. He planned to join his father and brothers at what he modestly calls "the family store": Smith Carpets and Flooring, which has five outlets in South Bend and nearby Mishewaka. Meanwhile Kemp enrolled at the prestigious Culinary Institute of America in Hyde Park, New York. She wanted to fulfill her dream of becoming a chef.

Smith and Kemp reunited on Nantucket Island in October 1992.

"Fiona had been working on the island for two years at that point," Smith says. "And she felt ready for her own place. She convinced me to visit, and once I saw the island, I decided to leave South Bend behind. I sold my interest in the business to my brothers and took the money and invested it in Fiona. I knew there was no way she would fail."

Indeed, not. Smith and Kemp bought a run-down restaurant on the beach that had formerly served burgers and fried clams, and they transformed it into the Blue Bistro, with seating for over a hundred facing the Atlantic Ocean. The only seats harder to procure than the seats at the blue granite bar are the four tables out in the sand where the Bistro serves its now-famous version of seafood fondue. (Or, as the kitchen fondly refers to it, the all-you-can-eat fried shrimp special.) Many of Ms. Kemp's offerings are twists on old classics, like the fondue. She serves impeccable steak frites, a lobster club sandwich, and a sushi plate, which features a two-inch-thick slab of locally caught bluefin tuna. Ms. Kemp relies on fresh local produce to keep her plates alive.

Ms. Kemp's cooking has been celebrated in such places as *Bon Appétit* and the *Chicago Tribune.* She was named one of the country's hottest chefs by *Food & Wine* in 1998. All this notoriety comes despite the fact that she is, in Thatcher Smith's words, "a highly private person. Fiona doesn't give interviews. She doesn't allow herself to be photographed. She doesn't believe in the new craze of 'chef as celebrity.' Fiona just wants to feed people. It has never been about the reviews or about the money, even. For Fiona, it's all about love; it's about giving back."

For Thatcher Smith, running the Blue Bistro is a dream come true—a dream he wasn't even aware he harbored. "I love every minute of my work," he says. "The fast pace, the high energy, the personal interaction, the management challenges. And yes, I love the food. Once I tried a plate of Fiona's steak frites, I learned the difference between tasting and eating. I knew I would never hit the drive-through at Burger King again. I became a person who lives to eat."

TO: Ade12177@hotmail.com
FROM: DrDon@toothache.com
DATE: June 7, 2005, 7:33 P.M.
SUBJECT: possible dates

How about the last week in July? Love, love.

Adrienne was so nervous when she woke up on Wednesday morning that her ears were ringing. *Where are we going? Where aren't we going?* The blue dress hung in the closet on a padded hanger that Adrienne had borrowed from Caren without her permission. When Adrienne had gotten home the night before, she went online and looked up the article about Thatcher in *Notre Dame* magazine. Then she lay in bed for nearly an hour thinking about it. It gave her a better sense of Thatcher than the other articles. He came from a family of men who worked in carpet and flooring. His mother had left, maybe for that very reason: too many men, too much carpet. Adrienne wondered about Fiona's "childhood illness," just as she wondered about everything else regarding Fiona. She had liked the story about the cheesecake. She could imagine Thatcher and his grubby twelve-year-old friends staring at the marbled cheesecake sitting in a bright pink raspberry pond as though it were a work of modern art they were being asked to understand.

Adrienne heard the swish of Caren's bare feet against the floorboards of the hall, then the espresso machine. She looked at her clock: It was nine. She had hoped to sleep in, but there was no chance—too much on her mind.

By the time Adrienne made it out to the kitchen, Caren was alone, sipping her short black, flipping through the pages of *Cosmo.*

"Where's Duncan?" Adrienne asked.

"I have no idea."

Adrienne eyed the glossy pages of the magazine. Caren was reading an article entitled: "Is Your Relationship on the Rocks? 10 Early Warning Signs."

"Are you fighting?" Adrienne asked.

"I have no idea," Caren said again.

"Oh," Adrienne said.

"You're off tonight?" Caren asked.

Adrienne poked her head into the fridge for some juice. "Yep."

"You're going out?"

Adrienne got a glass out of the cabinet, steeling herself. What was the first thing Caren had ever told her? *I know the dirt on every person who eats at the Bistro and every person who works there.*

"I am," Adrienne said.

"With Thatch?"

"Yes," Adrienne said. She let out a long exhale; it was a relief, having it spoken. "What do you think?"

"I'm psyched to work the front," Caren said. "It's such a breeze."

Adrienne recognized that as some kind of slight, but she let it go. "What do you think about me and Thatch?"

"I think you should be careful."

Adrienne poured her juice and sat down across the table from Caren. Caren was not exactly her friend, but Adrienne knew she wouldn't lie.

"Why?" Adrienne said. "Has he been with a lot of women?"

"No," Caren said. "He hasn't gone on a date in the twelve years I've known him." She slapped her magazine shut. "And that's why you should be careful."

Thatcher arrived at five to seven bearing a bouquet of red gerbera daisies. He looked like an old-fashioned suitor: He was dressed in a jacket and tie, holding out the flowers, and he had a very clean-shaven look about him. *Haircut,* she realized after studying him for a second. Adrienne was glad Caren was at work—she might have teased this version of Thatcher Smith. Earnest, fresh-faced, with flowers, on his first date in twelve years.

"Look at you," Adrienne said. She carried the flowers into the kitchen, where she hunted for a vase. No vase. She filled one of the unused sunflower canisters with water.

Thatcher followed her in. "Look at *you,*" he said. "That dress. I can't get over it."

"Good," Adrienne said, smiling. She grabbed a gray pashmina (borrowed from Caren, with her permission) and checked her silver-beaded cocktail purse (ditto): lipstick, dental floss, a wad of cash, just in case. "Let's go."

Thatcher took her to 21 Federal, in the heart of town. The building was one of the old whaling houses; inside, it had a lot of dark wood and antique mirrors. The woman working the front wore Janet Russo and had a professional manicure. She smiled when they came in and said in a flirty voice, "Thatcher Smith! The rumors are true!"

Thatcher put a finger to his lips, and the woman said, "You don't want anyone to know you're here? Would you like to sit in the back?"

"Even better," Thatcher said, pointing at the ceiling.

The woman led them up the staircase. "Siberia, it is," she said.

The upstairs of the restaurant was even more charming than downstairs, Adrienne thought. There was a darling little bar and a couple of deuces by the front windows that looked down onto Federal Street. Thatcher pulled out Adrienne's chair then seated himself. The hostess whispered in Thatcher's ear. He nodded. A second later, an elderly bartender appeared with their drinks: Veuve Clicquot for Adrienne and a club soda with lime for Thatcher.

"Our compliments, Mr. Smith," said the bartender.

"Thank you, Frank."

"The hostess forgot our menus," Adrienne whispered.

"No, she didn't," Thatcher said. "I've ordered for us already."

Adrienne tried to relax. She gazed out the window at the cobblestoned street below. "Okay," she said. "You're the boss."

Thatcher lifted his glass to her. "Thank you for coming out with me tonight," he said. "I don't do this enough."

Adrienne clinked his glass and sipped her champagne. "From what I hear, you don't do it at all."

"You've been talking to Caren?"

"Of course."

"She thinks she knows everything about me," Thatcher said. "But she doesn't."

The hostess approached the table again and whispered something else in Thatcher's ear. The whispering was in very bad taste; Adrienne would never do it.

Thatcher said, "Not tonight. Sorry. You'll tell them I'm sorry? But not tonight."

The hostess disappeared. Thatcher turned to Adrienne. "The chef wants to prepare us a tasting menu."

"That's nice," Adrienne said.

"It's a commitment," Thatcher said. "And I have other plans for us."

"Do you now?" Adrienne said.

"Yes, I do."

A few minutes later the bartender, who was keeping a shadowy profile behind the bar, presented two plates. "The portobello mushroom with Parmesan pudding," he announced.

Thatcher lit up. He spun the plates. "This is the best first course on the island," he said.

"If you're not eating at work," Adrienne said.

"Right," Thatcher said.

Adrienne brandished her knife and fork. She was used to eating family meal at five thirty and now, nearly two hours later, she was starving. She tasted a bite of the mushroom, then a little of the creamy, cheesy pudding. The dish was perfect. Thatcher stared at his plate, smiling at the mushroom as though he expected it to smile back. Was he nervous?

"I read an article about you this morning," Adrienne said.

"Which one?"

"*Notre Dame* magazine."

He raised his pale eyebrows. "You must have been doing research," he said. "I gather you're not a subscriber."

"No," she said. "I went to three colleges, but I wouldn't call any of them my alma mater."

"Where is your degree from?"

"Florida State," she said. "Psychology. I did my first two years in Bloomington, then a year at Vanderbilt, and I ended up at Florida State—and that's where I got into hotels. My adviser at FSU got me a job on the front desk at the Mar-a-Lago in Palm Beach."

"Starting your enviable life of resort-hopping."

"Exactly." Adrienne took another bite of her mushroom. "In that article, it said Fiona had a childhood illness."

"Now you know why I don't like journalists," he said. He twirled his glass then looked around the dining room—they were the only people eating upstairs. He hunched his shoulders and said, "Can we not talk about the article?"

Adrienne didn't care for his tone of voice; it was the same tone he used at work when he was telling her what to do. She was about to say something tart when the bartender appeared with a second glass of champagne. Adrienne drank half of it down, questioning her decision to come on this date. This was what had happened in her relationship with Kip Turnbull in Thailand; right before they broke up he was micromanaging her personal life, telling her how to defog her snorkel, insisting she condition her hair with coconut milk, feeding her psychedelic mushrooms without her knowledge. That was the problem with dating the boss; they couldn't get over themselves. Adrienne concentrated on her appetizer. It was pretty damn good, though she now resented the fact that Thatcher had ordered it for her, as though she weren't educated enough to select something on her own. She noticed Thatcher still wasn't eating. He was looking at her with a worried expression.

"I'm sorry," he said. "If you want to know something about me, you can just ask. You don't have to read about me in my alumni magazine. Most of what I tell reporters is baloney anyway."

Adrienne nodded once, but only to let him know she'd heard him. She finished her mushroom and her champagne in silence, and feigned interest in the photographs of sailboats on the walls. Then, when she could avoid conversation no longer, she reached for Caren's purse. "I'm going to the ladies' room," she said. "Where is it?"

"Down the hall," he said. He stood up when she left, just like Adrienne's father used to do for Rosalie. Adrienne gave him points for that.

The hall leading to the bathroom was adjacent to a back corridor that was used as a waiters' station. Adrienne noticed the folded food stands, the stacks of china and linen, the racks for the silver, the bud vases, and a plastic pitcher of white freesia stems. She eyed the computer where the waiters placed orders. Just as she was about to step into the ladies' room to check her teeth, she heard two female waiters talking as they trudged up the back stairs.

"He hasn't been here in, like, five years," one said. "And Fiona, you know, never eats anywhere."

"That's not Fiona he's with tonight?"

"No, it's some other chick. He's not married to Fiona or anything."

"Oh, I know."

Adrienne made sure the waiters got a good look at her before she entered the ladies' room. *Some other chick!*

When she returned to the table, Thatcher stood up again and remained standing. Their plates had been cleared.

"The female waiters were talking about you," Adrienne said.

"I'm not surprised," Thatcher said. "Whenever I leave the Bistro at night, it's news. Are you ready?"

"For what?" Adrienne said. "Where are we going?"

"Across the street," Thatcher said. "We've just begun."

They crossed Federal Street to the Pearl, a restaurant that made Adrienne feel as though she were underwater. There was a waist-to-ceiling fish tank filled with tropical fish and the tables and chairs were very modern and sleek. The dining room had a blue glow that gave it a peaceful, floaty feeling despite the fact that it was packed with people. Young, hip, well-dressed. The people smelled like money.

"This is see and be seen in town," Thatcher said. "Which isn't what we're after, but . . . I would have taken you downstairs to the Boarding House for pot stickers, except the Parrishes eat there every Wednesday and I couldn't risk running into them."

"No," Adrienne said. She would have ended up babysitting Wolfie on her date.

"Danger," Thatcher said. "Danger, danger." He put his hand up to shield his face, as though the paparazzi were after him.

"Who is it? Not the Parrishes?"

"Cat is at the four-top by the window," Thatcher said. "And Leon Cross is at a deuce in the corner with a woman who is not his wife. He asked me yesterday if I would hide them away and I said no. Why he would bring her *here* is beyond me."

"Since you don't want to be seen with me, I could ask you the same thing."

"I'm proud to be seen with you," Thatcher said. "I just don't want to work on my night off."

"Should we leave?" Adrienne asked.

Before he could answer, a woman with straight black hair all the way down to her butt emerged from the crowd and pulled Thatcher and Adrienne forward as though she was granting them entrance to a hot club. "Follow me," she said.

The woman was Red Mare, Spillman's wife. She seated them at a table tucked back in the corner. Within minutes, Red Mare brought their drinks: a passion fruit cosmo for Adrienne and a club soda with lime for Thatcher.

"You're Adrienne," Red Mare said. "John really likes working with you. Much better than with Kevin. Didn't you think Kevin had a pole up his ass, Thatch?"

Thatcher shrugged. "Sure."

"I'm glad you finally got smart and put a woman up front. An attractive woman." She touched Adrienne's shoulder. "Great dress."

"Thanks."

"Anyway, Thatch, I know you called in your request, but the kitchen knows you're here and chef wants to make you his six-course Asian seafood menu."

"Tell chef thanks," Thatcher said. "But we'll stick with our original plan."

Red Mare clapped her hands and held them together in front of her chest like a praying mantis. "You got it."

After she disappeared back into the beautiful crowd, Adrienne said, "Everyone knows you."

"I've been here a long time."

"Twelve years isn't that long."

"It is when you're young. Listen, twelve years ago you were still in high school. Am I right?"

"You're right."

"And it's a small island. The restaurant community is tight. Over the course of the summer we'll have all the chefs in on their night off. We take good care of them. They just want to do the same."

Adrienne saw Red Mare peek at them from her position by the door, checking up on them like Adrienne herself did eighty-two times a night. Now that she worked in a restaurant, she noticed the things that other guests wouldn't. For example, the number of glasses hanging from a rack over the bar was dwindling (a few seconds later, the bar back appeared with clean glasses) and a certain busser, in this case a tiny brunette, kept bumping into one of the male servers. (They were obviously having a fling.) Adrienne might have shared these insights with Thatcher but he, no doubt, had outgrown being amused by the behind-the-scenes of other restaurants.

"What do you do around here all winter?" she asked.

"Catch up on my sleep," he said. "And Fiona and I take a trip back to South Bend at Christmas."

Adrienne had worked the last six Christmases but just the thought brought the face of Doug Riedel to mind. Those damn shearling gloves! She drained her cosmo. At that instant, Red Mare appeared with a second cosmo and their food. "Two tuna martinis—this is seared tuna with wasabi crème fraîche."

Adrienne tasted it as soon as it hit the table. "The best second course on the island," she said.

"If you're not eating at work," Thatcher said. He sipped his club soda.

"I have a question," Adrienne said, a challenge in her voice. Just breathing in the vapors from the second cosmo sent her good judgment through the roof.

"Shoot."

She had many questions, all of them provocative: Why had he been to see the priest? Why was he closing the restaurant? Why no journalists in the kitchen? But the one she chose was: "How did you come to be an alcoholic?"

His laugh was so forceful it startled her. "Ha!" After two weeks, she still wasn't used to that crazy laugh. "You're trying to shock me with a direct hit," he said. "And it's working."

Adrienne speared a piece of tuna. Even the silverware here had a sleek design. "You don't have to answer," she said. "I'm at the mercy of alcohol now myself."

"That was my goal," Thatcher said. "Get you drunk so you forget I'm your boss."

"Why do you want me to forget you're my boss?"

"So you'll like me."

"I do like you."

He stared at her a minute then reached for her hand. She looked at the side of his face, at the clean pink skin around his ear, newly exposed from the haircut. With his other hand, he loosened his tie and undid his top button. He had barely touched his food.

"You're not eating," she said.

"I'm pacing myself," he said. "Remember, I know what's to come."

Adrienne reclaimed her hand to finish her tuna, and if Thatcher wasn't going to eat, she would finish his.

"I became an alcoholic as a result of the business," Thatcher said. "It's an occupational hazard."

"What happened?"

"I don't know that anything happened," he said. "I was just drinking a lot every night. A couple of cocktails, a bottle of wine, a glass of port. And by the time the hand bell chimed, I was sloshed. I did stupid things. Forgave all the tabs at the bar. Doubled the tips for the waitstaff. This made me very popular, mind you, but it was bad for our bottom line. I started AA four years ago. Fiona insisted."

"Did she?"

"My behavior was threatening the business. It had to stop."

"Isn't it hard, though, not drinking? Especially when you're around alcohol all the time?"

"At first, I tried to cut back. Have one cocktail, one glass of wine. But I couldn't do it. One cocktail wasn't an option. Alcoholism is a disease and I have it. But it's not so bad." He held up his drink. "I really love club soda."

Adrienne smiled and stared at Thatcher's tuna, ruby red in the frosted martini glass. She could stay here all night. She wanted to enjoy being waited on for a change. But Thatcher seemed antsy. He checked his Patek Philippe. "Time's up," he said. "We're going."

At a restaurant called Oran Mor, Thatcher and Adrienne hid at a tiny table tucked behind the horseshoe-shaped bar. The table had a view of the harbor and the ferry—the same ferry that Adrienne had arrived on two weeks, and another lifetime, ago. A male waiter brought Adrienne a glass of red wine followed by an enormous porterhouse steak topped with Roquefort butter. Thatcher got a shallow dish of lobster risotto.

"I couldn't decide between the two," he said. "So we got both." He watched Adrienne take a bite of steak. "Now taste your wine."

Adrienne bristled once again at being told what to do, especially since she knew he'd be right. The steak and wine were made for each other.

"How's the wine?" he asked.

"Incredible."

He picked up her glass and inhaled. "Big," he said. "Plummy. Just as they described it."

Adrienne offered her steak to Thatcher but he shook his head. "Go on," she said. "There can't be more after this." He relented, then hand-fed her a bite of his risotto, and all Adrienne could think was that it was a good thing no one could see them. Nothing brought more sarcasm from the waitstaff than a couple feeding each other.

Adrienne drank down her wine and another glass appeared. She was officially drunk; across the table, Thatcher was blurry. He was looking at her so intently that it took the place of conversation. *He's soaking me up,* Adrienne thought. *Whatever* that *meant.* The more Adrienne drank, the more it seemed like Thatcher himself was drunk. When she finished eating, Thatcher took her hand again.

"Who are you, Adrienne Dealey?" he said. "Who are you?"

She didn't have anything resembling a good answer. She couldn't say "I'm a dentist and a father." Or "I'm a restaurant owner." Or "I'm a chef." She couldn't even say "I'm a childhood friend of Fiona's. I've been a friend of hers since kindergarten." She had no identity. She lived in a place for a while, working a desk, skiing bumps, visiting Buddhist temples, sitting on a sugar-sand beach, making poor decisions, fudging the details of her past—and six months or a year later she was somewhere else. Someone else. New friends, new boyfriend, new job, new location. The most important thing in her life had been the money for her Future, the money saved up for . . . what? Some bigger plan that she had yet to identify. Her father was right. One of these days she was going to have to pick a place and stay there.

"I'm a student of human nature," Adrienne said. She was so drunk this didn't even sound corny. "I'm trying to absorb it all before I settle down."

"Do you think you'll ever settle down?" Thatcher said. "Get married?"

Adrienne pushed her plate away; she was absolutely stuffed. She reached for her wine and held the glass with two hands. "I don't know. I've had a lot of boyfriends. There was a guy on the Cape who asked me to marry him and I considered it for about a day and a half. Then I freaked out and flew to Hawaii. It was very immature behavior on my part."

"My mother bailed on us when I was nine," Thatcher said. "My three older brothers were sixteen, fourteen, and eleven at the time. There is no doubt in my mind that we drove her away; we would have driven Mother Teresa away. So I used to have an issue with women who run, but I got over it. I forgave my mother—that's one thing AA really helps with, forgiveness. She lives in Toronto now, but I never see her."

"Yeah," Adrienne said. "My mother died when I was twelve."

"I didn't know your mother died," Thatcher said. "Something you said earlier made me think . . ."

"I'm sorry about that," Adrienne said. "I have a hard time talking about it and sometimes it's just easier . . ."

"You don't have to apologize," Thatcher said.

"Maybe not to you," Adrienne said. "But I've lied to a lot of people about it. I pretend my mother is still alive. I want her to be alive."

"Of course."

Adrienne placed a fingertip at the corner of her eye. "I probably don't need any more wine."

Thatcher looked around the restaurant. "I was going to take you to Languedoc for the Sweet Inspirations sundae."

"It may interest you to know," said Adrienne, "that the key to dessert is not sugar." She bent her head close to the table and whispered, "It's eggs."

Thatcher groaned. "When a woman starts quoting Mario Subiaco, I know she's had too much to drink. No sundae for you. Let's go for a drive."

"I have to use the ladies' room," Adrienne said.

She nearly tripped on the uneven floor on the way to the bathroom and when she got inside, she looked at herself in the mirror. Her cheeks were bright pink. *I am drunk,* she thought. *Schnockered.* She splashed her face and pulled out her dental floss. Who are you, Adrienne Dealey? *I am a person who cares about dental hygiene.*

They climbed into Thatcher's silver pickup. His truck was impeccably clean and smelled like peppermint. Adrienne fell back into the gray leather seat while Thatch fiddled with the CD player. He put on Simon and Garfunkel.

"How old *are* you?" she asked.

"Old. Thirty-five." He rummaged through the console and brought out a tire gauge. "I'm going to take you up the beach," he said. "Do you have any objections to that?"

"None," Adrienne said. The clock in the car said ten thirty. She couldn't help thinking about the restaurant: Had Caren and Duncan made up? Would they be sneaking in gropes and shots of espresso, giddy with their freedom like kids whose parents were away for the weekend? Would they be playing techno on the stereo (which Thatch hated) and hogging all the crackers for themselves? "Do you miss work?" she asked. She noticed his cell phone sitting in the console next to the tire gauge, his ring of Bistro keys, and a tin of Altoids, but he hadn't so much as checked his messages.

"No," he said, starting the engine and pulling out of town. "Not at all."

When Adrienne next opened her eyes, she was alone in the truck. It was dark, and looking out the window she saw nothing but more dark.

"Thatcher?" she said.

She heard a hissing noise outside her window. When she opened her door, she saw Thatcher kneeling by the front tire letting out air. From the dome light she could see sand dunes covered with eelgrass.

"This is the last one," Thatcher said. He checked the tire with the gauge and stood up, wiping his hands on his pants. He had removed his jacket and tie and his shirt was open another button at the neck.

"Where are we?"

"Dionis Beach," he said. "Have you been here?"

Adrienne shook her head.

"Good," he said. "Hang on."

He drove the truck up over the dunes with abandon, bouncing Adrienne out of her seat. Thatcher whooped like a cowboy and Adrienne prayed she didn't vomit. (She had a worrisome flashback from twenty years earlier: the Our Lady of the Assumption carnival, cotton candy, kettle corn, and the tilt-a-whirl. Her mother holding back her hair in a smelly Porta-John.) Then, thankfully, they were on the beach, and the water was before them, one stripe shining from the crescent moon. The beach was deserted. Thatcher parked the truck then opened Adrienne's door for her. He spread a blanket on the sand.

"You came prepared," she said.

"Lie down," he said. "But keep your eyes open."

"Yes, boss," she said.

After getting gracefully to the ground in her dress, Adrienne looked at the stars. Thatcher lay on his side, staring at her. She closed her eyes. She could fall asleep right here. Happily, happily. Listening to the waves lap onto the beach. She heard Thatcher's voice in her ear.

"I'm going to kiss you if that's okay," he said.

"It won't be our first kiss," she said.

"No," he said. "I let one slip at the restaurant. I thought about apologizing to you for that, but I didn't feel sorry." And with that, he kissed her. One very soft, very sweet kiss. The kiss was fleeting but it left a big ache for more in its wake. Adrienne gasped, taking in the cool sea air, and then Thatcher kissed her again. Even softer, even shorter. The third time, he stayed. They were kissing. His mouth opened and Adrienne tasted his tongue, sweet and tangy like the lime in his drink. She felt like she was going to burst apart into eighty-two pieces of desire. Like the best lovers, Thatcher moved slowly—for right now, on the blanket, it was only about the kissing. Not since high school had kissing been this intense. It went on and on. They stopped to look at each other. Adrienne ran her fingertips over his pale eyebrows, she cupped his neck inside the collar of his shirt. He touched her ears and kissed the corners of her eyes, and Adrienne thought about how she had come right out with the truth about her mother at dinner and how unusual that was. And just as she began to worry that there was something different this time, something better, of a finer quality than the other relationships she had found herself in, she and Thatcher started kissing again, and the starting again was even sweeter.

Yes, Adrienne thought. *Something was different this time.*

How much time passed? An hour? Two? Of lying on the blanket kissing Thatcher Smith, the man who had handed her a new life on this island. Adrienne felt herself drifting to sleep, she felt him kiss her eyelids closed—and then suddenly, like a splash of icy water, like a bolt of lightning hitting way too close, like the foul smell that wafted from the restaurant garbage, there came a noise. From the car. Thatcher's cell phone.

He pulled away. Checked his twenty-thousand-dollar watch in the moonlight. And ran for the truck.

He took the call standing in the deep dark a few yards behind his truck. Which was smart, because if he'd been closer, Adrienne would have yelled at whomever was on the other end. *How dare you spoil my night!*

Thatcher snapped the phone closed as he walked back toward Adrienne who was now sitting up on the blanket, headache threatening.

"I don't want to hear it," she said.

"That was Fee."

"Fiona? What did she want?"

"It's twelve thirty. My dinner is ready."

"Your dinner is ready," Adrienne repeated flatly. "Your *dinner* is *ready*?"

"We eat together every night," he said.

"Yes, except tonight you're on a date with me. Tonight you ate with me." As soon as she said the words, she realized he *hadn't* eaten—he had barely touched his food. Because he knew all along that he was going back to the

Bistro. *To eat with Fiona.* "Take me home," Adrienne said. "Take me home right now."

"You're tired anyway," he said. "You were practically asleep." He tried to reach for her but she climbed into the truck and made a point of slamming the door in his face. She fastened her seat belt and when Thatcher got in, she stared out the windshield at the black water of the sound.

"Don't be mad," he said.

"This is weird," Adrienne said. "You going back to have dinner with her. It's *strange.*"

"I realize it must seem that way."

"She loves JZ," Adrienne said.

"What do *you* know about it?" he asked.

"I saw them together yesterday," Adrienne said. "She left with him. She loves him."

"She does love him," Thatcher said. "But what I asked was, what do you know about it?"

"Nothing," Adrienne admitted. "She was coughing and he picked her up and held her."

"Okay," Thatcher said, as if he'd made some very important point. He started the truck and eased them out over the dunes, the truck rocking gently this time, as gently as a cradle.

He pulled into her driveway by quarter to one.

"Don't bother getting out," Adrienne said. "I can see myself in."

"I'm walking you to the door," Thatcher said. He returned to his persona of old-fashioned suitor and took her arm. She had forgotten to leave on any lights and so the cottage was pitch-black. As they stood at the doorway, Thatcher touched the strap of her blue dress. Adrienne knew she should thank him for the date; he'd gone to a lot of trouble. But she was angry, incredulous, defiant. *His dinner was ready!*

He leaned in to kiss her and she let him. She thought maybe she could keep him. Maybe his dinner would go cold and Fiona would have to throw it away. They kissed and kissed; Adrienne had never felt such urgency.

"Stay with me," she said.

He pressed her against the door frame and for the first time she felt his body right up against hers and it was an even better feeling, if that were possible, than the kissing. She could feel herself winning, she could see the future: his shirt coming off, her blue dress dropping into a silk puddle on the floor, the two of them entwined in Adrienne's bed. Caren's shock the following morning at the espresso machine when Thatcher joined her for a short black. But then, just as Adrienne knew he would, he surfaced from the pull of her desire with a gulp of air like a man who had been drowning.

"Go," Adrienne said.

And he went.

6

The Wine Key

How did men do it?

It was ten minutes to six on Thursday night, 101 covers on the book, and Thatcher actually had the gall to knock on the door of the ladies' room where Adrienne was brushing her teeth and deciding whether or not to quit.

"Come on out," he said. "I need to talk to you."

Adrienne shut off the water, tapped her toothbrush angrily against the side of the sink, and flung open the door.

"You have some nerve," she said.

He held up a wine key. "I'm going to show you how to use this. Now. We've waited too long."

How did he manage to look better than ever on the one night (possibly of many) Adrienne had arrived at work prepared to hate him? It looked like he had gotten some sun—his face had that healthy golden glow. *Did you go to the beach?* Adrienne wanted to ask. But no, she wouldn't. Just as she wouldn't ask him, *How was your dinner?* (though she had practiced the exact tone of sarcasm and contempt).

How did he have the presence of mind to stand before her holding up the wine key as innocuously as a door-to-door salesman? Did he not remember pressing his body up against hers the night before? Did he not remember how tenderly he kissed her eyelids closed? How did men find the nerve the next day to act as though nothing had ever happened? (And it wasn't just Thatcher, Adrienne conceded. She'd seen it time and time again.)

Over Thatcher's shoulder, Adrienne saw Joe and Spillman lighting candles. Rex began to play "Old Cape Cod." Adrienne rolled her eyes. She would be a brick wall.

"Fine, the wine key," she said. She followed Thatcher into the wine cave. He closed the door behind them and Adrienne thought, *Okay, here it comes.* The wine key was a ruse. He was going to apologize.

Thatcher removed a bottle of red from the rack. Bin forty-one: Cain Cuvée—they sold it by the glass as well as from the list.

"First," he said, "you have to cut the lead."

She stared at him, trying to make her eyes as hard as the point of an awl.

"Some restaurants have a special tool for this," Thatcher said. "Not us. We use the very inexpensive, very user-friendly Screwpull. Wait until you see how easy this is." He used the sharp end of the key to cut the lead, which was the metal wrapper over the cork. He pulled it off. Then he set the plastic arms of the Screwpull over the cork, inserted the key, and turned the knob at the top. Turned and turned—and like magic, the cork appeared. "A third grader could do it," he said. He set the bottle aside and pulled out their most popular bottle of white—Menetou-Salon, from an area of France near Sancerre. Adrienne had heard Thatcher give the spiel on this wine before—the vintner was also the mayor of the town.

"You try," he said, handing her the bottle and the key.

She cut the lead, peeled it away (a little less seamlessly than Thatch, but she got it), set the Screwpull in place, and turned. Out came the cork. Piece of cake.

"Fine," she said.

"The waiters open their own wine," Thatcher said. "I open for VIPs, and I open when the waitstaff is slammed. Step in when you feel you're needed."

"Fine, fine." She dug her heel into the floor in a way that she hoped conveyed her impatience. She was wearing yet another pair of new shoes—buff-colored Jimmy Choo sling backs—that she'd bought that afternoon in an attempt to make herself feel better.

"And there's one more thing," Thatcher said.

Something in his voice made her look at him and their eyes locked. *I am a brick wall,* she thought. *I am a swan carved from ice.*

"What's that?" she said.

He held her gaze for whole seconds of precious time. Outside the door, Adrienne could hear Spillman's voice: "Has anyone seen the boss man?" Thatcher didn't move. He just held Adrienne captive with his eyes and when Adrienne thought it was inevitable—they were going to kiss—he snapped out of his daze.

"Champagne," he said. He opened the refrigerator and pulled out a bottle of Laurent-Perrier. He unfolded a towel from the Sankaty Head Golf Club. "Up front, you'll use a side towel, or even a dinner napkin," he said. He removed the foil from the cork, wrangled off the cage, and showed Adrienne the bottle with the naked cork. "You could push at the bottom of the cork until it shoots out, but champagne corks are unpredictable. You could take out someone's eye. Best-case scenario, the cork gets lost in the sand and one of our guests with an environmental conscience writes a letter to the *Inquirer and Mirror* about how we here at the Blue Bistro are littering Nantucket's pristine beaches. So." He covered the cork with the golf towel and twisted. "Twist while pulling up." The cork came free with a muted *pop.* Thatcher whipped off the towel. The lip of the bottle showed a wisp of smoky carbon dioxide; he tossed the cork in the trash. "Take this out to Duncan and have him pour you a glass," he said. "It's time to get to work."

So that was it. They were together in the wine cave with the door closed for six whole minutes and all she'd gotten was a deep stare and a lesson on the world's easiest tasks. Adrienne saw her options: quit or work as though nothing had happened. Life wasn't made any easier by the fact that everyone on the staff knew she and Thatcher had been out together—and likewise, everyone knew that Thatcher returned to the restaurant to eat with Fiona. Caren had said it best that morning while she and Duncan (reunited) drank espresso and Adrienne drank ginger lemon tea because, to add insult to injury, Adrienne had a killer hangover, the worst of the summer so far. Caren had said, "How was your date? It couldn't have been too wonderful."

And Adrienne said, "There is something very fucked up going on between Thatcher and Fiona."

Caren and Duncan had stared at her blankly but when they thought she wasn't looking, they exchanged an alarmed glance. Adrienne caught it and said, "And you two pissants know what's going on and you won't tell me."

Caren had nodded very slowly. "They're friends," she said.

And Duncan said, "I have to go. I'm sailing with Holt Millman at ten."

Adrienne tried to lose herself in the service. One hundred and one covers on the books, but first thing there was a walk-in party of four, dressed in workout clothes. They informed Adrienne that they had arrived on their bikes after a long ride to Sconset, and they wanted to know if they could eat dinner and get back into town before dark.

"Sure," Adrienne said. Table three was empty; it was a less desirable table, saved on slower nights for walk-ins. She sat the party, gave them the exact time of sunset along with their menus, and told them she'd have the kitchen on top of their order. The head biker palmed her fifty bucks.

"Thanks," he said. "We're really hungry."

Joe took the table; he was psyched. "Good work," he said. "How was your date last night?"

"What date?" she said.

She was a swan carved from ice.

First seating breezed by. She delivered three orders of chips and dip, and she opened four bottles of wine. She completely ignored Thatcher and, at a couple of points, she was so busy, she forgot him.

In between seatings, Thatcher called her over to the podium. "Can I brief you?"

While he talked, Adrienne stared at the ceiling.

Table eleven was a four-top under the awning, a good table: a local lawyer and her husband and their friends visiting from Anchorage, Alaska. The lawyer was not Thatcher's lawyer but she was a prominent Nantucket citizen—on the board of Hospice and the Boys & Girls Club—and a regular guest. VIP. Adrienne had delivered their chips and dip and opened their wine, the fantastic Leeuwin chardonnay from Western Australia. Now they were eating their entrées and Adrienne saw the lawyer glancing around the dining room in distress. Adrienne hurried over.

"What can I help you with?" she asked.

The lawyer beckoned Adrienne closer. "You won't believe this," she said. "But my friend swears her swordfish is overcooked."

"Overcooked?" Adrienne said.

"And I'll tell you what, it must be true because people from Alaska never complain."

Adrienne moved around the table to the Alaska woman and eyed the swordfish. It was black and shriveled; it looked like one of the pork chops that Doug used to murder in his cast-iron skillet before he doused it with ketchup.

"I'm sorry," the Alaska woman squeaked.

"I'm the one who's sorry," Adrienne said. "Let me bring you another piece. Believe me when I say this almost never happens."

She carried the swordfish to the kitchen, poking it once with her finger. It was completely dry; it had the texture of plaster. Adrienne was thrilled. Two weeks earlier a complaint about the doughnuts had nearly made her weep, but today a complaint about the food was a gift from God. She couldn't wait to confront Fiona with this hideous swordfish.

Adrienne slammed into the kitchen and dropped the plate on the pass with a clatter. No one was expediting.

"Where's Fiona?" she said.

"She's in the office lying down," Hector said.

Adrienne deflated. Her rage was overcooked, shriveled, dry, and yet she couldn't get rid of it.

"Well, where's Antonio, then?" she asked.

"It's his night off," Hector said. "Which reminds me, how was your date?"

"Fuck you," Adrienne said.

This set the platoon of Subiacos laughing. Adrienne picked the swordfish up off the plate and flung it at Hector, who was, conveniently, working grill. It hit him in the shoulder, smudging his white jacket.

"You killed the swordfish for eleven," she said. "The guest complained—in fact, she was practically in tears because it tasted so bad. Fire another one."

"Boo-hoo," Hector said, laying a swordfish steak across the grill.

Adrienne marched back out to table eleven. "Sorry about the swordfish," she said. "We're going to comp your bill this evening and I hope you'll forgive us."

The lawyer touched Adrienne's wrist. "You don't have to comp the meal," she said.

"Oh, yes," Adrienne said. "Yes, I do."

A few moments later, table six, a deuce, guests from the Nantucket Beach Club, called Adrienne over. No lobster on the lobster club. What they showed her was a twenty-nine-dollar BLT.

"Please," Adrienne said, picking up the plate. "Let me get you some lobster meat. And your dinner tonight is on the house."

The third table she comped because the top of the butterscotch crème brûlée was scorched. The guest hadn't even complained but Adrienne saw the desserts go out, and she saw the black spots. She had an infuriating vision of Mario back in his lair doing the bossa nova while he took a welding tool to the custard. The dessert was going to a table of six, which meant a tab of at least a thousand dollars. Adrienne bought their dinner. The revenge was so sweet it made her dizzy.

Later, Thatcher cornered her at the podium. It was eleven fifteen; she had a line of five people. The bar was packed but unusually quiet.

"You comped three meals," he said. "One tab was twelve hundred dollars. Because that six-top was drinking a Chateau Margaux."

Adrienne shrugged. "The food was bad tonight. Fiona wasn't expediting. You should have seen the swordfish at eleven. It was a piece of drywall."

"I understand the swordfish. And that was Leigh Stanford's table and I would have comped it myself. But a piece of lobster missing? A bad crème brûlée?"

"The lobster missing was a table Mack sent us, and the brûlée looked like it had the bubonic plague. At the beginning of the season you told me that close to perfect wasn't going to cut it."

"I did. But to *comp* a twelve-hundred-dollar dinner?"

"During first seating, I took a walk-in four-top that one of your other managers probably would have turned away because they weren't wearing

Armani. They drank two bottles of Cristal and had a thousand-dollar tab themselves. Take the difference out of my salary."

Thatcher sighed. "I'm not going to take it out of your salary," he said. "All three tables left huge tips so the waitstaff loves you. And I know you did what you thought was right." He nodded at the kitchen. "I'm going to eat."

Adrienne didn't answer. She was crushed. He didn't even care enough to fight with her.

TO: DrDon@toothache.com
FROM: Ade12177@hotmail.com
DATE: June 16, 2005 9:14 A.M.
SUBJECT: Surprise!

I sent you the last of the money I owe you—not bad for two weeks of work! And your "interest" should arrive at the office tomorrow morning. Bon appetit—and thanks for always being there for me. Love.

TO: kyracrenshaw@mindspring.com
FROM: Ade12177@hotmail.com
DATE: June 16, 2005 9:37 A.M.
SUBJECT: First date of the summer

I can honestly say I would rather go out with drug abuser and felon Doug Riedel than ever go out with my boss again. Doug may have stuck my life savings up his nose and robbed my place of employment, but at least he didn't leave me stranded for another woman!

Business Notes

The Inquirer and Mirror

Week of June 17, 2005

BLUE BISTRO UP FOR SALE

Harry Henderson of Henderson Realty, Inc. announced late last week that Blue Bistro owners Thatcher Smith and Fiona Kemp have put the popular waterfront restaurant on the market for $8.5 million. Mr. Smith was quoted as saying, "This is a classic case of quitting while we're ahead." Rumors have circulated that

> Smith and Kemp are looking for another property on the island, and that they have expressed interest in Sloop's on Steamship Wharf, which they hope to turn into a chic café called Calamari. "While we feel that space is currently underutilized," Smith says, "the rumors are absolutely untrue." The only certain plans Smith and his partner Ms. Kemp have in the works, he says, is a trip to the Galápagos Islands in October.
>
> Ms. Kemp could not be reached for comment.

For Father's Day, Adrienne bought her father a gas grill from the Williams-Sonoma catalog and a box of Omaha steaks. It cost her over seven hundred dollars but money, now, was the least of her worries. The balance in her bank account was steadily growing and she had paid off her thirteen-hundred-dollar debt to her father. If for the money alone, she was going to keep her job.

A week had passed and Thatcher hadn't said a word about their date. Of course, Adrienne hardly gave him a chance—she spoke to him in only the most perfunctory way, in only the most professional capacity, and he returned the favor. With each passing day the evening of their date faded into yesterday's news. Adrienne tried to regard it as a failed experiment. A fallen soufflé. She had broken Rule Three and she was paying the price. So now it was back to the straight and narrow. If she felt bruised—her heart, her ego—she was going to make sure that no one could tell.

She did a crisp, clean job on the floor. She handed out menus, delivered the chips and dip, ran food, opened wine, processed credit cards, and worked the door without compassion. Tyler Lefroy informed her that patrons of the bar called her the Blue Bitch. That made her smile for the first time since Dionis Beach.

What she needed, she told herself, was a life apart from the restaurant, and so she started jogging in the mornings. She ran to Surfside Beach, she ran to Cisco Beach, she ran along Miacomet Pond. She rode her bike to the rotary and ran along the Polpis Road. One day she ran to the restaurant—the Sid Wainer truck was in the parking lot and Adrienne saw Fiona and JZ sitting in the back of the truck talking, their legs dangling over the edge. She ran on Cliff Road past Tupancy Links and the water tower, out to Eel Point where the road turned to dirt.

Every way she went, Nantucket revealed its beauty. The rosa rugosa was blooming pink and white, the ponds were blue, the eelgrass razor sharp. The beaches were clean and still not crowded. The island had a lot more to offer, Adrienne told herself, than just Thatcher Smith.

One morning, Adrienne ran all the way out to Madaket Harbor, which was too far on a hot day. She bought a cold Evian at the Westender before she embarked on her limp home. She was on the bike path by Long Pond when a green Honda Pilot stopped; the tinted passenger window went down.

"Do you need a lift?" the driver asked.

It was a man, in his forties, with dark hair. The exact kind of person one imagined offering candy to an unsuspecting young girl.

"No, thanks," Adrienne said, waving the empty water bottle. "I'm fine."

"You sure?"

"All set."

"It's awfully hot. I can drop you in town. It'll take three minutes."

Adrienne looked at her dusty shoes. The soles of her feet burned. The guy was right: It was hot. She was out of water and she had three, maybe four, miles to go. She noticed a child's car seat in the back of the Pilot. So he probably wasn't a serial killer, and he couldn't exactly abduct her on Nantucket.

"Okay," Adrienne said. "Thanks." She climbed in. The air-conditioning was a blessing.

The man put up her window and hit the gas. "I'll just drop you in town," he said. "I'm headed in to pick up my mail."

"Fine."

He hummed along to a song on the radio. Adrienne sat up very straight to avoid sweating all over his car.

"You don't recognize me, do you?" the man said.

Adrienne fumbled with her Walkman and it fell to the floor. She bent over to retrieve it, trying not to panic. She slid in a sideways look. He looked familiar, but she met so many people on a nightly basis that . . .

"Drew Amman-Keller," he said.

Adrienne glanced up. Drew Amman-Keller? Adrienne studied his face. The lips she recognized, but the rest was different. Hadn't he had a beard? And an awful pair of glasses?

"I'm sorry," she said. "You look different."

"I shaved," he said. "My wife insists that I shave in the summer."

"You're married?" Adrienne asked.

"Three kids," he said.

Adrienne stared out the window. They were passing the landfill. She prayed to see another car, but they seemed to be the only one on the road. She tried to parse her fear. The guy was a freelance journalist, not a criminal. And it wasn't as though he was stalking her; he was on his way to the post office.

"You can just drop me off here, if you want," Adrienne said.

"At the dump?"

"I can walk home. It's not far."

"Did Thatcher tell you not to talk to me?"

A car approached, a red Jeep Wrangler with the top down—two very tan college boys with a couple of surfboards strapped to the roll bars. They were gone before Adrienne could think of how to signal for help. What, she wondered, would Thatcher do if he learned she'd accepted a ride from Drew Amman-Keller? And why did she care what Thatcher thought?

"I know what's going on with Fiona," he said. "I've known for years. What she and Thatcher don't understand is that I want to help. I have an offer on the table from the *Atlantic Monthly* if Fiona ever agrees to talk to me. Sometimes by writing a feature in a big magazine, you can create positive change."

Adrienne squeezed her water bottle in the middle, making a plastic crunch. This was the guy who had sent her to the Bistro in the first place. He'd set her up, maybe, hoping she'd spy on Fiona and report details back to him. But what kind of details was he after, exactly? "I have no idea what you're talking about," she said.

Drew Amman-Keller took his eyes off the road for a split second to look at Adrienne. She noticed something funny about the bottom half of his face. It was pink and raw-looking where he'd shaved, as though he'd stripped off a mask.

He downshifted and signaled to the left. "Here's Cliff Road," he said. "Is it okay if I drop you here?"

"I thought you were going to take me into town," Adrienne said. "Are you trying to get rid of me now?"

He laughed. "I'm happy to take you to town," he said. He pulled back onto the road and turned up the radio.

Adrienne collapsed back in the seat. "You're happy to take me to town, but you won't tell me what's going on in the restaurant where I'm the assistant manager. You must think I'm pretty naïve."

"I think no such thing."

Despite the air-conditioning, Adrienne was hot. And thirsty. And angry.

"I went on a date with Thatcher last week," she said. "But Fiona called at midnight and told Thatcher his dinner was ready and he left me at my front door." Adrienne watched Drew Amman-Keller for a reaction, but he had none. She kicked his glove compartment and left a mark with her filthy shoe. The restaurant was turning her into a lunatic, the kind of person who confided in strangers and disrespected their brand-new cars. "You told me if I ever wanted to talk, I should call you. You gave me your card. I still have it at home."

"Good," he said. "Hold on to it."

"I don't suppose you'll write an article about my date with Thatcher?"

"No," he said.

"No," Adrienne echoed. Girl likes boy, boy likes different girl. He'd heard it a thousand times before. Everyone had.

There were only two people in the restaurant whom Adrienne trusted, and one of those people was Mario. This might have seemed counterintuitive, as Mario's reputation among the staff was for being exactly the opposite—untrustworthy, fickle, a scoundrel. He had dumped Delilah by kissing another woman on the dance floor of the Chicken Box while he was there on a date with Delilah. Delilah had cried for three days, and she begged Duncan to defend her honor. Duncan said, "I told you not to go near the guy in the first place."

Mario was deadly as a lover, but as a friend he had a curiously golden touch. The afternoon of her ride with Drew Amman-Keller, Adrienne marched back into pastry.

"It looks like someone could use a Popsicle," Mario said. He pulled a tray out of the freezer and handed Adrienne a creamy raspberry-banana Popsicle then took one for himself. They licked the Popsicles leaning side by side against the marble counter.

"They're good, yeah?" Mario said.

"Yeah," she said. She bit off a big piece and it gave her an ice-cream headache. She moaned. Mario rubbed the inside of her wrist.

"This is supposed to help," he said.

"You just want to touch me," she said.

"You got that right."

She said, "Do you know what's going on between Fiona and Thatcher?"

He dropped her arm. "There's nothing going on."

Adrienne threw her Popsicle stick into the trash. "You're lying to me."

"No," Mario said. He moved down the counter to where the dough for the Portuguese rolls was proofing. He worked the dough with his hands. "I would not lie to you. There's nothing going on the way you're thinking."

"How do you know what I'm thinking?"

"I always know what the ladies are thinking."

"So if it's not what I'm thinking, then what is it?"

"I wish I could tell you," Mario said.

The other person Adrienne trusted was Caren, but only during certain times of the day: mornings after Duncan left, in the Jetta on the way to work, as they listened to Moby.

"I am not a jealous person," Caren said, one morning after four espressos, which was enough to make even her tremble. "You haven't known me very long, so you'll have to take my word for it. Usually, I eat men for breakfast."

"I can tell," Adrienne said.

"I'm a biting bitch."

"You're strong."

"Right. Except not with Duncan. I've known him twelve years and I've seen him do all kinds of outrageous things with women at the bar, and before it was always funny. But now it's awful. They all want to sleep with him, even the married ones. He says he's in it for the money, but I don't know, it's got to be an ego rush for him, right? This is driving me fucking nuts. But don't tell anyone, okay? Promise you won't tell."

"I promise," Adrienne said. She had sworn to herself that she wasn't going to tell anyone about her ride with Drew Amman-Keller, not even Caren. But at that moment Caren seemed vulnerable—pale, sweating, shaking from her mainline of caffeine—so Adrienne said, "I know I've beaten this subject to death, but I really want to know what's going on between Thatcher and Fiona."

Caren gathered up her hair and tied it into a knot. It stayed perfect like that, without a single pin. Adrienne was both fascinated by her manipulations and driven batty by her silence. Caren was deciding how much, if anything, to divulge. "It's a lot simpler than you think."

"Simpler how?"

"They're friends, like I said before. If you're ever going to have a relationship with Thatcher Smith, you need to accept that."

"I'm not going to have a relationship with Thatcher Smith," Adrienne said. She needed to accept *that.*

On the Sunday before the official start of summer, Caren announced from her post in front of the espresso machine that she and Duncan were going sailing on Holt Millman's yacht and that Adrienne was joining them.

"You're not allowed to say no," Caren said. "Holt is thrilled you're coming. We're leaving in thirty minutes and we'll be back at four."

Adrienne knew damn well that Holt Millman had no clue who she was but Caren seemed resolute and Duncan backed her up, saying, "Yep. Better get ready."

It was something different, a welcome change from running by herself and going to the beach by herself. Once she was heading down the docks of Old North Wharf, Adrienne felt excited. It was another gorgeous day and she liked being among the boats—the sailboats, the power yachts—and the people loading up coolers of beer and bags of sandwiches, getting ready for a day on the water. She hoped Thatcher was cooped up inside, the phone stuck to his ear like a tumor.

Holt Millman's yacht, *Kelsey,* was the biggest boat Adrienne had ever seen in person. It was, Duncan told her, 103 feet long with a ninety-foot main mast. It was modeled after the *Shamrock,* a 1930s era J-class racing yacht, but Holt's boat was made out of Kevlar and honeycombed fiberglass. It had clean lines up top, Duncan said, but below deck it was a mansion—with china in cabinets, a Jacuzzi, a washer and dryer.

Duncan paused. "I'm going to guess that you've never seen anything like this."

Adrienne had sailed on the Chesapeake when she was a child, she'd fished in blue water off the coast of Florida, hung on for dear life to a catamaran in Hawaii, and she island-hopped in an old junk during her year in Thailand. When she lived in Chatham, her boyfriend Sully had use of a seventeen-foot Boston Whaler and he'd even let her take the wheel. But none of that had prepared her for *Kelsey*.

They took their shoes off before they stepped onto the teak deck. Holt was standing in the cockpit talking to a man with broad shoulders who looked like the captain. Holt wore a green polo shirt with KELSEY on the pocket; he was drinking something pink and frosty in a Providence Puritans glass. (The Puritans, Duncan had informed Adrienne in the car, were an NHL expansion team that Holt had purchased the year before.) As soon as Holt saw Duncan and Caren, he raised his glass in greeting. Adrienne wished she knew something about hockey.

"Thanks for coming, thanks for coming," Holt said. He pumped Duncan's hand and kissed Caren on the cheek. "And you brought Adrienne. Good for you. This boat needs more pretty women."

Adrienne smiled. "Thanks for inviting us," she said, but Holt Millman didn't hear. He was calling below deck for "Drinks, more drinks," ushering Duncan forward, and introducing the rest of the guests with a sweep of his arm. There were five other people on the boat, some of whom Adrienne recognized. The woman who cut Thatcher's hair sat on a cushioned bench in the cockpit talking to the hostess from 21 Federal. There were two older bond-trader type men who rose to greet Duncan and ask him about his handicap. And out on the bow of the boat was a stunning blond woman in a red bikini. She sat up and waved at Adrienne; it was Cat, the world's most glamorous electrician.

"Cat is everywhere," Adrienne murmured to Caren.

"She could be a model," Caren said. "If she weren't busy wiring Millman's home theater."

Caren joined Duncan's conversation with the bond traders, leaving Adrienne to either sit alone or talk to the hostess and Thatcher's hairdresser. While the first option was infinitely preferable, the hostess—who must have been the social director for her sorority in college—waved Adrienne over.

"Come sit with us!" she called. She moved her tiny butt a fraction of an inch to indicate that she was making room. Holt popped up the stairs with a tray of pink frosty drinks. He held the tray out to Adrienne.

"This is my own recipe," he said. "It's called a Kelsey. I keep trying to get Duncan to make them at the restaurant."

Duncan lifted his head from his other conversation. "No blender drinks," he said. "Sorry."

Holt Millman laughed with his head thrown back, exposing his tan throat. Adrienne guessed he was nearing seventy, yet she sensed he went to great lengths and expense to keep himself looking younger. Spa treatments to erase the wrinkles from his face and neck and the like.

Adrienne accepted a drink and sat next to the hostess from 21. "Hi," she said. "I'm Adrienne."

The hostess clapped her hands. "We know who you are," she said. "Because remember, I seated you? When you were on your date with Thatcher?"

The hairdresser piped in. "I just love Thatch," she said. "That red-gold hair. I have clients who would sell their souls for hair that color."

"Have you two been dating long?" the hostess asked.

"We're not dating," Adrienne said. "It was a business dinner."

"Oh, stop," the hairdresser said. "I cut his hair that very afternoon and he told me he had a hot date. It didn't sound like business to me."

"Well, it was business," Adrienne said. She sipped her drink. It was delicious—watermelon, strawberry, club soda, and what she thought must be vodka. It went straight to her head. She removed her T-shirt so that she was in her bikini top and shorts. The sun felt terrific. *Hot date?* She was relieved when the motor revved and the captain steered them out of the harbor.

One hour and three Kelsey drinks later, Adrienne was happier. Caren had rescued her and now Adrienne, Caren, and Cat were lying in their bikinis on the teak deck near the bow. Above their heads the sails rumbled, the ropes snapped, and a crew of young men in green shirts like Holt's moved about—tightening, loosening, using jargon like "foredeck" and "power winches." Nantucket was a blur of green and gray in the distance. A young woman with an English accent brought a basket of wraps and refills for their drinks. The sandwiches were beautiful pinwheels of color: avocado, tomato and bacon, goat cheese and roasted red pepper, roast beef, cucumber, and horseradish cream. *Forget Fiona,* Adrienne thought. She was never getting off this boat.

Four drinks, five drinks. Then somehow, Adrienne found herself sitting in the cockpit with the rest of the guests passing around a joint. Adrienne smoked rarely but she was so relaxed that she didn't even blink. Everyone smoked except for Holt Millman, who just beamed as though nothing pleased him more than young people smoking marijuana on his boat. When Adrienne looked at him again, she thought maybe he was closer to sixty.

She went below deck for the first time a while later in search of the bathroom, and since she was the only one underneath (aside from whatever sandwich genius was working in the galley) she took a look around. There was a living room with an overstuffed sofa and chairs and a wall lined with books that were held in place by a brass rail. There was a formal dining room with a bouquet of Asiatic lilies and pink roses on the oval table, and eight Windsor chairs, and the promised china in cabinets. There were a couple of small sleeping quarters, the beds decked out in Frette linens. And then Adrienne peeked quickly—because she was pressing her luck snooping around like this—into the master suite. A queen-size bed with a green silk spread, photographs of Holt Millman with Bill Gates, Holt Millman with Bill Clinton, Holt Millman with Elton John, and a framed article from *Time* about Holt Millman and his myriad companies. The article had been written by Drew Amman-Keller.

"Adrienne."

Adrienne gasped; she'd been caught. Holt Millman himself stood in the doorway. This was, no doubt, the kind of situation that Adrienne's father composed in his mind, the kind that turned his hair silver: Adrienne, wearing only a bikini, standing in the bedroom of Holt Millman's yacht.

The pot made her feel like laughing; she bit her lip. "Sorry," she said. "I was looking for the bathroom."

"Use mine," he said. He opened a door that Adrienne had thought was a closet, but it was the master bath. Marble, of course, with the Jacuzzi.

"Okay," she said. "Thanks."

She closed the door behind her and peed—she really had to go—looking at the stacks of fluffy green towels and at the glassed-in shower. She felt the boat listing from side to side. She washed her hands with one of the cakes of sailboat-shaped soap and checked her teeth, hoping and praying that by the time she opened the door, Holt Millman would be gone. But he was right there, sitting on the edge of the bed, talking to someone on his cell phone. When she emerged, he snapped the phone shut.

"I just made a dinner reservation for two, tonight, eight o'clock, at the Wauwinet," he said. "I hope you'll join me."

Adrienne stared at him, unwillingly imagining a woman smoothing essence of sea cucumber on Holt Millman's neck to keep it taut. She wanted to laugh. She bowed her head. This was the eleventh richest man in the United States, asking her on a date.

"I can't," she said. "I have to work."

"Work?" he said, as though he'd never heard of the word. "Okay, then, what night are you free?"

The answer was Wednesday night, but Adrienne couldn't bring herself to tell him. She wished like hell that she was up on deck lying safely between Caren and Cat, picking at the leftover wraps, maybe indulging in one more cocktail since her mouth was dry and ashy.

"I'm dating someone," she said. And in her alcohol-saturated, drug-induced state, she thought, *I'm dating Thatch.*

Holt Millman didn't get to be so successful by being a jerk or by preying on young women in bikinis whom he found nosing around his personal quarters. He was, at all times, a model of graciousness. "Whoever he is, he is one lucky man," Holt said. He offered Adrienne his arm and escorted her up the stairs, back into the sun.

When Adrienne woke up from her nap, it was four o'clock, and the girl with the English accent was offering her a cold Coca-Cola, which Adrienne immediately recognized as the answer to her prayers. She had fallen asleep on her stomach and she could tell just from sitting up that her back was burned. She knocked back half the Coke and went in search of Caren and Duncan, whom she found standing at the stern on either side of the flapping Rhode Island flag. They were tan and laughing; they looked like models in a Tommy Hilfiger ad. Adrienne caught Caren's eye and pointed to her running watch. It was five after four, they were zero feet above sea level, and Nantucket was still a smudge on the horizon. Caren shrugged. Nonchalance was her middle name. Adrienne, on the other hand, was a realist. If they headed back now they might be in the harbor in half an hour.

Leaving twenty-five minutes to drop Duncan off, get home, change (there would be no time for a shower), and get to work. But who was she kidding? They were going to be late.

Adrienne tapped the captain on the shoulder. "I know I'm going to sound like a Providence Puritan," she said, desperately hoping he got the joke, "but there are three of us on this boat who have to be at work at five."

Even with both motors turned on full-throttle, they didn't reach the mouth of the harbor until ten of five. By this time, the effects of the alcohol and the pot were gone and in their place was the special anxiety that hit when Adrienne knew she was going to be fatally late. Her brain ticked like a clock, she checked her jogging watch eighty-two times, and finally—because everyone on the boat could sense she was about to have a nervous breakdown—Holt Millman pulled out his cell phone and told Thatcher that he had taken three of the Bistro's key employees hostage and that they would be to work by the stroke of six. Adrienne was dying to hear Thatcher's response to this, but Holt snapped his cell phone shut, as if closing the book on the problem of the time, and said, "There. Do you feel better?"

"I don't like to be late," she said.

When they finally docked, Adrienne hugged the eleventh richest man in the country and thanked him for a wonderful day, then she hauled ass to the car with Duncan and Caren trailing reluctantly behind. The next hour was a blur of activity: drive, drop off Duncan, drive, wash face, brush teeth, change into the diaphanous blouse, which hid her sunburn, stuff half an untoasted bagel with light veggie cream cheese into her pie hole since they were going to miss family meal (Caren ate the other half and spent four minutes brewing an espresso—Adrienne drank one also in the interest of staying awake through service), brush teeth again, drive. They walked into the Bistro at five fifty-six, trying to look like it was just another lovely day at the regatta. *Pshew!*

Thatcher was at the podium, going over the book. He seemed unperturbed by their late arrival. "How was the sail?" he asked.

"Fabulous," Adrienne said.

Why had they hurried? There were only sixty-two covers on the book and only twenty people for first seating, though Adrienne did have three parties walk in. Joe and Christo both had the night off, as did Rex, so instead of piano music the stereo played Vivaldi.

"It's dead," Adrienne complained.

"The calm before the storm," Thatcher said. "This is a notoriously slow weekend because people have other things going on—weddings, graduations. But I had a hundred calls today about the Fourth. It's going to be a circus."

This was the longest conversation they'd had since their date. The sail had put Adrienne in a more generous frame of mind. She could talk to Thatcher as though he was just another person.

"What was family meal tonight?"

"Grilled pizzas," Thatcher said. "Are you sorry you missed it?"

"I ate at home," Adrienne said, thinking, *Of course I'm sorry I missed it!* "The boat was fun. Holt Millman asked me out to dinner."

At first it appeared Thatcher hadn't heard her—either that or he was letting it go, like he did the time Adrienne asked if Fiona was his wife. But then he tilted his head and peered at Adrienne out of the corner of his eye. "What did you tell him?" he asked.

There was no mistaking his tone of voice: He cared. He cared! Adrienne did her best to keep the trumpet of victory out of her response.

"I told him no."

At seven o'clock, JZ came in with a little girl who had brown bobbed hair and a mouth full of chewing gum.

"Adrienne," JZ said. "I'd like you to meet my daughter, Shaughnessy. Shaughnessy, this is Adrienne Dealey."

"Big dealey," Shaughnessy said, then she giggled.

"You'll excuse my daughter," JZ said. "She's suffering from a cute case of being eight. We're going to sit at the bar."

Adrienne held out a hand. "Be my guest," she said.

But Shaughnessy remained at the podium, studying Adrienne. "We're going to eat caviar," she said. "And then I'm going into the kitchen to help Fiona make a pizza."

"Is that so?" Adrienne said. "Do you like to cook?"

She shrugged. "Of course."

JZ led Shaughnessy to the bar, where the two of them perched on stools. Since there was absolutely nothing else to do—Thatcher had left her to work the door in case of walk-ins while he romanced the floor—Adrienne watched them. Dad and daughter: The sight made Adrienne miss her own father who at that moment would be relaxing in a house Adrienne had never seen, hopefully enjoying a perfectly grilled Omaha steak and watching *60 Minutes.*

Duncan poured JZ a beer and made Shaughnessy a Shirley Temple with three cherries. Shaughnessy removed the gum from her mouth and parked it on her cocktail napkin. Adrienne decided to check in the kitchen; if the chips and dip were ready, she could run them out.

When she walked through the kitchen door she nearly crashed into Fiona, who was on her tiptoes at the out door, trying to see through the window. Behind the pass, the Subiacos were engrossed in the baseball game on the radio; the White Sox were at Fenway tonight. Adrienne had hardly seen Fiona since her date with Thatcher; Fiona had been hiding out a lot in the office. Adrienne certainly hadn't spoken to her. But she looked so funny trying to see out the window that Adrienne decided to excuse the fact that this was the woman who had sabotaged her date and caused her ten days of date-induced angst.

"You should go say hi," Adrienne said. "There's practically no one sitting down."

Fiona spun on the heels of her kitchen clogs. "The last time I went out during service, Ruth Reichl was sitting at table one. The month following there was a tidbit in *Gourmet* about how Chef Fiona Kemp does occasionally peek out of her shell. So I'm not going out. What do you need?"

"I saw JZ. I thought there might be chips for him. His daughter said she was going to eat caviar and then come in here and help you make a pizza."

Fiona's face softened. "She wants to be a chef," she said. "Isn't that crazy?" And then she yelled out, "Spuds, Paco!"

And Paco said, "Yes, chef."

Pfft, pfft, pfft, hiss.

"They'll be ready in three minutes," Fiona said. "Get back to your post."

Adrienne ran the chips, opened two bottles of wine, changed the CD to Bobby Short at the Carlyle Hotel. She saw JZ and Shaughnessy slip into the kitchen. Suddenly, in that way he had, Thatcher materialized at her side.

"She's a cute kid," Adrienne said. "Seeing her with JZ reminds me of me and my dad."

"Adrienne Dealey waxes sentimental," Thatcher said.

"Where's her mother? Is she alive?"

"I'm afraid so," Thatcher said.

"So JZ's divorced?"

"No."

"He's not divorced?"

"No. He's married."

"He's married?"

"Yes." Thatcher handed Adrienne a pile of menus to return to the podium, meaning: Get back to your post.

"But you said he was a nice guy." Thinking: *He brought his daughter to the restaurant to make pizza with his lover? Not nice.*

"Oh, Adrienne," Thatcher said. "Were the world so easy as you appear to believe it is."

Three women who walked in at quarter to eight asked for rolls and butter, giving Adrienne an excuse to poke her head in the kitchen. She had finally learned where the rolls were kept—in a burlap sack hanging from one of the oven doors so the rolls would keep warm. Adrienne fixed a basket of rolls and arranged the cake of butter on a glass pedestal, all while watching Fiona and Shaughnessy make their pizza. The dough was rolled out and Shaughnessy painted it with sauce, then she gathered up two handfuls of pepperoni.

"I want to make a face," she said.

"Not only a chef," Fiona said, "but an artist."

Shaughnessy laid out the pepperoni. Eyes, nose, mouth.

"Your face is frowning," Fiona said.

"Because I feel sad," Shaughnessy said.

Fiona had a handful of sliced fresh mozzarella poised over the pizza, but when Shaughnessy said this, she lowered her hand to the counter and glanced at JZ. JZ shrugged.

Fiona raised Shaughnessy's chin with her finger. Adrienne's attention was captivated by the look on Fiona's face. She recognized that look.

"Why are you sad?" Fiona said.

"Because I want everything to be different," Shaughnessy said. "I want you to be my mother."

Thatcher let Adrienne go early and she was glad; it had been the world's longest day. When she got home, she showered, then fell into bed in her towel with her hair wet. She thought she might have crazy dreams about Holt Millman or the girl with the English accent who worked on the boat or Shaughnessy and JZ and the absent wife/mother whom they both seemed so eager to replace. But Adrienne slept without dreaming at all. When she heard the knock at her door, that was the one thing she was certain of: She hadn't been dreaming and she wasn't dreaming now. There was someone knocking on her door.

She pulled her comforter up under her chin. Thinking, *Caren. But maybe Duncan—and how weird would* that *be?*

"Hello?" she said.

It was dark, but even so, she could tell that the person in the doorway was Thatch. A light from somewhere caught his hair and she knew the shape of him, his tread, his smell. Thatcher Smith was in her room. She checked her clock—one forty-eight—not so late, really. Not by restaurant standards. His presence was so bizarre that she didn't even know where to begin her thinking. She waited for him to speak.

He eased himself down onto the side of her bed. "Hi," he said. "It's me."

"Hi, me," she said. She worried what she looked like; she wondered if he could see her.

There was a long pause and then he sighed. "I'm sorry, Adrienne."

The words hung in the room in an odd way, as if they required more explanation, but they didn't.

"I know," she said.

"You may wonder why I'm telling you now, in the middle of the night."

"The middle of the night part doesn't bother me," Adrienne said. "Nor the fact that you seem to have broken into my house. But you made me wait ten days."

"There's a lot going on," Thatcher said. "Fiona's sick."

"I know," Adrienne said.

"She's very sick."

"I know," Adrienne said—because she *did* know, somehow. The coughing, the childhood illness Thatcher didn't want to talk about, Fiona's reclusiveness, her embrace with JZ, the last year of the restaurant, Drew Amman-Keller's cryptic words, Thatcher's slavish devotion—they had all added up in Adrienne's mind to an instinct she hadn't been able to acknowledge, even to herself. But then there was earlier that evening, the scene she witnessed; Shaughnessy in the kitchen with Fiona. There had been something in Fiona's face, a longing Adrienne had seen before in her own mother's face when Rosalie lay in the hospital bed, her pale head covered with a Phillies cap. So, yes, Adrienne knew: Fiona was sick.

"Do you want me to leave?" Thatcher said.

"No," Adrienne said. "I want you to stay. Do you want to talk about Fiona?"

"Not tonight," Thatcher said. "Is that okay?"

"Of course."

Thatcher removed his blazer and laid it across Adrienne's computer table. Then he shed his loafers and his watch and his belt and he climbed into bed. Adrienne was nude—her towel had long ago been mixed up with the covers—and when he realized this fact, he inhaled a sharp breath.

"Sorry," she said. "I showered when I got home, and . . ."

He kissed her and Adrienne was filled with awe. How had she survived ten days without his mouth on hers, his tongue, his lips, his body pressed against her body? How had she survived? It felt as though she had gone ten days without food, without water. Because she was hungry for him. She was starved.

7

Old Boyfriends

October 1, 2002

Dear Sully,

The one thing I remember my mother telling me about love was that you couldn't hunt it down or sniff it out. Like all great mysteries in the world, my mother said, it just happened.

This summer was the best summer of my life. But although I wished for it and wanted it, love didn't happen to me the way it happened to you. I can't explain it any better than that. I hope someday you'll forgive me for taking off like this, without warning, without good-bye. I thought this would be easiest—for me, certainly—but also for you.

If there was something else I could say, I would say it. Sorry, sorry, sorry.

Adrienne

Cystic Fibrosis

Cystic fibrosis is a genetic disease affecting approximately thirty thousand children and adults in the United States. CF causes the body to produce an abnormally thick, sticky mucus, due to the faulty transport of sodium chloride within cells lining organs—such as the lungs and pancreas—to their outer surfaces. The thick CF mucus also obstructs the pancreas,

> preventing enzymes from reaching the intestines to help break down and digest food.
>
> CF has a variety of symptoms. The most common is very salty-tasting skin; persistent coughing, wheezing, or pneumonia; excessive appetite but poor weight gain. The treatment of CF depends on the stage of the disease and which organs are involved. One means of treatment, chest physical therapy, requires vigorous percussion (by using cupped hands) on the back and chest to dislodge the thick mucus from the lungs. Antibiotics are also used to treat lung infections and are administered intravenously, via pills, and/or medicinal vapors, which are inhaled to open up clogged airways.
>
> The median life expectancy for someone with CF is thirty-two, though some patients have lived as long as fifty to sixty years.

Before she met Thatcher, Adrienne had been down the road and around the bend with three and a half other men. The first, chronologically, was her academic adviser during her fifth year of college. Adrienne was twenty-two years old, trying to earn enough credits to graduate from Florida State. Her transcript—with courses from IU Bloomington and Vanderbilt and AP credits from her high school in Iowa, not to mention two semesters at Florida State—looked like a patchwork quilt and smacked (so her father claimed) of a half-baked effort that was draining him of his savings. She had plenty of class hours and good grades but nothing that equaled a major. She had started out as elementary ed at IU, then at Vandy she switched to sociology with a minor in art history. Florida State didn't have a sociology major, though they did have anthropology, which she could qualify for with twenty-six more credits. Or she could go the route of art history, but she felt this wasn't a major that would ever present any career opportunities, and her father agreed.

Thus, the academic adviser.

The first time Adrienne met with Will Kovak, she barely noticed him. She was too agitated about her tattered state of affairs. Her father was right: She wasn't taking college seriously, she was flitting around, unwilling to commit to a major or even a school. Sure, some people transferred once, but twice? She hadn't made a lasting friendship or held on to a single interest since her mother died. She had toyed around with notions of law school (everyone she knew who didn't have long-term concrete goals applied to law school); she considered becoming a personal trainer; she had taken a course called African Drumming and really enjoyed it; she wondered if she should drop out of school and get a job. But where? Doing what? Her father and Mavis pelted her with possible vocations. Mavis thought she should teach the deaf. Her father thought she should take the hygienist's courses and join him in practice. Both of them thought she should see a shrink. With all these disturbing notions flooding her mind, Will Kovak registered only as a body behind a desk. His office was dark; the venetian blinds were pulled against the strong Florida sun. She could hardly see him. All Adrienne cared about was her transcript, which lay on his desk like a trauma patient. Could he save it?

"Psychology," Will said, after reviewing Adrienne's file for fifteen silent minutes, during which he referenced the college manual four times. "I can get you out of here in January with a degree in psychology if you take five classes this semester."

Psychology? Adrienne laughed. She could be her own shrink! But psychology had a scientific, even medical, sound that would please her father. Without stopping to think, Adrienne stepped behind Will Kovak's desk and hugged him around the shoulders. "Thank you," she said. "Thank you. Thank you."

He was stiff; he gave her an embarrassed smile. "You're, uh, welcome," he said.

Adrienne met with Will Kovak a second time to figure out what the five classes would be and then a third time to have him sign her add–drop slip. It was during this third visit that Adrienne began to wonder about him. He was an associate professor of world literature, but he was only twenty-nine. And he was cute, in a bookish way, with longish hair that curled at the neck and rimless glasses. Adrienne had hooked up with a few guys at beer parties, but these guys struck her as young and clueless, and because Florida State was as big as some developing countries, she never had to see them again. She hadn't been on a date since her first junior year at Vanderbilt, when Perry Russell took her out for fried chicken then talked her out of her virginity. She was ready for something different. She asked Will out for coffee, and after a very long, very awkward silence with Adrienne standing there in the near-dark and Will staring at his folded hands, he said yes.

In this way, the first real relationship of Adrienne's life began. She entered the peculiar universe of young academics. It seemed to Adrienne that in these circles the person with the most abstemious lifestyle was the most worthy of admiration. Adrienne and Will attended the free foreign film series sponsored by the university, they went to readings at the bookstore, they went for coffee, and, at Adrienne's insistence, splurged on the occasional beer at Bullwinkles. They studied together at the library and they spent every night making love on Will's futon in the condominium unit that his parents bankrolled. The condo had a tiled bathroom and a gourmet kitchen with an island and granite countertops, but it was as if Will were embarrassed by these amenities and, to make up for them, he kept the rest of the condo as spartan as possible. The living room was dominated by two card tables pushed together and covered with an Indian print tapestry and piled with books and Will's laptop computer (also bankrolled by the parents). The bedroom had just the futon mattress on the floor, a row of votive candles on the windowsill, and a boom box on which Will played his favorite kind of CD—the movie soundtrack.

Adrienne was out of place from the beginning. Amid all the older, unwashed, ramen–noodle eating, Edward Said–reading, quiet smart people, she was a dilettante undergrad who had a steady source of cash from her doting dentist father. She liked to sit by the pool, she liked to watch David Letterman, she had zero interest in grad school. Every so often, Will would drag Adrienne to a "party" thrown by one of his teaching assistant friends. These were usually held in an unair-conditioned studio apartment where graduate students and young professors, many of them foreign, drank very cheap Chianti, smoked clove cigarettes, listened to Balinese gamelan music, and talked about topics so erudite they might as well have been speaking another language. Adrienne hated these parties, and when she complained about them to Will, he confessed that he hated them, too, but the danger in not going was that they might gossip about him.

Will was quiet and shy and extremely concerned about what his older and more established colleagues thought about him, but he excelled at intimacy—at lighting the votive candles and putting on soft music and sharing things about himself. Adrienne knew he was an only child, that his parents lived in a Manhattan brownstone on Seventy-second and Fifth Avenue; she knew he occasionally smoked pot before lecturing because it helped him to relax;

she knew the names and complete histories of his six previous girlfriends (one of whom was his second cousin, who sometimes called late at night from her job as night auditor at Donald Trump's posh resort in Palm Beach); she knew the long and Byzantine road that led Will to his dissertation topic about *War and Peace*. It bothered Will that Adrienne never talked about herself. "Tell me about your childhood," he said.

"There's nothing to tell."

"What about your parents?"

"What about them?"

"What are they like?"

"Why are you asking me so many questions?"

"Because I want to know you," he said. "Tell me about your first kiss, your last boyfriend. Tell me *something*."

"I can't," she said. She was afraid if she opened her mouth, a lie would pop out. That was how it always happened.

"You can," Will said. "You just don't want to."

"I don't want to," she admitted.

"You don't trust me," Will said. He would usually end up leaving the bedroom and falling asleep on the bare wooden floor in front of his computer. These fights bothered Adrienne only slightly. It was a small price to pay for her privacy.

When the semester ended and Adrienne graduated, Dr. Don flew to Tallahassee for the ceremony. On the way to the airport to pick him up, Will asked, "Why isn't your mother coming?"

Adrienne could remember staring out the window at the hot, green Florida hills. She yearned to disappear in them. Adrienne's roommate at Vanderbilt had asked her this very same question when Dr. Don showed up alone for parents' weekend, and Adrienne had told the roommate that Rosalie stayed home because Adrienne's brother, Jonathan, was very sick.

"Well," Adrienne said. "Because she's dead."

"Dead? Your mother's dead?"

"This is your exit," Adrienne said.

Dr. Don took Adrienne and Will to Michelsen's Farm House for dinner, and in those three hours, Will mined Dr. Don for every conceivable detail of Adrienne's childhood—including, after two bottles of wine, the maudlin story of Rosalie's illness. Will gobbled up every word; Adrienne sat in astounded silence. She could not believe her father was emoting like this with a virtual stranger.

Dr. Don kept slapping Will on the back. "Professor at twenty-nine . . . really going places." Later, to Adrienne, he said, "Quiet guy, but he's got a strong handshake and a nice smile. And he is solely responsible for getting you out of this place before your thirtieth birthday."

"Funny, Dad."

"I give him credit. A professor at twenty-nine!"

"Don't get attached," Adrienne said.

"Why not?"

"I'm breaking up with him tomorrow."

"Oh, honey, no. Not because of me? If I said I hated him, would you stay together? I hated him."

Adrienne called Will the next day to tell him it was over, and she could hear the anguish in his voice reverberating through his near-empty apartment. "I thought after last night that our relationship was heading in a new direction," he said. "I feel like I know you so much better now."

"I'm sorry?" Adrienne said.

Ten minutes after she hung up, Adrienne called him back. She wanted his cousin's phone number.

"Why?" he said.

"Because," she said. "I want to work with her."

Once Adrienne crossed the bridge into Palm Beach and was escorted through the gates of Mar-a-Lago, her future became clear. There was a world filled with beautiful places and she wanted to live in them all.

On the twenty-eighth of June there were one hundred and ninety covers on the book, and lobster salad sandwiches for family meal. It was seventy-seven degrees in the dining room at the start of first seating, which was abnormally hot, but Thatcher pointed out that everyone would drink more. Adrienne wore the silk outfit in bottle green that matched her eyes or so she convinced herself in the bathroom while she was brushing her teeth. When she came out to the podium, Thatcher said, "I'm sitting down at table twenty to eat at first seating."

"What?" Adrienne said, in a voice that gave away too much. Dating only a few weeks and already her interest and fear were showing. Her mind scanned possible reasons why Thatcher would eat during first service at the most visible table in the room, instead of later with Fiona. Adrienne decided it must be Harry Henderson, the Realtor, who had been calling a lot lately with people who were interested in buying the property. Harry, she was pretty sure, was on the books tonight.

"Father Ott," Thatcher said. "The priest. And here he is now. So you're going to have to cover."

"Fine," Adrienne said.

"Are you Catholic?" Thatcher asked. It seemed like an oddly personal question to be asking fifteen seconds before work started, but among the things they'd agreed upon was that they were going to get to know each other slowly, bit by bit. Adrienne had told Thatcher the story about Will Kovak and he understood. They weren't going to stay up all night confiding their innermost secrets then wake up and claim they were soul mates.

"Lapsed," Adrienne said. Had they been alone in the dark, though, she might have added that the last time she set foot in a Catholic church was on the afternoon of her mother's funeral. As she followed the casket out of Our Lady of Assumption she crossed herself with holy water and left the Catholics behind. It was Rosalie who had been Catholic—and when Rosalie died, so, in some sense for Adrienne, did God. Dr. Don was a Protestant and whenever he and Adrienne moved to a new place they shopped around for a church—sometimes Presbyterian, sometimes Methodist—it hardly mattered to Adrienne's father as long as they had a place to go on Christmas and Easter. Dr. Don donated twenty hours of free checkups to needy kids and senior citizens in the congregation per year. It was nice, but somehow to Adrienne it never felt like religion. That, maybe, was how the Protestants preferred it.

"Hello, Thatcher Smith!" Father Ott was the tallest priest Adrienne had ever seen—six foot six with a deep, resonant voice and hair the bright silver of a dental filling. He wore khaki pants and a navy blazer. A pair of blue-lensed, titanium-framed sunglasses hung around his neck. Never in eighty-two years would Adrienne have pegged him as a priest; he looked like one of Grayson Parrish's golf partners. Thatcher and Father Ott embraced and Adrienne smiled down at the podium.

"Father Ott, please meet my assistant manager, Adrienne Dealey," Thatcher said.

Adrienne was overcome with shyness and guilt—she could feel the words "lapsed Catholic" emblazoned on her forehead.

"It's lovely to meet you," she said, offering her hand.

Father Ott smiled. "Likewise, likewise. Adrienne, you say? Like Adrienne Rich?"

"The poet," Adrienne said.

Thatcher raised his pale eyebrows. "You're named after a poet?"

"Not after," she said. "Just like."

Father Ott rubbed his hands together. "I'm starving," he said. "But I promised Fiona I would bless the kitchen before the holiday. Shall we get business out of the way?"

Thatcher led Father Ott into the kitchen. Adrienne turned around. Bruno and Elliott were checking over the tables, lighting candles. Rex started up with "Clair de Lune." Adrienne heard Duncan pop the champagne at the bar but since no one else had arrived, she decided to sneak into the kitchen. If a priest who wore Revos and knew about feminist poetry was going to bless the place, Adrienne wanted to see it.

When she walked in, the kitchen was silent. The radio had been shut off and all the Subiacos—including Mario, who had actually removed his headphones—were standing with their hands behind their backs, heads bowed. Fiona and Thatcher stood on either side of Father Ott as he placed his right hand on the pass.

"Oh, Heavenly Father, please bless this kitchen, that it may serve nourishing meals to the patrons of this fine restaurant. May we all serve with love and humility as your son, Jesus Christ, taught us to do. Grant us the strength and the patience to follow in his footsteps in this, and in all things. We ask this in the name of the Father, and of the Son, and of the Holy Spirit. Amen."

"Amen." Behind the pass, the Subiacos crossed themselves. Adrienne crossed herself for the first time in sixteen years. Father Ott kissed Fiona and she said something to him quietly while holding on to both of his forearms. Then Thatcher and Father Ott filed out past Adrienne, who was hiding next to the espresso machine. As soon as they were gone, Fiona tugged on her chef's jacket.

"Okay, people," she said. "You've been blessed. Now let's get to work."

Adrienne kept her eye on Thatcher and Father Ott throughout first seating and even checked on them once to see if they needed anything. Thatcher smiled at her like she was a child intruding on her parents' dinner party. In fact, she had hoped to overhear a bit of their conversation, but from what she picked up, it sounded like they were talking about Notre Dame football.

Father Ott ordered the crab cake; Thatcher the foie gras. Father Ott drank bourbon; Thatcher drank club soda with lime. Thatcher was eating and drinking in the dining room just like a regular guest.

"Is it weird?" Adrienne asked Caren. "Or is it just me?"

"He does it every year," Caren said. "Like sometimes an old girlfriend from South Bend will come in, or one of his brothers. And the padre comes in once a summer."

Old girlfriend? Adrienne thought, panic-stricken. Then she thought, *Oh, shit. It's happening.*

After Father Ott left, Thatcher said to Adrienne, "Can you go into the wine cave and count the bottles of Menetou-Salon? I'm worried we're low."

"Sure," Adrienne said.

No sooner had Adrienne entered the luxuriously cool wine cave and opened the big fridge—there were at least thirty bottles of the Menetou-Salon, she wasn't sure what Thatcher was concerned about—than Thatcher came in and shut the door behind him. He lifted Adrienne's hair and pressed his lips to the side of her neck.

They kissed, with Adrienne's back pressed up against the chilled door of the fridge. Adrienne could hear the bussers carrying their trays into the kitchen. Nice as it was to have Thatcher close, even for a minute, she far preferred having him to herself, away from work, in her bed, in the quiet wee hours.

"This is what you do the second the priest walks out the door?" she said.

"I couldn't help myself," he said.

■

Adrienne's second relationship was a few years after her escape from Will Novak. It took place on the other side of the world with Kip Turnbull, the British owner of the Smiling Garden Resort in Koh Samui, Thailand. That was the year that Adrienne's father worried about her the most, and for good reason. She was twenty-five years old, halfway across the globe, working in a bikini. She lived in the queen bee bungalow of the forty bungalows at the Smiling Garden Resort, sleeping alongside her boss who had a hash problem and who cheated on her, Adrienne was sure, during his monthly pilgrimages to the full moon parties on Koh Phangan.

Kip's biggest fault was that he was too handsome. Adrienne had been addicted to him physically, to the way he would untie the string of her bikini top at the end of her shift and make love to her on his desk in the back office. He rode a motorcycle and he had taken Adrienne for excursions around Koh Samui—to the hidden temples, to the waterfalls, to the giant gold Buddha on the north coast. He had bargained with a Thai woman at the market in Na Thon for the best papaya for a couple of bhat, then he sliced it open with a machete and fed it to Adrienne with his fingers.

Kip was older, too, ten years older, and he had told Adrienne stories about Eton and Cambridge, Hong Kong, Macao, Saigon, Mandalay. She had nothing to offer that could compare. She was provincially American, with only the gentle and studious Will Novak to claim as a past lover. She was plagued for the first time by jealousy. She wanted Kip to take her to one of the full moon parties on Koh Phangan.

"You won't like it," he said.

"Try me," she said.

Kip gave in, and at the end of the month, he and Adrienne were on an old junk cruising through the Gulf of Thailand toward Koh Phangan.

It was lying on the very soft, very white sand of Haad Rin Beach that Adrienne noticed she was the only woman around, except for four Thai girls who were offering massages for fifty bhat. The beach was packed with men—Israelis, South Africans, Germans, Australians, Danish, Americans. They were all eyeing Adrienne in her bikini, and she felt Kip's attention tighten around her. She wanted to stay in that spot forever. Kip called one of the masseuses over.

"For the lady." And he palmed the girl some bills.

"I don't want a massage," Adrienne said. "Really."

Kip said something to the girl in Thai that made her laugh. The girl knelt next to Adrienne in the sand and started kneading her back. It felt wonderful, and Adrienne closed her eyes, trying not to worry if this was some kind of turn-on for Kip or for the other men on the beach. The girl's hands were as soft as warm water.

Later, Kip took Adrienne to dinner. They hiked down a jungle path to a grass shack that had only three stools at a counter. "The vegetable curry," Kip said. "I order it every time."

Adrienne didn't care for curries, but it would have been useless to say so. The curry she was given was mild and sweet with coconut milk, cilantro, lime. She had left the mushrooms to float in a small amount of broth at the bottom of the bowl, and when Kip noticed, he laughed hysterically.

"Eat the mushrooms," he said.

She ate the mushrooms.

The rest of the night was a stew of paranoia and hallucinations. Kip took Adrienne back to their bungalow and somehow locked her in from the outside, claiming he had to meet some Americans to buy some hash. *When are you coming back?* Adrienne asked the already closed door. *Later, love, a little later.* Adrienne lay down on the embroidered satin bedspread. She was cogent enough to realize that the mushrooms had been drugs, and now the simplest tasks eluded her. She couldn't get the door open. She was freezing, but she couldn't turn down the air-conditioning. She had been dreaming of a hot bath since arriving in Thailand months earlier, and this room had a marble bathroom and a deep Jacuzzi. She turned on the water, and then she lost time. The next thing she knew she was lying on her face on the embroidered bedspread drowning in what felt like wave after wave crashing over her.

Kip returned at three o'clock in the morning, high on six different drugs and drunk on Mekong whiskey, to find Adrienne passed out and their entire bungalow ankle-deep with warm bathwater. They left on the first boat the next morning and neither of them said a word to each other. Adrienne was mortified about the water damage (it ended up costing Kip nearly five hundred pounds) and she was livid about everything from the massage to the mushrooms to being locked up like an animal. She couldn't deny the truth much longer: Kip was a control freak. And yet he was so handsome that when they returned to Koh Samui, and he said he forgave her, it took another month of Kip's obnoxious demands and e-mailed pleas from her father to make Adrienne leave. She wasn't even fully packed when Kip announced he'd hired an Australian girl to replace her.

By his own admission, Thatcher "hadn't exactly been celibate" over the past twelve years, but there had been no one special, he said, and Adrienne decided to believe him. The only other woman Adrienne wanted to talk about as they lay in bed late at night was Fiona.

"Fiona was never my girlfriend," Thatcher said. "I've never even held her hand. I tried to kiss her once when we were fifteen but she pushed me away. She said she didn't want me to kiss her because she was dying and she didn't want to break my heart."

Fiona had cystic fibrosis. It was a genetic disease; Adrienne had looked it up on the Internet. Mucus was sealing Fiona's lungs like a tomb. She was thirty-five years old, and losing lung function every year. Over the winter, she had decided to put herself on the transplant list, and that was why this was the final year of the restaurant. If she got a lung transplant, if she survived the lung transplant—there were too many ifs to worry about running a business. Thatcher had mentioned a doctor at Mass General, the best doctor in the country for this disease. To look at Fiona, Adrienne would never know a thing was wrong. She was a pistol, a short pistol with a braid like the Swiss Miss and freckles across her nose. A pistol wearing diamond stud earrings.

"What was it like being friends with her?" Adrienne asked.

"I'm still friends with her."

"Growing up, I mean. What was it like?"

"It was like growing up," Thatcher said. "She lived in my neighborhood. We went to school together. She cooked a lot and I ate what she cooked. We drove to Chicago for concerts in the summer. She had boyfriends, but they all hated me. One of them siphoned the gas from my car."

"Really?"

"They were jealous because we were friends. Because, you know, I would eat over there during the week and I walked into her house without knocking, that kind of thing. Once a month or so, she would go to the hospital—sometimes just to St. Joe's but sometimes up to Northwestern and I was the only one who she let come visit."

"And what was that like?"

"It was awful. They had her on a vent, and the doctors were always worrying about her O_2 sats, the amount of oxygen in her blood."

"Who knows that she's sick?"

"Some of the staff know, obviously—Caren, Joe, Duncan, Spillman, and everyone in the kitchen—but it's the strictest secret. Because if the public hears the word 'disease,' they shun a place, and in that case, everyone loses. You understand that."

"I understand," Adrienne said. She nearly told Thatcher that Drew Amman-Keller knew. He knew and was keeping the secret just like everybody else, but Adrienne was afraid to bring it up. She still had his business card hidden in her dresser drawer. "I won't tell anyone."

"Of course not. I trust you. I wouldn't be here if I didn't trust you."

"Does Fiona know about us?"

"Everybody knows about us," Thatcher said. "Which is fine. When the public hears the word 'romance,' they come in droves. The phone rings off the hook."

"We'll have to beat them back with a stick."

Thatcher tucked her under his chin and buried his face in her hair. "Exactly."

If Will Novak was too soft, and Kip Turnbull too hard, then Michael Sullivan, the third man Adrienne dated, was just right. Sully was the golf pro at the Chatham Bars Inn, where Adrienne worked the front desk. Unlike Will and Kip, Sully was Adrienne's age, he had a degree from Bowdoin College, and he, too, was living the resort life with the reluctant backing of his parents, who lived in Quincy, forty-five minutes away. Sully had valued one thing above all others for his entire life and that thing was golf. Adrienne first noticed him on the driving range smacking balls into the wild blue yonder. He was tall and freckled; he wore cleats and khakis and a visor. Adrienne met him a few nights later at a staff party where she tried to impress him by reciting the names of all the golfers she knew:

Adrienne was twenty-six. She understood that what Sully was suggesting—getting married, having children—was what people *did.* It was how life progressed. Adrienne didn't say anything further to Sully on the topic of marriage, but in his chirpy, good-natured way, he played through as though a decision had been made. In the following twenty-four hours, he called Irene and told her that a big announcement was coming, but first he wanted to ask for Adrienne's hand. He pestered Adrienne for Dr. Don's phone number, then with a shy smile, he said, "I have stuff to talk over with him."

Adrienne felt like someone was wrapping a wool scarf over her nose and mouth. She was hot and prickly; she couldn't breathe properly. She was terrified and, in a mindless panic, she ran: packed her stuff while Sully was at work, wrote him a letter, and had a short, teary conversation with her front desk manager. She cried through the cab ride to Logan, and through the flight from Boston to Honolulu. She was afraid to call her father. She knew he would assault her with the obvious question: *What is wrong with you?*

Within a week, Adrienne had a job on the front desk at the Princeville Resort on Kauai. She had photocopied the letter she wrote to Sully and every time she considered dating a man that winter, she read it. To keep herself from doing any more damage.

Before Thatcher there had been three and a half men, and the half a man was Doug Riedel. But that was just Adrienne being mean. It was more accurate to say that Doug and Adrienne had only had half a relationship, or a half-hearted relationship. Doug Riedel was a mistake, an accident; he was a one-night stand that lasted an entire winter. Adrienne met him right before Christmas while she was skiing on her day off. They skied together, they après-skied together, they après-après-skied together. The next thing Adrienne knew, Doug Riedel was showing up at the front desk of the Little Nell on Christmas morning with a gift-wrapped box from Gorsuch. Adrienne, who had been feeling sorry for herself for working on Christmas (she always worked on Christmas because she had no kids), opened the box that held a pair of shearling gloves and thought: What luck! Doug was darkly handsome, he had a great dog, he worked as one of the ski school managers at Buttermilk. He was a catch. She started meeting him after work to walk

Jax, he took her out for a day of cross-country, he was calling her before he went to the gym, after he got home, before he went out to the Red Onion, after he got home. He was, somehow, becoming her boyfriend.

Right around the busy February holidays, Doug lost his job at Buttermilk Mountain and, subsequently, his housing. *You're probably going to break up with me now,* he'd said. If Adrienne had been half paying attention, then this was exactly what she would have done, but instead she found herself fibbing to management so that he could move in with her and bring Jax. Then, his unevenness began to register. Sometimes he was funny and charming, but sometimes he was disparaging and negative. He hated Kyra (what a slut), he hated the Little Nell (a bastion of phony luxury), he hated Aspen in general. He spent more and more time in Carbondale with a mysterious friend. Adrienne thought he was sleeping with someone else, but she didn't care. He was a houseguest who had overstayed his welcome—he was grouchy, he had a constant head cold, he stayed up all night watching *Junkyard Wars,* and every morning he went to the Ajax Diner for scrambled eggs with ketchup. He did nothing about finding a new job, and yet he never seemed to be short on money.

Well, yeah! Adrienne shuddered with anger every time she thought of her empty Future box, her money gone, her prospects stolen, her master key card swiped. Doug Riedel was the devil himself. But if it hadn't been for Doug and his felonious ways, Adrienne reminded herself, she wouldn't be here on Nantucket, working at the Blue Bistro, with Thatcher.

Adrienne and Thatcher had been dating for less than three weeks and already this relationship was different. *Exercise good judgment about men!* her napkin screamed. Talk about your feelings, but give nothing away. Be careful, but don't act scared. Nothing she told herself helped. With Thatcher, she felt like a person afraid of flying: Was it safe to board the aircraft? Would the plane crash? Would she be left on the open sea with a broken leg and a flimsy flotation device? Would she die? Already her emotional investment was so great that complete devastation of the life she had worked so hard to cultivate seemed possible. This was all brand-new.

On July second, there were two hundred and fifty covers on the book, their first sellout of the year. It was eighty degrees at four o'clock and when

Adrienne sat down for family meal at five, she was uncomfortably warm. Thatcher was at an AA meeting; it was his second meeting that day. He had gone to one at ten that morning while Adrienne covered the phone. Now, as she ate, she worried about Thatcher. Was it normal to go to two AA meetings in one day, or was there something wrong? Then she worried about Mrs. Yannick.

Mrs. Yannick had called that morning with a trick question. "Is your restaurant child-friendly?"

"How old is your child?" Adrienne asked.

"Two."

Adrienne faltered. Thatcher, no doubt, had a smooth answer that would perfectly convey to Mrs. Yannick that while they did have one high chair in the back of the utility closet, it was covered with cobwebs, and seemed to be there only in case of emergency. Would it be grossly inappropriate to suggest Mrs. Yannick get a babysitter?

"We don't have a children's menu," Adrienne said. "And we don't have any crayons. This is fine dining."

"So you're not child-friendly."

"Well . . ."

"You allow children but don't encourage them."

"We do allow children." Adrienne thought of Shaughnessy—and Wolfie. "And I myself am not a parent. But it seems like you'd be asking an awful lot of a two-year-old to have her sit through a meal with wine and so forth. And the other guests . . . I think you might be more comfortable if . . ."

"We tried to get a babysitter," Mrs. Yannick said. "We tried and tried. But we're away from home and I don't want a stranger. I'm afraid I'm out of options."

"Maybe another night?" Adrienne said.

"Not possible," Mrs. Yannick said. There was a long pause. "We're bringing William with us." There was another long pause. "I'm really sorry about this in advance. I'd just cancel the reservation but the number-one reason why we come to Nantucket is to eat at your restaurant."

Ah, flattery! Adrienne still wasn't immune to it. "We'll see you at six," she said.

■

Adrienne had been too cowardly to mention the Yannicks' reservation at the menu meeting. She tried to tell herself it was no big deal. After family meal, Adrienne pulled the high chair out of the closet and wiped it down with a wet rag. She set it at table four, the least desirable table in the restaurant—the farthest away from the beach, the piano, and the glitz of table twenty. The waitstaff worked on a rotating schedule; Adrienne hoped table four would go to Elliott or Christo, who were too new to complain. But no such luck. Tonight, it was Caren's table.

At six o'clock, Thatcher still wasn't back. Adrienne sat parties, Rex played "You Make Me Feel So Young," and a very slight breeze from the water cooled the dining room down. At ten after six, the Yannicks arrived. They were a handsome, well-dressed couple and the two-year-old, William, was darling. He had strawberry blond hair and freckles that looked like they were painted on. He wore white overalls and little white sneakers. Adrienne congratulated herself for allowing such a cute little boy to come to the restaurant. When he saw her, he held out a plastic fire truck.

Adrienne smiled. "You must be the Yannicks." She snapped up two menus and a wine list. "Follow me." She led them to table four and stood aside as Mr. Yannick buckled William into the high chair. William was angelic. He chewed the top of his fire truck. "Caren will be your server tonight," Adrienne said. "Enjoy your meal."

Five minutes later, Caren stormed the podium. "I hate you."

"I'm sorry. They're sorry. They couldn't find a sitter."

"I don't like babies," Caren said. "Or toddlers. Or children in preschool."

"But he's cute," Adrienne said.

"I don't like anyone who isn't old enough to drink," Caren said.

"At least he's well-behaved," Adrienne said.

"They gave him a sugar packet to play with, which he spilled all over the tablecloth. And he got into the mother's water. They asked for doughnuts 'right away,' but the kitchen isn't making doughnuts tonight. Too hot. They asked for a plastic cup with a top. It seems they forgot his at home. Already it's too much work. Why didn't you refer them to the Sea Grille? It's perfect for families."

"I'm sorry," Adrienne said. "I'll take care of it."

But because Thatcher was gone, Adrienne had to seat fifteen more tables, open wine, run chips and dip, and answer the phone. She went to the bar to pick up her champagne and Duncan was so in the weeds that he couldn't pour it. "Get it yourself," he said. "You know how."

Adrienne didn't have time. She raced over to check on table four. William was gnawing on a piece of pretzel bread and there were little bits of pretzel bread all over the floor. And the floor was wet. Adrienne nearly slipped.

"Whoa," she said.

"Sorry," Mrs. Yannick said. She was valiantly trying to keep William occupied by reading a small, sturdy book called *Jamberry*. Mr. Yannick studied the wine list. Adrienne bent down to pick up the pieces of bread. The floor underneath the high chair was soaked.

"Please don't worry about the mess," Mr. Yannick said. "We'll get it before we go."

"William spilled his water," Mrs. Yannick said. "We're very sorry. Our waitress couldn't find a plastic cup with a top."

"I'll look in the back," Adrienne said. "Have you placed your order?"

Mr. Yannick looked at his wife. "What are you getting, honey?"

Mrs. Yannick slapped *Jamberry* down on the table. "I haven't exactly had a chance to read the menu."

William threw his pretzel bread and it landed in Mr. Yannick's water. Mr. Yannick laughed and fished it out.

"I'll get you fresh water," Adrienne said. She glanced about the dining room. Were people staring? William pushed himself up by the arms in an attempt to launch himself from his high chair.

"All done," he said.

"You are not all done," Mrs. Yannick said. "We haven't even started." She wiped the gummy bread from around William's mouth with her napkin and this made him angrier. "Just order me the steak, Carl. Steak, rare, nothing to start. He won't make it through two courses."

"Honey . . ."

"Honey, what?"

"What was the point of coming if . . ."

"If you can't order the foie gras? Fine, order the foie gras. I'll take William out to the parking lot and you can eat it in peace."

"Honey . . ."

"Let me get you the water," Adrienne said.

"All done!" William said in a more insistent voice. He kicked his feet against the underside of the table and then swept *Jamberry* to the floor where it landed in the puddle.

Adrienne cast around for a busboy. Roy was at table twelve refilling water. Adrienne waved him down. "We need a new glass here."

"The water is the least of our worries," Mrs. Yannick said. "Can you get our waitress so we can place our order?"

"Certainly," Adrienne said. She found Caren coming out of the kitchen with apps for table twenty-eight. Adrienne followed her. "Here, let me help you serve."

Caren eyed her. "Why? What do you want?"

"Table four," Adrienne said. "They'd like to place their order. William is restless."

"They made their bed," Caren said.

"So you won't go over there?"

"When I'm good and ready."

Adrienne heard a shriek. All the way across the dining room, she saw William red in the face, kicking, trying to free himself from his chair. Adrienne hurried over. Mrs. Yannick was trying to read *Jamberry* over William's screaming. Mr. Yannick raised his arm in a sign of distress; his ship was going down.

"Would you take our order, please?" he said.

"Certainly," Adrienne said.

"Foie gras and the duck for me and my wife will have the crab cake and the steak."

"Rare," Mrs. Yannick said.

"And a bottle of the Ponzi pinot noir," Mr. Yannick said.

"Really, Carl, wine?" Mrs. Yannick said.

"You love the Ponzi."

"You think we have time to drink a bottle of wine?"

"We'll just drink what we can," Mr. Yannick said. "The Ponzi."

"Very good," Adrienne said. William was temporarily mesmerized with a lipstick Mrs. Yannick had pulled from her purse. He took off the cap and put the lipstick in his mouth.

"For God's sake," Mr. Yannick said.

"At least he's quiet," Mrs. Yannick said.

William threw the lipstick to the ground and started to cry. Mrs. Yannick dug through her purse. "I thought I had a lollipop in here." Adrienne headed for the kitchen. She didn't have time for this, and yet she felt responsible. *Is your restaurant child-friendly?* No, it's not. The next time, Adrienne would just come right out and say it. No children under six. Why wasn't this a rule already? She tried to think about how to help the Yannicks. Maybe she should comp their dinner and insist they come back another night. *What,* she wondered, *would Thatcher do? Where was he?*

"Ordering table two: one bisque, one crab cake, SOS. Where's the duck for fourteen? Louis? Get your head out of the oven, Louis! Ordering table six: one frites, medium-well, one pasta. That's right, I said pasta, so Henry, you're going to work tonight after all. Ordering table twenty-one . . ." Fiona noticed Adrienne at her elbow. The kitchen was brutally hot even with two standing fans going. "What do you want?"

"I came to put in an order for table four."

"Who's the server?"

"Caren, but she's busy."

"News flash: We're all busy. What is it?"

"What?"

"The order!"

Adrienne thought for a second. If you gave Fiona the food in the wrong sequence, she got pissed. "Foie gras, crab cake, duck, frites rare."

Fiona scribbled out a ticket. "Fine."

"Can you rush it?" Adrienne said. "These people brought their two-year-old and he's *freaking* out."

"Ordering table four: one foie gras, one crab cake, pronto," Fiona said. Then to Adrienne, she said, "What's the kid eating?"

"He's not eating. But they would like a plastic cup with a top. I know Caren already asked, but . . ."

"Sippy cup, Paco," Fiona shouted.

Seconds later, a plastic cup with a bright blue plastic top whizzed through the air. Fiona caught it and handed it to Adrienne. "Go get him."

"Who?"

"The kid. Go get the kid and bring him in here."

Adrienne thought she had heard wrong. The kitchen with the grill and the fryer and four sauté pans going and the fans running was loud.

"You want me to bring William in here?"

"If you think it would help the parents enjoy the meal, then yes," Fiona said. And—surprise!—she smiled. "I keep some toys in the back office. I love kids."

Adrienne popped into the wine cave for a bottle of Ponzi. By the time she reached the podium, she noticed the dining room was not only cooler, but quieter. She looked at table four. Thatcher was standing by the table with William in his arms, William was chewing on the top of his fire truck. Adrienne felt a surge of tenderness and awe and whatever else it was a woman felt when she first saw her lover holding a small child. She hurried to the bar, where her champagne glass was waiting. She took a drink, then she set down the sippy cup.

"Orange juice, please," she said.

Duncan filled it without a word, and Adrienne took the sippy cup and the wine to table four. She handed the sippy cup to Mrs. Yannick who brightened, then Adrienne presented the Ponzi to Mr. Yannick.

"Juice!" William said.

Mr. Yannick nodded at the wine, visibly relaxed. Adrienne uncorked and poured, he tasted.

"Delicious."

"I put a rush on your order," Adrienne said as she poured a glass of wine for Mrs. Yannick. "Your appetizers should be out any second."

"Would it be all right if I took William into the kitchen?" Thatcher said. "I know our chef would love to see him."

"She has some toys in the office," Adrienne said.

"All right," Mrs. Yannick said. "You'll bring him back if he's any problem?"

"This guy, a problem?" Thatcher said. William was resting his head on Thatcher's shoulder, sucking noisily on the cup. Thatcher winked at Adrienne and vanished into the back.

Mrs. Yannick collapsed in her wicker chair. "I love this place," she said.

Fourth of July. Two hundred and fifty covers on the books, the maximum. Prix fixe menu, sixty dollars per person. First seating was at six; the guests were to eat then move out to the rented beach chairs in the sand to watch the fireworks. Second seating was at ten; those guests would watch the fireworks first, then sit down to dinner. Duncan was working the bar outside, and Delilah took over the blue granite, her first solo flight.

Everything was different and Adrienne was anxious. Thatcher asked her to arrive early, and she was there at quarter to four, but the front of the house was deserted. When she poked her head back into the kitchen it was 182 degrees—the deep fryers were going full blast with the chicken, and Fiona had the ribs in enormous pressure cookers. Adrienne checked in pastry to find Mario up to his elbows in fruit. He wasn't listening to music, and he didn't smile when he saw her.

"I have fifty pounds of peaches that need to be skinned. Everybody else gets a prep cook and I get left in the shit. One hundred twenty-five peach pies I have to make. I spent all morning with the blueberries. Look at my hands." He held up his palms. They were, of course, impeccably clean. "My nails are blue. I can tell you one thing. I'm gonna have nightmares tonight. You ever have a nightmare about stone fruit?"

"No," Adrienne said.

"Where you have a bushel of peaches looking as gorgeous as *Playboy* asses and then you break one open and it's brown and rotten inside? And the next one? And the next one? They're all that way?"

"I never had that dream," Adrienne said.

"Yeah, well, lucky you."

In the kitchen, Adrienne heard Fiona yelling about deviled eggs. She wanted five hundred deviled eggs.

Adrienne retreated to the empty dining room just as a man with a clipboard walked in saying, "I got two hundred and fifty folding chairs, sweetheart. Where do you want them?"

Some help would be nice, she thought. She had never done the Fourth of July thing on Nantucket before and she didn't know where on the beach Thatcher wanted the chairs or even which direction they should face. If she told this man the wrong thing then two hundred and fifty chairs would have to be moved. (Adrienne pictured herself slogging through the sand in her Jimmy Choo heels.) So better get it right the first time.

Adrienne called Thatcher's cell phone.

"Where are you?" she said. Then thought: *Try not to sound like a wife.*

"At Marine. I wanted to get flags for the tables."

"The gentleman is here with the chairs. He would like to know where to put them."

"On the beach."

"Right, but where?"

"Let me talk to the guy."

"Happily," Adrienne said. She handed off the phone to the chair man, then surveyed the dining room. What could she do to help? Set the tables? A roll of red, white, and blue bunting sat on top of the piano along with a book of music, *101 Patriotic Songs.* Deviled eggs, bunting, patriotic songs. These people really got into it.

A moment later, Caren walked in. It looked like she'd been crying.

"It's over," she said. "I'm finished with that rat bastard."

"Duncan?"

Caren glared at her. Adrienne tried to think: He had been there that morning. She'd heard them in the kitchen, though as a rule, she and Thatcher didn't fraternize with Caren and Duncan. Too much like work.

"What happened?" Adrienne asked.

"He's been cheating on me during the *day,*" Caren said. "This morning? He says he has golf at ten with the bartender from Cinco. Fine. I decide to do something different because of the holiday so I set myself up with a gorgeous Cuban sandwich from Fahey and then I go to the beach at Madequecham. And lo and behold, whose car is there? Who is lying on the beach with the hostess from 21 Federal?"

"The hostess?" Adrienne said. "You mean Phoebe?"

"Phoebe!" Caren spat. "So I saunter up to the happy couple and Duncan doesn't even blink. But I could tell he thought I followed him there or was spying on him or something. However, he pretended like it was no big deal and therefore I had to pretend like it was no big deal. He asked me to put lotion on his back, and I said, 'No way, motherfucker.' So then Phoebe pipes up and says she would love to put lotion on his back—and I have to sit there and *watch.*" Her eyes filled up. "What am I going to do?"

Adrienne put her arm around Caren, awkwardly, because Caren was so much taller. Duncan was a woman magnet; Caren had to learn to accept it. Before Adrienne could find a way to say this, Thatcher walked in, clapping his hands.

"Good, good, good," he said. "The two of you can hang the bunting. All the way around and try to make it even, okay? Joe's coming in at four thirty to set the tables—and look! I got flags." He waved a small flag in the air and his smile faded. "Is something wrong?"

Caren tucked in her shirt and sniffed. "I can't work with Duncan," she said. "Either he goes or I go."

Thatcher groaned. He yanked at his red, white, and blue necktie to give himself some air. Then, slowly, he said, "I told you . . ."

"I know what you told me!" Caren snapped, and she burst into tears.

Thatcher's hands hung at his sides. He gazed at Adrienne with longing. But what about Caren? Adrienne tried to make her eyes very round.

"You need to have an espresso and calm down," Thatcher said. "Or, hell, have a drink, I don't care. Just, please, pull yourself together because we have two hundred and fifty people coming and you are working and Duncan is working, and if tomorrow, July fifth, you two want to battle it out to see who stays and who goes, that's fine. It's fine on July fifth. It is not fine tonight. Tonight you have to be a brave soldier."

Caren pouted. She was lovely, really—Adrienne had a hard time believing that Duncan would ever prefer Phoebe. "I'll have an espresso martini," Caren said. "Kill two birds." She stepped behind the bar. "God, I feel like trashing his perfect setup."

"Well, please don't," Thatcher said. "Delilah is working back there tonight anyway. Duncan's on the beach. You'll barely have to see him."

Caren slammed a martini glass on the blue granite then poured generously from the Triple 8 bottle. "Brilliant."

Thatcher put his arm around Adrienne and kissed her ear. "You'll have to hang the bunting by yourself," he said.

"What are you doing?" Adrienne asked.

"Everything else."

By ten to six, the restaurant was ready. The bunting hung evenly all the way around the edge of the restaurant, and the tables were set with a tiny American flag standing in each silver bud vase. On the beach, two hundred and fifty chairs were set up in perfect rows. It was a beautiful night. Adrienne had wolfed down a plate of tangy, falling-apart ribs and three deviled eggs at family meal and then she rushed to brush her teeth. When she went to the bar to get her champagne, Duncan confronted her.

"I'm innocent," he said.

"Delilah, would you pour me a glass of Laurent-Perrier, please?" Adrienne asked.

Delilah, also wearing a red, white, and blue necktie, seemed harried. She studied the bottles in the well. "Where's the champagne?" she asked Duncan.

"In the door of the little fridge," he said. "You'd better learn quick; you only have ten minutes." And then, turning back to Adrienne, he said, "I know she told you."

Adrienne watched Delilah grapple with the champagne bottle. It took her forever just to unwrap the cork. Finally, Duncan wrested the bottle from his sister. He had it open in two seconds and he poured Adrienne's drink.

"Hey," Delilah said. "I'm supposed to learn how to do it myself."

Duncan ignored her. "She talked to you," he said to Adrienne. "So if she asks, you tell her I'm innocent. Golf got cancelled, I bumped into Phoebe in town . . ."

Adrienne picked up her champagne. "Tell her yourself," she said. "I'm not getting involved."

She walked to the podium to await the onslaught with Thatcher: 125 people arriving at once.

"What was your best Fourth of July?" Thatcher asked her.

This sounded like another getting-to-know-you question. Why didn't he ever ask her when she had time to answer?

"I'll have to think about it," she said.

"Tonight is going to be right up there," Thatcher said. "Nobody does this holiday better than we do."

By six thirty, 125 people were sitting down, including the Parrishes; the local author and her entourage; Holt Millman with a party of ten; Senator Kennedy; Mr. Kennedy the investor; Stuart and Phyllis, a couple who dined at the Bistro so often that their college-aged kids referred to the food as "mom's home cooking"; the Mr. Smith for whom the blueberry pie was named, and his wife; Cat, her sister, and their husbands; Leigh Stanford with friends from Idaho; and Leon Cross and his mistress. The place was hopping. Rex played "Yankee Doodle Dandy," followed by "Camptown Races." The busboys brought out the pretzel bread and mustard and when Adrienne poked her head into the kitchen, Paco and Eddie were frantically plating shrimp skewers. Adrienne ran the skewers out. Ten of the thirty tables were drinking champagne; the corks sounded like fireworks.

Adrienne saw Caren out by the beach bar. From the looks of things, Caren was letting Duncan have it, but in a quiet, scary way. Letting him have it while Adrienne ran Caren's apps and Delilah drowned in drink orders.

"Adrienne!" Delilah cried. "I need help."

Rex launched into "American Pie."

Adrienne ran to the wine cave for wine, she refilled Delilah's juice bottles, and went to the kitchen for citrus. It was even hotter in there than before—so hot that Fiona had taken off her chef's jacket. She worked in just a white T-shirt that had a damp spot between her breasts. It seemed like it took forever to get Delilah out of the weeds, yet Rex was still playing "American Pie," and half the restaurant was singing.

Adrienne walked by table fifteen, where Thatcher was chatting with Brian and Jennifer Devlin. She heard the word "Galápagos" and stopped in her tracks. A woman at the table behind had gotten up to use the ladies' room and Adrienne took great, slow pains in folding the woman's napkin so that she could listen to Thatcher.

"We leave on October ninth," he said. "Fly to Quito overnight then to the islands for ten days. We're on a fifty-foot ship. I'm really looking forward to it."

Adrienne returned to the podium. Rex finished "American Pie," and half the restaurant applauded. She thought back to her first breakfast with Thatch: *As soon as we close this place, I'm taking Fee to the Galápagos. She wants to see the funny birds.* He had told Adrienne right from the beginning that he was going away with Fiona. There was no reason for Adrienne to expect that he would change his travel plans just because he and Adrienne were now dating. But she did expect it. She had made peace, sort of, with the dinners. The dinners were business. They talked about the restaurant mostly, he said. The dinners were important.

Fine, Adrienne could live with the dinners. He came to her house afterward and always spent the night. But hearing him talk about ten days in the Galápagos with Fiona physically hurt. And yet what could she say? His best friend was sick and she wanted to see the funny birds. He would take her.

Caren came in off the beach and charged past the podium into the ladies' room. The ladies' room only accommodated one person at a time, so Adrienne knocked. "It's me," she said.

Caren cracked the door. "Men!" she said, leaving Adrienne with nothing to do but agree.

By quarter to nine, most of the tables had finished eating and Adrienne went crazy running credit cards. The guests moved out onto the beach to order more drinks and settle in their chairs. Adrienne ordered a coffee. She was exhausted and her red T-shirt dress was soaked with sweat.

Thatcher rallied the waitstaff. "We have an hour of peace and quiet. Once these tables are stripped and reset, you're free until the finale of the fireworks starts. Then I want you back in here ready for second seating."

The fireworks began at ten after nine. By that time, the guests for second seating had all arrived and the only people working out front were Duncan, who was pouring the drinks, and Bruno and Christo, who were serving them. Thatcher took Adrienne by the hand and led her out of the restaurant. She wanted to say something to him about the Galápagos, but she had yet to come up with the right words. *Please don't go? Take me with you?* Or how about this: *Would you at least not say you're looking forward to it?*

He led her into the sand dunes behind the restaurant. Adrienne took off her shoes and climbed after him. They plopped in the sand, hidden from the crowd by eelgrass. Thatcher held Adrienne in his lap like she was a child, and she pressed her face into his neck. She could feel his pulse against her cheek.

"How are you?" he asked. "Isn't this great?"

There was a bang, and a burst of red exploded in the sky, like a giant poppy losing its petals. The water shimmered with color. Then gold, blue, purple, white.

Adrienne's best Fourth of July, just like the other best moments of her life, had happened Before—before her mother got sick. Adrienne was eleven years old. In the morning, Rosalie and Dr. Don worked together in the kitchen preparing a salad for the potluck dinner while they watched Wimbledon on TV. Then, at four o'clock, they walked across the street.

(Adrienne remembered her old neighborhood in summer—the smell of the grass, the huge, beautiful trees, the grumble of lawn mowers and the whirring of sprinklers.) Seven families gathered at the Fiddlers' pool for swimming and croquet and a cookout. And Popsicles and flashlight tag and sparklers. Adrienne had been part of a family with the other kids, kids she hadn't seen or thought of for years and years: Caroline Fiddler, Jake Clark, Toby and Trey Wiley, Tricia Gilette, Natalie, Blake and David Anola. The girls lined up their Dr. Scholl sandals and lay back in the grass looking up at the stars and searching for any hint of the big fireworks being set off in Philadelphia. They talked, naïvely, about boys; Natalie Anola had a crush on Jake Clark. The world of boys at that point to Adrienne was like a wide, unexplored field and she was standing at the edge. At ten o'clock, Rosalie and Dr. Don, flush with an evening of Mount Gay and tonics, dragged Adrienne home where she fell asleep in her clothes. Happy, safe, excited about the possibilities of her life.

That one was the best, and Adrienne had spent all the interceding years mourning, not only the loss of her mother, but the loss of that happiness. Right this second she felt a glimmer of it—Nantucket Island, in Thatcher's arms, watching the colors soar and burst overhead, feeling a breeze, finally, coming off the water. *Forget the Galápagos,* she told herself. Forget that there were 125 people yet to feed. Forget that Fiona would have twice the amount of time alone with Thatcher that Adrienne had. Forget all that because this moment *was* great, great enough to make it into her memories. Adrienne savored every second, because she feared it wouldn't last.

8

Hydrangeas

July was true summer. It was eighty-five degrees and sunny—beach weather, barbecue weather, Blue Bistro weather. The bar was packed every night, and the phone rang off the hook. Florists came in to change the flowers in the restaurant from irises to hydrangeas. Hydrangeas like bushy heads, bluer than blue.

Adrienne was admiring the bouquet of hydrangeas on the hostess podium when the private line rang. It was a Monday morning and she was covering the phones while Thatcher met with a rep from Classic Wines.

"Good morning, Blue Bistro."

"Adrienne?"

"Yes?"

"Drew Amman-Keller. I'm surprised you're not out jogging. It's a beautiful day."

"Well, you know," Adrienne said, glancing nervously around the dining room, "I have to work."

"I'm calling to confirm a rumor," Drew Amman-Keller said.

Adrienne held the receiver to her forehead. Should she just hang up?

"What rumor is that?"

"Is Tam Vinidin eating at the bistro tomorrow night?"

"Tam Vinidin, the actress?"

"Can you confirm that she has a reservation?" he asked.

Adrienne laughed. *Ha!* "I wish she did. Sorry, Drew." She hung up.

A few minutes later, JZ's truck pulled into the parking lot. He rolled in the door with two boxes of New York strip steaks on a dolly.

"Hey, Adrienne!" he said.

"Hey," she said. "How's everything? How's Shaughnessy?"

"She's fine," he said. "She leaves for camp in two weeks."

"Is that good or bad?"

"It's good," he said. "I'm going to sneak over here for a vacation."

"That'll be nice," Adrienne said. "Fiona will be happy."

JZ backed up the dolly. Before he headed into the kitchen, he said, "I heard Tam Vinidin is eating here tomorrow night."

"You did?"

"Yeah. Guy on the boat told me."

"She hasn't called," Adrienne said. She flipped a page in the reservation book. "I hope she calls soon. We're almost full."

As JZ pushed into the kitchen, Hector popped out. Of all the Subiacos, Hector was Adrienne's least favorite. He used the foulest language and was merciless when he teased his brothers and cousins. Adrienne was not excited to see his tall, lanky frame loping toward her.

"Hey, bitch!" he said.

Adrienne rolled her eyes. "What do you want, Hector?"

"Special delivery," he said. He palmed a fax on top of the reservation book. "It's our lucky day."

Tam Vinidin was coming to eat at the Blue Bistro! She wanted table twenty at seven thirty and she wanted it for the night. She would allow one photographer, a woman almost as famous as she was, to take her picture while she ate. She was on the Atkins diet. She wanted Fiona to make her a plate of avocado wrapped in prosciutto and Medjool dates stuffed with peanut butter. She would drink Dom Pérignon.

Adrienne checked the book. Tuesday nights the Parrishes ate at table twenty first seating, and one of Mario's friends from the CIA was coming in with his wife at nine. Adrienne would have to bump them both for Tam Vinidin. She wondered about the photographer. Would she need a table, too?

And what about the Dom Pérignon? The bistro didn't carry it. Adrienne called Thatcher on his cell phone. Since he was with a wine rep, he could order a case. Her call went to voice mail. "Thatch, it's me," Adrienne said. She was so excited, she could barely keep from screaming. "Tam Vinidin is coming in tomorrow night at seven thirty. We need a case of DP. Call me!"

Adrienne loved Tam Vinidin with a passion. She was sexier than JLo and prettier than Jennifer Aniston. And she was eating at the Bistro! Adrienne would get to meet her, open her champagne, deliver her chips and dip. She reread the fax. She had to e-mail her father.

Adrienne took the fax into the kitchen. Hector was drizzling olive oil over a hotel pan of fresh figs, and Paco was shredding cabbage for the coleslaw.

"Where's Fiona?" Adrienne asked.

Hector nodded at the office. The door was closed. Adrienne knocked.

"Come in!"

Adrienne opened the door. Fiona was sitting at Thatcher's desk filling out order forms. She had plastic tubes up her nose; she was attached to an oxygen tank.

"Oh, sorry," Adrienne said.

Fiona looked up. "What is it?"

Adrienne tried not to stare at the tubes. "Tam Vinidin is coming in tomorrow night."

Fiona blinked. "Who?"

"Tam Vinidin, the actress?"

Fiona shook her head. "Never heard of her."

Never heard of her? She must be kidding. "You must be kidding," Adrienne said.

Fiona took a deep breath, then coughed. "What can I do for you, Adrienne?"

"This is a fax from her manager," Adrienne said. "She wants all this . . . stuff. She wants— Here, you can see." Adrienne let the fax flutter onto the desk.

Fiona read. "She can't have twenty tomorrow night and certainly not at seven thirty. It's Tuesday. She can't have a photographer. She can't have DP and I'm not making that ridiculous food." Fiona handed the fax back to

Adrienne. "If she wants to sit at table eight and drink Laurent-Perrier and eat off the menu like everybody else, then fine. Otherwise, send her to the Summer House."

"Wait a minute," Adrienne said. "This is Tam Vinidin, Fiona. You don't know who this person is."

"That's right," Fiona said. "Thank you, Adrienne."

Adrienne appealed to Thatcher when he returned from his meeting, but he backed up Fiona.

"She's right," he said. "We might be able to slide Mario's buddy to table twenty-one, but we can't move the Parrishes."

"Why not?"

"Because they're the Parrishes."

"But this is Tam Vinidin."

"I didn't order DP and Fiona won't make special dishes." He checked the fax. "Medjool dates? Is she kidding? And as for the photographer— Do I really need to go on?"

"No."

"She'll be happier at the Summer House," Thatcher said. "Sorry. Do you want to call her manager or do you want me to do it?"

"You do it," Adrienne said. "I'm going home."

On Tuesday, Tam Vinidin's visit to Nantucket rated a front-page story in the *Cape Cod Times* and the *Inquirer and Mirror,* and there was a two-column article in *USA Today* written by Drew Amman-Keller describing the house she rented (on Squam Road), naming all the shops where she dropped bundles of cash (Dessert, Gypsy, Hepburn), and disclosing where she ate (the Nantucket Golf Club, 56 Union, the Summer House). Mr. Amman-Keller made a point of noting that Ms. Vinidin's trip to the Blue Bistro had been cancelled because Chef Fiona Kemp "would not accommodate her strict adherence to Dr. Atkins's diet." One of the Subiacos had clipped Drew Amman-Keller's article out of the paper and taped it to the wall next to the reach-in. Under the picture of Tam Vinidin (sitting on the bench outside Congdon & Coleman Insurance in cut-off jean shorts) someone had written: "Feed me fondue."

Wednesday was Adrienne's day off, and she forgot about Tam Vinidin. Wednesday night, Thatcher took Adrienne to Company of the Cauldron for dinner and he ate every bite. After dinner they went back to Thatcher's house—a cottage behind one of the big houses in town. His cottage was only large enough to accommodate a bed and a dresser, and on top of the dresser, a TV for watching college football in the fall. There was a bathroom and a rudimentary kitchen. Not exactly impressive digs, but Adrienne was honored to be in his private space. She studied the pictures of his brothers, she flipped through his high school yearbook. In the back, on the "Best Friends" page, she found a picture of Thatcher, with a bad haircut and acne on his nose, and Fiona, who looked exactly the same as she did now, twenty years later.

Adrienne and Thatcher spent the entire next day together. They drove Thatcher's pickup to Coatue, where they found a deserted cove and fell asleep in the sun. Thatcher skipped rocks and built Adrienne a sand castle. At four o'clock, he'd dropped her at home so she could shower and change. She caught a ride to work with Caren, who informed Adrienne that she and Duncan were back together, though Duncan was on probation.

"One more fuckup and it's over," Caren said.

Adrienne tried to listen seriously, but she couldn't stop smiling. The sand castle Thatcher built had been as beautiful as a wedding cake.

There were 229 covers on the book. Family meal was grilled cheeseburgers and the first corn on the cob of the season. Thatcher was late, but all Adrienne could think of was how happy she was going to be when he came walking through the door.

The phone rang, the private line. It was Thatcher. "Is everyone there?" he said. Adrienne turned around to survey the dining room.

"Everyone except Elliott," she said. "It's his night off."

"Okay," he said. "Listen. I need you to listen. Are you listening?"

She heard the normal sounds of the restaurant—the swinging kitchen door, the chatter of the waitstaff, the first notes of the piano—but none of that could overtake the high-pitched ringing in her ears. She could tell he was about to say something awful.

"Yes," she said.

"Fiona isn't doing well. Her doctor wants her to go to Boston for at least three days. And I'm going with her."

Adrienne stared at the kitchen door. She hadn't realized Fiona wasn't in.

"You'll be in Boston for three days?" she said.

"At least three days," Thatcher said. "Antonio knows, and he's told the kitchen staff. They're used to it, okay? For them, this is no big deal. And you're going to cover for me." He paused. "Adrienne?"

"What?"

"You do a terrific job. On the floor, on the phone. Everything. The waitstaff knows how to tip out, so all you have to do at the end of the night is add up the receipts and make a deposit of the cash in the morning. The restaurant can run itself."

"What about reservations?"

"Just do the best you can."

"Can I call you? You're taking your cell?"

"Absolutely. I have a room at the Boston Harbor Hotel. You should call me there before you lock up at night. And I'll need you in at ten to do reconfirmations and answer the phone."

"Okay."

"I'll pay you."

"You don't have to *pay* me," Adrienne said. She felt like a tidal wave was crashing over the perfect sand castle of her life. Thatcher gone for three days. Fiona sick enough for a hospital. Adrienne left in charge of the restaurant in the height of the season. It was impossible, wasn't it, what he was asking of her? As though he had told her she had to land an airplane or dock an ocean liner. "You can pay me, but I'm not worried about money. I'm worried about you. And Fiona. Is she going to be all right?"

"I'll know more tomorrow," Thatcher said. "She has a lot of anxiety. Father Ott is sitting with her right now."

"Father Ott?"

"She's afraid she's going to hell," Thatcher said. He cleared his throat. "Listen, I have to go. Call me before you close, okay?"

"Okay," Adrienne said.

He hung up.

▪

Some time would have been nice, a few minutes to collect herself, to wrap her mind around what this phone call meant. But it was six o'clock, the waitstaff wanted confirmation that they were perfect—they were—and Rex played the theme from *Romeo and Juliet.* The first table arrived: a male couple who was staying at the Point Breeze. Adrienne sat them at table one, handed them menus, and told them to enjoy their meals, but when she said this, it sounded like a question, and in fact, as she looked at their perplexed tan faces, she was thinking: *Fiona is afraid she's going to hell.* Adrienne headed for the bar; she needed her drink.

"Where's the boss man?" Duncan asked.

How much was she supposed to say? Thatcher hadn't given her any guidelines. "He's not coming in tonight."

"Out last night *and* tonight?" Duncan said. "You need to take it easy on him."

"Funny," Adrienne said. "May I have my champagne, please?"

Duncan nodded at the door. "I'll bring it over to you," he said. "You have work."

Two couples were standing by the podium. Adrienne hurried over. "Good evening," she said. "Name?"

"You don't remember us?" asked a man with red hair and a red goatee. "We were in two nights ago? You talked us into a bottle of that pink champagne? We're from Florida?"

"Boca Raton," one of the women said.

Adrienne stared at the foursome, utterly lost. She would have sworn she had never seen them before in her life.

"You told us you used to work at the Mar-a-Lago," the red-haired man said.

"I did?" Adrienne said. She must have. Okay, she had to get a grip. Shake off this feeling of being stranded in the Sahara without any Evian. She scanned the book, looking for a familiar name. *Cavendish? Xavier?* She smiled. "Please forgive me. I can't remember what name the reservation is under."

"Levy," the man said. "But our feelings are hurt."

Adrienne sat them at table fifteen and made a mental note to send these people, whom she still did not remember, some chips and dip. She saw Leon Cross and his wife waiting by the podium. Leon's wife was a TV producer, a hotshot who recently tried to talk Thatcher into a reality show set at the Bistro. Initially, Adrienne had thought the Bistro would make a great setting for a reality show, but if a camera had filmed the last fifteen minutes no audience would believe it. Anxiety, death, and hell among the hardest-to-get reservations in town? Then there was Leon Cross himself, who sometimes came to the restaurant with his wife when he sat at table twenty (Adrienne led them there now), but just as often came with his mistress (who was older than his wife and a nicer woman) when he sat at table nineteen in a dark corner under the awning.

No one would believe it.

Party of eight from the Wauwinet, party of four waitresses from the Westender celebrating a birthday, party of five that was a single mom out with her two kids and their spouses. Then a series of deuces, then a four-top that was two couples celebrating the fact that they'd been friends for twenty years. The phone rang and rang. Adrienne checked each time to see if it was the private line—no. She didn't answer. Delilah ran her a glass of champagne and Adrienne took half of it in one long gulp.

She hurried into the kitchen to put in two orders of chips. The kitchen seemed the same except that instead of Fiona, Antonio was expediting.

"Ordering sixteen," he called out. "One foie gras, one Caesar."

"Yes, chef," Eddie said.

"Ordering twelve," Antonio said. "Two chowder, one beet, one foie gras killed, Henry baby, okay?"

"Yes, chef," Henry said.

Adrienne held up two fingers to Paco and he started slicing potatoes on his mandolin. Adrienne knew it would take six minutes and she should get back out front, but she lingered in the kitchen for a minute. Everything seemed way too normal. The Subiacos worked as though nothing was wrong. The baseball game was on. She poked her head back into pastry. Mario was pulling a tray of brownies out of the convection oven. Adrienne stared him down. They had never talked about Fiona's illness.

"What?" he said. "You want one?"

"Thatcher and Fiona are in Boston," Adrienne whispered. "They're going to be gone for three days. Fiona is in the *hospital.*"

Mario squeezed Adrienne's face to make fish lips. It hurt. "It's okay," he said. "This happens. They put Fiona on a vent and it clears things out. They pump her full of miracle drugs. It makes things better. Trust me. It's no big deal." He let Adrienne's face go.

"Really?" Adrienne said.

"Fifteen years ago, we're in Skills One together and the day before our practical, she goes into the hospital. Big hospital down in the city. So I know something's wrong. As soon as I finish my test, I take the train to see her and she tells me about her thing. And I think maybe I'm gonna cry but then I realize Fee is the toughest person I know. She's gonna survive. And, like I said, that was fifteen years ago. She goes back to school the next week, makes up her practical, scores a ninety-seven out of a hundred. I get a seventy-three. Suddenly, she's the one who's worried about me. And for good reason." Mario cut the crispy edges off the brownies. "She'll outlive us all. You watch."

"Okay," Adrienne said. That was what she wanted to hear. She smacked Mario's butt and walked back to the hot line.

Spillman burst into the kitchen. "Adrienne, can you open wine for table fifteen? I'm slammed, and they say they're friends of yours."

"Sure," Adrienne said. She returned to the dining room. Rex was playing Barry Manilow. She took the Levys' wine order, retrieved the bottle from the wine cave, opened the wine and served it, all in under five minutes, at which point she remembered the chips and dip. Adrienne delivered chips and dip to the Levys, then Leon Cross. She returned to the podium and finished her champagne. *Run the restaurant by herself?* she thought. *Piece of cake!*

Smack in the middle of first seating, two women walked in wearing baseball hats and jeans. Adrienne felt a headache coming on. The Bistro didn't have a dress code, she reminded herself. The best tippers were often the guests who were underdressed. One of the women was wearing giraffe-print Prada mules and Gucci sunglasses. She took the sunglasses off as she approached the podium.

"Is it all right if we eat at the bar?"

Adrienne was caught completely off-guard. She made a gurgling sound. It was Tam Vinidin.

"Sure," Adrienne said finally, her mind ricocheting all over the place. She wanted to shout, but she had to remain cool. She wanted everyone in the restaurant to know Tam Vinidin was there, yet it was imperative that no one found out. Did anyone recognize her? She was beautiful and all the more so because she wore no makeup and had her hair in a ponytail under a hat. Her friend was . . . no one Adrienne recognized. Sister, maybe.

"Follow me," Adrienne said. She plucked two menus and led the women to the bar.

"Duncan!" Tam Vinidin said.

"Hey, Tam," he said. "I heard you were on-island." They kissed. Adrienne stared at Duncan in genuine awe.

"This is my cousin Bindy," Tam said. "We decided to stay through the weekend. It's so relaxing here."

"Cool," Duncan said. "What can I get you ladies to drink?"

"Champagne," Tam Vinidin said.

"Laurent-Perrier?" Duncan asked.

Tam Vinidin took off her hat and let her fabulous black hair free of its elastic. "Sure."

"Adrienne, are you willing to share your bottle with these ladies?" Duncan said.

Adrienne realized she had been gaping. "Okay?" she said, then she beat it into the kitchen.

"Okay," she said to Paco ten seconds later. "Guess who's eating at the bar."

"I don't give a shit," Paco said. He was helping Eddie build club sandwiches. "I'm fucking busy."

"Tam Vinidin."

Paco yelled to Hector, who was grilling off steaks. "She's here. Eating at the bar."

Hector whooped then pleaded with Antonio. "Can I go out and see her, Tony? Please, man?"

Antonio wiped his forehead with a side towel. He was older than Fiona by at least ten years and it showed. He was sweating; he looked exhausted and second seating hadn't even started yet. "Tam Vinidin's here?" he asked Adrienne.

Adrienne nodded. "I came to put in a VIP order."

"Hers is in the reach-in," Antonio said. "Fiona ordered those Medjool dates, just in case."

"You're kidding," Adrienne said. She checked the reach-in and found a plate of dates stuffed with peanut butter.

Caren slammed into the kitchen. "Is Adrienne in here?"

Adrienne turned around, holding the dates. "Did you see who's—"

"You promised me you wouldn't," Caren said. She threw her hands up in the air. Her lovely neck was getting red and splotchy. "You put Tam Vinidin at the bar!"

"She asked to sit at the bar. She knows Duncan from . . ."

"You promised me you wouldn't do it!" Caren said. "You could have put her at table three."

"Put Tam Vinidin at table three?"

"Because now she's out there with Duncan!"

"She's a movie star," Adrienne said. "She's not interested in Duncan."

"He's interested in her."

"No, he's not . . ."

"Shit, yeah, he is," Hector interjected.

"Shut up!" Caren said.

"You're a bitch," Hector said. "You think he wants you instead?"

"You're a bitch, *bitch,*" Caren said.

"No fighting in the kitchen!" Antonio said. He clapped his hands and pointed to the door. "I don't want to hear anything else about the movie star. The dates, the organic peanut butter, fine. But not another word. And no more special treatment."

As it turned out, Tam Vinidin didn't want special treatment. She was thrilled about the dates and offered one to her cousin, one to Duncan, one to Adrienne, one to Leon Cross's wife who knew Tam from New York and popped over to say hello, and one to Caren who passed by the bar three times in two minutes to keep an eye on Duncan. Everyone refused.

"You don't know what you're missing," she said.

Rex played "Georgia, on My Mind." Adrienne forced herself to return to the podium. The phone rang and she realized she hadn't thought about

Thatcher for almost half an hour. She wanted to call him and thank him and Fiona.

Thank you for creating a restaurant so wonderful that people like Tam Vinidin want to come even without a reservation, even in their jeans. Thank you for ordering the Medjool dates and the organic peanut butter even though you never go to the movies or read People *magazine. You made someone happy tonight. You make people happy every night.*

You're going to heaven.

That night, Thatcher didn't answer his cell phone. Adrienne tried three times then called the hotel but he didn't answer in his room either. It was nearly two o'clock in the morning. Adrienne left a message in his room then called his cell phone a fourth time and left the same message.

"Hi, it's me. Everything went smoothly tonight. We made twenty-one six on the floor and another nineteen hundred seventy at the bar." Adrienne paused, thinking about how astounding those numbers were. Because she was the only one working, she herself had cleared over six hundred dollars in tips. And yet, under the circumstances, the money seemed very beside the point. "So I'll take it home and make a deposit at the bank on my way in tomorrow morning. Call me . . . I hope everything is okay . . . I'm thinking of you."

The first call that came in the following morning was on the private line. Adrienne punched the button, thinking *Thatcher, Thatcher, Thatcher.* There had been no message from him on the machine.

"Good morning," Adrienne said. "Blue Bistro."

"Harry Henderson for Thatcher, please."

Harry Henderson of Henderson Realty. Adrienne had sat the guy half a dozen times and he still didn't know her name.

"This is Adrienne, Harry," she said. "Thatcher won't be in today."

There was a big noise of annoyance on the other end of the line. "What are you talking about? Forget it! I'll call him at home."

"He's off-island," Adrienne said.

"No!" Harry cried out, as though he'd been shot. "Listen, I have a couple standing in my office this minute who are extremely interested in the property. I'm bringing them over."

"Wait," Adrienne said. She glanced around the dining room. The cleaning crew had been in but the restaurant had that dull daytime look. And Adrienne was in jean shorts and flip-flops. When she'd walked back into the kitchen upon her arrival, Eddie and Hector were having a contest to see who knew more curse words. "I don't think you should come now. Nothing's ready."

"You might not understand real estate, Amanda," Harry Henderson said. "We have to strike while the iron is hot. See you in ten." He hung up.

Adrienne dialed Thatcher's cell; she got his voice mail. Then she called the hotel. Ditto. She called his cell again. What was the point of taking his cell phone if he wasn't going to answer it? Then she pictured the hushed corridors of the hospital, the room where Fiona lay in bed hooked up to a ventilator, worrying about hell. She left a message.

"Harry Henderson is on his way over with some prospective buyers. I told him to wait but he couldn't be dissuaded. He thinks my name is Amanda. Call me at the restaurant."

Adrienne saw the Sid Wainer truck pull into the parking lot. JZ parked diagonally, taking up sixteen spots. He shut off the engine and climbed down from his seat. Instead of going around to open the back, he marched inside.

"JZ," Adrienne said. He stared at her and Adrienne could see he wasn't doing well. Just looking at him made Adrienne feel like a person with her act together.

"Have you heard anything?" he said.

She shook her head.

"You haven't talked to Thatch?"

"He's not answering his cell. And I couldn't reach him at the hotel."

"That's not good news," JZ said. "Either her O_2 sats are low or she has another infection."

"I saw her the other day hooked up to oxygen," Adrienne said. "But she seemed okay."

JZ took hold of the podium as though he planned to walk away with it. "I love her," he said. "I really fucking love her."

"I know," Adrienne said.

"I'm married," he said. "My wife and I are in love with other people."

Adrienne met this with silence. As interested as she was, she didn't have time for a confessional this minute.

"You're probably wondering why we don't get divorced," he said. "The reason is eight years old and four feet tall."

"Shaughnessy?"

He nodded. "Jamie says if I file for divorce, she'll take Shaughnessy away. And Jamie is just enough of a bitch that she means it. The guy she's been screwing for the last five years is married and won't leave his wife. And if she can't be happy, she won't let me be, either."

"Oh," Adrienne said.

JZ paced the floor in front of the restrooms. "I love Fiona but I can't lose my daughter."

The phone rang. The private line.

"I have to take this," Adrienne said. "It might be Thatch."

JZ nodded.

"Good morning," Adrienne said. "Blue Bistro."

"What in God's name is going on with this truck?" Harry Henderson asked. "We're in the parking lot and this truck is blocking the front view of the restaurant. Do you hear what I'm saying? We can't see the front."

"It's deliveries," Adrienne said.

"Well, tell him to move." With that, Harry Henderson hung up.

Adrienne smiled at JZ apologetically. Out in the parking lot, she heard Harry Henderson honking his horn.

"They want you to move," she said.

"They can fuck themselves."

"I'd agree," Adrienne said. "Except it's the Realtor with potential buyers. They want to see the front of the restaurant."

JZ ran a hand over his thinning hair. "Do you understand about Shaughnessy?"

"It doesn't matter if *I* understand," she said. "It only matters if . . ."

"I know. And she does understand. Or she claims she does. But she doesn't have kids. It's difficult to comprehend losing a child when you don't have one of your own."

Harry Henderson honked again.

"I'll move," JZ said. He took a Blue Bistro pencil and wrote a phone number on Adrienne's reconfirmation list. "Here's my cell. Will you call me if you hear anything?"

"Of course," Adrienne said.

"They're filthy rich."

This was what Harry Henderson whispered in Adrienne's ear while the prospective buyers wandered through the restaurant. Adrienne had been expecting a couple who *looked* filthy rich—an older couple, distinguished, like the Parrishes. Instead, Harry introduced Scott and Lucy Elpern. Scott Elpern was handsome despite his best efforts. He was tall and had a just-out-of-the-locker-room thing going in jeans, a dirty gray T-shirt, and a Red Sox cap. The wife, Lucy, wore a flowered muumuu that she must have picked up at Goodwill. She was hugely pregnant. Three days past her due date, she told Adrienne when they shook hands, as though she didn't want anyone around her getting too comfortable. Lucy herself could not have looked less comfortable. She was swollen and perspiring, her face was red, her hair oily. She resembled one of the cherry tomatoes the kitchen roasted until the skin split and the seeds oozed out.

"Technology billionaires," Harry Henderson said. "Nobody thinks there are technology billionaires anymore but I found two of them."

Adrienne looked out the window by the podium. JZ had swung the truck around so that it was perpendicular to the restaurant and now he was going about his business of unloading crates of eggs and peaches and figs. He moved sluggishly, plodding like he was being asked to carry gold bullion.

The Elperns stood by table twenty gazing out at the water. Lucy Elpern rested her hands on her belly. Harry Henderson gave them a moment to enjoy the view, then he gently led Lucy Elpern up the two steps and through the bar area.

"This is a blue granite bar," Harry said.

Lucy eyed her husband. "We could keep that."

"Of course!" Harry said. "And there's a state-of-the-art wine room and, naturally, an industrial kitchen."

"Can we see the kitchen?" Lucy asked.

"Of course!" Harry boomed. He looked to Adrienne for confirmation.

"I didn't tell anyone you were coming," Adrienne said.

"We'll just poke our heads in," Harry said. "Is Fiona back there?"

"No," Adrienne said.

"Too bad," Harry said to the Elperns. "You could have gotten a glimpse of the most famous chef on the island." He led Scott Elpern to the kitchen door.

"I have to use the ladies' room," Lucy Elpern said to Adrienne. "This baby is sitting on my bladder."

Adrienne pointed to the bathroom door.

Lucy rubbed her belly. Her fingers were swollen; the diamond wedding band she wore cut into her flesh. Her ankles looked soft and squishy, like water balloons. She had on a pair of turquoise flip-flops, the plastic kind you could buy at the five-and-dime. "I have to go every five minutes," she said.

Once Harry and Scott disappeared into the kitchen and Lucy closed the door of the restroom, Adrienne dialed Thatcher's number. Voice mail. She hung up. She heard water in the bathroom and a second later, Lucy emerged. Instead of heading into the kitchen, she wandered over to the podium, where Adrienne was pretending to review the reconfirmation list.

"You've worked here a long time?" Lucy asked.

"Not really," Adrienne said. "Only about six weeks."

"Harry told us that most of the staff has been here for years."

"Most of the staff has."

"But not you?"

"Not me."

Lucy Elpern inhaled. "This place has good karma."

"Are you in the restaurant business?" Adrienne said.

"No," Lucy said, and she laughed. "We're going to demolish and build a real house. But it would be nice if there were things we could keep. The bar, for example. We could put it in our family room, maybe."

"In your family room?"

"And then we could say this is the bar that used to be in a famous restaurant." She picked a pack of matches out of the bowl. "The Blue Bistro."

"You've never eaten here?" Adrienne asked.

"No. We've only been on Nantucket for a week. But we really want a second home on the beach. We live on Beacon Street in Boston. Nice, but very urban."

Adrienne checked her reservation sheet. There were 232 on the books for tonight, but she did have a couple of deuces left during first seating.

"Why don't you come in tonight on the house?" Adrienne said. "Around six?"

Lucy smiled, then ran a hand through her unwashed hair. "You're a doll to offer. That way we'd know what it might feel like to eat . . . in our new dining room. Let me ask Scott." She waddled to the kitchen door and with great effort, pushed it open.

Adrienne stared at the phone. She wanted to tell Thatcher that some people were here who wanted to demolish his restaurant but salvage the blue granite bar to put on display in their family room like a museum piece from a country they had never visited. She heard a noise and looked out the window. JZ was pulling out of the parking lot. *Don't go!* Adrienne thought. The feeling of abandonment returned and she picked up the phone to call Thatcher, but at that minute, Harry Henderson and the Elperns emerged from the kitchen.

"They weren't very friendly back there," Harry said.

Adrienne tried not to smile. She wondered if Hector had shared his seventeen words for copulation. "You support the wrong baseball team," Adrienne said, nodding at Scott's hat. "They're White Sox fans."

Scott shrugged. "Nice refrigerator," he said.

"We'd like to come to dinner tonight," Lucy said.

"And I'll join them," Harry Henderson said. "Amanda, you're a genius."

At five o'clock, Adrienne still hadn't heard from Thatcher. She led a very brief menu meeting, keeping her voice stern so that no one would be brave enough to mention the elephant in the room: *Thatcher is absent from class again today.*

It was Friday night and the first people in the door were the Parrishes. Earlier that afternoon, Adrienne had done the unthinkable: She had called the Parrishes to ask if they would give up table twenty.

"Just for tonight," Adrienne said. In a stroke of what she thought would be bad luck, she'd gotten Grayson on the phone, and hearing his gruff voice, she'd almost chickened out. "I can't tell you the reason, but believe me, I would never ask you to move if it wasn't critical."

Grayson had chuckled. "Sweetheart, Darla and I don't give a rat's ass where we sit. For the last twelve years we've had everyone thinking we're more important than we are. Put us wherever you want."

"Oh, thank you," Adrienne said. "Thank you, thank you."

Now she led Darla and Grayson to table eleven under the awning. It was a very warm night so she felt they would be happiest here.

Darla took her seat and looked around in amazement. "I feel like I'm in a whole other restaurant. And look! You've changed the flowers!"

Adrienne sent Bruno over and told him to comp the Parrishes' first round of drinks though she doubted they would care. Grayson never checked his bill. Once the Parrishes were squared away, Adrienne relaxed a wee bit. She had called Thatcher's cell phone four times over the course of the afternoon but she hadn't left a message. Too much to say.

Adrienne sat guests, handed out menus, opened the white burgundy for the Parrishes, delivered their chips and dip, and helped Christo rearrange seating to accommodate a hundred-year-old woman in a wheelchair. Then Adrienne spotted Harry Henderson's florid face at the podium and she hurried over. The Elperns stood behind him. Lucy's hair was damp and she had changed into a clean muumuu. Scott had thrown a white dress shirt over his gray T-shirt and traded in his jeans for khakis. Lucy was visibly dazzled.

"Look at this place," she said. "It is glam-or-ous." Rex was playing Frank Sinatra. "Can we keep the piano?" she asked.

Adrienne led the party to table twenty and Harry stopped along the way to shake hands with two gentlemen at table eight.

"Amanda," he said when she handed him his menu, "this was a really smart move on your part."

He sounded absolutely giddy. *And why not?* Adrienne thought. He was sitting down to a free dinner with a potential six-figure commission at the best table in the restaurant.

"My name," she said, "is Adrienne."

Harry smiled. He had no idea what she meant.

"My name is Adrienne, not Amanda."

"Like Adrienne Rich, the poet," Lucy said.

"Yes. Thank you," Adrienne said. "Now what can I get everyone to drink?"

■

Adrienne did a kamikaze shot at the bar before she delivered the Elperns' drinks. Unprofessional, possibly even unethical, but her stress level was so high that champagne wasn't going to cut through it and she told Duncan so and he put the kamikaze shot in front of her. It tasted like a bad night in college, though once she chased it with the Laurent-Perrier she regained her sense of humor. She went into the kitchen to put in a VIP order for the Elperns.

The restaurant can run itself. Joe walked by carrying two quesadilla specials. They looked delicious. Antonio was expediting with his usual avuncular charm, calling everyone baby. Everything was going to be fine.

Back in the dining room, Caren grabbed Adrienne's forearm. "Table twenty wanted the fondue. I told them no."

Adrienne peeked at twenty. Lucy Elpern had ordered a glass of Laurent-Perrier and from the looks of things, it had gone straight to her head. She was waving her champagne flute in the air, calling out to anyone who looked her way, "This bread is baked!"

"Let them have it," Adrienne said.

"Let them *have* it?" Caren said. "You bumped the Parrishes for Harry Henderson of all people, and now you're going to let them have the fondue first seating?" She gave an incredulous little laugh. "This isn't your restaurant, you know."

"Let them have it," Adrienne said. She walked away before she and Caren moved on to more sensitive topics, like how Caren was still pissed at Adrienne for putting Tam Vinidin at the bar, or how, technically, Adrienne was Caren's boss.

Adrienne thought Antonio might veto her decision about the fondue, but a little while later Caren passed by holding a pot of oil. She wouldn't meet Adrienne's eyes and Adrienne's confidence wavered. She had never even worked at Pizza Hut. What was she doing, breaking all the rules while Thatcher was away? Was it all in the name of selling the restaurant, or was it to exercise power in a situation where she felt utterly helpless?

A couple of minutes later, she checked on the Elperns again. Scott

Elpern lifted a golden brown shrimp from the pot and dragged it lavishly through the green goddess sauce, then the curry. Was it any surprise that the man had no table manners?

"How's everybody doing?" she asked.

"Adrienne," Harry Henderson said before he popped a shrimp into his mouth. It wasn't a response to her question so much as a demonstration that he had learned her name.

Lucy Elpern finished her glass of champagne. "Never better," she said.

Adrienne approached the Parrishes. They were eating in complete silence.

"Is there anything at all I can get you?" Adrienne asked.

"We love the new table," Darla said. "We like it better than the other table."

"You're kidding."

"At the other table, everyone watches you."

"Yes, they do," Adrienne said. She glanced at table twenty. The Elperns were having the time of their lives. There was no doubt in Adrienne's mind that this time next year the floor under her feet would be the Elperns' new living room.

Adrienne stopped at the bar to pick up her champagne.

"Another shot?" Duncan asked.

"Your girlfriend's pissed at me," Adrienne said. "She thinks I put too many pretty women at the bar."

"If you stop, I'll be pissed at you," Duncan said.

Elliott, who never said a word unless spoken to, chose this moment to interrupt. "Where's Thatcher?" he said. "Does he normally take a vacation in the middle of summer?"

Adrienne was saved having to answer when she spied Harry Henderson on his cell phone, which was a Blue Bistro no-no.

"Excuse me," Adrienne said, and she hurried back into the dining room.

Before she could scold Harry for using his phone, she sensed something was wrong. The atmosphere at the Elperns' table had altered. Lucy's face was screwed up and Scott hovered close, squeezing her hand. Darla was right.

Every other table in the restaurant had their attention fixed on the Elperns. The hundred-year-old woman in the wheelchair touched Adrienne's arm.

"I think that woman is having her baby."

Adrienne smiled. "She may have started labor. We'll get her to the hospital." She sounded preternaturally calm, thanks to the kamikaze shot, thanks to the fact that she'd prepared herself for this possibility. You didn't invite a woman three days past her due date to dinner and not consider the worst-case scenario.

Harry snapped his cell phone shut. "I called nine-one-one. An ambulance is coming."

"An ambulance?" Adrienne said, thinking: sirens and lights, the pall of emergency and doom. "The hospital is less than two miles from here. You could drive."

Scott Elpern glanced up. "We're in a rental car." These, Adrienne realized, were the only words she'd heard him speak other than *Nice refrigerator.*

"So?"

Lucy spoke through pursed lips. "My water broke," she said. "I'm sitting in a huge puddle of yuck."

Adrienne nearly laughed. Was this or was this not the theater of the absurd? She caught a whiff of something acrid: Three shrimp burning in the peanut oil. Adrienne fished them out, then she lassoed Spillman. "Let's get guests their checks. This could turn into a circus."

Unfortunately, it was too late. A minute later, Adrienne heard sirens in the distance, then lights flashed through the restaurant and three paramedics stormed in like they were rescuing a hostage. Conversation in the restaurant came to a dead halt; Rex stopped playing. Adrienne led the head paramedic, a woman with a long, scraggly ponytail, through the now-hushed restaurant to the Elperns' table.

"She just started labor. I really don't think there's any reason to panic . . ."

The paramedic knelt down and spoke quietly to Lucy Elpern. Adrienne wondered what to do in the way of damage control. They would need a towel. She retrieved the Sankaty Golf Club towel from the wine cave, and on her way back to the Elperns' table, she passed Darla and Grayson leaving.

"We loved the table," Darla whispered. "But we're going to get out of here before there's any blood."

"There won't be any blood," Adrienne whispered back. Would there? Grayson palmed Adrienne a hundred dollars.

The golf towel was very little help. The back of Lucy Elpern's muumuu was soaked and this seemed to be a cause of concern for her; she didn't want to leave the restaurant.

"Everyone will know," she whispered.

"Everyone already knows," Adrienne said. "And it's no big deal. It's perfectly natural."

"This is so embarrassing," she said.

The head paramedic called one of her guys for a blanket and once they had wrapped Lucy Elpern up, they led her out of the restaurant to the ambulance. The guests at the remaining tables applauded politely, much like they did when the sun set, and the decibel level rose back to normal. Adrienne trailed Lucy and the paramedic to the front door. The phone rang. Adrienne glanced over the top of the podium: It was the private line.

"Good evening," she said. "Blue Bistro."

"Hi," Thatcher said. "It's me."

Tears welled up in Adrienne's eyes so that when she looked out the window, the lights of the ambulance blurred and became a psychedelic soup. She didn't know exactly why she was crying though she imagined it was a combination of anxiety, relief, and the kamikaze shot. *Where the hell have you been?* she wanted to scream, but she held her tongue. She should ask about Fiona, about the hospital. However, there wasn't time to listen to the answers.

"Can I call you back?" she said. "In, say, fifteen minutes? I have to get first seating out of here."

"Sure," Thatcher said.

There was a long pause during which Adrienne tried to think of something else to say, but then she realized that Thatcher had hung up. She replaced the phone as the ambulance pulled out of the parking lot, sirens screeching. Tyler Lefroy was standing at the podium, a put-out expression on his seventeen-year-old face.

"Do I really have to clean that gross shit up?"

"Get a mop," Adrienne said.

■

Adrienne wanted to call Thatcher back, but she couldn't. Tables had to be turned; there were a hundred and twenty people sitting down at nine, and because of the Elpern spectacle, first seating was running behind. Adrienne monitored the progress of dessert and coffee; her foot was actually tapping. *Turn 'em and burn 'em,* she thought. The busboys were humping. Then Caren had a credit card war. Adrienne had heard about these but never seen one. Two men at table eight (by chance, the very men Harry Henderson had stopped to greet) wanted the bill. They were *fighting* over it. Adrienne's attention was called to the problem when she heard Caren's voice, much louder than it should have been.

"Gentlemen, I'm sure we can work this out! I am happy to split the bill."

The men were on their feet now, tugging at either end of the bill. Thankfully, this was one of the last tables in the dining room. Adrienne approached: The table was another Realtor and his wife and a local lawyer and her husband. The lawyer's husband was the louder of the two men, though the Realtor was physically bigger.

"I thought we agreed . . ." the lawyer's husband said.

"Please, I *insist,*" the Realtor growled.

Adrienne felt badly that she hadn't at least asked Thatcher how Fiona was doing; it was a big mistake that needed to be rectified as soon as possible. With a lightning quick movement, Adrienne snatched the bill from both men, then put her palm out.

"We don't have *time* for this," she said. Blue Bitch voice. "Cards."

They handed over their cards and Adrienne spun on her heels. Caren followed her.

"Impressive," Caren murmured.

Adrienne tried to call Thatcher back after everyone from second seating was settled, but just as she felt it was safe to pick up the phone, Hector appeared from the kitchen.

"The exhaust fan is out," he said.

"What does that mean?"

"It means the kitchen is getting smoky."

"Okay," Adrienne said.

"We need it fixed," Hector said.

"Fine."

"Tonight."

"Tonight?" Adrienne said. She checked her watch. "It's a quarter of ten."

"Cat," Hector said. "Call her on her cell phone."

"I will not," Adrienne said. "She's probably *asleep.*"

"If you don't call her, the fire alarms are going to go off and the fire department will show up."

"Take the batteries out," Adrienne said.

Hector readjusted his White Sox hat. "This is an industrial kitchen," he said. "Do you really think our fire alarms run on a couple of double As? You have to call Cat."

"You're kidding me, right? This is a joke?" Adrienne was *certain* it was a joke. A prank to go with Lucy Elpern's labor. A little laugh at her expense while the boss was away.

"I'm serious," Hector said. "Look." He pointed to the window of the kitchen door. Smoke.

"I can't believe this," Adrienne said. *The restaurant can run itself. Ha!* as Thatcher would say. *Ha ha ha!*

She found Cat's cell phone number on a list pasted to the front of the reservation book and Cat answered on the first ring. It sounded like she was in high spirits. Too high.

"Cat? It's Adrienne calling from the Blue Bistro."

"Hey, girlfriend!"

"Hi. Listen, I'm sorry to bother you, but we have an exhaust fan out."

There was a long pause. Adrienne feared she had lost the connection, but then Cat spoke up. "I just needed to step outside," she said. "I'm having dinner at the Chanticleer."

Adrienne groaned. The Chanticleer was in Sconset, on the other side of the island. "So you can't come fix it?"

"And leave behind the duck for two with pomme frites?" Cat said. "The bottle of 1972 Mouton Rothschild . . ."

"We could give you dinner here," Adrienne said. "Hector said if it's not fixed, the alarms will go."

"Well," said Cat. Another pause. "I'm with a party of ten and I know for a fact my husband can eat the duck for two by himself. I'll sneak out now and come back. They're so drunk, they might not even miss me."

Fifteen minutes later, the kitchen was filled with smoke such that Antonio could barely read the tickets. They had opened the back door of the office and the six narrow windows and they pulled the two oscillating fans out of the utility closet and Paco was yanked off his station—his new job was to stand in front of the smoke detector waving a large offset spatula. Adrienne returned to the front. She drank her third glass of champagne and contemplated another kamikaze shot. Every time one of the waitstaff emerged, he smelled like a barbecue.

"Whew! It's getting bad back there," Joe said. "Have you called Cat?"

"She's on her way," Adrienne said, praying that Cat didn't get stopped on Milestone Road for drunk driving. Adrienne considered calling Thatcher and asking quickly about Fiona, but she wouldn't be able to keep the panic out of her voice. As she finished her champagne, Cat walked in the door—black cocktail dress, Manolo Blahniks, tool belt.

"Praise Allah," Adrienne said.

Cat stuck out her lower lip. "The 1972 Mouton Rothschild," she said.

"We'll make it up to you," Adrienne said.

Cat disappeared into the kitchen and Adrienne called Thatcher.

"Hi," he said. "Is everything all right?"

"I was just going to ask you the same thing," Adrienne said.

"Her O_2 sats are back up for the time being," Thatcher said. "The doctors are worried, though."

"About what?"

"She's becoming resistant to the antibiotics, and there's a lot of other stuff going on that I don't even pretend to understand. The doctor nixed the trip to the Galápagos, and Fiona was crushed. Can you make a note in the book for me to cancel with the travel agent? We'll be home tomorrow night, Fiona will be back to work on Monday. Would you pass that on to Antonio?"

"Sure," Adrienne said, scribbling a note about the travel agent. No Galápagos, then. She thought she might feel relieved, but instead she just felt sad. "JZ was in this morning. He's worried."

"He should be here," Thatcher said. "She's been asking for him." He sighed. "I got your messages. Sounds like everything is going well there."

"Going well?" Adrienne said.

"Isn't it?"

At that moment, Adrienne heard a muted cheer from the kitchen and Cat stepped out, hoisting her tool belt in victory. Adrienne blew her a kiss as she ran out the door.

"Sure," Adrienne said.

"Good. I'll see you tomorrow night. We'll be on the four o'clock flight so I hope to make the menu meeting. How many covers are on the book?"

"Two thirty-five," Adrienne said.

"Whoa," Thatcher said. "It's July. Hey, would you call Jack at the flower shop in the morning and have him deliver fresh hydrangeas on Monday? I want it to look nice when Fee comes back."

"No problem," Adrienne said.

"I miss you," Thatcher said. "Do you miss me?"

"I do," she said.

She hung up the phone. She felt better, like she was the one whose exhaust fan had been broken, and now she sucked in clean, fresh air. The phone rang again, private line. Adrienne had to do rounds through the dining room, but she picked up the phone in case it was Thatcher with one last thing.

It wasn't Thatcher, but Adrienne was glad she took the call anyway. Harry Henderson informed her, in a voice both jubilant and humbled, of the birth of Sebastian Robert Elpern, nine pounds, twelve ounces, perfect in every way, and of an official offer on the Blue Bistro for eight and a half million dollars.

9

Phosphorescence

***The Inquirer and Mirror*, Week of July 15, 2005**
"Here and There" column

There have been several reports of phosphorescence in the water at beaches along the north shore this week. Phosphorescence is caused by a type of algae called dinoflagellates, which are capable of bioluminescence when the water they reside in is disturbed.

***Sports Illustrated* cover story:**
"The Heroes of America's Heartland: Can the White Sox Win the Pennant?"

TO: Ade12177@hotmail.com
FROM: kyracrenshaw@mindspring.com
DATE: July 13, 2005, 9:02 A.M.
SUBJECT: Things I can't believe

I can't believe you've traded in the cushy life of the hotel front desk for the restaurant business. I can't believe you're dating your boss. I can't believe you're living with my dreamboat Duncan. You should thank me for recommending Nantucket. You should remember me in your will.

TO: kyracrenshaw@mindspring.com
FROM: Ade12177@hotmail.com
DATE: July 13, 2005, 10:35 A.M.
SUBJECT: Thank you

Thank you for recommending Nantucket. I am in a much better place, following my new rules, feeling good about myself. I paid off both Mr. Visa and Ms. MasterCard and I have a positive bank balance. I am in a relationship with a real, live, grown-up man. I sing in the shower.

It is amazing, Kyra, the way that happiness changes a person.

TO: Ade12177@hotmail.com
FROM: kyracrenshaw@mindspring.com
DATE: July 14, 2005, 8:41 A.M.
SUBJECT: the way that happiness changes a person

Is happiness contagious? Can you send me some spores in the mail?

When Fiona returned from Boston, Adrienne studied her for signs of illness, but Fiona had never looked better. One very busy Thursday night, the kitchen was waist-deep in the weeds. The kitchen had so many tickets, there wasn't enough room for them above the pass. The Subiacos were sweating and cursing and busting their humps to keep up. Fiona slid behind the line to plate soups, sauce pasta, and sauté foie gras while singing "The Sun Will Come Out Tomorrow." Every time Adrienne peeked her head in, she found Fiona in soaring good spirits.

"One plate at a time," Fiona called out. She even helped Jojo, the youngest Subiaco, load the dishwasher. She was a general in the foxhole with her men, but singing, gleeful. It was strange. Adrienne thought maybe the hospital had given Fiona a personality transplant.

It didn't take Adrienne long to figure out that Fiona's improvement in attitude had nothing to do with the hospital or facing her own mortality. It had, very simply, to do with love. Right after first seating, JZ walked in.

Shaughnessy was away at camp and he had rented a house on Liberty Street. Today was Day One of a week's vacation.

Fiona and JZ were inseparable. By Day Three they had established a routine: They did yoga together on the beach in the mornings, and then JZ helped Fiona in the kitchen. One morning Adrienne found him pitting Bing cherries and joking with the Subiacos. (The Subiacos were in a collective good mood because the White Sox had won eleven straight and held first place by a game and a half.) Fiona and JZ escaped from the kitchen by noon with a picnic basket and off they would go in Fiona's Range Rover to secret, out-of-the-way beaches where no one would ever find them. JZ ate dinner at the bar and spent the hour after second seating in the kitchen—and Adrienne knew that after eating with Thatch, Fiona drove her Range Rover to the house on Liberty Street and spent the night.

Was happiness contagious? By Day Four, it was safe to say that the food at the Bistro had never been better and Adrienne wasn't sure how to explain that. How did the best get better? It just did. Every single guest raved about the food. *Perfectly seasoned, perfectly cooked, the freshest, the creamiest, the most succulent. The best I've ever had.* Adrienne noticed it, too, at family meal: the Asian shrimp noodles, the Croque monsieurs, the steak sandwiches with creamy horseradish sauce and crispy Vidalia onion rings. *Are you kidding me?* Adrienne thought as she stuffed her face. She thought: *JZ, never leave.*

On Day Five, Adrienne was working reservations when the private line rang. By this time, Adrienne realized the private line could be anybody: Thatcher (who was at an AA meeting), Cat, Dottie Shore, Harry Henderson, Ernie Otemeyer, Leon Cross, Father Ott.

"Good morning, Blue Bistro," Adrienne said.

A woman's voice said, "This is Jamie Zodl. I'm looking for my husband. Have you seen him?"

Adrienne found herself at a loss. "I'm sorry? Your husband?"

"Jasper Zodl. JZ. There's no need to play games. I know you know who he is and I know he's there. Or if he's not there now, he'll be there at some point and I want to speak to him."

Adrienne wrote JZ's name at the top of her reconfirmation sheet. She thought of Shaughnessy at summer camp and all the things that might have gone wrong: sunburn, mosquito bites, sprained ankle, homesickness. "He normally delivers here at ten," Adrienne said. "But he's on vacation this week."

"You can cut the crap," Jamie said. "I'm not stupid. Have him call me. His wife. At his house. He knows the number."

"Okay, if I see him—"

Jamie Zodl hung up.

Adrienne passed on the message that evening when JZ came into the bar for dinner. He was wearing a dolphin-blue button-down shirt and his face and forearms were very tan. He and Fiona had rented a Sunfish that afternoon and sailed on Coskata Pond. Adrienne delivered the bad news with his chips and dip.

"Your wife called this morning," she said.

"Here?"

Adrienne nodded. "She wants you to call her at home."

"It can't be important," he said. "Or she would have called me on my cell. I had it on all day. She probably just called to make a point. To let everyone know she knows I'm here."

"Okay, well," Adrienne said. "That was the message."

Later that night as they lay in bed, Adrienne asked Thatcher what he knew about Jamie Zodl.

"She's unhappy," he said. "She's one of those people who thinks the next thing is going to save her. When I first met her twelve years ago, she was desperate to marry JZ. They used to come into the restaurant all the time. He proposed to her at table twenty."

"Oh, you're kidding," Adrienne said.

"After they got married, Jamie wanted to be pregnant. That didn't happen right away and they went to Boston for fertility help and it worked, obviously, because they had Shaughnessy. But then Jamie realized how hard it was to be a mother. So to afford a live-in, she and JZ sold their house here and moved to Sandwich. Jamie had an affair with the guy who owned the gym that she joined, and JZ found out. Jamie promised to break it off, they went into counseling for a while, and JZ took a job driving for another company so he wouldn't have to be gone every day. We didn't see him here for two whole summers. But then he found out Jamie was back with the guy from the gym and he gave up. Got his old job back and he's been trying to file for divorce, but Jamie won't let him. She threatens to take Shaughnessy away and she disappears to her mother's in Charlottesville, and once she and Shaughnessy flew to London for the weekend. The only way JZ was able to find them was by calling his credit card company. Jamie has run them into mountains of debt on top of it all. Pretty woman, gorgeous, but what a disaster." Thatcher rubbed his eyes. "JZ used to talk to Fiona about the whole thing. It was strange because Fiona and I and the staff had watched the relationship from the beginning—the courtship, the proposal, the wedding, the child, the breakup, and the next thing I knew Fiona and JZ were in love."

"When was that?"

"Two years ago."

"So what do you think will happen, then?"

"What do I think will happen?" Thatcher repeated. He was lying on his back, arms folded over his chest like someone resting in a coffin. "Nothing will happen."

"What does that mean?"

"JZ won't leave Jamie. He's too cowardly."

"He's worried about his daughter."

"That's what he says."

"You don't believe him?"

"JZ is a good guy," Thatcher said. "But he's not going to risk anything for Fiona. Leave his wife and lose his daughter for someone who's going to die?" Thatcher rolled onto his side, away from Adrienne. "That would take a hero. JZ is nobody's hero."

Happiness might be contagious, but it was also fleeting, delicate, mercurial. On Day Six, Jamie called again, in the middle of second seating. The restaurant was loud, but Adrienne picked up a new tone in Jamie's voice.

She sounded manic and untethered, like someone who had pounded six shots of espresso.

"This is Jamie Zodl," she said. "ISJZTHERE?"

"Yes," Adrienne said. "Please hold on one minute."

"You hold on one minute," Jamie said.

"Excuse me?"

"I know Fiona's sick," Jamie said. "I know all about it."

Adrienne said nothing. Across the room, a table burst out laughing. Rex played, "In the Mood."

"Let me get JZ," Adrienne said.

"I have a phone number," Jamie said. "For a journalist who wants to write about her. He wants to talk to me about Fiona and JZ. The question is, do I want to talk to him?"

"Let me get JZ," Adrienne said again, though she was afraid to put Jamie on hold. Bruno swung by the podium.

"I need your help on ten," he said. "Can you pull a bottle of the Cakebread?"

Adrienne's ears were buzzing; she felt like she had a bomb threat on the phone.

"Get JZ," Adrienne whispered to Bruno. "His *wife* is on the phone."

Bruno wasn't listening closely—what he heard was Adrienne asking him for something in response to his asking her for something. He wagged a finger. "Honey, I'm slammed. Can you get the wine for me, please?"

Adrienne searched the dining room for Thatcher. Her eyes snagged on table ten, a deuce, a middle-aged couple, fidgeting, glancing around. They wanted their wine. Adrienne snapped back to her senses. This was a restaurant! She put Jamie Zodl on hold, zipped into the wine cave for the Cakebread, then she shouted into the kitchen, "JZ, call for you on line three!" By the time Adrienne opened the wine for table ten and made it back to the podium, the phones were quiet. Jamie had hung up.

Adrienne didn't see JZ on Day Seven, but she gathered he had packed up and left. Fiona took a day off; when she returned, she was back to her old sarcastic, scowling self. The White Sox lost a double-header to the Mariners. Adrienne stayed out of the kitchen.

TO: kyracrenshaw@mindspring.com
FROM: Ade12177@hotmail.com
DATE: July 21, 2005, 10:35 A.M.
SUBJECT: happiness

Not sending spores. You don't want them. Happiness is fickle. Plays favorites.

A couple of days later, Adrienne was working the phone when a man walked in dressed entirely in black. Black jeans, black shoes, black dress shirt open at the neck. Bulky black duffel bag. He was a young guy who had shaved his head to hide his baldness, so all Adrienne could see was something like a five o'clock shadow where his hair used to be. *New York,* Adrienne thought, and immediately her guard went up. The press. Who else dressed in black on a hot July day at the beach?

"Can I help you?" Adrienne said.

He offered her his pale hand. "Lyle Hardaway," he said. "*Vanity Fair* magazine."

Yep. Adrienne eyed her phone. If he didn't leave when she asked, she would call the police.

"I'm sorry," Adrienne said. "You don't have an appointment and our owner isn't here."

He held up his palm. "I have a meeting scheduled with Mario Subiaco. He said he'd be working. He said I should come here."

"He did?"

"Yeah. Mario, the pastry chef. This is the Blue Bistro?"

"It is." Blue Bitch voice. She pointed a finger at his raised hand. "You wait right here. Don't move. Is there a camera in that bag?"

"Yes," he said.

"No photographs," she said. "Understand?"

"Okay," he said, and he smiled like maybe this tough act of hers was supposed to be funny.

Adrienne marched into the kitchen. She heard Fiona's voice in the walk-in; she was making an order list with Antonio. Adrienne slipped into pastry. Mario was all gussied up in his houndstooth pants, washed and pressed, and his dress whites—the jacket with black piping and his name over the chest pocket. He was rolling out dough.

"You have a visitor," Adrienne said.

He didn't look up. "Do I?"

"Lyle somebody. From *Vanity Fair.*"

"Okay," Mario said.

"He's not coming back here," Adrienne said.

"Yeah, he is," Mario said. "He wants to watch me work. I'm making my own pretzels today. For chocolate-covered pretzels. It's a special on the candy plate."

"I thought there was no press allowed in the kitchen," Adrienne said. "I thought that was a law."

"This isn't the kitchen," Mario said. "It's pastry."

"Does Fiona know this guy is coming?" Adrienne asked.

"Not yet."

Adrienne watched Mario fiddle with the pretzel dough, twisting it into nifty shapes. "What's going on?" she said.

"They're doing an article about me," he said.

"Just about you?"

"Just about me. I hired a publicist."

"You did *what*?"

"I hired a publicist and she sent out my picture and my CV and *Vanity Fair* called. They're doing some article about sex and the kitchen. You know, sexy chefs. Rocco DiSpirito, Todd English, and me." He raised his face from his work and mugged for her.

"Now I've heard it all," Adrienne said. "You hired a publicist and you have a writer from a huge New York magazine in the bistro with a camera to take pictures of you making chocolate-covered pretzels because you're sexy."

"King of the Sweet Ending," he said. "They loved the name."

"Yeah, well, Fiona doesn't know. And guess what? I'm not telling her."

"No one was asking you to."

"So you'll tell her yourself?"

"Tell her why? It's my business."

"It's not your business," Adrienne said. "It's her business."

"Just send the guy back, please, Adrienne."

As Adrienne returned to the dining room—Lyle Hardaway was right where she'd left him—the phone rang. Darla Parrish, bumping her reservation to three people. Adrienne asked cautiously, hoping, praying, "Not Wolfie?"

"No, it's our youngest son, Luke. I can't wait to introduce you. Oh, and Adrienne, dear, will you put us at that new table?"

"Sure thing," Adrienne said. She made a note on her reconfirmation list. The writer was watching her every move. She hung up the phone, then said, "Follow me."

Adrienne and Lyle Hardaway made it three steps into the kitchen before Fiona stopped them.

"Whoa," she said. "Whoa. Who's this? Not a wine rep back here?"

"His name is Lyle Hardaway." Adrienne was afraid to say more.

"Is he a friend of yours?" Fiona asked.

"No," Adrienne said.

Suddenly, Mario appeared from the back. "He's here for me."

"What is he, your new dance instructor?" Fiona said. She glared at Lyle Hardaway. "Who are you?"

"I'm a writer for *Vanity Fair*," he said. He offered Fiona his hand. "You're Fiona Kemp? It's an honor to meet you."

Fiona pointed to the door. Her cheeks were starting to splotch and she bent her head and coughed a little into her hand. Antonio spoke up from behind the pass.

"Get him out of here, Adrienne," he said. And Adrienne thought, *Yes, get him out before he sees Fiona cough.*

"Fuck off, Tony," Mario said. "He's here for me."

Antonio said, "What are you, crazy?"

Fiona spoke to the floor. "I have to ask you to leave," she said. "I don't allow press in the kitchen."

"Come on, Fee," Mario said in a voice that normally got him whatever he wanted. "He's here to take pictures of my pretzels."

"No," Fiona said.

Lyle Hardaway held his arms in front of his face, like the words were being hurled at him. "Maybe I should wait out front while you work this out."

"Wait outside," Fiona said. "In the parking lot."

Lyle Hardaway disappeared through the door.

Fiona slammed her hand on the pass. "And now there will be a line in *Vanity Fair* or one of the other magazines they're sleeping with—you can bet on it—about what a bitch I am." She glared at Mario. "What were you thinking? You *invited* him into our kitchen?"

"He wants to write an article about me," Mario said.

"No," Fiona said.

"You can't tell me no," Mario said. "The article is about me. It's not about you, it's not about the Bistro."

"That's where you're wrong," Fiona said. "He told you the article is about you. But that was just so he could get through the door. Did you hear him a second ago? 'You're Fiona Kemp? It's an honor to meet you'? He's using you to get to me."

Mario laughed and looked around the kitchen at his cousins, and his brother Louis, who was filling ravioli and pretending not to listen. Only Adrienne was captive, rooted in the kitchen, afraid to leave lest she attract attention to herself, or worse, miss something.

"I cannot believe how self-centered you are," Mario said. "You think the world revolves around your tiny ass? It does not. You think people care so much about you? They do not. That man came here to interview *me.* And I'm going to let him. Because my career isn't over in September, Fee. I have to move on, I have to build my prospects, increase the value of my stock. So maybe I get investors and open my own place. Maybe my cousin Henry gets investors for his root beer. We have to move on, Fee. Move forward. We aren't quitting at the end of the summer."

"I'm not quitting, either," Fiona whispered.

"The Bistro is closing," Mario said. "That's a fact. The building is sold, it's torn down, it's rebuilt as somebody's fat mansion. There is no more Bistro. So what do you expect us to do, lie down and die with you?"

"Mario!" Antonio said.

"Get out!" Fiona shouted. She whipped around and caught Adrienne standing there, but she didn't seem to care. Her eyes were ready to spill over with tears. Was Adrienne going to see Fiona *cry*? "Get out! Get out of my kitchen!"

Mario ripped off his chef's jacket and threw it to the floor. "Fine," he said. "I'm finished with you."

He stormed out the door, leaving the kitchen in a stunned silence. Adrienne felt a strong desire to run after him. She liked Mario and she saw his point—once the Bistro closed, everyone had to fend for himself. Fiona would be four million dollars richer, but where would the rest of them be?

Fiona retreated to the office and slammed the door.

Adrienne heard the faint ringing of the phone. She went out front to answer it. That was her job.

That night, there were 244 covers on the book. Family meal was pulled pork, corn muffins, grilled zucchini, and summer squash. At the menu meeting, Thatcher announced that there would be no desserts. All Antonio had been able to find back in pastry were a few gallons of peanut butter ice cream, a tray of Popsicles, and the unfinished pretzels.

"I'll say one thing for my cousin," Antonio said. "He works fresh."

No one knew where Mario was; at last report, he hadn't checked in at the Subiaco compound. Adrienne wondered if he had flown off-island in search of another job. She wondered if she would ever see him again.

"What do you think?" Adrienne asked Thatcher at the podium as they awaited first seating.

"I stay out of the kitchen's business."

"Yeah, but what do you think?"

"Fee's afraid," he said quietly. "And fear does strange things to people."

"It's too bad," Adrienne said. "They've been friends a long time."

"They're still friends," Thatcher said. "This is just a fight."

"So you think he'll come back?"

"Where's he going to go?" Thatcher said.

"I don't know. Chicago?"

"Ha!" Thatcher gave her the laugh, and Adrienne felt better. She was smiling when the Parrishes walked in.

"Halloo," Darla called out. She was holding a young man by the hand, pulling him along like he was Wolfie's age. "Adrienne, this is my son, Luke Parrish. Thatcher, you remember Luke."

Thatcher shook hands with Luke and patted him on the back. Luke smiled shyly at the floor. He was the exact opposite of what Adrienne expected a Parrish son to look like: He wore tiny frameless glasses and had

"Just yourself, when you have a minute," Darla said.

Adrienne stopped at the bar to order another tequila and then met Thatcher at the podium. Everyone from first was down.

"I think Darla is trying to set me up with her son," Adrienne said.

"Oh, I know she is," Thatcher said. "For years she's been wondering if he's gay. She told me on Tuesday that it was her intention to introduce him to you."

"And what did you say?"

"I said, 'Good luck. I hear she's very picky.' "

Adrienne swatted him. "Not picky enough."

"I want to have a meeting after closing tonight," Thatcher said.

"A meeting?"

"On the beach outside my office."

"Because of Mario?"

"Morale booster," he said. "It's mandatory. Please spread the word."

No one on the staff expressed enthusiasm about a mandatory meeting at one o'clock in the morning. Joe looked at Adrienne cross-eyed; Spillman claimed he had a date with his wife at Cioppino's.

"Morale booster?" he said. "What are we going to do—have a sing-along around the campfire?"

Caren, who was standing right there, said, "Thatch likes to give a little speech when the first person burns out." She nudged Spillman. "Last year, remember, when Bruno lost his shit on that woman with the alligator shoes, Thatch gave us the talk and we all got a raise?"

"True," Spillman said.

Tyler Lefroy asked if there would be beer. Adrienne was too afraid to tell anyone in the kitchen about the meeting; she would make Thatcher handle that.

Between their appetizer and entrée, Adrienne visited the Parrishes again. She had to admit, Luke Parrish fascinated her, not because of anything he said or did, but because he was so different from Darla and Grayson. He was a revolutionary. He'd ordered the mixed green salad with beets, and the ravioli; he was a vegetarian. And now, after two beers and three shots of tequila, Adrienne could tell he was getting drunk. His posture was falling apart. He was slumped in his seat.

"How's everyone doing here?" Adrienne asked. Again, the empty glass of tequila had been pushed to the edge of the table, and Adrienne picked it up and held it discreetly at her side. "Would you like another?" she asked Luke.

"No more tequila," Grayson said.

Luke sank a little lower in his chair. Adrienne was afraid he might slip under the table. Darla, for the first time ever, seemed distressed. She looked at Luke imploringly, as though she wanted him to speak. He was not picking up whatever signal she was trying to send. She laughed.

"Well, I suppose I might as well say it. Adrienne, Luke would like to take you out to dinner on your night off. He'd like to take you to Cinco."

Luke put both his hands on the table and Adrienne noticed he was wearing a silver pinkie ring. What to say? That she didn't normally go out with men who had their mothers ask? Luke pushed himself out of the chair. "I have to piss," he said, and he propelled himself toward the men's room.

Darla pretended not to have heard this last declaration. She smiled at Adrienne. "I hear Cinco has wonderful tapas."

Adrienne glanced around the dining room. There were no emergencies calling her name, and there was no one available to save her. She lowered herself into Luke's vacant seat.

"Thank you for thinking of me," she said. "But I'm already seeing someone."

Darla put her hand to her throat. She looked stunned. "Who?"

Adrienne took another look around. She felt the way a criminal must feel just before breaking the law. She was going to tell Darla and Grayson the truth—tell them because she wanted to—even though she could feel indiscretion coating her tongue like a film.

"Thatcher."

"No!" This came from Grayson.

"Thatcher?" Darla said. "You and Thatcher?"

"That's a dead-end street, my girl," Grayson said. "A dead . . . end . . . street." He picked up his wineglass and swirled his white burgundy aggressively. "Let me ask you a question. Why would someone as beautiful and smart and *charming* as yourself pick someone like Thatcher? Don't you want stability? A house? Children? Don't you want, someday, to be one of these soccer moms with everything in its place?"

"I thought you liked Thatcher," Adrienne said. "I thought you loved him."

Darla put her hand on top of Adrienne's hand. "Thatcher is a dear, sweet fellow and one of our very favorites. But he's a restaurant person."

Adrienne felt her temper rear up, though she knew they had arrived at this place in the conversation because of her own stupidity. "So am I."

"Why, one of the first things you told us is that you've never worked in restaurants. You said this was just another adventure. You aren't like the other people who work here. You aren't like them at all."

"Restaurants are as risky as the theater," Grayson said. "They're as derelict as television. It's a volatile and transient life. It's goddamned make-believe."

"Honey, now you're being dramatic," Darla said.

"Am I?" Grayson pitched forward in his chair. "What do your parents think of this?"

"My parents?" Adrienne panicked. She didn't want to answer a question about her parents. She wanted to defend restaurant people and restaurant life and all the exciting, diverse, and enriching aspects of it. She wanted to tell them that she was as happy as she'd ever been in her life because of this restaurant. But instead, Adrienne did what any good restaurant person would have done. She salvaged the moment.

"I really love you two," she said. She flashed them her biggest, toothiest smile. "Thank you for the vote of confidence. And if I ever come across a good prospect for Luke, I'll let you know." She stood up and touched Darla's shoulder. "Your dinners will be out shortly."

Adrienne dropped off the empty glass at the bar, picked up her flute of Laurent-Perrier, and returned to the podium. The podium was her home.

At twelve thirty that night, Thatcher slipped through the throng at the bar holding the cash box and wad of receipts close to his chest.

"I'm going to eat," he said.

Adrienne had just finished a stack of crackers. Hector had brought them out to her, along with the news that Mario was still MIA.

"No news is good news," Hector said. "They find him in his Durango at the bottom of Gibbs Pond, that's bad news."

■

Forty minutes later, Duncan rang the hand bell. The decibel level in the bar increased; the frenzy for one more drink looked like the scenes shown on TV of the floor of the New York Stock Exchange. Guests' hands shot in the air, waving money. In her change purse, Adrienne had four hundred dollars in tips. Two hundred of it had been palmed to her by Grayson Parrish, possibly as an apology for his tirade, but more likely an apology for Luke's bizarre and ultimately miserable behavior. He hadn't returned from the men's room for a long time and Grayson was forced to check on him. Luke had vomited and was trying to clean up the mess with toilet paper. Adrienne sent Tyler Lefroy into the men's room with the mop (why did he get all the foul jobs, he wanted to know) and Grayson led Luke back to the table, where he stared down his ravioli but didn't eat a bite. *This is who you want me to go out with?* Adrienne thought. *This is your idea of stability?*

After last call, the bar crowd thinned and eventually disappeared. Duncan cashed out, tipped his sister, and poured drinks for the waitstaff and Eddie and Hector, who were waiting around for the meeting to begin. Eddie filled Adrienne in on the story circulating about JZ and Jamie: Jamie had found out from a Realtor friend on the island that the house JZ rented on Liberty Street went for three thousand dollars a week. In furious revenge, Jamie had bought a hot tub from Sears. Meanwhile, the director of Shaughnessy's summer camp called threatening to send Shaughnessy home because her tuition had yet to be paid. JZ was, in Eddie's words, "wickedly screwed" because Fiona had paid for the house on Liberty Street but JZ didn't want to admit that to Jamie, and Jamie had spent Shaughnessy's camp money on the hot tub. JZ had gone home to straighten out the mess and in the end, Fiona had paid the summer camp.

"Because she's cool like that," Eddie said. "She's the coolest."

Adrienne checked her watch. It was twenty of two. Her feet hurt. "Okay, people, let's go," she said. "Beach outside Thatcher's office."

They exited through the dining room and walked around the restaurant to the back door of the office. There they found Thatcher and Fiona eating Popsicles at a plastic resin picnic table. Fiona was wearing jean shorts and her chef's jacket. Her hair was down—it was lovely and wavy released from its braid—but her face looked drawn.

Adrienne and the rest of the staff plopped down in the sand and Thatcher called for the remaining kitchen staff—Antonio, Henry, Paco,

Jojo. When everyone was seated in the sand, he did a strange thing. He lifted Fiona up out of her chair and carried her toward the water.

"Follow me," he said.

The staff followed, including Adrienne, who couldn't help feeling stupidly jealous that Thatcher was carrying Fiona. Fiona screamed in protest, her head thrown back, her hair streaming in the breeze. It was a beautiful night, moonless, still. The staff trudged to the water's edge but Thatcher plunged right in until he was up past his knees. He let Fiona go and she splashed into the water and the water lit up around her like a force field.

"Whoa-ho," said Paco. (Adrienne knew he and Louis had been smoking dope back in pastry.) "That's cool."

Delilah was the next one in because she was young and unabashed about swimming in her clothes. She dove under, and again, the water illuminated around her.

Soon the whole staff, including Adrienne, was in the ocean, marveling at the way the water sparkled and glowed around their arms and legs.

"Phosphorescence," Adrienne heard Thatcher say. In the dark, she couldn't tell which body was his. "I didn't want any of you to miss it."

Thatcher had called this a morale booster, but Adrienne's heart was aching, for reasons unknown. She put her head under and opened her eyes as she waved her hands to light up the water around her. For weeks, she had been so happy she felt like her life was phosphorescent, like the space she moved about in glowed and sparkled around her. But now, this minute, that notion seemed silly and wrong. *You're not like the other people who work here. You're not like them at all.* The Parrishes were right, though Adrienne didn't know how she was different or why that bothered her. Her eyes stung from the salt water. She wanted to be swimming next to Thatcher, and what she really wanted was for it to be her and Thatcher out here alone. Just the two of them, floating in the sea of light. But Thatcher had brought them all out here for Fiona's sake. Fiona came first, and she should come first. She was a good person, better than anyone knew, paying for Shaughnessy's camp, tolerating JZ's manipulative wife. She was good. And she was sick.

The staff horsed around. Adrienne saw Duncan and Caren kissing. Paco grabbed Adrienne's ankle and tried to tip her over but she squirmed from his grip and dove under, feeling the material of her red T-shirt dress swirling around her. There was something about being underwater that made her feel lonely, even amid a group of people. When she surfaced, it was quiet, and Adrienne checked to see who was nearby. A man she didn't recognize was treading water next to her, and Adrienne became confused until she realized it was Bruno without his glasses. Bruno pointed at the shore and then Adrienne heard some of the Subiacos murmuring in Spanish.

A man stood on the beach, silhouetted by the light of the office. He just stood there at first, hands on his hips, menacing. *Police?* Adrienne thought. *JZ? Drew Amman-Keller?* But then, very slowly, the figure started to sway and the swaying became dancing. The figure was dancing in the sand and the Subiacos laughed and catcalled and Adrienne heard Fiona shout, "Get in here, Romeo!"

He came running toward the water, and Adrienne caught a glimpse of his face before he dove into the light.

Mario.

Dr. Don

TO: Ade12177@hotmail.com
FROM: kyracrenshaw@mindspring.com
DATE: July 24, 2005, 9:01 A.M.
SUBJECT: To Hell You Ride

The spores you didn't send me worked! I have officially Met a Man. Thirty-six, divorced, two kids. Sounds like my worst nightmare except I am falling, head over heels. Even worse, he is a landscape painter—but his work sells—some people pay more for his paintings than I paid for my last car. So although my mother is crying out about No Steady Income, he does just fine. In the winters he goes to Telluride and paints there and skis, and he's asked me to go with him. And I, in turn, will ask you (because I miss you, but also because I think you'd like it). Do you want to join us?

TO: kyracrenshaw@mindspring.com
FROM: Ade12177@hotmail.com
DATE: July 24, 2005, 11:22 A.M.
SUBJECT: It's July!

Since when do you plan more than one day in advance? You *must* be in love! I hate to admit it but I am not far from that pitiable state myself—this thing with

Thatcher is getting serious. Tomorrow he will meet the other man in my life—that's right, the good doctor. I'll let you know how it goes. As for this winter, I can't bear to think about it, but I'll keep Telluride in mind.

TO: Ade12177@hotmail.com
FROM: DrDon@toothache.com
DATE: July 24, 2005, 11:37 A.M.
SUBJECT: A quick (don't) pick-me-up

We fly in tomorrow—US Air flight 307, BWI to Philadelphia, US Air flight 5990 Philly to Nantucket arriving around three. We'll take a cab from the airport to the Beach Club and we'll meet you at the restaurant at six o'clock sharp. You'll eat with us? And what about this Thatcher person? Can't wait to see you, honey. Love, love, love.

TO: DrDon@toothache.com
FROM: Ade12177@hotmail.com
DATE: July 24, 2005, 11:40 A.M.
SUBJECT: Breakfast and lunch

Dad, I will *not* be able to have dinner with you. I have to work dinner—get it? As does Thatcher. So reorganize your expectations to include breakfast and lunch. Those are the meals for which I am available. Breakfast and lunch.

You guys are going to love the Beach Club. It's the best. Please tip generously as they know you're my father! Love.

"I shouldn't have invited them," Adrienne said to Caren on the morning of her father and Mavis's arrival. She and Caren were at the kitchen table, which, now that the weather was consistently nice, they had moved out into the backyard. They drank tea and espresso in the sun together on mornings like this one—when Duncan went sailing with Holt Millman and Thatcher left for the restaurant to give Fiona extra help. "No one else's parents come to visit."

"Mine certainly don't," Caren said. She had informed Adrienne early on that she was a casualty of the nastiest divorce in history.

Duncan and Delilah's parents lived in California and were too old to travel. Fiona's parents didn't like to fly. Thatcher's father was too busy with the stores. Spillman's parents were divorced like Caren's and remarried to other people with whom they had had more children (Spillman had a brother in kindergarten). Joe's mother, Mrs. Peeke, had come once years earlier and spent the whole time back in the kitchen teaching Fiona how to make the corn spoon bread that now was on the menu with the swordfish.

"In general, though," Caren said, "I think the restaurant business attracts people who, you know, want to escape their families."

"My father sort of invited himself," Adrienne said. "I couldn't tell him not to come."

"I thought you loved your father," Caren said.

"I do," Adrienne said. "More than anyone in the world."

"So you should be happy," Caren said. "Does he know about Thatch?"

"I told him we were dating," Adrienne said. "But there's a lot I didn't explain. He's going to ask why the restaurant is closing. He'll ask about Thatcher and Fiona. He'll ask about next year."

"Thatcher will be rich next year," Caren said. "That's an answer any father would love to hear."

"But what will happen between Thatcher and me?" Adrienne said. "My father will ask."

"Have you asked?"

"No," Adrienne admitted. "I'm too afraid." With Fiona's illness it seemed fruitless, not to mention unfair, to ask about the future of their relationship.

"Does he tell you he loves you?"

"No," Adrienne said. This was another thing she tried not to dwell on. "What about Duncan?"

Caren fired off a laugh that sounded like a shrill machine gun. "As far as Himself is concerned, I've resorted to desperate measures."

One desperate measure was this: At three o'clock that afternoon Caren was flying to Boston to meet her friend Tate for the second night of the Rolling Stones concert (they were playing three nights at the Fleet Center). Caren and Tate were then sharing a room at the Ritz Carlton. Tate was gay but Caren had not disclosed this fact to Duncan. Duncan, she said, was seething with jealousy—not only about Tate but about the sixth-row seats that Tate had procured from his very wealthy and influential friends. Duncan did not like being outdone in the wealthy and influential friends department, hence that morning's sail with Holt.

"It better work," Caren said. "I'm betting all my chips on this one." True enough—she had basically sold herself in slavery to Bruno to get him to switch nights off with her.

"Well, you're going to miss my father," Adrienne said. "Tonight's the only night he's eating at the Bistro." And that only because he insisted. The other two nights Adrienne had booked him at the Pearl and the Club Car. Thatcher had set Don and Mavis up in a hotel room at the Beach Club, where reservations in July and August had been booked for six months. Thatcher talked to Mack and Mack had a last-minute cancellation and so Dr. Don and Mavis were staying in a room on the Gold Coast. Adrienne had worried about the price, but her father seemed excited about paying six hundred dollars a night for a room. This was a very special vacation, he said, and there would be no skimping.

By the time she got to work, Adrienne's stomach was churning like Mario's Hobart mixer. There were 247 covers on the book. Family meal was shrimp curry over jasmine rice and a cucumber salad, but Adrienne couldn't eat. She begged Mario to make her some of his banana French toast with chocolate syrup—what she needed was some comfort food—and Mario bitched about the two hundred and fifty other people he had to feed that night. Since he had put the writer from *Vanity Fair* on a plane back to New York without a story, and since he had lost five hundred dollars for breaking his contract with his publicist, Mario had gotten good at bitching. He worked too many hours, he made too little money, he wasn't treated like the genius he knew himself to be. Still, Adrienne knew that he liked her.

"My father is coming in tonight with his . . . friend," Adrienne told him.

"Your father's gay?" Mario said.

"No," Adrienne said. "Why do you ask?"

"The way you said 'friend' sounded funny."

"It is funny," Adrienne said. "But he's not gay. The woman he's coming with is his . . . hygienist. She's his employee. Just please don't think it's my mother. Mavis is not my mother. My mother died when I was twelve."

Mario crossed himself then held up his palms. "I'll make the toast," he said.

But Adrienne couldn't eat the French toast either—her anxiety level rose to her eyebrows every time she reviewed the reservation book. The circle that stood for table twenty said "Don Dealey." Her father was coming to the restaurant tonight, stepping into her life for the first time since he'd flown to Tallahassee for her college graduation. Always she went to him. She liked it that way; it gave her control. This feeling she had now was a distinctly out-of-control feeling.

Thatcher joined her at the podium. "I missed you today," he said. "What did you do?"

"Sat on the beach and stressed."

"About what?"

"Do I really need to say it?"

"Your father?"

Adrienne nodded. She didn't want Thatcher to know how nervous she was because she wasn't sure she could explain why. Her father meeting Thatcher, Thatcher meeting her father. The disastrous dinner with Will Kovak years earlier festered in her mind. Why was her father coming to see her this year of all years? Why hadn't he come to see her in Hawaii when she was low on friends and spent most of her evenings wallowing in misery over her breakup with Sully? It seemed so much sager to follow the example of her fellow employees and keep family members out of the restaurant. She thought of how morose Tyler Lefroy had looked at the table with his parents and his sister. Tonight, that would be her.

"You haven't noticed my haircut," Thatcher said. "I had Pam squeeze me in because your father was coming."

Adrienne looked at him blankly. "You're right," she said. "I didn't notice." She checked her watch. "Five minutes until post time." She wandered over to the bar and Duncan slid her drink across the blue granite.

"So what do you think about Caren going to see the Stones with this Tate guy?" Duncan said.

Adrienne shrugged. "She's psyched about the concert."

"Yeah, but what about the guy?"

"He's loaded, I guess. He owns a villa on St. Bart's."

"She says they're just friends."

"Of course, they're just friends," Adrienne said. "You're not worried about Caren?"

"They're sharing a hotel room," he said.

"It has two beds," Adrienne said. "I'm sure that since the two of you are so happy together, nothing will happen with this Tate person, even if he is rich. And handsome."

"Handsome?"

Adrienne tried not to smile. "I saw his picture. The guy looks like George Clooney." She pointed to the row of bottles behind Duncan. "But I'll bet he can't make a lemon meringue pie martini."

"Thanks," Duncan said. "You're a pal. Hey, your parents are coming in tonight?"

Adrienne took a long sip of her champagne. "My father," she said. "And his hygienist."

Duncan looked at her strangely.

"My father's a dentist," Adrienne said. "He's coming with a woman who works for him. His hygienist."

Duncan smiled. "Sure."

Adrienne took another drink. This was more than half the problem—explaining about Mavis. There was no easy way to do it, and yet Adrienne had vowed that she was going to be honest. She would not pretend Mavis was her mother.

She heard Thatcher say, "You must be . . ."

Adrienne slowly turned around to see her father and Mavis standing by the podium. Dr. Don was a good six foot two, and he looked tan and handsome. He'd lost weight and he was wearing new clothes—a lizard green silk shirt and a linen blazer. Adrienne was suddenly overwhelmed with love for him. It was a love that had lasted twenty-eight years and had solely sustained her for the last sixteen. It was a love that was the ruling order of her life; she was able to exist only because this man loved her.

"Dad," she said.

He hugged her tight and kissed the top of her head, rocking her back and forth. "Oh, honey," he said. Adrienne hid her face in the soft material of his shirt. "I forget just how much I miss you." He held her apart. "Smile."

She had brushed and flossed when she first got to work because she knew he would ask. He always did. She smiled, but when she smiled she felt like she might cry. She took a deep breath and regarded Mavis, who was beaming at her. No, this was not her mother, but Mavis was, at least, familiar. She had the same haircut, the same frosted coral lipstick, the same minty smell as Adrienne kissed the side of her mouth. She wore a red dress with gold buttons—that was new.

"Mavis, hi."

"Hi, doll." The same vaguely annoying nickname: doll. Mavis called everyone by diminutives: doll, baby doll, sweetie, sugar, honey pie. Except for Adrienne's father whom she called "the doctor," when she was speaking about him, and "Donald," when she was speaking to him.

Adrienne felt a light hand on her lower back and she remembered Thatcher. Thatcher, the restaurant, her job.

"Daddy, Mavis, this is Thatcher Smith, owner of the Blue Bistro. Thatcher, my father, Don Dealey, and Mavis Laroux."

"We just met," Thatcher said. He glanced from Adrienne to Don and back again. "I wish I could say I saw a family resemblance."

Don laughed. "Adrienne looks like my late wife," he said. He turned to Mavis. "Doesn't she?"

Mavis nodded solemnly. "Spitting image."

Adrienne plucked two menus from the podium. "Okay, well," she said. "Since you're here, you might as well sit. Follow me." She walked through the dining room to table twenty, wobbling a little in her heels. Something felt off. She tried to think: Her father was definitely at table twenty. She would seat him, give him a menu, and have Spillman get him a drink. Thatcher would put in the VIP order. Fine. The restaurant was sparkling and elegant. Rex played "What a Wonderful World."

"This place is not to be believed," Mavis said. "And our hotel room! Adrienne, doll, you are a marvel. It's the nicest room I have ever stayed in."

"Good," Adrienne said. "I'm glad you like it."

"We don't like it," Don said. "We love it." He pulled a chair out for Mavis, then he sat. Adrienne stood behind them with the menus. Something still was not right; she felt artificial, like she was playacting. But no—this was her job. She was the assistant manager of this restaurant and had been for two months.

When she handed Mavis a menu, she saw the ring. One emerald-cut diamond on a gold band. Immediately, Adrienne thought: *Mavis is engaged.*

And then she nearly cried out. She closed her eyes. *Okay,* she thought. *It's okay.* She pictured her mother's face—one eyebrow raised suspiciously, the face Adrienne got when she had asked for permission to wear eye shadow. When Adrienne opened her eyes, her vision was splotchy and she was glad she hadn't eaten anything because suddenly it felt like someone was holding her upside down under water. She wavered a little and her father took her by the wrist.

"Are you okay, sweetheart?"

"Sorry," Adrienne said. In her peripheral vision, she saw Spillman approaching. "I haven't eaten anything all day."

"Good evening," Spillman said. "You're Adrienne's parents?"

Dr. Don stood up to shake Spillman's hand while Mavis smiled at her Limoges charger. Adrienne had lost language. *This is my father and his friend Mavis. His hygienist, Mavis. His fiancée, Mavis.*

"We'll have champagne," Adrienne heard her father say. "You'll sit and have a glass with us, Ade?"

"Actually . . . no," she said. They wanted to tell her. They had come all the way to Nantucket to tell her in person. Meanwhile, Adrienne wished her father had simply sent an e-mail. That way she could have digested the news privately. But no—they were going to make her sit through it here, in front of them, while she was supposed to be *working.* She turned around—there was a cluster of people at the podium. "I have to go," she said. "Because remember, Dad, I told you . . ."

Dr. Don smiled and shooed her off. "Go. I want to watch you."

Suddenly it was like Adrienne was twelve years old again, in the school play. Peppermint Patty in *You're a Good Man, Charlie Brown.* Adrienne's mother had been in the hospital so Dr. Don came to the play with—yes—Mavis. As if to make up for Rosalie's absence, the two of them had paid extra close attention. After the play was over, they commented on Adrienne's every gesture; they remembered each of her eight stiff lines.

Act natural, Adrienne had thought then, and now. Leigh Stanford and her husband were in with friends from Guam—where did they find these far-flung friends?—and Thatcher's hairdresser, Pam, was in with a date. Adrienne sat a party of six women, then a couple celebrating their twenty-fifth wedding anniversary. When Adrienne glanced over at her father and Mavis, they were sipping Laurent-Perrier, studying their menus. Her father

started slicing potatoes, muttering curses about Jojo. There was one order of chips and dip up. Adrienne took it.

"That's for your parents?" Fiona asked.

"My father," Adrienne said. The explaining was becoming tedious. "And his girlfriend."

"His girlfriend," Fiona said.

"Yes." There, she'd said it, and it sounded a lot less bizarre than hygienist. Girlfriend, fiancée, did it really matter? Adrienne's mother had been dead for sixteen years; her father deserved to be happy. Getting upset about this was as adolescent as partying too hard at the Rolling Stones concert and missing work.

"I'll cook for them myself," Fiona said. "They're on twenty, right?"

Adrienne was confused. "Right. But . . . you don't have to do that. You have other stuff. The expediting."

Fiona took a swig from an enormous Evian bottle. "When it's family, I like to do the cooking myself."

"Even my family?" Adrienne said.

"Of course," Fiona said. "Your family is our family."

Adrienne reentered the dining room slightly cheered. She liked the idea of her father as a shared responsibility. Maybe she could send Fiona to her father's wedding in her place. Adrienne delivered the chips and dip to her father's table.

"Hand-cut potato chips with crème fraîche and beluga caviar," she announced.

"Honey, this is too much," Dr. Don said.

"No, it isn't, Daddy," she said. "We do it for people a lot less special than you."

"Well, okay, then," he said, digging in. "Thank you."

Thatcher materialized at the table. "Everyone's down," he said to Adrienne. "You can have a drink with your dad and Mavis here. You can even order if you'd like."

"I ate already," Adrienne said tightly.

"You told me you haven't eaten anything all day," Dr. Don said.

"Sit and eat," Thatcher said. He put his hands on Adrienne's shoulders and pushed her into a chair. "I'm going to order you the foie gras and the club."

"Please don't," Adrienne said. "I want to work."

"You can work second," Thatcher said. "Right now you should enjoy your family."

Enjoy your family: For so many people this phrase was a paradox, as tonight it was for Adrienne. Still, she didn't want to throw a tantrum or make a scene in the middle of a very full restaurant so she sank into the wicker chair next to her father and Spillman brought over her drink.

"We should have a toast," Dr. Don said, raising his glass. "To you, sweetheart. You've done it again. This island is beautiful."

"And the restaurant," Mavis said. "I always thought restaurants were, you know . . . a seedy place to work."

"Risky, derelict, volatile, transient, goddamned make-believe," Adrienne said. "I've heard it all."

"But this place is special," Mavis said. "As anyone can see."

"Thank you," Adrienne said.

They clinked glasses. Adrienne helped herself to caviar. Across the dining room, she caught Leigh Stanford's curious eye. The curse of table twenty. Adrienne wished she had a big sign: THIS IS NOT MY MOTHER!

"Thatcher is so charming," Mavis whispered. "He really seems to like you."

"He does like me," Adrienne said.

"Do you have any long-term plans?" Dr. Don asked.

"Long term? No. Right now I'm celebrating my solvency. I paid you back, I paid my credit cards off, and I have money in the bank. You should be happy about that. I am."

"Oh, honey," Dr. Don said. "If you only knew how much I worried about you."

"You don't have to worry," Adrienne said. "I'm self-sufficient. Now."

"Of course you are," Mavis said.

"I keep your picture in my examining room," he said. "Everyone asks about you. And I tell them all about my beautiful daughter who lives in . . . Hawaii, Thailand, Aspen, Nantucket. They always ask if you're married or if you have children . . ."

"And you tell them no."

"And I tell them no."

"But you want to tell them yes. You want me to be a soccer mom with everything in its place."

"No, honey."

"Well, what then?"

"I want you to be happy," he said.

"I am happy," Adrienne snarled.

"Good," Mavis said, and Adrienne saw her hand land on Dr. Don's arm. As if to say, *Enough already, Donald!* This was a sad state of affairs. There was no one to come to Adrienne's defense except for Mavis.

"Anyway, how's Maryland?" Adrienne asked. "You like it?"

"Oh, yes!" Mavis said, clearly relieved at the shift in topic. "You're a doll to ask."

"Business is good," Dr. Don said. "And the eastern shore is something else, especially now that it's summer. A few weeks ago we went to Chincoteague to see the wild horses."

"We didn't actually see any," Mavis said.

"I think we might stay in Maryland awhile," Dr. Don said. "Settle in. I'm too old to keep moving around so much."

These words had the same effect on Adrienne as a drum roll. *Just say it!* she thought. She wanted it over with. Spillman approached with the appetizers. Foie gras for Adrienne, corn chowder for Dr. Don, the Caesar, no anchovies, for Mavis. Spillman twisted the pepper mill over everyone's plates.

"Can I bring you anything else right now?" he asked.

"Kamikaze shot," Adrienne said. She stared at him, thinking: *Get me out of here!* Then, finally, she smiled. "Only kidding."

Spillman's facade never cracked. The man was a professional. "Enjoy your food," he said.

The sun was a juicy pink as it sank toward the water. Rex played "As Time Goes By." The foie gras was good enough to shift Adrienne's mood from despondent to merely poor. It was deliciously fatty, a heavenly richness balanced by the sweet roasted figs. Who wanted to be married and have children when she could be eating foie gras like this with a front-row seat for the sunset? Adrienne forgot her manners. She devoured her appetizer in five lusty bites, and then she helped herself to more caviar. She was *starving.*

Dr. Don took soup into his spoon back-to-front, the way Adrienne's mother had taught her eighty-two years earlier. Adrienne tried to imagine what her mother would think about her father and Mavis getting married. It was impossible to imagine Rosalie feeling betrayed or hurt. *Sixteen years,* she would say. *What took you so long?* Adrienne couldn't stage a protest to the marriage on her mother's behalf. She would have to claim responsibility herself. She didn't want her father to get married because then he wouldn't belong to her anymore. By marrying Mavis, he would be calling an end to their sixteen-year mourning period. Rapping the gavel. *Time to move on!* Easy enough when it was your wife, but there was no way to replace your mother. Had he bothered to think of that? There was no way to replace your mother. The hole was there forever.

"How are the boys?" Adrienne asked.

Mavis dabbed her coral lips with a napkin. "Good, good. Graham is at Galludet getting his master's in education. Cole is in California working for Sun Microsystems."

"Girlfriends?"

"Graham is dating a girl named Charlotte who goes to Galludet with him."

"She's deaf?"

Mavis nodded, eyes wide. "And with Cole, I can't keep track of the girls from one week to the next."

Adrienne pressed the soles of her fabulous shoes to the floor. "Do they know that you're engaged?"

Mavis put down her fork slowly as though Adrienne were holding a gun to her head and had forbidden any sudden movements. "Yes," she said. "They do. We called them last week."

"Honey," Dr. Don said.

A few tears fell on to Adrienne's appetizer plate. Here it was, then: the scene where Adrienne cried at her father's happy news.

"Congratulations," she said. She couldn't look at either of them because she was afraid she'd break down, and so she studied the band of bright pink sky hovering above the ocean.

"Honey," Dr. Don said. He reached into her lap and squeezed her wrist. "Both Mavis and I have the utmost respect for the memory of your mother. And we have respect for you. We wanted to tell you in person."

Adrienne could feel the gazes of a hundred and twenty interested guests at her back. She took a deep breath and said, "When's the wedding?"

"In the fall," Dr. Don said. "Just Mavis and myself, the boys, and you, if you'll come. Small church, a nice dinner out afterward . . ."

Adrienne didn't have to answer because Roy appeared to clear their plates and crumb the table, and although Adrienne knew she should introduce him, she was silent until he left.

"We're sorry to spring this on you," Mavis said. "I told Donald we should give you the news in private."

"That's okay," Adrienne said. "I noticed your ring. It's beautiful."

"Thank you." Mavis held out her hand to admire the ring, then she fidgeted with one of the gold buttons on the front of her dress. "I think I'll go to the ladies' room."

"It's by the front door," Adrienne said.

Mavis left and Dr. Don tightened his grip on Adrienne's wrist.

"Don't say anything, Dad," she said. "Please. You'll make me cry."

"Even if I tell you how much I love you?"

"Yes. Please stop."

"And your mother loved you. She loved you, Adrienne, and she was so afraid you would grow up not remembering that."

Tears splashed onto Adrienne's charger. She held her napkin to her face. For two months she had watched guests eat dinner at these tables. She had seen guests laugh, cry, argue, declare their love, tell stories, hold hands, kiss, and in the case of Lucy Elpern, go into labor. From the safe distance of the podium, this all seemed well and fine. However, sitting at table twenty was turning out to be a keenly painful experience.

"I remember," Adrienne said. To avoid her father's gaze, she turned around. Charlie was waving at her from the bar. He pointed to his steak and gave her the thumbs-up. Out of the corner of her eye, Adrienne saw the red of Mavis's dress coming closer and behind her, Spillman with their dinner. Adrienne waited for the table to settle. Mavis sat, and a minute later Spillman served. Did they need anything else? *Nothing he could bring them,* Adrienne thought. The plates were gorgeous. Mavis had ordered the lamb lollipops.

"They're adorable," she said. "Donald, will you take a picture of my dinner?"

Adrienne shifted ever so slightly in her chair.

"We can't embarrass Adrienne like that," Dr. Don said.

Adrienne took a huge bite of her sandwich. Guests took pictures of the food all the time, but somehow Adrienne felt victorious about robbing Mavis of this one pleasure. There would be no toast celebrating the marriage and no pictures taken at the table. Adrienne licked a glob of mayonnaise from her lip and thought about Fiona constructing her sandwich. *Your family is our family. Yeah, right.* Adrienne couldn't wait to get back to work.

It wasn't until two o'clock in the morning when she and Thatcher were safely in bed that she told him the news. By that time, she had cultivated the offhand tone she wished she'd had access to at dinner.

"My father and Mavis are getting married," she said.

Thatcher lay on his back, and Adrienne was sprawled across his chest. Sometimes they fell asleep like this.

"Is this good news or bad news?"

"Bad."

"Yeah," he said. "I thought so."

They lay there in the dark and Adrienne cried, free at last, and freer than ever because Caren wasn't home. She could make as much noise as she wanted, she could scream and yell, but she just sobbed quietly, wallowing in the childish sadness she felt. Sad, sad, sad—and not even really about the marriage. It was all the old stuff, too. Thatcher rubbed Adrienne's back and touched her hair and when she quieted and her eyes were burning and her throat ached, he kissed her and her need for him was so deep and overwhelming that when they made love, she batted herself against him furiously. She grabbed his red-gold hair and clung to him, thinking, *Can you make this longing go away? Can you fill up the empty spot? Can you help me, Thatcher Smith? You who do so much for so many people night after night, granting wishes, fulfilling dreams, can you help me?* She put her hands around his neck while they thrust together and then Thatcher groaned and fell back against the mattress with a soft thud but Adrienne remained upright, even as he softened and slipped from her.

"I love you," she whispered.

As soon as the words were out, she hoped and prayed that he was asleep—he did that after sex, fell hard and immediately to sleep. But she didn't hear him breathing; if anything she heard him *not* breathing. She wondered what had made her say those words, words she had never said to anyone before, except, of course, her parents. Then she thought, stupidly, of a Norma Klein book she had once begged her mother for, a book called *It's OK If You Don't Love Me,* whose plot Adrienne had long forgotten though it certainly had a moment in its pages just like this one. *I'm sorry,* she almost said, *I'm sorry I said that.* Except she wasn't sorry. She did love him and she didn't feel like playing games to make him say it first. She was being honest with her feelings; no one would catch her in a room at the Ritz-Carlton with a sham lover. She was brave, like Kyra in Carmel, making plans four months in advance to move halfway across the country with her landscape painter.

And yet, she listened for the catch of his breath. The room was completely dark; they always pulled the shades against the morning sun, which rose at five. So she couldn't even tell if his eyes were open.

"I . . ." he said.

Her skin prickled, her sweat drying in the cool night air. *Shit!* she thought. *Shit, shit, shit!*

"I love you, too," he said. "I've loved you since the first second I saw you."

Adrienne tried to speak but the noise she made sounded like water trying to pass through a clogged drain. What was he saying?

Finally, she managed a whisper. "You mean, in the *parking lot*?"

"My heart fell on its knees in front of you. *I thought maybe I could wait tables. Someone told me it was a piece of cake.* Your purple jacket. Your rosy cheeks. And then you inhaled that breakfast like you hadn't eaten in three days. My heart was prostrate at your feet."

"You're kidding."

"I've loved you since that very first morning."

"I don't believe you."

"You can ask Fiona," Thatcher said. "After you left I went back into the kitchen and told Fiona that I had fallen in love with a woman named Adrienne Dealey and that everyone else would fall in love with her, too."

"You said that to Fiona?"

"I did."

Adrienne thought back to her first conversation with Fiona when Adrienne told her the Parrishes wanted her to bring their bread.

Thatcher was right about you, then.

Right about me how? I mean, what did he say . . .

"Caren loves you. The Parrishes. Mario. Mario wanted to ask you out and I told him if he did, I would fire him. He didn't speak to me for three days."

"Stop it," Adrienne said.

"You think I'm making it up," Thatcher said. "I am not making it up. I love you . . ." His voice trailed off and Adrienne sensed the other shoe about to drop.

"But?" she said.

"But," he said. He rolled onto his side so that he could look down on her. "The reason why I haven't had a relationship in twelve years is because of Fee. There hasn't been time to think about anyone else."

Adrienne was silent.

"And I never met the right person," he said, quickly. "You, Adrienne Dealey, are the right person. I love you. But I love Fee, too. Differently. She's my best friend and has been for a *long time.*"

"I know that," Adrienne said, trying not to let impatience creep into her voice.

"And sometimes, I don't know how to handle things. I don't know who to put first."

That's clear, Adrienne thought. She could tell Thatch was at a loss, like a teenager trying to figure it all out for the first time.

"I don't have to be first," Adrienne said, then she checked herself. Was she lying? Was she just trying to be brave? What had she learned earlier that night? That being first or second had nothing to do with love, really. Her father loved her, Thatcher loved her. Her father also loved Mavis, Thatcher also loved Fiona. That was okay, wasn't it? It would have to be okay. "I understand."

"You do?" Thatcher said. He sounded unconvinced, but hopeful. "Do you really?"

"I do really," Adrienne said. She lifted her head to kiss him, and then, deciding she didn't want to talk anymore lest she ruin the moment or change her mind, she closed her eyes, pretending to sleep.

■

The next morning at nine, Thatcher and Dr. Don went fishing on the *Just Do It, Too.* Dr. Don had offered the fishing trip up to Thatcher the night before and Adrienne was sure that Thatcher would decline, but instead he'd looked beseechingly to Adrienne. He could only go if Adrienne covered the phone in the morning.

"Go," she'd said, though, really, the last thing she wanted was her father and Thatcher alone for three hours on a boat when the only topic they had in common was her.

She dropped them off at the docks in the morning. Pulling out of the A&P parking lot in Thatcher's enormous truck, she almost ran over a family of four. Lack of sleep. Nerves.

She drove out to the airport to pick up Caren, who had called very early on a sketchy cell phone line and begged a ride. *I don't have a dime left for a taxi,* she'd said. Adrienne found her standing on the curb in front of the terminal. Caren was wearing the same outfit she'd left in—her white jeans and black halter top. Her hair was down but tangled and messy and her clothes were rumpled. She looked like a half-smoked cigarette. And when she climbed into the cab of Thatcher's truck, there was a horrible smell: spoiled wine, rotten meat, a bad fart. Adrienne cracked her window.

"So," she said. "How was it?"

"I drank too much. Smoked weed. Did a line of cocaine. Took X."

"Does that mean it was good or bad?" Adrienne said.

"The concert was good. Are you kidding me? Sixth row for Mick Jagger? But that was the great beginning of something bad. I never even saw the inside of the Ritz. We left the concert and went to Radius. I had three martinis for dinner. Then we went to Mistral. Then a party somewhere in Back Bay where we all did coke. Haven't been that stupid in many, many years. Then to Saint." She eyed the dashboard. "I left Saint at six."

"This morning?"

"Choked down a ricotta cannoli in the North End. I feel lousy."

"So you haven't slept."

"Half an hour on the plane. I need a shower and a Percocet. My bed. Room-darkening shades. Six cups of espresso before I go to work."

"That would be a start," Adrienne said.

"Did you talk to Duncan? Was he upset? He didn't call my cell."

Adrienne gnawed her lower lip. Before she'd left the restaurant the night before, she had one more conversation with Duncan as he cleaned up the bar.

"I guess I won't be seeing you at our house tonight," Adrienne had said. "It'll probably feel weird to sleep in your own bed."

"Who said I'm sleeping in my own bed?" Duncan said.

"Where else would you sleep?" Adrienne asked.

"We're going *out*," Duncan said. He nodded toward Charlie who, after seventeen beers, was staggering near the front door. "Last call at the Chicken Box. For *starters.* And when you talk to Caren, feel free to tell her so."

But Adrienne had no desire to tell Caren so. Adrienne had too much emotional work of her own.

"Well," Adrienne said, "he asked a lot of questions about Tate."

"What kind of questions?"

"Just about who he was."

"You didn't tell Duncan that Tate was gay?"

"Of course not." Adrienne glanced at Caren. It was a hundred degrees out and the woman was shivering in her seat. "What do you expect from Duncan, anyway?"

"The same thing every woman expects," Caren said.

"Which is what?" Adrienne was asking because she really wanted to know. Thatcher had said he loved her, but now what happened? Where did they go? What did they do?

"Which is this," Caren said. She pointed to a white van from Flowers on Chestnut idling in their driveway.

Adrienne parked alongside the van while Caren bolted for the house. By the time Adrienne got inside, Caren had her face buried in what must have been three dozen long-stemmed red roses.

For me, Adrienne thought. *Thatcher? Dad?*

But the card was addressed to Caren. She held it in the air like a winning lottery ticket.

"He loves me," she said.

By the time Adrienne was ready to leave for work fifteen minutes later, Duncan was carrying Caren down the hall toward the bedroom.

"Don't ever take off on me like that again," Duncan said. "You made me crazy. Wasn't I crazy, Adrienne?"

"You were crazy," Adrienne said. She inhaled the deep perfume of the roses. Proof that there was more than one way to skin a cat. Adrienne wondered if her father and Thatcher were talking about her. Two hours left.

At work, the phone rang off the hook. Now that summer was more than half over, she heard a new desperation in everyone's voice. Or maybe everyone else was the same and it was Adrienne with the desperation.

Jennifer Devlin: I heard you're *closing.* For *good*? How many nights can I get in this week? And what about next week? The week after that? Just book me for any night you have open between now and Labor Day. Party of four. No, six.

Mrs. Langley: Hello, honey. You don't know me but I am a very good customer even though I haven't managed to get in once all summer. I'd like a table for ten Saturday night at seven thirty. What do you mean you don't seat at seven thirty? You always used to before. Well, at six I'm just starting to think about cocktails and by nine I'm half asleep. Can't you make an exception just this once? We'll pay double.

Harry Henderson: We need Fiona to come in and sign the purchase and sale agreement. She's holding the whole deal up, and you know these new parent–types. They're so sleep-deprived, they're likely to back out without warning! I don't suppose Fiona will come to the phone?

Darla Parrish: Sorry, honey, about the scene with Luke. He's normally such a good boy. And sadly, we have to cancel our reservation for tonight. Grayson has business back in Short Hills. And just so you know, Grayson won't be coming in on Friday, either. I'll be in with my sister.

Mr. Mascaro: Five people at nine on Saturday night. Heard my secretary wasn't allowed to make the reservation, which is the dumbest thing I've ever heard. Do you people want to lose all your business?

Kevin Kahla: Hi, hi, hi! I used to be the manager there? Now I work at Craft in the city? I have two *very good customers* coming to Nantucket this week and I told them I'd get them a reservation for Saturday night, first seating. Last name Gibson. Can you put them at table twenty and VIP them? Thanks, you're a superstar. Love to Thatch and Fiona, and please, please tell Caren there isn't a woman in New York as bitchy as she is—and that's a compliment. Ta!

Lana, personal assistant to Dustin Hoffman: Mr. Hoffman would like a table where he won't be bothered. Is there a back entrance? And he'd like to chat with the chef after dinner. He's been trying to do this for three years and since we hear you're closing forever on Labor Day, it becomes imperative that we get it done this Saturday. Tell me I have your help on this.

Cat: My sister and her husband are coming in for their anniversary on Friday. Would you send them a bottle of Cristal from me? I'll drop off some cash later. Thanks, girlfriend!

Mack: I need a party of two at six o'clock for Saturday. Name Chang. A party of six for nine on Saturday—name, O'Leary—and a party of two at six on Sunday. Name Walker. Do you want me to repeat that?

Mr. Kennedy: I have to have Saturday and I have to have table twenty. Party of four. Very big clients. Book us for six but we'll probably be late because we'll be playing at the golf club all afternoon.

Red Mare: You want to send your father and his fiancée a bottle of Cristal? I see them here—Dealey at six thirty. Consider it done. What's your credit card number?

Mr. Lefroy: Please tell Thatcher I'll be in for an official visit one morning next week. This is standard operating procedure—he doesn't have to tell me it's stupid. I already know that. In twelve years I've never cited him for an infraction and if I did, what would I do? Shut him down? Ha!

Mme. Colverre: I'm calling from Paris, France. Table for six for Saturday at six, *s'il vous plait?*

Leigh Stanford: Rumor on the cobblestones has it that Thatcher isn't happy with his attorney on this real estate transaction. Would you, delicately, mention that I'd be happy to take it on in exchange for credit at the restaurant. Speaking of which, we have friends coming in from the Ozarks on Saturday. Can we do an early table of four?

Ms. Cantele: Do you have vegetarian dishes on your menu? What about vegan dishes? Can you just read me the whole menu? That's right, the whole menu.

Mack: It's me again. I have to change Simon O'Leary's party from Saturday to Sunday the thirty-first.

"The thirty-first is Saturday," Adrienne said. Her brain was a swarm of names, dates, and times, as pesky as gnats.

"No, the thirty-first is Sunday."

"No," Adrienne said, checking her reservation sheet. "The thirty-first is Saturday."

"Reference your calendar," Mack said. "I'll wait."

Adrienne flipped to the front of the book where the calendar was pasted inside the front cover. The hair on her arms stood up. She felt like she was the one on a boat, a boat precariously keeled to one side, threatening to dump her in with the sharks. Her book was all wrong. She had been booking reservations for Friday on Saturday's page. She flipped to Saturday and was horrified to find it was full—and so all the people who had called that morning asking for Saturday had to be called back. There was no room! Adrienne scrambled with her eraser. This was awful. A hideous mess. How many reservations had she made today? How many really were for Sunday? This was her worst fuckup so far. This was worse than skipping a line on her SATs and not realizing it until the end of the section when she had one more answer than space. Now she had to call back nearly everyone she had spoken to in the past hour to tell them, *Sorry, Saturday is booked.*

Adrienne hung up with Mack and tried to channel her thoughts. Paris, France. Kevin in New York. Kennedy could eat on Saturday night but not at table twenty, unless Thatcher wanted to move him. Who else? Dustin Hoffman? Adrienne walked away from the podium. The phone rang but she didn't answer. She went into the ladies' room and, out of habit, checked her teeth.

The two of them were out on the water, talking about her.

When Adrienne next saw her father and Thatcher, they were walking down the dock like lovers. Adrienne was quaking. She had managed to staunch the bleeding of her massive trauma that morning, but it wasn't pretty. In the end she gave the three tables she had left on Saturday night to Kennedy, Hoffman, and Leigh Stanford and she called everyone else back to renege with enormous apologies. Mrs. Langley screamed so loudly Adrienne had to set the receiver down. Kevin changed his party's reservation to Sunday but at the end of their conversation he said, "This kind of thing never happened when I worked there." Mascaro threatened to call the chamber of commerce.

"It was a *mistake*," Adrienne said.

Just as she thought she might fill her pockets with tablecloth weights and walk out into the ocean, Henry Subiaco emerged from the kitchen with a mug of his homemade root beer.

"This is the best root beer I've ever tasted," Adrienne said.

"Next year," he said, "you work for me."

Now Adrienne was confronted with her father's hand on the back of Thatcher's neck as they strolled toward her. Grinning, faces red from the sun. With his free hand, her father waved.

"Did you catch anything?" she asked.

"Thatch caught a thirty-nine-inch striper," Dr. Don said. "It was a thing of beauty."

"Family meal tonight," Thatcher said.

"Where's the fish?"

"First mate's cleaning it for me. How was work?"

"I quit," she said. "I'm going to work for Henry Subiaco."

"That bad?"

"Worse than bad." She looked at her father. "We're taking you back to the hotel?"

"Can you join Mavis and I on the beach?" Dr. Don asked.

Adrienne checked her running watch. Twelve fifteen, one foot above sea level, and sinking by the minute. "I can. After I go over some work stuff with Thatcher. Say two o'clock?"

"Thank you, sweetie."

"You don't have to thank me for spending time with you," she said.

They waited on the dock until the first mate delivered a huge plastic bag of filleted fish. Dr. Don clapped Thatcher on the shoulder. "This is a great guy, Adrienne."

Three hours on the water and they were best friends.

"You're the great guy," Thatcher said. "I haven't been fishing in years. Thank you for taking me."

Adrienne stifled a yawn. Nerves. Lack of sleep.

"Thatch seemed uncertain about his next step," Dr. Don said. "It hinges, I guess, on the girl."

"Girl?"

"Fiona."

"Yeah," Adrienne said.

"Which leaves you in a funny position."

"I've been in a funny position all summer," Adrienne said.

"In what way?"

"I don't know," Adrienne said, though she did know. She thought about it all the time. "Thatcher and Fiona have been friends since they were born. And Duncan has his sister Delilah. And the Subiacos, who work in the kitchen, are all brothers or cousins. And Spillman and Caren and Bruno and Joe have all been at the Bistro since it opened. I was worried when you and Mavis showed up because nobody on the staff seems to have a family. But that's because they're each other's family. And what I realized is that I don't have any relationships like that. Because we moved." She looked up to see her father swallow. "We moved and moved and then I moved and moved and so there's nothing in my life that's lasted relationship-wise. And that's strange, isn't it? I'm twenty-eight years old and there's no one in my life, you know, permanently."

"This may be pointing out the obvious," Dr. Don said, "but you have me."

"Yes," Adrienne said. "I have you."

Two days later when it was time for Dr. Don and Mavis to go to the airport, Thatcher insisted on driving them in Fiona's Range Rover. Mavis sat up front with Fiona's oxygen tank at her feet, and Adrienne sat in the back holding hands with her father. She didn't want him to leave. The Cristal had been a big hit—it brought Mavis to tears—and Adrienne felt saintly, bestowing her blessing.

At the airport, Thatcher stayed in the car while Adrienne walked into the terminal with her father. Mavis hurried ahead to get in line at the US Air counter. Adrienne's nose tingled. It was the school play again: teary good-bye scene.

"October?" her father said. Dr. Don and Mavis had chosen October sixteenth as their wedding day. Even though it was only two and a half months away, Adrienne wondered what she'd be doing. Would she be staying on this island or leaving?

"I'll be there," she said.

Her father put down his suitcase and hugged her. "I probably don't have to say this, but I will anyway because I'm your father. I want you to be careful."

"I will."

"He told me he loves you."

"Did he?"

"He did. And I took him at his word. But that doesn't mean . . ."

"I know."

Her father scanned his eyes over the scene in the terminal: the people on cell phones, the Louis Vuitton luggage, the golden retrievers. "I wanted you to get married first," he said. "I wanted you to be settled before I married Mavis. Do you forgive me for wanting that?"

"Yes," Adrienne said. "But I'm glad you didn't wait for me. I may never be settled."

"You will someday." He kissed her forehead. "I'm proud of you, honey. And so is your mother. You know that?"

"Yes," she said.

He picked up his suitcase and kissed her again. "Love."

"Love," Adrienne said. She watched her father join Mavis in line. Then he turned around and waved one last time, and only then did she let herself cry.

11

The Sturgeon Moon

Sign hanging next to the walk-in refrigerator:

35 DAYS UNTIL THE END OF THE WORLD

Adrienne had been hearing about August since her first day of work. When the bar was busy, Caren might say, "It's busy, but not as busy as August." When the dining room was slow back in mid-June, Thatcher had said, "You'll be longing for this once it's August." What was it about August? *Everyone* was on Nantucket in August—the celebrities, the big money, the old families. It was America's summer vacation. Thirty-one days of sun, beach, boating, outdoor showers, fireflies, garden parties, linen sheets, coffee on the deck in the morning, a gin and tonic on the patio in the evening.

In the restaurant business, August meant every table was booked every night. Thatcher and Adrienne were forced to start a waiting list. If a guest didn't reconfirm by noon, he lost his reservation. There was no mercy; it was simply too busy. It was too busy for anyone to take a night off; the staff was to work straight through the next thirty-five days until the Saturday of Labor Day weekend when the bistro would close its doors forever.

"You want a break," Thatcher said one night during the menu meeting, "take it then."

In the restaurant kitchen, August meant lobsters, blackberries, silver queen corn, and tomatoes, tomatoes, tomatoes. In honor of the last year of the restaurant, Fiona was creating a different tomato special for each day of the month. The first of August (two hundred and fifty covers on the book, eleven reservation wait list) was a roasted yellow tomato soup. The second of August (two hundred and fifty covers, seven reservation wait list) was tomato pie with a Gruyère crust. On the third of August, Ernie Otemeyer came in with his wife to celebrate his birthday and since Ernie liked food that went with his Bud Light, Fiona made a Sicilian pizza—a thick, doughy crust, a layer of fresh buffalo mozzarella, topped with a voluptuous tomato-basil sauce. One morning when she was working the phone, Adrienne stepped into the kitchen hoping to get a few minutes with Mario, and she found Fiona taking a bite out of a red ripe tomato like it was an apple. Fiona held the tomato out.

"I'd put this on the menu," she said. "But few would understand."

In August, it felt like someone had turned up the heat, bringing life to a rolling boil. It wasn't unusual to have nineteen or twenty VIP tables per seating; it wasn't unheard-of to have thirty-five people waiting in line for the bar. The Subiacos had never done a better job—they cranked out beautiful plates, they made a double order of crackers at the end of the night, and they kept a sense of humor. The staff in the front of the house, on the other hand, started to resemble prisoners of war. Adrienne actually heard Duncan say to Caren, "I can't have sex with you tonight. I'm too tired." For Adrienne, work started at five fifty-nine when she checked her teeth, and after a blur of Beluga caviar, Menetou-Salon, foie gras, steak frites, requests for Patsy Cline, compliments on her shoes, and the never-ending question, "So what's going to happen to this place next year?" it would end with six or seven hundred dollars in her pocket and Thatcher leading her at two o'clock in the morning out to his truck where she invariably fell asleep with her head against the window.

And it was in August that Adrienne's nightmares started, nightmares much worse than a bushel of rotten peaches. She forgot coffee for table ten. She threw the contents of her champagne glass in Duncan's face and only when his face started to melt did she realize she'd thrown boiling oil. She sat down at the piano to fill in for Rex, then panicked because every guest in the restaurant was silent, waiting for her to begin. It was a *recital,* but she didn't know how to play. She crammed ten two-year-olds in high chairs at table twenty. She sent Holt Millman to the end of the bar line. She went into the back office to find Thatcher and Fiona having sex on Thatcher's desk. She got locked, somehow, in the walk-in refrigerator and when she pounded on the door with the heel of her Jimmy Choo sling back, nobody answered. The restaurant was closed. She was alone. She was going to die.

When strange things started to happen at the restaurant, Adrienne thought she was suffering from sleep deprivation. Garden-variety fatigue.

August ninth: two hundred and fifty covers and an unprecedented twenty-six reservations on the wait list. Special: whole tomatoes stuffed with a crab, smoked corn, and Thai basil salad, dressed with a lime-shallot beurre blanc.

At the end of first seating, Adrienne had a complaint from Tyler Lefroy. On the Tuesday after Labor Day, Tyler was headed to the Citadel for four years of military college—his father's idea. Tyler was dreading the end of summer. He loved this job, he told Adrienne. She knew he loved it because of the money and the crackers and because he partied after work with Eddie, Paco, and Jojo at the Subiaco compound. The actual work left him cold, though, and he was forever complaining.

"The guests have been stealing the silverware," he said. "And the plates."

"Stealing?"

"Yeah." He held out his rubber bin. "This, for example, is what I just cleared from table twenty-seven. A four-top. And, as you see, I only have three chargers. I only have three dessert forks. And there was a cappuccino at that table, but I don't see the cup or the saucer. Seem strange?"

"Maybe Roy or Gage cleared them," Adrienne said.

"They never help me out," Tyler said. "Nev-er."

This was true. Roy and Gage didn't like Tyler. They thought he was a smart-ass. They thought he *deserved* four years of military college.

"Maybe they did it as a joke, then," Adrienne said.

"Okay," Tyler said. "Except it's not funny."

"So you're telling me you think someone at table twenty-seven stole dishes."

"Yes."

Adrienne checked the reservation book. Table twenty-seven had been two couples from Sconset with houses on Baxter Road, the oldest money on the island. What was the likelihood that they had *stolen* dishes?

"The one lady had a big purse," Tyler added.

"Okay, Nancy Drew," Adrienne said. "Let me know if you notice anything else."

The next evening after second seating, Gage approached the podium. "I saw a woman hide a wineglass under her blouse," he said. "She walked out with it."

Adrienne stared at him in disbelief. She didn't know exactly what to make of Gage. Sometimes she thought he was a wasted life and other times she thought he was a good, though unlucky, man trying to make the best of bad circumstances by taking a job suited for teenagers. "Why didn't you stop her?"

He shrugged. "I just bus."

The following night there was a third incident. A well-dressed, middle-aged couple who had languished on the waiting list three nights running agreed to come in and have their meal at the bar. When they were through, they left money for their bill and a good tip, but absconded with the leather folder that the bill came in. Duncan was sure of it, because—*Hello, Adrienne, it's missing and where the hell did it go?*

"We're all tired," Adrienne said. But that didn't explain it. At the podium, her bowl of matches had to be refilled every two days and her Blue Bistro pencils kept disappearing. A count showed that she was short five menus. Five! She confronted Thatcher.

"The guests are taking things," she said. "Silverware, plates, wineglasses. The matches, my pencils, the menus. They're stealing."

Thatcher looked upon her with weary eyes. Of everybody up front, Thatcher seemed the most exhausted. And not only exhausted but sad. The sign that hung in the kitchen seemed to speak straight from his heart. His world was ending in twenty-five days. "Can you blame them?" he said. "We close in three and a half weeks. Whatever they took, that's all they'll be left with."

August thirteenth: two hundred and fifty covers, twenty-one reservations on the wait list. Special: oven-roasted tomatoes with garlic and thyme, served with grilled peasant bread.

Thatcher and Fiona went to mass at St. Mary's and were not expected in the restaurant until after first service started.

"Is everything okay?" Adrienne asked Thatcher when he told her he was going to church.

"She wants to see Father Ott," he said. "She wants to take communion."

"Could you go tomorrow morning?" It was bold of Adrienne to ask, but the restaurant business did not lend itself to five o'clock mass on Saturday.

"She wants to go tonight," Thatcher said.

After family meal but before service, Adrienne snuck into pastry. Mario had the ice cream machine running (special tonight: blackberry sherbet); he was melting Valrhona chocolate over a very low flame and reading *Sports Illustrated.* He had a garish red-purple mark on his neck the size of a quarter.

"Really," Adrienne said. "A hickey?"

"Girl I met last night at the Muse," Mario said without lifting his eyes from his magazine. "She was crazy about me. Said I looked like Antonio Banderas."

"Well, you don't."

"Okay, thanks," he said. He stirred the chocolate with a wooden spoon. "What do you want?"

"They're at church."

"Who?"

"Thatch and Fiona."

"So?"

"So, do you think that's bad?"

"No."

"Do you think it means she's getting worse?"

"Hospital means she's getting worse," he said. "Church just means . . ." He looked up for the first time, slapping the magazine down on the marble counter. "It means she wants religion. It's August, for God's sake."

"Twenty-two days until the end of the world," Adrienne said, and suddenly she felt like she was going to cry. Even if they were the longest three weeks of her life, it wouldn't be long enough. "What are you going to do when it's over?" she asked Mario. "Will you and your cousins try to open your own place?"

"We're talking about it," he said.

This answer saddened her even more. They were making plans without her. Everyone was: That morning, Adrienne had heard Caren on the phone with a Realtor in Providence, Rhode Island.

"Providence?" Adrienne had said when Caren hung up, only slightly cowed by the fact that she'd been eavesdropping. "What happened to St. Bart's?"

"That part of my life is over," Caren said. "It's time to move on. I have to get a real job. I have a degree in biology, you know. I could work in a lab."

"You're a scientist? I thought you did ballet."

"I'm too old for ballet now. I'm almost thirty-three. I have to get some structure in place. Some health insurance."

"What about Duncan?" Adrienne said.

"He'll be in Providence, too," Caren said. "Providence is not a place I would have chosen on my own."

"What's he going to do in Providence?"

"Work for Holt Millman," Caren said.

"As a bartender?"

Caren laughed. "You're kidding, right?"

So Caren and Duncan were off to Providence and the Subiacos were talking about opening their own place. Henry Subiaco had his root beer. Spillman and Red Mare were moving to Brooklyn; they were going to work for Kevin Kahla at Craft and start trying to have a baby. To avoid being stranded out in the cold, Adrienne told herself she could always go to Telluride with Kyra and the painter—or she could put her finger on the map and pick a new place. But what Adrienne really wanted was to go where Thatcher went and do what he did. He had cancelled the trip to the Galápagos, but no plans appeared in its place. Adrienne was left to speculate: He would ride it out with Fiona, whatever that entailed.

While Adrienne was lost in this train of thought, Mario picked up his magazine and started reading again.

"I should get back to work . . ." Adrienne said, but he didn't answer. He wasn't listening.

Adrienne returned to the front to find Doyle Chambers pacing by the podium. Adrienne steeled her resolve, then breezed around him as if he weren't there. She checked her running watch, which she kept inside the podium: five fifty-five, three feet above sea level. She rechecked the reservation book.

"Adrienne," Doyle Chambers said.

She held up a finger—*One minute*—with the authority (she hoped) of the conductor of an orchestra. Doyle Chambers worked on Wall Street. He was intense, he was fastidious, he was busy. He and his mousy wife, Gloria, rented a house in Quaise, and flew to Nantucket on their jet every weekend. Doyle never requested reservations so much as demanded them. Adrienne had sat him at least six times over the course of the summer and each time he had made her feel increasingly menial. The world was Doyle Chambers's servant. But not tonight.

"I called you three times and left three messages on your cell phone," Adrienne said. She glanced up to see Gloria, wearing a fringed shawl like a rock diva of a certain era, slinking around by the front door. "I made myself clear. Call back to reconfirm or I give away your table."

"Adrienne."

"It wasn't like you," Adrienne said. "But you didn't call me back."

"A reservation is a reservation," he said. "Do you understand the meaning of the word? I *reserved* a table."

"It's the middle of August, Mr. Chambers," Adrienne said. She breathed in through her nose and if she could have breathed out fire, she would have. "I gave away your table."

"No!" he said. His voice reverberated through the restaurant. Adrienne turned around. It was empty except for the servers who looked up from their polishing and straightening, startled. When they saw it was just Doyle Chambers releasing testosterone, they resumed work.

In response to his raised voice, Adrienne lowered hers. "Yes," she said. "Those, I'm afraid, are our rules. However, since you're here early, you're more than welcome to sit at the bar."

"Sit at the bar?" he said. "Sit at the bar like I'm someone who doesn't have enough *pull* to get a real table?"

Adrienne wished she could blink herself back into pastry with Mario, love bite, indifference, and all. She could watch the ice cream machine churn liquid into solid. She peeked out the window, hoping that Thatcher and Fiona had skipped the last hymn and Thatcher's silver truck would be pulling into the parking lot any second. Doyle Chambers never spoke like this to Thatcher; he only bullied women. Caren had refused to serve him years ago.

"*Pull* has nothing to do with it," Adrienne said, her voice practically a whisper. "If you'd like a table, you have to make a reservation, then reconfirm. It's a Saturday night in August. I have a twenty-one-reservation wait list. I called your cell phone three times. You did not call me back. I waited until two o'clock, which is, incidentally, two hours past the deadline, then I gave away your table."

Doyle Chambers snatched a pack of matches out of the bowl and whipped them sidearm at the wall behind Adrienne's head. Gloria Chambers slipped out to the parking lot. Adrienne felt someone by her side: Joe.

"I can't believe this!" Doyle Chambers shouted. "What is the point of making a reservation if it doesn't reserve you shit!"

"Hey, man," Joe said. "Lower your voice. Please. And stop throwing things at the lady. She's just doing her job."

Doyle Chambers glared at Joe and took a step toward him. *Fight,* Adrienne thought. Duncan rushed over from the bar and grabbed Doyle Chambers's arm in a good-natured, break-it-up way.

"Doyle," he said. "Dude, you have to chill. I'd be happy to set you up at the bar."

Doyle Chambers shrugged Duncan off. "I'm not eating at the bar," he said. "I'm eating in the dining room. I have a reservation."

"You *had* a reservation," Adrienne said. She was shaking, but it felt good to be enforcing the rules, especially with a cretin like this. He beat his wife; there wasn't a doubt in Adrienne's mind.

Doyle Chambers looked at the ground and said nothing. His face and neck were red, the part in his sandy blond hair was red. Adrienne thought he was collecting himself. She thought maybe he would apologize and maybe he would agree to sit at the bar. Duncan, who prided himself on being a man's man, would buy him a round of drinks and put in a VIP order. But when Doyle Chambers raised his head, Adrienne could see nothing of the sort would happen. He lifted his hand and Adrienne thought he was going to strike her, but what he did was more devastating. He grabbed Adrienne's reservation book and ripped out the page for that night, crumpling it in his fist. "No!" Adrienne cried. But before she or Joe or Duncan could comprehend the full meaning of his action, Doyle Chambers was out the door, pushing past a party of eight that was on their way in. Adrienne darted out from behind the podium and made it to the doorway in time to see Doyle and Gloria Chambers tear out of the parking lot in their convertible Jaguar.

"There goes my night," Adrienne said. "Literally. *There goes my night.*" One of the men in the party of eight looked at her expectantly; she didn't know who he was or where he belonged. Joe and Duncan stared at Adrienne with dumb, shell-shocked expressions. "What am I going to do?" Adrienne asked them. Joe retreated to the dining room to pass the bad news on to the other servers.

Duncan repaired to the bar. "Let me get your drink," he said.

Adrienne returned to her post behind the podium. Her book was destroyed. In addition to Saturday, Doyle Chambers had ripped out half of Sunday. Adrienne tasted the grilled sausage she'd had for family meal in the back of her throat.

"I'm sorry?" said the man with the party of eight. "We have a reservation at six o'clock. The name is Banino. The Banino family from Oklahoma."

A glass of Laurent-Perrier materialized at the podium and Adrienne felt Delilah give her arm a squeeze. She could do this. She remembered that there were three eight-tops first seating and Adrienne sat Mr. Banino at the best of the three, handed out menus, and said, "Someone will be your server tonight. Enjoy your meal." On the way back to the podium she wondered if she could call the police and press charges against Doyle Chambers. Attempted assault with a pack of matches. First-degree rudeness.

Adrienne sat the restaurant as best she could on the fly. The local author and her entourage were one of the other parties of eight and the author told Adrienne, a bit impatiently, that Thatcher had promised her a table under the awning, the table that she had already given to the Oklahoma contingency. Adrienne was flummoxed; she nearly launched into the whole long story because an author would appreciate the drama. You couldn't even put a character like Doyle Chambers into fiction. He was too awful; no one would believe him. But as Adrienne was short on time she offered to put the author out in the sand at two of the fondue tables pushed together. This solved the problem temporarily. Adrienne just waited for those tables to show up and complain about being stuck inside on such a lovely night. Call Doyle Chambers, she would say.

Thatcher didn't show up until everyone from first was down. When Adrienne saw his truck pull in, she checked her watch: six forty-five. What a night to be late. She tried to summon words poisonous enough to describe what had happened. She had quelled some of her rage by writing across the top of Sunday's ripped page: "Doyle Chambers never allowed back." Never in the next twenty-one days. *So there,* Adrienne thought. Take that. She would throw the remainder of her fury against Thatcher the second he walked in. He should have a computer like every other restaurant! He should make a backup copy of the book! But most of all, he should have been here where he was needed and not at church.

When he stepped through the door, he looked somber, verging on mournful. Fiona and Father Ott trailed him in. Fiona gave Adrienne a weary glance then vanished into the kitchen with Father Ott in her wake. Adrienne dropped her load. There was no one like Thatcher and Fiona to make her feel like the restaurant business really was not all that important.

"How was mass?" she said.

"Good," he said dully. "Everything okay here?"

"Sure," Adrienne said. "Doyle Chambers absconded with tonight's page from the reservation book, but I got everybody down. It's not perfect, but . . ."

"Looks fine," he said, scanning the dining room with disinterested eyes. "Father Ott is going to sit with Fiona in the back office for a while. Her O_2 sats are low and she's afraid she's getting another infection. She's lost seven pounds since we got back from Boston. The doctors want her in the hospital."

"When?"

"Tomorrow."

"Tomorrow?"

He flashed Adrienne a look she had never seen before. He was angry. "Well, she can't breathe."

This was enough to push Adrienne over the edge into hysteria. Doyle Chambers, the precarious state of her future: job, relationship, and all. And she was premenstrual. But Adrienne simply nodded. "Okay, I understand."

Thatcher backed down. "Sorry," he said. "It's just . . ."

"It's all right," she said.

"So let me see the book," he said. He regarded Doyle Chambers's damage, then whistled. "In twelve years, this has never happened to me."

"He isn't allowed back," Adrienne said. "If you let him in, I'll quit."

"You'll quit?"

"Yep."

"Don't want that," Thatcher said. He squeezed Adrienne's hand. "Let's get out of here."

"What do you mean?"

"We were invited to a party."

"A party?'

"At Holt Millman's house."

Holt Millman's house. Duncan had told Adrienne about this party a few mornings earlier over espresso. Holt Millman threw a legendary cocktail party every August. Two hundred guests, vintage Dom Pérignon, flowers flown in from Hawaii, a full-blown feast by Nantucket Catering Company, and a band from New York City. Every year people got so drunk that they jumped in the pool with their clothes on.

"Are you going?" Adrienne had asked Duncan.

"No," Duncan said. "I never get to go anywhere."

Now Adrienne stole a glance at Duncan. He had four people eating at the bar and he was shaking up martinis.

"We can't go," Adrienne said. "Who's going to work?"

"Caren," Thatcher said.

"You've asked her?"

"I'll ask her right now."

"And who's going to take her tables?"

"The other waitstaff can cover. Heck, I'll give Tyler and Roy a table or two. They've been begging me for one all summer."

"They have?" Adrienne said. This didn't sound right. Tyler, especially, would not want more work. Adrienne looked around the dining room. The waitstaff was humping—it wasn't even seven o'clock and Christo was sweating. Every single table was packed, food was just starting to come out from the kitchen. Caren was at table seventeen opening champagne, Joe was delivering appetizers. Spillman was at the Baninos' table taking their order. Adrienne wondered if Thatcher saw what she saw. "I think it's too busy for us to just disappear."

"I'm the boss," he said. "I have to get out of this place for a little while."

"You go, then," Adrienne said. She could sense he was about to lose his cool. "I'll stay here and cover."

"I will not go without you," he said.

"Thatch."

"We're going," he said. "It's just down the road. We'll stay an hour. We'll be back before second seating. They won't even notice we're gone."

He sounded so irresponsible, Adrienne thought he must be joking. He grabbed her by the wrist.

"Wait," she said. "You have to tell Caren, at least."

He took a deep breath, then made a face like a judge deliberating.

"Okay, I'll tell her. Be right back."

He pulled Caren away from a four-top and whispered in her ear. Caren did not seem pleased. She glanced at Adrienne at the podium. Adrienne stared down at her ruined reservation book. Why did there have to be nights like these?

Thatcher dragged Caren back to the podium. Adrienne chose not to meet her gaze.

"I'll just stay here," Adrienne said.

"No," Thatcher said. "You won't. You're coming with me or you're fired."

Adrienne rolled her eyes for Caren's benefit, but Caren would have none of it. She was pissed. The first thing she did was march to the bar to tell Duncan. *They're going to the party.* Adrienne said, "Okay, let's get out of here, then." And they left.

Holt Millman's house was located on the harbor side of Hulbert Avenue. It was a thirty-second drive from the bistro.

"See?" Thatcher said as he pulled up to the white gates. A valet came out to take his keys. "We could have walked."

Adrienne tried to exude nonchalance. She had come to terms with Holt Millman's wealth during her sail on *Kelsey.* But she had never seen a house or grounds—or a *bash*—like this one. She and Thatcher walked through the white gates onto a expansive lawn bordered by lush flower gardens. A tent was set up in the middle and there were people everywhere—people and tables of food and waiters in white jackets with silver trays of hors

d'oeuvres and champagne. Adrienne took a glass and Thatch said, "I'm going to get a club soda."

"I'll come with you," Adrienne said.

She and Thatcher weaved between the clumps of laughing, chatting guests. The house loomed in front of Adrienne; it was the biggest house she had ever seen at this proximity. It had classic Nantucket features: gray shingles, climbing New Dawn roses on trellises, huge windows, and five brick chimneys. Adrienne snatched an hors d'oeuvre from a passing tray. She had eaten a sausage grinder for family meal but this food was too gorgeous to pass up. She stopped at the buffet table and dipped a crab claw in a lemony mayonnaise. Her champagne was ice cold; it was crisp, like an apple. Across the tent, she saw Darla Parrish and her sister Eleanor standing in front of a table where a man was slicing gravlax. Adrienne turned away; she wasn't in the right mood for Darla. She saw Brian and Jennifer Devlin talking to the manager of the Nantucket Golf Club and his pregnant wife. Everywhere Adrienne turned—guests! She looked for Thatcher but he was gone. She moved through the crowd to the bar hunting for his blue blazer. Nearly every man at the party wore a blue blazer, so she cast her eyes at the ground hoping to pick out his Gucci loafers.

Where was he? Adrienne experienced a twinge of panic, like when she had gotten lost as a child (the Christmas light show at Wanamaker's—her mother had been hysterical with worry). The panic gave way to guilt; she should leave now, escape, run down the road back to work. But mostly what Adrienne felt was curiosity, a pressure behind her eyes, urging her to see, to soak it in. Tomorrow, she would e-mail the details to her father.

Behind the tent, a slate walkway led to a tall privet hedge and through an archway was the pool area. The pool was a simple rectangle, dark and exotic-looking. There was a waterfall at one end. There were people surrounding the pool, another bar, more tables of food. Adrienne saw Mr. and Mrs. Kennedy talking to another couple and when Mrs. Kennedy saw her, Adrienne felt like she had no choice: She had to go over and say hello.

She positioned herself at Mrs. Kennedy's elbow. "Hello," she said.

The man Adrienne didn't know was telling a story. He paused when Adrienne spoke and looked at her briefly, then went back to telling his story. Something about a flight he had recently been on, an aggressive passenger, a pilot who had been sent back from the cockpit with pepper spray.

Adrienne was trapped at Mitzi Kennedy's elbow—it would be too awkward to walk away and yet no one in the circle had acknowledged her presence. So walk away. But then the man finished his story and there were *ohs* and *ahs* and then a brief silence. Adrienne touched Mrs. Kennedy's arm.

"Mrs. Kennedy, hello."

Mitzi Kennedy stepped back; it seemed Adrienne had caught her off-guard. She regarded Adrienne with a blank expression, and Adrienne thought, *I have sat you every week since the first of June, I have opened your champagne and chatted with you about your son's college applications, and I have bent over backward to give you a better table. Don't tell me you don't recognize me.* But sometimes, if you saw someone out of context . . . so Adrienne identified herself. "Adrienne," she said, "from the Blue Bistro."

"I know who you are," Mrs. Kennedy said. "I'm just trying to figure out what you're doing here."

"I . . ." Adrienne was at a loss for words. She smoothed the material of her dress and wished she was wearing something new. "We were invited. Thatcher and I. He's around here somewhere."

Mrs. Kennedy looked nonplussed. Adrienne considered drowning herself in the pool. She tried to catch Mr. Kennedy's eye—he was always friendly, friendlier than his wife. But he was deep in conversation with the man who had been telling the story about the airplane and he didn't notice Adrienne.

She drifted away in what she hoped was a graceful fashion, like a flower petal being carried off by the breeze. Who was she kidding? She qualified as staff to 99 percent of the people at this party and no one wanted to be caught chatting with the staff.

Her main objective now was to find Thatcher and convince him to return to the restaurant. She wasn't wearing a watch but it was nearly dark and she guessed it must be almost eight. They would have to be back by nine: thanks to Doyle Chambers, Caren didn't even have a book to work from to get second seating down. So Adrienne decided to return to the tent to track down Thatcher. Problem was, the Kennedys were standing on the slate path that led back to the tent and now, worse than almost anything Adrienne could imagine, they were talking to Drew Amman-Keller. Adrienne spun around and headed in the opposite direction, praying Drew hadn't seen her. She followed a path that led around the right side of the house—over a

white shell driveway, through an arbor hung with grapevines, toward the ocean. This was the front lawn, which had a stunning view of the harbor: sailboats, Brant Point lighthouse, the jetty. Adrienne wished she could enjoy the party instead of negotiating it like a live minefield.

There were fewer people on the front lawn: several couples who, like herself it seemed, had strayed from the heart of the party and wanted to get a look at the water. Then Adrienne heard a burst of joyous laughter and she knew a group of people was approaching behind her but she was afraid to turn around.

Someone took her arm at the elbow. "Adrienne? My God, it's you, it's really you."

A wave of relief and salvation rolled over Adrienne. She wished Mitzi Kennedy was nearby to see the look of delight on Holt Millman's face.

"You must meet my friends," he said. "Frank and Sue Cunningham. Jerry and Ann Longerot. And certainly you know Catherine."

Catherine. For the first time since she walked through the white gates, Adrienne smiled. It was Cat. Conservative tonight in a blue seersucker sundress and flats.

"I can't believe you're here," Holt said. "I'm honored. I'm thrilled. I want to give you a tour of my house. Would you like more bubbly?" He took Adrienne's glass and handed it to one of his friends. "Jerry, your job is to get that filled, pronto. And bring Adrienne one of those shrimp puffs. Those are good."

"I'm fine," Adrienne protested. "Actually, I have to find Thatcher. We just stopped in for a minute. We have to get back to work."

"Work?" Holt Millman said. "No, no, no, sweetie. I'm not willing to let you leave."

Adrienne turned her eyes to the house. They were now standing on a gorgeous semicircular deck—another bar, more food. Jerry Longerot handed Adrienne a filled champagne glass and a shrimp puff. A tour of the house would take forever. It was not an option.

"I must find the ladies' room," Adrienne said. She grabbed Cat's forearm. "Do you know where there's a ladies' room?"

"Follow me, girlfriend," Cat said. "I wired every inch of this house."

They left Holt Millman standing on the deck. "We'll be back," Adrienne said.

"Because I want to give you a tour!" he called out.

Adrienne followed Cat to the pool house. Adrienne was feeling happier. The eleventh richest man in the country—the owner of all *this* and more—loved her. And she had found Cat, who was ten times more glamorous than Mitzi Kennedy.

"Where's your husband?" Adrienne asked. "Is he out back?"

"He's in Montana," Cat said. "Fly-fishing."

"Oh," Adrienne said. "I have to find Thatcher. You haven't seen him?"

"I've never seen Thatcher at a party before in my life," Cat said. "I didn't think he went to parties."

"He doesn't," Adrienne said. "This is an aberration."

They opened the door to the pool house. Adrienne heard a strange noise; it sounded like a hurt kitten. Cat disappeared into the powder room and Adrienne poked her head into the changing room. A woman sat at an old-fashioned dressing table, crying into her hands. Adrienne said, "Oh, I'm sorry," and the woman looked up. Adrienne saw her face in the mirror. Darla Parrish.

Again, Adrienne wondered why there had to be nights like this. Why had she agreed to come to this party? And why, oh why, had she strayed from Thatcher's side?

"Darla," she said. "Is everything all right?"

"Adrienne, honey," Darla said. She held her arms out. "Give me a hug."

Adrienne bent down and embraced her. She watched herself in the mirror. From the back, she thought, Darla could have been her mother. They could have been mother and daughter hugging. Gently, Adrienne released her hold. She heard the toilet flush, then water, then Cat's face appeared in the mirror. Cat pointed at the door. Adrienne nodded and Cat left.

"Is everything okay?" Adrienne asked. She felt herself slipping back into restaurant mode. "Is there anything I can get you?"

"I need another drink," Darla said, though Adrienne could smell the Southern Comfort on Darla along with her Shalimar. She eyed the glass of melting ice on the dressing table. Did Darla expect Adrienne to fetch her another drink? Maybe she did. Adrienne considered it, but instead she said, "Let's go out. I'm trying to find Thatcher and we can look for your husband."

"Grayson isn't here," Darla said, and she started to weep again.

"Oh, right," Adrienne said. "You came with Eleanor?"

Darla nodded, face in her hands. Adrienne plucked a tissue from a box on a nearby table and held it out to Darla. It was getting later and later; it might be as late as eight thirty. Adrienne started to panic. She had to get back to the tent and find Thatcher—if she couldn't find him, she was leaving anyway. Either way, Caren was going to be bitter and with good reason.

Darla dabbed her eyes with the tissue. "He's having an affair," she said. "He's been having an affair for twelve years."

"Oh," Adrienne said.

Darla nodded firmly as though Adrienne had just said something she very much agreed with. "One of my bridge partners back home."

Back home was Short Hills, New Jersey. Darla had cancelled once, and another time come to the Bistro with Eleanor, because Grayson had business back in Short Hills.

"I'm sorry, Darla. That's awful. Shall we try to find your sister?"

Darla gripped Adrienne's arm in a way that made it clear she wasn't going anywhere.

"Promise me you won't marry Thatcher," Darla said.

"Excuse me?"

"You're as free as a bird," Darla said. "That's always what I think of when I see you. Drinking champagne, in your beautiful silks, flitting here, flying there—you're a bird. Free, free. I wouldn't want to see Thatcher or anyone else clip your wings. Promise me you won't marry Thatcher."

"I can't promise anything," Adrienne said. "Life has too many surprises."

"Oh, honey," Darla said. She had a smudge of lipstick on the bottom of her front tooth. Adrienne nearly pointed it out, but she didn't have the heart. She excused herself for the powder room. When she peeked back in a minute later, Darla was gone.

At ten minutes to nine, Adrienne found Thatcher standing at the main buffet table eating stuffed mushrooms. She took his arm. "Let's get out of here," she said. "How do we get the car from the valet?"

Thatcher smiled at her. Something was funny about him. Funny peculiar.

"What?" she said.

"I love you," he said. "I was just standing here thinking of you and how much I love you. And I was also thinking about Fiona. Fiona is really fucking sick."

Discreetly, Adrienne surveyed their surroundings. There was a man replenishing the buffet and a couple of guests lingering at the end of the table by the crab claws. "I wouldn't say that too loudly," Adrienne said.

"It's true," he said. "She's sick. She can't breathe. Her lungs are polluted. They're a junkyard."

"Thatcher?"

He grinned, then pulled her in close. "This is a great party. You know how many years I've been invited to this party? Twelve. And I've never come. You know, I heard the band warming up. They start playing at nine."

"That's nice," Adrienne said. "But we have to go back. Second seating. Caren has no book."

"I'm not leaving."

"What?"

"And you're not leaving, either. We're going to dance. I've been dying to dance with you all summer."

Adrienne picked up Thatcher's glass. She took a sip. It looked like club soda with lime but it was the tail end of a gin and tonic.

"You've been drinking," she said.

"Yep."

"How many of these have you had?"

"Several."

"Several?"

"Yep." Thatcher took the glass from her hand and emptied it into his mouth in one gulp. "Come on, let's find the dance floor."

"No, Thatcher."

"Yes." He kissed her. As angry and agitated as she was, she succumbed. She'd had two glasses of champagne herself, three including the one she drank at work to calm her Doyle Chambers–induced stress, and she had a little buzz. For the second that Thatcher kissed her, she let her mind wander. How bad would it be if she just went along with this reckless course of action? Allowing Thatcher to get drunk and dancing to this band from New York instead of heading back to the Bistro to work second seating.

Caren could get everyone down with a little creativity; she knew the guests as well as Thatcher and better than Adrienne. How bad would it be to blow off a little steam?

Bad, she decided. The bar would be packed. They still had the stealing problem. Fiona was sick and the priest was there. As for Thatcher's drinking, Adrienne didn't know what to think. He once told her that drinking, for an alcoholic, was like falling into a river filled with raging rapids. It was easy to get swept away, to drown. So should she stop him? Yes. Get him a Coke. Or a coffee.

"We're leaving," Adrienne said. At that minute, she heard Thatcher's cell phone ringing. She removed it from his blazer pocket. She didn't check the number; the only place that ever called him was the restaurant.

"We're on our way back," Adrienne said.

"Don't bother." It was Caren. "I'm calling to tell you that Chambers's wife came in with the page from the book. Is it me or does that woman look like Stevie Nicks? Anyway, she apologized and I can get second down. Fiona and the padre left—she went home to sleep and Antonio said everything was fine. The kitchen is cranking the plates. We're all set. You stay and enjoy yourself."

"No, we can't," Adrienne said.

"Sure you can." And Caren hung up.

Adrienne slipped the phone back into Thatcher's blazer. Now what to do? Thatcher didn't ask about the phone call. He was too busy attacking the buffet table—tenderloin, crab claws, gravlax, mushrooms, cherrystones on the half shell. He held one out to Adrienne.

"Eat this," he said.

"No, thanks."

"Come on."

"I'm not hungry."

"Not hungry?" he said. He piled his plate with Chinese spare ribs. "This food is incredible."

"Okay," Adrienne said. "We can stay. But you have to promise me you'll stop drinking. You have to promise, Thatch."

He gave her big eyes as he gnawed on a spare rib. "I don't need to stop drinking," he said. "Because I feel fine. I feel better than I have all summer.

When the restaurant is closed, this is what I'm going to do. Party like this."

Adrienne surveyed the tent. Across the lawn, she saw Eleanor leading Darla Parrish out of the party. Home for ice water, aspirin, and bed. Adrienne was relieved. Darla's news was still ticking in her brain like a bomb that had yet to go off.

"If you feel good now," Adrienne said, "you should stop drinking."

"What are you drinking?" Thatcher asked.

"I was drinking champagne," Adrienne said. "But I'm ready for coffee. Do you want coffee?"

"No."

"Okay. We don't have to drink anything. We can dance. There's the band over there. Come on."

"I have to use the bathroom," Thatcher said.

Adrienne regarded him. She had no idea if he was going to sneak another drink and she was too worn down to care. She remembered back to a time in high school, her senior year in Solon, Iowa, when she snuck out of her house to go to a party in one of the cornfields. She drank beer and smoked a cigarette and after the party she sat in the back of one of the kid's vans and played strip poker and drank more beer. To recall the events in this way made them sound like fun, but they hadn't been fun at all because the entire time, Adrienne experienced fear like a cold hand gripping the back of her neck. She was afraid that her father would find out, that he would call the police and start a manhunt. At five o'clock in the morning, the kids she was with wanted to go to the Egg and I for breakfast and at that point Adrienne finally relaxed. Sure enough, when her friends dropped her off at six thirty and Adrienne slipped back into the house, her father was asleep. He hadn't realized she'd been gone.

She convinced herself that this was a similar moment. It was a Saturday night in August, it had been weeks since she'd had a night off. And here she was at the fanciest party she could ever hope to attend with a man she loved. If she got swept away in the spirit of things, who would ever know—and who would blame her?

Adrienne drank and Thatcher drank.

They danced. Thatcher spun and dipped her, and through the crowd, Adrienne caught sight of Cat dancing with Holt Millman, and a few minutes later, Cat dancing with one of the handsome male waiters. Only Cat.

The band slowed down. They played "Wonderful Tonight." Adrienne clung to Thatcher; they were holding each other up.

Someone tapped Adrienne's shoulder. She turned, a flash went off. Drew Amman-Keller had snapped their picture.

Thatcher recoiled. "Hey," he said. He blinked. "Hey, fuck you, Drew."

Drew Amman-Keller smirked. "It's good to see you out, man." He held out his hand. Thatcher and Adrienne stared at it. "Hey, come on. Adrienne?"

"Don't talk to her," Thatcher said. "Don't talk to either of us, you fucking parasite."

"Thatcher," Adrienne said. Her mind was fuzzy, buzzing television snow. "Don't give him anything to write about. That's what he wants."

Drew Amman-Keller bowed and shuffled backward off the dance floor. "I'm still waiting for you to call me," he said to Adrienne. "Callmecallmecallme." He was drunk, too. Adrienne looked around. Everyone at the party was drunk.

"Let's get out of here," Adrienne said. "Let's go look at the water." They stumbled through the tent (where coffee and dessert were set up), past the pool (where people were indeed swimming with their clothes on), and out onto the small beach in front of Holt Millman's house. They fell over into the sand, Adrienne first and Thatcher on top of her. Adrienne felt a shell behind her ear, some damp seaweed under her left leg. Was anyone watching them? Was Drew Amman-Keller going to take a picture of them in this compromising position? Thatcher started to kiss Adrienne in a sloppy way. She struggled to sit up but Thatch pressed her down.

"We're not," she said. She lifted her knee between Thatcher's legs. "Thatch, I mean it."

She had sand in her hair and inside her dress. Thatcher fiddled with her bra; it came unhooked. "We're not going to do this," Adrienne said. She pushed him off her and he fell heavily to the side with a grunt. His eyes were closed, his features were blurry. He didn't even look like himself. Adrienne poked him in the ribs harder than she meant to. She reached inside her dress to shake out the sand and rehook her bra.

"I want to ask you something," she said. She was feeling so confrontational, she scared herself. Off to the right she saw the red light of Brant Point, warning, warning. She had read somewhere that the definition of elegance was restraint. Adrienne wanted to be elegant—what woman didn't?—but it was hard to be elegant when her skirt was hitched up and her bra was left of center and she had sand in her ears and under her fingernails. It was hard to be elegant when she was drunk. Restraint was a good idea, noble, but at that moment it was too flimsy to hold back the urgency of her question. "Are you and I going to make it past the summer?"

Thatcher opened his eyes for a second, then closed them again. "I don't know," he said.

Later, Adrienne would call a cab and have the driver take them to her cottage, where Thatcher would vomit until sunrise and then fall into a comatose sleep. Over espresso the next morning, Caren and Duncan would berate Adrienne for letting him drink. "Couldn't you see he was in a dangerous state when you went to that party?" Caren would ask. And Adrienne would counter that Caren had granted them permission to stay and that was when things had gotten out of hand. Duncan would concede that Thatcher was an adult and not Adrienne's responsibility. He and Caren would pump her for details of the party and various images passed through Adrienne's mind—the crab claws, the dark-tiled pool, the smell of the powder room, the distaste on Mitzi Kennedy's face, the smudge of lipstick on Darla Parrish's tooth, the semicircular deck—but all Adrienne would really retain, the only part of the night that had any meaning for her, were those three words spoken as she buried her feet in the cold sand and gazed out across Nantucket Sound. *I don't know.*

The next morning, Fiona was at work as usual. Adrienne went in early to answer the phones and generally atone for her many sins of the night before. The only two cars in the parking lot belonged to Fiona and Hector. Through the window of the kitchen door, Adrienne saw Fiona behind the pass portioning swordfish. The restaurant had a Sunday hush, which was a good thing since Adrienne was suffering from a dreadful hangover. She poured herself a Coke at the bar and sat down with the phone and the reservation book. There were two hundred and fifty covers and a fourteen reservation wait list. The two halves of Sunday's page had been smoothed out and carefully repaired with Scotch tape.

Adrienne jumped when the door to the kitchen opened and Fiona came out. Adrienne wanted to ask how she was feeling, but she was too afraid.

Fiona set down a plate of toast, a cake of butter, a Ball jar of apricot jam. The same toast that Adrienne had eaten at her first breakfast.

"You didn't have to . . ." Adrienne said. "I mean, how did you know I was here?"

"I heard the brakes of your bike. You should have those oiled."

"Oh." Adrienne looked at the toast. "Thank you for this. I really need it."

"Yeah." Fiona stared at her and Adrienne attempted a smile. Fiona didn't look sick. She was wearing white cotton drawstring pants, a white tank, clogs. She was tan, she wore lipstick.

"I want you to have dinner with me tonight," Fiona said.

"Tonight?"

"At the table out back. Around midnight. Thatcher can take the bar while we eat. I want to talk to you."

"About what?" Adrienne said.

"Stuff," Fiona said. "I'm tired of Thatcher. I'm tired of him worrying about me. He worries so much that I start to worry and I made a decision this morning that I'm done worrying. Whatever happens, happens. To think that I can control it, or the doctors, or the priest . . . no, it doesn't work like that."

Adrienne sat, speechless.

"So midnight?" Fiona said.

"Yes," Adrienne said. "Of course."

The special was a tomato salad with bacon, basil, and blue cheese. It was a work of art. Fiona had found a rainbow of heirloom tomatoes—red, orange, yellow, green, purple, yellow with green stripes—and she stacked them on the plate in a tower as colorful as children's blocks. It flew out of the kitchen; by the end of first seating, it was eighty-sixed.

Adrienne didn't see Thatcher until five, though he'd called her at noon to say he'd woken up and, first thing, cleaned the bathroom. Then he'd gone to an AA meeting.

"I'm sorry about last night," he said.

"I'm sorry, too," Adrienne said. There was no denying the regret she felt about letting Thatcher stay at the party and drink. It was monstrous of her. The worst thing was, she had *wanted* him to drink. She had wanted to see what he was like and she had hoped that with his guard down she might wheedle some promises out of him about the future. But all she had gotten was the truth: He didn't know.

At menu meeting, Thatcher looked and smelled chastened. He was clean-shaven, his red-gold hair held teeth marks from his comb. He wore his stone white pants and a new shirt from Thomas Pink with cuff links. He had shined his loafers. He was professional, in charge, sober. It was time to move on.

At family meal, Adrienne ate only a salad.

Caren said, "On a diet?"

"No. I'm eating tonight with Fiona."

Caren's eyebrows arched. She said nothing, though Adrienne knew she was curious. Adrienne was not only curious but worried. She expected to be chastised for running out of the restaurant and allowing Thatcher to drink. Adrienne had no words to offer in her own defense; she was going to take her punishment. She had to admit, though, that Fiona hadn't seemed angry or perturbed that morning when she invited Adrienne to dinner, and so what really worried Adrienne was that Fiona might not even know that Thatch had been drinking, but she was sure to find out over the course of the night. Every time Adrienne went back into the kitchen for chips and dip, she expected Fiona to cancel. But Fiona treated Adrienne normally, which was to say, with complete indifference. She was expediting, the kitchen was brutally hot—so hot they had the oscillating fans going—and they were too busy to gossip.

"Ordering table four," Fiona called out. "Two Caesars, one crab cake SOS. Ordering table twenty-three, three bisques, one foie gras, killed. Another person who doesn't know how to eat. Jojo, baby, I need more of those square plates. Stop the cycle now and finish them by hand, please."

Adrienne inhaled the smells of grilling and sautéing and frying. Three weeks until the end of the world.

Between seatings, Adrienne stood with Thatch at the podium. His hands were shaking.

"Are you okay?" she said.

"Fine."

"Fiona seems better."

"I just hope she isn't wearing herself down."

"She thinks you worry too much."

"Ha!"

"I'm eating with her tonight," Adrienne said.

"Yes. She told me."

Adrienne wished the news had come as a surprise to him. But Thatcher and Fiona were like an old married couple; they shared everything with each other first.

"What do you think she wants?"

"A woman's perspective."

"Why not Caren?"

"Do I really have to answer that?"

"I guess not." Caren wasn't exactly the girlfriend type. "I just wonder what she wants to talk about."

"She didn't tell me and I didn't pry. I assume it's something that I, as a man, wouldn't understand."

Christo approached the podium with a pepper mill. "This thing's empty. I twisted it over a Caesar at table fifteen for, like, five minutes until we figured there wasn't anything coming out. Unless it's white pepper. It's not white pepper, is it? Because if it is, that old guy eating the Caesar is going to croak."

"Your former boss told me you were smart, Christo," Thatcher said. "That's why I hired you."

"Yeah, I know."

"There are peppercorns in the pantry," Adrienne said. "They're black."

"I don't have time. I thought the busboys were supposed to do it. I thought they filled them every night."

Thatcher nodded at the kitchen door. Christo went, huffing.

"Are you angry?" Adrienne asked.

"You mean because it's August and one of my servers hasn't deciphered the pepper mill?"

"No, because I'm eating with Fiona."

"No."

"You're sure?"

"Yes."

By midnight, Adrienne was starving. The crackers came out and she could have eaten the whole basket. But she held herself to two, then two more the next time Louis passed by. She longingly contemplated two more, but then she saw Thatcher coming toward her with the cash box and receipts. He was smiling.

"Lots of expensive wine tonight. Table twenty-six ordered two bottles of the Chateau Margaux. I don't even know who those people are, do you?"

Adrienne checked the book. "Beach Club. Mack sent them."

"Guy knew his wine."

"Mack said he was a doctor in Aspen."

"You know him?"

"No. Duncan knows him. Can I go?"

"You can go."

"And what will you eat? Are they sending something out?"

"I'll be fine," he said. "Go."

"Are you sure, because . . ."

"Adrienne," Thatcher said. "Go."

It felt awkward, like a first date. Fiona was in the walk-in checking inventory, telling Antonio what she needed to get up at the farm and what they should order from Sid Wainer. Adrienne poked her head in and said, "I'm here."

Fiona looked confused, sweaty, and pale. Then, it seemed, she remembered. "What do you want to eat?" she said.

Adrienne was so hungry she would have eaten straight from the industrial-sized container of sour cream on the shelf in her line of vision. "I don't know," Adrienne said. "What are you having?"

"What I'm having is neither here nor there. You should order what you want. You know the menu?"

"Yes." Already, Adrienne felt like this was a test she was failing. *Think,* she implored her brain. *What did she want for dinner?* "Steak frites. Actually, no, the crab cake."

"Start with the crab cake. Then you can have the steak. What temp?"

"Rare."

Fiona looked sideways at Antonio. "Got that?"

"Yes, chef," he said. "You feel okay?"

"I'll just have some bisque," Fiona said. She wiped her forehead with a side towel. "I may not come in tomorrow."

"I'm making you a sandwich, too," Antonio said. "You have to eat."

Fiona shooed Antonio out of the walk-in. "All these men telling me what to do," she said. "Did you bring a drink from the front?" she asked Adrienne.

Adrienne held up her champagne. "Would you like anything?"

"I drink water," Fiona said. "Wait for me outside. I'll be just a minute."

Adrienne got a glass of ice water with lemon and carried it out to the plastic picnic table. It was another lovely night. The full moon lit up the whole beach; Adrienne could see her shadow in the sand. She sat in one of the plastic chairs. It was peaceful here. The noise from the bar was reduced to a faint bass line.

Adrienne waited for what seemed like an eternity—she was nervous and hungry—but then Fiona appeared holding two plates and two sets of silverware. She had taken off her chef's jacket to show a white tank top underneath and had let her hair down. Adrienne rose to help her.

"The crab cakes," Fiona said. "Go ahead and sit. I sent Jojo to the bar to get us a bottle of champagne."

"You did?"

"I decided I want some. I haven't had a drink in forever."

Adrienne sat down, staring at the two plump, golden brown crab cakes floating in a pool of Dijon cream. She restrained herself until Fiona sat, then she took a bite, and another. Then, she felt, she had to confess.

"Thatcher was drinking last night," Adrienne said.

"He told me."

"He started while I wasn't looking. I was . . . off somewhere."

"But once you got back, you asked him to stop?"

"I asked him. He didn't stop."

"Of course he didn't," Fiona said. "He's an alcoholic."

"I know."

"Do you know? It's a disease. Thatcher has a disease just like I have a disease."

"I wasn't sure what to do," Adrienne said. "I didn't know anybody at the party except for guests and I didn't feel like I could ask a guest for help."

"It's okay," Fiona said. "I don't mean to scold you."

"But I feel awful . . ."

"Don't," Fiona said. "It's not your fault. It's my fault. I'm the reason why he drinks. I'm the albatross around his neck."

"No, you're not," Adrienne said.

"Yes, I am," Fiona said, in a voice that ended the topic.

Adrienne took another bite of her crab cake and gazed at the water. Next to her, Fiona spooned soup in tiny bites. Adrienne looked at Fiona's hands. There was something funny about her fingers. They were clubbed on the ends and her nails were bluish. Fiona caught Adrienne staring, and Adrienne looked at the sky.

"Full moon," she noted.

"The Native Americans call it the sturgeon moon in August," Fiona said. "That's one of the useless things I happen to know."

Fiona was sweating despite the breeze; she looked sick for the first time to Adrienne, but sick like a normal person, like she might vomit or faint. She took a huge breath and Adrienne could hear the struggle it took to get air in. Then Fiona coughed. She coughed and coughed until her eyes were watering and it looked like her face was falling apart. Adrienne didn't know what to do. Was this the time to call the ambulance? Just then Jojo came out with a bottle of Laurent-Perrier. He set the bottle down and walloped Fiona on the back, like it was the most normal action in the world.

"You okay, chef?" he said.

She coughed a bit more then stood up, moved into the shadows, and spat. When she came back, her face was dark red. "Sorry," she said.

"Please don't worry," Adrienne said. "Would you like some water?"

Fiona chugged the whole glass of water. "Thanks for the bubbly," she said.

"No prob," Jojo said. He was the only Subiaco who was still boyish. Adrienne loved his long eyelashes and his slow smile. He was what a Subiaco looked like before he became smooth like Mario or capable like Antonio or gross like Hector. "I'm going to call it a night."

"Okay," Fiona said. "See you tomorrow."

Jojo left and Fiona reached for the champagne. Gently, Adrienne took the bottle from her, opened it with the softest pop, and poured two glasses.

It might be worse for Adrienne to drink with Fiona than it had been for her to drink with Thatcher. She had no idea. But Fiona seemed eager—she raised her glass in Adrienne's direction and took a long sip.

"How's JZ?" Adrienne asked.

"Married."

"Married," Adrienne agreed. "But you can't doubt that he loves you."

"Sure I can."

"He loves you."

"Yes. But it's not enough. I want him to marry me."

"Oh."

Fiona took another drink and pushed her soup bowl away; she'd barely eaten anything. "You will, no doubt, find this surprising, but I am a big believer in marriage."

"Are you?"

"My whole life that's all I've ever wanted—to be married and have kids. Probably because I've been told since I was young that those two things would never happen. No kids, certainly. My body couldn't handle it. And probably no marriage. No one wants damaged goods."

"Fiona . . ."

"It's true," she said flatly. "If JZ really wanted to, he would have gotten a divorce. He would have taken Shaughnessy and left that awful woman. *Jamie.* She's manipulative and dishonest. But she's not damaged. He doesn't make love to her like she might break."

"Fiona."

"Even if I get off the damn transplant list, there's no guarantee that I'll survive the operation, and if I do survive, they give me another five years. Five years is hardly worth leaving your wife over."

Antonio appeared at the table with their entrées. He set down the steak frites for Adrienne and a grilled cheese and tomato sandwich with frites and a dill pickle for Fiona.

"I'm going home, Fee," he said. "Take tomorrow off, if you want. I can do the special."

"What would you do?" she asked.

"Those tomato flans," he said. "With a red pepper coulis."

"Okay," Fiona said. "Thanks for dinner."

"Yes, thank you," Adrienne said.

Antonio kissed the top of Fiona's head like she was indeed someone who might break. He nodded at Adrienne and disappeared back into the kitchen.

"I don't want you to feel sorry for me," Fiona said. "Because I have things in my life other than JZ. I'm a damn good chef. I have a devoted staff. I've had my own restaurant since I've been twenty-four years old and I'm a woman, okay? It's unheard-of."

"You're the best," Adrienne said.

"You're trying to flatter me," Fiona said. "But I *am* the best. I never wanted to be famous. I never wanted to have my own TV show or my own cookbook or a line of salad dressings. I just wanted to be the best, pure and simple. Next year, when this restaurant is closed there won't be anyone on this island or anywhere else who does things the way we do them. It ends with us."

"You're right," Adrienne said.

"You're still trying to flatter me," Fiona said. "But I *am* right. And that's what I've always wanted, too. Immortality. When I die, I want people to say, 'Nobody cooks like Fiona Kemp anymore. Nobody makes foie gras like Fiona. Nobody makes shrimp bisque like Fiona.'" She slammed back the remainder of her champagne and narrowed her blue eyes. "All these years I've been claiming I cook out of love. But I don't. I've been cooking out of ambition."

"That's okay," Adrienne said. "Ambition is okay."

"Love would have been better," Fiona said.

Somehow they made it to the bottom of the champagne bottle. Adrienne couldn't believe her eyes when she saw Fiona empty the last drops into her glass. Suddenly, Adrienne became aware of certain things: she had finished her steak frites, though she barely remembered eating them. Behind her, the restaurant was quiet and dark, though she didn't recall seeing the lights go off and no one had come out to check on them. According to Adrienne's running watch, it was five past two. Everyone had gone home, including, Adrienne presumed, Thatcher. For the last who-knew-how-long, Adrienne had been talking about herself in a way that used to make her shudder. She was giving herself up, turning herself over. She wanted Fiona to know her.

On the subject of her mother, Adrienne said: *She was a lovely person. The loveliest. Gracious, kind, funny. She died when I was twelve of ovarian cancer.*

I'm sorry, Fiona said. *Do you worry that you'll get it?*

Get what?

Cancer.

No.

On the subject of her father: *He's getting married again after sixteen years. To the woman he brought here, Mavis.*

Will you go to the wedding?

Yes.

When will that be?

October sixteenth.

Oh, Fiona said. *That's my birthday. I'll be thirty-six.*

This was followed by a space of silence.

On the subject of her travels: *My favorite place aside from Nantucket has been Thailand.*

Never been, Fiona said. *Never been anywhere. Not going anywhere.*

Right before Adrienne became aware of the time, she had been regaling Fiona with the story of Doug, the cocaine, the theft of Adrienne's Future, the arrest. Fiona was shaking her head, coughing. She drank some water, then she poured the last of the champagne, and watching it dribble out of the bottle snapped Adrienne out of her reverie. And Fiona, too, because she said, "I think we should talk about Thatcher."

"Should we?" Adrienne said. She was drunk now—*again*—and talking about Thatcher sounded like a bad idea. And yet, the tone of Fiona's voice made it seem like this had been the point of the whole dinner: to talk about Thatcher.

"We should," Fiona said. Her long hair hung over the back of her chair and her face had regained its color—lightly suntanned with freckles across her nose. Adrienne felt her eyes drooping, but Fiona seemed as alert as ever. Alert, intense, focused. What was the first thing Thatch had ever said about her? *My partner, Fiona. She never sleeps.*

"Go ahead," Adrienne said with a grand sweep of her hand. "Talk."

Fiona fidgeted with the crusts of bread on her plate. She'd eaten nearly the whole sandwich and half the pickle. "I've never talked to one of Thatcher's girlfriends like this before," she said.

"He told me he didn't have girlfriends."

"He had a girlfriend in high school. Carrie Tolbert. She hated me," Fiona said. "And he had a girlfriend in college, Bridget, her name was. Hated me. And since he's been on Nantucket . . . the occasional one-night stand he never wanted me to find out about." She took a huge breath, like she was planning on going underwater. "Anyway, here's what I want to tell you, because I think it's only fair you should know. Thatcher and I have a special bond."

For whatever reason, these words incensed Adrienne. They made her as mad as a bee sting, or a glass of ice water in her face, or lemon juice in her eye. Something clicked in her, or unclicked.

"Why don't you tell me about it?" Adrienne said. "You can start by telling me how you've known each other since you were in diapers. Then you can tell me about how you walked together on the first day of kindergarten and about how he tried to kiss you on top of the slide the night before tenth grade started when you were out drinking on the elementary school playground. I've heard it. You pushed him away. But you never let him go. You invited him to Nantucket because you knew he would sell everything he had and hand it over to you. Now it's twelve years later and the man is as devoted to you as ever. You wonder why he never has girlfriends, and why the ones he did have resented you. You *wonder*!" Adrienne paused. She felt like a bottle of Laurent-Perrier that had been violently shaken and then opened, spewing everywhere. Restraint was a mountaintop on a faraway continent. She couldn't stop herself. "I can't believe you have the nerve to tell me you have a special bond like I am too *stupid* to have figured it out on my own. Where do you think I've been the last three months, Fiona? He's my boyfriend. I sleep with him every night. But you think I don't know that you're in bed with us, too? That you never leave his mind? I get it, Fiona. Your relationship is special. It is more special than my relationship with Thatcher. It is the most special."

Fiona was quiet, staring out at the moonlit water like she hadn't even heard. "I was afraid this would happen."

"What?"

"You're upset."

"I'm not upset," Adrienne shouted. "I'd just like some credit for understanding how things are. My first date with the man he ate exactly nothing and left me cold as soon as you called. The night he first told me he loved me he made sure he mentioned that he loved you, too. 'Differently,' he said, whatever that means."

"It means we're friends," Fiona said. "Nothing but friends."

"Nothing but friends!" Adrienne said incredulously. "Thatcher is yours and he's been yours all along."

"I've never seen him like he is this summer," Fiona said. "You changed him. He's different. He's happy."

"That may be," Adrienne said. "But it won't mean much in the end. You know it and I know it." She threw her napkin onto her empty plate and moved her chair back from the table. "This was a nice dinner. I enjoyed myself. But just now I can't figure out why you invited me here. Did you want to *gloat*?"

"No," Fiona said. In the moonlight, her tank top and pants looked very white, like she was an angel. Or a ghost. "I wanted to say I was sorry."

TO: DrDon@toothache.com

FROM: Ade12177@hotmail.com

DATE: August 16, 2005, 9:33 A.M.

SUBJECT: the sturgeon moon

The full moon in August is called the sturgeon moon by the Native Americans. There's a piece of useless trivia to share with your patients.

Did you know that the summer you sent me to Camp Hideaway I lied to all the girls in my cabin? I told them my brother was dying. Jonathan. I tried to tell myself that it wasn't exactly a lie because I did have a brother Jonathan who died. But for years I wondered what it was that made me say that. Why not just say Mom was sick? I wasn't okay saying she was sick and I've never been okay saying that she's dead. I never learned to deal with it, Dad. I never learned how to make it okay in my own mind.

I know the girls in my cabin had a reunion later that summer. Pammy Ipp told me about it in a letter. They all met at the Cherry Hill Mall and ate at the food court. She wrote to let me know I hadn't been invited.

Love.

TO: Ade12177@hotmail.com
FROM: DrDon@toothache.com
DATE: August 16, 2005, 10:27 A.M.
SUBJECT: none

Honey, are you all right? Love, love, love.

TO: kyracrenshaw@mindspring.com
FROM: Ade12177@hotmail.com
DATE: August 16, 2005, 9:42 A.M.
SUBJECT: Another season

I don't know how things got so messed up. I came here for money and money I now have. I thought that was what I wanted—money saved up for my Future. Then I fell in love and now my wanting is ten-fold but the problem is that what I want doesn't have a price. It's this big, important, shapeless thing—I want to be loved in return, I want my situation to be different, somehow, but I don't even know how. I thought I had problems in Aspen. Ha! I did not. In comparison, I did not.

TO: Ade12177@hotmail.com
FROM: kyracrenshaw@mindspring.com
DATE: August 16, 2005, 12:02 P.M.
SUBJECT: Another season

Adrienne, are you all right?

12

It's Okay if You Don't Love Me

Darla and Grayson Parrish were getting divorced. They had been married forty-two years, but twelve of those years were tainted by Grayson's adulterous relationship with Nonnie Sizemore from Darla's bridge group. Nonnie Sizemore was six months older than Darla and fifty pounds heavier. She was a clownish woman, Darla told Adrienne, jolly, she talked a lot, laughed a lot, ate and drank a lot. She smoked. Darla wouldn't say she had always pitied Nonnie Sizemore, who had been divorced from her husband since 1973, but she would say she had never envied her. And she certainly never believed Nonnie was capable of betrayal—but, in fact, Nonnie had been sleeping with Grayson for a dozen years. They had even snuck off for a week together some years earlier to Istanbul. Grayson had claimed business—the hunt for tile and stone—in Europe. But Istanbul! It was a place that held zero appeal for Darla, and she had to admit it was possible that she'd lost touch of how different her predilections were from those of her husband. They had practically nothing to talk about.

"I did notice your dinners this summer were a little . . . quiet," Adrienne said. She and Darla were sitting at table nineteen in the most secluded corner of the restaurant. It was occupied every night, but Adrienne always thought of it as the table where Leon Cross sat when he ate with his mistress. She thought of it as the table where Thatcher did the bills each night.

Now it was the table where Darla Parrish had bravely decided to eat alone. She wouldn't give up the standing Tuesday and Friday night reservations, not when the restaurant was less than two weeks away from closing. She could have invited other people to dine with her—her sister Eleanor, her best friend Sandy Beyrer—but that felt like denial somehow. She was to be a single woman; she would eat alone, with Adrienne as occasional company. Ten minutes here or there; Darla appreciated whatever time Adrienne could spare.

"Watching you gives me hope," Darla said. "When you leave this island for the next fabulous place, you call me. I'm going with you."

For three nights running, Thatcher had spent the night at Fiona's house. Fiona slept hooked up to an oximeter, and when her O_2 sats dropped, an alarm sounded. Thatcher was there to respond to the alarm, call an ambulance, get Fiona to the hospital, and although this hadn't happened, he wasn't sleeping. He showed up at work with his hair parted on the wrong side and his cuffs buttoned incorrectly. He misplaced his watch for twenty-four hours. In the days since Holt Millman's party, the only real conversation that Adrienne had had with Thatcher was about the lost watch. He bought it for himself with his profits from the Bistro the first year. The watch and the Bistro were linked in his mind. He received compliments on the watch every night; once, Charlie Sheen had tried to buy it right off his wrist.

Adrienne understood how certain objects could hold real value, though she didn't have anything herself that was worth anything—except now, a couple of great pairs of shoes. She offered to help Thatcher search Fiona's place, but when she suggested this, he backed up.

"Whatever," he said. "It's just a watch."

The following morning, however, when Fiona's cleaning lady found the watch on the windowsill of Fiona's bathroom, Thatcher's mood improved. He led Adrienne from the podium into the wine cave, where they made love standing up with Adrienne's back against the cooling unit. It seemed sneaky and cheap, and Adrienne thought miserably of the one-night stands Fiona had mentioned.

"I love you," Adrienne said.

Thatcher kissed her neck in response, then he laughed. "Ha!"

She could tell he was thinking about the watch, and sure enough, once Adrienne was back at the phone, Thatcher asked her to clear a table for Consuela, Fiona's cleaning lady—dinner for two, on him.

Three nights without Thatcher turned into five, six, seven.

"It's been a whole week," Adrienne said to Caren. It was another hot, sunny morning. They sat at the sawed-off table in the shade of the backyard, Adrienne drinking tea, Caren drinking espresso and poring over the Pottery Barn catalog. She needed furniture for her new apartment.

Caren looked up from a page of leather sofas. "Are you worried?"

"I'm furious," Adrienne said. She was in her running clothes, ready to put on her shoes and go. But now that she had Caren's attention, she wanted to keep it. "I know I should feel sorry for Fiona, but I can't."

Caren bit her thumbnail. "That's tricky."

"You think I'm horrible," Adrienne said. "I am horrible." She stared at her bare feet. They were tan with white lines from the straps of her flip-flops; her toenails were painted "ripe raspberry." These were the feet of a woman who had learned to stand for eight-hour stretches, and who had learned to walk in slides and sling backs with a four-inch heel. These were the feet of a woman who had kicked the bad habit of lying about her past and who had learned to trust a man and love him. The summer had been so brilliant. What was happening to her sense of peace, her happiness? What was happening to her?

Since her dinner with Fiona, Adrienne had tried to stay out of the kitchen, but she couldn't avoid the normal course of her job. She had to pick up the chips and dip; she had to help the waitstaff. The previous evening, when Adrienne walked into the kitchen to put in a VIP order for the owner of American Seasons, she found Fiona whipping a side towel against the pass like she was a jockey in the Kentucky Derby. The sweat streamed down her face, her hair was matted to her head.

"Ordering table one: one chowder, one bisque. Who are these people eating soup when it's so hot?" She glanced over at Adrienne. "And you, my dear, look as fresh as a fucking daisy."

Adrienne could not get past her fury. It was a boulder blocking her path.

Adrienne left Caren to her armchairs and ottomans. Caren couldn't handle Adrienne's anger. There was, perhaps, only one person who could.

Adrienne pulled Drew Amman-Keller's card out of the top drawer of her desk.

She thought he might sound smug, or victorious, but when Drew Amman-Keller answered the phone and learned it was Adrienne calling, he treated her like a friend.

"Adrienne, how's the summer going? I mean to come in one more time before you close, but, as you know, I'm at the mercy of Mr. Millman. That was some party last week, wasn't it?"

"Yeah," Adrienne said. She closed the door to her bedroom even though Caren was still outside. And Duncan—was he lurking around somewhere, or was he golfing? Adrienne hadn't even thought to ask. She was discombobulated. She had mustered the guts to call, but now what?

"So . . ." Drew said. "Is there something I can do for you or did you just call to chat?"

She pictured him licking his womanish lips.

"I called to talk to you about Fiona."

Drew Amman-Keller cleared his throat. "Would you like to talk in person? You could come here or I could come to you."

His voice was low and smooth, like a lover suggesting a rendezvous. Adrienne moved into the doorway of her closet.

"No," she said.

"Okay, then, the phone."

"The phone."

There was silence. Drew Amman-Keller was either feeling as awkward as she was or else his silence was a tactic to get her to talk. And what, exactly, was she going to tell him? Did she tell him about the concealed illness, the transplant list, the affair with the married delivery driver, the smothering friendship with Thatcher? What Adrienne needed was a friend—someone to take her side, someone to sympathize with her. She had shown up on this island with an empty Future box. Now she had plenty of money but she had nowhere to go and no plans. Her life was so devoid of people who cared that she was forced to talk to a reporter.

Drew Amman-Keller took a breath. "I can pay you," he said.

Adrienne hung up.

■

She spent the rest of the day feeling both proud of herself for shutting the lid on Drew Amman-Keller and ashamed of herself for calling him in the first place. She went to Dionis Beach and lay in the hot sun at low tide. She felt her anger wilting. On the way to work that night, she stopped at Pam's salon and bought Thatcher a gift certificate for a massage. She gave it to him before menu meeting.

"Ha! When am I supposed to use this?"

"I don't know," Adrienne said. "It only takes an hour."

"Ha!"

"What is wrong with you?" Adrienne said. She felt blood rise to the surface of her face; the hair on her arms stood up. They were going to fight, and she was glad. She wanted a fight. The phone rang, the private line. Tempting, but she ignored it.

Thatcher didn't even seem to hear the phone. "I'm tired," he said.

"That's a cop-out," Adrienne said. "We're all tired. I'm just trying to figure out what's going on. You don't . . ."

He pointed a Blue Bistro pencil at her nose. "I don't what?"

"You don't say you love me anymore."

"I love you."

"That wasn't very convincing."

"Why do I have to convince you?"

"Because!" she said. "Our sex life . . . you don't stay over . . ."

"I've been up for seven straight nights at Fiona's, hoping and praying that she doesn't stop *breathing*!" He snapped the pencil in half across the back of his hand, and the pieces sailed through the air, bounced off the wooden floor, and rolled under the podium.

"Father Ott said he'd spell you. Let him take a night or two."

"So I can focus on our sex life?"

"No," Adrienne said.

"No, my ass. That's what you want."

"I want you to get some sleep," Adrienne said.

"I thought you said my being tired was a cop-out."

The phone rang again. Private line. Adrienne watched the blinking light. *Pick it up?* She was getting nowhere with Thatcher.

"You've stopped caring about me," Adrienne said.

"You know that's not true."

"Do I?"

"I told you it was going to be like this," Thatcher said. "I told you I was limited in what I could give and you said that was okay. You said you understood. However, it sounds very much like you don't understand. Now, answer the phone, please."

Adrienne snatched up the private line, glaring at him. "Good evening, Blue Bistro."

"Harry Henderson calling for Thatcher, please."

Thatcher disappeared into the kitchen.

"He's not available right now, Harry."

"Not available? He and Fiona are supposed to sign the closing documents tomorrow morning. We have ten days to put this deal to bed. I expect them at noon, and I don't want to hear that they're too busy making bouillabaisse. Not *available*? Really, Adrienne, I expected more from you."

August twenty-fourth: two hundred and fifty covers on the book, thirty-two reservation wait list, and then Adrienne disconnected both of the public phone lines. The special was lobster ravioli with a charred tomato cream sauce. They served it at family meal and Adrienne ate until she felt heavy and lethargic.

The Elperns arrived at six o'clock with their new baby, Sebastian. Adrienne tried to exude enthusiasm when she gazed at Sebastian's chubby cheeks, but she contradictorily felt both stuffed and deflated. Scott held the baby in the infant car seat, and Lucy held out the blueprints for their fat mansion. They had been to Harry Henderson's office to sign the closing documents that morning and tonight was a celebration of that. In ten days, the restaurant would be theirs. Adrienne was the only person they knew at the Bistro; she had somehow become intimately involved in this new phase of their lives. They thought of her as a friend, and while she was flattered, it took all of her strength just to smile and coo at the baby appropriately. She envied them—not because they were technology billionaires and not because they were buying the building that Adrienne now loved better than any building on earth—but because of their family-ness: Mama, Papa, baby. They were smug without meaning to be, smug about the simplest and yet most enduring things in life—their love for each other, their love for their child.

Adrienne was amazed at the transformation in Lucy Elpern; only four weeks after giving birth, every part of her previously swollen body was now slender and tight, except for her breasts, which were alluringly large. Tyler Lefroy ogled Lucy when he walked past with a sweating water pitcher.

"You're under the awning tonight," Adrienne told the Elperns. She led them to the far edge of the awning, table twenty-two, where nobody would be bothered by a crying baby, or startled by the sight of Lucy Elpern's enormous, exposed breast as she nursed Sebastian.

"I just love this restaurant," Lucy Elpern said. "It seems such a shame to tear it down."

Scott Elpern locked eyes with Adrienne. He grinned. "But wait until you see the plans for our indoor pool!"

"Indoor pool!" Adrienne said to Duncan five minutes later at the bar. He slid her a flute of champagne that she was too full to drink. "They're building an indoor pool."

Duncan shrugged. "It's their house," he said. "They can do whatever they want."

"Indoor pool!" Adrienne said to Caren as they walked to the kitchen. Adrienne had to put in a VIP order for the Elperns.

Caren said, "Can you run apps for me? Table five?"

"Did you hear what I said? About the indoor pool?"

"I heard you. Did you hear me?"

"Indoor pool!" Adrienne said to Mario between seatings. The Elperns had further regaled her with details of their new house and had asked her if she wanted to hold the baby. She declined, claiming an oncoming cold. "They're building a six-thousand-square-foot house with an indoor pool. The HDC didn't bat an eye. They break ground September fifteenth."

"These people are loaded, right?" Mario said. "You think they want to invest in our new restaurant? You know them. It couldn't hurt to ask."

Adrienne thought she tasted blood in her mouth. Her eyes stung and she bowed her head. Only ten days left and nobody seemed to care. Everybody was already gone.

At midnight, Adrienne had a line forty people long and the bar was hopping. Duncan blared the CD player—no need to comply with the noise ordinance at this late date—he was convinced that the louder the music, the more people drank. Thatcher emerged from the dancing crowd with the cash box and receipts clutched to his chest. For the first time in days, he was smiling. On his way into the kitchen, he stopped and kissed Adrienne in a slow, searching way. Someone from the back of the line yelled, "Get a room!"

Adrienne felt a surge of hope. "What did I do to deserve that?" she asked.

Thatcher answered, but the music was so loud, she didn't hear what he said.

The kiss changed her channel. She let two people into the bar just for the heck of it, she sang along to the music. The questions in her brain melted away: *Are you okay? Am I okay? It's okay if you don't love me. Do you love me?*

When Thatcher ran out of the kitchen and grabbed both her wrists and shook her—he was shaking her and yelling, yelling! but she couldn't hear what he was saying—she knew that this was the beginning of the end. Bruce Springsteen was assaulting the room at ninety decibels and it took Adrienne several seconds to make out the words coming from Thatcher's mouth. *It's Fee. It's Fee. Get everybody out! Everybody out!*

Adrienne didn't know what to do. She picked up the phone. 911? Thatcher slammed the receiver back down. He raced to the bar and turned off the music; the crowd booed. Duncan whipped around. "Hey!"

"The bar is closing," Thatcher announced. "Right now. Tabs are forgiven, but I have to ask you all to leave immediately. We'll reopen tomorrow night at six."

There was a din of chatter. Adrienne could sense the guests' confusion, their resistance. Thatcher grabbed the hand bell and swung it through the air like a madman swinging a hatchet. Adrienne eyed the kitchen door. *It's Fee.*

People filed past her. "Sorry about this," she said, as calmly as she could. "We'll see you tomorrow." The stench of emergency was in the air—this was even before Adrienne heard the approaching sirens—and someone said the word "fire." There was pushing. One woman stumbled; the heel broke off her shoe and the people behind her piled up, yelling, "Get up! Get out!"

"There's no fire," Adrienne said loudly. "But you have to go. No fire. Please go. See you tomorrow."

Because there was still a crowd in the parking lot—guests lingering, trying to figure out what was going *on*—the paramedics took Fiona out through the back door. Adrienne saw her on the stretcher, and she rallied the staff to act as a barrier to the public. Adrienne stood shoulder to shoulder with Caren and Joe and next to Joe was Spillman and next to Caren was Duncan and Elliott and Christo and Louis and Hector and young Jojo on the end, crying. And Delilah was crying. Fiona was unconscious, her face ashen, her lips blue. The paramedics slapped an oxygen mask on her face and they did a lot of shouting, numbers, a code. Thatcher climbed into the back of the ambulance and the doors slammed shut behind him. Adrienne felt an arm around her—Mario. The ambulance cut a path through the crowd and sped off, sirens wailing.

Adrienne turned to Mario. "Now what?" she said. "What do we do?" She wanted to hitch a ride to the hospital. She wanted to be with Thatcher, but Mario steered her back toward the Bistro.

"Close out the bar," he said. "Get the money. Go home."

"Go home? But what about . . ."

"They'll medevac her to Boston," Mario said. "She'll be at Mass General in less than an hour. It's okay."

"I don't know how you can say that," Adrienne said, and she went inside.

■

August twenty-fifth: two hundred and fifty covers on the book, twenty reservation wait list. There was no tomato special; Antonio was too distraught to put one together. Adrienne had received a phone call from Thatcher at five o'clock that morning. He talked, Adrienne listened.

"Keep the restaurant open. No matter what happens, keep it open. She's in and out of consciousness. She wants the restaurant open. That's all she asks, *Is the restaurant open?* I tell her yes. The answer has to be yes."

Adrienne swallowed. Her voice was thick with sleep. "Should I call JZ?"

"I already called him."

"Is he coming?"

"No."

"Why not?"

"She says she doesn't want to see him."

"She's lying."

"That's not for you to say." Thatcher paused. "It's really not."

"Okay," Adrienne said. "Sorry."

"You don't know what this is like for me," he said.

"Sure I do," Adrienne said. "I watched my mother die."

"How is that the same thing?"

"Because . . ."

"Because Fiona is dying. Is that what you mean? It just so happens, they're trying another drug today, okay? Another drug!"

"Why are you fighting with me?" Adrienne said. "Thatcher, I love you."

"I have to go," he said. "I'll call you later." And he hung up.

At ten o'clock, Adrienne fielded phone calls, including a call from the *Inquirer and Mirror* with a reporter asking about the emergency vehicle the night before. Adrienne offered no comment. She was edgy, distracted. After she'd hung up with Thatcher she'd lain awake until the sun rose. Adrienne felt like she had just thrown something of enormous value into the ocean and watched it sink. Lost forever.

When the Sid Wainer truck pulled into the parking lot, she went to the door, her heart knocked around. She would talk to JZ. But the driver wasn't JZ; it was some young kid, blond, tan, too good-looking.

"Where's JZ?" Adrienne asked.

"He's out," the kid said. "Sick."

That night, family meal was ten pizzas from the Muse. Adrienne wanted to say something at menu meeting, but what to say? Fiona's left lung had collapsed, she was coughing up blood, her O_2 sats were very low. The lung infection she'd been battling all summer was back, but they were trying a new drug. That, and praying for a lung donor. Thatcher had given Adrienne these stark details but had asked her not to share them. And so, Adrienne sat quietly at the twelve-top while the staff ate pizza. She watched Tyler stuff half a piece in his mouth like a healthy eighteen-year-old boy who was ten days away from having every freedom of his young life rescinded at military college. She watched Caren, who was eating a bowl of lettuce that she had swiped from the reach-in. She watched Joe, who ate his pizza neatly, with a knife and fork. The staff looked tired, worried, uninspired. Adrienne lifted a slice of pepperoni off the greasy paper plate, but she couldn't eat. She was starving, ravenous, but food wasn't going to help. She was hungry for something else: the phone ringing, Thatcher's voice, good news, love.

And yet, the restaurant opened at six and service began: the pretzel bread, the mustard, the doughnuts, the VIP orders, the crab cakes, the steak frites, the fondue. Antonio expedited, the kitchen sent out impeccable plates, Rex played the piano, Duncan poured drinks, Tyler Lefroy complained that he was working twice as hard as Gage who, he informed Adrienne, had gotten *stoned* before work. The guests laughed, talked, paid their bills, left tips, raved about the food. No one could tell there was a single thing wrong.

Holt Millman was in, table twenty, party of four. *Better than ever,* he said. *Tell Fiona I said so.*

Thatcher didn't call. Adrienne left him a message with the totals from the floor and the bar. She said nothing else.

August twenty-sixth: two hundred and fifty covers, thirty-six reservation wait list. The special was an inside-out BLT: mâche, crispy pancetta, and a round garlic crouton sandwiched between two slices of tomato, drizzled with basil aioli. Adrienne's stomach growled at the sight of it, but she couldn't eat.

Cat was in, having fondue at one of the four-tops in the sand. They polished off a magnum of Laurent-Perrier, then ordered port. So Cat was tipsy and then some when, at the end of the night, she pulled Adrienne aside.

"There are rumors going around," Cat said.

"Really?" Adrienne said. "What's the word?"

"The word is that Fiona is dead."

Adrienne laughed; it was a strange sound, even to her own ears. "No," Adrienne said. "She's not dead."

The next morning, Adrienne called her father at work. She got Mavis on the phone, who said, "Adrienne, doll, he's with a patient. Can I have him call you?"

"I have to speak with him now," Adrienne said.

Mavis put Adrienne on hold to some awful Muzak and Adrienne stared at the calendar in the front of the reservation book. One week left. That was it. She took a deep breath. Well, there was always Darla Parrish, who kept insisting she was going to accompany Adrienne into the next chapter. Adrienne couldn't decide if that made her feel better or worse.

Her father came on the phone. "Honey, is everything all right?"

When Adrienne took a breath to answer, a sob escaped. She cried into the phone and imagined herself facedown on a childhood bed she had long forgotten—her father and her mother, too, smoothing her hair, patting her back, telling her not to worry, telling her everything was going to be just fine.

August twenty-seventh: two hundred and fifty covers, twenty-three reservation wait list. Special: whole ripe tomatoes cut into quarters and served with salt and pepper. Antonio decided on this simple preparation as a tribute to Fiona. A man at table two complained that it wasn't fancy enough. "I've been hearing all about these tomato specials," he said. "And this is what you give me?"

Adrienne removed his plate. “Don’t you get it?” she said. “The tomato is perfect as it is.”

He didn’t get it. He ordered the foie gras cooked through.

That night, at quarter to three, the phone rang. Adrienne had just gotten home. Caren and Duncan were opening a bottle of Failla pinot noir that they had stolen from the wine cave.

Caren said, “Who calls at this hour?”

Adrienne had a funny feeling and she snapped up the phone.

“Hello?” she said.

“Adrienne?” It was Thatcher, but something was wrong with his voice. Then she realized he was crying.

“Thatcher?” she said.

The line clicked. She held a dial tone. She called Thatch back on his cell phone but it went to his voice mail. “It’s me,” she said. “Call me back.”

Caren glanced up from the Pottery Barn catalog. She and Duncan were talking drapes.

“Thatch?” she said.

Adrienne managed a nod.

“Did he say anything?”

“Nothing.”

“Want a glass of wine?” Caren said.

“Yes,” Adrienne said.

She didn’t sleep. She finished the bottle of wine and opened another, then she sat at the kitchen table and listened to the muted sounds of Caren and Duncan’s lovemaking. She called Thatcher three more times—all three calls went to his voice mail, but she didn’t leave a message. Caren came out to use the bathroom and when she saw Adrienne sitting at the table, she offered her a Percocet. Adrienne took it. It made her loopy and vague, but it didn’t put her to sleep. At five thirty, the sun rose. Adrienne watched the light through the leaves of the trees in the backyard, and when she couldn’t wait another second, she hopped on her bike and rode to the restaurant.

The red Durango was in the parking lot. Mario was in way too early for work. The door to the Bistro was swinging open; when Adrienne stepped through, she saw him sitting at the bar with a drink, a Scotch. He looked at her.

"She's dead?" Adrienne said.

He tossed back the last of his drink, then brought the glass down so hard that it cracked in his hand. He left the damaged glass on the bar and walked toward Adrienne. Adrienne was numb; she had no thoughts.

"There's something else you have to know," Mario said. He hugged her.

"What's that?" Adrienne asked. Her fingers and toes were tingling. She pressed her tongue into the fibers of Mario's cotton shirt. She wanted to taste something.

"Thatcher married her yesterday afternoon. Father Ott was there. He married them in the hospital chapel at two o'clock. Fiona slipped into a coma at nine. She died at two this morning."

"Thatcher married her?"

"He married her."

Adrienne waited to feel something. She thought of Thatcher carrying Fiona toward the phosphorescent ocean, carrying her the same way a groom carries a bride over the threshold. Adrienne had been so jealous then, so typically sorry for herself, as she wondered, *Who is going to carry me?* But now she didn't feel jealous or sad or lonely. She didn't feel anything.

She sat next to Mario on a bar stool and rested her cheek on the cool blue granite. Her eyes fell closed. She felt her mind drifting away.

When she awoke, with a crick in her neck and a flat spot on her face, it was because the phone was ringing. She went to the podium. Line one. Adrienne checked her watch: nine o'clock. *Reporter,* she thought. *Drew Amman-Keller.* She hadn't told him anything. In the end, she hadn't told him a thing.

She pushed open the kitchen door. It was quiet except for the hum of the refrigerators, and it was clean. The floors had been mopped the night before, the pass buffed to a shine, the trash had been emptied, there was a stack of clean side towels on the counter. Adrienne picked one up and pressed it to her face. This was Fiona's kitchen without Fiona. Fiona was dead.

Adrienne found Mario in pastry, surrounded by his usual tools: the mixing cups, the measuring spoons, the stainless-steel bowl that was as big as a wagon wheel. He had flour out, baking powder, butter, and a brick of Gruyère cheese. "Good, you're awake," he said. "You can help me."

"You're cooking?"

"I want to make crackers."

"Crackers."

"We have to call the staff in at eleven," he said. "We have to tell them the restaurant is closing. I want to have the crackers. You know, as something nice."

"The restaurant is closing?" This, somehow, pierced her. No more restaurant. Dead, like Fiona.

"Oh, honey," Mario said. He patted a high stool where she sat like a child to watch Mario work. He measured flour, grated the Gruyère with his microplane rasp until the brick was a fluffy mound, cut in the butter, mixed up a dough. He rolled the dough into three logs, wrapped them in plastic, and put them in the reach-in to chill. He made Adrienne an espresso, which she threw back joylessly. That, she vowed, would be the last espresso of her life.

"How do you make yourself do it?" she asked him. "Cook at a time like this. Aren't you sad?"

"Sad?" he said. "My compadre, my mentor, my *friend,* she's dead. I'm more than sad, honey. I'm something else, something I don't even have a word for. But cooking saves me. It's what I do, it's who I am. I stop cooking, I'm the one who dies."

"I want something like that," Adrienne said. "I want something to do, someone to be. I don't have that. I've never had that."

"You're good at being beautiful."

She knew he meant this as a compliment, but it only proved her point. She was nothing. She had nobody.

Mario retrieved the dough from the walk-in and sliced the logs into thin discs, then laid them out on three cookie sheets. He handed Adrienne a jar of dried thyme and showed her how to lightly dust the crackers, then he put the cookie sheets in the oven.

"I'm going to have a cigarette," he said.

"You don't smoke," she said.

"I do today. You want to come?"

"I'll stay here," she said. She sat on the stool and felt the heat rise from the oven; minutes later, pastry was filled with the smell of the cheese and the thyme. Mario reappeared. He pulled the cookie sheets out of the oven.

The crackers were crispy and fragrant. *Ninety-nine percent of the world think that crackers only come out of a box . . .*

Mario offered her one and Adrienne let him place it on her tongue like a Communion wafer.

"This," he said, "was the easy part."

As Adrienne returned to the dining room, the Sid Wainer truck pulled into the parking lot. She hoped and prayed for the blond kid, but no such luck. JZ walked in. The phone rang, Adrienne ignored it. She was frightened when she looked at JZ. He was filled with something and about to burst from too much of it. Grief, rage, and the something else that nobody had a word for. She stepped out from behind the podium and hugged him.

"I'm so sorry, JZ."

"No one is as sorry as I am." Adrienne let him go. His eyes were watering and Adrienne held out the side towel, but he just stared at it. "You're closing?" he said.

"Yes."

He picked up the bowl of matches and Adrienne feared he might smash it against the wall, but he just held it for a few seconds, then put it back down. "I bought that bowl for her in Boston two years ago," he said. "She was at Mass General then and I went to visit her. We'd just started dating."

"I can't imagine how awful this must be for you," Adrienne said.

"She wouldn't let me come this time," he said. "I didn't get to see her."

"JZ . . ."

JZ stared into the bowl. "Thatcher married her."

"I know."

"She really wanted to be married. I should have done it a long time ago."

"I would have liked that better," Adrienne said.

"But I couldn't. My hands were tied."

"So you've said."

"She never believed that."

"I'm sure she understood."

"She said she did, but she didn't. And now she's dead."

Adrienne nodded.

"I wanted to see her. But Thatch is taking her body . . ." Here, JZ paused, put his hands over his eyes. His left leg was shaking. "He's taking her body back to South Bend. Her parents want a family-only service at their church." He looked at Adrienne, tears falling down his face. "I can't even go to her funeral."

Adrienne held out the side towel again, but JZ didn't take it. The phone rang. Line one. Adrienne wanted to smash the phone against the wall. She still had to call everyone on the staff and have them in here in an hour. The ringing phone seemed to keep JZ from careening into the abyss of his own sadness. He straightened, cleared his throat.

"I should go. I'm making deliveries today. Today's my last day."

"You're quitting?"

"I need to be closer to my family. Shaughnessy."

"That makes sense," Adrienne said. Suddenly, she felt angry at JZ. She guessed being "closer to my family" meant that he would get back together with his wife. So Thatcher had been right. JZ had never risked anything for Fiona at all, not really. He was nobody's hero. Sorrow flooded Adrienne's stomach; she couldn't even fake a smile. "I guess I'll see you later?"

"No," he said. "I'm never coming back."

At eleven, the staff sat around table nine much as they had at the very first menu meeting of the summer: Delilah next to Duncan, Joe, Spillman, Elliott, Christo, Caren, Gage, Roy, Tyler. The Subiacos sat at the adjoining table—Antonio, Hector, Louis, Henry, Eddie, Paco, Jojo. Bruno was in the kitchen brewing espressos and Adrienne stood with Mario holding the baskets of crackers. The place was silent. Everyone knew Fiona was dead, and yet Mario took it upon himself to announce it.

"Fiona died at two o'clock this morning at Mass General. Thatcher was with her."

There was crying. The loudest crying was from Delilah, but the men cried, too—Spillman and Antonio and Joe. Adrienne didn't cry and neither did Caren. Adrienne squinted at the ocean. It was an exquisite day, which seemed so wrong. Everything was wrong.

"Are we staying open?" Paco asked.

"No," Mario said. "We're closing."

"So that's it, then?" Eddie said. "It's over?"

"It's over."

Mario had a sheaf of envelopes and he handed one to each staff member.

Checks. Five thousand dollars for each year employed at the Blue Bistro. Caren's check was for sixty thousand dollars; Adrienne's was for five. Adrienne studied her name typed on the light blue bank check: *Adrienne Dealey.* She remembered back to her first morning, the breakfast. She had taken a gamble, and she had lost. *It's okay if you don't love me,* she thought. But it wasn't okay.

There was still work to do. Adrienne had to call every guest who was on the books for the next five days. It took several hours and she was worried her voice would falter, but it didn't. *The restaurant is closing early. All reservations are cancelled. We're sorry for the inconvenience. I'm sorry . . . that's all I can tell you.* Mario brought her a pile of crackers on a napkin. The rest of the staff was getting drunk at the bar—Duncan was pouring—though some, like Tyler, Elliott, and Christo, had left right away. Adrienne cancelled with Holt Millman's secretary, Dottie Shore, she cancelled with Darla, she cancelled with Cat, the Devlins, the Kennedys, Leon Cross, and the local author.

What happened? Darla asked, Dottie Shore asked, the local author asked.

I'm sorry, Adrienne said. She felt badly because she liked these people, she felt she knew them though she probably didn't and they certainly didn't know her. They would never understand the blow she'd been dealt: *Thatcher married Fiona before she died.* They would never know how her heart felt stripped and exposed, like the yolk of an egg separated from its whole, like a child without a mother.

I'm sorry, she said. *That's all I can tell you.*

The last person Adrienne called was Mack Peterson. Guests from the Beach Club held thirty-seven reservations in the last five nights. Thatcher had been right about Mack: He was good for business.

"We're closing early," Adrienne said. "Please convey to your guests how sorry we are for the inconvenience."

"They'll get over it," Mack said. "The important thing is that everyone there is all right. Is everyone all right?"

"I'm sorry," Adrienne said. "All I can tell you is that we're closing. But thank you, Mack, for all the business you sent us."

"Half my staff leaves on Labor Day and we're open another six weeks," Mack said. "If you're looking for a job, call me. I would love to hire you."

"That's very kind," Adrienne said. "Thank you."

She crossed the last names from the reservation sheet and double-checked her list to make sure she hadn't forgotten anyone. She called Bartlett Farm to cancel their vegetable order, she called East Coast Seafood, she called Caviarteria in New York, she called the mushroom company in Kennett Square, she called Classic Wines, she called Flowers on Chestnut, she called the cleaning crew. Closing, closing, closing. And then it was done.

Mario walked out of the back carrying two steaming plates: omelets.

"You want?"

"No," she said.

"Come on, you have to eat something."

"Something," she said. "But not that."

"I'll tell you a secret," Mario said. "Me and Louis and the cousins are looking to buy Sloop's down on Steamship Wharf. Maybe this fall if we can get the money. Open it up next summer as Calamari Café, Italian with Cuban accents. Antonio as chef. We want you to work the front."

Adrienne shut her eyes. She was shocked that Mario would mention his new restaurant on the very morning that Fiona had died. And yet, wasn't that human nature—the desire to move forward, to move away from the bad, sad news? Wasn't that what Adrienne and Dr. Don had been doing their whole lives? Hadn't they always hoped that grief was something they could run away from? Adrienne imagined the Italian-Cuban café that the Subiacos would open next June. It would be a great place. Another great place.

"Sorry," Adrienne said.

Mario cocked his head. "Come on, you think about it."

"Thank you," she said. "But no."

"Okay," Mario said, holding out the omelets. "I'll give these away to somebody else."

■

Caren, Bruno, and Spillman sat at the bar, drinking, and eating omelets.

"Fiona was like my sister," Caren said. "I didn't always like her, but I always loved her."

"She knew we loved her," Bruno said.

Spillman set his beer down on top of his check. "I don't even want this money," he said.

"You could give it to charity," Duncan said.

"Red would kill me," Spillman said.

Caren glanced at Adrienne then reached out for her hand. "Are you all done?"

"Yeah."

"So have a drink. Champagne?"

"I can't," Adrienne said. "I don't care if I ever drink champagne again."

"How about something else?" Caren asked. "Martini?"

"No," Adrienne said.

"You look awful. Sit down. How about a Coke?" Duncan pulled out a glass and hit the gun. He slid the Coke across the bar.

"I don't feel like it," Adrienne said. "I'm tired."

"You can sleep for the rest of the week," Caren said. "This is going to be the last time to sit with all of us."

Joe came out of the kitchen. He put his arm around Adrienne and kissed her temple.

"Thatcher married her," Adrienne said. She gazed at the surprised faces of Spillman and Bruno, the downcast eyes of Duncan and Caren who had probably suspected as much all along. Joe tightened his grip on Adrienne's shoulder.

"It was the right thing to do," Adrienne said. This was the only way she could bear to think of it: as a generous gesture on Thatcher's part. A good deed. But she knew it was just as likely that Fiona did it as a favor to Thatcher, that he'd begged her. He loved Fiona more than any woman in the world. Not romantically, maybe, but he loved her just the same. "I don't feel much like hanging out."

"No," Caren whispered.

"I'm going home to get some sleep," Adrienne said.

Caren passed her the keys to the Jetta. "Take my car," she said.

"And take this," Duncan said. He held aloft the brass hand bell that he used each night to announce last call.

"No, I can't," Adrienne said.

"Take it," Duncan said. "You earned it."

"You earned it," Bruno said.

"You earned it," Joe said.

"Take the bell, Adrienne," Spillman said.

She took the bell. It was heavier than she expected. Her eyes filled with tears and she couldn't bring herself to look at anyone, or worse yet, utter words of good-bye, so instead she rang the bell and listened to its deep metallic thrum. The Bistro was quiet then except for the distant sound of the ocean, and the resonant note of the bell.

Adrienne rang the bell again, then again, as she walked out of the restaurant. Its tone was pure and holy, a benediction.

The New York Times, **Sunday, August 28, 2005**

Chef Dies at 35; Landmark Restaurant Closes

by Drew Amman-Keller

Nantucket, Mass.

Fiona Kemp, 35, chef/owner of the popular beachfront restaurant the Blue Bistro, died at Massachusetts General Hospital early yesterday morning from complications arising from cystic fibrosis. Ms. Kemp was frequently portrayed in the food press as quiet and reclusive. She did not give interviews, she did not allow her photo to be taken, and she rarely set foot in the dining room of her own restaurant. Still, she was widely acknowledged to be a talent without peer in New England kitchens. Her focus on simple, fresh, "fun" foods (such as sandwiches, fondue, and whimsically named entrées like "lamb lollipops") earned her top accolades from the critics and loyal devotion from the restaurant's customers.

In a conversation via cell phone from Logan Airport, Ms. Kemp's partner, Thatcher Smith, denied that Ms. Kemp kept a low profile intentionally to conceal her illness. "Fiona's illness was genetic," Smith said. "She battled symptoms since she was a child. But the illness never took center stage—her career did. Fiona stayed in the kitchen because she didn't want to draw attention away from her food." Mr. Smith did acknowledge that their plans to close the restaurant at the end of the month were, in part, due to Ms. Kemp's health. She was on the list for a lung transplant. "We decided in the spring that this would be our last year. Fiona needed a rest. So, quite frankly, do I." Mr. Smith declined to talk about his plans for the future. "Right now I want to mourn Fiona—an excellent chef, a beautiful person, my best friend."

The Blue Bistro closed its doors yesterday, nearly a week earlier than planned. News of Ms. Kemp's death broke yesterday afternoon in a press release sent to the AP, and since then, according to Mario Subiaco, pastry chef, the restaurant has been deluged with phone calls and over a hundred bouquets of flowers have been left outside the now-locked front entrance.

"She had a lot of fans," Mr. Subiaco said. "She will be missed, most keenly by those of us who worked alongside of her."

Inquirer and Mirror, Week of August 26, 2005
Property Transfers

Fiona C. Kemp and Thatcher E. Smith to the Sebastian Robert Elpern Nominee Trust: 27 North Beach Extension, $8,500,000.

South Bend Tribune, Monday, August 29, 2005
Obituaries

Fiona Clarice Kemp of Nantucket, Massachusetts, and formerly of South Bend, died on Sunday at Massachusetts General Hospital in Boston. She was 35.

Ms. Kemp was born at St. Joseph's Hospital in South Bend to Clarice Mayor Kemp and Dr. Hobson Kemp, a professor of engineering at the University of Notre Dame. She graduated from John Adams High school in 1987 and attended the Culinary

Institute of America in Hyde Park, New York. In 1991, she moved to Nantucket, where she worked for two years as a line cook at the Wauwinet Inn before opening her own restaurant, the Blue Bistro, in 1993.

Ms. Kemp collected many accolades as a chef. Her cuisine was featured in such publications as *Bon Appétit, Travel & Leisure,* and *The Chicago Tribune.* She was named one of America's Hottest Chefs 1998 by *Food & Wine* magazine.

She is survived by her parents and her husband, Thatcher Smith.

A private memorial service will be held at Sacred Heart Chapel, the University of Notre Dame. Memorial contributions may be made in Fiona's name to the Cystic Fibrosis Foundation, 6931 Arlington Road, Bethesda, Maryland 20814.

13

Last Call

Because he is twelve, and in middle school, and because Fiona is a girl, Thatcher always takes friends along when he stops by Fiona's house, and most of the time these friends are Jimmy Sosnowski and Philip St. Clair. This particular day in May, Fiona has slipped Thatch a note in the hallway between history and music class, a scrap of paper that says, simply, "cheesecake." *Last week, she passed him notes that said* "quiche" *and* "meatballs," *and the week before it was* "bread pudding" *and* "veal parmigiana." *Most of the time the word is enticing enough to get him over right after school—for example, the veal parmigiana. Thatcher and Jimmy and Phil sat at Fiona's kitchen table throwing apples from the fruit bowl at one another and teasing the Kemps' Yorkshire terrier, Sharky, while Fiona, in her mother's frilly, flowered, and very queer-looking apron, dredged the veal cutlets in flour, dipped them in egg, dressed them with breadcrumbs, and then sautéed them in hot oil in her mother's electric frying pan. The boys really liked the frying part—there was something cool about meat in hot, splattering oil. But they lost interest during the sauce and cheese steps, and by the time Fiona slid the baking pan into the oven, Jimmy and Phil were ready to go home. Not Thatcher—he stayed until Fiona pulled the cheesy, bubbling dish from the oven and ate with Fiona and Dr. and Mrs. Kemp. His father worked late and his brothers were scattered throughout the neighborhood (his two older brothers could drive and many times they ate at the Burger King on Grape Road). Thatcher liked it when Fiona cooked; he liked it more than he would ever admit.*

So cheesecake. Thatcher figures it will be easy to get Jimmy and Phil to come along for a dessert, but Phil has gotten a new skateboard and so, after school, two hours are spent in the parking lot of the Notre Dame football stadium with the three of them trying stunts (none of them particularly impressive). Every twenty minutes or so, Thatcher reminds Jimmy and Phil about the cheesecake. He knows Fiona will be, at these very minutes, making it. Her cooking fascinates him. She is the only twelve-year-old Thatcher knows who has her own subscription to Gourmet *magazine. Cooking is something Fiona does, Mrs. Kemp told him once, because Fiona is sick. Really sick, the kind of sick that puts her in the hospital in Chicago for weeks at a time. Fiona's illness makes Jimmy and Phil uncomfortable, on top of the fact that she's a girl. They don't want to catch anything. How many times has Thatcher told them? "She doesn't have anything you can catch. She was born sick."*

"You know," Phil says, front wheels of his skateboard in the air. "I think you like Fiona. Really like her."

"I think so, too," Jimmy says.

"Shut up," Thatcher says. He is sweating. It's a true spring day, where even the air in the asphalt parking lot smells like cut grass and forsythia. "I'm just hungry."

They reach the Kemps' house at five o'clock, dangerously close to dinner time, and making the situation more precarious is Dr. Kemp's brown Crown Victoria in the driveway.

"I don't know about this," Phil says.

"Come on," Thatcher says.

When they walk into the side door of the Kemps' kitchen, Sharky's bark announces their arrival. Much to Thatcher's relief, Fiona is alone in the kitchen, wearing her apron, drying dishes. Thatcher is looking at her, but Phil, with his skateboard tucked under his arm, and Jimmy, with his hair sticking up in sixteen permanent cowlicks, are looking at the kitchen table. In the center, where the fruit bowl usually is, the cheesecake rests on a pedestal. It's beautiful—perfectly round and smoothed, creamy white with chocolate swirls on a chocolate cookie crust, sitting in a pool of something bright pink.

"You didn't make that," Phil challenges.

"Sure I did," Fiona says.

"What is it?" Jimmy asks.

"Chocolate swirl cheesecake with raspberry coulis." She holds up the June issue of Gourmet*; the very same cake is pictured on the cover.*

The three of them stare at the cake like it's an alien spaceship landed on the table. Thatcher feels enormously proud of Fiona. He wants to hug her, but then he remembers Phil's words in the parking lot and he tightens his expression.

Dr. Kemp saunters into the kitchen in his professor's clothes—brown suit, bow tie, half-lensed reading glasses, South Bend Tribune *tucked under one arm. He has an imposing academic look, but really, he's very friendly.*

"What do you think of that cake, boys?" he says. "Isn't it something else?"

Phil and Jimmy nod nervously. Thatcher thinks how "something else" is exactly the right phrase. He can't believe that someone he knows has made such a cake.

"Um, I have to go," Phil says.

"Me, too," Jimmy says.

They are frightened by the cake, maybe, or by Dr. Kemp, or by Fiona. They leave abruptly, the screen door banging behind them.

"Do you want a slice, Thatch?" Fiona asks.

Dr. Kemp rinses out a coffee mug in the sink. Thatcher does want a slice, and in the years since his mother left, there has been no one to stop him from eating dessert before dinner. And yet, he hesitates. He's worried by how much he wants to taste the cheesecake, by how he craves it, craves Fiona's eyes on him as he brings the first bite to his lips; he's worried that what he really craves is Fiona. He feels himself reddening as Fiona gazes at him expectantly, awaiting an answer, and then Dr. Kemp looks at him from the sink. Suddenly the pressure of the question—Does he want a slice?—is more than he can bear.

Thatcher turns toward the door. "I have to go, too," he lies.

Labor Day, 1984. They are fifteen now, about to be sophomores in high school. Fiona left home by herself for the first time over the summer, to a culinary camp in Indianapolis, but Thatcher knows she's also interested in the things other fifteen-year-old girls are interested in. She spends whole days sunning herself on the roof of her house; she has rigged the telephone so that the cord reaches her perch.

Sometimes, if the wind is right, Thatcher can hear her from his front porch four doors down: Fiona, deep in conversation with her friend Alison.

Thatcher has spent the summer working at his father's carpet store—mostly moving the big-ass Persian rugs off the trucks into the showroom. As his father says, the Persians sell like winter coats on the day hell freezes over, and so there are always rugs to move. His father also has him steam-cleaning the two-by-three-foot samples of wall-to-wall, deep pile, and shag, because nothing ruins sales like a dirty sample. Thatcher moves Persians and steam-cleans samples and makes coffee and runs errands and stands around smiling so that his father can drape an arm over Thatcher's shoulder and say to his customers, "This is my youngest son, Thatcher. Big help to his old man." Thatcher hates carpet, hates wood flooring and linoleum and tile, and he really hates Persian rugs. His brothers hate it, too. His two oldest brothers, Monroe and Cal, work as lifeguards at the community swim club and his brother Hudson, just two years older, is a musical genius (drums) and has spent all summer at a music camp in Michigan. For Thatcher, Labor Day comes as a huge relief; school starts the next morning.

It's Phil St. Clair's idea to sneak out that night and meet at the playground of the elementary school, and it's Thatcher's idea to invite Fiona and convince his brother Monroe, now a junior at IUSB and still living at home, to buy them a six-pack of beer. Thatcher calls Fiona from the carpet store; he pictures her sitting on her roof in her powder-blue bikini. She's all for the plan. Thatcher's next call is to Jimmy Sosnowski, who suggests Thatcher ask for two six-packs. He does, Monroe extorts a price of thirty dollars, which Thatcher pays from his savings of the summer, and at ten o'clock that night, Thatcher walks out the front door of his house with twelve beers in his backpack. Thatcher wishes it could have been more like sneaking, but his father isn't home yet and when he does get home, he won't check on Thatcher; he never does.

Phil is already at the playground when Thatcher arrives. Phil sits on one of the swings. His whisper cuts through the darkness.

"Hey, did you get it?"

"Yeah." Thatcher shifts the backpack; there's a promising clink.

"Jimmy can't get out," Phil says. "His parents are having a barbecue and they're staying up late."

"That sucks."

"Truly," Phil says. "Give me a beer."

Thatcher's experience with beer is limited, and he panics because he hasn't thought to bring an opener, but the beer Monroe bought, Budweiser, are twist-offs. Thatcher gives one to Phil, then opens one for himself and drinks. The beer is lukewarm (after Monroe brought it home, Thatcher hid it from his other brothers in the closet) but it tastes good anyway. It tastes adult.

"Sophomores tomorrow," he says.

Fiona's voice catches him so by surprise that he chokes on his second swallow, sending a spray of beer down the front of his shirt.

"Hey, you guys!" she says. She laughs at Thatch. "Amateurs." She plucks a Budweiser from Thatcher's backpack, flips the top off, and chugs half the bottle. Thatcher is impressed; Phil just shakes his head.

"Fiona, what are you doing here?"

"Thatch invited me."

Phil glares at Thatcher. Thatcher shrugs.

Fiona says, "Get over it."

"It was supposed to be a guy thing," Phil says.

"We didn't decide on that," Thatcher says.

"We didn't decide on it, but . . . I mean, when you're sneaking out to drink beer the night before school starts, that's a guy thing."

Fiona expertly polishes off the rest of her beer and belches. "Excuse me."

"Do you want another one?" Thatcher asks.

"In a minute." She climbs to the top of the slide and comes flying down. She's wearing some kind of one-piece terry-cloth sun suit. Next to Thatcher, Phil huffs.

"Dude . . ."

"Relax," Thatcher says. "She's lots of fun."

"Whatever," Phil says. He stands up from the swing and sets his nearly full beer down on the asphalt. "I'm going home. This beer isn't even cold."

"Come on," Thatcher says. "Don't be a dope."

"You're the dope," Phil says, nodding his head toward Fiona. "I'll see you tomorrow." He strolls away.

Fiona climbs back up to the top of the slide. "Where's he going?" she says.

"Home."

Fiona coughs. Thatcher holds his breath; he hates it when she coughs. He drinks down his beer, then he's overcome with a loose, tingly feeling. He's happy that Phil's gone.

"I'm coming up after you," he says.

"Do what you want."

He climbs the ladder of the slide, hands over feet. When he's almost at the top, Fiona slides down and runs back to the ladder. Thatcher slides down. By the time he's made it to the bottom of the slide, she's at the top of the ladder. They chase each other like this for a while. Fiona's breath is labored; Thatcher can hear it, and he slows down on purpose. Then he climbs the ladder and she doesn't slide down. She sits at the top and he sidles in next to her. It's cramped, their thighs are touching but Fiona doesn't move.

"Go ahead," she says.

"You go ahead."

"I don't want to go ahead."

"Me, either."

Fiona turns her face, carefully it seems, to look at him. Is she thinking what he's thinking? The beer emboldens him. He leans in to kiss her.

She puts her palm on his face and pushes him away.

"Don't you dare."

"Why not?"

"Because I can't have you falling in love with me."

"I won't fall in love with you."

"You will so," Fiona says. "And I don't want to break your heart."

This, he realizes, is what she and Alison spend all day talking about: falling in love, breaking hearts. "You're nuts," he says.

"I'm going to die," she says.

He sits with this for a second. Even when he first learned about her illness, it was never phrased this way. No one has ever said anything about dying.

"We're all going to die," he says.

"Yes," she says. "But I'm going to die first." And then, with a great big breath, she pushes off and swoops down the slide. She disappears into the dark.

Adrienne doesn't cry about Fiona and she doesn't cry about Thatcher. One day, a gust of wind catches the screen door of her cottage and it whacks her in the side of the face, surprising her, stinging her. A different day, she orders a BLT from Something Natural and after a fifteen-minute wait in the pickup line, a college-age Irish girl tells Adrienne they've lost her order. The Irish girl flips to a fresh page on her pad. "What was it you wanted again, love?" These things make her cry.

Adrienne throws away the Amtrak napkin with her three rules on it. They didn't protect her. Her bank account has five digits in it for the first time in her life, but she doesn't care. It is almost impossible to believe that when she got here money was her only objective. Now money is nothing. It's less than nothing.

She gets a new job working at the front desk of the Nantucket Beach Club and Hotel. She can't believe she ever enjoyed hotel work. It's ho-hum eight-to-five stuff: check the guests in, check the guests out, run American Express cards, send the bellmen to the rooms with more towels, an ironing board, a crib. Adrienne works alone, while Mack pops in and out of an office behind the desk. There are hours when it is just her, the opera music, the wicker furniture, the quilts, and the antique children's toys in the lobby. She starts bringing a book so she won't think about Thatcher or Fiona. She tells herself that her mind is a room, and Thatcher and Fiona aren't allowed in.

Caren pays her rent through the fifteenth of October, but she and Duncan leave a week after the restaurant closes and so Adrienne lives alone in the cottage. Caren is kind upon leaving, offering to hook Adrienne up with her connections in St. Bart's: *You could rent my villa,* she says. *You could get a job. My friend Tate, you know, owns a spa, you could work for him maybe . . .* But Adrienne isn't ready to commit to winter plans, not when it's still so hot and sunny and heartbreakingly beautiful on Nantucket.

Adrienne goes out at night, though not to any of the places she went with Thatch. She favors the Brant Point Grill at the White Elephant because it's spacious and on certain nights has a jazz combo, and because she found it herself and she likes the bartender. He's older than Duncan and more seasoned, more refined. He doesn't act like he's doing her a favor to pour her a drink. She orders Triple 8 and tonics because they pack a quiet punch—three, four, five of those and something light off the bar menu, and for hours she floats around in a state of near-oblivion. She loses the haunting pain where she feels as though the best time of her life has come and gone in three short months.

One night she sees Doyle Chambers at the end of the bar, but he pretends not to recognize her. Ditto Grayson Parrish who comes in with a rotund, florid-faced woman whom Adrienne guesses is Nonnie Sizemore. But one awful night, she feels a hand on her shoulder, which shocks her. She realizes at that moment that she has gone weeks without anyone touching her. She turns around to see Charlie, Duncan's friend, wearing the marijuana leaf necklace. His face is stripped of his usual smugness. He looks as lonely as she feels.

"Hey," he says, and that one word conveys a sense that they are the two lone survivors from some kind of fallout.

"Hey."

"Have you seen Caren?" he asks. "Or Duncan?"

"They moved," Adrienne says, surprised that Charlie isn't aware of this fact, as chummy as he was with Duncan. "They live in Providence now. Duncan works for Holt."

Charlie takes a sip of beer and looks Adrienne over. "And what are you doing?"

"Working," she says. "At the Beach Club."

"Oh." Charlie reaches for his gold marijuana leaf and moves it along its chain wistfully, like a teenage girl. "Do you miss the restaurant?"

"Not really," she says.

"No," he says. "Me neither."

The next day on her way to work, Adrienne stops by the Bistro. An excavator is out on the beach tearing down the awning skeleton; it is as awful as watching somebody break bones. A Dumpster sits in the parking lot, filled with boards from the deck. Adrienne runs her hand over one and imagines she feels divots from her spike heels. Then she peeks in the front door. The restaurant is empty. The tables and chairs have been taken to the dump; Thatcher donated the dishes and silverware and glasses to a charity auction. The piano and the slab of blue granite have been moved to storage until the Elperns are ready for them. Someone has dragged the dory away, but its ghost remains: a boat-shaped patch of dry brown dirt.

Mack never asks personal questions. Compared to life at the Bistro, where everyone's business polluted the air like smoke, working at the hotel is bloodless, boring. It's just a job. But one day, shortly after Adrienne watched the bulldozers demolishing the bistro, Mack calls her into his office.

"The Harrisons said they saw you last night at the Brant Point Grill," he says.

"Did they?"

"They said you didn't recognize them."

"I try not to fraternize with guests outside of work," she says. "That was your suggestion."

"It was," Mack says. "They told me you were drunk. They were worried."

The Harrisons are an older couple from Quebec. Mrs. Harrison is another woman who wants to be Adrienne's mother; she fusses and clucks and makes a big deal about her every time they set foot in the lobby. Adrienne really liked the Harrisons until this very second.

"There's no reason for anyone to worry about me," she says. "I'm fine."

It takes fifteen late-night phone calls, several long letters, and Fiona's weak but charming attempt to write up a business plan for Thatcher to agree to come to Nantucket to look at this restaurant she's been talking about. He's hesitant on several fronts: Fiona is young and relatively inexperienced; he, Thatcher, knows nothing about the restaurant business or the business of living on an island. He fears Fiona is asking him to be her partner because he's the only person she knows who has access to real money. He can, with ease, sell his fifth of the carpet business. His brothers are greedy for it; Smith's Carpet and Flooring has become an empire.

He expresses his concerns to Fiona. She, repeatedly, expresses her concerns to him: She hates cooking on the line, the male cooks harass her, they won't stop talking about blow jobs, she has to get her own place, she has to be the boss.

"You're not talking to a normal person," she finally says over the phone late one night after her shift. "I can't put in eight or nine years before I strike out on my own. I don't have that kind of time."

She has never, in the long history of their friendship, invoked her illness as an excuse or a reason for special treatment and the fact that she does so now makes Thatcher see that she is serious. He agrees to come out to the island, sleep on the floor of Fiona's spartan cottage, and meet with the Realtor at the ungodly hour of six in the morning to see the place she's found. It's a burger shack, plain and simple: picnic tables in the sand sheltered by half-walls and an awning. The only things properly inside are the kitchen, the bathrooms, and a meager counter where one places an order, and yet the young, exhausted-looking real estate agent tells them the current owners want seven hundred thousand dollars for it. Fiona loves the place; she loves the way it sits on a beach all by itself like a restaurant on a deserted island. Thatcher remains skeptical; it's still too dark for him to even see the water.

"It's not close to anything," Thatcher says. "It's not in town. How will people know to come here?"

"It will be a destination restaurant," Fiona says. "Ever heard of the Michelin guide?"

"It doesn't even have floors," Thatcher says. How will he explain to his father that he's investing nearly three quarters of a million dollars in a building without floors?

"Let's look at the kitchen," Fiona says. She's skipping, giddy, as happy as he's ever seen her, already dressed in her whites for her other job. She is so small she looks like a child dressed up as a chef for Halloween. The kitchen is, at least, clean, and the appliances are impressively large and modern. Fiona opens the walk-in: it's stocked with burger patties and bags of French fries and tubs of mayonnaise.

"Have you ever eaten here?" Thatcher asks.

"Of course not," Fiona says.

They return to the dining room, where the real estate agent sits forlornly at one of the picnic tables, fiddling with a packet of ketchup. She has, she informed them on the drive out, shown the restaurant almost sixty times between the hours of six and seven A.M. *or after eleven at night. In her opinion, it's overpriced.*

"Don't you see it?" Fiona says.

"See what?"

"We'll get a piano player, and one of those zinc bars like they have at the bistros in Paris. We'll have white linen tablecloths, candlelight. We'll have new lives, Thatch. Me in the kitchen with a civilized crew, you up front greeting the guests. I can make crackers."

"You can make crackers?" He has no idea what she's talking about. She wants to spend all of his inheritance and then some on a fancy restaurant and make crackers? Still, he feels himself succumbing. If she makes crackers, they will be the best crackers on earth, he knows it.

She smiles at him. She has a burn mark on her cheek from a sauce that bubbled up the night before at work; the burn is round, the size of a dime. "This will be a great place."

"It has no floors," Thatcher says in a last ditch effort to escape his fate.

"The doctors gave me ten years," Fiona says. "Maybe fifteen."

"Maybe fifty," Thatcher says. He sighs, digs a toe in the sand, and nods toward the glum Realtor. Outside, the sky is lightening. "Let's do it, then. Let's make this lady's day."

TO: Ade12177@hotmail.com
FROM: DrDon@toothache.com
DATE: September 26, 2005, 7:01 P.M.
SUBJECT: wedding and worries

I will start by telling you what you already know which is that I am sick with worry about you. I wish you would call. I try you every night at the number you gave me for the cottage but you never answer and you are the last person in America without an answering machine. Please call me soon or I will mortify you by calling you at the hotel. You don't have to pretend to be happy. I just want to make sure you're breathing, eating, brushing.

The wedding has ballooned to include a few of the friends we've made here and some of Mavis's family from Louisiana, so now it's sixty people for sure with the possibility of seventy-five so we've gone and booked a banquet room at this wonderful restaurant in St. Michael's. You will love St. Mike's, and in fact, I think you should consider staying here in Maryland for a while, through the holidays at least. You can get a job if you want, though I would be happy to bankroll my little girl again for a few months so that you can simply relax and reflect and have some quiet time. That way I will see for myself that you're breathing, eating, and brushing.

I'm not sure, Adrienne, what you're still doing there. I worry.

Love love love.

Autumn arrives at the end of September. The weather grows cool and misty, the trees in town turn yellow and orange and red; at the end of her shift each afternoon, Adrienne lights a fire in the lobby's fireplace. Adrienne takes comfort in all this; it's been a long time since she experienced fall. On a rare excursion into town on her day off, she ventures into Dessert to buy herself a sweater. The woman with the red hair isn't in, and Adrienne feels both sorry and relieved. Part of her wants to be recognized as the hostess from the Blue Bistro, Thatcher's girlfriend, and part of her wishes the three months of summer never happened.

She spends a lot of time thinking about the summer before her mother died, her summer at Camp Hideaway. She had grown to love the smell of her cabin, and the soft flannel lining of her sleeping bag. She loved the certainty of flag raising and oatmeal with just-picked raspberries and Pammy Ipp who was her partner in everything from canoeing to late-night trips to the bathhouse. The summer at Hideaway was an escape to a place where the rules for the real world didn't apply. Her mother wasn't sick—her mythical brother was. But Adrienne had realized even then that it wouldn't last forever. The bubble would pop: She would leave behind the days of swimming in the cold green water of Lake Sherwood and sitting around the campfire singing "Red River Valley" as the very cute Nick Boccio strummed his guitar. She would confess the truth to Pammy Ipp and return home to spend August watching *General Hospital* in the air-conditioned dens of her regular, at-home friends, and visiting her mother in the hospital. In many ways it was as though Camp Hideaway had never happened, except it had, and now, so many years later, she was still thinking about it with longing and regret.

One night at the Brant Point Grill, a very quiet Monday night, Adrienne drinks too much. She received an e-mail from her father about his wedding, less than three weeks away, and she realizes she has to make a decision. Her lease at the cottage ends the day after Columbus Day. What *is* she still doing here? She's passing the time, filling up hours, waiting. The thought of not waiting, of going to Maryland or St. Bart's or some other place panics her. So she drinks her vodkas steadily and evenly, with purpose. She forgets to order food. It's the regular bartender's night off, and there's a young brunette woman in his stead. This girl pours with a smile so fake that Adrienne orders more often just to study her insincerity.

Next thing she knows, she's in the bartender's arms, inhaling the wholesome Aveda scent of her hair.

"Here we go," the bartender directs. "Toward the door."

Adrienne stares down at her feet (she is wearing a pair of red suede driving moccasins, a holdover from Aspen). She's doing some kind of dance step—stumbling, weaving, buckling.

"We're almost there," the bartender says. "I called you a cab, though you might need an ambulance." This is said with concern, probably more for her job than for Adrienne's well-being, though maybe not. The bartender's arms are strong and she handles Adrienne firmly but carefully, like she's a child.

"Do you have children?" Adrienne hears herself ask.

The bartender nods. "Three."

Adrienne tries to say something about how she hardly looks old enough but her words come out slurred and mangled and there isn't time to start the thought over because a cab whips into the circular driveway. The cabbie, who looks familiar somehow, accepts Adrienne from the bartender and pours her into the backseat of the cab.

She wakes up at four in the morning with her face stuck to the linoleum floor of the kitchen, but she's powerless to move. At seven thirty, when the sun comes up, she crawls to the phone and calls Mack.

Not coming in today, she says. *Too sick to work.*

Two days later, she agrees to work a double as penance. Tiny, the night desk person, wants a break, and Adrienne volunteers to cover for her. In addition to getting Adrienne out of the doghouse with Mack, it will keep her away from the bars. She has promised herself she will never drink again, and she wonders how long it will be until she wants to.

Adrienne has never worked the night desk before and she finds that she likes it. Between six and seven o'clock, the hotel guests meet cabs out front or walk into town for dinner. All the other great places are still open: Club Car, Boarding House, 21 Federal, American Seasons, Company of the Cauldron, Le Languedoc, Blue Fin, 56 Union, the Pearl, Cinco. Then, when most of the guests have wandered out, Adrienne puts on some opera and makes herself a cup of tea and enjoys the fire.

She is a person with a broken heart. That hardly makes her special. It happens to everyone. She herself broke Michael Sullivan's heart less than three years earlier. How does she think he felt banging around Chatham after she fled for Hawaii? He probably felt like she does now. Adrienne considers calling him up to apologize. Then she thinks about calling Pammy Ipp.

St. Michael's might not be so bad, she thinks. It's another charming resort town that probably needs help through Christmas. She can attend her father's wedding and simply stay with him and Mavis in their new home. In January, she can try St. Bart's, maybe, if she feels up to it. Then in the spring she might join Kyra and the landscape painter in Carmel. So there it is: An entire year of possibility. Adrienne feels better than she has since Fiona's collapse. She feels clean and right-headed and warm, in her new sweater in front of the fire. Her heart is broken, but it will heal. That's what hearts do.

And then, she feels a blast of cold air. The door opens and Mario walks in.

At first, Adrienne mistakes him for a late check-in: a handsome, dark-haired man in a black silk shirt, jeans, tweed blazer. Her newfound optimism blooms, because maybe what she needs is a mild flirtation to carry her even farther from her sadness. But as the man approaches, Adrienne's mind whispers, *Mario. Is it him? No. Yes, it is. No. It is so. It's him.*

She stands perfectly still, her left hand wrapped around the now-cold mug of tea. She wonders if he's heard about her poor showing at the Brant Point Grill. (She finally figured out that the cabbie who drove her home that night was the same one who had picked her up from the Subiacos' first party, because she didn't remember giving him her address, and yet she arrived home safely.) Maybe Mario is here to suggest AA. Or maybe he's come to declare his love for her, and how will Adrienne feel about that? Will she be able, in the face of all her pain and rejection, to turn him down? She takes a shallow breath. Maybe he's here to ask her again about working at his new restaurant, or to show her the piece that has finally been run in *Vanity Fair* (Adrienne has the issue at home but can't bring herself to read it). Or maybe he's just here to catch up because they had, after all, been friends. But his stride is purposeful and his black eyes are intent and Adrienne is petrified. She clenches the mug. He doesn't try to kiss her or hug her; he doesn't even greet her. But he does, with two swift words, cut the rope that ties Adrienne to the heavy load of her uncertainty. She's finished waiting.

Mario's voice is low and husky, barely audible over the crackling fire and the Andrea Bocelli.

"Thatcher's back," he says.

Fiona hasn't been off the vent for more than an hour at a time since they got to the hospital, and when she does come off, the nurses have warned her not to talk—talking uses up too much oxygen. The corners of Fiona's mouth are cracked and bleeding from all the times she's been intubated. Her O_2 sats are very low, the new drug has failed; Fiona won't be getting any better. The doctors suggested Thatcher *call Fiona's parents. They're on their way. This is it—Thatcher knows it and Fiona knows it and yet neither of them can speak.*

All along, Thatcher has had a plan: Marry her. He's talked about it with Father Ott. For months, they've gone over the sticky emotional territory. Fiona yearns to be married, and what she really wanted was to marry JZ. But JZ is already married; he had a chance to make things right with Fiona and he blew it. So that leaves Thatcher, who wants to make a pledge of his devotion to this person—his friend, his partner, his first love. She is more his family than his own family. He has planned to marry her all along and she agreed to it only by saying, "At the very end. If nobody else wants us."

How ironic, and awful, that this was the summer Thatcher fell in love. He didn't think it was possible—at age thirty-five, as solitary as he liked to be, as devoted to his business and Fiona, as impermeable to romance—and yet, one morning, just as he was wondering where he was going to find the kind of help that would enable him to make it through the summer, there she was. Adrienne Dealey. Beautiful, yes, but he loves Adrienne not because she is beautiful but because she is different. He has never known a woman so free from conceit, vanity, ambition, and pretense. He has never known a woman so willing to show the world that she is a human being. He has never known a woman with such an appetite—a literal appetite, but also an appetite for adventure—the places she's been, unafraid, all by herself. Thatcher loves her in a huge, mature, adult way. He loves her the right way. Now he has to hope that God grants her patience and understanding and faith. Whenever he prays these days, he prays for Adrienne, too.

He calls the hospital chapel and reserves it for two hours. He orders flowers from the gift shop near Admitting. They aren't prepared to outfit a wedding, but they can put together a bouquet. One of the nurses in oncology plays the piano; Thatcher discovers her lunch hour is from one thirty to two thirty. He phones Father Ott who is staying at the rectory of St. Ann's, then he takes Fiona's hand. Her hands are so important to her for chopping and dicing and mixing and blending and stirring and rolling and sprinkling, and yet she's always been so self-conscious about her swollen fingers and her discolored fingernails that he's never been allowed to touch them. There's a scar across her left palm from the day she picked up a hot sauté pan without a side towel. She went to the emergency room for that burn, and for the stitches she got when she cut herself while boning a duck breast—fifteen stitches across the tips of her second and third fingers. There are other marks and scars that Thatcher can't identify; if he could, he'd ask her about each one.

She's off the vent but her eyes are closed.

"Fiona," he says.

She opens her eyes.

"We're getting married at two o'clock."

The words terrify him, because he knows that she'll know what they signify. At the very end. If nobody else wants us.

Fiona's lips are cracked and bleeding, and although it must hurt, she smiles.

In this ward of the hospital there isn't much in the way of good news, but everyone is excited about a wedding. Thatcher goes back to his room at the hotel to shower, shave, and change, and he spends a full, precious five minutes considering the telephone.

Call Adrienne? And say what?

When he returns, the nurses have put Fiona back on the vent—just until she's ready to go—and they have changed her into a fresh white johnny and brushed her hair so that it flows down over the top of the sheet. The gift shop has done a beautiful job with the bouquet of roses and Fiona holds it as they unhook her from the ventilator and wheel her down the corridor toward the chapel. Thatcher tries to be present in the moment, he tries not to peer behind the half-open doors they pass, he tries not to listen to the dialogue of the soap operas on TV. The attending nurse, a woman named Ella, chatters about her own wedding twenty-eight years earlier at the steepled Congregational Church in Acton.

"Do you have rings?" Ella whispers to Thatcher.

He has rings, expensive rings purchased that morning from Shreve, Crump & Low. As Ella and Thatcher wheel Fiona's gurney into the chapel, he checks his shirt pocket for their delicate presence—two circles wrapped in tissue paper. The chapel is a brown room, dimly lit, with sturdy, functional-looking wooden benches and a large plain wooden cross hanging over the carpeted stairs of the altar. Father Ott waits there, all six foot six of him, in his flowing white robe. Oncology nurse, Teri Lee, a diminutive Korean woman, waits for Thatcher's signal, and then she starts to play Pachelbel's Canon in D. On this piano, in this chapel, under these circumstances, the music is plaintive. A third nurse named Kristin Benedict is sitting in the first row; she has spent a great many hours caring for Fiona, and what makes her even more special is that she's eaten at the Bistro (in the summer of 1996, while she was on vacation with her husband). Thatcher has asked her to be a witness. Kristin is a crier; she sobs quietly as Teri plays the piano, as the gurney moves down the aisle, Thatcher on one side, Ella on the other. Once they reach the altar, the music subsides, Thatcher takes Fiona's scarred hand and Father Ott raises his arms and proclaims in his resonant voice: "We gather here today in the name of the Father, and of the Son, and of the Holy Spirit."

Thatcher crosses himself and out of the corner of his eye, he sees Fiona lift her hand and cross herself. She is smiling.

Father Ott leads them, briskly, through the age-old wedding vows. He is hurrying, Thatcher suspects, because no one knows how long Fiona will last without oxygen. Thatcher tries, tries, to stay present in the moment, and not to think of how Father Ott will, at some point, give Fiona the sacrament of Last Rites, he will anoint her with oil, he will whisper Psalm 23 into her deaf ear. Fiona's parents are to land at Logan at six o'clock. Thatcher offered to pick them up but Mrs. Kemp doesn't want Fiona to be alone, even for a second. Thatcher is shaking. Fiona will die, she will be cold to the touch, gone from Thatcher in every human sense, even though she is alive now—she is alive and he is marrying her and she is marrying him. They are getting married, honoring the thirty years that they've been best friends—through the chocolate swirl cheesecake, and the beer on the playground, and the day they bought the restaurant, and every moment in between and since.

Fiona is smiling. She takes a deep breath and whispers, "I do." Thatcher slips a ring on her finger. It's way too big and he's crushed because he wants her to take the ring with her when she goes. She holds it in place with her thumb. Thatcher puts on his own ring; he swears he will never take it off. Father Ott bestows a blessing and they cross themselves again, but not Fiona; her eyes are glazing over, she's checking out. But not yet! Not yet!

"You may kiss the bride," Father Ott says. Teri Lee starts in with the piano and Kristin Benedict sobs and Thatcher kisses Fiona, his new wife, on her cracked lips. For the first time ever, he kisses her.

Adrienne doesn't sleep.

She was able to wheedle only the most basic information out of Mario before he checked his watch and claimed he was late meeting Louis and Hector at the Rope Walk and left. The basic information was this: Thatcher was back, Mario had bumped into him at the airport, Thatcher asked if Mario had seen Adrienne and Mario said no. Thatcher asked Mario to find Adrienne and let her know that he, Thatcher, wanted to talk to her.

Talk to me about what? Adrienne asked.

He didn't say.

This is not something she bargained for: Thatcher, here, on Nantucket, looking for her. The restaurant is gone, Fiona is dead, and Adrienne is most comfortable placing Thatcher in a similar category: disappeared, vanished, nonexistent. Easier that way to banish him from her mind. Not so easy now that she knows he is asleep (or not) on this tiny island.

She gets home from work at eleven thirty and sits in her kitchen with all the lights off contemplating a glass of wine. But no, she's promised herself, no. She tries to read, she tries turning off the light and closing her eyes. She gets up and looks out into her backyard—the one big tree is swaying. It's windy, but not particularly cold. She throws on a fleece and goes outside. She feels better being outside.

She rides her bike to Thatcher's cottage, the cottage behind the big house in town. There is a light on. She feels like if she opens her mouth, something awful will come out. He's right there, ten feet away, in that cottage, and she panics because she can't face him, she can't deal with closure; it will kill her, and those words are so wrong, so harsh in light of what he's just been through, but they will kill her in a sense. Closure will destroy her fragile sense of okay-for-now. Seeing him will ruin every step toward healing that she's made in the last month.

She rides her bike home and makes a decision. She has to leave. Tomorrow.

She spends the rest of the night packing up her clothes, her new pairs of beautiful shoes, the hand bell. Mack will not be happy that she's leaving him with two weeks until the hotel closes for the season, but what else can she do? At first light, she writes out a note of apology and hops back on her bike. Cowardly girl, she thinks, quitting by note. She will never be able to use Mack or Thatcher as a reference. This is a summer that will be missing from her résumé. The summer that didn't count. The summer that was a mistake.

Nantucket is too beautiful to be a mistake, however, especially this morning. The sun comes up and the sky is pale at first with the promise of that brilliant blue; the air is crisp and rich with smells of the water. She pedals down the road toward the Beach Club, trying to correct her thinking. Nantucket was not a mistake. She learned so much about food, about wine, about people, about herself. Because it is so early and she still has lots of time, she takes the turn in the road that she made the first day here—the stretch that leads to the spot where the Bistro used to be. From a hundred yards away, she sees the frame of the Elperns' new house. It's impressively large, as large as Holt Millman's house. She is so amazed that something so tall and grandiose could be built in two short weeks that she doesn't notice the silver truck in the parking lot until it's too late. But then, once she does see the truck, right there, his truck, a strange thing happens: She keeps going, propelling herself closer to the very thing she's running away from.

Thatcher stands in the parking lot wearing his red fleece jacket, his hands in his pockets, staring at the house. Adrienne has plenty of time to turn around, a more than good chance of leaving undetected. But she is drawn to him. She wonders what it feels like to be looking at the thing that is standing in the place where your life used to be. Is it awful? Is it a relief?

"Thatcher," she says.

He whips around; she's scared him. Good. She wanted to scare him. He stares at her a second, and she dismounts her bike. He squeezes her so tightly she cries out and then, before she knows it, they're kissing. They're kissing and Adrienne starts to cry.

"I'm sorry," Adrienne says. "About Fee. I'm so sorry."

He holds her face in his hands. She can feel his wedding band against her cheek.

"I love you," he says. "I know you don't believe it, but I do."

She does believe it, but she's afraid to say so.

"I wanted to call, but . . . it's been so . . . I was in South Bend for three weeks . . . I wasn't sure if you'd understand . . . I felt like, God, if I got back and you were still here . . ."

"I was going to leave today," she says. She holds up the note, which she has been crushing in her palm since she left her house. "I was about to tell Mack and go."

"Because of me?"

She nods; there are more tears. She can't predict what's going to happen: Is it good, is it bad? Will he come with her to her father's wedding? And what on earth will they do after that? Another restaurant? Another business? Will he marry her and be a man who wears two wedding rings? Maybe he will. And since when is she the kind of person who needs so many answers?

While she was packing her bags she took a minute and inspected the hand bell that Duncan bequeathed to her, the one he rang each night for last call. Inside the bottom rim, she found an inscription: "To Thatcher Smith with appreciation from the Parish of St. Joseph's, South Bend, Indiana." It had alarmed her that she was taking Thatcher's bell, but at the same time she felt she had a right to it; she felt she had earned that small piece of Thatcher. She is not sure she deserves more than that small piece; she is not at all sure she deserves what she has now: his whole self in her arms, declaring his love.

"I want to talk to you," Thatcher says. "So I can tell you I love you. What time do you have to be at work?"

She crumples the note to Mack in her hand. "Eight thirty."

"That's in two hours," he says, checking his beautiful watch.

"What should we do?" she asks.

Thatcher turns her so that she is facing the Elpern house; it will be a lovely house when it is finished. He takes her hand and leads her to his truck and he picks up her bike with one hand and lays it down in the back.

Adrienne doesn't ask where they are going; she already knows.

They are going to breakfast.

Acknowledgments

This one, especially, took a village.

I could never have written this book without the support of the restaurant community on Nantucket.

Robert Sarkisian, H.H. at 21 Federal, talked with me for hours, fed me, allowed me to "work" during Christmas Stroll 2002, and gave me access to his staff, all of whom were honest and charming. Special thanks to Chris Passerati, Dan Sabauda, Russell Jaehnig, and Johnny Bresette, bartender extraordinaire, who very much wanted me to change the name of the bartender in this book from Duncan to "Johnny B."

Al and Andrea Kovalencik, of the exquisite jewel-box restaurant, Company of the Cauldron, shared hours of stories with me from their rich and varied experience in the "resort life."

Joanna Polowy, pastry chef, taught me about the sweeter side of the restaurant business.

Angela and Seth Raynor, owner and chef/owner of The Boarding House and the Pearl, told me more stories than I could possibly include in one book. Angela also inadvertently gave me the idea for this book. In the summer of 2000, when my novel *The Beach Club* was released, Angela said to me, "We decided in the back [of the house] that you could never write a restaurant book. Too scandalous." Thank you, Angela!

Finally, I am indebted to Geoffrey, David, and Jane Silva of The Galley, who for the twelve years as my friends have demonstrated how to gracefully run a successful beachfront restaurant.

I read comprehensively about restaurants, culinary schools, and food and wine. The following publications were especially helpful: *The Art of Eating* by M. F. K. Fisher, *Becoming a Chef* by Andrew Dornenburg and Karen Page, *Cosmopolitan: A Bartender's Life* by Toby Cecchini, *The Fourth Star* by Leslie Brenner, *The Making of a Pastry Chef* by Andrew MacLauchlan, *Waiting: The True Confessions of a Waitress* by Debra Ginsberg, *The Making of a Chef* and *The Soul of a Chef* by Michael Ruhlman, *If You Can Stand the Heat* by Dawn Davis, *Kitchen Confidential* by Anthony Bourdain, *The Last Days of Haute Cuisine* by Patric Kuh, and what felt like hundreds of issues of *Bon Appétit* and *Gourmet.*

Thank you to my early readers: Mrs. Pat van Ryn, Tom and Leslie Bresette, Amanda Congdon, Debbie Bennett, and, as ever, Heather Osteen Thorpe. Thank you to Wendy Hudson of Bookworks and Mimi Beman of Mitchell's Book Corner. It is a lucky writer who has two stellar independent bookstores on her home island. In New York, as always, thanks to Michael Carlisle, Jennifer Weis, and Stefanie Lindskog.

Finally, thank you to the people who gave me the time, space, and support to write. My sitters (who are also friends): Becca Evans, Julia Chumak, Kristen Jurgensen, Jennifer Chadwick, and Dan Bowling. My friends (who are also, occasionally, sitters): Amanda Congdon, Anne Gifford, Sally Bates Hall, Margie Holahan, Susan Storey Johnsen, and Wendy Rouillard. My sons' school: The Children's House of Nantucket. The sanest hour of my week: the Thursday morning parenting group. My mother, Sally Hilderbrand, and my husband, Chip Cunningham.

Chip shines his light on my every page. In this instance, I am especially grateful to him for sharing the details of his beautiful and unique friendship with Katie van Ryn, who died from complications of cystic fibrosis in 1995 at the age of thirty.

The Love Season

For Margie Holahan—
a friend for all seasons
XO

Part One

Provisions

August 19, 2006 • 6:30 A.M.

Marguerite didn't know where to start.

Each and every summer evening for nearly twenty years, she had cooked for a restaurant full of people, yet here she was in her own kitchen on a crystalline morning with a seemingly simple mission—dinner for two that evening at seven thirty—and she didn't know where to start. Her mind spun like the pedals of a bicycle without any brakes. Candace coming here, after all these years. Immediately Marguerite corrected herself. Not Candace. Candace was dead. Renata was coming tonight. The baby.

Marguerite's hands quivered as she brought her coffee mug to her lips. The grandfather clock chimed just as it had every fifteen minutes of its distinguished life—but this time, the sound startled Marguerite. She pictured a monkey inside, with two small cymbals and a voice screeching, *Marguerite! Earth to Marguerite!*

Marguerite chuckled. *I am an old bat,* she thought. *I'll start by writing a list.*

The phone call had come at eleven o'clock the night before. Marguerite was in bed, reading Hemingway. Whereas once Marguerite had been obsessed with food—with heirloom tomatoes and lamb shanks and farmhouse cheeses, and fish still flopping on the counter, and eggs and chocolate and black truffles and foie gras and rare white nectarines—now the only thing that gave her genuine pleasure was reading. The people of Nantucket wondered—oh yes, she knew they wondered—what Marguerite *did* all day, hermited in her house on Quince Street, secreted away from the eyes of the curious. Although there was always something—the laundry, the garden, the articles for the newspaper in Calgary (deadline every other Friday)—the answer was: reading. Marguerite had three books going at any one time. That was the chef in her, the proverbial more-than-one-pot-on-the-stove. She read contemporary fiction in the mornings, though she was very picky. She liked Philip Roth, Penelope Lively, as a rule no one under the age of fifty, for what could they possibly have to say about the world that Marguerite hadn't already learned? In the afternoons, she enriched herself with biographies or books of European history, if they weren't too dense. Her evenings were reserved for the classics, and when the phone rang the night before Marguerite had been reading Hemingway. Hemingway was the perfect choice for late at night because his sentences were clear and easy to understand, though Marguerite stopped every few pages and asked herself, *Is that all he means? Might he mean something else?* This insecurity was a result of attending the

Culinary Institute instead of a proper university—and all those years with Porter didn't help. *An education makes you good company for yourself,* Porter had liked to tell his students, and Marguerite, when he was trying to convince her to read something other than *Larousse Gastronomique.* Wouldn't he be proud of her now.

The phone, much like the muted toll of the clock a few seconds ago, had scared Marguerite out of her wits. She gasped, and her book slid off her lap to the floor, where it lay with its pages folded unnaturally under, like a person with a broken limb. The phone, a rotary, continued its cranky, mechanical whine while Marguerite groped her nightstand for her watch. Eleven o'clock. Marguerite could name on one hand the phone calls she'd received in the past twelve months: There was a call or two from the editorial assistant at the Calgary paper; there was a call from the Culinary Institute each spring asking for a donation; there was always a call from Porter on November 3, her birthday. None of these people would ever think to call her at eleven o'clock at night—not even Porter, drunk (not even if he'd split from the nubile young graduate assistant who had become his late-in-life wife), would dare call Marguerite at this hour. So it was a wrong number. Marguerite decided to let it ring. She had no answering machine to put the phone out of its misery; it just rang and rang, as pleading and insistent as a crying baby. Marguerite picked it up, clearing her throat first. She occasionally went a week without speaking.

"Hello?"

"Aunt Daisy?" The voice had been light and cheerful; there was background noise—people talking, jazz music, the familiar clink and clatter of glasses and plates—was it *restaurant* noise? It threw Marguerite off. And then there was the nickname: *Daisy.* Only three people had ever used it.

"Yes?"

"It's Renata." There was an expectant pause. "Renata Knox."

Marguerite's eyes landed across the room, on her desk. Taped to her computer was Renata Knox's e-mail address; Marguerite beheld it every day as she binged guiltily on the Internet for an hour, but she had never sent a single message. Because what could she possibly say? A casual hello would be pointless and anything more, dangerous. Marguerite's eyes skittered from her desk to her dresser. On top of her dresser were two precious framed photographs. She dusted them carefully each week, though she rarely lingered over them anymore. Years ago she had scrutinized them so intensely that they imprinted themselves on her brain. She knew them by heart, the way she knew the streets in the sixth arrondissement, the way she knew the temperament of a soufflé. One picture was of Marguerite and Candace taken at Les Parapluies on the occasion of Renata's christening. In it, Marguerite was holding Renata, her goddaughter. How well she remembered that moment. It had taken a magnum of Veuve Clicquot and several glasses of thirty-year port to get Dan to relinquish his grip on his newborn daughter, and when he did, it was only to Candace so that the baby could nurse. Marguerite sat with Candace on the west banquette as the party thundered around them. Marguerite knew little of babies, or lactation; she fed people every day, but nothing was as captivating as watching Candace feed her daughter. When Candace finished, she eased the baby up over her shoulder until the baby burped. Then Candace passed her over to Marguerite casually, like she was a loaf of bread.

Go see your godmother, Candace said to the baby.

Godmother, Marguerite had thought. The last time she had been inside a church before that very morning was for Candace and Dan's wedding, and before that the Cathedral of Notre-Dame in Paris the year she met Porter, and so her notion of godmother came mostly from fairy tales. Marguerite had gazed down at the baby's tiny pink mouth, which still made the motion of sucking even though the breast was gone, and thought, *I will feed you your first escargot. I will pour your first glass of champagne.*

"Aunt Daisy?" Renata said.

"Yes, dear," Marguerite said. The poor girl probably thought Marguerite was as crazy as the islanders said she was—*self-mutilation, months in a psychiatric hospital, gave up her restaurant*—or worse, she thought Marguerite didn't know who she was. How surprised the child would be to find out that Marguerite thought of her, and of Candace, every day. The memories ran through her veins. *But enough of that!* Marguerite thought. *I have the girl on the phone!* "I'm sorry, darling. You caught me by surprise."

"Were you sleeping?" Renata asked. "It's awfully late."

"No," Marguerite said. "Not sleeping. In bed, reading. Where are you, darling? Are you at school?"

"I don't start back for three more weeks," Renata said.

"Oh, right," Marguerite said. "Silly of me." Already she felt like the conversation was a dog she'd agreed to take for a walk, one that yanked on its chain, urging Marguerite to catch up. It was August now; when Renata went back to college she'd be a . . . sophomore? Marguerite had sent Renata five thousand dollars for her high school graduation the spring before last—an outrageous sum, though who else did Marguerite have to give her money to? Renata had graduated first in her class, and although she'd been accepted at Yale and Stanford, she'd decided on Columbia, where Porter was still chairman of the art history department. Renata had sent Marguerite a sweet little thank-you note for the money in loopy script with a lot of exclamation points—and Dan had dashed off a note as well on his office stationery. *Once again, Margo, you've done too much. Hope you are well.* Marguerite noticed he had not actually said thank you, but that would have been hoping for too much. After all these years, Dan still hadn't forgiven her. He thought she sent the money out of guilt when really she had sent it out of love.

"Where are you then?" Marguerite asked. In his annual Christmas letter, Dan had written about Renata's infatuation with her literature classes, her work-study job in the admissions office, and her roommate, but he had hinted nothing about her summer plans.

"I'm here on Nantucket," Renata said. "I'm at 21 Federal."

Marguerite suddenly felt very warm; sweat broke out on her forehead and under her arms. And menopause for her had ended sometime during the first Clinton administration.

"You're *here*?" Marguerite said.

"For the weekend. Until Sunday. I'm here with my fiancé."

"Your *what*?"

"His name is Cade," Renata said. "His family has a house on Hulbert Avenue."

Marguerite stroked the fraying satin edge of her summer blanket. Fiancé at age nineteen? And Dan had allowed it? *The boy must be rich,* Marguerite thought sardonically. *Hulbert Avenue.* But even she had a hard time believing that Dan would give Renata away while she was still a teenager. People didn't change that fundamentally. Daniel Knox would always be the father holding possessively on to his little girl. He had never liked to share her.

Marguerite realized Renata was waiting for an answer. "I see."

"His parents know all about you," Renata said. "They used to eat at the restaurant. They said it was the best place. They said they miss it."

"That's very nice," Marguerite said. She wondered who Cade's parents were. Had they been regulars or once-a-summer people? Would Marguerite recognize their names, their faces? Had they said anything else to Renata about what they knew, or thought they knew?

"I'm dying to come see you," Renata said. "Cade wants to meet you, too, but I told him I want to come by myself."

"Of course, dear," Marguerite said. She straightened in bed so that her posture was as perfect as it had been nearly sixty years ago, ballet class, Madame Verge asking her students to pretend there was a wire that ran from the tops of their heads to the ceiling. *Chins up, mes choux!* Marguerite was so happy she thought she might levitate. Her heart was buoyant. Renata was here on Nantucket; she wanted to see Marguerite. "Come tomorrow night. For dinner. Can you?"

"Of course!" Renata said. "What time would you like me?"

"Seven thirty," Marguerite said. At Les Parapluies, the bar had opened each night at six thirty and dinner was served at seven thirty. Marguerite had run the restaurant on that strict timetable for years without many exceptions, or much of an eye toward profitability.

"I'll be there," Renata said.

"Five Quince Street," Marguerite said. "You'll be able to find it?"

"Yes," said Renata. In the background there was a burst of laughter. "So I'll see you tomorrow night, Aunt Daisy, okay?"

"Okay," Marguerite said. "Good night, dear."

With that, Marguerite had replaced the heavy black receiver in its cradle and thought, *Only for her.*

Marguerite had not cooked a meal in fourteen years.

8:00 A.M.

Marguerite left her house infrequently. Once every two weeks to the A&P for groceries, once a month to the bank and to the post office for stamps. Once each season to stock up at both bookstores. Once a year to the doctor for a checkup and to Don Allen Ford to get her Jeep inspected. When she was out, she always bumped into people she knew, though they were never the people she wished to see, and thus she stuck to a smile, a hello. *Let them think what they want.* And Marguerite, both amused and alarmed by her own indifference, cackled under her breath like a crazy witch.

But when Marguerite stepped out of her house this morning—she had been ready for over an hour, pacing near the door like a thoroughbred bucking at the gate, waiting for the little monkey inside her clock to announce that it was a suitable hour to venture forth—everything seemed transformed. The morning sparkled. Renata was coming. They were to have dinner. A dinner party.

Armed with her list and her pocketbook, Marguerite strolled down Quince Street, inhaling its beauty. The houses were all antiques, with friendship stairs and transom windows, pocket gardens and picket fences. It was, in Marguerite's mind, the loveliest street on the island, although she didn't allow herself to enjoy it often, rarely in summer and certainly never at this hour. She sometimes strolled it on a winter night; she sometimes peered in the windows of the homes that had been deserted for fairer climates. The police once stopped her; a lone policeman, not much more than a teenager himself, started spinning his lights and came poking through the dark with his flashlight just as Marguerite was gazing in the front window of a house down the street. It was a house Marguerite had always loved from the outside; it was very old, with white clapboard and wavy leaded glass, and the people who owned it, Marguerite learned from nosing around, had fine taste in French antiques. The policeman thought she was trying to rob it maybe, though he had seemed nervous to confront her. He'd asked her what she was doing, and she had said,

Just looking. This answer hadn't satisfied the officer much. *Do you have a home?* he'd asked. And Marguerite had laughed and pointed. *Number Five,* she'd said. *I live at Number Five.* He'd suggested she "get on home," because it was cold; it was, in fact, Christmas. Christmas night, and Marguerite had been wandering her own street, like a transient, like a ghost looking for a place to haunt.

Marguerite reached Centre Street, took a left, then a quick right, and headed down Broad Street, past the bookstore, past the French bistro that had absorbed all of Marguerite's old customers. She was aimed for Dusty Tyler's fish shop. Marguerite's former restaurant, Les Parapluies, had been open for dinner seven nights a week from May through October, and every night but Monday Marguerite had served seafood from Dusty Tyler's shop. Dusty was Marguerite's age, which was to say, not so young anymore. They'd had a close professional relationship, and on top of it they had been friends. Dusty came into the bar nearly every night the year his wife left him, and sometimes he brought his ten-year-old son in for dinner. Dusty had gotten very drunk one night, starting at six thirty with vodka gimlets served up by Lance, Marguerite's moody bartender. He then ordered two bottles of Mersault and drank all but one glass, which he sent to Marguerite back in the kitchen. By the time dinner service was over, the waitresses were complaining about Dusty—he was out-of-bounds, obnoxious, bordering on criminal. *Get him out of here, Margo,* the headwaiter, Francesca, had said. It was a Sunday night, and the fish shop was closed on Mondays. Marguerite overruled the pleas of her staff, which was rare, and allowed Dusty to stay. He stayed long after everyone else went home, sitting at the zinc bar with Marguerite, sipping daintily from a glass of Chartreuse, which he had insisted he wanted. He was so drunk that he'd stopped making any kind of sense. He was babbling, then crying. There had been spittle in his beard, but he'd smelled salty and sweet, like an oyster. Marguerite had thought they would sleep together. She was more than ten years into her relationship with Porter at that point, though Porter spent nine months of the year in Manhattan and—it was well known to everyone—dated other women. It wasn't frustration with Porter, however, that led Marguerite to think of sex with Dusty. Rather, it was a sense of inevitability. They worked together every day; she was his first client every morning; they stood side by side, many times their hips touching as they lifted a bluefin tuna out of crushed ice, as they pried open sea scallops and cherrystones, as they chopped the heads off shrimp. Dusty was destroyed by the departure of his wife, and Marguerite, with Porter off living his own life in the city, was lonely. It was late on a Sunday night; they were alone in the restaurant; Dusty was drunk. Sex was like a blinking neon sign hanging over the bar.

But for whatever reason, it hadn't happened. Dusty had rested his head on the bar, nudged the glass of Chartreuse aside, and passed out. Marguerite called a taxi from a company where she didn't know anyone, and a young guy wearing an Izod shirt, jeans, and penny loafers had dragged Dusty out to a Cadillac Fleetwood and driven him home. Marguerite felt—well, at first she felt childishly rejected. She wasn't a beauty, more handsome than pretty, her face was wide, her bottom heavier than she wished, though certain men—Porter among them—appreciated her independence, her God-given abilities in the kitchen, and the healthy brown hair that, when it was loose, hung to the small of her back. Dusty had sent sunflowers the next day with just the word *Sorry* scribbled on the card, and on Tuesday, when Marguerite and Dusty returned to their usual song and dance in the back room of the fish shop, she felt an overwhelming relief that nothing had happened between the two of them. They had been friends; they would remain so.

Marguerite felt this relief anew as she turned the corner of North

Beach Street, passed the yacht club, where the tennis courts were already in use and the flag was snapping, and spied the door to Dusty's shop with the OPEN sign hanging on a nail.

A bell tinkled as she walked in. The shop was empty. It had been years and years since Marguerite had set foot inside, and there had been changes. He sold smoked bluefish pâté and cocktail sauce, lemons, asparagus, corn on the cob, sun-dried tomato pesto, and fresh pasta. He sold Ben & Jerry's, Nantucket Nectars, frozen loaves of French bread. It was a veritable grocery store; before, it had just been fish. Marguerite inspected the specimens in the refrigerated display case; even the fish had changed. There were soft-shell crabs and swordfish chunks ("*great for kebabs*"); there was unshelled lobster meat selling for $35.99 a pound; there were large shrimp, extra-large shrimp, and jumbo shrimp available with shell or without, cooked or uncooked. But then there were the Dusty staples—the plump, white, day-boat scallops, the fillets of red-purple tuna cut as thick as a paperback novel, the Arctic char and halibut and a whole striped bass that, if Marguerite had to guess, Dusty had caught himself off of Great Point that very morning.

Suddenly Dusty appeared out of the back. He wore a white apron over a blue T-shirt. His hair was silver and his beard was cut close. Marguerite nearly cried out. She would never have imagined that she had missed people or that she missed this man in particular. She was shocked at her own joy. However, her elation and her surprise were nothing compared to Dusty's. At first, she could tell he thought he was hallucinating. For as much of an old salt as Dusty believed himself to be, he had the kind of face that gave everything away.

"Margo?" he said, his voice barely above a whisper.

She smiled and felt a funny kind of gratitude. There were people you knew in your life who would always be the same at base, hence they would always be familiar. Marguerite hadn't seen Dusty Tyler in years, but it might have been yesterday. He looked so much like himself that she could almost taste the ancient desire on her scarred tongue. His blue eyes, his bushy eyebrows, white now.

"Hi," she said. She tried to sound calm, serene, as if all these years she'd been away at some Buddhist retreat, centering herself. Ha! Hardly.

" 'Hi'?" Dusty said. "You disappear for damn near fifteen years and that's all you have to say?"

"I'm sorry." It was silly, but she feared she might cry. She didn't know what to say. Did she have to go all the way back and explain everything? Did she have to tell him what she'd done to herself and why? She had been out of the public eye for so long, she didn't remember how to relate to people. Dusty must have sensed this, because he backed off.

"I won't ask you anything, Margo; I promise," he said. He paused, shaking his head, taking her in. "Except what you'd like."

"Mussels," she said. She stared at the word on her list, to avoid his eyes. "I came for mussels. Enough to get two people off to a good start."

"Two people?" he said.

She blinked.

"You're in luck," he said. "I got some in from Point Judith this morning." He filled a bag with green-black shells the shape of teardrops. "How are you going to prepare these, Margo?"

Marguerite poised her pen above her checkbook and looked at Dusty over the top of her bifocals. "I thought you weren't going to ask me any questions."

"I said that, didn't I?"

"You promised."

He twisted the bag and tied it. Waved away the checkbook. He wasn't going to let her pay. Even with real estate prices where they were, two pounds of mussels cost only about seven dollars. Still, she didn't want to feel like she owed him anything—but the way he was looking at her now, she could tell he wanted an explanation. He expected her to wave away his offer of no questions the way he waved away her checkbook. *Tell me what really happened. You clearly didn't cut your tongue out, like some people were saying. And you don't look crazy, you don't sound crazy, so why have you kept yourself away from us for so long?* A week or two after Marguerite was sprung from the psychiatric hospital, Dusty had stopped by her house with daffodils. He'd knocked. She'd watched him from the upstairs window, but her wounds—the physical and the emotional wounds—were too new. She didn't want him to see.

"I could ask you a few questions, too," Marguerite said, figuring her best defense was an offense. "How's your son?"

"Married. Living in Cohasset, working in the city. He has a little girl of his own."

"You have a granddaughter?"

Dusty handed a snapshot over the refrigerator case. A little girl with brown corkscrew curls sitting on Dusty's lap eating corn on the cob. "Violet, her name is. Violet Augusta Tyler."

"Adorable," Marguerite said, handing the picture back. "You're lucky."

Dusty looked at the picture and grinned before sliding it back into his wallet. "Lucky to have her, I guess. Everything else is much as it's always been."

He said this as if Marguerite was supposed to understand, and she did. He ran his shop; he stopped at Le Languedoc or the Angler's Club for a drink or two or three on the way home; he took his boat to Tuckernuck on the weekends. He was as alone as Marguerite, but it was worse for him because he wanted company. The granddaughter, though. Wonderful.

"Wonderful," Marguerite said, taking the mussels.

"Who is it, Margo?"

"I'd rather not say."

"Not the professor?"

"No. God, no."

"Good. I never liked that guy. He treated you like shit."

Even after all that had happened, Marguerite didn't care to hear Porter spoken about this way. "He did the best he could. We both did."

"What was his name? Parker?"

"Porter."

Dusty shook his head. "I would have treated you better."

Marguerite flashed back to that night, years earlier. Dusty with his head on the bar, drooling. "Ah, yes," she said.

They stood in silence for a moment, then two; then it became awkward. After fourteen years there were a hundred things they could talk about, a hundred people, but she knew he only wanted to talk about her, which she wasn't willing to do. It was unfair of her to come here, maybe; it was teasing. She shifted the mussels to her other hand and double-checked that her pocketbook was zipped. "Oh, Dusty," she said, in a voice full of regret and apology that she hoped would stand in for the things she couldn't say.

"Oh, Margo," he mimicked, and he grinned. "I want you to know I'm happy you came in. I'm honored."

Marguerite blushed and made a playful attempt at a curtsy. Dusty watched her, she knew, even as she turned and walked out of his shop, setting the little bell tinkling.

"Have a nice dinner!" he called out.

Thank you, she thought.

Marguerite had been in the fish store all of ten minutes, but those ten minutes were the difference between a sleepy summer morning and a full-blown August day on Nantucket. One of the ferries had arrived, disgorging two hundred day-trippers onto the Straight Wharf; families who were renting houses in town flooded the street in search of coffee and breakfast; couples staying at B and Bs had finished breakfast and wanted to rent bikes to go to the beach. Was this the real Nantucket now? People everywhere, spending money? Maybe it was, and who was Marguerite to judge? She felt privileged to be out on the street with the masses; it was her own private holiday, the day of her dinner party.

There was a twinge in Marguerite's heart, like someone tugging on the corner of a blanket, threatening to throw back the covers and expose it all.

Dusty had let her off easy, she thought. But the girl might not. She would want to hear the story. And Marguerite would tell her. The girl deserved more than five thousand dollars. She deserved to hear the truth.

8:37 A.M.

The sheets were white and crisp, and the pillows were so soft it was like sinking her head into whipped cream. The guest room had its own deck with views of Nantucket Sound. Last night, she and Cade had stood on the deck kissing, fondling, and finally making love—standing up, and very quietly, so that his parents, who were having after-dinner drinks in the living room with their absurdly wealthy friends, wouldn't hear.

Once you marry me, Cade had whispered when they were finished, *all this will be yours.*

Renata had eased her skirt and her underwear back into place and waited for the blinking red beacon of Brant Point Lighthouse to appear. She would have laughed or rolled her eyes, but he was serious. Cade Driscoll wanted to marry her. He had presented her with a diamond ring last week at Lespinasse. (The maître d' was in on the plan in advance: drop the ring in a glass of vintage Dom Pérignon—he didn't realize Renata wasn't old enough to drink.) They set out, cautiously, to inform their families. This meant Cade's parents first—and then, at some point later, Renata's father.

The announcement to the Driscolls had taken place the previous morning, shortly after Cade and Renata arrived on the island. Miles, a drop-dead gorgeous hunk of a man who was spending his summer as the Driscolls' houseboy, had picked up Cade and Renata at the airport, then delivered them to the house on Hulbert Avenue, where the cook, Nicole, a light-skinned black girl with a mole on her neck, had prepared a breakfast buffet on the deck: mimosas, a towering pyramid of fresh fruit, smoked salmon, muffins, and scones (which Mrs. Driscoll wouldn't even look at, being on Atkins), eggs, sausage, grilled tomatoes, coffee with hot frothy milk.

"Welcome to Nantucket!" Suzanne Driscoll said, opening her arms to Renata.

Renata had bristled. She was nervous about announcing the engagement; she was afraid that the Driscolls, Suzanne and Joe (who had early-stage Parkinson's), would notice the ring before Cade was able to tap his silver spoon against his juice glass, and she had to abide another display of the Driscolls' wealth in the form of the house, Vitamin Sea.

Renata tried to view the circumstances through the eyes of her best friend, Action Colpeter, who was cynical about the things that other people found impressive. *Houseboy? Cook?* Action would say. *The Driscolls have servants!* Action had traced her ancestors back to slaves in Manassas, Virginia; she was touchy about hired help, including her own retarded brother's personal aide and her parents' cleaning lady. She was touchy about a lot of other things, too. She would be horrified to learn of Renata's engagement; she would pretend to vomit or, because she tended to get carried away with her little dramatizations, she would vomit for real. Faint for real. Die for real. Renata was spared her dearest friend's reaction for three more weeks—Action was working for the summer as a camp counselor in the mountains of West Virginia, where there were no cell phones, no fax, no computers. More crucially for the inner-city kids who attended the camp, there were no TVs, no video games, no Game Boys. In her most recent letter, Action had written: *We are completely cut off from the trappings of modern culture. We might as well be in the Congo jungle. Or on the moon.* She had signed this letter, and every other letter she sent Renata, *Love you like rocks,* which Renata understood to mean a great and rarefied love. Ah, Action. Good thing she wasn't here to see.

Miles had whisked Renata's luggage to her guest quarters; she was presented with a mimosa and encouraged to eat, eat, eat! If either of the Driscolls noticed the whopper of a diamond on Renata's left hand, it was not mentioned until Cade pulled Renata into the sun, placed his arm tightly around her shoulders, and said in his resonant lacrosse-team-captain voice, *I have an announcement to make.*

Suzanne Driscoll had shrieked with delight; Mr. Driscoll, his left hand trembling, made his way over to clap Cade on the back. It was for Mr. Driscoll's sake that Cade had proposed to Renata after only ten months of dating. No one knew how quickly the Parkinson's would progress. Cade was an only child; he was older than Renata, a senior to her freshman when they'd met, and now, with his degree from Columbia in hand, he would start a job with J. P. Morgan the Tuesday after Labor

Day. His parents had bought him an apartment on East Seventy-third Street; "a little place," they called it, though compared to Renata's dorm room on West 121st, it was a castle.

Once you marry me, all this will be yours. The castle on Seventy-third Street, the house on Nantucket, the servants, a life of grace and ease. Action would accuse Renata of wanting all this, of finding it impossible to refuse—but what Renata had found impossible to refuse was Cade himself. He was the kindest, fairest person she had ever known; he was principled; he did the right thing; he thought of others; he was a leader in the best sense; he was princely, presidential. A real, true good egg. He adored Renata; he loved her so earnestly and had proposed with such old-fashioned good intentions that Renata overlooked the obvious objections: It was too soon. She was too young.

I'm only nineteen years old, Renata had said when the ring appeared in her drink. She wasn't sure how she wanted her life to unfold, though she and Action had spent many nights talking about it in the minutes before they drifted off to sleep. Renata wanted to finish college, travel, visit museums, drink coffee, forge friendships, make connections, select a career path, a city (maybe New York but maybe not)—and then, once the person of Renata Knox was sufficiently cultivated, she would consider a husband and children.

Renata felt strangely cheated by Cade's proposal. She'd had the misfortune to meet the perfect man at eighteen years of age, and they were to be married. As Renata languished in the guest room bed, she felt surprised that no one in the Driscoll family had seen the shame in this. No one said (as Renata had hoped), *You two should wait a few years. Let your love steep, like tea; let it grow stronger.* However, Renata was certain her father would put his foot down and that all the current celebrating would be for naught.

Renata wandered downstairs in her bathrobe. It was not quite nine, but already everyone in the house was awake and showered and fed. Renata found Nicole in the kitchen doing the breakfast dishes and Suzanne Driscoll in her tennis clothes leaning against the marble countertop, telling Nicole everything that needed to get done that day. There were lobsters being delivered, but Nicole would have to run up to the farm for corn and tomatoes and salad greens.

When Suzanne saw Renata, she stopped. "And here comes Little Miss Sleepyhead!" This was said with enormous affection, the same tone of voice, Renata noted, that Suzanne used with the family's Siamese cat, Mr. Rogers. Renata heard Action's voice in her head: *There you go, girl. You're the new pet.*

On their third date, Cade had taken Renata to meet his parents. The Driscolls lived on the ninth floor of a building on Park Avenue—the entire ninth floor. Renata had tried to talk herself out of being intimidated—she was smart, her high school's valedictorian; she was worthy of anyone, including Cade—and yet she trembled with inadequacy the whole evening. She had knocked over her glass of wine, staining the tablecloth. Suzanne and Joe had laughed musically, as though nothing could be more charming. Renata got the feeling that it didn't matter who she was or what she was like; if Cade liked her, loved her, married her, the elder Driscolls liked her, loved her, and would overlook her obvious shortcomings. Renata, who had grown up without a mother, had hoped for a real connection with Suzanne; however, her exchanges with the woman were pleasant but artificial, like a bouquet of silk flowers.

"Good morning," Renata said. She felt a stab of guilt as Nicole peeled off her rubber gloves in order to fetch Renata a cup of coffee. "Where's Cade?"

"Sailing with his father," Suzanne said.

Renata's heart sank. "When will he be back? We were supposed to go to the beach."

"Well, you know Joe," Suzanne said, though, of course, Renata didn't know Joe Driscoll, not really. She did know that if Cade had abandoned her, it would only have been to please his father. "They were out the door at seven. We're having lunch at the yacht club at noon. The Robinsons are coming at six for cocktails followed by lobsters on the deck. You do like lobster, don't you?"

"I like lobster," Renata said.

Suzanne sighed as if her day had hung in the balance. "Oh, *good.*"

"But I won't be here for dinner."

Suzanne stared, nonplussed. Was it a bad sign that already Renata enjoyed stymieing her future mother-in-law?

"I'm having dinner with my godmother," Renata said. "Marguerite Beale."

"Of course," Suzanne said. "Marguerite Beale." She said this in a quasi-patronizing way, as if Marguerite Beale were an imaginary friend Renata had invented. "You've spoken to her, then?"

"Last night," Renata said. "After you and Joe left the restaurant, I called her."

"And you're having dinner?"

"That's right."

"Are you going out? Or . . . you'll eat at her house?"

"Her house." Renata sipped her coffee.

"Is she cooking?" Suzanne said. "I hate to sound nosy, but I've heard . . . from friends who have friends who live here year-round, that . . ."

"That what?"

"That she doesn't cook anymore."

Renata set down her coffee cup more forcefully than she meant to and tugged at the sash of her robe. There was a way in which the Driscoll family could not get over themselves. They believed, for example, that they held exclusive rights to the island of Nantucket. And yet how many times had Renata mentioned her own family's history here? Her uncle Porter had been coming since the fifties; he had been Marguerite's lover for seventeen years. Renata's mother, Candace, had worked at the Chamber of Commerce; she and Marguerite had been best friends. Renata's father, Daniel Knox, had owned the Beach Club down the street; he sold it a few months after Candace died, right around the time that Marguerite closed Les Parapluies. Renata herself had been born here and christened here, but the most important fact about Nantucket within the Knox family history was that Candace had died here. Hit by a car, on the road that led to Madequecham Beach. Somehow, Renata felt this gave her the strongest connection to the island; it trumped everyone else. And yet the only tie Renata could claim anymore was Marguerite. Marguerite, her godmother, whom she had been forbidden from seeing her whole life. There had been letters, checks, a distant paper presence. Renata had studied photographs of Marguerite; she had overheard snatches of the old stories. She had only one memory of the woman—a cold day, snow, a grandfather clock, a cup of tea with honey. The tea had burned Renata's tongue. She cried, and arms wrapped around her. She sat on a soft, flowered couch.

"She's cooking," Renata said, though she had no idea if this were true or not, and quite frankly, she didn't care. Pizza was fine, or peanut butter toast. Renata just wanted to talk.

Suzanne sniffed, smoothed her tennis skirt. Her face was at once unbelieving and envious.

"Well," she said. "Aren't you lucky?"

9:14 A.M.

Marguerite smoked the mussels herself. She debearded them and placed them in a smoker that a fellow chef had sent her for Christmas several years ago. She had never used the smoker and remembered thinking when she unwrapped it that she would never use it. But now she had grown old enough to prove herself wrong.

The smoker required a pan of water and wood chips. Marguerite set the contraption up, got it smoking like a wet campfire, and left it on the patio to do its thing. The clock chimed quarter past the hour. Marguerite looked longingly at her sofa, where a collection of Alice Munro stories beckoned to her like a middle-aged siren. Not today. Marguerite checked her list.

Call for the meat
Herb Farm
Tart crust
Bread!!!
Pots de crème
Aioli
Polish silver
Champagne!!!

Back in the day, Marguerite had worked from lists all the time. She had made daily pilgrimages to Dusty's fish shop, and to the Herb Farm for produce; the meat had been delivered. She had prepared stocks, roasted peppers, baked bread, cultivated yogurt, rolled out crusts, whipped up custards, crushed spices. Les Parapluies was unique in that Marguerite had served one four-course menu—starter, salad, entrée, dessert—that changed each day. Porter was driven mad by the simplicity of it. *People want choices,* he'd said. *They want to come in when they're hungry. You're telling the customer what they will eat and when they will eat. You can't run a business that way, Daisy!*

Marguerite triaged her list. *Bread.* If she started it now, the dough would have ten hours to rise. She took a jar of yeast from the fridge and found sugar, salt, and flour in the pantry. The acquaintances Marguerite happened across at the A&P never failed to inspect the contents of her shopping cart—she noticed they did this ever so subtly, skimming their eyes over her groceries the way one ran a white glove over a shelf to check for dust. On any given week, they would find cans of corn, packaged soups, occasionally a hunk of expensive French cheese because the texture pleased her, and basic staples: sugar, salt, flour. But nothing fresh, nothing exotic. There was no pleasure in food for Marguerite anymore. She could taste nothing. She ate only to stay alive.

She missed cooking as profoundly as an amputated limb. It felt odd, sinful, to be back at it; it felt like she was breaking some kind of vow. *Only for her,* she thought. And it was just the one meal. Marguerite bumbled around at first; she moved too fast, wanting to do everything at once. She took three stainless-steel bowls from the cabinet; they clanged together like a primitive musical instrument. The bowls were dusty and needed a rinse, but first, Marguerite thought, she would get warm water for the bread (a hundred degrees, as she'd advised in the column she'd written about bread baking for the Calgary paper). There used to be a rhythm to her process, one step at a time. *Slow down,* she thought. *Think about what you're doing!* She proofed her yeast in the largest of the bowls; then she mixed in sugar, salt, and a cup of flour until she had something the consistency of pancake batter. She started adding flour, working it in, adding flour, working it in, until a baby-soft batch of dough formed under her hands. Marguerite added more flour—the dough was still sticky—and she kneaded, thinking, *This feels wonderful: this is like medicine, I am happy.* She thought, *I want music.* She pushed the play button of her stereo, leaving behind a white, floury smudge. When she dusted the smudge away in three or four days, would she remember this happiness? It would have evaporated, of course, transmogrified into another emotion, depending on how the dinner party went. What Marguerite was thriving on this second was the energy of anticipation. She had always loved it—the preparation, getting ready, every night a big night because at Les Parapluies the evenings when the numbers were the smallest had been the best evenings, the most eventful. The locals came, and the regulars; there was gossip flying from table to table; everyone drank too much.

Ella Fitzgerald. Marguerite felt like singing along, but even shuttered inside her own house she was too shy—what if her neighbors heard, or the mailman? Now that it was summer, he came at irregular hours. So instead, Marguerite let her hands do the singing. She covered the bread dough with plastic wrap and put it in the sun, she pulled out her blender and added the ingredients for the *pots de crème:* eggs, sugar, half a cup of her morning coffee, heavy cream, and eight ounces of melted Schraffenberger chocolate. What could be easier? The food editor of the Calgary paper had sent Marguerite the chocolate in February as a gift, a thank-you—Marguerite had written this very recipe into her column for Valentine's Day and reader response had been enthusiastic. (In the recipe, Marguerite had suggested the reader use "the richest, most decadent block of chocolate available in a fifty-mile radius. Do not—and I repeat—*do not* use Nestlé or Hershey's!") Marguerite hit the blender's puree button and savored the noise of work. She poured the liquid chocolate into ramekins and placed them in the fridge.

Porter had been wrong about the restaurant, wrong about what people would want or wouldn't want. What people wanted was for a trained chef, a real authority, to show them how to eat. Marguerite built her clientele course by course, meal by meal: the freshest, ripest seasonal ingredients, a delicate balance of rich and creamy, bold and spicy, crunchy, salty, succulent. Everything from scratch. The occasional exception was made: Marguerite's attorney, Damian Vix, was allergic to shellfish, one of the selectmen could not abide tomatoes or the spines of romaine lettuce. Vegetarian? Pregnancy cravings? Marguerite catered to many more whims than she liked to admit, and after the first few summers the customers trusted her. They stopped asking for their steaks well-done or mayonnaise on the side. They ate what she served: frog legs, rabbit and white bean stew under flaky pastry, quinoa.

Porter had pressed her to add a seating to double her profits. *Six thirty and nine,* he said. *Everybody's doing it.*

Yes, said Marguerite. *And when I left high school all the other girls were becoming teachers or nurses. University was for boys; culinary school was for Europeans. I don't do what other people do. If people want to eat at Les Parapluies, they will come at seven thirty. In return for this inconvenience, they will get their table for the entire night.*

But the profits, Porter said.

I will not send Francesca out to breathe down somebody's neck in the name of profits, Marguerite said. *This restaurant is not about profits.*

What? Porter said.

We're in love, Marguerite had said, nodding at the dining room filled with empty chairs. *Them and me.*

The song came to an end. The clock chimed the hour. Ten o'clock.

Marguerite retreated to the bedroom to phone the A&P and order the meat. A three-pound tenderloin was the smallest available.

"Fine," Marguerite said. It would be way too much, but Marguerite would wrap the leftovers and send them home for the fiancé on Hulbert Avenue.

There was another startling noise. Marguerite, who had been sitting on the bed next to the phone, jumped to her feet. In the last twelve hours, the noises had come like gunshots. What was that high-pitched ringing? The CD player gone awry? Marguerite hurried out to the living room. The CD player waited silently. The noise was coming from the kitchen. Aha! It was the long-forgotten drone of the stove's timer. The mussels were done.

10:07 A.M.

Renata hadn't counted on being alone, and yet that was exactly what had happened. Cade and his father were sailing and Suzanne was off for tennis, leaving Renata with two blank hours until she was expected at the yacht club. She wanted to go running; it was the coffee, maybe, combined with the antsy-weird feeling of being alone in the house. As Renata climbed the back stairs—she had never stayed in a house that *had* back stairs—to the guest room to change, she found Mr. Rogers weaving deftly between the spindles of the banister. So she was not alone after all.

She dressed in her exercise clothes and gathered her hair into a ponytail. On a scale of one to ten, her guilt was at a six and a half and climbing. Before she embarked on this weekend trip to Nantucket, she had promised her father only one thing: that she would not, under any circumstances, contact Marguerite. But how could Renata resist? She had been dreaming about contacting Marguerite since she and Cade boarded the plane yesterday morning; she had been dreaming of it since the day, ten months earlier, when Cade told her his parents had a house on Nantucket.

Nantucket? she'd said.

You know it?

Know it? she said. *I was born there. My parents' life was there. My godmother is there.*

But Renata didn't really know Nantucket, not the way Cade did, coming every summer of his life.

I'll take you this summer, Cade had said.

That was back in October; they had been dating for two weeks. But even then, Renata had thought, *Yes. Marguerite.*

To Renata, Marguerite was like a shipwreck. She had, somewhere within her hull, a treasure trove of information about Candace, information Renata had never been privy to. And now that Renata was an adult, now that she was a *woman* about to be *married,* she wanted to hear stories about her mother, even silly, inconsequential ones, and who better to tell her than her mother's best friend? The fact that Daniel Knox had forbidden Renata from contacting Marguerite—had, in fact, kept them apart since Candace's death—only fueled Renata's desire to see the woman. There was something her father didn't want her to learn, possibly many somethings. *She's crazy,* Daniel Knox had said. *She's been institutionalized.* But Marguerite hadn't sounded crazy on the phone. She had sounded just the way Renata always imagined—cultivated, elegant, and delighted to hear Renata's voice. As if she couldn't believe it, either: They were finally going to be reunited.

Renata jogged down the back stairs (*Service stairs!* Action's voice cried out), brushing by Mr. Rogers, who was still intent on his acrobatics, and burst out the side door. Beautiful day.

"Hey," a voice said. Renata whipped around. She had thought that she and the cat were the only ones home, but there, among the hydrangeas, was Miles, holding a hose.

"Oh, hi!" Renata said. She had been awed by Miles's good looks when he came to fetch her and Cade at the airport, and once she'd acknowledged this attraction to herself, she was doomed to be tongue-tied in his presence.

"Where're you off to?" he asked.

"Oh . . . ," Renata said. "I'm going running."

"Perfect day for it."

"Yep," Renata said. She bent down and touched her toes; then she lifted her leg to the railing of the porch and touched her toes, hoping for a ballerina-in-a-Degas-painting effect, but she felt like a complete idiot. "What are you doing?"

"Watering," he said, and then in a whispered falsetto he added, "the precious hydrangeas."

"Are you in school?" Renata asked. He looked older than her but younger than Cade. Though maybe not. Cade could already pass for thirty.

"School?" Miles said. "No. I graduated from Colby three years ago."

"So what do you do now?" Renata asked.

"Work my ass off for these people," Miles said. "And in the winter I travel."

"Travel where?"

"You name it."

"Tell me where," Renata said.

"I've been to South Africa, Botswana, Mozambique, Kenya, and Tanzania. I climbed Kilimanjaro twice in one week."

"You did?"

Miles laughed.

"You did not."

"Enjoy your run," Miles said.

Renata set off down the white shell driveway, hoping and praying that Miles wouldn't watch her. She turned around to check. He was staring right at her ass. Renata was mortified and thrilled. She waved. Miles waved back. On a scale from one to ten, her guilt was at an eight.

She headed down the street toward the Beach Club, her father's former business. Daniel Knox had started his career in Manhattan, trading petroleum futures in the 1970s, which, he liked to tell people, was akin to striking oil himself. In five years he had a bleeding ulcer and had made enough money to retire. He took a sabbatical from the business of petroleum futures and moved to Nantucket for the summer to relax. He bought the Beach Club on a whim; he had played tennis with the son of the man who was selling it. At that time, the club was long on history and short on charm. Dan proceeded to renovate, restore, upgrade.

He added a fitness center—the first of its kind on Nantucket—and a hot tub, a sauna, a room for massage. He bought a hundred and twenty beach umbrellas from the company that supplied the most exclusive establishments on the Cap d'Antibes. He built a lunch shack, where families could sign for grilled hamburgers and ice-cream bars. For seventy-five years the members of the Beach Club had packed sandwiches wrapped in plastic; they had suffered with cold-water-only showers; they had lounged on rickety beach chairs and threadbare towels. Many of the members liked things this way; they were reluctant to embrace the improvements and the rate hike that came with them. But Daniel Knox won in the end. Not a single member quit, and, in fact, many had clamored to join. To hear him tell it on a night when he'd had a few scotches (which was what it took to get him to talk about Nantucket at all), he had single-handedly saved the Beach Club.

These endeavors ate up a good chunk of his capital, but he was happy. His bleeding ulcer healed. He had told Renata of the members' attempts to marry him off—to their single niece visiting from Omaha, to a career girl they knew from Boston. He'd endured five hundred blind dates in his estimation—dinners at the Club Car, picnics on Dionis Beach, movies at the Dreamland Theater—all a complete waste of time. The members concluded that he was too picky, or gay. And then one summer he noticed a young woman who would jog past the club every morning. He started saying hello; she would only wave. He began to ask around and heard varying reports: Her name was Candace Harris; she worked for the Chamber of Commerce. Her half brother, Porter Harris, was part-owner of the restaurant Les Parapluies. From someone else Dan heard that Porter was not part-owner at all; he was merely involved with the chef, a woman named Marguerite Beale. Candace hung out at the restaurant every night. She was to be seen with older men, drinking champagne. She was to be seen alone, always alone, or palling around with her brother and the chef. She was training for the New York Marathon or no, not the marathon. She ran for fun. *The best way to see her, man,* someone finally said, *is to go to the restaurant. The food's pretty damn good, too.*

Renata had heard this part of her parents' history plenty of times. Her father went to the restaurant without a reservation, and after a scotch at the bar he insinuated himself at a table with Candace, Marguerite, and Porter. They, having no idea who he was aside from another man in love with Candace, proceeded to punish him by drinking him under the table. He crawled out of the restaurant and claimed he couldn't even think the words *Les Parapluies* without vomiting. Ten days passed before he forced himself to return; when he did, Candace agreed to go out with him. The problem was, the only place she wanted to eat was Les Parapluies. *She* lived *at that restaurant,* Daniel said. *It was her second home.*

As Renata approached the Beach Club, her heart beat wildly. (She was also still thinking of Miles—he *had* been staring at her; she was sure of it.) The club was glorious. The blue, green, and yellow umbrellas were lined up in rows on the beach, and the water glinted in the sun. She spied some children digging with shovels at the shoreline and a solitary figure, swimming. There was a pavilion shading five blue Adirondack chairs and a low shingled building she assumed was the bathhouse. *This could have been mine,* Renata thought, and she pined for it for a minute—a place on Nantucket that would have been hers and not Cade's. She wished that her father could see the club at that moment, with the sun just so, and the water, and the breeze. He would have been forced to admit that he was shortsighted for selling; he would have wanted it back. Renata had heard the possibility of this in his voice in their final conversation before she left. He had been excited for her to see the club. *My old darling,* he said. There was a tone to his voice that sang out, *Those were the good old days,* and this made Renata think that maybe, after all this time, he was healing. But he'd ended the conversation by making her promise not to contact Marguerite. So no. Not healing. Never.

Renata slowed down, then stopped. Then wished for water, the cooling spray of Miles's hose. Cade's parents had been trying to join the Beach Club for years, but they were stuck on the waiting list, a fact that secretly thrilled Renata. She felt a connection to the place, probably more imagined than real. How many years had it been since it was not her but her mother running down this road? Twenty-three years. Renata imagined her father loitering in the parking lot with a clipboard, pretending to check the wind indicator as he waited for Candace to jog by. *Hi,* he would have said. *How are you this morning?* And the mother Renata could barely remember would smile to herself and give a little wave.

Renata loved her father, and she pitied him. His life since Candace died had been comprised of a safe new career—insurance—and his daughter. The career's primary purpose was to provide income for Renata's private high school, her tennis lessons, gymnastics, horses, French, the Broadway shows followed by dinner at One If by Land, Two If by Sea, the vacations to Bermuda and Tahoe and Jackson Hole, with Renata in her own hotel room from the time she was ten because that was, according to her father, the age when she stopped being a little girl and started becoming a young woman. It was around the age of ten, too, when Renata's view of her father changed. When she was a small child, his love had been a blanket, her security, her warmth. But then one day it became a heavy, itchy wool sweater that she was forced to wear in the heat of the summer; she wanted to shrug it off. *Lighten up, Dad,* she'd say. (He'd become "Dad," not "Daddy.") *Back off. Leave me alone.* The light of his interest only intensified; Renata felt like a bug he was torturing under a magnifying glass.

He had taken her to buy her first bra. She was a few months past her eleventh birthday, the other girls in the sixth grade wore bras, and Renata had to have one. *I want a bra,* she said. Her father had looked shocked at this pronouncement, and his eyes flickered over her chest—where, it had to be admitted, not much was happening.

Renata could still remember the trip to Lord & Taylor, the orange carpeting, the fluorescent lights, the soft dinging of the elevators. She and her father walked, not touching, not speaking, to Lingerie.

This is the place? her father asked incredulously, eyeing the mind-boggling array of bras and panties. The bras on display right in front of them were 36 triple-D—beige, black, lacy, and leopard print. Renata wasn't sure this *was* the place; she had never been bra shopping before. She wanted her mother, or any mother at all, and at that moment she hated her father for not remarrying, for not even dating.

They found a saleswoman. GLENDA, her name tag said, like the good witch from *The Wizard of Oz.* She took one look at Dan and Renata—embarrassed father and skinny eleven-year-old daughter who bleated like a lamb, "Bra?"—and whisked Renata into the dressing room while she discreetly snuck over to Juniors to fetch an assortment of training bras. Renata emerged, twenty minutes later, with three bras that fit; she wanted to wear one home. Her father, in the meantime, sat slumped in a folding chair until it was time to pay. On the way out, he started to cry. Renata didn't ask what was wrong; she couldn't bear to hear the answer. His little girl was growing up, and where was Candace?

Where was Candace?

When Renata and Cade started dating, Renata told him the story of bra shopping. *That,* she said, *sums up the way things are between me and my father. He loves me too much. He feels too responsible. He is weighing me down. I am weighing him down. I have been his daughter* and *his wife, you know what I mean?*

But you don't mean . . . ? Cade said.

No, Renata had said; then she wondered if her relationship with her father was too nuanced to explain to another human being or simply too nuanced to explain to Cade. She was pretty sure that Cade's relationship with his parents was cut-and-dried; it was normal. *They* took care of *him;* it was a one-way street. Cade didn't feel the need to escape them. What Cade wanted, more than anything in the world, was to be just like them.

Renata gazed out across Nantucket Sound. Her guilt was eating her for breakfast. She blew the Beach Club a kiss, then turned and ran for home.

10:40 A.M.

She was out again, on foot. It was unheard of: Marguerite Beale out of her house, twice in one day. And that was just a start; later she would have to go to the Herb Farm. She would have to *drive.*

But for now, the meat. Picked up, directly, from the butcher at the A&P. And while Marguerite was in the store, she bought olive oil, Dijon mustard, peppercorns, silver polish, toilet paper. It all fit in one bag, and then it was back out into the August sun. Marguerite was wearing a straw hat with a pink satin ribbon that tied under her chin. She felt like Mother Goose. The liquor store was next.

She went to the liquor store on Main Street, steeling herself for interaction; she had known the couple who owned the store for decades. But when she entered, she found a teenager behind the cash register and the rest of the store was deserted.

Marguerite wandered up and down the aisles of wine, murmuring the names under her breath. Chateauneuf-du-Pape, Chassagne-Montrachet, Semillion, Sauvignon, Viognier, Vouvray. She closed her eyes and tried to remember what each wine had tasted like. Wine in the glass, buttery yellow, garnet red, jewel tones. Candace across the table, her shoulders bare, her hair loose from its elastic.

"Can I help you?" the teenager said. He moved right into Marguerite's personal space. He stood close enough that she could see the white tips of his acne; she could smell his chewing gum. Instinctively she backed away. She was browsing the wine the way she browsed for books; she wanted to be left to do so in peace.

"Do you know what you're looking for?" the teenager asked. "Red or white? If it's red, you could go with this one," He held up a bottle of something called ZD. Marguerite had never heard of it, which meant it was from California—or, worse still, from one of the "new" wine regions: Chile, Australia, Oregon, upstate New York. Even fifteen years ago, she had been accused of being a wine snob because she would only serve and only drink wines from France. Burgundy, Bordeaux, the Loire Valley, Champagne. Regal grapes. Meanwhile, here was a child trying to peddle a bottle of . . . merlot.

Marguerite smiled and shook her head. "No, thank you."

"It's good," he said. "I've tried it."

Marguerite raised her eyebrows. The boy might have been seventeen. He sounded quite proud of himself, and he had an eager expression that led Marguerite to believe she would not be able to shake him. Which was too bad. Though maybe, in the interest of time, a good thing.

"I've come for champagne," Marguerite said. "I'd like two bottles of Veuve Clicquot, La grande Dame. I hope you still carry it."

Her words seemed to frighten the boy. Marguerite found herself wishing for Fergus and Eliza, the proprietors. They used to rub Marguerite the wrong way from time to time—a bit pretentious and very Republican—but they were profoundly competent and knowledgeable wine merchants. And they knew Marguerite—the champagne would have been waiting on the counter before she was fully in the door. But Fergus and Eliza were curiously absent. Marguerite worried for a minute that they had sold the store. It would serve her right to squirrel herself away for so long that when she surfaced there was no longer anyone on Nantucket whom she recognized. It was scary but refreshing, too, to think that she might outlast all the people she was hiding from.

The boy loped over to the wall of champagnes, plucked a bottle from the rack, and squinted at the label. Meanwhile, Marguerite could spy the bottles she wanted without even putting on her bifocals. She sidled up next to the boy and eased the bottles off the shelf.

"Here it is," she said, and because she was in a beneficent mood she lifted a bottle to show him the label. "When you're a bit older and you meet a special someone, you will drive her out to Smith's Point for the sunset with a bottle of this champagne."

The tips of his ears reddened; she'd embarrassed him. "I will?"

She handed him the bottles. "That's all for today."

He met her at the register and scanned the bottles with his little gun. "That will be two hundred and seventy dollars," he said. He shifted his weight as Marguerite wrote out the check. "Um, I don't think I'll be buying that champagne any time soon. It's *expensive.*"

Marguerite carefully tore out the check and handed it to him. "Worth every cent, I promise you."

"Uh, okay. Thanks for coming in."

"Thank you," she said. She picked up the brown bag with the bottles in one hand and the groceries in the other. Back out into the sun. The champagne bottles clinked against each other. Should she feel bad that she hadn't selected a Sancerre to drink with the tart and a lusty red to go with the beef? It was grossly unorthodox to drink champagne all the way through a meal, though Marguerite had done it often enough and she'd noticed any person in the restaurant who was brave enough to do it. But really, what would her readers in Calgary think if they knew? Champagne, she might tell them, was for any night you think you might remember for the rest of your life. It was for nights like tonight.

Her hands were full, true. She had a pile of things to do at home: The aioli, the marinade for the beef, and the entire tart awaited, and Marguerite held out hope for a few pages of Alice Munro and a nap. (All this exercise—she would pay for it tomorrow with sore muscles and stiff joints.) But even so, even so, Marguerite did not head straight home. She was out and about in town, which happened exactly never and she had done so much thinking about . . . and if she had really wanted to escape her past, she would have moved away. As it was, she still lived on the same island as her former restaurant, and she wanted to see it.

She lumbered down Main Street and took a left on Water Street, where she walked against the flow of traffic. So many people, tourists with ice-cream cones and baby strollers, shopping bags from Nantucket Looms, the Lion's Paw, Erica Wilson. Across the street, the Dreamland Theater was showing a movie starring Jennifer Lopez. Marguerite harbored a strange, secret fascination with J.Lo, which she nourished during her daily forays into cyberspace. Marguerite surfed the Internet as a way to keep current with the world and to combat the feeling of being a person born into the wrong century; she needed to stay somewhat relevant to life in the new millennium, if only for her Canadian readers. And cyberspace was alluring, as addictive as everyone had promised. Marguerite limited herself to an hour a day, timing herself by the computer's clock, and always at the end of the hour she felt bloated, overstimulated, as though she'd eaten too many chocolate truffles. She gobbled up the high-profile murders, the war in Iraq, partisan politics on Capitol Hill, the courses offered at Columbia University, the shoes of the season at Neiman Marcus, the movie stars, the scandals—and for whatever reason, Marguerite considered news about J.Lo to be the jackpot. Marguerite was mesmerized by the woman—her Latin fireworks, the way she shamelessly opened herself up to public adoration and scorn. *Jennifer Lopez,* Marguerite thought, *is the person on this planet who is most unlike me.* Marguerite had never seen J.Lo in a movie or on TV, and she had no desire to. She was certain she would be disappointed. After a second or two of studying the movie poster (that dazzling smile!) she moved on.

Down the street, still within shouting distance of the movie theater, on the opposite side of Oak Street from the police station, was a shingled building with a charming hand-painted sign of a golden retriever under a big black umbrella. THE UMBRELLA SHOP, the sign said. FINE GIFTS. Marguerite's heart faltered. She ascended three brick steps, opened the door, and stepped in.

If what the girl wanted was the *whole* story, the unabridged version of her mother's adult life and death and how it intersected with Marguerite's life and how they both ended up on Nantucket—if that was indeed the point of tonight—then Marguerite would have to go all the way back to Paris, 1975. Marguerite was thirty-two years old, and in the nine years since she'd graduated from the Culinary Institute she had been doing what was known in the restaurant business as paying her dues. There had been the special hell of her first two years out when she worked as *garde manger* at Les Trois Canards in northern Virginia. It was French food for American congressmen and lobbyists. The chef, Gerard de Luc, was a classicist in all things, including chauvinism. He hated the mere idea of a woman in his kitchen, but it was the summer of 1967 and he'd lost so many men to Vietnam that, quite frankly, he *had* to hire Marguerite. She had been, if judged by today's standards, egregiously harassed. The rest of the kitchen staff was male except for Gerard's mother, known only as *Mère,* an eighty-year-old woman who made desserts in a cool enclave behind the kitchen. Initially, Marguerite had thought that *Mère*'s presence might help ameliorate Gerard's wrath, his demeaning tirades, and his offensive language. (The worst of it was in French, but there were constant references to the sexual favors he would force Marguerite to perform if every strand of her hair wasn't caught up in the hair net, if the salad greens weren't bone-dry.) But after the second day, Marguerite deduced that *Mère* was deaf. Gerard de Luc was a fascist, an ogre—and a genius. Marguerite hated him, though she had to concede his plates were the most impeccable she had ever seen. He made her instructors at the CIA seem slack. He knew the pedigree of every ingredient that entered his kitchen—which farm the vegetables were grown on, which waters the fish were pulled from. *Fresh!* he would scream. *Clean!* He inspected their knives every morning. Once, when he found Marguerite with a dull blade, he threw her *mise-en-place* into the trash. *Start over,* he said. *With a sharp knife.* Marguerite had been close to tears, but she knew if she cried, she would be fired or ridiculed so horribly that she'd be forced to quit. She imagined the dull blade slicing off Gerard de Luc's testicles. *Yes, Chef,* she said.

Sometimes, staying in a less-than-optimal—or in this case a savage and unsafe—situation was worth it because of what one could learn on the job. In the case of Les Trois Canards, Marguerite became tough; any other woman, one of the cooks told her, would have left the first time Gerard pinched her ass. Marguerite's tolerance for pain was high.

She left Les Trois Canards after two years, feeling seasoned and ready for anything, and so she moved to restaurant Mecca: Manhattan. During the summer of 1969, she worked as *poissonier* at a short-lived venture in Greenwich Village called *Vite,* which served French food done as fast food. It folded after three months, but the *sous chef* liked Marguerite and took her with him down a golden path that led into the kitchen at La Grenouille. Marguerite worked all of the stations on the hot line, covering the other cooks' days off, for three magical years. The job was a dream; again, the staff were mostly Frenchmen, but they were civilized. The kitchen was silent most of the time, and when things were going smoothly Marguerite felt like a gear inside a Swiss watch. But the lifestyle of a chef started to wear on her. She arrived at work at nine in the morning to check deliveries, and many nights she didn't leave until one in the morning. The rest of the staff often went out to disco, but it was all Marguerite could do to get uptown to her studio apartment on East End Avenue, where she crashed on a mattress on the floor. In three years she never found time to assemble her bed frame or shop for a box spring. She never ate at home, she had no friends other than the people she worked with at La Grenouille, and she never dated.

Marguerite left Manhattan in 1972 for a *sous chef* position at Le Ferme, a farmhouse restaurant in the Leatherstocking District of New York. The restaurant was owned by two chefs, a married couple; they hired Marguerite when the woman, Annalee, gave birth to a daughter with Down's syndrome. For the three years that Marguerite worked at Le Ferme, the chefs were largely absent. They gave Marguerite carte blanche with the menu; she did all the ordering, and she ventured out into the community in search of the best local ingredients. It was as ideal a situation as Marguerite could ask for, but Le Ferme was busy only on the weekends; people in that part of New York weren't ready for a restaurant of Le Ferme's caliber. Marguerite even did her own PR work, enticing a critic she knew in the city to come up to review the restaurant—which he did, quite favorably—but it didn't do much to help. The restaurant was sold in 1975, and Marguerite was left to twist in the wind.

She considered returning home to northern Michigan. Marguerite's father had emphysema and probably lung cancer, and Marguerite's mother needed help. Marguerite could live in her old room, bide her time, wait to see if any opportunities arose. But when she called her mother to suggest this, her mother said, "Don't you dare come back here, darling. Don't. You. Dare."

Diana Beale wasn't being cruel; she had just raised Marguerite for something bigger and better than cooking at the country club or the new retirement community. What were the ballet lessons for, the French tutor, the four years of expensive cooking school?

I'm sending you money, Diana Beale said. She didn't explain where the money came from, and Marguerite didn't ask. Marguerite's father had worked his whole life for the state government, and yet all through Marguerite's growing up Diana Beale had magically conjured money with which to spoil Marguerite: weekend trips to Montreal (they had bought the grandfather clock on one trip; Diana Beale spotted it in an antique store and paid for it with cash), silk scarves, trips to the beauty parlor to shape Marguerite's long hair. Diana Beale had wanted Marguerite to feel glamorous even though as a child she'd been plain. She wanted Marguerite to distinguish herself from the girls she grew up with in Cheboygan, who taught school and married men with factory jobs. And so the mystery money. Only then, at the age of thirty-two, did Marguerite suspect her mother had a wealthy lover, had had one for some time.

What should I do with the money? Marguerite asked. She knew it was being given to her for a reason.

Go to Europe, her mother said. *That's where you belong.*

Marguerite could barely remember the person she had been before April 23, 1975, which was the day she stepped into Le Musée du Jeu de Paume in Paris and found Porter fast asleep on a bench in front of Auguste Renoir's *Les Parapluies.* She could remember the facts of her life—the long hours working, the exhaustion that followed her everywhere like a bad smell—but she couldn't recall what had occupied her everyday thoughts. Had she been worried about the stalling of her career? Had she been concerned that at thirty-two she was still unmarried? Had she been lonely? Marguerite couldn't remember. She had walked across the museum's parquet floor—it was noon on a Tuesday, the museum was deserted, and the docent had let her in for free—and she'd found Porter asleep. Snoring softly. He was wearing a striped turtleneck and lovely moss-colored linen trousers; he was in his stocking feet. He was so young then, though already losing his hair. Marguerite took one look at him, at his hands tucked under his chin, at his worn leather watchband, and thought, *I am going to stay right here until he wakes up.*

It only took a minute. Marguerite paced the floor in front of the painting, bringing the heels of her clogs firmly down on the parquet floor. She heard a catch in his breathing. She moved closer to the painting, her feet making solid wooden knocks with each step; she swung the long curtain of her hair in what she hoped was an enticing way. She heard muted noises—him rubbing his eyes, the whisper of linen against linen. When she turned around—she couldn't wait another second—he was sitting up, blinking at her.

I fell asleep, he said, in English, and then he caught himself. *Excusez-moi. J'ai dormi. J'etais fatigué.*

I'm American, Marguerite said.

Thank God, he said. He blinked some more, then plucked a notebook out of a satchel at his feet. *Well, I'm supposed to be writing.*

About this painting? Marguerite said.

Les Parapluies, he said. *I thought I was going to London, but the painting's on loan here for six months so I find myself in Paris on very short notice.*

That makes two of us.

You like it? he asked.

Paris?

The painting.

Oh, Marguerite said. She tilted her head to let him know she was studying it. She had been in Paris for two weeks and this was the first museum she'd visited, and here only because the Louvre was too intimidating. The little bald man who owned the hostel where she was staying had recommended it. Jeu de Paume. *C'est un petit gout,* he'd said. A little taste. The hostel owner knew Marguerite was a *gourmand;* he saw the treasures she brought home each night from the *boulangerie,* the *fromagerie,* and the green market. Bread, cheese, figs: She ate every night sitting on the floor of her shared room. She was in Paris for the food, not the art, though Marguerite had always loved Renoir and this painting in particular appealed to her. She was attracted to Renoir's women, their beauty, their plump and rosy good health; this painting was alive. The umbrellas—*les parapluies*—gave the scene a jaunty, festive quality, almost celebratory, as people hoisted them into the air.

It's charming, Marguerite said.

A feast for the eyes, Porter said.

When Marguerite entered the gift shop, she was overpowered by the scent of potpourri. *Mistake,* she thought immediately. It was a special corner of hell, standing in a space that used to be her front room, that used to have a fireplace and two armchairs, walls lined with books, and a zinc bar with walnut stools. Now it was . . . wind chimes and painted pottery, ceramic lamps, needlepoint pillows, books of Nantucket photography. Marguerite tried to breathe, but her sinuses were assaulted by the scent of lavender and bayberry. Her groceries and the champagne weighed her down like two bags of bricks.

"Can I help you?" asked an older woman, with tightly curled gray hair. A woman about Marguerite's age, but Marguerite didn't recognize her, thank God.

"Just looking," Marguerite squeaked. She wanted to turn and leave, but the woman smiled at her so pleasantly that Marguerite felt compelled to stay and look around. *It's nobody's fault but your own,* Marguerite reminded herself. *Your restaurant is now one big gingerbread house.*

Porter Harris, his name was. An associate professor of art history at Columbia University, on his spring break from school, working on an article for an obscure art historian journal about Auguste Renoir's portraits from the 1880s—how they were a step away from Impressionism and a step toward the modernist art of Paul Cézanne. Marguerite nodded like she knew exactly what he was talking about. Porter laughed at his own erudition and said, "Let's get out of here, want to?" They went to a nearby café for a beer; Porter was thrilled to find another speaker of English. "I've been staring at the people in Renoir's painting for so long," he said, "I was afraid they would start talking to me."

The beer went right to Marguerite's head as it only could on an empty stomach on a spring afternoon in Paris when she was sitting across from a man she felt inexplicably drawn to.

"Marguerite," he said. "French name?"

"My mother is an avid gardener," she said. "I was named after the daisy."

"How sweet. So what brings you to Paris, Daisy? Vocation or vacation?"

"A bit of both," she said. "I'm a chef."

He perked up immediately. Marguerite had always found it odd that when she first met Porter he was asleep, because his most pronounced trait was that of abundant nervous energy. He was exceptionally skinny, with very long arms and slender, tapered fingers. His legs barely fit under the wrought-iron café table. Marguerite could tell he was the kind of person who loved to eat but would never gain a pound. He lurched forward in his seat, his eyes bulged, and he lit a cigarette.

"Tell me," he said. "Tell me all about it."

Marguerite told. Les Trois Canards, *Mère, vite frites,* La Grenouille. Before she could even brag about her crowning achievement, Le Ferme, he was waving for the check.

I am boredom on a square plate, she thought. *And that is why I am single.*

It would be a lie to say that Marguerite had not entertained any romantic notions about her trip to Paris. She had fantasized about meeting a man, an older man, a married man in the French tradition, with oodles of money and a hankering for young American women to spoil. A man who would take her to dinner: Taillevent, Maxim's, La Tour d' Argent. But what happened was actually better. Porter paid the check, and when they were back on the street he took both of her hands in his and said, "I have a question for you."

"What?"

"Will you make dinner for me?"

She was speechless. *I love this man,* she thought.

"I'm being forward, yes," he said. "But all I've eaten for the past three days is bread, cheese, and fruit. I will buy the groceries, the wine, everything. All you have to do is—"

"You have a kitchen?" she whispered.

"My own apartment," he said. "On the boulevard St.-Germain."

Her eyebrows shot up.

"It's a loaner," he said. "Last minute, through the university. The owners are in New York for two weeks."

"Lead the way," she said.

Now that *was a dinner party,* Marguerite thought. Beef *tartare* with capers on garlic croutons, *moules marineres,* and homemade *frites,* a chicory and endive salad with poached eggs and *lardons,* and crème caramel. They drank two bottles of Saint Emilion and made love in a stranger's bed.

All week she stayed with Porter, and part of the following week, since he didn't have to teach until Friday. Porter was funny, charming, self-deprecating. He didn't walk so much as bounce; he didn't talk so much as bubble over like a shaken-up soda pop. As they zipped through the streets of Paris, he pointed out things Marguerite never would have noticed on her own—a certain doorway, a kind of leaded window, a model of car only manufactured for three months in 1942, under the Nazis. Porter had found himself in Paris on short notice, and yet he knew a tidbit of history about every block in the city. "I read a *lot,*" he said apologetically. "It's the only thing that keeps my feet on the ground." Marguerite liked his talking; she liked his energy, his natural verve, his jitters, his nervous tics; she loved the way he was unafraid to speak his bungled, Americanized French in public. She liked being with someone so zany and unpredictable, so alive. He raced Marguerite up the stairs of Notre-Dame; he bought tickets to a soccer match and patiently explained the strategy while they got drunk on warm white wine in plastic cups; he bought two psychedelic wigs and made Marguerite wear hers when they visited Jim Morrison's grave in Père Lachaise Cemetery.

Every night she cooked for him in the borrowed apartment on the boulevard St.-Germain and he stood behind her, actively watching, drinking a glass of wine, asking her questions, praising her knife skills, fetching ingredients, filling her glass. While the chicken roasted or the sauce simmered, he would waltz her around the kitchen to French music on the radio. Marguerite, at the advanced age of thirty-two, had fallen in love, and even better, she *liked* the man she was in love with.

He made her feel beautiful for the first time ever in her life; he made her feel feminine, sexy. He would tangle his hands in her long hair, nuzzle his face against her stomach. They played a game called One Word. He asked her to describe her mother, her father, her ballet teacher, Madame Verge, in one word. Marguerite wished she had spent more time reading; she wanted to impress him with her choices. (Porter himself used words like *uxorious* and *matutinal* with a wide-eyed innocence. When they visited Shakespeare and Company, Sylvia Beach's bookstore opposite to Notre-Dame on the Ile de la Cité, Marguerite raced to the *First Oxford Collegiate* to look these words up.) In the end, she said *savior* (mother), *diligent* (father), *elegant and uncompromising* (Madame Verge).

"That's cheating," he said. Then he said, "And how would you describe yourself? One word."

She took a long time with that one; she sensed it was some kind of test. *Charming,* she thought. *Witty, talented, lonely, lost, independent, enthralled, enamored, ambitious, strong.* Which word would this man want to hear? Then, suddenly, she thought she knew.

"Free," she said.

Even as she looked back from this great distance, it was nothing short of miraculous—the way that meeting Porter Harris had changed the course of Marguerite's life. But then, as suddenly as it began, it ended: He flew back to New York. Marguerite traveled all the way out to Orly, hoping he would ask her to come back to the States with him, but he didn't, which crushed her. She had his telephone number at home and at his office. He had no way to reach her. She stayed in Paris.

But Paris, in the course of ten days, had changed. The place that had been so mysterious and full of possibility when she arrived was unbearable without Porter. She wondered how long she had to wait before she called him and what she would say if she did. She had given him the word "free," but she wasn't free at all, not anymore. Love held her hostage; it made her a prisoner. She returned to her bed at the hostel; she went back to eating bread, cheese, figs. April turned into May; Paris was warm. Before he left, Porter had given her a copy of *The Sun Also Rises.* She hung out in the Tuileries and read and slept in the afternoon sun.

And then, after two excruciating weeks, the owner of the hostel knocked on the door of her room. A telegram. *DAISY: MEET ME IN NANTUCKET, MEMORIAL DAY.—PH*

Marguerite moved through the shop into the back room, the saleswoman on her trail. This had been the dining room. Eighteen tables: On a crowded night, a Saturday in August when every seat was taken, that meant eighty-four covers. Marguerite closed her eyes. There was Muzak playing, a rendition of "Hooked on a Feeling" on the marimba. But in Marguerite's mind it was laughter, chatter, gossip, whispers, stories told and told again. In Marguerite's mind the room smelled like garlic and rosemary. A spinning card rack stood where the west banquette used to be, next to a display of scented candles, embroidered baby items, wrapping paper.

Porter had found the space; he'd been looking around the island for a place to put an art gallery. He brought Marguerite to the building as soon as he picked her up from the ferry dock. He kept saying, *I want to show you something. You're really going to love it. Really, really, really. I can't wait to show you.* Marguerite was a bundle of nerves. Did Porter know what she would like or not like after only ten days together in what now seemed like a fairy-tale city on the other side of the Atlantic? She was so ecstatic to be back in Porter's presence that she didn't care. On her first ride through town she didn't notice a single detail about Nantucket other than the weather: It was gray and drizzling. Porter pulled his Ford Torino up onto the curb and ran around to open Marguerite's door.

You're going to love this, Daisy, he said. And up the three brick steps they went, hand in hand. Porter pulled out keys and swung the door open.

A narrow room, empty. A bigger room behind it, empty. A lovely exposed brick wall, two big windows.

What is it? Marguerite said.

Your restaurant, he said.

In that moment, Marguerite had many times mused, lay the conundrum of Porter Harris. They had been in each other's presence for less than two weeks and he was making the gesture of a lifetime, offering that space to her. And yet Porter's commitment to her began and ended with the space. The restaurant had, in many ways, taken the place of a marriage, taken the place of children. The space was what Porter had to offer (and, little did she know then, *all* he had to offer). At the time it had seemed a miraculous thing. Marguerite had dreamed of her own restaurant, she was ready, certainly, and she would ask her mother for the down payment. (It was unfathomable, but the building had cost only thirty thousand dollars.) Her life was starting over. That was how Marguerite felt when she'd stood in this room for the first time: She felt like she was being born.

Marguerite returned to the front room. Time to go. She was being self-indulgent; she had to get home. But her conscience prickled; she didn't feel she could leave without purchasing something. A refrigerator magnet quipped, *HOW TO LIVE ON AN ISLAND: EXPECT COMPANY.* No, no. But then Marguerite saw them by the door, in a brass stand. Umbrellas. She wished they were classic black with wooden handles, like the umbrellas in Renoir's painting. Instead, they were blue and white quarter panels, and on the white it said, *NANTUCKET ISLAND,* in blue block letters. Marguerite shifted her parcels and plucked one from the stand.

"I'll take it."

The saleswoman beamed. Marguerite pulled out her checkbook. She had no use for an umbrella, as she never left her house in the rain, and she had a visceral aversion to any piece of merchandise that shouted the name of the island. She had lived here for more than thirty years. Why would she need to announce the name of her home on her umbrella? Still, she wrote a check out to the tune of . . . seventeen dollars.

"The Umbrella Shop," Marguerite said. "A curious name. Do you know where it came from?"

The saleswoman folded down the top of the shopping bag and stapled Marguerite's receipt to it. "Quite frankly," she said, "I have no idea."

10:53 A.M.

It was the powers-that-be in the student life office of Columbia University that had brought Renata Knox and Action Colpeter together in Finnerty 205, although Renata suspected another force had been at work: Fate, or the hand of God. The name on the letter Renata received two weeks before she left for Columbia was *Shawna Colpeter.* "Freshman," it said, and it gave a home address of Bleecker Street, New York, New York. Renata pictured *Shawna Colpeter* as a girl raised one of two ways in Greenwich Village. She was either a child of traditional hippies or a child of extraordinarily wealthy hippies. Any which way, Renata was intimidated. The people she knew who grew up in Manhattan went to private school (Trinity, Dalton, Chapin) and they prided themselves on attending fashion shows, rave clubs, charity benefits of which their parents were cochairs. They were grown-ups in teenage bodies; they were cynical, world-weary, impossible to impress. They looked down on suburbia, the Home Depots and Pizza Huts, cheerleaders, beer parties in the woods, driver's licenses. With ten thousand cabs at one's disposal, who needed a driver's license?

When Renata reached Finnerty 205 with her father in tow—hauling boxes and milk crates and all of her hanging clothes in six separate garment bags—Shawna was on her cell phone, crying. Renata was grateful for this for several reasons. First of all, Renata was positive that she, too, would cry when it came time to say good-bye to her father (and *certainly* her father would cry). Second, it showed Renata right off the bat that the person she was going to share a room with for the next nine months had a soft spot somewhere. Third, and most important, it gave Renata a chance to get over her shock at Shawna Colpeter's physical appearance. Shawna Colpeter was black, and although it mattered not one bit, there was still an adjustment to be made in Renata's mind, because Renata had not been thinking black. She had been thinking pale and unwashed and Greenwich-Villagey looking. She had been thinking ennui and devil-may-care; she had been thinking pot smoker; she had been thinking orange glass bong on top of the waist-high refrigerator.

Shawna Colpeter smiled at Renata apologetically and wiped at her eyes.

"My roommate's here," she said into the phone. "Gotta go. Okay? Okay, honey? Love you. Gotta go, Major. Bye-bye." She hung up.

Immediately Renata protested. "Don't mind us."

Daniel dropped the load he was carrying onto the bare mattress that was to be Renata's bed, then he offered Shawna a hand. "Daniel Knox. I'm Renata's father."

She shook his hand, then fished a raggedy tissue from her pocket and loudly blew her nose. "I'm Action Colpeter."

"Action?"

"It's a nickname my parents gave me as a baby. Supposedly, I wore them out."

Another adjustment. Not Shawna but Action, which sounded like a name for an NFL running back. The girl, when she stood up, was six feet tall. She had long, silky black hair that flowed all the way down to her butt. She wore purple plaid capri pants and a matching purple tank top. No shoes. Her toenails were painted purple. She wore no makeup and even then had the most exquisite face Renata had ever seen: high cheekbones, big brown eyes, skin that looked as soft as suede.

"That was my brother on the phone," she said. "My brother, Major. He's ten, but with the mind of a three-year-old. He doesn't understand why I'm leaving home. I explained it, my parents explained it, but he does nothing but cry for me. It's breaking my heart."

Daniel cleared his throat. "I'm going down to get more stuff from the car." He disappeared into the hallway.

Renata didn't know what to say about a ten-year-old brother with the mind of a three-year-old. She could ask what was wrong with him—was it an accident or something he was born with?—but what difference would it make? It was sad information, handed to Renata in the first minute of their acquaintance. Renata decided that since her father was out of the room it would be a good time to explain something herself, in case Action started asking where the rest of her family was.

"My mother is dead," Renata said. "She died when I was little. I don't have any brothers or sisters. It's just me and my dad."

Action flopped backward on her bed. "We're going to be okay," she said to the ceiling. "We're going to be fine."

Renata was too young to understand the reasons why two women clicked or didn't click, though with Action, Renata believed it had something to do with the way they had opened their hearts before they unpacked a suitcase or shelved a book.

They did everything together: classes and parties, late-night pizza and popcorn, attending the football games all the way uptown, writing papers, studying for exams, drinking coffee. Action knew the city inside out. She taught Renata how to ride the subway, how to hail a cab; she took her to the best secondhand shops, where all the rich Upper West Side ladies unloaded their used-once-or-twice Louis Vuitton suede jackets, Hermés scarves, and vintage Chanel bags. Action gave Renata lifetime passes to the Guggenheim and the Met (her mother was on the board at one and counsel to the other); she instructed Renata never to take pamphlets from people passing them out on the street and never to give panhandlers money. "If you feel compelled to do something," Action said, "buy the poor soul a chocolate milk." Action was so much the teacher and Renata so much the student that Action took to asking, "What *would* you do without me?" Renata didn't know.

Every Sunday, Renata and Action rode the subway downtown to eat Chinese food with Action's family in the brownstone on Bleecker Street. Action's family consisted of her father, Mr. Colpeter, who was an accountant with Price Waterhouse, her mother, Dr. Colpeter, who was a professor at the NYU law school, and her brother, Major, whom Renata had pictured all along as looking like a three-year-old. But in fact, Major was tall and skinny like Action. He wore glasses and he drooled down the front of his Brooks Brothers shirt. (Whenever Renata saw Major he was dressed in a button-down and pressed khakis or gray flannels, as if he had just come from church.) Miss Engel, Major's personal aide, also lived in the house, though she was never around, Sunday being her day off. Her name was constantly invoked as a way to keep Major in line. "Miss Engel would want you to keep your hands to yourself, Major."

The front rooms of the brownstone had been recently redone by a decorator, Action said, because her parents did a lot of entertaining for work. The living room was filled with dark, heavy furniture, brocade drapes, and what looked like some expensive pieces of African tribal art, though when Renata asked about it, Action said it had all been picked out by the ID; her parents had never been to Africa. The dining room had the same formal, foreboding, special-occasion look about it—with a long table, sixteen upholstered chairs, open shelves of Murano glass and Tiffany silver. The back of the house—the kitchen and family room—was a different world. These rooms were lighter, with high ceilings and white wainscoting; every surface was covered with the clutter of busy lives. In the kitchen was a huge green bottle filled with wine corks, a butcher-block countertop that was always littered with cartons of Chinese food, stray packets of duck sauce and spicy mustard, papers, books, pamphlets for NYU Law and the Merce Cunningham dance cooperative. The Colpeters' refrigerator was plastered with various schedules and reminders about Major's life: his medication, his therapy appointments, the monthly lunch menu from his special school. Every week Dr. Colpeter apologized for the mess, and she always reminded them that Mrs. Donegal, the cleaning lady, came on Mondays. "This is as bad as it gets," she said.

Renata grew to love Sundays at the Colpeters' house because it was a whole family—noisy, messy, relaxed—enacting a sacred ritual. They always ate in the den with the football game on TV; always Mr. Colpeter opened a bottle of wine, dropped the cork into the green bottle, and poured liberally for Renata and Action so that Renata had a glow by the time the food arrived. The food was always delivered by a young Chinese man named Elton, who always came into the living room to chat for a minute about the game, his heavy accent obscuring what he was saying, and Mr. Colpeter always tipped him twenty dollars. Always Major insisted on sitting with Action in the plush blue club chair. Renata watched them closely, Action trying to eat her egg rolls while Major wiggled next to her, studying a lo mein noodle, winding it around his tongue. Dr. Colpeter wore sweatpants and T-shirts on Sunday nights; she cheered voraciously for the Jets; she hogged the whole sofa lying facedown after she ate. Renata knew she was one of the most esteemed legal minds in the country, but on Sunday nights she was loose and melancholy as she watched her kids nestled in the armchair.

"Action is more that child's mother than I am," she told Renata once.

Always on the subway home Action complained about the very evening Renata had found so comforting. Action accused her parents of being too absorbed with their careers; she accused them of neglecting Major emotionally.

"Why do you think he wants so much love from me?" she said. "Because he's not getting it from them. They dress him up like a junior executive to make the world think he's normal, instead of letting him be comfortable. Ten years old and that boy does not own a pair of jeans. And then there are the servants." Renata braced herself; she already recognized the tone of Action's voice. "Miss Engel and Mrs. Donegal. One young and Jewish, one old and Irish, but servants just the same. Those women do the work my parents should be doing. The dirty work."

"You're being kind of hard on them," Renata said.

"Please don't take their side against me," Action said. She stood up and grabbed the pole next to the door, as though threatening to step off the train at the wrong station. "I wouldn't be able to bear it."

When Renata got back from her run, she was hot and dying of thirst. She stood inside the refrigerator and poured herself half a glass of fresh-squeezed orange juice cut with half a glass of water. The sweat on her skin dried up and she shivered. She gulped her juice and poured more.

On the marble countertop next to the fridge was a list written out in Suzanne Driscoll's extravagant script. At first, Renata thought it was a list for Nicole—the lobsters, salad greens, and whatnot. But then Renata caught sight of her own name on the list and she snapped it up.

Priorities: Pick date! Check Saturdays in May/June '07.
Place: New York—Pierre or Sherry Neth.
(Nantucket in June? Check yacht club.)
Invites: Driscoll, 400. Knox side?
Call Father Dean at Trinity.
Reception—sit-down? absolutely no chicken!
Band—6-piece min., call BV for booking agent.
Renata—dress: VW? Suki R?

Also: flowers—order from K. on Mad.
Cake—Barbara J.'s daughter-in-law, chocolate rasp, where did she get it?
Favors—Jordan almonds? Bonsai trees?
Honeymoon—call Edgar at RTW Travel, Tuscany, Cap Jaluca

"Okay," Renata said. Her breath was still short from the run. This was a list for the *wedding,* her wedding. Suzanne's list for Renata's wedding. A little premature organization from a woman who was, quite clearly, a control freak, right down to the Jordan almonds.

Renata looked around the kitchen. She was in foreign territory. This was nothing like the kitchen in the house where she grew up, which had a linoleum floor, a refrigerator without an ice machine, and a spice rack that Renata had made in her seventh-grade industrial arts class. (How many times had Renata begged her father to remodel? But no—this was how the kitchen had looked when Renata's mother was alive; that was how it would stay.) Nor was the Driscolls' kitchen anything like the Colpeters' kitchen in the Bleecker Street brownstone. The Driscolls' kitchen was a kitchen from a lifestyle magazine: marble countertops, white bead board cabinets with brushed chrome fixtures in the shape of starfish, a gooseneck bar sink in the island, a rainwood bowl filled with ripe fruit, copper pots and pans gleaming on a rack over the island. Renata knew she was supposed to feel impressed, but instead she decided this kitchen lacked soul. It didn't look like a kitchen anyone ever cooked in or ate in. There was no sign that human beings lived here—except for the list.

Something about the Driscolls' kitchen in general—and the list in particular—made Renata angry and uncomfortable. Sick, even, like she might spew the juice she'd drunk too quickly into the bar sink. There was a telephone over by the stainless-steel dishwasher. Renata dialed Cade on his cell.

Three rings. He was sailing. *Can you hear me now?* Renata looked through the glass of the double doors that led to the deck, the lawn, a little beach, the water. Sailboats of all shapes and sizes bobbed on the horizon. Renata might have better luck shouting to him, *Your mother is al-*

ready planning our wedding! She's calling booking agents! She's arranging for our honeymoon in Tuscany!

The ringing stopped. It sounded like someone had picked up. But then a crackle, a click. No reception out at sea. Renata hung up and called back. She was shuttled right to Cade's voice mail.

"It's me," she said. Her voice sounded tiny and meek, like a girl's voice, a girl too young and incompetent to plan her own wedding. A girl without a mother to help her. "I'm at the house. Call me, please."

Because, really, the nerve! Renata hung up. Here, then, was one of life's mysteries revealed. How and when did a woman start resenting her mother-in-law? Right away, like this. Renata crushed the list in her palm. She couldn't throw it away; it was her only evidence.

Renata reached for a banana from the fruit bowl, thinking, *Replace potassium,* but she was so angry, so worried that her wedding might be commandeered by Suzanne Driscoll, that as soon as she picked up the banana she flung it into the cool, quiet atmosphere of the kitchen. It hit a bud vase on the windowsill that held a blossom from the precious hydrangea bushes; the bud vase fell into the porcelain farmer's sink and shattered.

"Shit!" Renata said. She retrieved the banana, peeled it savagely, and ate half of it in one bite, surveying the damage. She was tempted to leave it be and suggest later that Mr. Rogers had knocked the vase over, though of course Mr. Rogers was far too graceful a creature for such an accident. If something had broken while Renata was alone in the house, it would be assumed that Renata was responsible. Thus she did the only reasonable thing and cleaned up the mess—the bud vase was in three large shards and myriad slivers. She threw the shards away with the flower—maybe no one would remember it had even been there—and washed the slivers down the disposal. She had covered her tracks; now all she had to do was eat the evidence.

"Hey."

Renata gasped. Her nipples tightened into hard little pellets. Miles sauntered into the kitchen with Mr. Rogers asleep against his chest. "How was the run?"

"Fine," Renata said, sounding very defensive to her own ears. "Hot." She stuffed the rest of the banana into her mouth. "I'mgngupstshwrnw."

"Excuse me?" Miles said.

Renata finished chewing and swallowed. Her father liked to point out that when she was angry or distracted her manners reverted to those of a barnyard animal.

"I'm going upstairs to shower now," she said.

"Okay," Miles said with a shrug. It was clear he couldn't care less where she went or what she did.

The guest bathroom's shower—unlike the dorms at Columbia where Renata had been living all summer while she worked in the admissions office—featured unlimited hot water at a lavish pressure. It was soothing; Renata tried to calm herself. One of the traits she had inherited from her father was a propensity for flying off the handle. Daniel Knox was famous for it. The sister story to the bra-shopping story was the stolen-bike story. When Renata was nine years old, she forgot to lock up her bike in the shed. She and her father lived in Westchester County, in the town of Dobbs Ferry, which was a safe place, relatively speaking. Safer than Bronxville or Riverdale, though burglars and other derelicts did travel up from the city on the train, plus there was the school for troubled kids, and so the rule with the bike was: Lock it in the shed. The one day that Renata forgot, the one day her pink and white no-speed bike with a banana seat, a woven-plastic basket, and tassels on the handlebars was left leaning innocently against the side of the house, it was stolen. When Daniel Knox discovered this fact the next morning, he sat down on the front steps of their house in his business suit and cried. He bawled. It was the mortifying predecessor to the crying in the department store; this was the first time Renata had seen her father, or any grown man, cry in public. She could picture him still, his hands covering his face, muffling his broken howls, his suit pants hitched up so that Renata could see his dress socks and part of his bare legs above his socks. Her father's reaction was worse than the stolen bike; she didn't care about her bike. At that time, because she was younger, or kinder, than she was during the bra-shopping trip, she clambered into her father's lap and apologized and hugged his neck, trying to console him. He wiped up, of course—it was just a bike, replaceable for less than a hundred dollars—and everything was fine. Renata, over the years and despite her best intentions, had sensed herself about to overreact in the same embarrassing way. The scene downstairs in the kitchen, for example. What if Miles had walked in and seen her throw a banana and break the vase? How to explain that? *I'm angry about Suzanne's list.* It was just a *list,* just a collection of thoughts, of good, generous intentions, which now sat crumpled on the side of the guest bathroom's sink, the words blurring in the shower steam.

And yet something about the list bugged her.

Renata dried off, moisturized, and slipped into her bikini. She wanted to have a swim and lie on the small beach in front of the house until it was time for lunch. But first she sat on the guest room bed—which had, miraculously, been made. (*Made?* Renata thought. She hadn't bothered. *Oh, maid. Nicole.*) Renata yearned for Action, who at that very moment would be doing what? Canoeing down a cold river? Gently dabbing calamine lotion on a camper's mosquito bites? Action would be able to deconstruct Suzanne Driscoll's list; she'd turn it into mincemeat, into dust. She would render it meaningless. Either that or she would become indignant; she would put Renata's outburst to shame with her ranting and raving. *Who does that woman think she is? The Sherry Netherland? Bonsai trees?* Action was unpredictable—at once both passionate and unflappable, always smart, always funny, always exciting. Would Action Colpeter feel comfortable in this house? Would she be *welcome* in this house? Renata seethed with guilt. Her own best friend didn't know about her engagement. Renata had tried to call her the second she got home from Lespinasse, the ring burning on her finger, but when Action's cell phone rang Major had answered. Action's cell phone had been left behind in her parents' brownstone on Bleecker Street. And so Renata was stuck with her guilt. The one person who should know about her engagement—who should have known before everyone else—didn't.

Or no, not the one person. One of two people.

Renata fished her cell phone out of her bag, stared at it for a few long seconds, then dialed her father.

She was so nervous she thought she might gag. This was, most definitely, not in the game plan that she and Cade had devised. They had planned to tell Daniel Knox of their impending nuptials together, in person, in Manhattan—on their turf, either over cocktails at "the little place" that now belonged to Cade on East Seventy-third Street or at a dinner that Cade would pay for, in a restaurant that Cade would select.

It doesn't matter how we tell him, Renata said. *He's going to say no. He'll forbid it.*

Don't be silly, Cade said. *Your father loves you. If you tell him you want to get married, he'll be happy for you.*

Renata was tempted to inform Cade of just how wrong he was, but Cade was a born diplomat. He accepted everyone's point of view, and then, by virtue of his patience and tolerance and goodwill, he inevitably won everyone over to his side. But not this time.

Still, Renata had agreed to wait. She was relieved that telling Daniel would be left until the last possible minute and that Cade would be the one to break the news. Renata couldn't pinpoint what was making her press the issue on her father now. Was it Suzanne's list or a general sense of propriety? Either way, her father needed to know.

Daniel Knox picked up after the first ring. Eleven o'clock on a gorgeous summer Saturday: Renata felt dismayed that he was at home. He would be alone, working, or catching up on *Newsweek,* when he should be at a Yankee game, or playing golf.

"Daddy?"

"Honey?" he said. "Is everything okay?"

"Everything's great!" Renata said. She wished she were wearing clothes. She felt exposed in her bikini. "I'm on Nantucket. At the Driscolls'. It's sunny."

"You're having fun?"

"Yep. I ran down to the Beach Club this morning."

"You did? Oh, geez." He paused. Which, of a hundred things, was he thinking? "I hope you stayed on the bike path. That's why it's there."

"I stayed on the path," she said.

"Okay, good. How was it then? The club, I mean."

"Beautiful."

"Did you go inside? Talk to anyone?"

"No."

"I don't even know if the same people own it," Daniel Knox said.

"I don't know, either," Renata said. She felt like she was spinning; she was dizzy and nauseous. "Daddy? Listen, I have something to tell you."

"You've called Marguerite," he said. His voice oozed disappointment. "Oh, honey. I told you, she's not—"

"No," Renata said, though this was in response to his digression and not to the accusation, which was true. "I mean, yes, I did call Marguerite, but that's not what—"

"She's not in her right mind," Daniel Knox said. "I don't know how to make you understand. She may sound cogent, but she has serious mental and emotional problems, and I don't want you talking to her. You're not going to try and see her, are you?"

"Tonight," Renata said. "For dinner."

"No," Daniel said. "Oh, honey, no."

"You can't stop me from having dinner with my own godmother," Renata said. "I'm an adult."

"You're my daughter. I would hope you'd respect my wishes."

"Well, I have something else to tell you and you're not going to like it any better."

"Oh, really?" Daniel said. "And what is that?"

"I'm getting married."

Silence.

"To Cade, Daddy. Cade and I are getting married. He proposed and I said yes."

Silence.

"Daddy? Dad? Hello? Say something, please."

There was nothing, save the steady sound of breathing. So he hadn't hung up. He was reeling. Or strategizing. What was the phrase he'd repeated all her life, to anyone who asked him how he did it, raising a daughter alone? *I spend all my spare time trying to stay one step ahead of her.* Everyone always chuckled at this declaration, understanding it to be a comical, fruitless effort on his part. But this silence was unsettling. She had expected shock, anger, an "over my dead body." This would mellow into an insistence that she wait. *Please finish college. Graduate. You're too young. I'll talk to Cade myself. I'll take care of it.*

But the silence. Weird. Dread sat in her stomach like a cold stone. Regret. Should she have waited, adhered to Cade's plan?

"Daddy?"

"Yes?" he said, and now his voice sounded . . . amused. Was that possible? Did he think she was kidding? She fiddled with her ring. That was another reason to tell him in person: He would be confronted by the reality of twelve thousand dollars on her finger. This was not something he could laugh off; he couldn't turn his head and hope it would go away.

"Did you hear me? What I just said? Cade and I are getting married."

"I heard you."

"Well, what do you think?"

He laughed in a way that she could not decipher. He *sounded* genuinely happy, delighted even. Had he spent all his spare time practicing that laugh? Because it threw her off-balance; she felt like she was going to fall.

"I think it's wonderful, darling. Congratulations!"

After she hung up, she sat on the bed as still as a statue. She felt the air on her skin. Another girl would be jumping for joy or, at the very least, wallowing in sweet relief. Renata, however, felt outsmarted, tricked, and yes, betrayed. It wasn't that she wanted her father to keep her from marrying Cade; she had been so sure that he would, so certain that she could predict his very words, that she had never considered the engagement to be real. But now it was real. She wore a real diamond and had what sounded like her father's real blessing.

The phone in the house rang. Cade? She couldn't bear to talk to him.

She picked up her monogrammed canvas beach bag—a welcome-to-Nantucket present that Suzanne Driscoll gave to all of her overnight guests—and stuffed it with a striped beach towel, her sunglasses, her book—and, as an afterthought, Suzanne's list. Then she raced downstairs. She had to get out of the house.

When she walked into the kitchen, she found Miles at the counter making a ham sandwich.

"Hey," he said. His favorite syllable. Employable in any situation, Renata now understood.

"Hey," she said. "I'm on my way out."

"Where to?" he said.

"Beach."

"Here?"

"I have no wheels," she said. "So, yes."

"That little beach is crap," he said. "And the water isn't clean. You notice Mr. D. keeps his Contender anchored offshore."

"It's not clean?" Renata said. "Are you sure?" More than anything, she wanted to swim.

"You should come with me," Miles said. "I'm just about to head out. I have the afternoon off."

"Well, I don't," Renata said. "I'm supposed to meet the family at the yacht club in an hour."

Miles rolled his eyes, and even then he was dazzling. Tall, broad shouldered, tan, with brown hair lightened by the sun, blue eyes, and a smile that made you think he was born both happy and lucky. "Blow off lunch," he said. "Cade and Mr. D. won't be there."

"You don't think?"

"Day like this?" Miles said. "Mr. D. will sail all afternoon. He won't have many more days on the water if he gets any worse."

Renata checked the horizon. She wished she was sailing herself, but she hadn't been invited. Cade had hung her out to dry this morning—but would he really stick her at lunch with only his mother? Renata could imagine nothing worse, today of all days, than lunch alone with Suzanne Driscoll.

"Where are you going?" Renata asked.

"The south shore," he said. "Madequecham."

"Made—" Renata tripped over the word; she had never actually spoken it out loud. Madequecham was the Native American name for a valley along the south shore, but to Renata the word meant her mother, dead. She nearly said this to Miles. *My mother was killed in Madequecham. So no thanks, I think I'll pass.* Except it was turning out to be a strange day, unpredictable, and Renata found that a trip to Madequecham satisfied many, if not all, of her immediate needs. She wanted out of this house. She wanted to bask in the friendly attention of Miles, however perfunctory, and on a more serious and substantial note, she wanted to see for herself the place where her mother had been killed. Was that morbid? Maybe. It was a secret desire, part and parcel of a larger belief: that somehow once Renata understood her mother's life and death, a fog would lift. Things that had been obscured from her would become clear.

"Come on," Miles said. He dangled a piece of sliced ham over the bread in a dainty way, like the queen with her handkerchief. He was trying to be funny. "I'll have you back here before Cade even gets home. Say, three o'clock."

"I'd like to go," Renata said apologetically. Strangely, what was holding her back was a factor she would have claimed in public not to care about: Suzanne Driscoll's disapproval.

"Whatever," Miles said. "Suit yourself."

Renata was getting a headache. Only eleven o'clock and already so much pressing down on her. Suzanne and her list, her father and his bizarre endorsement. They thought they could manipulate her. Well, guess what? They could not. And Cade, perhaps, was the worst perpetrator of all. He had told her they would be going to the beach together today, and yet he'd deserted her. Resolution must have fixed itself on her face, because Miles said, "Do you want me to make you a sandwich?"

"Yes," Renata said. "I'm coming."

11:45 A.M.

Almost noon and still so much to do! And Marguerite was exhausted. She put away the groceries and the champagne. She tucked her new, ridiculous umbrella into the dark recesses of her front closet. She checked on her bread dough—it was puffed and foamy, risen so high that it strained against the plastic wrap. Marguerite floured her hands and punched it down, enjoying the hiss, the release of yeasty stink. She had several things to do before she headed out to the Herb Farm. She would delay that trip for as long as possible, because she was afraid to see Ethan. He fell into the category of people she loved, but the connection between them was too painful. Maybe, like Fergus and Eliza at the liquor store, he would be out, leaving a teenager, a college student, someone Marguerite didn't know, in his place. She could always hope.

But for now, the aioli. Garlic, egg yolks, a wee bit of Dijon mustard. In her Cuisinart she whipped these up to a brilliant, pungent yellow; then she added olive oil in a steady stream. Here was the magic of cooking—an emulsion formed, a rich, garlicky mayonnaise. Salt, pepper, the juice of half a lemon. Marguerite scooped the aioli into a bowl and covered it with plastic.

She barely made it through the marinade for the beef. Her forehead was burning; she felt hot and achy, dried up. She whisked together olive oil, red wine vinegar, sugar, horseradish, Dijon, salt, and pepper and poured it over the tenderloin in a shallow dish. Marguerite's vision started to blotch; amorphous yellow and silver blobs invaded the kitchen.

I can't see, she thought. *Why can't I see?* The grandfather clock struck noon, the little monkey inside having a field day with his cymbals. As the twelve hours crashed around Marguerite like Ming vases hitting the tile floor, she realized what her problem was. She hadn't eaten a thing all day. All that walking on only two cups of coffee. So her symptoms weren't due to brain cancer or Alzheimer's or Lou Gehrig's disease, three things Marguerite feared only remotely, since there was very little to keep her clinging to life—though somehow, the event of tonight's dinner had sparked promise and hope in Marguerite in a way that made her relieved that she wasn't sick, only hungry. She pulled a box of shredded wheat from the pantry and doused it with milk. It was cool and crunchy, pleasing. The clock stopped its racket; Marguerite tried to coerce her vision clear by blinking. She might have sunstroke, despite the valiant efforts of her wide-brimmed hat. She drank a glass of water, slowly made inroads on her cereal. The journey out to the Herb Farm intimidated her; she could sacrifice quality, maybe, and simply return to the A&P for the herbs and goat cheese, the eggs, the asparagus, the *fleurs.* Then she laughed, derisively, at the mere thought.

Forget everything else for now, she thought. *I need to lie down.*

She was so warm that she stripped to her bra and underpants, double-triple-checking the shutters to make certain absolutely no one could see in. (It was the mailman she was worried about, with his irregular hours.)

And even then she felt too odd lying on top of her bed like a laid-out corpse, and so she covered herself with her summer blanket.

Too much walking around in the August sun. That and not enough food, not enough water. And then, too, there was all the thinking she had done about the past. It wasn't healthy, maybe, to go back and float around in those days. In fourteen years she hadn't indulged in the past as much as she had in the last twelve hours. It hadn't seemed productive or wise, because Marguerite had assumed that thinking about the things she had lost would make her unbearably sad. But for some reason today the rules were suspended, the logic reversed. Today she thought about the past—the whole big, honest past—and how she might, tonight, explain it to Renata, and it made her proud in a strange way. Proud to be lying here. Proud that she had survived.

The restaurant had been open for four summers before Marguerite felt the floor stabilize under her feet. She meant this both figuratively and literally. She had spent thousands of dollars getting the restaurant to look the way she wanted it to—which was to say, cozy, tasteful, erudite. She wanted the atmosphere to reflect a cross between Nantucket, whose aesthetics were new to her—the whaling-rich history of the town, the wild, pristine beauty of the moors, the beaches, the sea—and Paris with its sleek sophistication. Marguerite had decided to keep the exposed brick wall at Porter's insistence (this very feature was a major selling point for Manhattan apartments), and she refurbished the fireplace in the bar, installing as a mantelpiece a tremendous piece of driftwood that Porter had found years earlier up at Great Point. (He'd kept it in the backyard of his rental house, much to the chagrin of the house's owners, as he waited for a purpose to reveal itself.) To balance the rustic nature of the driftwood,

Marguerite insisted on a zinc bar, the only one on the island. But threatening to throw the whole enterprise off were the floors. They slanted; they sloped; they were tilted, uneven. She had to fix the floors. She couldn't have waitstaff carrying six entrée plates on a tray over their heads walking across this tipsy terrain, and she didn't want people eating their meals in a room that felt like a boat lurched to one side. The floors were made of a rare and expensive wormy chestnut; she was afraid she would damage them if she pulled them up and tried to level the underflooring, and so Marguerite opted for the longer, more arduous process of lifting the building and squaring the foundation.

Marguerite's efforts paid off. The space evolved; it became unique and inviting. She loved the bar; she loved the fireplace and the two armchairs where very lucky (and prompt) customers could hunker down with a cocktail and one of the art history books or Colette novels that Marguerite kept on a set of built-in shelves. She loved the dining room, which she'd painted a deep, rich Chinese red, and she hoped that customers would fight over the three most desirable tables—the two deuces in front of the windows that faced Water Street and, for bigger parties, the west banquette.

However, even with all this in place and precisely to Marguerite's specifications, it took a while for the people of Nantucket to *get it.* At first, Marguerite was viewed as a wash-ashore—some fancy woman chef with a checkered background. Was she French? No, but she peppered her conversation with pretentious little French phrases, and she spoke with some kind of affected accent. Was she from New York? She had worked in the city at La Grenouille—some people pretended to remember her from there, though she had never once set foot in the dining room during service—and she had been educated at the Culinary Institute in Hyde Park, but somehow she didn't quite qualify as a New Yorker. Her only saving grace seemed to be her connection to Porter. Porter Harris was a much-appreciated fixture on the Nantucket social scene; he had rented the same house on Polpis Road since graduating from college in the early sixties. When Porter spoke, people listened because he was charming and convivial, he could single-handedly save a cocktail party, and he was famous for his extravagant taste in art, in food, in women. He liked to tell people that he could look at Botticelli and Rubens all day and move on to Fragonard and the French Rococo all evening. Nothing was too rich or too fine for him. He claimed to have "unearthed a jewel" on a trip to Paris, and that "jewel" was Marguerite. The restaurant Les Parapluies was named after a Renoir painting. (For the first two summers, a good-quality reproduction hung over the bar, but then it came to seem obvious and Marguerite replaced it with a more intriguing piece, also of umbrellas, by local artist Kerry Hallam.) The restaurant served only one fixed menu per day at a price of thirty-two dollars not including wine, and this confounded people. How could one meal possibly be worth it? Porter was instrumental in those early years in filling the room. He lured in other Manhattanites, other academics, intellectuals, theater people on break from Broadway, artists from Sconset with sizable trust funds, and the wealthy people who looked to the aforementioned to set the trends. These people realized after one summer, then two, then three of unforgettable meals that anyone who worried they wouldn't like the food was worrying for no reason. This woman whom no one could figure out wasn't much to look at (or so said the women; the men were more complimentary, seeing in Marguerite's solid frame and long, long hair an earth mother)—but *boy, could she cook!*

It hadn't been easy to win Nantucket over, but at some point during that fourth summer it all came together. The restaurant was full every weekend, Marguerite had a loyal group of regulars who could be counted on at least twice during the week, and the bar was busy from six thirty when it opened (and sometimes a line formed outside, people who wanted to vie for the armchairs) until after midnight. Marguerite's questionable pedigree flipped itself into a mystique; the local press came sniffing, asking for interviews, which she declined, enhancing her mystique. People started recognizing Marguerite on the street; they claimed her as a friend; they announced Les Parapluies as the finest restaurant on the island.

People grew accustomed to her unusual accent (it was a combination of her childhood in Cheboygan and the lilting French-accented English she mimicked from her ballet teacher, Madame Verge, which was later reinforced by so much time in French-speaking kitchens)—but increasing speculation surrounded her relationship with Porter. As the rumors went, he had lured her to Nantucket from Paris and he had bought her the restaurant. (On this last point, Marguerite liked to set the record straight: She bought the restaurant alone; hers was the only name on the deed.) People knew that Porter and Marguerite lived together in the cottage on Polpis Road, and yet summers passed and no ring appeared; no announcement was made. The inquiries and critical glances of the clientele made Marguerite uneasy. The relationship between her and Porter was nobody's business but hers and Porter's.

The summers in the cottage on Polpis Road were good and simple. Marguerite and Porter slept in a rope bed; they used only the outdoor shower, whose nozzle was positioned under a trellis of climbing roses. They ate cold plums and rice pudding for breakfast, and then Marguerite left for work. Porter went to the beach, played tennis at the yacht club, read his impenetrable art history journals in the hammock on the front porch. He stopped in at the restaurant frequently. How many times had Marguerite been working at the stove when he came up behind her and kissed her neck? She had the burns to prove it. When Porter couldn't stop by, he called her—sometimes to tell her who he'd seen in town, what he'd heard, what he'd read in *The Inquirer and Mirror.* Sometimes he used a funny voice or falsetto and tried to make a reservation. They spent an hour or two together at home between prep and service—they tended a small vegetable garden and a plot of daylilies; they listened to French conversation tapes; they made love. They showered together under the roses; Porter washed her hair. They had a glass of wine; they touched glasses. "Cheers," they said. "I love you."

They were lovers. Marguerite adored the word—implying as it did a flexible, European arrangement—and she hated it for the same reason. Despite all the days of their idyllic summers, Porter could not be pinned down. When autumn arrived, Porter went back to Manhattan, back to work, back to school, back to his brownstone on West Eighty-first Street, back to his life of students and research and benefits at the Met, lectures at the Ninety-second Street Y, dinners at other French restaurants—with other women. Marguerite knew he saw other women, she suspected he slept with them, and yet she was terrified to ask, terrified of that conversation and where it might lead. On a spring afternoon in Paris, she had given him the word *free,* and she felt obligated to stick with it. If Porter discovered that freedom was not what she wanted, if he found out that what she craved was to be the opposite of free—married, hitched, bound together—he would leave her. She would lose the beautiful summers; she would lose the only lover she had ever had.

Marguerite's childhood contained one lasting memory, and that was of her ballet lessons with Madame Verge. Marguerite took the lessons in a studio that had been fashioned in Madame Verge's large Victorian house in the center of town. The studio was on the second floor. Walls had been knocked down to create a rectangular room with floor-to-ceiling mirrors, a barre, and a grand piano played by Madame Verge's widowed brother. Marguerite started with the lessons when she was eight. For three years, on Friday afternoons, she ascended the stairs in her black leotard, pink tights, and scuffed pink slippers, every last strand of her hair pinched into a bun. Madame Verge was in her sixties. She had dyed red hair, and her lipstick bled into the wrinkles around her mouth. She was not a beautiful woman, but she *was,* because she was completely herself. She wanted all her girls to look the same, to hold themselves erect, shoulders back, chins up. Feet in one of five positions. She did not tolerate sloppy feet. Marguerite could easily picture herself as a girl in that room on a Friday afternoon—some days were muggy with autumn heat; some days had ice tapping on the windows. She stood with the other girls in front of the mirrored wall, deeply pliéing as Madame Verge's brother played Mozart. She danced. There was a sense of expectation among the girls in Madame Verge's class that they were special. If they kept their chins up, their shoulders back, if they kept their feet disciplined, if their hair was caught up, every strand, neatly, then they would earn something. But what? Marguerite had assumed it was adoration. They would be darlings; they would be cherished, loved by one man for the rest of their lives; they would become someone's star.

Free, Marguerite had told Porter. But she had been lying, and the lie would cost her dearly.

During the first autumn of Porter's absence, Marguerite traveled to Manhattan to surprise him. She showed up on a Wednesday when she knew he didn't have classes. It was November, chilly, gray; the charms of autumn in the city were rapidly fading. Marguerite had paid a king's ransom on cab fare from LaGuardia; she was dropped in front of Porter's brownstone just before noon. The brownstone was beautiful, well kept, with a black wrought-iron fence and a mighty black door. On the door was a polished brass oval that said: HARRIS. Marguerite rang the bell;

there was no answer. She walked to the corner and called the house from a pay phone. No answer. She called Porter's office at the university, but the secretary informed Marguerite that Professor Harris did not teach or meet with students on Wednesdays. Once Marguerite revealed her identity, the secretary disclosed the fact that on Wednesdays Professor Harris played squash and ate lunch at his club. These lunches, the secretary said, *sotto voce,* sometimes included four or five men, sometimes got a bit out of hand, sometimes lasted well into the evening. Marguerite hung up, thinking, *What club?* She hadn't even known Porter belonged to a club. There was no way to locate him. She set about entertaining herself with lunch at a hole-in-the-wall Vietnamese restaurant while reading the *Post,* followed by a substantial wander around the Upper West Side. She was sitting, hunched over and nearly frozen, on the top step of Porter's brownstone when up strolled Himself, in his camel-hair coat and Burberry scarf, his bald pate revealed in the stiff breeze, the tips of his ears red with the cold. Marguerite almost didn't recognize him. He looked older in winter clothes, minus his tan and aura of just-off-the-tennis-court good health. Porter, under the influence of who knew how many martinis, took a bumbling step backward, squinting at Marguerite's form in the gathering dark.

"Daisy?" he said. She stood up, feeling cold, tired, and utterly stupid. He opened his arms and she went to him, but his embrace felt different; it felt brotherly. "What on earth are you doing here? You should have called me."

Of course he was right—she should have called. But she had wanted to take him by surprise; it was a test, of sorts, and she could see right away that he was going to fail or she was or they were.

"I'm sorry," she said.

"You don't have to be sorry," he said. "How long can you stay?" The question contained a tinge of worry; she could hear it, though he did his best to try to make it sound like excited interest.

"Just until tomorrow," she said quickly. In truth, she had packed enough clothes for a week.

His face brightened. He was relieved. He wheeled her toward the front door and held on to her shoulders as they trudged up the stairs. "I have just enough time for a celebratory drink," he said. "But then, unfortunately, I have to make an appearance down at Avery Fisher. I can't possibly get out of it. And I don't have a spare ticket." He squeezed her. "I'm sorry, Daisy. You should have called me."

"I know," she said. She was close to tears, thirty-three years old and as naïve as she had been at eight, with her knobby knees, standing in front of Madame Verge's mirrored wall. She felt she would break into pieces. Did he not remember the one hundred days of their summer? The one hundred nights they had spent sleeping together in the rope bed? They had made love everywhere in that cottage: on the front porch, on the kitchen table. He was always so hungry for her; those were his words. The only thing that kept Marguerite together was the keen interest she felt when the door to his brownstone swung open. This was his home, a part of him she'd never seen.

Porter's house was all she imagined. It was both classic and eclectic, the house of an art history professor—so many books, so many framed prints, and a few original sketches and studies, perfectly lit—and yet scattered throughout were Porter's crazy touches: a vase of peacock feathers, an accordion lying open in its case.

"Do you play the accordion?" Marguerite asked.

"Oh yes," he said. "Very badly."

Marguerite wandered from room to room, picking up *objets,* studying photographs. There were two pictures of her and Porter: one of them in

Paris in their wigs at Père Lachaise Cemetery (the picture was blurry; the boy who had taken it had been stoned) and one of them in front of Les Parapluies on its opening night. There were pictures of Porter with other women—but only in groups, and no one face appeared more than any other. Or was Marguerite missing something? She didn't want to appear to be checking too closely. Porter appeared with a drink, a flute of something pink and bubbly.

"I've kept this on hand for a very special occasion," he said, kissing her. "Such as a surprise visit from my sweet Daisy."

She wanted to believe him. But the fact was, things were stilted between them. Porter, who had never in his life run out of things to say, seemed reserved, distracted. Marguerite tried to fill the void, she tried to sparkle, but she couldn't quite capture Porter's attention. She talked about the restaurant—it felt like the only thing they had in common but also sadly irrelevant, here in the city—then she told him she'd been reading Proust (which was a bit of a stretch; she'd gotten through ten pages, then put it down, frustrated)—but even Proust didn't get Porter going. He was somewhere else. As the first glass of champagne went down, followed quickly by a second, Marguerite wondered if they would make love. But Porter remained seated primly on the divan, halfway across the room. And then, he looked at his watch.

"I should get ready," he said.

"Yes," she said. "By all means."

He vanished to another part of the house, his bedroom, she presumed, and she couldn't help but feel crushed that he didn't ask her to join him. They had showered together under the roses; he had washed her hair. Marguerite finished her second glass of champagne and repaired to the kitchen to fill her glass a third time. When she opened the refrigerator, she found a corsage in a plastic box on the bottom shelf.

"Oh," she said. She closed the door.

A while later, Porter emerged in a tuxedo, smelling of aftershave. Now that he was about to make his escape, he seemed more himself. He smiled at her, he took her hands in his, and rubbed them like he was trying to start a fire. "I'm sorry about this," he said. "I really wish I'd had a moment's notice."

"It's my fault," Marguerite said.

"What will you do for dinner?" he said. "There's a bistro down the street that's not half-bad with roast chicken. Do you want me to call right now and see if I can reserve you a seat at the bar?"

"I'll manage," she said.

He kissed her nose, like she was a child. Marguerite nearly mentioned the corsage, but that would only embarrass them both. He would pick up flowers on the way.

That night, afraid to climb into Porter's stark king-size bed (it was wide and low, covered with a black quilt, headed by eight pillows in sleek silver sheets) and afraid to use one of the guest rooms, Marguerite pretended to sleep on the silk divan. She had purposefully changed into a peignoir and brushed out her hair, but when Porter came home (at one o'clock? Two?) all he did was look at her and chuckle. He kissed her on the forehead like she was Sleeping Beauty while she feigned deep, peaceful breaths.

In the morning, Marguerite knocked timidly on his bedroom door. (It was cracked open, which she took as a good sign.) He stirred, but before he was fully awake, she slid between the silver sheets, which were as cool and smooth as coins.

I want to stay, she thought, though she didn't dare say it. *I want to stay here with you.* They made love. Porter was groggy and sour; he smelled like old booze; his skin tasted ashy from cigarettes; it was far from the golden, salty skin of summer. He wasn't the same man. And yet Marguerite loved him. She was grateful that he responded to her, he touched her, he came alive. They made love; it was the same, though he remained quiet until the end, when a noise escaped from the back of his throat. Might she stay? Did he now remember? But when they were through, Porter rose, crossed the room, shut the bathroom door. She heard the shower. He was meeting a student at ten, he said.

For breakfast, he made eggs, shutting the refrigerator door quickly behind him. While Marguerite ate all alone at a dining-room table that sat twenty at least, he disappeared to make a phone call. Corsage Woman? Marguerite was both too nervous to eat the eggs and starving for them; she had skipped dinner the night before. When Porter reappeared, he was smiling.

"I called you a car," he said. "It will be here in twenty minutes."

What became clear during Marguerite's scant twenty-four hours in Manhattan was that she had broken some kind of unspoken rule. She didn't belong in Porter's New York; there was no niche for her, no crack or opening in which she could make herself comfortable. This wounded her. Once she was back on Nantucket, she grew angry. She hacked at the driftwood mantelpiece with her favorite chef's knife, though this effort ended up harming the knife more than the mantel. She had closed the restaurant for the winter; there weren't enough customers to justify keeping it open. Without the restaurant to worry about and with things as they were with Porter, Marguerite ate too much and she drank. She had bad dreams about Corsage Woman, the woman who sat next to Porter at Avery Fisher Hall. He held her hand, maybe; he bought her a white wine at intermission. She was slender; she wore perfume and a hat. There was no way to find out, no one to ask, except perhaps Porter's secretary. Marguerite gave up on Proust and started to read Salinger. *An education makes you good company for yourself.* Ha! Little had she known when Porter said those words how much time she would be spending alone. She considered taking up with other men—Dusty from the fish store, Damian Vix, her suave and handsome lawyer—but she knew they wouldn't be able to replace Porter. Why this should be so she had no idea. Porter wasn't even handsome. He was too skinny; he was losing his hair; he talked so much he drove people mad. He farted in bed; he used incredibly foul language when he hurt himself; he knew nothing about football like other men did. Many people thought he was gay. (No straight man was that educated about art, about literature, about Paris. No straight man wore pocket handkerchiefs or drank that much champagne or lost at tennis so consistently.) Porter wasn't gay, Marguerite could attest to that, and yet he wasn't a family man. He didn't want children. *What kind of man doesn't want children?* Marguerite asked herself. But it was no use. Marguerite was a country Porter had conquered; he was her colonist. She was oblivious to everyone but him.

Porter, meanwhile, called her every week; he sent her restaurant reviews from *The New York Times;* he sent her one hundred daisies on Valentine's Day. His attentions were just enough to sustain her. She would make up her mind to end the relationship, and then he would write her a funny love poem and go to the trouble to have it delivered by telegram. The message was clear: *It's going to work this way, Daisy.* That was how it went the first winter, the second, the third, and so on. He promised her a trip each spring—to Italy or a return to Paris—but it never worked out. His schedule. The demands on him, he couldn't handle one more thing. *Sorry to disappoint you, Daisy. We still have summer.*

Yes. What got her through was the promise of summer. The summer would never change; it was the love season. Porter rented the cottage on Polpis Road; he wanted Daisy with him every second she could spare. For years it was the same: nights in the rope bed, roses in the outdoor shower, kisses on the back of the neck as she sauteéd mushrooms in clarified butter. The first daylily bloom was always a cause for celebration, a glass of wine. "Cheers," they said. "I love you."

Porter was private about his family, referring to his parents only when he was reminiscing about his childhood; Marguerite assumed they were dead. He did on one occasion mention that his father, Dr. Harris, a urological surgeon, had been married twice and had had a second set of children rather late in life, but Porter never referred to any siblings other than his brother Andre in California. Therefore, on the night that Porter walked into Les Parapluies with a young blond woman on his arm, Marguerite thought, *It's finally happened. He's thrown me over for another woman.*

Marguerite had been in the dining room, lured out of the kitchen by the head waiter, Francesca, who said, "The Dicksons at Table Seven. They have a present for you."

It was the restaurant's fourth summer. Yes, Marguerite was popular, but the phenomenon of gifts for her as the chef was novel, touching, and always surprising. The regulars had started showing up like the Three Wise Men with all kinds of treasures—scarves knit in Peru from the wool of baby alpacas, bottles of ice wine from Finland, a jar of fiery barbecue sauce from a smoke pit in Memphis. And on this day the Dicksons at Table Seven had brought Marguerite a tin of saffron from their trip to Thailand. Marguerite was thanking the Dicksons for the tin—*Such a thoughtful gift, too kind; I so appreciate*—when Porter and the young woman walked in. Porter had told Marguerite when she left the cottage at five thirty that he'd have a surprise for her at dinner that night. She had been hoping for tickets to Paris. Instead, she faced her nightmare: another woman on his arm, here in her restaurant, tonight, without warning. Marguerite turned away and, lest any of the customers perceive her reaction, rushed back into the kitchen.

How dare he! she thought. *And he's* late!

Thirty seconds hence, the kitchen door swung open and in walked the happy couple. The woman had to be fifteen years Porter's junior. *Contemptible,* Marguerite thought, *embarrassing for him, for me, for her.* But the woman was lovely, exquisite, she was as blond and blue-eyed and tan and wholesome looking as a model in an advertisement. She had a face that could sell anything: Limburger cheese, industrial caulking. Marguerite barely managed to tear her eyes away. She searched her prep area for something to do, something to chop, but her kitchen staff had everything under control, as ever.

"Daisy," Porter said. "There's someone I'd like you to meet." He had the trumpet of self-importance in his voice. He'd had a cocktail or two, someplace else. Marguerite busied herself selecting the words she would use when she threw him out.

Marguerite summoned enough courage to raise her eyes to the woman.

"My sister, Candace Harris," Porter said. "Candace, this is Marguerite Beale, the woman solely responsible for my happiness and my burgeoning belly."

Sister. Marguerite was an insecure fool. Before she could straighten out her frame of mind, Candace came swooping in. She put her hands on Marguerite's shoulders and kissed her. "I have been dying to meet you. What Porter told me in private is that he thinks you're pure magic."

"Candace is moving to the island," Porter said. "She has a job with the Chamber of Commerce and she's training for a marathon."

"Really?" Marguerite said. The Chamber of Commerce rubbed Marguerite the wrong way. She had paid the membership fee to join just like everybody else, and yet the Chamber was hesitant to recommend the restaurant to tourists; they felt it was too expensive. And Marguerite's heart wasn't that much warmer toward people who engaged in any kind of regular exercise. They eschewed foie gras, filet of beef, duck confit; they tended to ask for sauces without butter or cream. (How many times had she had been forced to explain? A sauce without butter or cream wasn't a sauce.) Exercisers, and especially marathon runners, ate like little birds. And yet despite these two black marks against the woman right away, Marguerite felt something she could only describe as affection for this Candace person. She was relieved, certainly, by the word "sister," but there was something else, too. It was the kiss, Marguerite decided. Candace had kissed her right on the lips, as though they had known each other all their lives.

Marguerite led Candace to the west banquette while Porter stopped to chat with friends. She pulled a chair out for Candace. As she did this, she noticed a subtle shift in the conversation in the dining room. The decibel level dropped; there was whispering. Marguerite's back burned like the scarlet shell of a lobster from the attention she knew was focused on her and this newcomer. *It's his sister!* Marguerite was tempted to announce. A half sister, she now deduced, from his father's second marriage. Marguerite slipped onto the red silk of the banquette, where she could keep a stern eye on her customers. She held out the tin of saffron.

"Look," she said. "Look what I've been given." She opened the tin to show Candace the dark red strands, a fortune in her palm, dearer than this much caviar, this many shaved truffles; it was for spices like this that

Columbus had set out in his ship. “Each strand is handpicked from the center of a crocus flower that only blooms two weeks of the year.” She offered the tin to Candace. “Taste.”

Candace dipped her finger into the tin, and Marguerite did likewise. The delicate threads smeared and turned a deep golden-orange. This was how Candace and Marguerite began their first meal together: by licking saffron from their fingertips.

Marguerite wasn’t really asleep. She was resting with her eyes closed, but her mind was as alert as a sentry, keeping her memories in order. First this, then that. Don’t step out of line. Don’t digress, wander down another path; don’t try to flutter away as you do when you’re asleep. And yet, for a second, the sentry looks away, and Marguerite is set free. She sleeps.

And awakens! It might have been an internal alarm that woke her, one saying, *There isn’t time for this! The silver! The Herb Farm! The blasted tart! (If you’d wanted to sleep, you should have chosen something easier!)* It might have been the sluicing sound of the mail coming through the slot. But what stunned Marguerite out of sleep was a noise, another blasted noise. It was the phone. Really, the phone again?

Marguerite held the summer blanket against her bare, flushed chest. She took a deep breath. She had a funny feeling about the phone ringing this time; she imagined some kind of memory police on the other end. She would be charged with reeking of nostalgia. She thought it might be Dusty, calling to ask her on a date, or perhaps it was someone Dusty had talked to that morning, a faceless name that would bounce around Marguerite’s consciousness like a pinball, knocking against surfaces, trying to elicit recognition. *We heard you're back among the living.* An old customer who wanted to hire her as a personal chef, a reporter from *The Inquirer and Mirror* seeking a scoop on her Lazarus-like return. Marguerite dared the phone to ring as she buttoned her blouse. It did. *Okay,* she thought. *Whoever this is must know I'm here.*

"Hello?" she said.

"Margo?" Pause. "It's Daniel Knox."

Marguerite's insides shifted in an uncomfortable way. Daniel Knox. The memory police indeed. Marguerite tried to decide how surprised she should sound at his voice. He sent a Christmas card every year, and the occasional scrawled note on his office stationery, but not once had he called her. Not once since the funeral. However, the fact of the matter was, Marguerite was not surprised to discover his voice on the other end of the line, not at all. He'd obviously found out Renata was coming to dinner and would try, somehow, to prevent it.

"Margo?"

Right. She had to do a better job on the telephone.

"Hello, Dan."

"Are you well, Margo?"

"Indeed. Very well. And you?"

"Physically, I'm fine."

It was a strange thing to say, provocative; he was cuing Marguerite to ask about his emotional well-being, which she would, momentarily, after she stopped to wonder what a "physically fine" Daniel Knox looked like these days. Marguerite didn't keep his picture around, and the snapshots that arrived at Christmas were only of Renata. She imagined him shaggy and blond gray, an aging golden retriever. He had always reminded Marguerite of a character from the Bible, with his longish hair and his beard. He looked like an apostle, or a shepherd.

"And otherwise?" Marguerite said.

"Well, I've been dealt quite a blow today."

Quite a blow? Was he talking about Marguerite, Renata, the dinner? This dinner should have taken place years ago; it would have, Marguerite was sure, if it weren't for Dan. *The girl wants to find out the truth about her mother. And can we blame her?* Dan had kept Renata away from Marguerite—from Nantucket altogether—for fourteen years. Marguerite couldn't scorn his parenting skills because anyone with one good eye could see he'd done a brilliant job just by the way Renata had turned out, all her accomplishments, and Dan had done it single-handedly. But Marguerite suspected—in fact she was certain—that on the subject of Marguerite, Porter, and Les Parapluies, Daniel Knox had been all but mute. Curt, dismissive, disparaging. *It's nothing a girl your age needs to know.* Except now the girl was becoming a woman and it was difficult to complete that journey without a clear image of one's own mother. There were photographs, of course. And Dan's memories, which would have been idealized for the sake of his daughter. Candace had been presented to Renata as angel food cake—sweet, bland, insubstantial, without any deviling or spice or zing.

"Renata's coming to me tonight," Marguerite said. "Is that what you mean?"

"No," he said. "No, not that. I knew she'd come to you. I knew it the second she said she was off to Nantucket."

"You didn't forbid her?" Marguerite said.

"I advised her against it," Dan said. "I didn't want her to bother you."

"Ha!" Marguerite said, and just like a clean slice through the tip of her finger with a sharp knife, she felt anger. Daniel Knox was a *coward.* He was too much of a coward to tell his own daughter the truth. "You hate me."

"I do not hate you, Margo."

"You do so. You're just not man enough to admit it."

"I do not hate you."

"You do so."

"I do not. And listen to us. We sound like children."

"You resent me," Marguerite said. It felt marvelous to be speaking aloud like this. For years Marguerite had dreamed of confronting Daniel Knox; for years his words had festered, hot and liquid, inside of her. *All you got in the end was her pity. She pitied you, Margo.* With time, however, Marguerite's convictions desiccated like the inside of a gourd; they rattled like old seeds. But now! "You've always resented me. And you're afraid of me. You want Renata to be afraid of me. You told her I was a witch. As a child, to scare her. You told her I was insane."

"I did no such thing."

"Oh, Daniel."

"Oh, Margo," he said. "I admit, it's complicated. What happened, our history. I asked her not to contact you, but she did anyway. So you won. You should be happy."

"Happy?" Marguerite said. Though secretly she thought, *Yes, I am happy.*

"Anyway," he said. "That wasn't why I called. I called because I need your help."

"My help?" Marguerite said. And then she thought, *Of course. He never would have called unless he needed something.*

"Renata phoned me a little while ago," Dan said. "She told me she was coming to you, and then she told me about the boy."

"The boy?"

"You don't know? She says she's getting married."

Ah, yes. The fiancé. Hulbert Avenue. "You just found out?" Marguerite said.

"This morning."

"I wondered when she said 'fiancé.' I wondered about you."

"I can't allow it."

"Well . . ." Marguerite saw where this was headed. Dan wanted Marguerite to be his mouthpiece. *Talk her out of it. Explain how hasty, how naïve, how reckless, she's being.* As if Marguerite had any influence. If she did have influence, would she waste it talking about the fiancé? "She's an adult, Dan."

"She's a teenager."

"Legally, she could go to the Town Building on Monday and get married by a justice of the peace."

There was a heavy sigh on the other end of the line. "I can't allow that to happen, Margo. I will get on a plane to come up there right now. If she marries him, it'll last a year, or five, and then she'll be the ripe old age of twenty-four and maybe she'll have a child or two and then—you know it as well as I do—something will happen that makes her see she missed out on the most exciting time of her life. She'll want to ride elephants in Cambodia or join the Peace Corps or go to culinary school. She'll meet someone else."

"She's in love," Marguerite said. "Some people who fall in love get married." She spoke ironically, thinking of herself and Porter. *Some people fall in love and dance around each other for years and years, until one partner tires, or dances away.*

"If he's knocked her up, I'll kill him," Dan said.

"She didn't sound like she was in that kind of trouble," Marguerite said. "She sounded blissful."

"Nineteen is too young to get married," Dan said. "It should be illegal to get married before you've traveled on at least three continents, had four lovers, and held down a serious job. It should be illegal to get married before you've had your wisdom teeth out, owned your own car, cooked your first Thanksgiving turkey. She has so many experiences ahead of her. I didn't spend all that time and energy—fourteen years, Margo, every single day—to stand by and let her ruin her life this way. Marry some spoiled kid she's known less than a year. If Candace were here, she'd—"

"Talk her out of it," Marguerite said.

"Flip," Dan said at the same time.

Marguerite cleared her throat. "If Candace were here, Renata wouldn't be getting married."

"Right," he said softly. "She's getting married to escape me."

"She's getting married because she thinks it will fill the empty space she has inside of her."

"It won't," Dan said. "That space is there forever."

"I know it as well as you do," Marguerite said. "Don't I?"

They were both silent for a second, thinking of the whistling gaps a person leaves behind when she dies, and how natural it would be for someone young and optimistic like Renata to believe that this hole could be filled with a substance as magical and exciting as romantic love.

The receiver slipped in Marguerite's hand. The bedroom was hot; she was sweating. She had so much to do, and yet she couldn't make herself hang up. *You always made her feel like she owed you something.* Dan blamed Marguerite for Candace's death and she accepted that blame; she had tried for years to wash the blood from her hands. Now he was asking her for help. *Save my daughter.* Marguerite wished she could. But the fact of the matter was, she had one person to save tonight and that was herself.

"It might work out just fine," Marguerite said. "Plenty of people who get married young stay married. Some do, anyway. You've met the boy?"

"Yes," Dan said. "He's not good enough for her. But he thinks he is. That's what really gets me. He *thinks* he is."

"For you, though," Marguerite said, "nobody would be good enough."

"I'm not going to argue with you, Margo," Dan said. "I'm just going to ask you for your help. Will you help me?"

"I don't think I can."

"Will you try?"

"I'll ask her about him," Marguerite said. "See where she is, how she's feeling, why she wants to make so serious a decision. I would have done that even without this call. I want to know her, Dan. You've kept her from me."

"I wanted to keep her life simple. Knowing a bunch of stuff about the past won't help her, Margo. Her mother is dead. That's a fact she's had to deal with her whole life. How she died, why she died—knowing those things will only confuse her."

"Confuse her?"

"You want to confess everything to make *yourself* feel better," Dan said. "You aren't thinking of Renata."

"Aren't I?"

"No."

"Well, now it sounds like you're arguing with me. I have things to say to the girl and I'm going to say them. After fourteen years, I deserve to have a turn."

"Fine," Dan said. "I'm asking you to think of her. And to be careful. That's all I can do." He was quiet for a moment, and against her wishes Marguerite had a vision of Dan's face, contorted with anger, grabbing the child from her arms. *She pitied you, Margo.* The child had turned back to Marguerite, reached out for her. Those pink overalls. Marguerite shook her head. A guttural noise escaped her throat. Daniel said, "She's coming to you because she thinks you have the answers. You're like Mata Hari to her, Margo. She's going to listen to what you say."

"I hope so," Marguerite said. Her voice was very soft, so soft she knew Dan wouldn't hear. "I hope so."

Dead noon

The wind whipped Renata's hair into her face as she roared down Milestone Road in Miles's convertible Saab. She could never have predicted that defiance would be this fun. Pure defiance! She'd left the Driscoll house without a note, and she did not bring her cell phone. No one knew where she was, who she was with, or how to get ahold of her, no one except for Miles, who was so capable and self-assured it was making her dizzy. He had grabbed a twelve-pack of beer from his apartment over the Driscolls' garage, and now they were driving too fast in the midday sun. Renata unbuckled her seat belt and eased the seat into recline position. She wore only her bikini and a little skirt. Miles glanced over at her and she wondered what he was thinking. Did he like what he saw, or did he think she was being obvious and silly? Renata saw his eyes catch on her diamond ring. She was engaged. Did this make her more desirable to him or less so? She wanted to believe it made her more desirable; a girl of nineteen who was already engaged must be the most desirable woman on earth.

It was too loud for conversation, and that was for the best. If they had talked—about Miles's job, the Driscolls, Cade—Renata's guilt would seize her like a fever and make her sick. As it was, they were two actors in a silent movie. Two kids on a summer day headed for the beach.

Miles hit the brake, hard. Renata gripped the sides of the seat. *Police?* He downshifted, hit his turn signal, and whipped a right so tight that Renata pictured the car tilting, turning on only its right tires. *Screech.* She sat up, readjusted the seat, buckled her seat belt. An airplane took off right over them.

"This is the way to Madequecham?" she said.

"We're picking up a friend."

Renata smiled mildly, as her spirits plopped at her feet. He hadn't said anything about a friend when he invited her, or when they left. It felt like a deception. She had thought they were going alone. This was probably better; Renata could only imagine what Cade and Suzanne Driscoll would say if they found out Renata had disappeared with Miles alone.

Miles headed down the road toward the airport. The planes were so low in the sky, Renata could see their pale underbellies; she could taste the fumes. To her and Miles's left was a massive storage facility, some baseball fields, a lot of construction machines.

"I didn't know anybody lived out here."

"Not everyone on Nantucket is rich," Miles said. "Some of us have to work."

"Right," Renata said. "Sorry."

"No need to be sorry," Miles said. "I can tell you're just an innocent bystander to the great spectacle of the Driscolls' wealth."

"Not so innocent today," Renata said.

"No?" Miles said. He gave her a sneaky sideways look and grabbed her leg with two fingers, right above the knee. She yelped and started laughing. She felt like something was going to happen, and she tried to quell her exhilaration. She turned her diamond ring so that it caught the rays of the sun. *Cade,* she thought. *Cade, Cade, Cade.*

Miles slowed down and turned onto a bumpy dirt road bordered on both sides by scrub pines. A mosquito bit Renata's arm, then her neck.

"Where are we going?" she said. "I'm getting eaten alive."

"Almost there," he said.

Another fifty yards down, he turned into a gravel driveway. There was a small gray-shingled cottage with two dormer windows. The front door was painted a very feminine pink, and the window boxes were planted with spindly pink geraniums. The front lawn had just been mowed; it was shaggy with dried clippings and littered with big-kid toys: two mountain bikes on their sides, a white surfboard, a brilliantly colored box kite. Miles honked the horn. A few seconds later, the pink door opened and a girl came out. Renata thought *girl,* but really she was a woman. She was striking—tall, slender, with long auburn hair cut in angles around her face. She wore a black bikini top and black and pink board shorts. She had a dark green tattoo around her right ankle, silver rings on her toes; a tiny round mirror dangled in her pierced navel. She picked up the surfboard as she walked toward the car. Renata was stunned. He had said *friend* and she had thought male, not female, not a queen bee like this.

"Hey," Queen Bee said, in a sexy-scratchy voice. She was smiling at Miles. Renata felt invisible. This was not better at all. This was awful, a travesty. Ten minutes ago, Renata was perched on a decadent mountaintop, as self-satisfied as she'd ever been in her young life. Then boom, just like that: eclipsed.

Miles turned to Renata. "Can you climb in back?"

"Huh?" Renata said. He was asking her to *move*? "Sure," she said, fumbling with her seat belt, trying to keep dismay from painting itself on her hot cheeks. As she crawled between the seats, her bag snagged on the gearshift and her tiny skirt hiked up, revealing her backside. She was making an ass of herself quite literally, while Queen Bee waited with an expression somewhere between amused and impatient.

Renata settled into the very cramped backseat. It was so tight that she had to sit on the right side of the seat and put her feet on the left side. There was no seat belt even if she'd wanted one, and to make matters worse, Miles used his backseat as a trash can—there were crumpled Dorito bags, empty CD cases, and lots of sand.

"Here comes the board," Queen Bee said. It seemed she was addressing Renata because suddenly the fin side of the surfboard was shoved into her face. What was she supposed to do with it? There was no room.

"There's no room," Renata squeaked.

"Like this," Miles said, and he balanced one end of the surfboard on top of the windshield and the other end on the back trunk. It sliced right through the backseat, making it impossible for Renata to see Miles, or her own feet. She could turn a few inches to the right to see outside of the car, or she could stare straight ahead at the back of Queen Bee's auburn head. "Now hold on to it."

"Yes, hold on to it," Queen Bee said, as if that were the reason Renata had been invited along: to hold the surfboard.

"I'm Renata," Renata said, thinking that maybe an introduction would make this situation more bearable, but as she spoke, Miles turned the radio up full blast for an old Sublime hip-hop anthem and backed out of the driveway. Renata's words were left behind, overturned in the yard, like the bikes.

This was, she thought a minute later when they were back on the Milestone Road rocketing along at unsafe speeds, a bed of her own making. No sooner had she digressed from her proscribed course than punishment was meted out. She should be at the yacht club picking at a BLT while Suzanne Driscoll stopped every other passerby to introduce Renata. ("Cade's new fiancée . . . we're so excited!") She should be with Cade, holding hands, whispering, instead of here, trying to keep a ten-foot surfboard from becoming a projectile missile and decapitating the people in the Audi TT behind them. Up front, Miles and Queen Bee were chatting easily—Renata could hear them talking, though she couldn't make out a single word they said. She ached for Action, who would have handled Queen Bee and Miles in just the right way. For one thing, Action would never have agreed to climb into the backseat. *Where do you think we are, Alabama 1961?* She might even have asked Queen Bee, right off, if she dyed her hair. Action would, however, be proud of Renata for escaping Hulbert Avenue. Vitamin Sea, *bah!* And yet Renata could not cultivate this devil-may-care attitude. Each minute at celestial speed on this road was taking her further and further from where she was supposed to be. She was at Miles's mercy; she was at the mercy of her own idiotic decision. With her free hand she reacquainted herself with the contents of her bag. No money, no phone, no lotion, no bottled water. *No brain,* she thought. *No common fucking sense.* All she had brought was a towel, her sunglasses, her book, and Suzanne's list, which was crumpled into a little ball. Renata was captive, a hostage, stranded with two people she didn't know. What was Miles's last name? She had no idea.

He slammed on the brake again and took another turn at breathtaking speed. Renata held on to the surfboard, but she was no match for the forces at work. *It's going to fall,* she thought. She didn't care. Queen Bee's hair was flying backward, stinging Renata between the eyes. Miles let out a whoop and Queen Bee grabbed the front of the surfboard, her slender arms tensing, revealing taut, toned muscles. Renata was mesmerized by the arms and by the side of Queen Bee's breast, perfectly round and pale and smooth. Renata didn't see the surfboard swing back. It smacked her in the jaw.

Renata yowled. Pain, mixed with rude, rude surprise. Her jaw was broken; it felt like her back teeth had been jarred loose. Renata's vision was blurred by tears. She let them fall. What did those two care if she cried? They wouldn't even notice.

They were driving down another dirt road; each rut and bump stabbed at Renata's jaw.

"Slow down!" she called out. She tasted blood.

Miles sped up; they careened down a road that was ridged like a washboard. Renata panicked. She wanted to escape, but she would never be able to make it back to Vitamin Sea by herself; now she wasn't even sure which direction they had come from. She could hitchhike maybe, pray for some kind person who might deliver her to the Nantucket Yacht Club by twelve thirty. But as they rumbled farther and farther from the main road, Renata's hopes plummeted. The sun burned her shoulders; she hadn't thought to put on lotion. This was awful; this was hell.

And then, for some reason, Miles slowed down. Queen Bee said something; she was pointing. Something on the side of the road. An animal? Renata looked out. A white cross stuck out of the low brush. Renata's jaw pulsed.

"Look," Queen Bee said. "Someone died right there. I think it's so morbid, those crosses, don't you?"

"Stop!" Renata said. She wedged an arm under the surfboard and managed to make contact with Miles's shoulder. "Stop the car!"

He hit the brake. Dust enveloped the car. "What?"

"Stop," Renata said. "I'm getting out."

"*What?*" he said.

Renata extricated herself from the backseat. Dust coated the inside of her mouth. She hopped down onto the road and walked back to the cross, watching her feet as she went. Her toenails, painted "Shanghai sunset," became filmed with dust.

It was just a white cross, just two pieces of wood nailed together; the paint was peeling. Renata stared at it. Was this it? The marker for her mother? There was a grave in New York, a large, simple granite stone that said: *Candace Harris Knox, 1955–1992, Wife, mother, friend.* Renata's father put flowers on the grave every week; he took a pumpkin in the fall, a wreath at Christmas. But this cross spoke more loudly to Renata. It screamed, *Here!* Here, on a pocked and rutted dirt road, among blueberry bushes, brambles, and Spanish olives. Here is where it happened. Candace was hit, in February of 1992: It was icy; the electric company truck had been going too fast; the driver had been drunk at ten o'clock in the morning. Candace had slipped, or the truck had skidded; it had never been made clear to Renata what had happened. But now at least, she knew where it had happened. If this was indeed a cross for Candace. Renata supposed there might have been other deaths out here; it was impossible to tell if the cross had been there fourteen years or two years, or forty years. There was no writing on it, no hint or clue, except for Renata's intuition. This was it. Would Marguerite know for sure? Would Daniel?

"What are you *doing*?" Miles called out. "Come on; we're going."

"You guys go," Renata said.

"*What?*" Miles said. "You have to stay with me. If you get lost or whatever, the Driscolls will *kill* me."

"No," Renata said. She sounded preternaturally calm, firm, confident. *This is what I was looking for. Part of it, anyway.* She knelt down in front of the cross. She felt like praying. She had been motherless for so long, it had come to define her. It was like being blind or deaf, or mentally retarded. She was missing something essential, something everyone else in the world had. Growing up there had been no one to braid Renata's hair, no one to bake muffins with, no one to shop for the bra or the nylons or the dress for her confirmation, her prom. There had been no one to read her *A Little Princess* or take her to *The Nutcracker,* no one to buy the Kotex, no one to tell about her first kiss, no one to tell about Cade. There had been no one to rebel against. The mothers of Renata's friends tried to reach out, to fill in. They picked Renata up from riding lessons when Dan worked late; they offered to take her jodhpurs home and launder them. Once, Renata's tenth-grade art teacher took offense to a skirt Renata was wearing. *It's see-through!* she said. But the next day, the teacher came into class with an apologetic look on her face and a brand-new slip in a Macy's bag. *For* you, she said as she handed the bag to Renata. *I'm sorry, I didn't know.* When Renata was little the kids teased her; one girl called her an orphan. Then, once Renata's friends were old enough to understand, they asked nervous questions. *How did it happen? What is it like, just you and your dad?* As they grew even older, they claimed to envy Renata. *My mother is such a pain, such a drain, such a bitch. I don't even talk to her anymore. I wish* she *were dead.* After Renata gave her valedictory speech in front of a hundred graduates and their families, her father alone walked to the podium with a bouquet of roses. He received a deafening round of applause. *So smart, so accomplished, and her mother died when she was little. . . . A beautiful woman,* people whispered when they caught sight of Candace in pictures. *Such a shame.*

The poor girl, Renata imagined Suzanne Driscoll saying. *She has no one to help her plan this wedding.*

Renata's father had given her few details about Candace. Why was that? Was he consumed with his own grief, or was he worried that talk of Candace would upset Renata? Either way, he said very little; all Renata had felt or known for sure was her mother's absence. Renata had never felt as connected to any object as she did to this white cross. It was for her mother, as unlikely as that might seem, out here in the middle of nowhere. *This cross is a part of me, a part of my history.*

In the dusty grass next to her she saw a pair of feet, the silver-ringed toes. Renata looked up; she was crying, she realized.

Queen Bee spoke kindly. "Was this someone you knew?"

"My mother."

"Your *mother*?"

"She was killed out here. Hit by a truck."

"When?"

"A long time ago."

"Oh, geez. I can't believe it."

"Hey!" Miles called out.

Renata stared at the cross, but no words came. She kissed the cross; it pricked her dry lips. *My mother.* They would think she was nuts, but it was true. It was true.

Renata stood up. Queen Bee held out her hand; the mirror in her navel winked in the sun.

"I'm Sallie," she said.

Together they walked back to the car.

12:49 P.M.

The bread dough had risen again. Warm and humid, this was the perfect day for baking bread. Marguerite punched the dough down, then drank a glass of water, took a vitamin, surveyed her list. Just the silver, and . . .

As she had feared. She couldn't procrastinate much longer.

She tied the ribbon of her hat under her chin. *Keys,* she thought. *Where are the keys?* She searched around the house—on the table by the front door? In the soup tureen that served as a junk drawer? On the hook drilled into the wall expressly to hold these very keys? No. She stumbled across a pile of mail on the floor by the front door. She bent to pick it up, thinking, *When was the last time I drove anywhere?* To the doctor in May? It seemed more recent than that. She had a memory of herself in late afternoon, the streets slick from a rain shower. She had been out near the airport—but why? She never had houseguests. Upstairs, five bedrooms waited like bridesmaids. They received attention once every two weeks, when Marguerite dusted. Would the keys be upstairs? Not likely.

Marguerite flipped through the meager envelopes. Did anyone receive less interesting mail than she? Bill for the high-speed Internet, bill for the propane gas, circular from the A&P—and then something thicker, addressed in handwriting: clippings of last month's columns from the Calgary paper. The editor was good about sending them so that Marguerite could appreciate her words in print.

It had kept her alive, that column. When she was released from the psychiatric hospital in Boston after Candace's death, she had to endure something nearly as painful—closing the restaurant. Marguerite had been unable to speak and refused to meet with anyone in person; therefore, her lawyer, Damian Vix, had set up conference calls, on which Marguerite remained mute. The conference calls had made her feel like she was locked with Damian and the gift shop people in a dark closet. The other side had thought—because of her "accident," her "incarceration," her "mental illness"—that they could take advantage of her, but Damian had extorted quite a price. (He negotiated brilliantly, motivated by the memory of a hundred exquisite meals, the bottles of wine Marguerite had saved for him, the shellfish allergy she worked around every time he dined.) At the time, Marguerite had thought money would make her way easier, but she had been wrong. It was, in the end, the newspaper column that had saved her. A call came from out of the blue the very week that Marguerite felt comfortable speaking again. It was the food editor from *The Calgary Daily Press: Someone gave me your number, we'd love to have you write a weekly food column, explain techniques, include recipes. Calgary?* Marguerite had thought. She consulted an atlas. Alberta, Canada? But in the end, how rewarding she found it—thinking about food again and writing about food for a place where she knew no one and no one knew her. Her editor, Joanie Sparks, former housewife, mother of three grown daughters, was officially Marguerite's biggest fan, and the closest thing she'd had to a friend in the past fourteen years. And yet they communicated primarily by yellow Post-it note. Today's note said: *Everyone loved the picnic menu. Hope you are well!*

Someone had given Joanie Sparks Marguerite's name long ago—but Marguerite never discovered who. It was Porter maybe: One of the daughters could have been a student. Or it was Dusty: He liked to fish in Canada on vacation. Or it was one of the regulars from the restaurant who wanted to reach out when they heard about Candace's death. Joanie had never said who passed on Marguerite's name and Marguerite never asked. Now it would seem strange to do so, though Marguerite had always wondered.

The grandfather clock struck one, forcefully, like a blow to the head. Picnic menu, yes. Lobster club sandwiches, coleslaw with apples, raspberry fizz lemonade. Marguerite had been late sending the column (she debated for too long about whether it was reasonable to put lobster on the menu when her readers were hundreds of miles from the sea)—and *that* was when she was last in the car. Right? Racing out to Federal

Express like the Little Old Lady from Pasadena. It was June, after a thundershower; there had been little rainbows rising up from the wet road. She had made it in the nick of time, and this self-generated drama had left her breathless, flustered. Which meant the keys were probably . . .

Marguerite's "driveway" consisted of two tasteful brick strips with grass in between. Her battered 1984 Jeep Wrangler, olive green with a soft beige top, was a classic now; every year some family or other called to see if they could drive it in the Daffodil Parade. But the Jeep, like Marguerite, was a homebody. She asked very little of it—less than fifty miles a year—and it kept passing inspection. Marguerite opened the car door. The keys were dangling from the ignition.

Marguerite eased out of her driveway and puttered down Quince Street toward the heart of town. The Jeep had no air-conditioning and it was too hot to drive with the windows up; already it felt like she had a plastic bag over her head. She unzipped the windows, thinking that this was the perfect weather not only for baking bread but also for riding with the top down—but no, she wouldn't go that far. Marguerite didn't want anyone to recognize her. She wore her enormous hat and round sunglasses like an incognito movie star. Even so, she worried someone would recognize the Jeep. When she bought the Jeep, Porter had given her a vanity plate: CHIEF. (He had meant for it to read CHEF, but someone at the DMV misunderstood; hence CHIEF, and since it wasn't inappropriate, it stayed.) When everything else went out the window, so did the vanity plate—now the Jeep was identified by numbers and letters that Marguerite had never bothered to memorize—and yet she still felt that the soft-top olive green Jeep itself was a dead giveaway. *Marguerite Beale, out on the street!*

She felt better once she was out of town, once she was headed down Orange Street toward the main rotary, and even more at ease once she was safely around the rotary and driving out Polpis Road. Wind filled the car and tugged at the brim of her hat. She felt okay. She felt fine.

How to describe Polpis Road, midafternoon, on a hot summer day? It shimmered. It smelled green and sweet in some places, like a freshly picked ear of corn, and green and salt-marshy in other places, like soft mud and decay. Polpis was, quite literally, a long and winding road, with too many turnoffs and places of interest to explore in one lifetime. On the early left was Shimmo—houses in thick woods that became, down the sandy road, houses that fronted the harbor. Shimmo was old money: At the restaurant, Marguerite had often heard people described as "very Shimmo," or "not Shimmo enough." Just past Shimmo on the right was the dirt road that led to Altar Rock, which was, at 104 feet, the highest point on the island. Marguerite swallowed. She had been to Altar Rock only once, with Candace. Suddenly Marguerite felt angry. Why was it that any memory that mattered led back to Candace or Porter? Why had Marguerite not opened herself to more people? Why had she not made more friends? All of her eggs had gone right into that family's basket; she had put them there herself, and they had broken.

It had been autumn when Marguerite and Candace hiked to Altar Rock, the autumn after they met, perhaps, or the autumn after that. Porter was gone, and Candace came to the restaurant every night by herself. (Had it really been every night, or did it only seem that way?) Candace came late and sat at one of the deuces in front of the window with Marguerite. They ate together; Candace was her guest. That was how their real friendship had started.

"I can't believe my brother leaves you here all winter," Candace said. "And you let him. Why do you let him?"

Marguerite sighed. Sipped her champagne. She had been drinking champagne that night with the aim of getting very drunk because, the previous Sunday, Porter had appeared on the society page of *The New York Times* with another woman on his arm. The photograph was taken at a gala for Columbia's new performing arts center. The caption underneath the picture read: *Professor Porter Harris and friend.* Marguerite had stumbled across the picture on her own; she had been alone, in her newly purchased house on Quince Street, drinking her coffee. Porter's face had jumped out at her from the sea of faces. He was smiling in the picture; he looked positively delighted, smug; he was the cat that ate the canary. He would never have admitted it, but he *wanted* to be on the *Times* social page and had wanted it his whole life—and if he was captured with an attractive escort, so much the better. The woman on Porter's arm—and how many hours had Marguerite wasted scrutinizing that damn picture, cursing the fuzziness of the newsprint, to see precisely *how* Porter was holding the woman's arm—was a brunette. Her hair was in a chignon; she wore a pale, sparkling dress with a plunging neckline. Her face was pleasant enough, though something was off with her mouth, crowded teeth, maybe, or an overbite. Overbite Woman, Marguerite named her. That Sunday the phone rang and rang, but Marguerite didn't answer. It was someone, many someones, calling to tell Marguerite about the picture, or it was Porter himself with an explanation, an apology. Marguerite ignored the phone. She considered calling Porter to tell him she couldn't do it anymore; she didn't want to be treated like a possession he kept in storage and dusted off at the start of every summer. Marguerite took a small comfort in the fact that the woman had not been identified by name. She was "friend," a newspaper euphemism for someone unimportant, someone nobody knew. It could simply have been a woman Porter happened to be standing next to when they were caught by the photographer. But it was humiliating nonetheless; it was a symptom of a larger illness.

Candace had said nothing about the photograph. She had seen it, no doubt, the whole world had seen it, but Candace fell into the category of people who wished to protect Marguerite from it. Now, as they ate dinner five days later, Candace was rallying against Porter in a general way. *Why do you let him go every autumn? Why don't you go to New York? Why don't you leave him?* Marguerite was stumped by these questions; she had never had a friend who cared enough to ask. She was grateful for someone to parse the relationship with, to help her analyze it. But things were complicated by the fact that Candace was Porter's sister. Candace loved to talk about how Porter had refused to indulge her as a child, even though he was fifteen years older. He was, Candace said, stricter and less fun than her parents. Always so self-important with his *art,* his books, his articles for the journals that only a handful of people ever read.

"He takes advantage of you," Candace said.

"Or I take advantage of him," Marguerite said. "I like things this way."

"Do you?"

"No," Marguerite said.

"No, I didn't think so," Candace said, swirling her champagne and studying the glass for legs. (She was charmingly naïve about wine.) "Bastard. He's a bastard; he really is."

"Oh, Candace."

"To not realize what he has in you. Look at this restaurant. The ambience, the food. All Daisy. This place is yours. It's you."

"Some days I wish I had something more," Marguerite said. "Or something different."

"You need to get out of the restaurant for a while," Candace said. "It would take your mind off things. How long has it been since you've been to the beach? Or taken a walk through the moors?"

"Long."

"Tomorrow we'll go together," Candace said. "To see the moors."

And go they did. It was a mercy trip; Marguerite understood that. A feeble attempt to get Marguerite's mind off the photograph she couldn't bring herself to throw away. (It was sandwiched in her copy of Julia Child on her kitchen counter.) But Marguerite knew she had to do something different, no matter how small, and so she laced up a pair of hiking boots that she hadn't worn since her years at Le Ferme. She followed Candace along the winding sand paths that climbed through conservation land to Altar Rock.

"This feels a lot higher than a hundred feet," Marguerite said. "This feels like the Alps." She was breathing heavily, cursing butter and cream, but she plodded along behind Candace to the top. From Altar Rock they gazed out over the moors, which were crimson with poison ivy. Tiny green ponds dotted the moors, and beyond lay the ocean. Marguerite could hear the eerie, distant cries of seagulls.

Candace flung her arm around Marguerite's shoulders. She was not even a little winded; this was nothing but a walk through the park for her. She let out a great yell, a yodel, a howl. "Come on," she said to Marguerite. "It's good for you. Let it all out." When Marguerite regained her breath, she shouted; she bayed. *He's a bastard. He really is.* The words seemed easy and true with Candace at her side. Blood was thicker than water or wine, and yet Candace always sided with Marguerite. As she yelled, Marguerite imagined her anger, her embarrassment, and her longing, floating over the land like mist or smoke and being carried away by the sea. She and Candace howled together until they were hoarse.

A few miles up Polpis Road, Marguerite passed the rose-covered cottage—featured on every third Nantucket postcard—in its second full bloom of the summer. Then Almanack Pond Road, the horse barn, the turnoff for the Wauwinet Inn and Great Point. Marguerite slowed down. She lived so resolutely in town that she had forgotten all this was out here, all this *country.* Sesachacha Pond spread out silvery blue to her left, and directly across the street was the white shell driveway that led to the cottage that Porter had rented for so many years. She would love to turn down that driveway and take a peek. Why not? This day had taken on the quality of the moments before death: her whole life passing before her eyes. She wanted to see if the hammock still hung from the front porch, if the roses still dangled over the outdoor shower, if the daylilies she and Porter planted had survived. But there was no time to waste, plus she didn't know who owned the property anymore. Mr. Dreyfus, who had rented it to Porter, had long been dead; one of his children owned it now, or someone new. The last thing Marguerite needed was to be caught trespassing. She drove on, but not too far. One mailbox, the stone wall, and then she turned right. A dirt path led deep into what guidebooks called the enchanted forest. Not so enchanted, however, because the skinny scrub pines were strangled with underbrush, pricker bushes, and poison ivy and the bumpy path leading through the woods held water, which meant mosquitoes. One could live on Nantucket one's whole life without going to the Herb Farm or even knowing it was there, which had suited Marguerite just fine for the long time that she had avoided it.

Like so much else on this island, the Herb Farm had been Porter's discovery. Every other restaurant provisioned at Bartlett's Farm, a far larger and more sophisticated enterprise, closer to town, and with a farm truck that was a steady presence on Main Street each summer morning. Marguerite held nothing against Bartlett's Farm except that she had never made it her own. She had, from the beginning, woken up in Porter's cottage and walked with an honest-to-goodness wicker basket down the dirt path. The Herb Farm reminded Marguerite of the farms in France; it was like a farm in a child's picture book. There was a white wooden fence that penned in sheep and goats, a chicken coop where a dozen warm eggs cost a dollar, a red barn for the two bay horses, and a greenhouse. Half of the greenhouse did what greenhouses do, while the other half had been fashioned into very primitive retail space. The vegetables were sold from wooden crates, all of them grown organically, before such a process even had a name—corn, tomatoes, lettuces, seventeen kinds of herbs, squash, zucchini, carrots with the bushy tops left on, spring onions, radishes, cucumbers, peppers, strawberries for two short weeks in June, pumpkins after the fifteenth of September. There was chevre made on the premises from the milk of the goats; there was fresh butter. And when Marguerite showed up for the first time in the summer of 1975 there was a ten-year-old boy who had been given the undignified job of cutting zinnias, snapdragons, and bachelor buttons and gathering them into attractive-looking bunches. Ethan Arcain, with his grown-out Beatle hairdo and saucer-sized brown eyes. Marguerite adored the child from the moment she saw him because that was the way she was with people—everything right away, or nothing.

Ethan Arcain worked at the Herb Farm every summer that Les Parapluies was open, and so for a hundred days a year Ethan's face was one of the first Marguerite saw each day. Their relationship wasn't complicated like Marguerite's relationship with Dusty. Ethan was a boy, Marguerite a woman. She thought of him as a little brother, although she was old enough to be his mother. *The son I never had,* she sometimes joked. Ethan's family life was a shambles. Dolores Kimball, who owned the farm in those days, once described Ethan's parents' divorce to Marguerite as a grenade explosion: *Destroyed everyone in the vicinity.* Years later, Ethan's mother remarried and Ethan fell in love with his stepsister and when they were old enough they got married, which people on the island whispered about, because people on the island whispered about everything. Ethan's father, Walter Arcain, worked for the electric company and was a well-known abuser of alcohol. The one time he had tried to come into the bar at Les Parapluies, Marguerite had asked Lance to see him out to the street.

It was Walter Arcain who had been driving the truck that killed Candace. Ten o'clock in the morning and he was three sheets to the wind, out joyriding the snowy roads of Madequecham for no good reason; there weren't any power lines down that road.

At Candace's funeral, Ethan had sat in one of the back pews—by that time a strong young man in his twenties—and cried bitter tears of guilt, atoning for the actions of his derelict father.

I feel responsible, Ethan had said to Marguerite as he left the church. *Dirty and responsible.*

Marguerite couldn't take anyone's guilt seriously but her own, and therefore she didn't grant him the absolution he was looking for. Now, from a greater distance and a clearer perspective, she felt sorry about that. Ethan eventually bought the Herb Farm from Dolores Kimball; once in a great while, Marguerite saw him in town, and he was always a gentleman, holding open doors for her, touching her arm or her shoulder. But the words unsaid polluted the air between them; she felt it and assumed he did, too.

There was a freckled boy working the register in the greenhouse, a boy about the same age Ethan had been when Marguerite met him. His son? Anything was possible. Marguerite just felt relieved that she didn't have to deal with Ethan head-on; she needed time to get her bearings.

Things in the greenhouse had stayed more or less the same, though the prices had tripled, as had the choices. Marguerite had read in the newspaper that the Herb Farm was supplying not only many Nantucket restaurants now but also several high-end places in Boston and New York. Marguerite was glad for this, she wanted Ethan to succeed, but she was pleased, too, that the trough filled with cool water and bunches of fragrant herbs was right where it had always been. Marguerite picked out bunches of basil and dill, mint and cilantro, and inhaled their scents. This was how Ethan found her, sniffing herbs as if they were her first dozen roses.

"Margo?" he said. The reaction she was getting was universal. Ethan's brown eyes widened as Dusty's had, like he couldn't . . . quite . . . *believe* it. Ethan's face was sunburned and his hair, longer than ever, was tied back in a ponytail.

"Hi," she said, though her voice was so quiet, it was inaudible to her own ears. She took a few steps toward him and opened her arms. He hugged her, she kissed his warm, stubbly cheek, and they parted awkwardly. This was what she had dreaded; the angst of this very second was what had nearly kept her from coming. What to say? There was too much and nothing at all.

"I thought I recognized the Jeep in the parking lot," he said. "But I wouldn't let myself believe it. What are you doing here? I thought—"

"I know," Marguerite said. She self-consciously drew her list out of her skirt pocket, checked it, and bent over to select a bunch of chives, which were crisp and topped with spiky purple flowers. Asparagus, she thought. Chevre, butter, eggs, red peppers, and flowers. If only she could get out of here without explaining. Although deep down she wanted to tell someone, didn't she? She wanted to tell someone about the dinner who would understand. This man. And yet how painful it would be to acknowledge their tragic bond. It would be far more couth, more polite, to ignore it and move on.

"You're cooking," he said. It sounded like an accusation.

"Yes," she said. "A chevre tart with roasted red peppers and an herb crust. You do still have the chevre?"

"Yes. God, of course." He glanced around the greenhouse, eager to change roles, to be her provisioner. He would recognize some kind of special occasion, but unlike Dusty, he wouldn't ask. He wouldn't want to know.

Ethan rushed to a refrigerated case, right where the chevre and the butter had always been kept; she could have found it herself with ease. He was stopped at the cheese case by another customer, and Marguerite was grateful. She wandered among the wooden crates, picking up tomatoes, peeling back the husks on ears of corn, adding two red peppers to her shopping basket and a bunch of very thin asparagus, a bouquet of zinnias for the table, and seven imperial-looking white and purple gladiolas to put in the stone pitcher that she kept by the front door. She was loaded down with fresh things, beautiful, glorious provisions. Could she stop time and stay here, with her basket full, surrounded by organic produce? Could she just die here and call it a happy end?

Ethan appeared at her side with the chevre, just the right amount for her tart. He held the cheese out; his hands, if she weren't mistaken, were trembling. Marguerite cast her eyes around. The woman he had been talking to at the cheese case was now at the counter. The freckled boy scanned her purchases, weighed her produce, and put everything in a used brown paper bag from the A&P. There was no one else in the greenhouse. Marguerite wondered if Ethan was still married to the stepsister. She wondered how marrying someone you were not at all related to could be considered by so many people as incest.

"Thank you," Marguerite said. She, too, could proceed to the checkout and walk across the sunny parking lot to her Jeep, drive home without another word, but for some reason she felt that would be cheating.

And yet she didn't want to knock him over with the force of an out-and-out testimonial. Conversation, she thought. She used to be, if not a master, then at least a journeyman. Able to hold her own with stranger or friend. And Ethan was a friend. What did friends say to one another?

"How *are* you?" she said. "Really, how are you?"

He smiled; his red face creased. He was sun-wrinkled like a farmer, but the hair and the soft eyes and the knowledge of his sensitive soul had always made Marguerite think *poet, philosopher.* "I'm good, Margo. Happy. I'm happy."

"The place looks wonderful."

"It keeps me busy. We're doing all kinds of new things. . . ." He sounded ready to launch into an explanation of heirloom varieties, hydroponics, cold pasteurization, which Marguerite, as a former chef, would appreciate, but he stopped himself. Backed up. "I'm happily married."

"To . . . ?"

"Emily, yes. And the boys are growing up too fast."

"That's one of them over there?" Marguerite asked.

"Yes."

They both looked at the boy, who, now that the greenhouse was empty of customers save for the one his father was talking to, had started reading a book. Marguerite felt proud of him on his father's behalf. Any other kid, it would have been one of those horrible handheld video games.

Ethan cleared his throat. "So you found everything you need? Everything for the tart?"

"Everything for the tart and then some," Marguerite said. She closed her eyes for a second and listened. Was she about to make a colossal mistake? She heard the goats maahing and the refrigerator case humming. She met Ethan's eyes and lowered her voice. "Renata is coming for dinner tonight."

His expression remained unchanged and Marguerite faltered. Did he not remember Renata? She had been just a little girl, of course. "Renata is Candace's—"

"Yes," he whispered. "I know who she is."

"She's nineteen."

He whistled softly and shook his head.

"I'm sorry," Marguerite said. "I shouldn't have—"

He grabbed her protesting hand. "Don't be sorry," he said. "I figured as much. If you were cooking again, I figured it was the girl. Or Dan. Or Porter."

"The girl," Marguerite repeated. "Renata Knox."

"If I could, I would prostrate myself at her feet," Ethan said. "I would beg her forgiveness."

"You don't have to beg her forgiveness," Marguerite said. "You did nothing wrong."

"Yes, but Walter—"

"Walter, exactly." Marguerite's voice was so firm she startled herself. She glanced at the boy, Ethan's son, but his gaze was glued to the page. "Walter isn't you and you aren't Walter. You never had to carry his load."

"But I did. I do."

"But you do," Marguerite said.

"When I had kids, I promised myself . . ." Here he paused and Marguerite saw him swallow. ". . . that I wouldn't *do* anything that would ever make them feel anything but proud of me."

"Right," Marguerite said. "And they are proud of you, I'm sure. This place is holy, your work is noble, you are a good, good person, and you always have been. Since you were that age." She nodded to the son. "I didn't tell you about Renata to awaken your old, useless guilt. I told you because I knew you would understand about tonight's dinner. How important it is to me. How you will be a part of it."

"I want to be a part of it," he said. "Thank you for coming all the way out here. In my wildest dreams, I never expected to see you today." Ethan took Marguerite by the arm and led her to the counter. "Margo, I'd like you to meet my son Brandon. Brandon, this is Marguerite Beale, an old friend of mine."

Marguerite offered Brandon her hand. "Your father feels no shame in calling me old."

"My apologies," Ethan said. "I meant 'longtime friend.' We've been friends a long time."

Brandon took Marguerite's hand, uneasily glancing between her and his father. Marguerite nearly laughed. She felt unaccountably happy. Relieved. This was almost over; the hard part was through. It would end well. Brandon began to unload Marguerite's purchases, but before he could weigh or scan anything, Ethan said, "It's on the house. All of it."

"Ethan," Marguerite said. "No. I can't let you do that."

"Oh yes, you can," Ethan said. "This is for the best chef on Nantucket and her esteemed guest."

Brandon bagged everything with extreme care as Ethan and Marguerite watched him in silence. Marguerite was grinning; the boy looked so much like his father. When she picked up her bag, Ethan touched her head and Marguerite remembered a priest, long ago, bestowing a blessing. "Now go," he said. "Cook. And enjoy your dinner."

1:14 P.M.

Madequecham Beach was just beautiful enough to improve Renata's attitude. It was a party, a carnival, a scene from *Beach Blanket Bingo.* No wonder her mother had come running down this road. Even in the dead of winter, the beach would have been breathtaking. At the edge of a dirt parking lot was a bluff, and spread out before them the blue, blue ocean and a wide white swath of beach. Renata descended a flight of rickety stairs while holding on to the ass end of Sallie's surfboard. Sallie held the top of the surfboard like a mother dragging an unruly child by the neck. Renata, in addition to watching her step and engineering the descent, was soaking in the action below her: the beautiful young people with their Frisbees and dogs and brilliantly colored beach towels and umbrellas, the radios playing Jimmy Buffett and U2, the beer cans popping open in a sound of serious Saturday celebration. Sallie, meanwhile, was focused only on the waves.

"Hurry up, Renata!" she said. "The surf is screaming my name!"

Renata quickened her step as she felt the surfboard being tugged from her grip. Miles was somewhere behind her. She didn't care where he was. She had left her good sense back on Hulbert Avenue and her heart back at the white cross in the road, and without those two things she felt curiously clean and empty, as though she didn't have a care in the world.

Once they reached the soft, hot sand Renata let go of the surfboard and Sallie raced for the water. Somebody called to her; she waved and pointed at the waves. She stopped suddenly and jogged back to Renata. She handed Renata her sunglasses.

"Hold these," she said. She kissed Renata on the jaw.

"Whoa-ho!" Miles said as he came up behind Renata with the towels and the cooler of beer and sandwiches. "I think she likes you."

She feels sorry for me, Renata thought. Together she and Miles watched as Sallie lay down on her board and paddled out. Renata slipped Sallie's sunglasses into her bag.

"Is she your girlfriend?" Renata asked.

Miles laughed. "She likes women," he said.

"Really?"

"Really."

Renata felt funny in a way she couldn't name. "Where do you want to sit?" she asked. "Do you know anybody here?"

"A few people," he said. "This is where I hang out when I'm not working. But I don't feel like getting into it all today. Let's just sit here." He plunked the cooler down on a plot of unclaimed sand, several yards away from four girls, tanned and oiled, lined up on a blanket like so many sausages across a grill. Renata stood by as Miles spread out a towel for her; then she slipped out of her skirt and lay down. Miles dug two beers out of the cooler and opened one for her. Renata didn't normally drink in the middle of the day, but she was dying of thirst and today, it was becoming clear, was not a normal day. She took a taste from the sweating bottle and instantly her mood improved. Miles lay down next to her on a second towel. He removed his shirt and every one of Renata's impure thoughts returned. His body was gorgeous—not pretty, like a model or a movie star, but muscular and rugged. Renata's experience with male bodies was limited to Cade, who was lankier than Miles. Cade had long, skinny legs and knobby knees. He had big feet and freakishly long toes that Renata teased him about; as a result, he'd stopped wearing flip-flops. Cade had a farmer's tan. He'd spent the summer with Renata in the city, working at Columbia's business school, and the only time he spent outside was the occasional lunch hour on the steps of Uris Hall and weekend afternoons, when he and Renata ate take-out food in Sheep Meadow, waving away the gnats. It wasn't at all fair to compare Miles to Cade or vice versa, and yet Renata found herself wondering what it would feel like if Miles leaned to his left and then leaned again so that he was lying on top of her. Would his weight feel different? How would he taste if she kissed him? Would sex feel different?

Renata drank her beer with purpose until it was gone. Miles had his eyes closed. Renata raised her head an inch off the towel and became light-headed. She scanned the water beyond the breaking waves for Sallie. There were a lot of people surfing and Renata thought she saw a woman with long hair, but it could just as easily have been a man.

"So," she said. "I'm missing lunch at the yacht club."

Miles didn't open his eyes. "That you are."

"Suzanne will be mad."

"Quite possibly."

"Have you worked for them a long time?"

He opened his eyes and looked at her. Was he annoyed? Was she keeping him awake? She was about to tell him to relax, she would be quiet, when he did half her bidding and leaned to his left, propping himself on one elbow so that he was gazing down at her. He sipped his beer. Renata felt a wave of desire so strong she nearly fainted away. She closed her eyes. *Oh,* she thought. *Oh, oh.* An engaged person should not feel this kind of insane hunger for the houseboy of her fiancé's family. There was something wrong with her.

"Three years," he said. "This is the first summer I've lived with them, though. Suzanne loves it because I'm always around."

"You live there by yourself?"

"No," he said. "I have a roommate."

"Who?" she said.

He licked his lips and twisted his beer into the sand.

"Let me ask you something," he said. "Why do you want to get married?"

"I don't," she said. She sat up and squinted at the water. The surfers were fun to watch once they finally decided a wave was worth pursuing. Renata located the person she thought was Sallie—long hair, bare midriff—and saw her crouch on her board, then stand, shifting her weight, steadying herself with her arms as the board careened along the smooth inside wall of the wave. Then crash. Time to start over. Renata wondered how surfing could possibly be worth all the time spent waiting for a decent wave. Were those seconds of riding just unbelievably rewarding? Was it like the thrill of a first kiss? "I think I'll have another beer," Renata said. "Please."

"Sandwich?" Miles said.

"Not yet."

Miles flipped the top off another beer for Renata and one for himself. Renata's guilt was at a ten; surely it couldn't get any worse than this. She had denied her own fiancé.

"It's not that I don't want to marry *Cade,*" she said. She nearly added, *I love Cade,* but at the last minute she changed her mind. "Everybody loves Cade."

"He's a great guy," Miles said. "Very upstanding. Very upwardly mobile. Lots of money."

"That's not why—"

"Oh, I know. That's not why I work for them, either. I work for them because I like Mr. D., and he's sick."

"He's sick," Renata said. "Cade wants to get married before anything happens to him. Before he's too sick to enjoy a wedding."

"Like I said, upstanding fellow."

"He was president of the student body at Columbia," Renata said. "And captain of the lacrosse team. He graduated Phi Beta Kappa."

"All very admirable."

"All very admirable," Renata repeated. Cade Driscoll was a catch, and she had spent the past ten months in a daze of pride and disbelief that he had chosen *her,* a lowly, motherless freshman, a relative nobody. And yet now the awe she'd felt had been displaced by something else. She feared him a little bit, his permanence in her life, the *finality* of it all. Marriage. "I guess I'd rather just stay engaged for a while."

"How old are you?" Miles asked.

"Nineteen."

"You're *kidding,*" he said. He looked genuinely aghast. "I'm going to have to confiscate that beer."

"How old are you?" Renata asked.

"Twenty-four," he said. He gazed at Renata's chest. "You're getting pretty red."

"No lotion," she said. She pressed her fingers against her skin and the fingerprints turned white. She was frying like bacon.

"Take my shirt," he said. He tossed it to her and it landed in her lap, soft and cool. She put it on. It smelled like a man, but like a man other than her fiancé. Cade wore cologne. This shirt smelled like bleach and sweat and piney soap. Renata felt all muddled; she yearned for clarity. She loved Cade—what woman wouldn't?—but the more she was forced to confront the reality of getting married (Suzanne's damn list, her father saying, *I think it's wonderful, darling. Congratulations!*) the less sure she was that marriage was what she wanted. Telling her father was one thing, but Renata was growing more and more afraid of telling Action. Action would pitch a French fit; she might even threaten to divorce Renata as her best friend, and Renata wouldn't be able to bear that. If she was forced to make a choice between Cade and her father, Cade would win. But if she was forced to pick between Cade and Action, Action would win. What did that say? Renata watched the surfers, keeping her eye on Sallie. *She likes women.* There was an intensity to Renata's relationship with Action that was missing from her relationship with Cade. There was a thrill, an excitement, a passion to their friendship; they were giddy with it half the time and smug the other half. They held hands, many times, walking to the dining hall.

We in love, Action liked to say.

There was a shout from down the beach. "Miles!" Some guys were setting up a volleyball net. A tall, dark man, hairy like a bear, punched the volleyball on top of his fist. "Want to play?"

Miles called out no, but the man didn't seem to hear. He waved his arm like a windmill. Miles shook his head. "No, man, sorry." Then he huffed. "We should have sat farther down," he said. "I'm going to have to go over there. I'll be right back."

"Whatever," Renata said. "Play if you want. You don't have to babysit me." She leaned back and closed her eyes, trying to turn the day back into what she thought it might be when she woke up that morning: a day on Nantucket, a day at the beach. Instead, she pictured the white cross, a piece of her mother up there on the bluff. Renata would ask Marguerite about the cross, first thing.

A few minutes later, Renata felt something land in the sand next to her. She opened her eyes to see Sallie sitting on Miles's towel. Her hair was wet and slick, revealing a small, white ear, which was punched with six identical silver hoops. Renata's father had spent hours of precious breath warning her about the dangers—not the tackiness or flamboyance but the *dangers*—of piercings and tattoos, and in this unique case, Renata had chosen to agree with her father and obey. But the effect of these "dangers" on Sallie was dazzling. There was a city block near Columbia where the residents had pressed colored glass and seashells and silvery stones into the sidewalk—Renata loved to walk that block because it was different; it turned the ordinary cement into a celebration—and Sallie with her earrings and toe rings and mirrored navel and the army green spiral twist of leaves and vines around her right ankle struck Renata in much the same way. She could barely tear her eyes away. Sallie was dripping wet; her eyelashes stuck together in thick clumps.

"How was the surfing?" Renata asked.

"It's wild out there," Sallie said. Her chest heaved; her breasts rose and fell. "It doesn't look that bad from here, but there's a wicked rip. I came in because I'm starving. Did Miles make lunch?"

"Sandwiches," Renata said.

Sallie opened the cooler and dug a sandwich out. "Roadkill," she said. "Another person would have thought to put the sandwiches *on top of* the beer. Ah, men." She said this conspiratorially, and Renata laughed a little, then remembered what Miles had said. *She likes women.* Renata watched Sallie unwrap the sandwich and take a lusty bite.

"Do you want a beer?" Renata asked.

"No, thanks," Sallie said. "I'm going back out in a minute." The offer, though, seemed to train Sallie's attention back on Renata, and Renata couldn't tell if she was flattered by this or worried. "So your mother died on that road back there. That honestly blows my mind. I'm sorry for what I said about the cross before. I hope I didn't offend you."

"No, it's fine—"

"I never thought about those crosses being for real people, you know? I just thought the Department of Public Works stuck them there to keep people from driving too fast. I never thought of them as being for someone's *mother.*"

"It's okay," Renata said.

"How old were you?" Sallie asked. "When she died?"

"Five."

"Noooooooo," Sallie said. "Tell me no."

"I was five."

Sallie reached out for Renata's hand and squeezed it. Renata felt grateful and silly. She didn't know what to say. Sallie swallowed the last of the sandwich.

"How do you know Miles?" Sallie asked. "He didn't pick you up at a bar, did he?"

"No," Renata said quickly. "I'm staying with the family Miles works for."

Sallie creased her eyebrows. Her nose seemed to wiggle.

"The Driscolls," Renata said.

"You know, I've never met them."

Renata nearly said, *Consider yourself lucky,* but she checked her swing. They were, after all, her future in-laws. "I . . . date the son. He's my boyfriend. His name is Cade."

Sallie nodded distractedly; her attention was back on the water, with the other surfers. Maybe she was put out by this pronouncement of Renata's heterosexuality. "I assumed you were with Miles."

"I assumed *you* were," Renata said.

At this, Sallie hooted. "That guy?" she said. She nodded down the beach at Miles, who was walking back toward them. "Want to hear something funny?" Sallie called out. "She thought I was your girlfriend."

"Get your ass up," Miles said. "You're sitting on my towel."

"Such a gentleman," Sallie said. She didn't move an inch.

"I mean it," Miles said. "Get up."

"Sit on my board if you're afraid of the sand," Sallie said.

"Never mind," Miles said. He plopped down on the other side of Renata. "So what were you two talking about?"

"None of your business," Sallie said. "Who is that down there?"

"Montrose. Couldn't shake him."

"And what did you two talk about?"

"None of your business."

Sallie looked at Renata and rolled her eyes. *Men.*

"Renata's engaged, you know," Miles said.

"What?" Sallie said. She moved her face so that it hovered directly over Renata's face, blocking out the sun. "I thought you said 'boyfriend.'"

"Well . . . ," Renata said. She realized she had her left hand, her ringed hand, tucked under her butt, and she kept it there.

"I'm trying to talk her out of it," Miles said. "She's only nineteen."

"You're trying to talk me out of it?" Renata said. "Suzanne won't like that."

"Who's Suzanne?" Sallie said.

"The woman I work for," Miles said.

"My future mother-in-law," Renata said. Something about the beer and the pure lawlessness of the afternoon made Renata want to throw Suzanne under the bus. She reached for her bag. "Look what I found this morning," she said. She pulled out the list and did her best to smooth it flat. "Suzanne is trying to plan my wedding without even asking me."

Sallie took the list and read it. Renata hoped she might share her outrage, but instead Sallie got all dreamy eyed.

"Weddings are a sick fantasy of mine," Sallie said. Miles guffawed, but she didn't seem to notice. "I love to think about this kind of stuff. The dress, the flowers, the champagne, a hundred and fifty people standing up when you walk into the church, band or DJ, sit-down or buffet. I've always wanted a big wedding."

"You have got to be kidding me," Miles said.

"Don't you?"

"I haven't given it a second's thought," Miles said.

"Me, either," Renata admitted.

"My parents eloped on Antigua," Sallie said. "They were pregnant with my oldest brother."

"That's romantic," Renata said. "Isn't it?"

"Well, they're still married," Sallie said. "My mother regrets not having a big to-do. She's pinned all her hopes on me, poor woman."

"You'll get married?" Renata said.

"No," Sallie said. "Not in any way that they'd approve of."

There were a few seconds of silence. Staying on this topic was like sitting bare butted on a barnacled rock; Renata wanted to get off. She gently reclaimed the list from Sallie, folded it up, and tucked it back into her bag.

"May I have another beer, please?" she asked.

Miles jumped up. "I'll get it." He opened the cooler and flipped the top off a bottle. "Sandwich?" he said.

"Not yet."

"Look at you, catering to her every need," Sallie said. "How sweet."

"I'm a sweet guy." He sat back down next to Renata, even closer than last time. Meanwhile, Sallie laid a hand on Renata's bicep; her fingers grazed the side of Renata's breast.

"I'm going back out for a beating," Sallie said. "Will you keep an eye on me?"

"Since when do you need a spotter?" Miles said.

"Since today. It's hairier out there than it looks."

"I'll keep an eye out," Renata said, though she had no idea what this entailed. If Sallie did get caught in a rip current, Renata would never be able to save her. All she had wanted from the afternoon was a swim, and yet the waves were pounding the shore so brutally that Renata was afraid to go in, lest she lose her top or get knocked on her ass.

Sallie pointed a finger and smiled. "Don't go getting married while I'm gone," she said, and with that she picked up her board and paddled out.

"Yep," Miles said, once Sallie was past the first set of breaking waves. "She likes you."

Renata sipped her beer. "Shut up."

"What?" he said.

There had been something familiar about it, Renata thought. Miles on one side, Sallie on the other, competing for her attention. It was like all the hours she spent, early on, in the company of Cade and Action—until they realized they didn't like each other that much, they were jealous of each other, they resented each other. Boyfriend, best friend: It didn't work out that well. Renata had spent the last year juggling, compromising, trying to keep them both happy. She sipped her beer and closed her eyes.

"Are you okay?"

"Huh?" Renata said. Miles was on her towel now, or part of his leg was. He had stretched out, and his lower leg and foot were on her towel. And when he spoke, he leaned closer and his right elbow sank into the sand next to her towel and his left hand was on her towel.

"I asked if you were okay."

She nodded, confused. She was lying: She wasn't okay. She felt lost. Cade, Action, her father, Marguerite, her mother, Suzanne. And now Miles, who, if she wasn't hallucinating, was leaning down to *kiss* her. She closed her eyes. Was this happening? He kissed her. He scooted closer and kissed her again, really kissed her, with his tongue. He tasted different from Cade, though she couldn't say how. She didn't have time to think about it; she was too busy worrying about the three hundred witnesses to this treachery—the four girls sunbathing near them, the hairy beast Montrose on the other side of the volleyball net, and most crucially Sallie: What on earth would Sallie think if she saw Renata and Miles kissing only seconds after she had discovered that Renata was engaged? Renata propped herself up on her elbows and did a quick scan—the girls were asleep, the volleyball game was its own spectacle, it had drawn a crowd, and Sallie was indistinguishable from the other surfers. No one had seen them, thank God. Miles took hold of her chin. "Hey," he said. "I'm over here." He kissed her again.

I'm trying to talk her out of it.

Stop! Renata screamed at herself. *Stop right now!* But all she could think was: *I want more. How do I get more?* Miles was turned on, she could tell through his bathing suit that he was hard, and her mind rooted out possibilities: the dunes, the water, his car? Her body was begging for more—she wanted him to reach inside her bikini top and fondle her breast; she wanted him to slip his hand between her legs. *Look what you've done to me.* Wait a minute! *Cade,* she thought. *Cade, Cade, Cade.* Thinking about Cade didn't help. He'd said they would go to the beach together today, but he had vanished without so much as a note. He would expect her to understand; he was sailing with his sick father. How could she argue with that? She couldn't. Cade was, as always, doing the right thing, whereas she, in her anger and confusion, was doing the wrong thing.

Renata broke free for a second, checked around them again. The girls, the volleyball game—on someone's radio, John Mellencamp sang "Jack and Diane." Miles probably kissed girls on this beach all the time. He was a predator; she should escape from him now, while she had the chance. Renata narrowed her eyes and tried to pick Sallie out of the water. If Sallie would only come back, she'd be safe.

"You want to get out of here?" Miles asked.

This was her chance to turn him down, to prove she was pure of soul, worthy of three karats, worthy of Cade, upstanding fellow—but instead, Renata nodded mutely. Miles wrapped a towel around his waist and led her away from the girls and the game, past an older couple, an anomaly in this thirty-and-under crowd, the woman heavyset and topless, lying facedown, reading a novel, the man even heavier in a webbed lawn chair with his binoculars trained on the surfers. They didn't move as Renata and Miles snuck past.

Up a second, smaller staircase, up to the bluff, into the dunes. There was nothing behind them—no road, no houses, nothing but eel grass and bowls of soft, white sand, some with circles of ash where people had lit bonfires, some with empty beer cans and condom wrappers. Renata followed behind Miles, every so often turning around to look at the beach. No one was shouting after them; no one would notice they were gone. Cade was on the other side of the island, possibly still sailing. He would never know.

If you did a bad thing and no one ever found out, Renata asked herself, *was it still a bad thing?*

Just as Miles led her into a deep bowl, deep enough so that they would never be seen and as wide as a king-size bed, Renata's head began to clear. What was she *doing*? Miles unwrapped the towel from his waist and laid it down in the sand. He sat.

"Come here," he said.

She could have run, or claimed she had to pee and *then* run; she could have started to cry, owning up to her guilt—any of these strategies would have worked. But she wasn't strong enough or mature enough to turn down something she wanted so badly. She'd wanted him since the first second she'd seen him at the airport, when his forearms flexed as he lifted their luggage into the back of the Driscolls' Range Rover. And then with the hose. And then making the sandwiches. Now here he was, offering himself up on a platter.

As she stepped down into the bowl, her feet sank into the soft sand.

He reached out and pulled her onto the towel. If he had been any bit rougher or more insistent, she would have stopped him. But he kissed her slowly and gently in a way that made her think *love.* This was a trick, of course; she hadn't been kissed by that many men, but she recognized his tenderness as a trick, a lure. He took his shirt off her body and his hands went where she had willed them to go earlier. She was panting; she wanted his bathing suit off; she wanted him right on top of her. He was taking his good old time, going slower and slower to maybe see if he could get her to think *love* again. But who was he kidding? She cried out softly in frustration, *"Oh, come on!"*

He stopped. His bathing suit was uneven around his hips, his cock strained through the nylon. He was sweating. It was blistering hot in the bowl of white sand, blocked from the ocean breeze. By now Renata's bathing suit top was off, discarded, buried somewhere, she didn't care where. She didn't care! She wanted to scream the words: *I DON'T CARE!* About Cade or her father, or even, at that point, her mother, and the sad little white cross that marked her demise.

"I'm thinking of you," Miles said. He had his hands by her ears; he was holding himself above her, shading her, his knees resting between her open legs. "You're about to burn your whole house down."

She thought of Sallie kissing her jaw and Cade kissing her last night on the guest room's deck and Action, who had kissed her on the mouth and each of the palms the day she left for the woods of West Virginia. She thought of her father kissing her good night on the forehead every night for fourteen years that she could recall. She thought of Suzanne kissing her upon the announcement of her engagement, kissing her with reverence and pride, like a mother would. Renata did not have a single memory of kissing her own mother.

"Burn it down," she said.

2:40 P.M.

The tart was a new recipe, flagged in a copy of *Bon Appétit,* June 1995, so not really new at all, but new to Marguerite because she had never tried it. She had marked the page and cataloged the magazine, however. Just in case.

Marguerite turned on different music: Tony Bennett singing Cole Porter. Happy songs, sad songs, love songs, lovesick songs. Marguerite whistled and, now that the mailman had come and gone, she hummed.

The first thing she did was tackle the tart crust. This was a pastry skill, and pastry skills had never been her strong suit. She loved to bake bread, but crusts were different from bread. Bread could take a beating, whereas crusts wanted to be handled as little as possible. Bread liked warmth and humidity, whereas crusts liked the cold. The butter had to be cold; the egg had to be cold. Marguerite minced the herbs, relishing the feel of her ten-inch Wusthof in her hands—a knife older than her dinner guest—and the sound of the blade against her cutting board. Dicing, chopping, mincing, all like what they said about riding a bike. Marguerite had always been gifted with a knife; she had cut herself only once, in the early days at Les Trois Canards. Gerard de Luc had been screaming at her in French, something she didn't understand, and Marguerite, who was aiming for a perfectly uniform *brunoise* of carrots, put the knife through her second and third fingertips to the tune of fifteen stitches. After that, she worked to achieve a kind of zen with her knife. When she held it, she blocked everything else out.

The scent of the herbs intensified once they were minced—minty, peppery, pickly. For some reason, this smell got to her. Marguerite started to cry. She wasn't tearing up like she might over an onion but crying. Crying so that she had to leave the herbs in a wet green pile on the cutting board next to the carefully measured flour and salt, crying so that she had to return the butter to the fridge, where it would stay cold, and find a place to sit down. Not the kitchen table, the chairs were too hard; not the bedroom, the bed was too soft. She wandered like Goldilocks through her own house, her eyes blinded by tears, to the sofa in the sitting room where, on any other day, she would have been reading her Alice Munro stories. She settled in a way that felt like collapsing.

Okay, what was it? What was wrong? She was sobbing, gasping, wheezing for air. Classic hysterics. And yet she was curiously detached. Part of her was watching herself cry, thinking, *Go ahead, get it out, get as crazy and as dramatic as you want now, better now than the second the girl walks in; we don't want to send her running back down Quince Street with the news that you actually have lost your mind.* The rational part of Marguerite did the watching. The irrational part of her, the part fully engaged in the sobbing, was feeling all the things she had forbidden herself to feel for the past fourteen years, because she might have wailed like this each and every day. She had been thorough and adamant about stripping her life of all sensory reminders from her old life, like the smell of those herbs, so that she wouldn't be tempted to dwell on what she had lost. It wasn't only her taste buds that had been numbed; it was her heart, too. But now, just for a minute, with snot and tears dripping down her face, she felt.

It was practically legend, the way that Daniel Knox had stormed into their lives. He appeared one night in July, a busy Friday night, around nine thirty. Marguerite, Candace, and Porter had just settled down on the west banquette to dinner. There were still a few tables lingering over dessert; this was usual. What was unusual was the man who approached from the bar, a full drink in his hand, and pulled out the fourth seat, the seat next to Candace, and said, "I know I'm being awfully forward, but—"

Candace looked up and said, "Oh! Hello."

Marguerite and Porter exchanged glances. Candace received a lot of attention from men. Drinks were sent to the table all the time. A few men waited at the bar until Candace rose from dinner; they thought they could trap her there, like an insect in their web. The men were usually older, graying, wealthy; some had accents. They were all full of promises, of ideas; they had a big boat, a big house, a big party the following night. Would Candace join them? Sometimes the answer was yes, and a few nights later Marguerite and Porter would hear about the big boat, the big house, the big party—but most of the time the answer was no. No one had ever been bold enough to approach the table. It was the chef's table, the owner's table. Marguerite ate after everyone was finished for a reason. She wanted a modicum of privacy, at least as much as she afforded her guests. She would never have sat down at one of *their* tables uninvited. The way Candace said, "Oh! Hello," however, made both Marguerite and Porter think that this man with the dark blond hair and the untrimmed beard was someone Candace knew. When the man sat down, Candace fumbled with the introduction.

"This is Marguerite Beale, the chef/owner, and my brother Porter Harris. And Marguerite, Porter, this is—"

"Daniel," he said. "Daniel Knox." They shook hands over and around their drinks.

Candace laughed nervously and said, "And my name is Candace Harris."

"I know," Daniel said.

"You're the man I see when I'm running, right?" she said. "Down at—"

"The Beach Club," Daniel said. "Yes. I own it. I bought it five years ago."

"Aha!" Porter said. He could talk to anyone, given a foothold. "So you're the chap who made all the changes."

"Capital improvements," Daniel said.

"You raised the dues, I hear."

"Had to."

"You must not be very popular," Porter said.

"More popular than one might think," Daniel said. "The place looks a hell of a lot better. You should come see it sometime."

"I'd love to," Porter said.

Francesca approached the table with three appetizer plates. "You have a fourth?" she said. Her voice barely concealed her annoyance; serving Marguerite was her last duty before tipping out.

Marguerite shook her head ever so slightly and tried to send Francesca a distress signal. *We don't know who this man is or where he came from.*

"Oh no," Daniel said. "I wouldn't want to impose."

Candace put a hand on his arm. "Stay," she said. "We'd love it." She looked to Marguerite.

"We'd love it," Marguerite said, though nothing was further from the truth. "A fourth! Francesca, would you ask Lance to bring Mr. Knox another drink. Scotch, is it?"

"Scotch," Daniel said. "But really, I have a full one here—"

"And a bottle of the 1974 Louis Jadot cabernet from the cellar. Two bottles."

"Well," Porter said. "Daisy is pulling out the big guns tonight."

Francesca nodded, then swept away from the table. She was back a second later with another plate of the wild mushroom ravioli and the Scotch and the wine.

"More bread?" she asked.

"No, thank you," Marguerite said. She smiled wickedly at Porter and nudged his foot under the table. Together they made sure that Daniel Knox always had a full scotch as well as one waiting, and a full glass of wine. *Drink,* they encouraged him. *Drink!* Daniel Knox talked about the Beach Club; then he talked about living in New York, trading petroleum futures, his retirement at age thirty. Candace seemed interested. She was good at that; she practiced patience all day long at the Chamber of Commerce, fielding phone call after phone call of people asking if there was a bridge to Nantucket. Daniel asked what Candace did for work, she told him, he asked about her running, and she talked about the New York Marathon. *This year for sure.*

By the time the entrées arrived, Daniel Knox was intoxicated. He slurred his words, he stared at his swordfish woefully, and Marguerite knew he was done for. He didn't eat a single bite. Candace chattered along; Porter talked about Nantucket as it was in the fifties when he first started coming there; Marguerite watched over Candace's shoulder as the kitchen was cleaned and closed up for the night. The conversation proceeded as if Daniel Knox weren't there—and a few seconds later, he wasn't. He excused himself for the men's room. Porter chuckled as he filled Daniel's wineglass for the tenth time.

"You two are awful," Candace said; then she smiled.

"Don't I know it," Marguerite said. "I'm sure he's not used to the likes of us."

"He seems like a nice man," Candace said.

"Does he?" Marguerite said.

"Yes!" Candace said, peeved now. "I'm going to check on him."

It took ten days for Daniel to resurface and ask Candace out on a date. He made a hearty campaign for Ship's Inn or the Club Car; he even offered to cook himself, in the small apartment behind the Beach Club where he lived. Candace sweetly declined. *I like to eat at Les Parapluies,* she said. *Sorry. That's what I like.*

And so Marguerite fed Candace and a very reluctant Daniel Knox at the regular seven thirty seating, just like everyone else. Cedar-planked salmon and potatoes Anna. Daniel Knox, despite the fact that he drank almost nothing and did not take his eyes off Candace, cleaned his plate. The following morning, Candace cornered Marguerite in the kitchen.

"Daniel wants to know what you put in our food," she said. "He swears it made him fall in love." Candace kissed Marguerite on both cheeks. "So whatever it was, thank you."

They came in together a lot that summer, though some nights they took sandwiches to the beach, or they went to the movies, or they attended a party thrown by one of the Beach Club members. At first Candace referred to Daniel as "the man I'm dating," and Porter and Marguerite followed her lead. "Daniel Knox," they said, when people asked who he was. "The man Candace is dating." Candace still came to the restaurant without Daniel, though less and less frequently. Marguerite asked, as casually as possible, if things were getting serious. Candace would smile and tilt her head. "Serious?" She was being coy and it drove Marguerite mad. The one time Marguerite tried to talk about it with Porter, they ended up arguing, which almost never happened. It was late at night, they were at Marguerite's house on Quince Street. Marguerite was sitting at her dressing table, unpinning her hair. Porter lay in bed reading a biography of John Singer Sargent.

"Candace is acting strangely," Marguerite said. "When I ask her about Daniel, I can't get a straight answer."

"I think that's probably a good sign," Porter said. "They're falling in love."

"Falling in love is a good thing?" Marguerite asked.

"It was for us," Porter said. He laid his book down on his chest. "Come here."

Marguerite spun on her stool. "I don't think Daniel is right for your sister."

"Because you don't like him."

"I do like him."

"Oh, Daisy, you do not. But then I suspect you wouldn't like anyone Candace dated. You're more protective than a mother."

"I'm not protective."

"Okay, then, you're jealous."

"Jealous? You've *got* to be kidding."

"Right," Porter said. "Why should you be jealous? You have me."

"It's just not like her to be so secretive," Marguerite said. "Your sister and I tell each other everything. And now there's this . . . thing, this big thing, that she won't talk about."

"Probably because she senses that you don't really want to hear about Daniel. Because you don't like Daniel. Because you're jealous."

"Please shut up," Marguerite said. "You're giving me a headache."

"You brought it up," Porter said. "And I'm certain you don't want my advice, but if I were you, I'd get used to the idea of Candace and Daniel together. In fact, I wouldn't be surprised if they got married."

"Oh, for heaven's sake, Porter."

"I heard her call him her boyfriend."

"You did not."

"I did. 'My boyfriend, Daniel Knox.' "

"You're just saying that to annoy me."

"I am not. You have to face the facts, Daisy. She's not going to belong to us forever."

Marguerite had not responded. She'd sat at the dressing table, looking at her reflection in the mirror, lost in thought. Porter called her to bed twice, then gave up and turned off the light.

That conversation had disturbed her deeply, but why? Why shouldn't Candace and Daniel be happy? Why shouldn't they get married? Was Marguerite being overly protective? *Was* she jealous? Was Candace keeping Marguerite at arm's length, or was Marguerite pushing Candace away by not accepting Daniel? Because the fact of the matter was, Marguerite *didn't* like Daniel. She was afraid of him, and she couldn't stifle a growing sense of resentment.

In the fall, once Porter left, Candace came into the restaurant to eat with Marguerite, and Daniel would plant himself on one of the benches outside the Dreamland Theater across the street, thinking they wouldn't see him among the movie crowds. It was weird, wasn't it? Daniel was stalking Candace. But no, Candace said, he was just waiting there so he could walk her home. Why didn't she just call him, then, when she was finished dinner? Why did Daniel have to be a spy, a silent, unwelcome witness to the most intimate moments of Candace and Marguerite's friendship? Daniel had come into their lives to whisk Candace away. Soon enough, Marguerite thought, she would be gone.

Matters weren't helped by the fact that, in the spring, Porter announced he was taking a trip to Japan. Four years he had promised Marguerite a spring trip, and four years he had backed out. Now he was off to Japan. For work, he said. Research about how the Orient influenced the art of Claude Monet.

Marguerite asked him if he was going alone.

"Alone?" he said, and right then she knew the answer was no. There was a pause. "Actually, no. I'm going with colleagues."

"Colleagues?"

"One colleague. From the department. An expert on Japanese art."

"A woman?"

"Yes, actually," Porter said. "Professor Strickland. A real battle-ax."

A real battle-ax? Marguerite thought. Like Corsage Woman? Like Overbite Woman? She felt helpless with rage; she trembled with jealousy. This was the last straw; he was daring her to confront him. Would she be brave enough? Angry enough? No. She couldn't. She was seething but paralyzed. She confronted Candace instead, over a pot of Darjeeling tea and a plate of macaroons.

"Your brother is off to Kyoto with a woman from his department. Teahouses, he said, pagodas, bridges, gardens. It's like a mystery, he claims, trying to locate Japanese artists who would have been contemporaries of Claude Monet. It all sounds very scholarly, but I'm being an idiot, right? Traveling with one woman alone. He's telling me something without coming right out and telling me."

Candace quietly munched and sipped. She agreed to do some detective work, find out what she could about Professor Strickland. "I'm the first one to condemn my brother," Candace said. "But this could be for real. She could be eighty years old for all we know. I have a hard time believing he would go on vacation with anyone but you. All the way to Japan?"

"It's not like him," Marguerite said.

"Not like him at all," Candace said. "His vacation is Nantucket. It's you. The rest of the year is work, work, work. This trip is work."

"Right," Marguerite said.

The second part of the conversation took place in the middle of town. Candace called Marguerite from the Chamber and said, "I found out who she is. I'm coming to you."

And Marguerite said, "No, I'm coming to you."

They met on the corner of Centre and India Streets, in front of a guesthouse that was closed for the winter. There was a crust of dirty snow on the curb; the wind was merciless.

"Thirty-five years old," Candace said. "Head coach of the tennis team. Blond. Unmarried."

"Japanese art?" Marguerite said.

"She's not a professor at all, Daisy," Candace said. "She's the tennis coach."

"So he lied," Marguerite said.

"He lied."

"He lied." To Marguerite's knowledge, Porter had never lied to her before. Withheld the truth, perhaps, but never lied.

"I don't know why you stay with him, Daisy," Candace said. "How many years has it been now? Six? Seven? Tell him you're done with him—that'll wake him up. Tell him to go straight to hell."

Marguerite played this out in her mind. *I'm sorry, Porter. It's over.* This was what she should do. Otherwise, she was allowing herself to be stepped on, abused; she was asking for it. Tell him to go straight to hell. *Go to hell, Porter.* She pictured his spidery legs, his tapered fingers; she pictured him asleep in the hammock with an art journal spread open on his chest; she pictured him asleep on the bench, in the Musée du Jeu de Paume. She pictured him practicing his accordion.

"I can't," Marguerite said. "I don't have anybody else."

"You have me," Candace said.

"Yes . . ." Marguerite said tentatively. What she was thinking was,

You belong to Daniel. This was now an ironclad fact. Candace and Daniel were a couple. Whenever Marguerite wanted to get together with Candace, Candace said she had to check. What she meant was that she had to check with Daniel. They had date nights, movies, a TV show they both adored that they couldn't miss, they had their own friends, other couples, dinner parties—a whole social life that did not include Marguerite. *You have me,* Candace said. It was a sweet lie, but a lie just the same. Candace and Porter were both lying to Marguerite, but she didn't dare call them on it. It was beyond her.

"Yes," she said. "I have you."

Porter returned from Japan in very high spirits. He brought Marguerite a pink silk kimono embroidered with butterflies and lotus flowers. It was the most gorgeous thing she had ever set eyes on, and yet when he gave it to her upon his arrival on Nantucket late in May she threw the box across the room; it was the closest she'd come to a tantrum, to addressing the real issue between them. She thought, *It's going to take more than this to win me back.* Porter retrieved the box, smoothed the folds of silk inside. His movements were calm, his face unsurprised, as though he'd been expecting this reaction. He kissed her and wrapped her in his arms. "Next year, Paris," he said. "Next year for sure."

Marguerite blew her nose and blotted her eyes in an attempt to pull herself together. She returned to the kitchen and eyed the pile of chopped herbs warily, like an enemy. She mixed up the dough, rolled it out, and pressed it into her nine-inch fluted tart pan. Marguerite covered the tart with foil, weighed it down with ceramic pie beads, and slid it into the oven. She hated to turn the oven on in the heat of the afternoon, but she had no choice. The monkey in her grandfather clock banged his cymbals together every fifteen minutes, time was slipping away, and the tenderloin had to roast, the bread had to bake and later, once Renata was here, the asparagus.

Marguerite polished her grand old oak table with five leaves that she'd bought at an estate sale in Cobleskill, New York. She left it fully extended for no good reason other than she liked the way it looked, although, as with the five bedrooms upstairs, she found it unsettling to rattle around in a house meant for ten. She brought out china service for herself and Renata, but she couldn't bring herself to set down the tarnished silver.

The tart shell came out; Marguerite cranked the heat on her old, reliable Wolfe stove (the salesman had said it would last forever, and he was correct) and slid in the tenderloin. She fixed herself a cup of tea and carried the mahogany chest that held her silver outside to her small patio.

It was a hot afternoon, but Marguerite's glass-topped table and wrought-iron chairs sat partially in the shade. She loved her garden, small though it was. Along with reading, the garden gave her constant pleasure—her rosebushes, the hydrangeas, her daylilies, each blooming for only one day, then withering. Marguerite snapped off the dead blossoms every morning, though she hadn't that morning, so she did it then, and when she finished, her hands were stained pink, red, orange. She cut a few dahlias to round out the bouquet of zinnias that she'd bought at the Herb Farm.

Finally, she sat down with her tea and her silver. She and Renata each would need a butter knife, a steak knife, a dinner fork, a salad fork, and a spoon for the *pots de crème*. Ten pieces of silver in all and yet, when Marguerite sat down, she remembered about a ladle for the béarnaise, tongs for the asparagus, a serving fork for the meat. She decided to polish it all:

120 pieces. It was soothing work—smearing the utensils with the bruise-colored polish, then wiping them clean with a flour-sack towel. The pieces shone like new dimes. Marguerite looked at her distorted reflection in the bowl of the big serving spoon; she dug the polish out of the crevices of the intricate designs on the handles. The white flour-sack towel became smudged with black, evidence that her efforts were paying off. How satisfying, how symbolic, wiping away the tarnish, the grime from the past. Marguerite cleaned her hands and sipped her tea.

It would be nice to have Ethan and his wife and his boys for dinner, she thought. It would be nice to have Dusty. Or Daniel, Renata, and the fiancé, even the fiancé's parents. It would be nice, in short, to call an end to her house arrest, to her pointlessly austere lifestyle; it would be nice to interact with real people, in person, rather than via a computer screen for an hour each day, rather than reading about made-up lives in stories and novels, rather than visiting with the people she had loved—the people who had both lifted her up and disappointed her—in her mind, her memory. She would never reach out, she knew, but on such a lovely summer afternoon in her garden with a cup of tea and half her silver yet to polish, there was no harm in imagining how nice it would be.

2:41 P.M.

As Renata scavenged through the sand for the components of her bathing suit, she decided that her real mistake wasn't what had happened five minutes ago in the sand, nor was it the events a week ago at Lespinasse. Her real mistake occurred last October when Renata allowed herself to fall in love with Cade Driscoll in the first damn place. Looking back, Renata realized how vulnerable she'd been—six weeks into her freshman year, drinking warmish beer at the Delta Phi house—when she'd met Cade. He had been wearing a beautiful blue button-down shirt with faint blue stripes and his monogram on the pocket; she had instantly turned away, mistaking him for an adult who might confiscate her beer. Renata was feeling unsure of herself; she and Action had been informed that this was a party "honoring" freshman girls, and yet many of the fraternity brothers wore T-shirts that said, *FRESHMAN GIRLS: GET 'EM WHILE THEY'RE SKINNY!* Cade separated himself from these peers by his sumptuous shirt; he approached Renata and Action and asked them what sounded like substantial questions: Which dorm? Which classes? Which professors? He sipped his beer slowly, thoughtfully, as he listened to their answers. He seemed like an ambassador, a gentleman—he took their plastic cups and refilled them, and when he handed them back he apologized for the quality of the beer.

Is this your party? Renata had asked.

He smiled. He wasn't attractive so much as successful looking. Clean, pleasant, well-heeled, athletic. *Only in the most tangential way,* he said. And then he checked his watch. Renata figured they were boring him to tears while Action (she later confessed) was thinking, *What is a college student doing with a Brietling watch?*

Let's get you out of here, Cade said to them both.

Where are we going to go? Renata asked. They had only arrived at the party ten minutes earlier and Renata was hesitant to leave, despite the pervasive aura that this was a dinner party and girls like Action and Renata were the first course. This, after all, was what she'd dreamed college would be like: a dark room with strobe lighting, Eminem at nearly unbearable decibels, the keg, the swarming boys.

Downtown, Cade said. *There's a band called Green Eggs playing at the Savannah.*

Renata had to beg Action to come along; she was wary of going anywhere with "Watch Boy." In the cab on the way downtown Cade told them he'd grown up in the city.

So did Action, Renata said.

Where? Cade said, leaning over Renata to look at Action.

Downtown, she said. *Bleecker Street.*

High school?

Stuyvesant.

Impressive.

Action snorted. *I gather you went somewhere uptown?* she said. *Let me guess. Collegiate?*

I went to boarding school, actually, he said. *Choate.*

Ah, Action said, as though she should have expected as much.

Renata, sensing the building tension, said, *I like your shirt.*

Thanks, Cade said. *I had a bunch of shirts made when I was in London last semester.*

Renata felt Action's hand press against the side of her thigh. *Right,* Renata thought. Boarding school, London, custom-made shirts. Renata knew Action was sneering, thinking, *privileged, pompous, why are we wasting our time?* But Renata couldn't help being impressed. And he seemed like a nice guy.

Cade paid for the cab ride (twenty-one dollars), he paid for Action and Renata to get into the club (twenty dollars), and he bought them cosmopolitans, which they sloshed all over the dance floor. The band was fantastic; Action and Renata started dancing right away. They screamed along to the music, tossing their hair, feeling their own sexual power. Action got something going with the lead singer; he was leaning down into the crowd toward her, practically devouring his microphone. Renata loved the feeling of slipping out of control; they were both sweating and laughing. Renata spilled a bit of cosmopolitan down her front; she had to go to the bathroom. She turned and saw Cade standing out among the crowd, and she felt a wave of gratitude. Action could say what she wanted, but to Renata, Cade was like a genie who had appeared from a bottle and granted them the three wishes of a good buzz, a great band, enormous fun. He smiled at her and crooked a finger. *Come here.* She went to him and he kissed her. Her stomach dropped away; it felt like a rushing chute down a roller coaster. Cade wanted to leave the bar, he said something about a poker game on the Bowery, he was meeting someone there, and he wanted Renata to come along. Despite the incredible kiss, Renata had no desire to leave the bar, and she knew she would never be able to peel Action away. She would stay with Action.

I'm going to stay, Renata said to Cade.

He had looked at her in a searching way; he was clearly expecting another answer.

Fine, he said. *Can I bring you another drink before I go?*

Sure, Renata said. She looked longingly at the dance floor. Action was still in the front row, going full tilt. Renata wanted to get back out there. *Actually, never mind.*

Cade shrugged, and ever the gentleman, he smiled. *Okay, I'll see you around, I guess.* He turned sideways and disappeared into the crowd.

Renata stood for a moment, looking after him. She felt guilty, though she didn't know why. Renata fought her way back to the dance floor, but her heart wasn't in it. It was as if Cade had taken her good mood with him—or maybe, she thought, she was only having fun because he was around.

Someone grabbed Renata's waist from behind. She turned. It was an older man, with gray hair in a buzz cut and high, prominent cheekbones. His tie hung loosely at his neck. When Renata turned, he smirked at her.

Dance?

No, she said, pulling away.

I'll buy you a drink, he said.

No, Renata said. *Thanks.* Somehow she managed to weave her way up front and grab ahold of Action.

I'm leaving with him, she said.

Who?

Cade.

Watch Boy? Action said. *Shirt Boy?*

Renata nodded.

Action crossed her eyes. *Pathetic,* she said.

Well . . . In the course of only a month, Action and Renata had become such good friends that Renata mistakenly assumed they were exactly alike. But no, they weren't. Action wanted a man like the lead singer—who had black hair to his shoulders, who wore a Mexican poncho and a hammered silver cuff bracelet. Renata wanted Cade with his tailored shirts. Action thought Cade was typical, stereotypical. Renata would never be able to explain her attraction and especially not here. She squeezed Action's arm. *You'll be okay getting home?*

I live here, remember?

Renata wended her way back through the frenzy, thinking it could all be for naught; Cade was probably already gone. She panicked at the thought and pushed, prodded, poked, until she was free and running for the door. *Please,* she thought. He was right there when she stepped outside—standing on the curb, eating a piece of pizza folded in half.

He didn't seem at all surprised to see her; it was as if he knew she'd follow him anywhere.

Want a bite? he said.

Sex with Miles was over before it began, but that was okay; that was how Renata liked it. She liked it that Miles got so excited he couldn't hold back. He was bigger than Cade, and now, as Renata moved about, she felt a dull ache between her legs. She wanted to find her suit and go for a swim, big waves or no. When Sallie was finished surfing, which Renata hoped was soon, she would make Miles take her back to Hulbert Avenue, where she would shower and nap before scurrying off to Marguerite's house. She could, with luck, avoid Cade until the morning, and by then, she hoped, things would make more sense than they made now.

"Here you go." Miles handed Renata her bathing suit.

"Thanks."

"Do you regret it?" he said.

"No," she said. "Do you?"

"No," he said. "God, no."

She looked at him and saw something in his eyes. Love, or what he mistakenly assumed was love. She smiled at her feet and felt triumphant. She could have him again right now, or tonight in the guest room.

"Hey!"

The voice was faint but insistent, floating up the bluff.

"Hey!"

Renata adjusted her bathing suit. Had someone seen them? She looked past Miles to the stairs. A head popped up, the overweight man from the webbed lawn chair. He was huffing and puffing as he climbed the stairs, waving his binoculars. He looked uncomfortable and agitated, like he was suffering from indigestion.

"Vo-tra-mee," he said.

"What?" Miles said.

"Vo-tra-mee," the man said, pointing at the water.

"He's German or something," Miles said. "French."

Renata looked down at the beach. A group was gathering by the waterline—the girls from the blanket, the people from the volleyball game. They were yelling and pointing offshore. Miles scrambled over the dunes and Renata followed, the towel draped over her burning shoulders. Miles raced down the stairs and along the beach back to their stuff. Renata was thinking, vaguely, *Shark, somebody thought they saw a shark,* though what were the chances? Still, she hurried along to see what was happening; she wondered what time it was and if anyone at Vitamin Sea had realized she was gone, if Suzanne was pissed about lunch, if Cade would be able to tell when they made love that she'd been with someone else. She was so wrapped up in her own thoughts that she didn't notice the two men in wet suits carrying a body out of the water. Or, rather, she noticed it but in a way that made it separate from herself, as though she were watching it happen on TV. The men laid the body in the sand and Miles, who had run far ahead, knelt by the body and started mouth-to-mouth. As Renata grew closer she felt her vision narrow; dread closed in. *Noooo!* she thought. *Tell me no.* She recognized the board shorts, the tattoo, the silver rings on the toes.

Renata stumbled to Miles's side, shoving people out of the way. A girl was screaming into a cell phone. "She's dead! She's dead!"

The girl's boyfriend was trying to rip the phone out of her hand. "She is not dead," he said. "Will you please shut up?"

The hairy beast, Montrose, said, "I called nine-one-one. The EMTs will be here in ten minutes, they said. Ten minutes."

Miles started CPR, pumping Sallie's chest, then blowing into her mouth. He was mumbling to himself, counting. Sallie's skin was the color of putty, grayish and goose pimpled. Her hair was plastered to her head; the mirror in her navel was dull.

Queen Bee, Renata thought, *Sallie. A person I've known for an hour.*

A complete stranger who accompanied me to my mother's cross, who kissed me on the wound she inflicted with her surfboard. The surfboard—Renata looked down the beach and saw it floating just offshore. She dashed into the water to get it, a gesture that other people might have found very beside the point, but Renata knew Sallie only well enough to know that she would want her surfboard back. This, then, became Renata's rescue mission. She waded out, savoring the cool water on her legs. The waves were as unforgiving as they looked. Twice Renata nearly toppled over as she waded out, farther and farther, in pursuit of the surfboard. The ocean seemed to be teasing her—the surfboard would be inches from her grasp and then the waves would snatch it back. The undertow was fierce; Renata fought to keep her legs planted. If she tried to swim, she would be pulled out to sea. But she wanted the surfboard. She had known Sallie for only an hour or two, maybe, by now. Renata liked her. *Don't go getting married while I'm gone.* Renata's stomach churned on her beer and her guilt. *Will you keep an eye on me? Since when do you need a spotter? Since today. I'll keep an eye out.*

Renata turned back to shore. The other people on the beach were looking at Renata with strange, fearful expressions, but nobody spoke to her. The girls were all crying and the men tried to look both strong and sympathetic; everyone on the beach was touching someone. Renata heard Miles say, "I can't get a pulse. Where are the damned EMTs?"

Renata let a huge wave break over her head. She was knocked down and her face was filled with cold, salty water—in her mouth and her ears, up her nose, stinging her. Miles sounded panicked—and worse, he sounded guilty. If he was guilty, she was guiltier still. *She asked me. And I was up in the dunes.* Renata got to her feet and lunged for the surfboard. She got her fingers on it and a swell brought the ass end into her arms. She clung on tight, thinking she would turn it around, point it toward shore, but it was impossibly heavy; it seemed to want to go the other way—out, to open ocean. Renata was about to let it go when she noticed blood at the top of the board. That was all it took: Renata vomited beer in one gross, powerful stream. It sullied the water. Renata spit. Dear God, no.

Renata heard shouting. She turned to see a force of men and women in black uniforms come charging down the steps to the beach. She pulled the surfboard against her hips as another wave surged, and she managed somehow, to pull herself on top of it. Then she paddled the way she'd seen Sallie do. She got the surfboard pointed toward the beach and propelled herself forward. She rode the next wave all the way in, and then she stood on wobbly legs and dragged the surfboard over to where the EMTs were gathered around Sallie, shouting numbers. They had covered her with a blanket; Renata heard a tall man with a crew cut say, "She's in shock. But she's breathing now. Slap a mask on her and let's get her in. Who is she here with?"

Renata hurried over, lugging the bloody surfboard. Miles was sitting on his towel, yards away from the action, with his head in his hands.

"Me!" Renata said. "She's here with me!"

The paramedic didn't hear her. "Let's take her in." He spoke into his walkie-talkie and surveyed the beach. Renata grabbed his arm.

"She's here with me," Renata said. "Me and Miles, that guy over there."

"We're taking her to the hospital," the paramedic said. "She received quite a blow to the head. And nearly drowned. Will you gather her personal effects, please, and bring them to the hospital? We'll need you to give us some information."

"Okay," Renata said. Sallie's personal effects consisted of the surfboard and the sunglasses. Renata snatched up her bag and nudged Miles with her foot. "Come on," she said. She ran toward the sound of the sirens.

3:32 P.M.

Check, check, check.

Marguerite's list was dwindling. The tenderloin had been roasted and was resting on the stove top. The tart had been filled with goat cheese and topped with roasted red peppers. The smoked mussels, the aioli, the chocolate *pots de crème,* all in the fridge, waiting. Marguerite had slipped two champagne flutes and her copper bowl into the freezer. She softened the butter she had gotten at the Herb Farm. The asparagus still needed attention, and the baguettes and the béarnaise. Marguerite debated setting up coffee and decided against it, then changed her mind; if they didn't drink it tonight, she'd have it in the morning. The morning: It would come, despite the fact that the day already seemed as stretched out as a piece of taffy, filled with as much activity as Marguerite engaged in in a whole year. She ferreted a wine cooler out from underneath the kitchen sink. The cooler was filled with cobwebs and mouse droppings. Marguerite washed it, then washed it again. The wine cooler was silver, sturdy, and unadorned, a leftover from the restaurant. There had been twenty such buckets and twenty iron stands, enough to post at every table, plus two spares. It was curious, Marguerite thought, the way some things survived and some did not.

The clock struck the half hour. Marguerite added items to her list, tasks that would come naturally to another person but that she, in her excitement, might forget. Shower. Hair, face, outfit. What to wear? The kimono stuck sorely in her mind like a porcupine quill. The damned kimono. Still, if she had a spare minute, she might try to find it. She tidied the kitchen, wiped down the countertops, rinsed the sink, cleaned the smoker, and returned it to its Styrofoam braces, closed it up in the box. This was all busywork, but Marguerite found it soothing. It allowed her to think of other things.

Since the day of Dan and Candace's wedding, there had been talk of going to Africa. The wedding was held at the Catholic church, St. Mary's, on Federal Street. Candace wore a strapless white satin gown with a tulle skirt and ballet slippers that laced up her calves. She was more Grace Kelly than Grace Kelly. She was captivating. Marguerite had been coaxed into preceding Candace down the aisle in a periwinkle dress with matching bolero jacket, despite her ardent pleas to sit with everyone else.

"I'm more matron than maid," Marguerite had said. "But I'm not married, so I can't be called matron. And no one thirty-nine years of age should be called maid. I don't belong in this wedding, Candace."

"I'm not willing to have anyone else."

"I need to be at the restaurant anyway, supervising before the reception."

"I will not have anyone else."

Marguerite had stood at the altar, opposite Dan's roommate from college, holding a cluster of calla lilies while Dan and Candace pledged their eternal love, while they promised to pass this love on to any children they might have, while they swore in front of a hundred-plus people to strive through good and bad, through windfall and famine. Porter had given Candace away, and he sat in the front row next to his brother Andre, in from California. On Andre's other side was Chase, Candace's full brother, whom Marguerite had just met that morning. Porter reveled in the role of patriarch, leaning against the back of the pew with his arm stretched out behind his brother and half brother, his eyes dewy, a proud and resigned smile on his face. Marguerite could picture him like it was yesterday. He'd winked at her and she blushed. In the end, she had felt proud to be standing up there next to Candace, despite the dress that most closely resembled a tablecloth from a Holiday Inn banquet hall; she had felt proud that Candace would not consider asking anyone else to wear the dress, to hold the flowers and Dan's ring, to stand by her side as she wed. Marguerite did not, however, stay for the receiving line. Instead, she negotiated the cobblestones in her inane dyed-to-match heels back to Les Parapluies, where she supervised the prep of the crab and mango canapés and the prosciutto-wrapped Gorgonzola-stuffed figs that would be offered to the wedding guests along with flutes of La grande Dame.

Marguerite had few memories of the reception. (Had she even sat to eat? Had she changed into her regular clothes? She had no recollection.) The after-reception, however, Marguerite recalled vividly. Everyone had gone home except for Marguerite and Porter, Andre, Chase, the college roommate (whose name was Gregory and who expressed, in no uncertain terms, his wanton desire for Francesca, the headwaiter), and, to Marguerite's surprise, Dan and Candace. They were all gathered around the west banquette with cigarettes and a 1955 bottle of Taylor Fladgate. Marguerite had set a plate of chocolate caramel truffles on the table to a smattering of applause, and then finally she relaxed, amazed that Dan and Candace hadn't beelined to the Roberts House, where they had a suite. They both seemed content to sit and drink and eat and talk, holding hands under the table.

They're married, Marguerite thought. There was nothing left to do but accept it. Daniel Knox would be a permanent part of their lives. He continued to irritate Marguerite—he was forever challenging her within her area of expertise, arguing with her about the quality of American beef or a certain vintage of Chablis, as though he believed he could do a better job of running the restaurant than she did. He had tried his best to sabotage the friendship between Marguerite and Candace. He disliked it when they spent time alone; he teased Marguerite about how often she and Candace touched each other, their kisses, their hugs; he pointed out how Marguerite never failed to choose the seat closest to Candace; he badgered Candace about what the two of them talked about when they were alone—were they talking about him? A hundred times Marguerite could have murdered the man—sardonically she thought all it would have taken was a little rat poison in his polenta—but Candace worked to keep the peace. She gave one hand to Daniel and one to Marguerite. "I love you both," she said. "I want you to love each other." While up at the altar, Marguerite vowed to herself to try her best to get along with Daniel. It was either that or tear Candace in half.

Across the table, Dan was proselytizing to Candace's brothers about how, if he hadn't come along to save the Beach Club, that waterfront would be a chain of garish trophy homes by now.

Candace grabbed Marguerite's hand. "Come with me to the loo," she said. "I need help with my dress."

Thus it was in the cramped, slanted-ceilinged women's bathroom at Les Parapluies, with Marguerite holding seventeen layers of tulle and averting her eyes as Candace peed, that Africa was first mentioned.

"I want to go to Africa."

Marguerite thought she was talking about her honeymoon. As it was, Candace and Dan had decided to wait until winter to take a trip and Marguerite believed discussion was hovering around Hawaii, Tahiti, Bora-Bora. She'd had too much to drink to make the leap across the globe.

"I'm sorry?"

"Dan asked me what I wanted to do," Candace said. "With my life. If I could go anywhere or do anything. And I want to go to Africa."

Marguerite narrowed her eyes. Above the sink, a peach-colored index card was taped to the wall: *Employees must wash hands before returning to work.*

"You mean, like, on safari?" Marguerite said.

"No, no, no. Not on safari."

Marguerite didn't get it. She was uncomfortable thinking of Candace starting a new, married life in Africa.

"It's awfully far away," Marguerite said. "I'd miss you."

"You're coming with me, silly," Candace said.

In the weeks and months that followed, Candace's vision of them all in Africa crystallized. She wasn't thinking of Isak Dinesen in Kenya, or trekking the Ugandan jungles in search of gorillas, or righting the evils of apartheid in South Africa—she was thinking of deserts, siroccos, sandstorms, of souks and mint tea and the casbah. She was thinking of Bedouins on camels, date palms, nomads in tents, thieves in the medinas. She had been reading *The Sheltering Sky* and begged Marguerite to make *tagines* and couscous.

Night after night after night, so many summer nights strung together like Japanese lanterns through the trees, Candace and Dan and Marguerite and Porter sat at the west banquette and talked and talked and talked until they were too drunk or too tired to form coherent sentences. They talked about Carter and Reagan, Iran, Woody Allen and Pink Floyd, Roy Lichtenstein, Andy Warhol, and the new Musée d'Orsay in Paris. Porter talked about a colleague accused of making a pass at a female student, who turned around and *pressed charges.* Marguerite talked about the bluefin tuna Dusty had caught and how he'd sliced it paper thin and eaten it raw right there on the dock of the Straight Wharf. And always, at the end of the night, like a punch line, like a broken record, Candace talked about Africa. She wanted the four of them to open a French restaurant somewhere in her make-believe North Africa.

"I can see it now," Porter had said, the first time she mentioned it. "A culinary Peace Corps."

"A restaurant in the middle of the desert," Candace said. "I've always dreamed of running barefoot through the Sahara. What would the restaurant be like, Daisy, if it were up to you?"

"If it were up to Reagan, it would be a McDonald's," Dan said. "Talk about cultural imperialism."

"I asked Daisy," Candace said. "So hush. She's the only one of us who would know what she was doing."

Marguerite gazed around Les Parapluies. This was how she loved it best—empty except for the four of them, lit only by candles. The staff had cleaned up and gone home for the evening, but there was still the lingering smell of garlic and rosemary and freshly baked bread. There was still plenty of wine.

"Just like this," Marguerite said. "I would want it to be just like this."

"Except it wouldn't be like this at all, would it?" Candace said. "Because it wouldn't be Nantucket. It wouldn't be thirty miles out to sea; there wouldn't be fog. We'd be surrounded by sand instead of water. It wouldn't be the same at all."

"Spoken like a true Chamber of Commerce employee," Porter said, raising his glass.

"I'm serious," Candace said. She turned to Marguerite with her cheeks flushed and her hair falling into her face. One of her pearl earrings was about to pop out. Marguerite reached for Candace's ear—all she had meant was to gently hold the earlobe and secure the earring in place before it fell and got lost in Candace's blouse or bounced across the wormy chestnut floors and got caught in a crack somewhere—but Candace swatted Marguerite's hand away. Smacked it in anger. Marguerite recoiled, and the energy at the table changed in an instant.

Candace's mouth was set in an ugly line; her eyes were glassy and wild. Marguerite was confused, then frightened. Had Candace had too much to drink?

"No one takes me seriously," Candace said. "Nobody listens when I talk. You treat me like a child. Like a china doll. Like an imbecile!"

Dan and Marguerite reached out for Candace simultaneously, but Candace locked her arms across her chest. Porter chuckled.

"It's not funny!" Candace said. She glared at them all. "You are all so smart and accomplished and that's fine, that's great. I support all of you in your work. But now it's my turn. I want to go to Africa. I mean it about this restaurant. It's a dream I have. You may think it's stupid, but I don't." She turned to Marguerite. "Now reimagine. What will the restaurant look like?"

Marguerite was stunned into silence. She couldn't bring herself to imagine a restaurant different from the one she had, especially one on a continent she had never visited.

"I can't reimagine," Marguerite said. "I want to stay here, where I am. I want everything to stay just as it is."

Yes, it was true: If she could have kept the four of them seated at the west banquette for all eternity—with meals appearing like Sisyphus's boulder—she would have. But then autumn came and Porter returned to Manhattan—to Corsage Woman, Overbite Woman, the blond, unmarried tennis coach. One unfortunate night that fall, Marguerite found herself standing in the restaurant's dark pantry with her lawyer, Damian Vix. Ostensibly, he had been in search of dried porcini for a risotto he wanted to make at home, but they had both had too much to drink and the foray into the dark kitchen and darker pantry was followed by kissing and some lustful groping. *Kid stuff,* Marguerite thought afterward. It gave her none of the satisfaction she'd been hoping for.

In the new year, Nantucket suffered one of the worst winters on record—snowstorms, ice storms, thirty-two hours without power, a record three hundred homes with burst pipes according to the claims man at Congdon & Coleman Insurance. Marguerite tested out new recipes in her kitchen on Quince Street, Candace was still working at the Chamber of Commerce, as assistant director now, and Dan monitored the weather—the wind gusts, the inches of snow—and he checked on things two or three times a day at the shuttered-up Beach Club. The three of them gathered occasionally, but mostly it was Candace and Marguerite meeting for lunch at the Brotherhood, or hunkering down in front of the fire at Marguerite's house on Quince Street with cheese fondue or pot-au-feu. It was during one of these fireside dinners that Candace proposed the trip: seven nights and eight days in Morocco. They would scout a location for their restaurant.

"Just the two of us," Candace said. "Me and you."

"I couldn't possibly," Marguerite said.

"I already have the tickets," Candace said. "We're going."

"Go with Dan."

"You'd send me to scout a location for a restaurant with *Dan*? You trust him to find the right place?"

Well, no, Marguerite didn't trust him. But Marguerite thought she had made her feelings more than clear: The restaurant idea was delusional.

"Anyway, I don't want to go with Dan," Candace said. "I want to go with you. Girl trip. Best friends and all that. We've never taken a trip together."

"I can't go," Marguerite said.

"Why not?"

"Porter promised me Paris," Marguerite said. "After his trip to Japan last year. He swore on a stack of Bibles."

"A stack of Bibles?" Candace said.

Well, a stack of Marguerite's bibles: *Larousse Gastronomique,* her first-edition M. F. K. Fisher, her Julia Child. At the end of August, before he returned to the city, Porter had laid his right hand on the cookbooks and said in a solemn voice, "In the spring, Paris."

"It's not going to happen," Candace said. "He'll back out. He'll find some reason."

Marguerite flinched. She stared at the dying embers of the fire and nearly asked Candace to leave. How dare she say such a thing! But perhaps it was tit-for-tat. She thought Marguerite was delusional.

"I'm sorry," Candace said, though her voice couldn't have been less apologetic. "I just can't stand to see you get hurt again. He's my brother. I know him. He promised you Paris to get himself out of a tight spot. But he won't follow through. You should just come to Morocco with me."

"I know him, too," Marguerite said. "He promised me Paris. There's no reason to doubt him."

Candace stared. "No reason to doubt him?"

Marguerite stood up and poked at the fire; it had gone cold.

"Porter is taking me to Paris."

"Okay," Candace said kindly. "Okay." Her tone of voice infuriated Marguerite; it was patronizing. Marguerite had never fought with her friend, though she was ready to now. The only thing that kept her from doing battle was the fear that Candace may be right.

And so, the following week, when Porter phoned, Marguerite pressed him on it.

"Your sister wants me to go with her to Morocco."

"For her restaurant idea?"

"Mmmhmm."

"She's crazy," Porter said. "God love her. Are you going?"

"No," Marguerite said. "I told her we were going to Paris."

Porter laughed.

Marguerite steeled her resolve. She could picture Porter's face when he laughed—his eyes crunching, his head thrown back—but she couldn't tell what this laugh meant.

"Have you checked your schedule?" she asked. "Decided on a week? If we want the Plaza Athenee, we have to book soon."

There was a pause. "Daisy . . ."

She only half-heard the rest of what he said. Something about a paper he was presenting, a week as a guest curator at the Met, a conference they were hosting at Columbia. Marguerite took the phone from her ear and poised it over the cradle, ready to slam it down. She thought of begging, of laying her heart out on the chopping block. It didn't have to be Paris. It could be the Radisson on Route 128 for all she cared. She wanted something from him, something that proved she was more than just his summertime. But in the end, all she could bring herself to do was cut him off in midsentence.

"Never mind; never mind," she said. "Candace will be thrilled. The casbah it is."

As Marguerite formed the bread dough into loaves, laid them down in her oiled baguette pan, as she snipped the tops of the loaves with kitchen shears and rinsed the loaves with water so they would have a sheen to them when they came out of the oven, she could say that the eight days in Morocco with Candace had been the best eight days of her life. It was when everything changed.

They had started out in a town on the coast, seven hours by car from Casablanca. The town was called Essaouira. It had a long, wide, magnificent crescent of silver sand beach where men in flowing robes offered camel rides for ten dirhams. Candace, who was in for every "authentic" experience she could find, insisted they try it. Marguerite protested, and yet she ended up eight feet off the ground crushed with Candace against the hump of a dromedary named Charlie. Riding a camel, Marguerite soon realized, was like sitting on a rocking chair without any back. Marguerite held on to Candace for dear life as they ricocheted forward and careened back with each of Charlie's steps down the coastline. Candace was shaking with laughter; Marguerite felt her gasping for air. The camel smelled bad, and so, for that matter, did the soft mud-sand at the waterline. Marguerite buried her nose in Candace's hair.

When they dismounted, Candace made the man in the flowing robe take their picture. Marguerite smiled perfunctorily, then said, "I need a drink."

They sat outside at a little café and drank a bottle of very cold Sancerre. They touched glasses.

"To Morocco," Candace said. "To the two of us in Morocco."

Marguerite tried to smile. She tried not to wish she were in Paris.

"Do you wish you were in Paris?" Candace said.

Marguerite looked at her friend. Candace's blue eyes were round with worry.

"You were right," Marguerite said. It was a relief to admit it. "About Porter, about Paris. You couldn't have been more right."

"I didn't want to be right," Candace said. "You know that, don't you?"

"Yes."

"I feel like I twisted your arm to come here," Candace said. "I feel like you'd rather be at home."

"Home?" Marguerite said. Home on Nantucket, where the beaches were frozen tundra, home where she could wallow in the misery of being disappointed again? "Don't be silly."

The heart of Essaouira lay in the souks, a rabbit warren of streets and alleys and passageways within the city's thick, whitewashed walls. Over the course of four days, Candace and Marguerite wandered every which way, getting lost, getting found. Here was the man selling jewelry boxes, lamps, coat racks, coffee tables, and backgammon boards from precious *thuya* wood, which was native to Essaouira. Here was a shop selling the very same items made from punched tin; here was a place selling Berber carpets, here another place selling carpets. Everyone sold carpets! Marguerite sniffed out the food markets. She discovered a whole square devoted to seafood—squid and sea bass, shrimp, prawns, rock lobsters, octopus, sea cucumbers, and a pallet of unidentifiable slugs and snails, creatures with fluorescent fins and prehistoric shells, things Marguerite was sure Dusty Tyler had never seen in all his life. In Morocco, the women did the shopping, all of them in ivory or black burkhas. Most of them kept their faces covered as well; Candace called these women the "only eyes." They peered at Marguerite (who wore an Hermés scarf over her hair, a gift from one of her customers) and she shivered. Marguerite's favorite place of all was the spice market—dozens of tables covered with pyramids of saffron and turmeric, curry powder and cumin, fenugreek, mustard seed, cardamom, paprika, mace, nutmeg.

Who wouldn't open a restaurant if they had access to these spices? Not to mention the olives. And the nuts—the warm, salted almonds sold for twenty-five centimes in a paper cone—and the dates, thirty varieties as chewy and rich as candy.

In the mornings Candace ran, and sometimes she was gone for two hours. The first morning Marguerite grew concerned as she drank six cups of café au lait and polished off three croissants and one sticky date bun while reading the guidebook. She found the hotel manager—a short, trim, and immaculately groomed Arab man—and explained to him, in her all-but-useless kitchen French, that her friend, *une Americaine blonde,* had gone missing. Marguerite worried that Candace had made a wrong turn and gotten lost—that wouldn't be hard to do—or someone had abducted her. She was, obviously, not a Muslim, and unlike Marguerite, she refused to cover her head with anything except for Dan's old Red Sox cap. Someone had stolen her for political reasons or for sexual ones; she was, at that very moment, being forced into a harem.

Just as the hotel manager was beginning to glean Marguerite's meaning, realizing she was talking about *Candace,* whom he himself had given more than one admiring glance, in Candace came, breathless, sweating, and brimming over with all that she'd seen. Fishing boats with strings of multicolored flags, the fortress with cannons up on the hill, a little boy with six dragonflies pierced on the end of a spear.

Marguerite got used to Candace's long absences in the mornings. When Candace returned, they ventured out into the medina to look for a restaurant. The restaurant business was alive and well in Essaouira—there were French restaurants, there were Moroccan restaurants, there was tapas and pizza and gelati, and there was a row of open-air stands along the beach selling fish that Marguerite and Candace picked out before it was grilled in front of their eyes.

They meandered and shopped. Marguerite bought an enamel pot for *tagine* with a conical top and a handcrafted silver platter for fish. Marguerite and Candace always stopped for lunch at one o'clock, gravitating toward the Moroccan places, which were dim, with low ceilings. They sat on the floor on richly colored pillows and, yes, stacks of carpets and ate lamb *kefta,* couscous, and *bisteeya.*

After lunch, they returned to their hotel for silver pots of mint tea, which they drank by the small plunge pool in the courtyard. Men in white pajamas brought the tea, then took it away; they brought the day's papers—the *Herald Tribune* and *Le Monde* as well as the Moroccan paper, which was written in Arabic—they brought fresh towels, warm and cool. There might have been other guests at the hotel, but Marguerite noticed them only peripherally—a glamorous French couple, a British woman and her grown daughter—it felt like Marguerite and Candace were existing in a world created solely for their benefit. Marguerite discovered she was having fun, all of her senses were engaged, she felt alive. She was *glad* she was here with Candace instead of in Paris with Porter, and who could have predicted that? Morocco, Marguerite declared, was heaven on earth! She never wanted to leave.

Several times during their week in Morocco, Marguerite revisited the moment when Candace first walked into the kitchen at Les Parapluies on Porter's arm and kissed Marguerite full on the lips. *What Porter told me in private is that he thinks you're pure magic.* The more time they spent together, alone, in this foreign and exotic country, the more Marguerite began to feel that *Candace* was pure magic. She was not only beautiful; she emitted beauty. Everywhere they traveled in Morocco, the people they met bowed to Candace as though she were a deity. The baseball hat, which might have been offensive on another American, was adorably subversive on Candace.

"These American women," one of their taxi drivers said. "They like everyone to know they are free."

On the fifth day, they traveled to Marrakech. The hotel in Marrakech was even lusher than their jewel in Essaouira. L'Orangerie, it was called, after the museum in Paris. The architecture was all arches and intricate tile work, open courtyards with sumptuous gardens and fountains, little nooks with flowing curtains and silk divans, bowls of cool water holding floating rose petals. Marguerite and Candace shared a two-bedroom, two-floor suite with an outdoor shower and their own dining table on a roof patio that overlooked Marrakech's famous square, Djemaa el-Fna. Marrakech had a cosmopolitan feel to it, a kinetic energy—this was where everything was happening. The Djemaa el-Fna was mobbed with people every night: jugglers, snake charmers, acrobats, pickpockets, musicians, storytellers, water sellers, street vendors hawking orange juice, dates, olives, almonds—and tourists snapping it all up. The call to prayer from the mighty Koutoubia Mosque came over a loudspeaker every few hours and several times Marguerite felt like dropping to her knees to pray. Marrakech had done it; she was converted. She started making notes for a menu, half-French, half-Moroccan; she wanted to attempt a *bisteeya* made with prawns, a *tagine* of ginger chicken with preserved lemon and olives. She looked in every doorway for suitable retail space.

And yet as Marguerite's enthusiasm flared, Candace's flagged. Her stomach was bothering her; she got quiet at dinner their first night in Marrakech, and the second night she went to bed at eight o'clock, leaving Marguerite to wander the chaos of the souks alone. Marguerite slouched and frowned; shopkeepers didn't give her a second look. Candace missed Dan—Marguerite was sure that was it—she was going to try to call him from the front desk of the hotel. Marguerite was crestfallen. *Girl trip,* she thought. *Best friends and all that.* For the first time in years she felt free of the grasp of Porter Harris—and yet that night, without Candace, she ended up buying Porter a carpet. It was a glorious Rabat-style carpet with deep colors and symbols hidden in the weave, but Marguerite was too gloomy to engage the shopkeeper in a haggle, despite the shopkeeper's prodding. "What price you give me? You give me your best price." Marguerite gave a number only fifty dollars less than the shopkeeper's first price, and he was forced to accept. It was unheard of: a transaction for something so valuable over and done with in thirty seconds. The shopkeeper threw in a free fez, a brimless red velvet hat with a tassel. "You take this, special gift." The hat was too small to fit anyone Marguerite knew; it would fit a baby or a monkey.

The following day, their next-to-last day of the trip, Candace arranged for them to visit a hammam, a traditional bathhouse. She had seemed excited about it when she described it a few days earlier to an ever-skeptical Marguerite. "It's like a spa. An ancient spa." But as they sat at breakfast, Candace picked at her croissant and said she was thinking of canceling.

"I'm just not myself," she said. "I'm sorry. It's something I ate, maybe. Or too much wine every night. Or it's the water."

"Well," said Marguerite. "It's nothing an ancient spa won't be able to cure. Come on. You're the one who wanted authentic experiences. We'll be home in forty-eight hours, and if we miss this, we'll be sorry."

"I thought you said you didn't want to sit in a room with a bunch of naked old women," Candace said. "I thought you said you'd rather eat glass."

Marguerite tilted her head. "Did I say that?"

The hammam was in the medina. It was a low whitewashed building with a smoking chimney and a glass-studded dome. A sign on the door said: *AUJOURD'HUI—LES FEMMES.* Marguerite pulled the door open, with Candace shuffling morosely at her heels. Truth be told, Marguerite was nervous. She wasn't used to working outside her comfort zone. She had no experience with ancient Moroccan women-only communal bathhouses, where, no doubt, there were rituals one was supposed to follow, rules one was supposed to know, gestures to be made. She wished for Porter, who was worldly enough to finesse any situation, or for the old Candace, Candace as she'd been only the day before yesterday—ready to throw herself into any experience headfirst with daring gusto.

There was a desk, ornately carved and inlaid, and a woman behind the desk in an ivory burkha. She was only eyes. Marguerite was wearing the Hermés scarf, Candace the baseball hat.

We don't know what we're doing, Marguerite wanted to say. *Please help us.* But instead, she just smiled in a way that she hoped conveyed this sentiment.

"Deux?" the woman said.

"Oui," Marguerite said. She reached into her money belt, which was hidden under her blouse, and pulled out a wad of dirham. Candace slumped against the beautiful desk. She was pale, listless, chewing a stick of gum because, along with her other symptoms, she couldn't rid her mouth of a funky, metallic taste. The only-eyes woman plucked three bills from Marguerite's cache, then paused and said.

"Avec massage?"

"Oui," Marguerite said. "Avec massage, s'il vous plaît."

The woman extracted two more bills. Was it costing three dollars, a hundred dollars? Marguerite had no idea. The only-eyes woman slid two plush towels across the desk and pointed down the hall.

The hallway had marble floors, thick stone walls, arched windows with translucent glass. The windows were on the interior wall, which led Marguerite to believe there was a courtyard. The overall aura of the hallway, however, reminded Marguerite of a convent: It was hushed, forbidding; their footsteps echoed. At the end of the hallway was a set of heavy arched double doors. Marguerite pulled one side open and stepped through, holding the door for Candace. *I'm not doing this without you.*

They entered a cavernous room with a high, domed ceiling. The floor was composed of tiny pewter-colored tiles; there were platforms at different levels around a turquoise pool. Women lay on mats around the pool in various stages of undress. There were naked teenagers; there were women older and heavier than Marguerite in underpants but no bras. There was one very blond girl who looked Western—she was American, maybe, or Swedish—wearing a bikini. Along the wall were pegs where the women had hung their clothes.

Okay, Marguerite thought, *this is it.* She looked at Candace, who gave her a wan smile.

"Here we are," Candace said, and in her voice Marguerite was relieved to hear the playful tease of a dare: *You go first.*

Marguerite stepped out of her shoes. Okay. She peeled off her socks. She stared at the wall as she unbuttoned her blouse. Her initial instinct had been correct. This was not the place for her. She hated the thought of all these women, and especially Candace, seeing her naked. She was too voluptuous, a Rubens, Porter called her, but that was him being kind. Her breasts hung heavily when she stripped to her bra. She thought of Damian Vix ushering her forward into the dark pantry. He had swept her hair aside so he could kiss her neck; then his hands had gone to her breasts. He had pressed against her and moaned. Marguerite laughed. If she had endured the embarrassment of being groped by her attorney in a pantry, she could endure this. She took her bra off next, then her slacks, but left on her underpants.

Candace had stripped completely, and she'd let her hair out of its rubber band. Her body was a museum piece: healthy American woman. Strong legs, small, shapely ass, flat stomach, and breasts a bit larger than Marguerite would have guessed.

"Nobody is swimming," Candace said, and she giggled.

"Right," Marguerite said. She was baffled. What was the point of lying around an indoor pool, naked, with other women? How did this make a person feel anything but anxious? She watched the Swedish girl exit through a door marked with an arrow. Marguerite nodded her head. *Follow her.*

They entered *la chambre froide,* the cold room, which was an elongated room with three domes in the ceiling. There was a pool in this room also, but the Swede bypassed it and so did Marguerite and Candace. The room itself was not particularly cold, but it was empty and inhospitable. The next room was noticeably warmer and more ornate—there were carved wooden pillars around the outside of the pool, and niches where women reclined like odalisques. *Like Ingres,* Marguerite thought. *Porter would love this.* There were attendants in this room with buckets and scrub brushes, loofahs and combs. Someone was having her hair washed; someone was getting a massage; someone was rubbing herself down with what looked like wet cement. Marguerite wondered if they should stop—they had, after all, paid for massages—but the Swede kept going and Marguerite decided to follow her.

They ended up in the warmest room of all; *LA CHAMBRE CHAUDE,* the sign said. The hot room. The room was filled with steam. It was a sauna. Candace breathed the steam in appreciatively and sat down on a tile bench. Marguerite sat next to her. The Swede popped into what looked like a very hot shower. The sound of water was loud and since they were the only three people in the room, Marguerite felt okay to speak.

"How do you feel?" she asked.

Candace gazed at Marguerite and started to cry. Because of the heat and the steam, however, it looked like she was melting.

Marguerite reached out. It might have been awkward, an embrace with both of them naked, but to Marguerite it felt natural, elemental; it felt like they had been friends since the beginning of time, like they were the first two women put on earth. Eve and her best friend. Candace cried with her head resting on Marguerite's shoulder, her hair grazing Marguerite's breast. It was absurdly hot, their bodies were being poached like eggs, and yet Marguerite couldn't bring herself to move. She knew she would never have Candace closer than she was right that second. Marguerite wanted to touch Candace, but she wasn't sure where. The knee? The face? Before she could decide, Candace reached for Marguerite's trembling hand and placed it on her taut, smooth stomach.

"I'm pregnant," she said.

Marguerite prepped the asparagus by chopping off the woody ends and peeling the skins. She drizzled it with olive oil and sprinkled it with *fleur de sel* and freshly ground pepper. Nearly two decades later and a hemisphere away, it was astounding how well she remembered those minutes in the hammam. Her best friend was pregnant. Marguerite had found she didn't know how to respond. She should have been ecstatic. But she felt offended by the news. Betrayed.

You're pregnant, Marguerite said. *Pregnant. I can't believe it.*

Candace blotted her eyes with her towel. *I thought I was sick.*

You're pregnant, Marguerite said.

Pregnant, Candace said with finality.

They returned to the center room. An attendant asked them, *Massage?* In a daze, Marguerite remembered to nod. They were led to mats and instructed to lie down. Marguerite had never been massaged by anyone other than Porter and she was anxious about a massage out in the open, in public, so she closed her eyes. The attendant's hands were both firm and soft; it felt wonderful.

Marguerite let her mind wander. A baby. She should have been relieved. She had thought perhaps Candace was homesick, missing Dan—or sick of Marguerite. But a baby. It was the best news a person had to give. It would be, Marguerite told herself, more of Candace to love.

And yet, as the hour wore on, as Marguerite peeked at Candace—on her stomach with an attendant kneading her shoulders, and later in the pool, her hair caked with greasy clay, her hair rinsed by the same attendant and smoothed with a comb—Marguerite experienced a jealousy that left her breathless. Candace's body would bear a child, and as Marguerite glanced about the room she guessed that most, if not all, of the bodies surrounding hers had borne children. They were, in some unspoken way, more of a woman than Marguerite would ever be. She thought back to her eight/nine/ten-year-old self in leotards and tights in front of the mirror of Madame Verge's studio. The reason she had never graduated to toe shoes, the reason she quit Madame Verge altogether, was that with adolescence came the cruel understanding that she was not pretty, she was not graceful, she would not dance the *pas de deux,* she would never be someone's star. Promises would go unfulfilled. She would not marry and she would never reproduce. The real shame of her body was that it contained some kind of an end. She would die.

Marguerite decided not to wash her hair—it was far too long and it took hours to dry—though the attendant seemed to enjoy touching it, admiring its length and its thickness. Marguerite waited by the side of the pool, dangling her feet in the water, until Candace was finished, and then they walked, wrapped in their towels, back to the room where they had gotten undressed.

Marguerite made what felt like a Herculean effort to be upbeat. *Success?* she said.

Success, Candace said. She beamed. *I'm so glad we came.*

They drank mint tea and ate dainty silver dishes of watermelon sherbet in the courtyard of the hammam. Candace talked, gaily, about names. She liked Natalie and Theodore.

What names do you like? Candace asked.

Inside, Marguerite was dissolving. Candace was married to Dan; she would bear Dan's child. She would form her own family. Marguerite could feel Candace separating herself, breaking away.

Names? Marguerite said. *Oh dear, I don't know. Adelaide? Maurice?*

Candace hooted. *Maurice?* she said.

Candace was right across the table, laughing, and yet to Marguerite she had already started to vanish.

They boarded the plane the following evening. While rummaging through her carry-on bag for her book, Marguerite found the notes for her half-French, half-Moroccan menu. She read the pages through, wistfully, then tucked them away. There would be no restaurant in Africa.

4:06 P.M.

Patient's full name.

Renata peeled her sunburned thighs off the vinyl waiting-room chair and eyed Miles. He wasn't doing well. His hands were shaking so badly that Renata had had to drive the Saab to the hospital while he clumsily grappled with the surfboard. (Renata had stopped, for just a second, at the white cross in the road and said a little prayer—for Sallie, for her mother, for herself.) Now she was filling out the admittance form, even though Sallie was already upstairs, hooked up to oxygen and an IV, awaiting someone's decision as to whether or not she should be mede-vaced to Boston. It was unclear as to whether that decision would be made by the doctors here or by her parents. Renata felt, absurdly, like she knew Sallie's parents: She could picture them standing on a beach in Antigua with a black preacher, Sallie's mother with flowers in her hair, wearing a white flowing sundress to hide her burgeoning belly. Renata could picture this, but she didn't know where the parents lived, and Miles had shrugged when she asked him. They had called Sallie's house, but none of the room-mates answered, so they left a message, which felt woefully inadequate.

Patient's full name.

"Sallie," Miles said. "With an *i-e.* Her last name is Myers. But I don't know how she spells it."

Renata wrote: *Sallie Myers.*

Address.

Miles exhaled. "She lives on Mary Ann Drive. I don't know which number."

"Do you know *anything*?" Renata asked impatiently.

"Do you?" he snapped.

Renata wrote: ______ *Mary Ann Drive, Nantucket.*

Phone number. Miles started reciting numbers. Home and cell. He had them memorized.

"You're sure she's not your girlfriend?" Renata said. She meant this to be funny, but Miles didn't crack a smile. He had let Renata wear his shirt into the hospital since she had agreed to take care of all the official stuff like talking to the doctors and filling out the forms, and he, in turn, had plucked a zippered tracksuit jacket out of the abyss of his car's backseat. The jacket was wrinkled and covered with crumbs; it smelled like old beer. He had it zippered all the way up under his chin. His teeth were chattering. The air-conditioning was cranked up. Renata herself was freezing, in no small part because her entire body was red and splotched with sunburn; however, you didn't see *her* shivering.

Miles didn't answer Renata. His blue eyes were glazed over. Renata gathered this was the worst thing that had ever happened to him. He wasn't used to accidents, to bad luck, to tragedy. He hadn't lived with it, maybe, the way Renata had.

She scanned her eyes down the form. "Age?" she said. "Date of birth?"

"No idea."

When they'd arrived at the hospital, Renata explained to the admitting nurse that they were friends of the young woman who'd had the surfing accident at Madequecham Beach. The nurse slid them the clipboard with the form and Renata had stared at it, wide-eyed, like it was a test she hadn't studied for.

"Just do the best you can," the admitting nurse had said.

"Occupation?" Renata said. "Place of employment?"

"She's a bartender at the Chicken Box," Miles mumbled.

"Really?" Renata said. She had pictured Sallie owning something, a surf shop maybe; she had pictured Sallie as the manager of a hotel or as one of the charming, witty guides on a tour bus. She had envisioned Sallie in a starched white shirt, with pearls replacing her six silver hoops, as the sommelier at a restaurant like 21 Federal.

Renata wrote in: *Bartender.*

She wrote in: *The Chicken Box,* wishing for something that sounded more dignified.

"Phone number of the Chicken Box?"

Miles rattled it off from memory. Renata gave him a look.

"I go there a lot," he said. "That's how I know her."

"Does she have a boss?" Renata said. "Maybe we should call her boss."

"Why?"

"We have to call someone," Renata said. Her voice was so loud that the admitting nurse looked up from her desk. A few chairs down, a woman was breast-feeding a feverish infant. Past the row of chairs was the large automatic sliding door of the emergency room, and on the other side of the door was bright sunlight, fresh air, the real world. It was after four o'clock. Renata felt a strong pull of responsibility to be here, and just as strong a desire to find someone who knew more about Sallie than they did, someone who could take charge, make decisions. But for the time being, Sallie belonged to them. Renata had promised to keep an eye on Sallie in the water and had failed miserably, but Renata was not going to fail now. She was going to handle this. "Listen. We're going to call her boss. Maybe he knows how to reach her parents."

"Maybe," Miles said.

Renata could see Miles was going to be absolutely no help. How had she ever found him attractive enough to sleep with? Only an hour later, it was a mystery. "Do you know the boss's name?"

"Pierre."

"Pierre what?"

"I don't know. People just call him Pierre. That's his name. If you call the Chicken Box, there's only one Pierre."

"Fine," Renata said. She had no money; she was at the mercy of the admitting nurse—who, much to Renata's grateful surprise, offered to dial the number for her.

The phone rang and rang. Finally, someone answered. A man. There was loud rock music in the background.

"Hello?" Renata said. "Is this Pierre?"

"What?"

Renata cleared her throat. "Is this Pierre? May I please speak to Pierre?"

"He's not here."

Renata sighed. She had a vision of Sallie upstairs, plugged into ten machines, with only Renata to advocate on her behalf. Renata said, "Is there another way to reach him?"

"His cell phone."

"Great," Renata said. She reached over Admitting Nurse's desk in search of a pen. "Can you give me the number, please?"

"Who is this?"

"My name is Renata Knox," she said. "I'm a friend of Sallie, the bartender."

"Do you know Pierre?"

"No," Renata said. "I'm calling because—"

"I can't give you the number."

"But I'm calling because Sallie—"

"Doesn't matter. He doesn't want his number passed out. There are too many psycho chicks in this world."

"I'm calling about Sallie Myers? The bartender?" Renata said. "You know her?"

"I know her, but—"

"She had a surfing accident," Renata said. "She's in the hospital."

"She is?"

"She is."

"But she's okay, right? She's supposed to be in tonight at seven. It's *Saturday* night."

"I promise you, she won't be coming in. She's in the hospital. She's unconscious."

"Dude."

"When you see Pierre, will you tell him?" Renata asked. "Will you tell him to come to the hospital? In fact, will you call him on his cell phone and ask him to come right now, this second? We need his help."

"Sallie's not going to die or anything, is she?"

"No," Renata said. Renata didn't care if she had to donate a lung herself; Sallie was not going to die. "But it's serious, okay? Tell Pierre to come; tell him it's serious."

"Okay," the man said. "Dude."

Renata hung up. She thanked the admitting nurse and returned to her chair. Miles didn't look the least bit curious about her conversation. He looked like he might need to be admitted any second himself. He had lost his tan, and the shivering had turned into convulsions.

Renata picked up the clipboard and delivered the sparsely filled-out form to the admitting nurse, who checked it over while sucking on her lower lip.

"No date of birth?" she said.

"Sorry," Renata said. She lowered her voice. "I don't know Sallie very well. I just met her today."

The admitting nurse's mouth formed an O. Her face was sympathetic, though, and Renata felt like she might be able to confess: *I told her I'd keep an eye on her. But I didn't. I was up in the dunes cheating on my fiancé.*

"We called the house where she lives and left a message, but her roommates weren't home. So that's why I just called her boss. I thought maybe he would know more than we do."

At that second, Admitting Nurse's phone rang. She held up a finger to Renata and answered the call, speaking in such a low murmur, it was impossible to hear. Renata turned her back so as not to seem too interested. The skin on her chest was throbbing, but the tops of her thighs had taken the worst of it—they were red and shiny and very hot to the touch. How was she going to explain this hideous sunburn to Cade? How was she going to explain any of this? She raised her head to see a very tall, very dark-skinned black man walk through the automatic door.

Pierre, she thought.

He stopped, surveyed the room, took in the woman breast-feeding, Renata at the desk, and the admitting nurse. Pierre wore tiny rimless glasses that seemed like toy glasses on his wide face. He pushed the glasses up with a long finger and surveyed the scene suspiciously, like maybe this was all a hoax. But then he saw Miles and his shoulders jumped in recognition. He jogged over. Miles, miraculously, stood up and shook Pierre's hand.

"What happened?" Pierre said. His voice had the lilt of a flowery accent. From the Caribbean, Renata thought.

"Hit in the head with her board," Miles said. "She went down and it took a while for someone to find her. She was under for almost three minutes, they think. But she's breathing now. Unconscious, though, and they said maybe brain damage." At this, Miles teared up. Pierre put a hand on his shoulder.

"Hey, man, it's okay." "Okay" sounded like "okee."

Renata joined them. "Hi," she said. "I'm Renata. I'm the one who called you."

Pierre and Renata shook hands. Renata watched their two clasped hands, one huge and dark, one skinny and sunburned. Her qualms subsided a bit. Pierre seemed very capable.

"They need her date of birth, her age, stuff like that," Renata said. "And do you know how to reach her parents?"

"I have it all in my files," he said. "At the bar. I have her tax information and her emergency contact. I'll go get it."

"Thank God," Renata said. "Thank God you came."

"Don't thank me. I love the girl." He said this simply and sincerely, and Renata was helpless to do anything but nod along in agreement. One hour she had known the woman and she had felt Sallie's pull.

"Excuse me!"

The three of them turned. Admitting Nurse had come out from behind her desk and was approaching in what looked like an official way. Her face said nothing good. "I have something to tell you."

She's dead, Renata thought. The floor under her feet moved and she fell toward the chairs. Pierre caught her arm.

"Whoa!" he said.

"Ms. Myers is being helicoptered to Boston," the admitting nurse said. "She needs help we aren't equipped to give her here."

"Where in Boston?" Pierre said.

"Mass General."

"Okee," he said. He pulled out his keys. "I'm going to get the information. Her emergency contact. Okee? I'll be back in five."

Miles sank into a chair. "Boston?" he said.

Admitting Nurse repeated herself, using different words. "The care is much better there . . . the equipment more sophisticated . . . not even in the same league . . ."

Renata followed Pierre out the automatic door, but whereas he headed into the parking lot and climbed into a Toyota Land Cruiser, Renata just stood on the hot sidewalk and turned, slowly, in circles.

She heard the helicopter before she saw it—a great roar followed by a hammering. It sounded like machine-gun fire. And then, several seconds later, Renata saw it rising, straight up, as though it were being pulled by an invisible hand. It hovered above the hospital for a few seconds, long enough for Renata to think, *Sallie.* And then, like a dog following a scent, the helicopter dipped its nose and flew away.

Even with Sallie gone, Renata was hesitant to leave. If she stayed at the hospital, there might be something else she could do. Miles sat slumped in the chair like he was planning on making it his permanent home.

"What should we do?" Renata asked.

"Once Pierre comes back, we'll call her parents," he said. "That's all we can do."

"We could go to Boston. We can be there when she wakes up," Renata said.

"Are you kidding?" Miles said. "Why would you want to do that? You don't even know her."

Renata took the seat next to his and lowered her voice. "She asked me to keep an eye on her," she said. "And I didn't."

Miles crossed his arms over his chest. "Even if you had seen her go down, there was nothing you could have done. You weren't going to be able to find her any faster than the guys who were out there did."

This sounded like an easy answer, but Renata was grateful for it. "You don't think?"

"There was nothing we could have done," Miles said. "And there's nothing we can do now except call her parents."

"Right."

"You should go," he said. "I'll wait for Pierre."

"Go where?" Renata said.

"Back to the house."

"I'll just wait for you," she said.

"I'm not going back there," he said.

"What does that mean?"

"It means I quit."

"What?" Renata said.

Miles had his chin tucked to his chest and wouldn't meet her eyes. "Just go home," he said. "Please."

"How?" Renata said.

"Call your boyfriend," Miles said. Renata had already realized that her love affair with Miles was over, but his words stung nonetheless.

"Fine," Renata said. "Do you have money for the phone?"

He wiggled a finger into the tiny Velcro pocket inside his bathing suit and produced fifty cents. He told her the number of the house.

Renata didn't want to call the house, she was afraid to talk to Cade, she wanted to quit, like Miles, but she had no choice in the matter. She located a bank of phones and made the call.

An unfamiliar voice answered the phone. "Driscoll residence."

Renata paused. Who was it? Then she thought, *Nicole.* "May I please speak to Cade?" Renata said. "This is Renata calling."

Ten minutes later, Cade pulled up to the emergency room entrance in the family's Range Rover. Renata had spent those minutes trying to piece together a plausible story, but in the end she decided to just tell him the truth, minus the part where she had sex with Miles. Cade got out and opened the passenger door for Renata, though he didn't speak to her or touch her. She hadn't seen him since the night before—it seemed like years. She was startled by how handsome he was, how upright with his military-school bearing, his perfect posture. He had taken a shower. His hair was damp and freshly combed, and he was wearing one of his beautifully tailored shirts, blue, with a white windowpane pattern. His mouth was a grim line. Renata felt like she had skipped school and now had to face the truant officer, the principal, her father. She was afraid that once she started to speak, she would never stop. *I'm sorry, I'm sorry, I'm sorry.*

He pulled out of the hospital parking lot, the only sound in the car the ticking of the turn signal. Cade's window was down; the air felt good. Renata tried to imagine what Action might say in this situation. *What are you feeling* sorry *for? He doesn't* own *your ass!*

In her nervousness, Renata selected exactly the wrong words. "I'm starving."

Cade turned to her with a look on his face like he just could not believe it.

He's not the boss of you, Renate heard Action say. *Why is he all of a sudden acting like he's the boss of you?*

"Well, I am," Renata said. "I haven't eaten anything all day."

"You ate a banana," he said. His voice was barely above a whisper.

"True," she said. "I ate a banana." She wondered how he knew this. Did Suzanne *count* her bananas? Did she hunt through the trash for the peel? Was there closed-circuit TV footage that showed Renata throwing the banana and breaking the bud vase? On the road, they passed a group of bikers wearing fluorescent yellow T-shirts. Cade slowed down, then stopped at the intersection so the bikers could pass. Ever the gentleman. He took a left when Renata suspected that home was to the right.

"Where are we going?" she said.

"For a drive," he said. "I'd like you to explain yourself."

Now Renata was the one with the incredulous face. Explain herself? He spoke like he was indeed her father, like he did indeed own her ass. She had to give him something, some reason for her absence, some excuse. She'd had a plan a minute ago, but that was before he pulled up and she had to confront the disappointment on his face. What had her plan been? To tell him the truth? Was she nuts?

"I don't know what you mean," she said.

"That's bullshit!" he shouted. The veins in his forehead were popping. Renata had never seen him this angry before, and certainly not at her. In fact, in the ten months of their dating, they'd had only one argument. There was a night when Cade's parents had asked them for Sunday dinner at the apartment on Park Avenue—Cade's aunt and uncle were visiting from California—but Renata decided to go with Action to her parents' house for Chinese food instead. Cade had pleaded, and when Renata turned him down he was exasperated and disappointed; a long conversation about Renata's priorities ensued. But there hadn't been any shouting. "You never showed up at lunch! You left my mother *stranded* at the yacht club."

Renata nearly laughed. It was impossible to strand Suzanne Driscoll; the woman had three thousand friends.

"So when we got back from our sail, my mother went on and on about how you'd stood her up, how you never showed and never phoned to explain. But she was worried, too, and so we all went home to figure out *where Renata was,* and Nicole informed us that she passed you and Miles on the road in Miles's Saab. She told us it looked like you were going to the *beach.*" He smacked his hands against the inside of the steering wheel so violently that Renata feared the air bag would explode. "How do you think it made me feel to know that my girlfriend, my *fiancée,* blew off lunch with my mother so she could gallivant around the island with the *help*?"

The help? Renata could hear Action's voice loud and clear. *The Driscolls have servants. They have slaves.*

"You went sailing," Renata said. Her voice was calm and even. How this was possible she had no idea, but she was grateful. "I figured you'd be gone all day."

"Not all day," he said. "We were back at two. Two thirty."

"You didn't tell me you were going," she said. "You didn't leave me a note. You just took off."

"Well, I'm sorry," he said, though he didn't sound at all sorry. Renata let the words hang in the air of the car so he could hear his insincerity. "It was important to my father."

"What about what was important to me?" Renata said. "You brought me to Nantucket and then you left me to fend for myself."

"We spent yesterday together," Cade said. "All day yesterday. And it's not like I *abandoned* you. My mother said she'd take you to lunch."

"You said we were going to the beach. I was looking forward to it. I didn't want to have lunch with your mother."

"Nice," Cade said.

"Well, I'm sorry, but it's true. You should have told me you were going sailing."

"I didn't know until this morning."

"You could have left me a note."

Cade snapped his fingers fiercely, like a magician breaking a spell. "It's not going to work, Renata."

"What?"

"You're trying to make it seem like *I* did something wrong. *I* did not do anything wrong. You are the one who disappeared."

They were quiet for a while as they rolled down the street. The story of Renata's day filled her until she thought she would burst. Cade prided himself on being reasonable, tolerant, on being able to place himself in other people's shoes. That was what he did best. That was why she loved him. And yet she knew there was no way to explain her afternoon to Cade so that he'd understand.

"Why did you go with Miles?" Cade asked. He swallowed; his Adam's apple bobbed in his throat. Another man would have been jealous, but Cade had skipped over jealous and gone right to hurt. He was hurt.

"I wanted to go to the beach," she said. "He was going. He invited me to join him. He said we'd be back by three. But things happened."

"What kind of 'things'?" Cade said.

"We picked up a girl. Sallie Myers. She's a friend of his. She came to the beach with us and she went surfing."

"What did you and Miles do?" Cade asked.

"Sat on the beach and watched her."

"Is that his shirt you're wearing?"

"Yes."

"Why are you wearing his shirt?"

"Because I was getting sunburned. I forgot to put on lotion."

"That wasn't too smart."

"I know," Renata said. She nearly said, *Nothing happened between me and Miles.* But Renata couldn't bring herself to lie. Only when Cade out-and-out accused her would she out-and-out deny it. She sighed. The sunburn hurt, she felt like she had a fever, she was suffering from guilt at a ten, she was hungry, her throat was dry and sore from vomiting, and she was tired. She had a headache. "Sallie got hit in the head with her board. She went under. It took a few minutes to find her. When they brought her out, she wasn't breathing. The paramedics came. They took her to the hospital. They asked Miles and me to follow with Sallie's stuff. We didn't know how to reach her parents. I called her boss and he showed up. Then they sent her in a helicopter to Mass General in Boston. Miles decided to stay at the hospital until everything was settled. I should have stayed, too, but I didn't. I called you. End of story."

"Is it?" he said.

"No," she said. "Actually, it's not. There's something else I have to tell you."

He took his eyes off the road to look at her.

"We went to Madequecham Beach. And on the road that leads to the beach, we saw a white cross. It was a cross for my mother."

Cade knit his eyebrows. "What?"

"There was a white cross on the side of the road. Marking where someone had died. My mother was killed in Madequecham. The cross was for my mother."

"Are you sure about that?" Cade said.

"I'm sure."

"Did the cross say anything?" Cade asked. "Did it have your mother's *name* on it?"

"No, but it was for her."

"How do you know?"

"I could tell," Renata said. "I could feel it."

"Oh, honey," he said. "Okay. I'm sorry."

Was he sorry? His sympathy sounded forced to Renata, just as it did every time she brought up her mother's death. Like when she told him the story of her high school graduation, her father walking up to the podium with an armful of American Beauty roses to thunderous applause. *Everyone felt sorry for me, because I had no mother,* Renata said. *Why do you look at it that way?* Cade said. *They clapped because they were proud, and impressed.* He didn't get it. He could cluck and apologize all he wanted, but he didn't understand what it was like to be her and he never would. Even now, he couldn't get that patronizing look off his face, as though Renata had told him she believed in UFOs, or Santa Claus. She was prepared to hate him at that moment. *Hate* him. She was ready to put down her window and throw her twelve-thousand-dollar diamond ring into the high brush at the side of the road, to spit the truth in Cade's direction: *I had sex with Miles in the sand dunes. He was bigger than you.* But then, in an instant, Cade turned back into his usual, princely self.

"You look tired," he said. He turned the car around. "Let's get you home."

Renata closed her eyes.

When they reached Vitamin Sea, Renata expected both of the elder Driscolls to be stationed on the front porch exuding their disapproval, their suspicion, their disgust. But the house was quiet. Cade pulled into the white shell driveway, right alongside Suzanne Driscoll's precious hydrangea bushes, the ones Miles had been watering that morning. Suddenly Renata felt contrite. The day had gotten away from her; it had turned into something she couldn't control. She had acted irresponsibly, immaturely, immorally. There was no other way to look at it.

"I'm sorry," she said. "I am so, so sorry."

Cade took the key out of the ignition. He sighed in that way he had, like he understood the rest of the world would fall short of his expectations, but that he was full of grace and willing to forgive. He was, maybe, willing to forgive her.

"My parents are . . . confused by your behavior today. So I'm going to suggest something."

"Yes," Renata said. "Anything." She would apologize to Suzanne Driscoll, beg her forgiveness, and cry doing it. Because along with everything else, Miles was going to quit. That, somehow, was Renata's fault.

"I'm going to suggest that you call Marguerite and cancel dinner. My mother wants you here. The Robinsons are coming and she went to all this trouble with the lobsters and stuff."

Renata was silent. She couldn't believe Cade would suggest such a thing. He didn't realize how important the dinner with Marguerite was. He didn't realize that Renata, at base, knew exactly nothing about her dead mother and this was her one opportunity to find out. He didn't get it. He didn't care about Renata's mother; he cared only about his own mother, who had made it clear without saying a word that she didn't want Renata to eat at Marguerite's.

"No," Renata said.

"Go see her tomorrow," Cade said. "We're not leaving until four."

"No," Renata said.

"I wouldn't ask you unless it was a really important dinner."

"My dinner is important, too," Renata said. "Very important." *More important,* she thought.

"I just don't know what my parents will think. You've been gone all day and you're disappearing again tonight. You're supposed to be joining this family."

"I'm not *disappearing,*" Renata said. "Your mother knows about my dinner with Marguerite."

"She does," Cade said. "But she still wants you to eat with us."

"Can't you say something to her?" Renata said.

"I did my best to smooth things over this afternoon," Cade said, and his meaning was clear.

Renata trained her eye on Cade's right knee, knobby as it was, and covered with fine blond hairs. This was the knee she was going to spend the rest of her life with.

"I won't ask you anything else about Miles," Cade said. "Quite frankly, I don't want to know. I'm not going to bring it up and I won't allow my parents to bring it up."

"Thank you," Renata said. "I'd appreciate that."

"But I'd like you to cancel dinner."

She stared at him. He had a faint white mask where his sunglasses had been. He was negotiating, playing diplomat. *I slept with him,* she thought. *He was bigger than you.*

"You can go tomorrow, first thing. You can stay all day. But please cancel for tonight. My mother wants you home, and so do I. I feel like I haven't seen you."

At that moment, Renata heard a door slam. She looked up. Nicole was descending the stairs from the apartment over the garage. *Tattletale!* Renata thought. *Snitch!* Nicole glared at Cade and Renata. Cade waved lamely; Renata lowered her eyes. Once Nicole entered the house, Renata got out of the car. She should have known it from that first night with Cade at the dance club; she should have known it from the way he'd drawn her out onto the street, away from the music, and her dearest friend, without a word. She should have understood that things always—always, *always*—went the way Cade Driscoll wanted them to.

It was not quite five o'clock, and yet Suzanne Driscoll was showered, dressed in Lilly Pulitzer pants and a pink silk shell, drinking a glass of white wine. She was lounging across the sofa with Mr. Rogers in her lap. Renata heard banging in the kitchen: Nicole, the little narc, preparing dinner.

"Oh, there you are, dear," Suzanne said. "We were beginning to wonder what had become of you."

"I'm sorry I missed lunch," Renata said sullenly.

"Don't give it a second's thought," Suzanne said, smiling. Suzanne Driscoll had red hair that she combed back over her head; the ends turned up under her ears. Every time Renata saw her, the hair always looked exactly the same. "I'll just bet you had fun with Miles. He is such a doll."

Renata studied Suzanne for signs of sarcasm but found none, which meant Suzanne was more slippery than Renata ever could have imagined. Before Renata could respond with an, "Oh yes, I had *lots* of fun," Cade spoke up.

"Renata's going to call Marguerite and cancel, Mom. She's going to eat here tonight with us."

Suzanne Driscoll squealed in such a grating way that Mr. Rogers jumped off her lap and left the room.

"Oh, good," Suzanne said. "Good, good, good. The Robinsons are coming at six for cocktails. They are dear friends and they really want to meet you. What can I get you? How about a big glass of ice water? How about some crackers and cold grapes? How about some aloe for your skin? If you go upstairs right now, you'll have time for a nap."

I will not play into this woman's hands, Renata thought, but she found she was too tired to rebel, too hungry and thirsty and sore to stand her ground. Too guilty to do anything but nod yes.

5:00 P.M.

The stove's timer buzzed again, making awful music in concert with the monkey in the clock as he announced the hour. Five o'clock. *Quitting time,* Marguerite thought, though this notion was from some long-ago life—five o'clock had been quitting time for her father. He was always home, without fail, at five fifteen and Diana Beale had dinner on the table by five thirty. Later, after culinary school, Marguerite would view this early dinner as middle-class, provincial, midwestern. For most of her professional life, five o'clock was the hour when she returned to work—after a full morning of prep and an all-too-short afternoon break, a glass of wine with Porter, lying in the unmade rope bed.

The timer insisted. Marguerite took the bread out of the oven and checked it off her list. She considered preparing the béarnaise and letting it sit in a warm-water bath until dinnertime, but she never would have done that at the restaurant and she wouldn't do it now. Marguerite set out the polished silver and then she moved the place settings across from each other. She wanted to look Renata in the eye.

So now the table was set, the china and water glasses buffed to a gleaming shine, the zinnias and dahlias crowded cheerfully in a crystal vase. The gladiolas were in the stone pitcher by the door. Marguerite had located cocktail napkins in a kitchen drawer that she hadn't opened in ages. The napkins had, at one time, been red with white polka dots, though the red was faded to pinkish-gray and they curled up slightly at the edges like burnt toast, but they would do. Marguerite changed the CD to, of all people, Derek and the Dominos, because "Bell Bottom Blues" had been Candace's favorite song. It was her anthem. Marguerite would tell Renata this.

All day Marguerite had been aware of time pressing down on her, and yet she suddenly found herself with two unclaimed hours. She wandered through her house. She had dusted on Wednesday and vacuumed on Thursday. The house looked fine. There was time for a few pages of the Theodore Roosevelt biography, her afternoon reading, there was time for the Internet, but Marguerite would never be able to concentrate on either. Renata, her goddaughter, was coming here for dinner. Marguerite had had the whole day to digest this fact, but still it struck her as unbelievable. In the bedroom, Marguerite picked up the photograph of Candace and herself and baby Renata, four weeks old, newly christened.

Marguerite didn't often pray. On those occasions when she'd found herself at church—Candace's wedding, Renata's christening, Candace's funeral—she'd bowed her head along with everyone else, and when required she moved her lips, spoke the words she'd memorized as a child. But she didn't feel anything. Marguerite was certain God existed and just as certain that God knew she existed, but for sixty-three years they had ignored each other. Marguerite had had no use for faith until the day Candace was killed, at which point Marguerite found her spiritual reserve empty. There was nothing to draw on, and rather than being angry at God for not appearing in her time of need the way he seemed to for so many others, rather than hating him for not providing her with a tool to make her way easier, Marguerite accepted his absence as her due.

Once Candace was gone, Marguerite frequently spoke out loud as she moved through her days alone. *Would you look at the bloom on that Jacques Randall? Elizabeth Taylor in rehab again! A wholly unsatisfying ending on the last story by Mr. Salinger, anyone would agree.* Marguerite assumed this was a symptom of her "insanity," a consequence of her decision not to allow anyone into her day-to-day life, but every once in a while she recognized her mumblings as prayer. She was talking to Candace.

As Marguerite gazed at the photograph, she echoed the words she'd said on the altar the afternoon Renata was baptized. "*Will you, Marguerite, as godmother, do the best that you can to . . ."* The priest went on to say something about guiding the child in the ways of the Lord, something about seeking truth, goodness, humility, grace, something about maintaining faith. Marguerite had agreed to do all these things, but only because she was relieved by the gentle phrasing of the question: *Will you do the best that you can?*

Yes, she thought. *I will do the best I can.*

Candace was pregnant through the summer. Her breasts swelled first; then her belly popped. Her hair grew at an amazing rate; at one point, it was nearly as long as Marguerite's. Her left hand became numb with carpal tunnel; she suffered from debilitating heartburn when she lay down; she had to pee every twenty minutes. And yet still she worked, climbing the steep stairs to the Chamber of Commerce office each day; still she ran—five, six, seven miles—even though people would stop in their cars, roll down the windows, and tell her to get on home.

One day at noon, she showed up at Les Parapluies and found Marguerite elbow deep in prep work: roasting peppers, reducing stock, marinating tuna steaks. Candace kissed Marguerite on both cheeks and demanded lunch.

"This is not a diner," Marguerite grumbled. "You know I don't make lunch. Half the time, I don't even eat lunch."

"You don't have to make lunch for me," Candace said. "But what about the baby?"

Candace came in almost every day for ten weeks. She was used to bringing soda crackers to work, carrot sticks, a hard-boiled egg, which she ate at her desk, but it wasn't matching her voracious appetite. Marguerite made quiches, Caesar salads, *croque monsieurs* like the ones she'd eaten in Paris; she made gazpacho, BLTs, tuna salad. She began to feel like a part of the pregnancy. She liked having Candace in her kitchen while she cooked. She liked having Candace to herself. They talked, really talked, and it was almost like the old days, before Dan. Candace expressed her concerns about the baby.

"I can't become somebody's mother," Candace said. "I don't know what I'm doing."

"Who does?" Marguerite said.

"I don't have the warm, fuzzy maternal feelings that other women have," Candace said.

"They'll come," Marguerite said. "When the baby's born."

"I don't even like babies," Candace said. "I think other people's babies are boring."

"They say it's different when it's your own," Marguerite said.

"How do you know so much?" Candace said.

Marguerite laced her fingers through Candace's and said, "You're going to be a wonderful mother."

"You think?"

Candace had given up alcohol and she was easily tired, but still Candace and Dan came to the restaurant to have dinner with Porter and Marguerite two or three times a week. Marguerite insisted on it.

"You're coming in tonight?" Marguerite would ask at lunch.

"Oh," Candace would say. "I don't know. I'm so tired."

"You should come while you can," Marguerite said. "Once the baby arrives, things will be different."

In the end, Candace always agreed. "Okay, we'll come. Nine o'clock. See you then."

Candace's belly was impressive—perfectly round and hard as a rock. Customers of the restaurant couldn't help themselves from stopping by the west banquette. "Boy," one said. "The way you're carrying, it's definitely a boy." The interruptions came so frequently, it annoyed them all.

"No one has any sense of boundaries," Dan complained. "Everyone has something to say to a pregnant woman."

"I know they're excited for us," Candace said. "But I feel like public property."

Candace drank mineral water while Dan and Porter and Marguerite carried on with cocktails and wine—two bottles, three bottles, four, followed by a glass of port or a cordial. The three of them drank more heavily, perhaps, while Candace was pregnant. There were dozens of conversations about Reagan, who might succeed Reagan, did the Democrats have a chance, and if they were to have a chance they needed to run somebody who would make a better showing than Walter Mondale did the last time around.

One night, Candace stopped conversation with a hoot. "Baby's kicking," she said.

Marguerite reached over and laid her hand on the smooth sphere of Candace's belly. The instinct to do this was perfectly natural, she thought. She, who would never have a child, wanted to know what it felt like, if only from the outside. She sensed the light but insistent tapping—*tap, tap, tap,* like the baby was trying to send her some kind of coded message. Without thinking, Marguerite moved her hand in a circle, as though Candace were a crystal ball.

Dan snorted. "That's my wife you're fondling," he said. "I will ask you kindly to remove your hand."

Marguerite lifted her hand. She looked at Candace. Always, when Marguerite and Dan bickered, Candace was the peacemaker. But now she just gazed into her lap. Marguerite's face burned with shame. "I feed that child," she said.

"Oh, Marguerite and her fabulous cooking," Dan said. "Where would we be without it?"

There was a terrible silence at the table. Marguerite looked to Porter. Confrontation made him cringe, but she couldn't believe he would let Dan talk to her that way. Porter glanced at her in a way that let her know he was embarrassed for her; then he tried to smooth things over by hoisting the last third of the bottle of Sauternes.

"Maybe we need some more wine," he said. "How 'bout it? Daisy?"

"I'm all done," Marguerite said. She threw her napkin onto her plate and stood up. "I have things to do in the kitchen. Good night." She addressed the centerpiece of hydrangeas because she couldn't bear to meet anyone's eyes.

The following morning Candace came into the kitchen looking as plain as Marguerite had ever seen her. Her hair was lank and unwashed; there were bruise-colored crescents under her eyes.

"Croque monsieur?" Marguerite asked, doing her best to smile. "Or is it a tuna fish day?"

Candace twisted a strand of hair around her finger. "I'm not hungry," she said. "I just wanted to apologize for last night."

"It's my fault," Marguerite said. "What I did was inappropriate." She said this, though she didn't quite believe it. Her touch had been innocent, curious. Had she crossed a line? Was she no longer able to touch her best friend? It pained her to think so.

"I have to stop coming in at night," Candace said. "It's too much for me. I'm too tired."

"No!" Marguerite said. "You can't stop coming." She heard the desperation in her voice and suddenly she saw herself the way other people must see her: As a woman terrified of being abandoned, of being left alone. She, who had prided herself on strength, on independence; she, who had chosen the word *free.* What was happening to her? "I mean, fine," Marguerite said. "Fine, yes. By all means, stay home."

Candace walked to the sink where Marguerite was seasoning a striped bass and put her hand on Marguerite's back. "There's going to be enough baby for all of us."

"It's you, though," Marguerite said. "There's not enough you for all of us."

The clock chimed the half hour. *Shower,* Marguerite thought. Hair, face, outfit. These were the only unchecked items left oh her list, and for some reason this made her apprehensive. She went to the refrigerator and eyed the champagne. Candace had always insisted on a dressing drink, and now Marguerite knew why. All those years with Porter, and Marguerite had never felt a nervous anticipation as keen as this very moment. She took one of the bottles out, popped the cork, poured herself three fingers in a jelly jar.

She took a sip. She couldn't taste it in any kind of proper way, though there was a cold, fizzy crispness that brought back memories of Porter's arched eyebrows, his bulging eyes, the feel of the zinc bar under her bare elbows, the sound of forks scraping plates, laughter, voices (Candace's voice sifting through all the rest), Marguerite closing her eyes at any point during the dinner service and knowing that she was responsible for everything that happened in that restaurant. *She* was God. Then, incongruously,

Marguerite thought of the pimpled boy in the wine shop that morning, his discomfort with the price of the champagne, with the whole idea of the champagne, and she laughed.

Right, she thought. *Shower.*

It was as she was stepping out of the shower that the phone rang. The bathroom door was closed, the overhead fan humming, and despite her promise to herself to be moderate, Marguerite had slugged back the champagne all at once, like a shot of tequila. It went straight to her head. She heard the phone, but even after the day she'd had, she couldn't quite identify the sound. She cracked open the door. It was indeed the phone.

Before the shower, she had located the pink silk kimono that Porter brought her from Kyoto; it had been at the far edge of her closet, the very last thing, beyond her five embroidered chef's jackets, which were pressed and vacuum-packed in dry cleaner's plastic. *Wallflower,* Marguerite thought as she wrapped herself up in the kimono. She stepped into the bedroom. The room was dim, though the sun had not set; there was liquid gold light slanting through her bedroom windows. The phone rang, and rang again. Marguerite was so preoccupied by the sight and feel of herself in the kimono (as though whoever was on the phone could see her) and with the circumstances under which Porter had given it to her (it was the consolation prize—he had taken a trip with the blond, unmarried tennis coach instead of her; he had lied *and* cheated) that she never considered who might be calling. She supposed, if pressed, she would have said it was Dan again, with another petition. Or Ethan, wishing her luck.

"Hello?" she said.

"Aunt Daisy?"

"Yes, darling, hello. How are you? Had a good day, I hope?" Marguerite was thinking, *She needs directions, after all. Would she be walking or taking a cab? Or would someone from the house on Hulbert Avenue be dropping her?* Marguerite was just about to ask when she realized a reasonable amount of time had passed and Renata hadn't answered. There was breathing on the other end, labored breathing, which Marguerite identified as weeping. Weeping, but no words.

"Are you all right?" Marguerite asked. "Darling?"

"Aunt Daisy?" Renata said.

The girl's voice was so despondent, so transparently on a mission to deliver bad news, that it was all Marguerite could do to find the edge of her bed.

"Yes?"

"I can't come," Renata said.

"You're not coming?" Marguerite said. She felt ambushed and stunned, like the victim of a surprise attack. How stupid she was! How daft! Because never once this whole day had it occurred to Marguerite that Renata might cancel.

"My boyfriend's parents," Renata said. "They want me here. They're being weird about it. And I'm in no position to argue with them because I did an awful thing today."

Awful thing? Marguerite knew she was supposed to ask about the awful thing, but her mind struggled like a weak flame. She was thinking about the boyfriend's parents, former customers who missed her restaurant. These people were asking Renata to forgo dinner with her own godmother who, because of a set of complex circumstances, Renata hadn't seen in fourteen years. The boyfriend's parents didn't understand the situation, its importance. Awful thing? Nothing could be so bad that it warranted the boyfriend's parents taking Renata from her. However, Marguerite said nothing. *Not coming,* she thought. The term "crushing blow" came to mind, the term "heartbreak." How would Marguerite be able to step into the other room and see the table set for two people, one across from the other? How would she deal with all the food she'd prepared? Her mind was running amok now. It was the champagne; she should never have allowed herself. God knows if she let herself do whatever her heart desired she would drink a bottle, or two, every night, and turn herself into a drunk. She would give herself cirrhosis of the liver. Marguerite squeezed the phone's receiver. She was in a conversation, she reminded herself; she had a responsibility to the person on the other end of the line to move the conversation, however unpleasant, forward.

"Awful thing?" Marguerite said.

"I ran away."

"You ran away?"

"I went to the beach without telling anyone where I was going. I went with this . . . *guy* who works here."

The way she said "guy" seemed significant. But how to respond?

"We went to Madequecham," Renata said.

Marguerite hissed involuntarily, like a balloon losing air. Madequecham. The poor girl.

"You saw the cross?" Marguerite said.

Renata started weeping again. "Yes." She snuffled. There was a pause, the sound of a tissue being pulled from a box. "It's for her, right?"

"It's for her. Your mother." Marguerite had made the cross herself. She bought the wood at Marine Home Center, painted it with three coats of heavy-duty white primer, nailed it together. She had done this as busywork, really, the whole time in a numbed daze, three days after

Candace's death and the day before her funeral. Marguerite had softened the ground with a thermos of boiling water and pounded the cross into the sandy mud with her kitchen mallet. And then she drove away. She had thought she might visit the marker like a grave, lay down flowers each week or some such, but she had never once gone back to see it.

"I knew it was for her," Renata said. "I saw it and I knew."

Good, Marguerite thought. She wasn't exactly sure why she had put the cross there. At least not until this very second.

"I'm sorry you can't come," Marguerite said. "Deeply sorry." *Devastated,* she thought. *Stupefied.* She felt like crying herself, like throwing a childish tantrum. She nearly listed the efforts she had made on behalf of the meal, but that would be selfish and rude. And yet she couldn't help herself from wondering if the situation could be salvaged or manipulated. "Would it help at all if I spoke to the boy's parents?"

"Oh no," Renata said. "God, no. I wouldn't want to drag you into all this."

"Are you sure, darling? Because I could explain—"

"Thank you, Aunt Daisy, for offering, but *no.*" The "no" was so emphatic, it wounded Marguerite's ego. Maybe the boyfriend's parents were an excuse, then. Maybe Renata simply didn't want to come. Maybe the boyfriend's parents or someone else had made a comment about Marguerite; maybe they'd perpetuated the worst of the rumors.

"Okay," Marguerite said. She felt ashamed for pressing the issue. This was rejection, another broken promise. She should be used to it by now.

"They said I'll have time for a visit tomorrow," Renata said. "I could come for lunch, maybe? Or breakfast?"

"Breakfast?" Marguerite said. A person less rigid than she would snap up this opportunity and start thinking about eggs, or crepes filled with fresh peaches. But Marguerite couldn't help feeling that something would be lost from their conversation if it took place in the bright, unforgiving sunlight of morning. An intimacy would be sacrificed; Marguerite felt that the confessions she had to make would only come across properly with candlelight, with wine, with nothing to stop them from talking but sleep. Marguerite felt annoyed, and resistant to changing her plans like this. After all the work she'd done, the way she'd choreographed the evening in her mind, she didn't want to accommodate. The girl would have to learn, eventually, that she couldn't go about disappointing people like this. But in the end, Marguerite decided, she wasn't willing to turn the girl away altogether. So eggs it would be. Crepes with fresh peaches.

"Breakfast is fine. Or lunch." They could have cold tenderloin sandwiches, asparagus salad.

"Breakfast," Renata said. "I'm coming over as soon as I wake up."

Marguerite surprised herself. She was able to laugh. "We'll see you in the morning, then."

"Thank you, Aunt Daisy," Renata said. "Thank you for understanding."

"Anything for you, darling." Marguerite said, and she meant it.

The sun set. Marguerite's windows shone pink, then darkened. Even here, in the heart of town, she could hear crickets. She did not turn on any lights and she did not get dressed. She sat on her bed through two chimes of the stodgy, unforgiving old clock and then she moved through her house as nimbly as if she'd lived in it all these years as a blind woman. She let the tenderloin sit, and the bread; she didn't have the heart to wrap everything up and put it away just yet. She took one of the chilled flutes from the freezer, filled it with champagne, and carried both the flute and the bottle to the dining-room table. There she lit the candles. The light was such that she could see herself in the dark window opposite, a woman drinking alone. She raised her glass to her reflection.

Part Two

The Dinner Party

August 19, 2006 • 6:32 P.M.

Suzanne Driscoll said, "The Robinsons just pulled in."

She and Renata were standing at the bottom of the staircase, a few steps to the right of the open front door. Suzanne touched her hair, her earrings, and then, reassured that she looked perfect, she inspected Renata. "My God, what is that mark on your chin? You look like you've been in a prize fight."

Renata's hand flew to her jaw. She had noticed it herself only a few minutes ago: a garish purple bruise where the surfboard had smacked her. The spot throbbed with dull pain, as did the sunburn across her nose and cheeks. Suzanne had given her a tube of aloe mask, and she had applied it liberally, then lain down for twenty minutes of dreamless sleep. When Renata washed the mask off, her face felt fragile, like if she smiled, it would crumble and fall apart in chunks. There was no way to explain the bruise without explaining about Sallie, so Renata said nothing. She was hurt that this was what Suzanne had chosen to notice, because she had tried to make an effort with her appearance: She wore a white T-shirt with a scoop neck and a short pink skirt. She wore pink thong sandals embossed with the letter *R*. And yet now Renata felt that what she was missing was the bag for over her head.

Attention was drawn from Renata's wound with the appearance of the Robinson family in the Driscolls' foyer. Renata had thought the Robinsons would be a couple, but there were three of them; they had brought along a daughter who was about Cade and Renata's age. Someone Renata, no doubt, would be expected to make friends with. Joe Driscoll came out to the foyer to greet the Robinsons, as did Cade. Everyone kissed, shook hands, thumped backs, grasped arms, and then Renata was ushered forth—Suzanne placed a light but insistent hand on her lower back and moved her forward into the center of a circle they'd all unconsciously made.

"And this," Suzanne said, "is the future Mrs. Cade Driscoll."

Renata tried to smile, though being introduced in this way offended her. She had been reduced to an announcement in *Town & Country*. Her face felt like plastic. She held out her hand. Mr. Robinson who was tall and balding, wearing Ben Franklin spectacles and a bow tie, was the first to take it.

"Pleasure to meet you. Kent Robinson."

"Renata Knox," Renata said, because for all the pomp and circumstance of the introduction, Suzanne had neglected to mention her name.

Mrs. Robinson, a short-haired brunette who was as thin and made up as Renata's future mother-in-law and as cheerful with the same kind of questionable sincerity, hugged Renata quickly but fiercely, kissed her burning cheek, and said, "Oh, Suzanne, you are so lucky!"

"Aren't I?" Suzanne said. She beamed as if standing before her were not a sunburned, bruised, delinquent, vase-breaking, list-stealing, lying, cheating Renata but someone else entirely. "And Renata," Suzanne said in the fetching voice she reserved for the cat, "this is Kent and Kathy's daughter, Claire. Claire and Cade went to Choate together. They are old, old friends."

Renata smiled at the Robinsons' daughter, trying to remember that first impressions were just that. Look how things had turned around with Sallie. But Claire Robinson had failed even more miserably with her appearance than Renata had. She wore a long peasant skirt and a man's white T-shirt, and a pair of leather sandals that had been mended with white medical tape. She had long, dark hair on its way to becoming dreadlocks, and the whitest skin Renata had ever seen—as white as a geisha under layers of powder—so that the freckles on her nose and cheeks looked like the black beans in vanilla ice cream. Renata looked at her and thought, *Ragamuffin, waif*—she reminded Renata of a street urchin from a Dickens novel—though her blue eyes were bright and overexcited. Renata wondered if she was on drugs.

"Hi," Renata said. And in case Claire had missed the earlier introduction, she added, "I'm Renata."

Claire was staring at Renata in a way that bordered on rude. Then she offered a limp, moist hand. "It's nice to meet you. I couldn't believe it when I heard Cade was engaged."

"Right," Renata said. "We're kind of young."

"Claire and Cade went to Choate together," Suzanne said again. She took a sharp breath. "Let's go to the big room and get a drink."

They repaired to the big room in three groups: Mr. Robinson, Joe Driscoll, and Cade led the way, slowly, accommodating Joe's occasional stutter step. (He was using a cane tonight because the sailing had worn him out.) Suzanne, Mrs. Robinson, and Claire followed behind, and Renata, feeling like a Sunset Boulevard streetwalker with her short, tight skirt and ugly bruise, brought up the rear. At least she thought she brought up the rear, but then she sensed a light, whispery presence behind her—Mr. Rogers, perhaps? She turned and was startled to find Nicole, dressed in black pants, a black shirt and black apron, quietly shutting the door and tucking away Mrs. Robinson's turquoise wrap. Renata felt angry at Nicole—she was a snitch—and yet this anger was mixed with an odd sense of kinship. Nicole was a black woman, as was Renata's best friend, whom she missed keenly, especially in these strange and compromised circumstances, and Nicole worked for the Driscolls, as did Miles, whom Renata still considered vaguely, though she might never see him again, to be her lover. On the strength of these two imagined connections, Renata felt it was okay to linger until she and Nicole were in step next to each other. She wasn't sure what to say, but she wanted to let Nicole know that she, Renata, wasn't like the rest of these people. As the future Mrs. Cade Driscoll (God, it made her shiver just to think it) she was as much Suzanne's pawn, Suzanne's servant, as Nicole was.

"You've worked hard today," Renata said. "I hope you're off soon?"

Nicole didn't deign to meet Renata's eye. "Miles was supposed to spell me at six. He phoned to say he wasn't coming." Nicole had a light and crisp British accent. It surprised Renata until she realized that this was the first time she had heard Nicole speak more than two words. The loveliness of her voice was poisoned by the disgusted look she shot Renata. "But you, I'm sure, know *all about that.*" She quickened her step and Renata hurried to keep up.

"His friend Sallie, you know," Renata said. "She had a surfing accident and went to the hospital."

Nicole dismissed this with a wave of her hand. "I have to fetch drinks," she said.

Even as mentally anguished and physically battered as Renata was, she had to admit there was no room as perfect for entertaining on a balmy summer evening as the Driscolls' living room. The room was lit only by candles and by a soft fluorescent light over the wet bar. The white couches had been connected to create a semicircle facing the out-of-doors. The coffee table had been cleared of Suzanne's collection of porcelain eggs and her copies of *Travel + Leisure* and was now laden with platters of food—bluefish pâté, crackers, grapes, cheese straws, nuts, olives. The glass doors had been flung wide open to the night. The deck was festooned with tiki torches; the teak table had been covered with a red checkered cloth and set with butter-warmers and lobster crackers, cocktail forks and plastic bibs. Just seeing the table costumed like this made Renata pine for the dinner she was not having with Marguerite. The white cross! Beyond the deck, Renata could see the moon shining on the water; she could smell the water; she could hear the water lapping against the side of Joe Driscoll's boat. *Once you marry me,* Cade had said, with the promise of a game show host, *all this will be yours.*

Renata tried to decide which of the two groups to join. She would be most comfortable with Cade at her side, though the second she had called Marguerite to cancel she had filled with a fury that could only be directed at him. She had thrown him several frosty looks since descending from her room (where, earlier, he'd knocked timidly, no doubt looking for sex, and Renata had told him brusquely and without opening the door that she was busy getting ready and to please go away)—but Cade didn't look as apologetic or as distraught as he should have. He seemed oblivious to her, and he had done nothing to acknowledge the sacrifice she made so that she could have lobsters with the Robinsons. Renata also felt put out by Claire Robinson's presence, primarily because it hadn't been mentioned and thus felt like something secret, something the Driscolls were trying to pull over on her. If an old friend of Cade's from boarding school was coming for dinner, why wouldn't anyone have mentioned it? And yet Cade didn't seem interested in Claire Robinson; Renata didn't remember seeing them even greeting each other. At this moment, Cade was talking to Kent Robinson about his new job at J. P. Morgan while Joe Driscoll leaned on his cane with one hand and tried to discreet away his other hand, which shook violently.

Renata, unable to place herself comfortably with the gentlemen, stood with Suzanne, Mrs. Robinson, and Claire. Suzanne and Mrs. Robinson were as thin as blades and Renata could imagine them working a crowded room, alternately smoothing and cutting. They were talking about a third woman, a friend of theirs maybe, but maybe not, who had breast cancer. The cancer had metastasized; the woman was the mother of three small children.

"In the end, I can't help but feel it's her own fault," Mrs. Robinson said. "All it would have taken was a yearly mammogram!"

At this, Claire gasped. "I can't believe you just said that. Really, Mother!"

"Those poor children," Suzanne said.

It was Renata's least favorite kind of story—those poor, motherless children. Just as she thought, *I can't be a part of this,* and made the slightest movement toward the men, Nicole appeared holding a tray of drinks.

"White wine spritzers," she said. She smiled warmly at the women and especially at Renata. Renata couldn't decide if Nicole had forgiven her or if she was being grossly insincere. Was there, Renata wondered, a genuine person in the room, including herself? She took a glass from the tray.

"Thank you," she said.

Mrs. Robinson also took a glass, though Claire and Suzanne declined. Claire asked for a hot chai ("if it's not too much trouble"), which Nicole assured her it wasn't. Renata noticed a very full glass of white wine resting on a side table just below Suzanne's fingertips, which, now that other guests had drinks, she felt free to pick up.

"Cheers," Suzanne said. "Here's to the end of the summer. And to Cade's engagement. And to being together."

The three of them clinked glasses while Claire stood among them, beaming, and cheerfully mimed as though she had a glass. Renata drank down quite a bit of her fruity, fizzy wine punch, hoping Nicole hadn't poisoned it. She glanced at Cade, who was drinking a Stella, still deep in conversation with Kent Robinson about his future on the buy-back desk. Joe Driscoll had availed himself of the sofa—he couldn't lean on his cane and hold a drink—and he smiled benignly at Cade and Kent's conversation, though he wasn't really a part of it any longer. Renata considered joining him. If there *was* a decent person in the room, it was probably Joe Driscoll. She could ask him about the sailing.

"We're lucky to have Renata with us tonight," Suzanne said. "She originally made other plans."

"Really?" Mrs. Robinson said. She smiled as though she couldn't imagine such a thing.

"I was supposed to have dinner with my godmother," Renata said. "Marguerite Beale."

"Marguerite Beale?" Mrs. Robinson said. "Marguerite *Beale*? The chef? From Les Parapluies?"

Suzanne smirked and nudged her friend's elbow. All of a sudden she seemed about to burst with pride and excitement, as if she'd just announced that Renata was related to the queen of England. "Her godmother."

"But why?" Mrs. Robinson said. "How?"

"She was my mother's best friend," Renata said. "Candace Harris Knox?"

"Renata lost her mother when she was terribly young," Suzanne said, clucking. "Joe and I used to go to the restaurant all the time, of course."

"Of course," Mrs. Robinson said. "So did we. God, that seems like ages ago."

"I think I remember your mother," Suzanne said. "Though maybe not. I only ever caught glimpses of Marguerite Beale. She used to sit down to eat with friends after everyone else went home, or moved into the bar. I have to admit, I wasn't really part of her crowd."

"Nor was I," Mrs. Robinson said. She sounded sad about this for a moment; then she cleared her throat. "So, Marguerite Beale. She's better then? You heard the strangest stories, right after the restaurant closed."

"Yes," Suzanne murmured. She sipped her wine and touched Renata's arm. "You must know all about it. Marguerite's trouble?"

Renata's face burned; her jaw pulsed. She sipped her drink and resolved to say nothing, to give nothing away. She glanced at Claire, who was staring at her again.

"It was rather like Vincent van Gogh cutting off his ear," Mrs. Robinson said. She tittered nervously. "At least that was what one heard. I'm sure she's better now; I'm sure she's just fine. Your godmother! That's simply extraordinary."

To keep from slapping Mrs. Robinson or telling her to fuck off, which was what the Action-voice in Renata's head was advising her to do, Renata made a move for the food on the coffee table. She had eaten nothing but the damned banana all day. She slathered a cracker with bluefish pâté and shoved it in her mouth. She could hear Suzanne and Mrs. Robinson whispering behind her. She heard Claire say in an aggravated whisper, "Mother, please! You're a terrible gossip!" Cade appeared at Renata's elbow.

"Are you okay?" he said.

Vincent van Gogh? she thought. She hated Mrs. Robinson. But before Renata could express this sentiment to Cade, Nicole appeared with a tray of fresh drinks.

"Renata?" Nicole said.

Renata slammed back the rest of her spritzer, placed the empty glass on Nicole's tray, and took another.

"Thank you," she said to Nicole. "I think you're the only person in the room who knows my name."

"Oh, come on," Cade said. "I know your name."

She glared at him. Nicole walked away. The four adults mingled in a group and then strolled out to the deck. Joe Driscoll leaned on his wife; he was moving without his cane.

Renata took a pull of her wine spritzer. She was feeling more dangerous every second.

"What's wrong?" Cade said. "Tell me."

Burn it down, she thought. But she was too afraid. If she told Cade about what had happened with Miles, he might forgive her. That was her fear. If she told him and he forgave her, she would never be free; she would always be indebted to him.

"Nothing's wrong," she said. She picked up a handful of mixed nuts. "I'm just hungry."

"Are you sure?" he said. He was asking her, but his voice was revved up with a false playfulness; he sounded like he was acting. And then Renata realized why: Claire Robinson was standing a few steps behind them, alone, chuckling to herself over the witticisms needlepointed on Suzanne's throw pillows. *LORD, DO NOT LEAD ME INTO TEMPTATION. I CAN FIND IT JUST FINE BY MYSELF.* She was listening to every word they said, and now that the adults were outside it was rude not to include her in the conversation. Cade, with his brilliant breeding, should know that.

Renata turned, forced her stiff face into a smile. "So you and Cade went to Choate together," she said to Claire. "That's exciting. I never met anybody that Cade went to Choate with." This wasn't strictly true. There was a girl at Columbia who had graduated from Choate a year behind Cade. She wore black capes and a lot of eye shadow. She had dyed her hair white, and when she saw Cade and Renata on campus she wolf-whistled and yelled out, "Cay—dee! Cay—dee, bay-bay!" The girl, her name was Esther, scared Renata; Renata wondered if Claire knew her; maybe they were friends.

"Yeah," Claire said, twisting her dirty hair. "We've known each other a long time."

"A long time," Cade echoed. "My dad and Mr. Robinson went to business school together. And Claire and I grew up here together summers."

Claire smiled at Cade over the top of her mug of tea. "All those JYC dances."

"Right," Cade said.

Renata bent over for another cracker. She was picking up an awkward vibe. Claire had a crush on Cade; she'd probably suffered from it her whole life.

There was a burst of laughter from outside. Renata, Cade, and Claire looked out at the two couples. Suzanne and Joe were arm-in-arm, as were the Robinsons, all of them gazing at the water. From here, they looked like nice people. How difficult would it be to just play along with this fantasy—to indulge Cade and Claire as they reminisced and used acronyms she didn't understand, to drink more wine, to eat lobster drenched in lemon butter, to laugh and chat and revel in being one of the most privileged people on earth out on the deck of Vitamin Sea? Could Renata make herself do it? Could she pretend she was someone else entirely?

"So where did you go to college, then?" Renata asked.

"Bennington," Claire said, and this sounded right to Renata. There seemed to be a lawlessness to Claire, starting with a blatant disregard for how to dress for this dinner party. Claire wasn't wearing a bra; her nipples poked right through the threadbare white T-shirt. Action probably would have loved the girl, and Renata tried to love her, too—she was the exact opposite of her mother and Suzanne. But there was something about Claire that irritated Renata, a cool knowingness, a sense of superiority. She moved around the house with confidence, even a sense of ownership—as though, someday, it would all be *hers.* "Vermont's a long way from New York City," Claire said. "So I barely saw Cade at all during college. Except for the semester in London, spring before last."

"You went to London, too?" Renata said. By Cade's account, the semester abroad had been overrated, yet he went because *that was what one did.* One attended the London School of Economics and bought a closetful of hand-tailored shirts. Renata supposed that, being a married woman, a semester abroad would be out of the question for her, though she and Action were desperate to go to Barcelona. They wanted to stroll the *Rambles* at midnight, drink sangria, learn to flamenco dance. It would be so much better than Cade and Claire stuck in cold, fussy London. "That's a coincidence. Both of you there at the same time."

Cade and Claire just stared at Renata like she had two heads. She gingerly touched her bruise; it reminded her of Sallie.

"Claire and I went to London together, actually," Cade said.

"Huh?" Renata said. There was some meaning to be extracted from the way he said "actually." Renata looked at them, side by side now, as though they were standing at a front door, about to welcome Renata into their home. Then she got it. They had dated, been lovers. Really? It struck Renata as funny and sweet—almost. A part of her recognized how much they had in common: Their parents were friends; they had all that shared history. Cade could play the flaming liberal when he wanted; had he been antiestablishment when he was with Claire? Renata could picture him holding Claire in his arms. She was tiny, doll-like, featherlight; he could pick her up with one hand. Had he liked that? Had he touched her nipples? Had he kissed her nose, with freckles so dark and distinct he could count them?

Renata twisted her ring to the inside of her hand; for the umpteenth time today it made her feel ashamed. And to make matters worse, Claire was staring at her again. What *was* her problem? Renata recalled the childhood retort: *Take a picture, it lasts larger.*

"I have to go to the ladies' room," Claire said. She disappeared into the front of the house.

Cade took Renata's arm a bit more forcefully than was necessary.

Somewhere in the house, the phone rang. Renata wrested her arm free and snarfed another handful of nuts. Manners of a barnyard animal, but she didn't care. Nicole rushed from the kitchen to the deck with a significant glance at Renata. Even Nicole knew about Cade and Claire; that was why she had suddenly been so friendly. It was amusing to see Renata made a fool of. Nicole fetched Suzanne from the deck and Suzanne sailed past, leaving Joe to plop in a teak chair.

"Renata," Cade said. "Listen to me."

"You dated her?"

"Renata—"

"She's your ex?"

He sighed. "Yes. We were together, off and on, for a long time. Since we were freshmen in high school."

Renata did the math. "Seven years?"

He nodded. "We broke up after London. But Renata—"

"But what?" Renata said; then she held up her hand. "On second thought, don't say anything. Don't explain. Please." She felt like Cade had just handed her something precious—a legitimate reason to be angry. She could be angry because at no time during the ten months of their courtship had Cade mentioned his seven-year relationship with Claire Robinson. There had been occasional references to a "girlfriend in high school"; Renata thought there had been more than one. She could be angry because she had been tricked into giving up dinner with Marguerite so that she could stay here and suffer through lobsters with Cade, his ex-girlfriend, and his ex-girlfriend's parents. She could even be angry on Claire's behalf; this couldn't be pleasant for her, either.

There were murmurs about the phone call. Who was it? Was it Miles? Had Sallie died? Renata nixed this last thought; she wouldn't be able to bear it.

"You've got quite a bruise on your chin," Cade said. "Miles didn't . . . *hit* you, did he?"

"Go to hell," Renata said.

"I was going to explain it all when I came upstairs earlier," he said. "But you told me to go away."

"Please," Renata said. "Don't."

"Don't what?"

"Don't pursue this. I am not willing to talk about it right now."

Suzanne approached, holding a fresh glass of wine. Renata doubted she needed it; her eyes were bright and wild, and she seemed unhinged.

Her always-perfect hair was mussed, which was to say a thick strand fell across her forehead, into her eyes.

"Renata?" she said.

Renata raised her eyebrows, a gesture that hurt, physically, because of her face.

"That was your father on the phone."

Renata's heart plummeted and skipped at the same time, like a stone scudding across the road.

"He's here, on Nantucket!" Suzanne said. "He's joining us for dinner!"

7:18 P.M.

Everyone was in a hubbub about Daniel Knox's arrival. Suzanne had given Nicole instructions to set another place at the table—thank God she'd had the foresight to order extra lobsters—and then make up the west guest room.

"He won't have much sun in the morning," Suzanne said. "But if we give him enough wine, he'll be grateful for that."

Cade was pacing. "We're going to have to tell him as soon as he gets here," he said to Renata quietly. "Maybe I should run out to the airport to get him myself; that way I could tell him alone. I should have asked him for your hand. People still do that, you know. If I hadn't been so sure he would say no—"

"He knows already," Renata said flatly. "I told him."

"What?" Cade said. "You told him when?"

"This morning," she said. "While you were sailing. I called him and told him."

"I thought we were going to wait," Cade said.

"I couldn't just have him not *knowing.* He's my father."

"So that's why he's here, then," Cade said. "He came to take you back."

"You may find this hard to believe," Renata said, "but I am an adult woman. A human being with my own free will. I'm not an object that can be handed over or taken back."

"I never implied you were," Cade said.

"You imply it all the time," Renata said. "Just because we're engaged doesn't mean you own me."

Claire appeared from the powder room. Her face looked dewy, like she had splashed it with water. "I finally figured it out," she said. "Where I've seen you before. It was today, at the beach. You were at Madequecham, right? You were there with Miles? When they pulled that girl out of the water?"

Now it was Renata's turn to stare. Claire had been at Madequecham? Claire had seen Renata there?

"Renata was there with Miles," Cade said quickly, as though he sensed Renata might deny it. "He kidnapped her for the afternoon."

"Lucky you," Claire said. "I've always thought Miles was hot."

"So what's the deal with that chick, anyway?" Cade said. "Is she going to be okay?"

"Yeah," Claire said, turning to Renata. "Did you *know* her?"

"My sunburn is bothering me," Renata said. "I may run up and put on some more aloe before Daddy gets here."

Outside, she heard Kent Robinson ask, "So what's this fellow Knox's business, anyway?"

"Insurance," Joe Driscoll said. "Or reinsurance."

"I'll be down in a few minutes," Renata said.

Once she was upstairs, she had to remind herself to breathe. She turned on the light in her room and threw all of her belongings into her duffel bag. She started whispering to Action, *I am getting out of here. You could not pay me enough money to stay.* She threw her damp bathing suit in, and the aloe mask, though she decided to leave behind the monogrammed beach bag, Miles's shirt, and Suzanne's list. Renata inhaled, exhaled. Her father, Claire, Sallie. On the one hand Renata couldn't believe the way things were turning out, and on the other hand it made all the sense in the world. She was going to get caught, but it hardly mattered. No one could tell her what to do.

She heard the Driscolls and the Robinsons below her on the deck. Suzanne said, "I've never had this happen before, at the last minute like this. He said he'd get a hotel—"

"But really," Mrs. Robinson said. "It's August! What was he thinking? We have extra room, Suzanne, if—"

"Oh, we have *room,*" Suzanne said.

Renata did not hear Cade or Claire. They were, no doubt, huddled in the living room, where Claire was describing Renata's treachery. *And then she followed Miles up into the dunes. They were gone for a while.* Renata looked long and hard at her engagement ring. Three karats, twelve thousand dollars. She had owned it now for seven days, but not for a second had it felt like it was hers. The ring came off easily. Renata left it on top of the dresser.

Renata checked the hallway. Clear. She hitched the strap of her duffel bag up over her shoulder and took off down the hall toward the back staircase. A light was on in one of the bedrooms. Renata stopped and peered in. She was so nervous, so giddy with her crime-movie escape tactics that she nearly laughed. Nicole was in the room, making up the bed. She snapped out the fitted sheet and it billowed. Renata watched her for a second, studying her face. It was grim, disgusted, and melancholy. Renata felt like she had X-ray vision; everything that had once been hidden in this house was now crystal clear. Nicole and Miles shared the apartment above the garage. *I have a roommate.* But he never said who it was. Miles and Nicole were sleeping together. *I'm sorry,* Renata thought. *I am truly sorry.* She snuck past, her bag bumping against her hip. At least she knew the kitchen was empty. She tiptoed down the back stairs (*The Driscolls have servants,* Action's voice said; *they have slaves*) and out the side door. Renata's sunburned skin puckered in the night air. She was standing in gravel by a row of trash cans next to the tall hedge that shielded Vitamin Sea from the western neighbors. Renata waited in the near dark until she heard the Range Rover start up and saw the headlights looping round.

Now, she thought. *Now!*

She heard a sound. Mr. Rogers was at the side door, mewing. He wanted to come with her, maybe.

"Good-bye," Renata whispered.

And she ran.

7:33 P.M.

Four glasses of champagne and nothing to eat—no wonder the room seemed off-kilter—and yet Marguerite couldn't bring herself to move. She poured another glass of champagne, already dreading the headache she would have in the morning. She should go get the mussels from the fridge, the aioli. She should tear off a hunk of bread; it might act like a sponge. The problem with having no sense of taste was that food held zero appeal and eating fine, beautiful food was an exercise in frustration. Marguerite would know, intellectually, that the mussels tasted like the ocean and that the aioli was heady with garlic and Dijon, and yet in her mouth it would be mush. She didn't dwell on the loss of this sense much anymore—after fourteen years it was a fact of life—though she often wondered what it felt like to be blind, or deaf. Was it as disheartening to imagine a painting by Brueghel or Vermeer, or a sunset on a winter's night, or your own child's face, but be trapped in darkness, even with your eyes wide open? Was it as ungratifying to remember the exultant tones of the "Hallelujah Chorus" on Christmas Eve, or a guitar riff of Eric Clapton, or the sound of your lover's voice, but be wrapped in baffling silence?

The grandfather clock went through its half-hour spiel. Seven thirty: the very moment this whole tumultuous day had been about. *Can I feel sorry for myself now?* Marguerite wondered.

There was a knock at the door. Surely not. But yes, Marguerite heard it: three short, insistent raps. She looked in the direction of the front hall but was too petrified to move. She sat perfectly still, like a frightened rabbit, well aware that if someone looked through the proper window at the proper angle, she would be fully visible.

Another knock, four raps, more insistent. Marguerite didn't fear someone trying to hurt her as much as someone trying to help her. She rose slowly, got her bearings with the room, eyed a path from her seat at the dining-room table to the front door. She cursed herself for not getting dressed; she was still wearing the kimono. She thought about all the brilliant minds who had written about drinking—Hemingway a master among them with his wine bags made from the skin of animals and the simple repetition "He was really very drunk." And yet no one had ever captured the essence of four glasses of champagne on an empty stomach. The way the blood buzzed, the way the eyes simultaneously widened and narrowed, but most of all the way one's perception of the world changed. Everything seemed strange, funny, outrageous; the situation at hand became blurred, softened—and yet so clear! Someone was knocking on the door and Marguerite, drunk, or nearly so, rose to answer it.

There had been many, many nights of serious drinking at the restaurant. The cocktails, the champagne, the wine, the port, the cordials—it was astounding, really, how much the customers drank, how much Marguerite herself had consumed on a nightly basis. Lots of times she had stumbled home, leaning on Porter, singing to the empty streets. Lots of times her judgment had been compromised—she had said things that were indiscreet, unwise, and possibly even cruel; she had done things she regretted (the episode in the pantry with Damian Vix came to mind), and yet she kept on drinking. She loved it to this day; she thought it was one of God's marvelous gifts to the world—the sense of possibility alcohol inspired. As her hand turned the doorknob, she conceded that she had been lucky; alcohol had never gotten the best of her the way it had, say, Walter Arcain. She had never tipped back whiskey at ten in the morning and then hit an unsuspecting jogger from behind while driving erratically over the speed limit on icy roads. The mere thought sobered Marguerite so that when she swung open the door, heedless of who it might be—hell, it could be the mailman with his irregular hours—she was frowning.

"Aunt Daisy?"

Marguerite heard the words before she focused on the face. *She came after all,* Marguerite thought, and then checked to see if it was true. Renata Knox, her godchild, stood before her—red in the face, panting, sweating, with a plummy bruise to the left of her chin. Her white-blond hair was in a ponytail, she wore a white shirt and a pink skirt, and slicing through her small breasts was the strap of an unwieldy duffel bag. It looked like she had run in her sandals all the way from Hulbert Avenue;

it looked like she was trying to escape the Devil himself—and yet she was utterly beautiful to Marguerite. She was Candace.

"Darling!" Marguerite said.

"Can I come in?" Renata asked. "I'm kind of on the lam."

"Yes," Marguerite said. "Yes, of course." She ushered Renata into her hallway, still not quite believing it. Was this really happening? She came anyway? Marguerite shut the door, and when Renata kept a steady, worried gaze on the door, Marguerite locked it.

"Thank you," Renata said.

"Thank *you,*" Marguerite said.

Marguerite pulled the second champagne flute from the freezer and filled it to the top. Meanwhile, Renata dropped her heavy bag.

"Is it all right if I stay the night?" she asked.

"Of course!" Marguerite said. She was so happy for herself, and for whichever of the upstairs bedrooms that would finally be used, that it took her a moment to realize something must have gone terribly wrong at the house on Hulbert Avenue. Marguerite handed the champagne to Renata, who accepted it gratefully. "Go right ahead and drink. You look like you need it. We'll have a proper cheers in a minute." Marguerite had planned to serve the hors d'oeuvres in the sitting room, but it suddenly seemed too stuffy; the grandfather clock would watch over them like an armed guard. So, the kitchen table. Marguerite fetched the polka-dotted cocktail napkins, the toothpicks, the mussels, the aioli. She decided to stay in her kimono. She didn't want to leave Renata for even a minute; she might disappear as quickly and unexpectedly as she had come.

"Sit, please, sit!"

Renata collapsed in a kitchen chair. Her face was still a bright alarm.

Sunburn. She impaled a mussel on a toothpick and zigzagged it heavily through the aioli.

"Can you tell me what happened?" Marguerite said, settling in a chair herself. This was supposed to be an evening when Marguerite did the talking, and she had worried about how she would negotiate the requisite small-talk-to-start. Now there was no need.

Renata didn't seem keen on explaining right away. She was too busy feasting. She brought the mussels successfully to her mouth a third of the time—otherwise, dollops of aioli landed on the table, which she didn't notice, or on the front of her white shirt, which she did. She swabbed those drops with her cocktail napkin, leaving behind pale smudges.

"Sorry," Renata said. "I'm starving."

"Eat!" Marguerite said. "Eat!"

"These are delicious," Renata said. "They're divine."

She finished her glass of champagne, burped quietly under her breath, and tried to relax. She was safe, for the time being, though her whereabouts wouldn't be a secret for long. Someone would come sniffing around shortly, but Renata wasn't leaving. They couldn't make her.

"Darling?" Marguerite said.

Renata had seen pictures of Aunt Daisy in her parents' wedding album. In these pictures, she wore a purple dress; her hair was in an enormous braided bun that sat on top of her head like a hat. There were different pictures of Marguerite in the back of the album, pictures taken during the reception. In one photograph, Marguerite's hair was down—it was long and wavy, kinked from the braiding—she had changed into a black turtleneck and black pants; she was holding a cigarette in one hand, a glass of red wine in the other. Renata's parents were also in the photograph, her uncle Porter, her uncle Chase, and one of the restaurant's waitresses. It looked like a photograph from a Parisian café—everyone was half-smiling and sexy and smoky. Marguerite, though she wasn't pretty like Renata's mother, appeared very glamorous in these pictures, and that was the image Renata had clung to. Her godmother, a famous chef with sophisticated sensibilities, her mother's best friend.

The Marguerite sitting next to Renata now had a short, shaggy haircut (truth be told, it looked like she'd cut it herself) and she seemed much older than she had in the pictures. She was wearing a pink silk kimono, an article of clothing that intrigued Renata; it was exactly the kind of thing Action would have picked out of a vintage shop and boldly made her own. The kimono looked like it had history, character; if Suzanne Driscoll owned such a kimono she would have stored it in the attic, pulling it out only for costume parties, Halloween. But here was Marguerite wearing it to dinner. Despite the haircut and the aging, Marguerite had style. And more important, most important, the thing Renata had counted on, was that she exuded generosity, tolerance, acceptance. Renata felt she could confide everything, just from the way Marguerite had said, *Can you tell me what happened?* Just from the way she said, *Darling?*

"Well," Renata said. "I ran away. Again."

Marguerite nodded, and gave a little smile. "So I see."

Renata wondered what kind of scene was enacting itself back at Vitamin Sea. Had her father arrived yet? Had anyone noticed she was missing? How long would it be until the phone rang? By leaving, Renata hoped she had made herself clear: She wasn't going to marry Cade. She wasn't going to conform to Cade's idea of her, or the Driscolls' idea, or her father's idea. She was going down another road entirely.

"I cheated on my fiancé today," Renata said. "I had sex with someone else."

Marguerite's eyebrows arched. The secret smile faded. Renata felt a wave of regret. Did Marguerite disapprove? Renata felt guilty about Miles, but mostly because she had been up in the dunes with him when Sallie had her accident. The act of sex bothered her less—though there were Cade's feelings to consider, and now Nicole's. The sex had seemed predestined, somehow, the inevitable result of the bizarre circumstances she found herself in today.

"If I tell you about it," Renata said, "you won't judge me, will you?"

"No," Marguerite said. "Heavens, no." She sipped her champagne, nibbled a mussel, and nodded her head. "Go ahead," she said. "I'm listening."

The clock ticked; it ding-donged out quarter till the hour, then the eight strokes of the hour. The number of mussels diminished as the number of used toothpicks piled up on the side of the platter. When the mussels were gone, Marguerite brought Renata a hunk of bread to wipe up the aioli. The girl remembered her manners from time to time, placing her hands daintily in her lap—then, as she got swept away by her own storytelling, she would forget them, downing her champagne in thirsty gulps, polishing the inside of the aioli bowl to a shine. Meanwhile, Marguerite tried to predict the girl's needs—more champagne, more bread, a fresh napkin—while trying to keep track of the tale she was spinning. Renata started with the engagement only a week earlier—a diamond ring in a glass of vintage Dom Perignon at Lespinasse. Impossible to say no to, Marguerite had to agree. Then Renata moved on to the house on Hulbert Avenue, and the boy's parents, Suzanne and Joe Driscoll. Did Marguerite remember them? Marguerite couldn't say that she did. Renata described the mother, Suzanne, very carefully: the red hair swept back and curled under the ears, the big blue eyes, the skinny forearms jangling with gold bracelets. Marguerite didn't remember anyone like this—or rather, she remembered too many people like this, so many years in the business, so many nights in the summer, it was impossible to keep track. Marguerite felt like she was letting Renata down by not recalling the couple who were to be her in-laws, but then Renata smiled wickedly and it became clear she was glad Marguerite didn't remember them.

"How about the Robinsons?" Renata said. "She's short with dark hair, weighs about eighty pounds. His first name is Kent; he wears half spectacles."

"No, darling. I'm sorry. If I saw them, maybe . . ."

Again, the look of someone who had just won a secret point.

Marguerite heard about Renata's jog to the Beach Club, the discovery of Suzanne's wedding list, the conversation in which Renata told her father of her engagement, followed by the decision to go with this boy, Miles, to Madequecham Beach.

"I can see how that would be hard to resist," Marguerite said.

"You don't even know," Renata said.

And then there was a change in Renata's tone. Her voice grew somber; the words came more slowly. Marguerite heard about a girl named Sallie, decorated like a Christmas tree with tattoos and piercings. Sallie had a surfboard in the car; it got loose and smacked Renata in the jaw, hence the bruise. Renata disliked Sallie. But then came the discovery of the cross Marguerite had fashioned so long ago (she could remember pounding it into the ground with a mallet meant for tenderizing meat, her bare hands freezing) and Sallie was there, next to Renata as Renata knelt before the cross and kissed it. Next Marguerite heard about heavy surf, Sallie handing Renata her sunglasses, Sallie kissing Renata on the jaw. Marguerite heard about the volleyball game, sandwiches smushed by beer bottles, Sallie and Miles sitting on either side of Renata, making her feel, somehow, like she had to choose sides. Marguerite heard the girl Sallie's words, *Will you keep an eye on me?* And, *Don't go getting married while I'm gone.*

"I said I'd keep an eye on her," Renata said. "But as soon as she was back in the water I disappeared into the dunes with Miles."

Marguerite nodded.

"And she went down. Hit her head on her board and went under and when they found her, when they brought her out, she wasn't breathing."

"Oh," Marguerite said.

"It was like I caused the accident," Renata said. "I said I would watch her and then I didn't, I was off doing this other horrible thing, and I feel . . . not only like I was negligent, but like it happened because of me."

"You feel responsible," Marguerite said. "Guilty."

"God, yes," Renata said.

Marguerite stood up to slide the asparagus into the oven. Guilt, responsibility—these were topics Marguerite knew intimately. She should be able to offer some words—*things just happen; we don't have any control; we can't blame ourselves for the fate that befalls others*—but Marguerite didn't believe these words to be true. Guilt lived in this house with her; it was as constant as the clock.

"I understand the way you must be feeling," Marguerite said. She cut two pieces of tart and set them down on the table.

Renata blinked her eyes; tears fell. Marguerite replenished their champagne and touched Renata's hand.

"Is the girl all right?" Marguerite said. "She went to the hospital?"

"She went to the hospital here," Renata said. "Then they flew her to Boston in a helicopter. I don't know if she's all right. I have no way of knowing."

Marguerite sniffed the air, as if she *were* a witch, or an intuitive person, capable of divining things.

"She's all right," Marguerite said. "I can feel it."

"Really?" Renata said.

For a second, Marguerite felt cruel. The conversation with Dan seemed like aeons ago, but she did recall his words: *You're like Mata Hari to her, Margo. She's going to listen to what you say.*

"Really," Marguerite said. "But if it makes you feel better, we can call someone. We can call the hospital in Boston and ask."

Renata searched Marguerite's face. More tears threatened to fall and Marguerite panicked. She wasn't prepared for any of this. But then Renata's features settled and she picked up her fork. She gazed at the tart. "This looks delicious," she said. She took a bite, then eyed the dark glass doors that led to Marguerite's garden, as though she expected the bogeyman to appear.

She started talking again—about Cade demanding that Renata stay for dinner, about the Robinsons, their daughter, Claire, the ex-girlfriend no one had mentioned to Renata, about the shared semester at the London School of Economics.

"The semester before he met me," Renata said. "And he never said a word."

Marguerite forked a bite of tart. The pastry was flaky, the cheese creamy, and although she registered no flavor at all, she could tell the tart was a success. Renata devoured hers, then pressed the pastry crumbs into the back of her fork. Marguerite cut her another piece, a small piece, because there was more food to come.

"Oh, thank you, Aunt Daisy," Renata said. "Thank you just for listening. It has been the weirdest day. Nothing was as I expected it to be."

"Indeed not," Marguerite said. She marveled at Renata's story. And Marguerite thought *her* day had been extraordinary—because she left the house, visited old friends, stopped by her former place of business, because she drove to the country side of the island and back, because she had telephone conversations, because she polished silver and drank tea, because she looked at old photographs, because she sacrificed her Alice Munro stories in favor of the old, useless stories of her own life, because she cooked a meal for the first time since Candace's death. Ha! That was nothing.

"I'm glad you escaped," Marguerite said, only a little ashamed at herself for lauding the girl for leaving a dinner party without any excuse, warning, or word of good-bye. Marguerite was being horribly selfish. "You're safe here."

"I haven't told you the real reason I left," Renata said.

"You haven't?"

"No."

"Okay," Marguerite said. The champagne had officially gone to her head. She had lost her wits, or was about to. *Water,* she thought. She fetched a tall glass of ice water for herself, and one for Renata, who simply stared at it. "What is the real reason you left?"

"My father is here."

Marguerite hiccupped, then covered her mouth and closed the top of her kimono with her other hand. "Here where?"

"On Nantucket. He flew in tonight. When I snuck out, Cade was leaving to pick him up at the airport."

Marguerite let her eyes flutter closed. She remembered Dan's promise to show up if he thought that was what it would take to save his daughter. *But look, Dan,* Marguerite thought as she gazed at Renata—bruised from the surfboard, sunburned, her two ringless hands pushing her corn silk hair back from her forehead—*she saved herself.*

"Daddy will call," Renata said. "Once he realizes I'm gone. He'll come here."

"Yes," Marguerite said. How it panicked her, knowing she didn't have much time, knowing she still had a story of her own to tell. "I'm afraid you're right."

8:11 P.M.

Claire Robinson was the first one to notice Renata's absence. She figured Renata was upstairs in her bedroom, pouting like a child, because no one, it seemed, had told her that Cade and Claire had been a couple for seven years. Either that or she was hiding, afraid Claire would tell Cade about her frolic with Miles in the dunes. Claire chuckled; this was just too good. She had battled her parents about coming tonight—haw could they possibly ask her to share a meal with Cade and his new fiancée? But when Claire saw Renata, a bell sounded. It took her a while to be sure—but sure she now was—Renata was the same girl that everyone playing volleyball at Madequecham that afternoon had watched Miles lure into the dunes. Eric Montrose had pointed it out. "There goes Miles with another Betty. Young one this time."

Claire tiptoed up the stairs, grinning with the stupid pleasure it gave her to be privy to this scandalous information.

To the left, Claire spied the dark doorway of Cade's room, a room she knew intimately. How many nights had she sneaked up and slept with Cade, both of them naked and salt-encrusted from a late-night swim, arms and legs and hair entwined until one of them woke up to the sound of the early ferry's horn or the cry of seagulls. Claire sighed. She had thought, for certain, that she and Cade would be married. Now she was headed to graduate school at Yale to study Emily Dickinson, and she should be grateful she hadn't married Cade Driscoll. Hell, if Miles had looked at *her* twice, she would have followed him into the dunes herself. She might even tell Renata this; they would conspire. *Don't worry, I won't tell a soul.*

Claire tapped on the guest room door. Light spilled out from the bottom of the door, but Claire heard no noise. Maybe Renata had fallen asleep; Claire noticed the way she had been pounding back the drinks. Claire knocked again. Nothing. She cracked the door. "Renata?" Claire hated to admit how much she loved the name; it was a poetic name, both harmonic and sensual. It meant "reborn."

Claire peeked into the room. It was empty. The bed was made, though a bit rumpled; there was a head-shaped indentation in the soft, white pillow. One of Suzanne Driscoll's canvas beach bags lay on its side on the floor among a scattering of sand. Inside the bag, Claire found a damp beach towel and a piece of folded-up paper. Did she dare? She checked the bathroom, empty, and the deck, deserted. Renata must have slipped downstairs.

Carefully Claire smoothed out the paper. It was a list, written out in Suzanne's hand. Wedding stuff. Claire sniffed. The list was silly—flowers, cake, party favors—and yet Claire felt a pang of . . . what? Regret? Jealousy? She reminded herself of her disastrous reunion with Cade in London: He admitted that he felt nothing for Claire anymore, nothing but a great fondness, a brotherly love. Claire was quick to agree. *Of course. I feel the same way.* This wasn't true, but at least she'd escaped with her pride.

Claire laid the list on top of the dresser. As she did so, she gasped. Sitting there all by itself like someone's forgotten child was Renata's engagement ring. The stone was huge, square, in a Tiffany setting; the stone must have been close to three karats. Claire turned the ring in the light.

The diamond was clear, flawless. Claire's hands were trembling. Did she dare? Why not? It was obvious at that moment, though perhaps only to Claire, that Renata was gone for good.

Claire slipped the ring onto her finger. It fit perfectly.

The ride from the airport to Hulbert Avenue was a quarter hour of hell for Daniel Knox, forced as he was to listen to Cade, a kid with a shirt and a watch and a car more expensive than Daniel's own, make a twenty-point case about why he should be allowed to marry Renata. Daniel said very little during this presentation, figuring silence was the best way to put Cade on edge. Daniel had given his "blessing" to Renata that morning, in a panic. Never in fourteen years of raising his daughter had he used reverse psychology, but for some reason the announcement of her engagement cried out for it. If Daniel said yes when she expected him to say no, it would frighten her. And it must have worked, because clearly Renata had said nothing to Cade about Daniel's cheerful response. Despite the tedium of listening to Cade describe how he would care for Renata, Daniel felt triumphant. He knew his daughter better than these people.

It was very dark, and Nantucket, out of town, had few streetlights, but Dan peered through the window nonetheless. It was a singular experience, returning to the place where your life had once been. He had *lived* here—alone at first, running the Beach Club, then he lived here with Candace, and then with Candace and Renata. He knew the streets, cobblestone, paved, dirt, and sand; he knew the smells of bayberry and of low tide on a still, hot day; he knew the sounds of the ferry horns and the clanging bell at the end of the jetty. This had once been his home, but now he was very much the visitor.

Cade hit the turn signal and pulled into a white shell driveway. The house loomed in front of them—it was huge, bedecked, terraced, landscaped, a castle of a place, and every light in the house was on; it was as bright as a Broadway stage. Dan couldn't help thinking that this looked suspiciously like new construction; they had probably bought the lot and then torn down the fine old summer cottage that stood here in order to build this monstrosity. *VITAMIN SEA,* the quarterboard said.

"So I hope, Mr. Knox, that Renata and I have your blessing," Cade said. "I know she's young, but we wouldn't be getting married until the spring."

"Spring?" Daniel said, to show he was listening.

"Yes, sir. After school is out."

Daniel Knox said nothing else, though he was dying to utilize his "one shouldn't get married until one's traveled on three continents" speech. He was cognizant of the fact that he had shown up without warning and would be relying on Cade's family and their good graces for a place to sleep tonight. And dinner—Daniel wasn't particularly hungry, but he'd gathered from something Cade said walking from the terminal to the parking lot that there was a dinner party in progress. Lobsters or some such, with family friends, and that was what had, miraculously, kept Renata from going to Marguerite.

A woman with red hair and the tight face of someone who'd had plastic surgery appeared in the door, waving a glass of wine.

"Welcome!" she called out. "Welcome, welcome!"

"My mother," Cade whispered.

Uh-huh. Dan felt a familiar disappointment. Why was it that women his own age went to so much trouble to beautify that they ended up erasing any natural beauty they might have possessed in the first place? It was one of the things that had kept Dan from dating again after Candace's death: the way women tried so hard. Cade's mother, for example. Clearly a pretty woman, if you could get past the fact that she was fifteen pounds underweight, had suffered a chemical peel, colored her hair, wore too much makeup and too much jewelry. Women like this made Daniel long for Candace, who had looked her most beautiful first thing in the morning when she woke up, or after she got home from a run—when she was sweaty, sticky, and the picture of all-natural glowing good health. Candace would never have done these things to herself. Her idea of glamour was a shower and a clean dress.

Daniel Knox ascended the stairs and shook hands with the woman, Cade's mother. She planted a wet kiss on his cheek, which seemed awfully familiar, though she was probably under the impression they were soon to be family—and what, really, was more familiar than showing up unannounced?

"I'm Daniel," he said. "It's nice to meet you."

"Suzanne," she said in an exaggerated way, as though she weren't trying to tell him her name so much as sling it at him. *Sha-zaam!* "I'm so glad you could come."

"I'm sorry it was last-minute," Daniel said. He had no good reason to offer these people for why he'd shown up out of the blue, and he was counting on them being too polite to ask.

"Come in; come in," Suzanne said. "Your timing is perfect. Nicole is just putting dinner on. And you must meet our dear friends the Robinsons. They've been so charmed by Renata that to meet you is just icing on the cake."

"Icing," Daniel repeated. He was ushered into the foyer, where there was a black-and-white parquet floor and a Robert Stark painting hanging on the wall—the lone sailboat with the flame red sail; every house on

Nantucket must have that painting. There was a curving staircase to the left; down the stairs came a pale milkmaid of a girl with messy dark hair. She smiled at Daniel.

"Hello!" she said.

"Claire, this is Daniel Knox, Renata's father. Daniel, this is Claire Robinson, a dear friend of the family. Claire and Cade went to Choate together."

"I see," Daniel said. He extended a hand to the girl, then began to wonder after the whereabouts of his own daughter. It didn't surprise him that she'd skipped the airport run; Cade had obviously seen that as an opportunity for a man-to-man chat. However, now that Daniel was in this enormous house with perfect strangers, he wanted to set eyes on his own flesh and blood. Renata was not going to be happy to see him; she would be decidedly unhappy, angry, mortified. That was the risk he had taken.

They moved into the living room, which was decorated in seventeen shades of white. Suzanne asked what he was drinking.

"Scotch," he said. "Straight up."

"You and my husband will get along just fine," Suzanne said. She did not make the drink herself but called a young black woman in from the deck and asked her to make it. "Mr. Knox would like a scotch straight up."

The woman nodded. Daniel grew warm around the neck. He hated to see people accept orders on his behalf.

"And how is dinner coming along?" Suzanne asked.

"All set, ma'am."

"Okay, then, please bring Mr. Knox's drink out to the deck. Cade? Claire? We're ready to sit."

"Yes, Mother," Cade said.

They moved out to the deck. It was a stunning evening, warm but breezy, with a black velvet sky and a clear crescent moon. And to be on the water like this, with Nantucket Sound spread out before them like a kingdom—well, overdone house aside, Daniel Knox was impressed. He introduced himself to the father, Joe Driscoll, who did not stand to shake hands but merely nodded and said jovially, "So glad you could join us!" His hands were clasped in his lap, one hand was rattling around like a Mexican jumping bean, and it was then Daniel remembered that Renata had mentioned that Joe Driscoll was sick. Parkinson's. Daniel bowed to him.

"Thank you for having me."

Next, Daniel met the elder Robinsons, Kent and Kathy.

"We hear you used to own the Beach Club," Kathy said.

"Years ago."

"We've been languishing on the wait-list for what seems like forever," Kathy said.

"Same here," Joe Driscoll said. "It's quite the exclusive place."

"We belong to every club on the island," Kent Robinson said. "Except for that one. So naturally that's the only one my wife cares about."

"Mmmmm," Daniel said. They were talking like he was somehow responsible for their exclusion from the club. "I don't have a thing to do with it anymore. I sold it in '92, the year my wife died."

The group nodded mutely, Joe Driscoll tipped back the ice in his drink with his good hand and they all listened to the clink of it in his glass. Suzanne came out, waving her wine. "Okay, everybody sit! Kathy, you're next to Daniel, and Kent, you come over by me. Claire, you're right there, and Cade—"

Daniel watched the Robinsons sit. Joe Driscoll stayed where he was, turning in his chair and raising an arm with his empty glass toward the young black woman, who whisked it away to be refilled. Claire sat, and Suzanne. Only Daniel and Cade remained standing, presumably wondering the same thing. The table was laden with a feast: A shallow bowl at each place held a two-pound lobster; there was a platter with twenty ears of steamed corn, an enormous bowl of green salad, Parker House rolls. But there was no Renata.

Daniel shot Cade a questioning look. Cade said, "She went upstairs to put some aloe on her face. She got quite a sunburn at the beach today."

"Who?" Suzanne said.

"Renata."

Suzanne glanced around the table as if double-checking each person's identity. "My word," she said. "Renata!"

"She's upstairs?" Daniel said.

"She wanted to fix her face," Cade said. "But that was a while ago. Maybe she fell asleep."

Claire coughed into her napkin.

"I'll go get her," Cade said.

"I'll go get her," Daniel said. "If she's hiding from anyone, it's me."

"Hiding?" Suzanne said. "Don't be ridiculous. You both sit. Nicole will go up and get Renata, won't you, Nicole?"

"Certainly," Nicole said.

"Wonderful," Suzanne said. "Thank you. The rest of us should start before everything gets cold." She lifted her wineglass and waited with a pointed gaze until Daniel and Cade took their places. "Cheers, everyone!"

Nicole trudged up the back stairs. She felt cranky and venomous, like a snake ready to strike. She had worked nearly fourteen hours today, she had not had a moment to take her dinner break, and she was pretty certain that, despite all the beautiful promises he had made in order to lure her to Nantucket from South Africa, Miles was leaving her. It would be unfair to say this was all Renata's fault. Things between Nicole and Miles had been strained all summer—he constantly asked her to take his shifts so he could hang out at the Chicken Box or go to the beach with the lesbian surfer girl. Since one of them was responsible round-the-clock for meeting Suzanne Driscoll's needs and desires, there was no time to be alone together, no time for sex except the wee hours (when, quite frankly, Nicole was too tired), no time to enjoy each other's company or even plan their winter escape—a three-month kayaking trip to Irian Jaya. No, it wasn't Renata's fault, though Nicole suspected they had slept together. Nicole heard it in Miles's voice that afternoon when he'd called to say he wasn't coming back. Miles had wanted Nicole to pack his stuff up and leave it hidden in the bushes at the end of the driveway; he wanted Nicole to tell Suzanne he was quitting. Nicole was incredulous. *I am not going to do your dirty work. Come pack your things yourself. Come tell Suzanne to her face, like a man.* But he claimed he couldn't—he told her the whole sob story about the lesbian surfer girl hit in the head with her board, nearly drowned, and then he confessed that the real reason he couldn't return to Vitamin Sea was because of a bad judgment call he'd made in regard to Renata. He'd kidnapped her for the afternoon; he'd convinced her to skip lunch with the madame. *And you know what Suzanne will think,* he'd said. Oh yes. It was what Nicole thought herself, it was what Cade thought, it was what everyone thought when they heard that Miles and Renata had slipped away together for the afternoon. Bad judgment indeed. Nicole had hung up on him, midsentence. She would never again trust an American.

Nicole knocked on the guest room door with authority, as though she were a dormitory proctor, or the police. "Renata?" she said. "Please open up, Renata. I'm afraid your absence has been detected downstairs." She knocked again, with such force the door rattled in its frame.

Renata had had . . . three wine spritzers? She was probably passed out facedown, drooling all over the linens. Nicole knocked once more for propriety's sake, then opened the door. Simply telling Suzanne that Renata wasn't answering wouldn't be good enough; Suzanne liked tasks completed.

Nicole was no detective, but she was able to put two and two together and draw a conclusion in a matter of seconds—the room was empty; the duffel bag that, only that morning, looked as though it had exploded everywhere was gone; the much-celebrated engagement ring sparkled on top of the dresser. On the floor lay Miles's shirt, his white polo with the small rip in the collar. Nicole picked it up. Sure enough. *The little bitch,* Nicole thought. *Gone with Miles.* Nicole hissed with anger. What a day. The worst of her life.

8:50 P.M.

They didn't sit down to their proper dinner until nearly nine o'clock, and by that time they had emptied both bottles of champagne. Marguerite suggested a trip to the basement for a third bottle, and Renata, because she was younger and more sure-footed, led the way down the stairs. The basement wasn't as scary as she imagined. There was a washer and dryer, a folded-up card table, a basic box of tools, and a wall rack that must have held five hundred bottles of wine.

"My secret cache," Marguerite said. "What I took from the restaurant when it closed."

"Geez," Renata said. Marguerite slid a bottle of 1990 Pommery off the shelves, and they went back upstairs.

They decided to be brave and eat in the dining room, where the table was set and waiting. Marguerite pulled all the shutters on the front of the house closed and yanked the curtains firmly across.

"No one can see in," she said.

Renata settled into a chair while Marguerite served pieces of rosy tenderloin ladled with béarnaise, crispy asparagus, and slabs of homemade bread served with the butter from Ethan's farm. Marguerite filled their flutes to the top and set the bottle of Pommery in the wine cooler. She eased herself down across from Renata and raised her glass. Derek and the Dominos played in the background. Yes: This was what Marguerite had been dreaming of when she woke up this morning.

"Salud," she said.

Their flutes clinked like a tiny bell. The clock struck nine.

"I feel so at home here," Renata said. "Nothing at all like I felt on Hulbert Avenue. I feel so peculiarly at home."

"I'm glad," Marguerite said.

"Will you tell me about my mother?"

"Yes," Marguerite said.

"I don't have anyone else to ask," Renata said. "Dad won't talk about it."

Marguerite cut a small piece of meat. "Have you thought to ask your uncle Porter?" This was something she'd been wondering. Porter had been there for nearly all of it; he could have shed a lot of light.

"Caitlin doesn't let him see us," Renata said. "She doesn't like my dad, I guess, and she doesn't like Uncle Chase. She has no use for anybody in Porter's family."

"That's too bad," Marguerite said. She wished she could say she was surprised, but Porter had gone against all good sense when he decided to marry Caitlin. "Surely you see him at school?"

"Never," Renata said. "He only teaches graduate students now, and every time I stop by they say he's busy."

"Right," Marguerite said. She cleared her throat. "Well, let's see. Your mother."

As Marguerite talked, Renata ate slowly. She laid her knife and fork down while she was asking a question; otherwise she savored every bite of the meat, the rich, lemony sauce, the asparagus, the chewy bread, thick with butter. When the clock struck the quarter hour, the half hour, the hour, Renata straightened, arched her back, stretched her legs under the table. Marguerite poured what seemed like an endless stream of champagne into Renata's glass, which she didn't need. She was very drunk—and yet, instead of impeding Renata's concentration, it enhanced it. Renata absorbed every word: Marguerite and Porter meeting at the Musée du Jeu de Paume under Renoir's *Les Parapluies,* Marguerite's first minutes on Nantucket when Porter brought her to the new restaurant, the wormy chestnut floors, the driftwood mantelpiece, the prix-fixe menu, the night Porter first brought in Candace, the kiss, the tin of saffron. The walk with Candace through the moors after Porter's picture appeared in *The New York Times* with another woman, the dinners when Candace and Marguerite sat by the fireplace in the very next room talking until well after midnight, the night in July when Daniel Knox first set foot in Les Parapluies and made it clear he wasn't leaving until Candace agreed to go out with him. Their first meal alone together, Marguerite said, was one that she cooked them: cedar-planked salmon and potatoes Anna.

"I'll bet your father never told you that," Marguerite said.

"Never," Renata said. "Do you think he even remembers?"

"He remembers," Marguerite said. "He swore I put something in the food that made him fall in love."

Renata smiled. She was wallowing in this talk like a pig in mud; she was sucking it in like a dog with his snout stuck out a car window. Her parents together, her parents in love—it was Renata's own history she was hearing about.

"Your father thought I was back in the kitchen stirring potions in my cauldron, my uncut hair graying in its braid. Even before your mother died, he never fully trusted me."

Renata kept quiet; she sensed this was probably true. She marveled that it was growing so late and no one from Vitamin Sea had called—not her father, not Cade.

"No one has called," she said.

"I unplugged the phone," Marguerite said.

"And no one has come by."

"Not yet," Marguerite said. She sipped her water and took a rejuvenating breath. She enjoyed telling Renata about the good times: the restaurant open, Marguerite and Porter together, Candace alive. Was she making herself clear? Could the child see her mother as Marguerite saw her—showered after a long day of exercise and sun, in one of the cocktail dresses that left her shoulder bare. Her blond hair freed of its elastic and spilling down her back. Her easy manner, like the best women of that time, full of simplicity and grace.

"She desperately wanted to go to Africa," Marguerite said. "She wanted to open a restaurant in the Sahara."

"She did?"

"We went to Morocco together, your mother and I."

"You did?" In her mind, Renata heard the metallic rain of coins falling from a slot machine. Jackpot. This was something she never would have known about her mother if she weren't sitting right here. Her mother had been to Morocco. She had gone running through the medina in a Boston Red Sox cap; the men who owned the carpet shops, the men who carved *thuya* wood, the men who served conical dishes filled with *tagine,* the men who drove the taxis, the men who pressed juice out of oranges on the Djemaa el-Fna, they had called after Renata's mother in wonder. It was her blond hair, her smile, her sweet and awkward French—the whole country fell in love with her.

"Your mother was one of those people," Marguerite said. "Everyone was drawn to her—friends, perfect strangers. She could do no wrong; she could get away with anything. I can't tell you how many times I wished I could be like that. I wanted to . . . *be* Candace." Marguerite arranged her silverware carefully at an angle on the side of her plate and folded her napkin. She had never admitted this to anyone; she hadn't even thought it all the way through in her own mind—but yes, it was true. When Marguerite stood in front of Madame Verge's mirror she thought she would grow up to be like Candace. Marguerite smiled. "I'm going to guess you take after your mother."

Renata's first instinct was to deny it. Her father loved her unconditionally, of course, and Action and Cade. She attracted people easily—like Miles and Sallie. Renata wasn't sure what all these people saw in her; she wasn't sure who they thought she was—she didn't even know herself yet. Her mother had had a magnetism, something natural she emitted from her heart: love, maybe, patience, understanding. Whereas Renata felt like she was constantly giving pieces of herself away, she was engaged in a juggling act to keep everyone in her life happy. *Yes, I'm being careful; yes, you're my best friend; yes, I love you the most.*

Renata shook her head. *No, not me. I'm not like that.* "Whatever happened with the restaurant in Africa?"

"Nothing happened," Marguerite said. "While we were in Morocco, your mother discovered she was pregnant."

"With me?"

"With you."

"So I ruined her dream, then?"

"No, no, darling. It would never have worked out anyway, for a million reasons. It wasn't meant to be."

"You could still do it," Renata said.

Marguerite laughed. "That time has come and gone."

"No, really," Renata said. "You could open a restaurant over there like you and Mom wanted. You could leave this place for a while." Renata's voice sounded concerned and Marguerite wondered if it contained any pity. The last thing she wanted was for the child to pity her.

"Leave?" Marguerite said, as though the thought had never occurred to her. It had, of course. Sell her house and move to Paris. Or Calgary. Start over someplace new, like she was nineteen instead of sixty-three. "I'll have to think about that."

Marguerite cleared away the dinner plates and left Renata in the dining room to enjoy the champagne, the flowers, the ticking of the old clock. All this information at once, it was a lot for a person to process; Renata could use a few minutes of quiet. As Marguerite rinsed the dishes she pondered the girl's words. Out of the mouths of babes. *You could still do it.* Marguerite thought about the night Candace first mentioned the restaurant. She remembered Candace's anger with her, her frustration. *I want you to reimagine.* She could reimagine now, with ease: A restaurant with walls of canvas, swathed like the head of a Bedouin. A place in the middle of the desert that would be hard to reach, where some nights it would be just Marguerite alone, enjoying enough romantic atmosphere for fifty people. She would wait those nights for the ghost who left footprints in the sand.

Before she set out dessert, Marguerite retreated to her bedroom to fetch the photographs from her dresser. There were only the two that Marguerite had to show, though there were hundreds of others—pictures from the restaurant opening, benefit nights, pictures from Candace's wedding, from Morocco—that Marguerite kept in a wooden wine crate in the storage space of the smallest of the five upstairs bedrooms. Maybe one day down the road she would have the courage to pull that box out and sift through it, but for now there were just these two pictures. Marguerite set them down in front of Renata. Renata picked up the christening picture first and squinted. Admittedly, there wasn't much light in the dining room, but Marguerite didn't want to spoil the atmosphere by making it brighter.

"That's me?" Renata said. "The baby?"

"That's your christening party."

"It was at the restaurant?"

"Of course. You're my godchild. The one and only."

Renata gazed at it with the most heartbreakingly earnest expression Marguerite had ever seen.

"You don't have pictures of Candace at your house?" Marguerite asked.

"Oh, we do," Renata said. "Just not this one."

"Right," Marguerite said. The girl's life had more holes than Swiss cheese. But here was a hole Marguerite could fill. Renata, Marguerite, and Candace at the party following Renata's christening. "It was probably the most glamorous christening party any child ever had. We had foie gras, black truffles, champagne, thirty-year port, Cuban cigars, caviar—"

"Really?" Renata said. "For me?"

"Really. For you." Daniel had insisted on footing the bill for everything, though Marguerite had given a case of champagne and Porter had, somehow, conjured up the cigars. "It was a big deal, your arrival in the world."

"I love this picture," Renata said.

"Yes, so do I." Marguerite studied it, trying to see with fresh eyes. Both she and Candace looked so proud, so awestruck, that they might have been the baby's parents: mother and godmother.

The other photograph was black-and-white. It was taken one long-ago autumn; it was just Candace and Marguerite sitting at one of the deuces facing Water Street. Neither of them was looking at the camera; they had plates of food in front of them, but they weren't eating. Marguerite was saying something, and Candace's head was bent close to the table, listening. Marguerite doesn't remember the moment the photo was taken or even the night; it was snapped by one of the photographers from *The Inquirer and Mirror.* It ran the week of October 3, 1980, on the Seen on the Scene page. Marguerite had been furious; she'd called the newspaper and threatened to sue, though the editor of the paper had laughed and said, *The picture's completely innocuous, Margo, a slice of life, and it's a damn attractive shot of you both, I might add.* The caption under the picture read: *Chef Marguerite Beale engages in tête-à-tête with friend Candace Harris at French hot spot Les Parapluies.* Marguerite never quite came around to the editor's point of view—to her the picture was an invasion of privacy; it reminded her uncomfortably of the picture of Porter with Overbite Woman in *The New York Times.* It put Marguerite and Candace's intimacy on display—however, it was this very thing that eventually endeared the picture to her, and she asked that the editor send her a print.

"Dessert?" she said. She spoke the word brightly, though inside she panicked. Dessert, no matter how sweet, meant the end. Marguerite would have to tell about the end.

"I'd love some," Renata said.

Marguerite disappeared into the kitchen.

9:30 P.M.

The young black woman came out onto the deck with her eyebrows knit together and her mouth pressed into a flat line. Even in the night air, lit only by candles and tiki torches, Daniel could tell she was a few shades paler than she'd been when she left. Daniel stood up and the table grew quiet. They had just been talking about the Opera House Cup sailing race, and an old boat they all remembered called *Christmas.*

"Renata?" Daniel said. "She's asleep?"

"She's gone," Nicole said.

Cade whipped around in his chair. "What?"

"The guest room was empty," Nicole said. "Her things are gone."

The Robinsons were quiet, except for Claire, who coughed into her napkin, in order to keep from laughing. She wasn't sure why but she found this very funny. All except for Cade, who looked like he was fourteen years old again, dropped off for his first day of boarding school, abandoned by his parents, separated from his friends. He had been so forlorn that first day, whereas Claire had felt free at last.

Suzanne laughed, too, but shrilly. "That's ridiculous," she said. "Where did she go?"

Nicole felt like Suzanne was daring her to come right out and say it: *She left with Miles.* But Nicole couldn't stand to think the words, much less speak them out loud to a tableful of people, and furthermore, she hated being the center of attention. *Don't shoot the messenger,* she wanted to say, though she knew they would anyway. That was why she'd left the ring right where it was, on top of the dresser. There was no use bringing down all the bad news at once; they could find the ring themselves when they went upstairs to investigate.

"You're sure her stuff is gone?" Cade said.

"I'm sure."

"I know where she is," Daniel said.

"Where?" Cade said.

"Where?" Nicole asked, forgetting herself. Then she thought, *You don't know where she is. You're only her father.*

"She's with her godmother," Daniel said. "Marguerite Beale."

"No," Cade said. "She called Marguerite to cancel."

"That's where she is," Daniel said. "Trust me." Faces around the table seemed unconvinced, or uncaring, but what these people didn't understand was the allure Marguerite held. Daniel had kept Renata away from her for fourteen years. He didn't want Renata to have to hear Marguerite's side of the story, her teary admissions, her apologies. But Renata had sought it out on her own. In a way, Daniel felt proud of her. She hadn't been taken in by these people; she hadn't been hypnotized by their wealth; she had kept her eye on what was important to her—seeing Marguerite, and learning about her mother.

Suzanne exhaled loudly and cradled her pink cheeks in her hands. She looked completely deflated. Daniel thought he might feel gratified by this, but instead he was ashamed. He very calmly sat back down. The poor woman had put a lot of work into tonight's dinner party and Renata had poked a hole in it. Despite Daniel's overwhelming desire to see his daughter, he wasn't willing to shred the evening further; he would salvage what he could. Renata wasn't going anywhere; she was safe. Daniel buttered a Parker House roll and took a bite.

Cade glared at him. "I'm going over there to get her."

Daniel swallowed the bite of roll and sipped his scotch. "Leave her be, son."

"What do you know about leaving her be?" Cade said. "She left because you showed up. I'm sure that's why she left."

"I'm sure you're right," Daniel said.

And because she doesn't want to marry Cade, Claire thought.

And because she had sex with Miles, Nicole thought. *She was swept along by his beautiful promises.* Just the way Nicole had been last winter when she was working as a breakfast waitress on the harbor front in Capetown. Miles had suckered her in with promises of love and money. Nicole was encouraged, however, by the confidence of the father's words. Maybe Renata did go to whatshername Beale's house. Hadn't she been talking about it with Suzanne that morning in the kitchen? Nicole sensed a filament of hope. Maybe Renata didn't go with Miles after all. For the first time all day, Nicole felt relieved. She felt almost happy.

"Let's just eat," Joe Driscoll said in a voice that would not be argued with. He held the end of an ear of corn with one hand and his butter knife with the other. Neither hand was shaking.

Cade noticed this, but he was too agitated to let it register. He threw his napkin onto his plate. "I'm going up to see for myself," he said.

"Cade," Suzanne said. "Listen to your father, please. Eat your dinner."

The Robinsons returned to their dinner plates; Kathy Robinson murmured something complimentary about the salad dressing. Joe Driscoll buttered his corn. Claire Robinson sipped her tea, which had grown cold. She knew, as did Nicole, who slipped into the kitchen, as did Daniel Knox, as did the others deep down in their hearts, what Cade was going to find.

9:42 P.M

Nine thirty was Lights-Out at Camp Stoneface and had been all summer. The twelve girls in Action Colpeter's cabin were doing their nighttime-whisper thing, which sometimes lasted until midnight if Action didn't lay down the law. However, tonight, for some reason, Action was antsy, eager to wash her hands of Camp Stoneface and the million and one rules she hand to enforce. What she wanted more than anything was to be *alone,* so she could *think.*

"I'm going to be right outside on the stoop," Action announced to her campers. "So do not attempt any funny business." Such as drawing with indelible marker on the girl who fell asleep first, such as telling stories, real or made up, about doing drugs or having abortions.

Action took her flashlight and her pen and notebook and sat on the top step right outside the cabin door. If they thought they were escaping tonight to raid the mess hall for stale potato chips or to make mooning noises through the screens of the boys' cabin, they were mistaken. Action started a letter to Renata. *Hola, bitch-ola!* But this sounded too cavalier. The truth was, Action was worried about Renata. Action had been born with nearly perfect instincts, and her instincts about Renata this second rang out: *Doomsday.*

Action heard a noise coming from the grass nearby. Even after eight weeks in the thick woods of all-but-forgotten West Virginia, Action was still freaked out by the wildlife—the bullfrogs, the owls, the bats, the mosquitoes. Action had grown up on Bleecker Street; her experience with wildlife had been limited to the freaks she'd seen on Christopher Street and in Alphabet City. The noise in the grass sounded suspiciously like a bullfrog. It made a buzzing, thrumming sound at regular intervals. Action shined her flashlight in the frog's direction; if she kept her eye on it, it wouldn't land on her—*plop!*—wet and slimy. She was wearing jeans and running shoes. She could step on it or nudge it away. The noise persisted. Action climbed down off the steps and hunted through the grass for the frog.

Her flashlight caught a glint of something silver. What was this? Action bent down, peering at the thing that was making the noise as if it were as unlikely as a moonstone. Ha! She snapped it up, triumphant. It was a cell phone, the ringer set to vibrate.

Eight weeks ago, discovering a cell phone in the grass would have made Action livid. Cell phones—and all other treasures from the world of IT—were strictly *verboten* at Camp Stoneface. Action and her fellow counselors took great joy in stripping campers of their cell phones, Game Boys, iPods, and laptops. But now, in the third week of August, discovering a cell phone in the grass, at night, while she was alone, was like a sign from the Virgin Mary herself. Action was supposed to call somebody.

She flipped the phone open. It was a Nokia, sleek and cool in her palm. And—would wonders never cease?—she got a signal.

Action felt a flash of guilt. *Hypocrite!* she screamed at herself in her mind. She hadn't even let twelve-year-old Tanya, who was the youngest and best-behaved child at the camp, call her mother on her mother's fortieth birthday. However, Action's presiding sentiment was that enough was enough and she had had enough of West Virginia unplugged. If she had to sing "Take Me Home, Country Roads," one more time, she would have a Tourette's-like outburst. *"Blue Ridge Mountains, Shenandoah River."* No, sorry.

One call, she thought. *I'll only make one call.* The call should rightly go to her brother, Major. Action received a letter from him every single day, written out in Miss Engel's neat block script. He wrote about how he went to Strawberry Fields, ate ice cream, watched some kid fly a kite that looked like a parrot. It was hot, he wanted to go on vacation to the ocean the way they did when Action was at home, but Mom had work and Dad had work. *I miss you, Action. I love you miss you love you.* He always signed his own name, and this was what hurt Action the worst. His name in wobbly capitals, a smiley face drawn into the O. Action had never gone eight weeks without seeing him, and what she missed the most was him needing her. Of course, she had twelve needy cases evading sleep inside the cabin, but it wasn't the same.

Action should have called Major—woken him up if he was asleep—but she didn't. She'd had a Doomsday instinct about Renata all day long in the front of her mind. Action was worried that something terrible had happened—she'd gotten hurt, or she died. The girl never looked both ways before she crossed the street; she was constantly getting her foot stuck in the gap between the subway car and the station platform; in nearly every way, Renata Knox acted like a person who didn't have a mother. However, that was one of many things that Action loved about her. Renata was her best friend, the sister she never had; she was special. Their friendship couldn't be explained any easier than one could explain peanut butter and jelly. Why? Just because.

Action dialed Renata's cell phone number, praying she wasn't sleeping over at Watch Boy's new apartment on Seventy-third Street. The phone rang. Action stepped away from her cabin and closer to the bordering woods, despite the hoots of owls. She didn't want her girls to hear. The phone rang four, five, six times; then Renata's voice mail picked up. *Hi! You've reached the voice mail of Renata Knox.* Action grinned stupidly. Voice mail was still the old girl's voice, which Action hadn't heard in eight weeks. *I can't answer my phone right now—*

Because I'm being held up at gunpoint, Action thought. But suddenly that didn't feel right. *Because I'm cuddling up with Watch Boy.* Yep, that was probably more like it.

Action cleared her throat; then after the beep, she whispered, "Hi, it's me." Action had never had a friend whom she could say those three words to. Before she met Renata, Action had never imagined having a *Hi, it's me,* friend; she never realized how important it was—to be recognized by another person, known instinctively, whether she was calling from down the street or the Tibetan Himalayas, whether she was calling from the woods of West Virginia or the D train. Action hoped that for the rest of their lives they would be each other's *Hi, it's me.* "I found a cell phone in the grass and I decided to break the first commandment of Camp Stoneface and call. I've been thinking of you all day. I hope you're all right. I have a funny vibe, like something is happening. Maybe you joined the circus today, maybe you found religion, but something is happening; I can feel it. Don't call me back. I'm about to turn this phone over to the authorities where it rightly belongs. So . . . write me a letter. Tell me you're all right. I'll be wait—" Action was cut off by the second beep. Renata always accused her of leaving the world's longest messages. Action thought to call back, to finish, but she had promised herself only one phone call.

I love you, she thought. *Love you like rocks.*

10:10 P.M.

In Room 477 of the Trauma Unit of Massachusetts General Hospital, Sallie Myers opened her eyes.

Ohhhkay, she thought. *Very strange.*

She registered *hospital,* herself pinned to a bed, stuck in both arms and attached to machines that blinked and beeped; she noted a white curtain to her right, shielding her from someone else, or someone else from her. She tried not to panic, though she had no idea why she might be in a hospital. *Think back,* she told herself. *Slowly. Carefully.* But there was nothing.

She was afraid to move; she was afraid she would try and find herself unable. So she remained still, except for her eyes, which roamed the room, and thus it was that she discovered a figure huddled in a chair off to the left, at the edge of her field of vision. She turned her head. Her neck was stiff, but it worked. It was . . . *Miles* in the chair. He was asleep, snoring.

Ohhhhhkay, she thought. What did she do to deserve waking up in a hospital room with Miles? Miles, Miles. She was still drawing a blank.

A minute passed, or maybe not a full minute but fifty or sixty beeps of the machine, which might have been counting the beats of her heart. Her heart was beating. Sallie figured she might as well try her arms. She turned her wrist. The right one moved just fine, but her left side felt fuzzy and not quite attached, like it was a prosthetic arm. Sallie gazed down. It was her arm. She touched it with her right hand. She could feel her own touch but she couldn't make the arm move.

At that second, some people walked in. There was a gasp from one of the people—a woman, Sallie's mother. Sallie's father followed right behind, and then a dark person, who towered over Sallie's parents like they were little children. Pierre. Pierre was here? Sallie couldn't recall ever seeing Pierre anywhere but at the bar.

Sallie's mother rushed to the side of the bed and took hold of Sallie's leaden arm. "You're awake!" she said. "The nurses told us it sounded like you were awake. They can tell from the way they monitor the machines out there."

Sallie's father clapped his hands in a rallying way. He was the head football coach at the University of Rhode Island. "I knew you'd snap out of it."

Pierre approached next, timidly. He was out of his element, away from the noise and the beer and the grime of the bar, away from his back office with the black leather couches and his computer where he played Tetris while the kids out front got smashed and slam-danced. "Hello, gorgeous," he said.

Sallie turned her attention back to her mother, her beautiful mother, who taught classical music at Moses Brown, who wore bifocals when she read a grocery list, who had fretted and worried so much over Sallie's three older brothers that she had been content to just let Sallie be. Bartending? *Fine.* Surfing? *Good for you.* A pontoon boat down the Amazon River? *You only live once.* Sallie's eyes filled with tears. She'd had a dream that her mother had died. In the dream, Sallie was driving down a dusty road and she spotted a white cross in the brush. She stopped, checked it out. The cross was for her mother. Sallie had screamed when she saw the cross, *Wait! Mom, wait! I'm getting married!*

"Honey?" Sallie's mother said. "How do you feel?"

"Confused," Sallie said. The cross hadn't been a dream. It was real. But how? Sallie's mother stood right in front of her. "What am I doing here?"

"You had a surfing accident on Nantucket," her father said. "You hit your head. They say you were underwater for a while."

"Just a little while," her mother said.

"And where am I now?"

"At Mass General. In Boston," her mother said. "Pierre called us. And your friend . . ." She nodded at the chair where Miles slept. ". . . was here when we arrived."

"Miles," Sallie said. It all came back to her like something that fell from the sky and landed in her lap. Miles picking her up at the house with the girl, Renata, who was the cutest, sweetest thing Sallie had ever seen. So innocent, so young, so clean. It was *her* mother the cross was for. She had knelt before it. Kissed it.

"The doctors say they expect you to be fine," Sallie's mother said. "You may feel stiff and numb for a while, but there's been no brain damage."

"Thank God for that!" Sallie's father said.

"You're going to be fine, doll," Pierre said.

"Did Renata come?" Sallie asked. "Did she come to the hospital with Miles?"

"Who?" Sallie's mother asked.

Sallie watched Miles snoring in the chair. *Wake him up!* she wanted to say. *Ask him if Renata came!* But Sallie knew the answer was no. After all, why would she?

10:25 P.M.

Ethan Arcain couldn't sleep. His wife, Emily, was dozing heavily beside him, her breathing deep and regular. His boys were asleep in their respective rooms; the house Ethan had built himself was solid and quiet. Out their open bedroom window Ethan could hear the occasional bleat of one of the goats. He and Emily had eaten grilled steaks for dinner with a fresh corn salsa and heirloom tomatoes drizzled with pesto. Such were the feasts when one lived on a vegetable farm. Ethan had drunk too much—he and Emily split a bottle of Shiraz from the Barossa Valley—and then he'd opened a second bottle to drink alone, despite Emily's warning eyebrows.

He hadn't been able to tell Emily about Marguerite coming to the farm that afternoon, despite Brandon announcing, "Dad introduced me to an old friend of his today."

Emily had been pulsing basil and garlic and pine nuts in the Cuisinart. "Oh yeah, who was it?"

Brandon conveniently chose that moment to leave the kitchen. "Nobody," Ethan said. "Someone who used to come to the farm back in Dolores's day, when I was just a kid."

"Someone you had a crush on?" Emily said.

"Oh God, no," Ethan said. "Nothing like that."

He hadn't been able to tell Emily, and then he drank too much and now both things weighed on his mind. He had lived on Nantucket his whole life; lots of people knew his history: his parents' brutal split, his father's drinking. And yet no one brought home the guilt and the shame of being Walter Arcain's son like Marguerite.

You never had to carry his load, Marguerite said. But he did. Despite the fact that he had worked hard to create a decent, peaceful, productive life, he did.

It had happened during the first week of February. Ethan had graduated the year before from Penn State with a degree in agriculture; he had confessed to his mother that he was in love with her new husband's oldest daughter, Emily; he was working as a waiter at the Jared Coffin House to make money. He had a deal all worked out with Dolores Kimball; he was going to buy the farm from her when she retired. Everything was moving forward—not quickly, maybe, but in the right direction. And then, just before service for the weekly Rotary luncheon, Ethan's mother came into the dining room to say that Walter had killed someone and not just someone but Candace Harris Knox. She was jogging out in Madequecham; Walter was driving the company truck, drunk out of his mind.

To a young man who had helped put vegetables and flowers on the table at Les Parapluies since he was ten years old, Candace Harris Knox was a living legend. She was much older than Ethan but captivating nonetheless. The blond hair, the way she could run for miles without ever looking tired, the successful husband, the adorable young daughter. Candace was royalty on the island; she was a goddess among women, Ethan knew it just from the way she carried herself, just from the genuine ring of her laugh. And Walter Arcain, Ethan's father, had run her down like she was a frightened rabbit.

Ethan pulled the quilt up under his chin. He was freezing, and a headache was starting from the wine. When he rolled over, he checked the red numbers of the digital clock. Ten thirty. He figured Marguerite's dinner with Renata must be nearly over.

10:41 P.M.

Cade Driscoll was nothing if not disciplined. He was nothing if not obedient. And so, in the end, he suffered through the world's longest dinner—through lobster cracking, corn munching, and people talking just to cover up the obvious awkwardness of Renata's desertion. Then he endured dessert—blueberry pie with ice cream, coffee, and port. He sent mental pleas to his mother: *Let the Robinsons go home! Set them free!* But his mother seemed to feel that the longer the Robinsons stayed, the less likely it was that they would remember the night as a disaster. Finally, finally, at nearly eleven o' clock, Kent Robinson stood up and offered to get his wife's wrap. Good-byes were said. Claire kissed Cade on the mouth and said, "She wasn't good enough for you, anyway." As if she knew something Cade didn't.

As soon as the Robinsons' car pulled out of the driveway, Joe Driscoll excused himself for bed. When he shook Daniel Knox's hand he said, "Any chance you'll be up for sailing tomorrow?"

"Let's see how things go."

"Yes, yes," Joe said. "Let's." He grabbed Cade's elbow before going up, but he said nothing. Suzanne, in a moment of mercy, set her wineglass on the lowboy and said, "I'll worry about cleaning up in the morning. Good night, all." And she followed Joe up the stairs.

Once his parents were gone, Cade turned to Daniel Knox. "How about you?"

"I'm a night owl," Daniel said. "I may sit on the deck for a while."

"Okay," Cade said. "Good night, then." He marched up the stairs, as if dutifully going to bed.

He had sneaked out of dinner, just for a minute, pretending to use the bathroom, and he'd called Marguerite's house, but he got no answer—the phone rang and rang. Then he called Renata's cell phone. Voice mail. He hung up without leaving a message. He wanted to believe Renata's disappearance had nothing to do with *him* per se. It was just a nineteen-year-old girl doing as she wished without thinking her actions through. She was upset with Cade for making her cancel dinner, and the whole thought of her father showing up freaked her out. So she bolted.

Cade pushed open the door to the guest room, thinking maybe she had left him a note. He turned on the light. He was looking for a piece of paper—and that was what drew his eyes to the list. He snapped it up, but seeing that it was just something in his mother's handwriting, he balled it up and threw it on the floor. He looked out on the deck, the deck where only the night before he and Renata had made love while his parents entertained friends below them. But the deck was deserted. Ditto the bathroom. It wasn't until Cade was ready to leave the guest room—and, quite possibly, make a surreptitious run over to Quince Street—that he noticed the ring. It was right on top of the dresser, as obvious as the nose on his face, so maybe he had seen it a minute ago and just not admitted it to himself.

He picked up the ring, squeezed it in his palm, and sat on the bed. *Renata.* He thought he might cry for the first time since who knew when. People had said he was crazy to propose to a nineteen-year-old girl. *She's too young*—his own parents had warned him of that—*she hasn't had time to get started, much less be finished.* And then there was Claire's parting shot: *She wasn't good enough for you, anyway.* Claire was jealous—either that or she suspected Renata had been indiscreet with Miles, which was, Cade had to admit to himself, entirely possible. Even so, Cade loved Renata fiercely. Yes, she was young, but she was going to grow into an amazing woman, and he wanted to be there for that.

He rocked back and forth on the bed. She didn't want him. Cade had the urge to knock on his parents' bedroom door and, like a three-year-old, crawl into their bed, have his mother smooth his hair, have his father chuck him under the chin. But his parents weren't like that; they weren't nurturing. They had given him every possible advantage and they expected him, now, to make his own way. He would have better luck seeking comfort from Daniel Knox. Yes, Cade thought, he would go down, pour himself a scotch, and confide in the man who might have been his father-in-law. Daniel knew Renata better than anyone. Maybe he could tell Cade something that would make him understand.

Cade walked down the hall, past the west guest room, in case Daniel had come upstairs. But the door to the west guest room was open; the room was dark and empty. Cade stumbled down the back stairs into the kitchen—it had been cleaned by somebody, Nicole probably—and into the living room. Empty. Cade walked out onto the deck. The table had been cleared, the tiki torches extinguished. The deck was deserted. Cade gazed out at the small front lawn, and down farther to the beach.

"Daniel?" Cade whispered into the darkness.

But he was gone.

11:00 P.M.

At eleven o' clock, with the old clock's grand recital of the hour, its eleven ominous bongs, Marguerite brought out dessert. Two *pots de crème,* topped with freshly whipped cream and garnished with raspberries. Renata was fading; Marguerite could see it in the way her pretty shoulders were sagging now, her eyes staring blankly at her own reflection in the dark window. Marguerite set the ramekins down with a flourish. This was it. There was no more champagne to pour. Nothing left to do but tell her. Marguerite's heart hammered away. For years she had imagined this moment, the great confession. Many times Marguerite had considered going to a priest. She would sit in the little booth, face-to-face with the padre, and confess her sins—then allow the priest to touch her head and grant her absolution. But it would have made no difference. Marguerite knew that God forgave her; his forgiveness didn't matter. Forgiveness from the girl in front of her, Candace's child, that did matter.

Marguerite had imagined this moment, yes, but she still couldn't believe it was about to happen. Her chest felt tight, like someone was squeezing her windpipe. Heart, lungs—her body was trying to stop her.

"I'd like to talk to you about your mother's death," she said.

"You don't have to tell me," Renata said. "You don't have to say anything else."

"I'd like to anyway. Okay?"

"Okay."

"A couple of years after you were born, your parents bought the house in Dobbs Ferry. They wanted a place to spend the winter. Your father thought maybe Colorado, but your mother wanted to be close to the city. She loved New York, and Porter was there. She wanted to put you in a good school; she wanted to be able to take you to the museums and the zoo. It made sense."

Renata nodded.

"They bought the house when you were four."

Renata swirled her whipped cream and chocolate together, like a child mixing paints. She had yet to take a bite.

Marguerite paused. Her task was impossible. She could speak the words, relay the facts—but she would never be able to convey the emotion. Candace had spent months preparing Marguerite for the news—saying that she and Dan were looking at houses off-island, saying they'd found a house in a town they liked, Dobbs Ferry, New York, less than four hours away. Marguerite never responded to these announcements; she pretended not to hear. She was being childish and unfair—they were all adults, Candace and Dan were free to do as they liked, they had Renata to think of, and Nantucket in the winter had few options for the parents of small children. The warning shots grew nearer. One day Candace had the gall to suggest that Marguerite join a book group or a church.

You need to get out more, she said. *You need to make more friends.*

What she was saying was that she couldn't carry the load by herself. She was going to be leaving. But Marguerite, stubbornly, would hear none of it.

You can't leave, Marguerite said. She picked Renata up, kissed her cheeks, and said, *You are not leaving.*

But leave they did, in the autumn, a scant three weeks after Porter returned to Manhattan. In the final days, Candace called Marguerite at the restaurant kitchen every few hours.

I'm worried about you.

Dobbs Ferry isn't that far, you know.

We'll be back for Columbus Day. And then at Thanksgiving, you'll come to us. I can't possibly do the dinner without you.

We're leaving nearly everything at the club. Because we'll be back the first of May. Maybe April fifteenth.

On the day that Candace left, Marguerite saw them off at the ferry. It was six thirty in the morning but as dark as midnight. Dan stayed in the car—Renata was sound asleep in the back—but Candace and Marguerite stood outside until the last minute, their breath escaping like plumes of smoke in the cold.

It's not like we'll never see each other again, Candace said.

Right. Marguerite should have been used to it, sixteen years Porter had been leaving her in much the same way, and yet at that moment she felt finally and completely forsaken.

"Your mother leaving was painful," Marguerite said.

Candace had phoned every day during Renata's nap and Marguerite—despite her claims that she would be fine, that she was very, very busy—came to rely on those phone calls. After she hung up with Candace, she poured her first glass of wine.

"I traveled down to the new house for Thanksgiving like your mother wanted. We cooked three geese."

"Geese?"

"Your uncle Porter took the train up from the city. It was a very big deal. That was the only time in seventeen years that I ever celebrated the holidays with him."

Marguerite closed her eyes for a second and was gone again. Three geese stuffed with apples and onions, served with a Roquefort sauce, stuffing with chestnuts, potato gratin, curried carrots, brussel sprouts with bacon and chives—Marguerite made everything herself, from scratch, while Candace did her best to help. Porter, bald and with a belly, did his old stint of lingering in the kitchen all day, drinking champagne, shaving off pieces of the exotic cheeses he'd brought in from the city, providing a running commentary on the Macy's parade, which played on TV for Renata, who stacked blocks on the linoleum floor.

At the dinner table, they all took their usual spots: Marguerite next to Candace, across from Porter. It was a careful imitation of their dinners at Les Parapluies, though Marguerite keenly felt the difference—the strange house, the evanescence of the occasion—in three short days, she would be back on Nantucket alone, and Porter, Dan, and Candace would return to the lives they had made without her.

Later, though, Porter cornered her in the kitchen as she finished the dessert dishes—Dan was in the den watching football; Candace was upstairs putting Renata to bed. He pushed Marguerite's hair aside and kissed her neck, just like he used to all those years ago in the restaurant. She nearly broke the crystal fruit compote.

I have something for you, he said. *Call it an early Christmas present.*

Marguerite rinsed her hands and dried them on a dish towel. Christmas used to mean pearls or a box from Tiffany's, though in the last few years Porter's ardor had mellowed or matured and he sent an amaryllis and great bottles of wine that he picked up at one of the auctions he attended in New York.

Marguerite turned to him, smiling but not happy. Porter sensed her misery, she knew, and he would do anything short of performing a circus act to get her to snap out of it.

He handed her an envelope. So not the amaryllis or vintage Bordeaux after all. Marguerite's hands were warm and loose from the dishwater, too loose—she fumbled with the envelope. Inside were two plane tickets to Paris. It was like a joke, a story, something unreal, but when she looked at Porter his eyes were shining. She grabbed his ears and shrieked like a teenager.

"Just after the first of the year, your uncle took me back to Paris," Marguerite said to Renata. "Finally. After nearly seventeen years."

"How was it?" Renata said. "Was it like you remembered?"

"No," Marguerite said. "Not at all as I remembered."

Marguerite had convinced herself that Paris was the answer to her prayers, the key to her happiness; her expectations were dangerously high. There was, after all, no way to re-create their earlier time in Paris: Too much had happened; they were different people. Marguerite was nearly fifty years old, and Porter was beyond fifty. They were professionals; they were seasoned; they had money and tastes now. Instead of being caught up in the throes of fresh love, they were comfortable together; they were, Marguerite thought, a pair of old shoes. And yet she held out for romance—a promise from Porter, a proposal. She believed the trip to

Paris was a sign that he was finished with his bachelor life in New York; he was done with his string of other women; the sparkle had worn off; the effort wearied him; he was ready for something lasting, something meaningful. Marguerite had won out in the end for her perseverance. She would finally belong to someone; she would finally be safe.

No, it wasn't the same, though still they walked, hand in hand. Marguerite had compiled a list of places she wanted to visit—this *fromagerie* in the sixth, this chocolatier, this home-goods store for hand-loomed linens, this wine shop, this purveyor of fennel-studded salami, which they ate on slender *ficelles,* this butcher for roasted *bleu de Bresse.* It was January and bitterly cold. They bundled up in long wool coats, cashmere scarves, fur hats, leather gloves, boots lined with shearling. Despite the temperature, Marguerite insisted they visit the Tuilieries, though the gardens were brown and gray, dead and dormant—and afterward Le Musée du Jeu de Paume. The museum was smaller than either of them remembered; it was overheated; the bench where Porter had fallen asleep was gone, replaced by a red circular sofa. They revisited the Cathedral of Notre-Dame. When they opened the door, the draft licked at the flame of five hundred lit prayer candles. Marguerite paid three francs to light one herself. *Please,* she thought. At Shakespeare and Company, Marguerite lingered among the Colette novels and picked one out for Candace while Porter, to her astonishment, bought something off the American best-seller list, a thriller penned by a twenty-five-year-old woman.

"All my students are reading it," he said.

They were staying in a suite at the Plaza Athenee—it was all red brocade and gold tassels; it had two huge marble bathrooms. It was sumptuous and decadent, though a far cry from showering together under the roses. One afternoon, while Porter worked out in the new fitness center, Marguerite lounged in the bubble bath and thought, *I should feel happy.*

Why aren't I happy? Something was missing from this trip. An intimacy, a connection. When she got out of the tub, she called Candace.

"Why are you calling me?" Candace said, though she sounded happy and excited to hear from Marguerite. "You're supposed to be strolling the Champs-Elysées."

"Oh, you know," Marguerite said. "I just called to say hello."

"Just hello?" Candace said. "This must be costing you a fortune. Is everything okay? How's Porter?"

What could Marguerite say? Suddenly, with Candace on the phone, her worries seemed silly, insubstantial. Porter had brought her to Paris; they were staying in a palace; Porter was sweet, attentive, indulgent. He hadn't so much as called his secretary. She couldn't possibly complain.

"Everything's great," she said.

Each night, they dressed for dinner—Porter in a tuxedo, Marguerite in long velvet skirts or the silk pantsuit Candace had sent her from Saks. They went to the legends: Taillvent, Maxim's, La Tour d'Argent. The service was intimidating; the food was artwork; the candlelight was flattering to Porter's face as Marguerite hoped it was to hers. She worried that they might run out of things to talk about, but Porter was as manic and charming as ever; he was so filled with funny stories that Marguerite was surprised he didn't burst from them. And yet she couldn't combat the feeling that he felt it was his job to keep her amused.

One night, at a bistro that had been written up in *Bon Appétit,* they drank three bottles of wine and when they got in the cab they spoke to the driver in fluent French. When they reached the hotel, they were laughing and feeling extremely pleased with themselves. Porter looked at Marguerite seriously, tenderly; he seemed to recognize her for the first time during the trip and maybe in years. They were standing outside the door to their suite; Porter had the old-fashioned iron key poised above the lock.

"Ah, Daisy," he said. He paused for a long time, searching her face. Marguerite felt something coming, something big and important. She wanted him to speak, though she was afraid to prompt him; she was afraid to breathe.

"This is the life," he said.

This is the life? Marguerite nodded stupidly. Porter unlocked the door on his third try; then he shed his tuxedo and called her to bed. They made love. Porter fell asleep shortly thereafter, leaving Marguerite to brush her teeth alone among so many square feet of marble and turn off the lights.

As she climbed into bed she realized she felt like crying. She was too old for this kind of rushing emotion, this kind of searing disappointment, and yet the sorrow persisted; it lay down and embraced her.

"A few weeks after your uncle Porter and I returned from Paris, something happened that took me by surprise. Porter called to say that he had fallen in love with his graduate assistant. Caitlin. She was twenty-four years old. Now, I knew he dated other women in New York. It was a source of enormous heartache for me. He took other women to plays and dances and benefits and restaurants. Once, he took a woman to Japan. He wasn't exactly open about this, but I knew it and he knew that I knew. I never learned a single woman's name except for the woman he took to Japan; that was a favor he granted me. I presumed they weren't important enough to be named. He told me he loved me; he used to say I hung the moon. But he would not commit. I thought maybe when we were in Paris . . . but no. Paris was good-bye. He already belonged to somebody else; every hour he spent with me, he was thinking of this other person. This girl. But I didn't know that. Until."

Until the phone call. Marguerite sensed something wrong immediately. Porter's voice, always booming and upbeat, had been resigned and sorrowful. *You're the greatest friend I have in all the world, Daisy,* he'd said. *And I'm afraid I'm about to hurt you very badly.*

Marguerite had listened, without comprehending a word he said. Back in September, he'd fallen in love with his graduate assistant, twenty-four-year-old Caitlin Veckey from Orlando, Florida. She was red haired and freckled, fresh faced, naïve, she was young enough to have grown up in the shadow of Disney and Epcot. Marguerite imagined her as a cartoon character, a two-dimensional, Technicolor fairy like Tinkerbell. It was all wrong. If Marguerite was going to lose Porter, finally, after so many years, she wanted it to be to a worthier opponent—a sultry, dark beauty who spoke seven languages fluently, a sophisticate, someone with European sensibilities. Or even one of the women Marguerite had imagined Porter with over the years: Corsage Woman, Overbite Woman, Japan Woman. An aging ballerina or show jumper with a degree from Vassar and a trust fund, a closetful of shoes. But it was not to be. Porter had been stolen away by a child, a Lolita. He was in over his head, he said, in love beyond reason, and the only way he could make things right—with the university, certainly, but also in his own heart—was to marry Caitlin.

I'm getting married, Daisy, he said.

She thought of Paris and felt deeply betrayed, embarrassed even. All the usual signs had been absent. There had been no mysterious phone calls, no suspect gifts purchased that she knew of. There was the book he'd bought, and the way he'd worked out religiously at the hotel's fitness center. Twice he'd skipped dessert and he had passed up the Cuban cigars. *Are you getting healthy on me?* she'd asked him, teasing. Now she saw.

Marguerite held the receiver long after Porter hung up, staring out her bedroom window. Snow was falling, blanketing Quince Street. She remembered back to the first moment she saw him, she remembered the quiet sounds of him waking up on that bench in the Jeu de Paume, the way he'd blinked his eyes rapidly, unable to place himself for a moment. She remembered his worn leather watchband, and the first time his long, tapered fingers touched her hair. That was a Porter Harris this Caitlin person would never know, never understand.

"Your uncle Porter called to say he was marrying Caitlin," Marguerite said. "He called to say our relationship was over."

"You must have been devastated," Renata said.

It was like learning of her own death; she'd always known it was coming, but so soon? In this ridiculous way? She was shocked, incredulous; her ego was like an egg found cracked in the carton; she was angry, insulted—and worried for Porter's sake. He'd been tricked by beauty and youth, by sex. He didn't know what he was doing. The end of a seventeen-year relationship seemed too fantastical to Marguerite to be taken seriously. Porter said it was over, he said he was getting married to this young girl from Florida, and he promised he would never bring the girl to Nantucket, meaning he would never return himself. So Marguerite would never see him again. It couldn't just end, she reasoned; their relationship couldn't go from a rich and layered creation to *nothing.* Her way of life, her identity, her whole world, was threatening to shift, to tilt, to dump her into cold, unfamiliar water. She and Porter were no longer together? It was impossible. So yes, *devastated* was a fair choice of words. But the hurt was located in distant parts of her—her brain, her reason, her nerves. (Her hands shook for hours; she remembered that.) Her heart cried out for one person, the way a hurt child called out for her mother, and that person was Candace.

"I called your mother to tell her what happened," Marguerite said.

"The weather was bad, it was snowing, it was horrible weather for traveling, and yet I asked her to come up. She wanted me to come to Dobbs Ferry, but I couldn't move. I was immobilized."

I want to come, Daisy, she said. *Believe me, I do. But Dan is in Beaver Creek looking at a second property and so I'd have to bring Renata—*

By all means, bring her.

I'm worried about traveling with her in this weather. Have you looked at the TV? It's awful. Is it snowing there?

Snowing, yes. Quietly piling up outside.

Okay, Marguerite said. *It's okay. I'm okay.*

Are you?

No, she said, and she dissolved into tears. *Of course not.*

Daisy, don't cry.

Do you understand what's happened? Marguerite asked. *You cannot reasonably tell me not to cry.*

Okay, I'm sorry. There was a long pause, the sound of shuffling papers, the sound of Candace's sighing. *Okay, we'll come. We're coming.*

Marguerite should have backed down at that point; she should have listened to the reluctance in Candace's voice. What did another day or two days or a week matter? It was blizzarding. Asking anyone to travel in that weather was absurdly selfish, cruel even. And yet those words, *we'll come, we're coming,* were the words Marguerite craved. She needed to know there was someone in the world who would do anything for her. That person had never been Porter.

"That night, your mother was on my doorstep, holding you in her arms."

"I came here?"

"I remember it like it was yesterday. You were wearing pink corduroy overalls."

Marguerite had been pacing her house for hours when the knock finally came. She opened the door and found Candace and Renata, bundled in parkas, dusted with snow. As soon as she saw them she felt ashamed. She had guilted her best friend into traveling three hundred miles through a blizzard with a child. Candace had caught a flight from White Plains to Providence, where she hired a car to take her to Hyannis, where she caught the freight boat, which was the only boat going. And yet, in her gracious way, she made it sound like an adventure.

It's a miracle, Candace said. *But here we are.*

"I remember being embarrassed that I didn't have dinner ready. All that jangling around the house, I could have been making a stew. Instead, we ordered a pizza, but the pizza place refused to deliver, so your mother trudged down Broad Street to get it. All those years I had cared for her, but she had turned into a real mother hen. She set the table, whipped up a salad, made me a cup of tea—I wanted wine, of course, but she said no, alcohol would only make things worse—and she stared us down until we'd eaten a proper dinner, you and me."

Renata smiled.

"Your mother brought a prescription of Valium with her, thank God. She gave me two, tucked me into bed, and I fell asleep. I woke up at four in the morning and made a pot of coffee. Your mother woke up, too, and sat with me in the dark kitchen, but neither of us spoke. We didn't know what to say. It was like we'd known all along the sky was going to fall and then it fell and we pretended to be taken by surprise. Then Candace's face brightened like she'd had some inspiration, like she'd devised some foolproof way to get Porter back, to make everything right again. But she did the strangest thing. She insisted on cutting my hair. My hair hadn't been cut since I was a child. Candace said, *'Time for a new look.'* Or a new outlook. Something like that. She'd cut her own hair that winter—it was short and she wore a bandanna to push it off her face. She wouldn't let me say no. We pulled a chair over by the kitchen sink and your mother wrapped me up in an old shower curtain."

Marguerite sat in the makeshift salon chair. As Candace wet her hair, massaged her scalp, combed the length, and snipped the ends, holding them up between two fingers, something dawned on Marguerite. Something transpired. Marguerite could barely breathe; the truth was so obvious and yet so startling. *This* was what she wanted, all she wanted, Candace here, her warmth, her voice in Marguerite's ear. Marguerite filled with longing. It wasn't Porter's love she sought, and it hadn't been, maybe, for years. Marguerite wanted Candace; she loved Candace. With Candace fussing and clucking around her, with Candace touching her, Marguerite experienced a new realm of emotion. It was terrifying but glorious, too.

"When she was finished, your mother blew my hair dry and styled it, and when she handed me the mirror I started to cry."

Candace's face had fallen apart. *You hate it.*

"I was crying; then I was laughing," Marguerite said. "I put down the mirror and I took your mother's hands and I told her that I loved her."

I love you, too, Candace said. *You're the greatest friend I have.*

The greatest friend I have. Marguerite faltered. Those had been Porter's exact words and Marguerite thought, *These are the words the Harrises use when they are leaving you.*

I don't care about Porter, Marguerite said. *I loved the man dearly at one time, and we were intimate. Yes, we were.*

You're better off without him, Candace said. *I've been wanting to say that since I arrived. You* will *be better off.*

It doesn't matter, Marguerite said. *Because when I heard, when Porter told me, my heart cried out for you. You are the one person I cannot bear to lose. I love you. You are the one that I love. Do you hear what I'm saying? Do you hear?*

Confusion flickered across Candace's face. Marguerite saw it, though it only lasted a second. Did Candace understand what Marguerite was saying?

You're the best person I know, Candace said. *I can't believe what my brother has done to you.*

Say you love me, Marguerite said. *Please say it.*

Of course I love you. Daisy, yes.

I want you to love me, Marguerite said. *I don't know where this can lead. I don't know what I'm asking. . . .*

Candace's hands were cold. Marguerite remembered that. She remembered the cold hands; her friend was frightened. Marguerite dropped the hands, and as soon as she did so Candace turned away.

I think I hear Renata, she said, though the house was silent.

You don't want me, Marguerite said.

I don't even know what those words mean, Candace said. *What are you asking me for? You're upset about Porter. He hurt you. You asked me to come and here I am. What else do you want me to say?*

You don't feel the same way that I do, Marguerite said.

What way is that? Candace said. *Are you saying you're in love with me?*

Marguerite looked at herself in the mirror. The short hair now. She was a stranger to herself. What *was* she saying? Did she want to take Candace to bed, do things neither of them could imagine? Did love fall into categories, or was it a continuum? Were there right ways to love and wrong ways, or was there just love and its object?

I can't help the way I feel, Marguerite said.

You don't know how you feel. Right? Porter hurt you. You're confused. Aren't you confused?

I don't feel confused, Marguerite said. *I'm as sure about this as I've been about anything in my whole life. Since the second I met you, when you kissed me. I thought you were Porter's lover, but you kissed me.*

I kissed you, Candace said quickly, *because I knew we were going to be friends.*

Friends, yes. But more than friends. The hundreds of dinners, their mingled laughter, the walk through the moors, the winter evenings by the fire, the trip to Morocco. Candace there, that was all Marguerite had ever wanted.

It's been since the second I met you, Marguerite said. *This feeling.*

You're upset, Daisy. You don't know what you're saying.

You don't feel the same way, Marguerite said. *I'm an idiot to think you would. You have Dan. Dan and Renata. You belong to them.*

Yes, Candace said. *That's right. But you're my best friend and you have been for a long time. Things don't have to change between us just because Porter's gone. Don't make them change, Daisy. Please. Do not.*

Marguerite didn't know what to say. Things had already changed. Marguerite had crossed a boundary; she'd handed herself over, a gift to someone who didn't know what to do with it. No, not a gift, a burden. A woman nobody wanted. The girl in the mirror with the knobby knees.

"It was a big mess," Marguerite said now, to Renata. "The messiest mess. I said things to your mother I should never have said. I loved her so immensely—and I wanted her to love me. She tried her best, but things were different for her. So she found herself stuck in this house with her best friend and this huge, unwieldy confession. Your mother would have done anything for me—she'd proved that just by showing up—but there was no way I could make her feel as I felt. There was no way. She tried to pretend everything was okay, that everything could go back as it was before, but we both knew it was impossible."

Yes, Candace tried. She wiped Marguerite's face gently with a dish towel, like Marguerite was the five-year-old. Then she gave Marguerite a long and beautiful hug. Looking back, Marguerite could see there was a good-bye in the hug, but she didn't understand it then. She didn't understand. Renata had started crying upstairs, and Candace went to her.

She needs me, Candace said.

Fourteen years spent thinking about it and yet there was no way to convey to Renata what had happened that morning. Marguerite said, "Here is the thing you need to know about your mother. Everyone loved her, everyone was drawn to her, but no one more than me. I loved Candace with my whole being. Do you have someone like that? The fiancé, maybe?"

"I thought I loved Cade," Renata said. "I do love Cade. But it's not like you described. Not with my whole being. I don't even know who my whole being is."

"You're so young," Marguerite said.

"I love my roommate, Action," Renata said. "My best friend. I know it's not the same. We've only known each other a year. But still, I feel like I would die without her."

Marguerite could see the girl trying to process what she'd just heard, trying to relate. Marguerite wasn't sure, however, if Renata was intuiting what Marguerite was telling her. *I loved your mother too much, and the love destroyed her.*

Marguerite looked down at her dessert. It was beautiful enough for a magazine shoot, and yet she couldn't bring herself to eat a single bite. "Your mother brought you downstairs and she made the three of us breakfast. Tea and toast. Cinnamon toast, cut into squares. She did all this but she didn't speak, except to soothe you. She didn't speak to me; we didn't speak to each other. What to say? Then, once we were finished eating and the dishes were washed, dried, and put away, she started talking about a run."

You can't run, Marguerite said. *Look outside. The weather.*

Candace had stared, said nothing, disappeared upstairs. She came down bundled in workout clothes.

Is it okay if I take the Jeep? she said.

Where are you going?

I need air, she said. *I need to clear my head. I feel like you, like I . . .*

What?

I need to get out of the house for a while. Is it okay if I take the Jeep?

Candace . . .

Please, Daisy? You'll watch Renata? If not, I'll take her with me. . . .

You can't take her with you. It's too cold. You shouldn't be going at all. I'll bet the roads are a sheet of ice.

I have to get out, Candace said. *I need to get out of this house!* She was yelling now. Renata was scared, hugging her around the knees. What else could Marguerite have said?

Okay, yes, the Jeep. Take it. The keys are on the hook by the door. Renata will be fine. I'll take care of her. We'll have fun. And you'll . . . be careful? It's not the car I'm worried about, it's you. . . .

"But Candace didn't answer; she was halfway out the door. She couldn't wait to leave. She wanted to escape me."

Renata nodded.

"I helped you crayon in a coloring book, I got down on my hands and knees and played with blocks, and when Candace still didn't return I put you down in front of *Sesame Street,* where you fell asleep. I made myself a cup of tea. I swept up the hair trimmings; I started a stew."

"Were you worried about her?" Renata asked.

"I tried to tell myself I was being silly. Your mother used to run for hours."

"I remember being here," Renata said. "That must be what I remember. I drank tea with honey and burned my tongue. You sang to me in French, or we read in French. I remember the pattern of flowers on the sofa."

"Yes," Marguerite said.

When Renata woke from her nap, she was crying. Her hair was tangled. She was thirsty. Marguerite fixed her a small cup of tea and added honey. Together they sat on the sofa and read from *Babar.* When the phone rang the first time, Marguerite ignored it.

Renata set her spoon down in her empty ramekin. *Ching!* Marguerite flinched.

"The roads were covered with ice. Walter Arcain was drunk; he was out on the very same road you were on today, joyriding, doing doughnuts, going way too fast. He claimed he didn't see Candace at all; he claimed he felt a thump, he thought he'd hit a deer. He stopped the truck and found Candace underneath."

Renata's breath caught. Her mother. "It was his fault," Renata said. "He went to jail."

"For ten years," Marguerite said. "And yes, technically, it was his fault. But it was my fault that Candace was here in the first place. I guilted her into coming. And then the things I said that last morning . . . undid her. She was not herself when she left here. I had scared her; I had created a rift, a horrible awkwardness. I had pushed our friendship beyond its limit. Your mother would have been thinking that it was all Porter's fault; he had hurt me, made me needy; he had left me for her to sweep up; she would have been screaming at him in her mind. She would have wondered if the Valium was a mistake; she would have chastised herself for bringing it. I guarantee you she was thinking of these things, some, if not all, of them. She didn't hear Walter Arcain's truck; she didn't sense the rumble on the road. She was preoccupied, muddled, distracted. By me." Marguerite put her hand to her forehead. It was hot and damp, like she had a fever. "I should never have let her leave the house. But she wanted to get away from me. She said she needed air. She wanted to go." Marguerite searched for words that would soften the blow, but if the girl had been listening, she would see the truth, plain as day. "I have always felt responsible for your mother's death, Renata."

Renata blinked. Marguerite hadn't been driving the electric company truck, she wasn't the one who was drunk at ten in the morning, and yet Renata could see why Marguerite blamed herself. *She was here because I guilted her into coming. I abused our friendship. I upset her. She left the house upset....* *God,* Renata thought. *Yes.* Marguerite had admitted to Candace what few people would ever be honest enough to say, even to themselves. *I love you more. I need you more.* Was it wrong to love someone too much, to love them in a way you knew they could never return? Was it possible to kill someone by loving them? Clearly, Renata's father thought so, and that was why she'd been forbidden to see Marguerite, banned from this house, from hearing this story. Was Renata supposed to feel angry at Marguerite? Was she supposed to hate her, to shun her, to judge her the way Daniel had? Maybe she was; maybe she should. But strangely, Renata didn't feel angry. She felt relieved that there was someone else in the world as confused, as guilty, as flawed, as Renata herself was. That very day she had taken her eyes off of Sallie; she had cheated on Cade, then deserted him. Was it possible to kill someone by not loving them? Renata's head swam.

"I don't know what to say," she admitted.

"I'm sure not."

"What if she wasn't thinking about you?" Renata said. "What if it was just an accident? What if Walter Arcain ran her down on purpose? Or what if it's all part of some predestined plan that we can't control? It might not have had anything to do with you. Have you considered that?"

"No," Marguerite said.

"In which case, all you'd be guilty of is telling her you loved her before you left. I wish I had told her I loved her before she left."

Marguerite twirled the stem of her empty champagne flute. If anyone could have kept Candace from going running that morning, it was the little girl in pink overalls. Renata had wrapped her arms around her mother's legs and refused to let go until Candace bent down, kissed her, and gently pried her arms away. *You stay with Aunt Daisy,* she said. *I'll be back in a little while.*

At that moment, Marguerite understood why Renata had skipped out on Hulbert Avenue, why she ran all that way with a heavy bag, in her sandals. She had come not to hear Marguerite's confessions but for another reason altogether. *I feel so peculiarly at home.* Home: The last place she felt her mother's touch.

"You did," Marguerite said. "You did."

She could have stopped there, maybe. It was late, nearly the start of a new day, but Marguerite was determined to finish.

"You've heard people say I'm crazy," Marguerite said. "Your father, and other people?"

Renata wanted to deny it, but the words were too fresh in her mind. *Not stable,* her father had said. *Rather like Vincent van Gogh,* Mrs. Robinson had said. And then there were all the things Renata had picked up in the past: *She lost it, complete mental breakdown, miracle she didn't kill herself, no one in her right mind would have . . .*

Renata shrugged.

What words did Marguerite have left at her disposal to describe the days after Candace died?

Daniel flew in from Colorado. Marguerite picked him up at the airport, and during the twenty-minute ride in the dark car, she tried to explain what had happened.

This whole thing with Porter, she said, *took me by surprise. . . .*

You made her feel like she had to come here, Daniel said. *With my daughter. In the middle of a goddamned blizzard. Who does that?*

Marguerite didn't answer. They were in the Jeep, with the wind whining through the zippered windows like an angry mosquito. Even with the heat turned up full blast, it was freezing. Marguerite's face was frozen, her fingers were frozen to the steering wheel. Her heart was frozen.

Daniel repeated himself in a louder voice. *Who does that, Margo? Who asks her best friend and her godchild, age five, to travel in a blizzard?*

I'm sorry, Marguerite said.

You're sorry? Daniel said. He spat out a mouthful of air, incredulous. *You spent all these years making her feel like she owed you something, but what you got in the end was her pity. She pitied you, Margo.*

The words were awful to hear. But how could Marguerite deny them? *You're right,* she said. *She pitied me. And I frightened her.* Here, she swallowed. If he were going to condemn her, he should condemn her for all of it. Someone should know what Marguerite had done, and a part of her held out hope that Daniel would understand. And so she told him about how she'd confessed her love, how confused Candace was by the confession, how addled. *She was desperate to get out of the house,* Marguerite said. *There was no stopping her.*

That's twisted, Daniel said. *It's sick. You made her sick. You make me sick.*

There was nothing sick about it, Marguerite said. *It was a revelation to me—how I felt, how important she was to me. I wanted her to know.*

Revelation? Daniel said. *Revelation? She's* dead, *Margo. My wife. Renata's mother. Candace is dead. Because of you.*

Yes, Marguerite said. It was almost a relief, hearing it spoken out loud. Marguerite blamed herself, others who learned the whole story or part of the story would blame her silently, but Daniel was angry enough to blame her openly. It was like a slap in the face—it hurt, but she deserved it.

When they reached the house on Quince Street, Dan snatched Renata away from the babysitter and marched upstairs, returning with Candace's suitcase.

Every last thing that belonged to her, he said. *Put it in here. You will keep nothing for yourself.* He bundled up Renata and hurried her out the door. Marguerite believed she would never see the girl again.

She had lost everyone who mattered, making it that much easier to give up. After the funeral, she saw no one, spoke to no one—not Porter, not Dusty, not Ethan. . . . She decided immediately that she would close the restaurant, but that didn't seem like enough of a sacrifice.

"After your mother died," Marguerite said, "I considered suicide. I did more than consider it. I tried it on like it was a dress, imagining how I would do it, and when. Eating the Valium was too much like falling asleep. I wanted to drive my Jeep into the ocean, or throw myself off the ferry with a weighted suitcase chained to my leg. I wanted to set myself on fire, like the women in India. I felt so *guilty,* so monstrous, so bereft, so empty. And then at some point it came to me that dying would be too easy. So I set out to destroy the part of myself that I valued the most."

"Which was?" Renata was almost afraid to ask.

"My sense of taste." Marguerite brought a spoonful of creamy chocolate to her mouth. "I can taste nothing. This could be pureed peas for all I know."

"So how . . . ?"

"I branded my tongue." She had been very scientific about maiming herself; she had been meticulous. She made a fire of hickory, which burns hotter than other woods, and she set one of her prized French utensils among the embers until it glowed pinkish white. "I burned my taste buds so profoundly that I knew I would never taste a thing again."

"Didn't it hurt?" Renata asked.

Hurt? Marguerite hadn't been concerned about the pain; nothing could hurt more than . . . But there had been nights in the past fourteen years when she'd awoken, terrified of glowing metal, of the hiss, the stink.

"When it happened, my tongue swelled up. I can remember it filling my mouth, suffocating me. I nearly lost consciousness, and if I had, I probably would have died. But I got to a phone, dialed the police. I couldn't speak, but they found me anyway, took me to the hospital." Insidious pain, yes, she remembered it now, but also a kind of numbness, the numbness of something newly dead. "A day later, stories were everywhere. Some people said I'd cut my tongue out with a knife; others said I went into convulsions and swallowed my tongue. Everyone said I had lost my mind. Some believed Candace and I were lovers; others thought I'd done it because of Porter. Self-mortification, they called it at the hospital. They weren't willing to release me. They said I was a danger to myself. I spent three months in a psychiatric hospital in Boston. Posttraumatic stress disorder—that's what they would call it now. Eventually, the doctors realized I was sane. My lawyer helped a lot; he fought to get me released. But even once I returned home, I couldn't go back out into the world. I sold the restaurant and made a fortune, but I knew I was destined to spend my days alone and dreadfully misunderstood. And I was right.

My life"—here Marguerite lifted a hand—"is very small. And very quiet. But that is my choice. I am not insane. Some days, believe me, I wish I were."

Renata didn't know how to respond, but like everything with Marguerite, this seemed to be okay. Silence seemed preferable; it seemed correct. And so, they sat—for a few minutes, fifteen minutes, twenty; Renata wasn't sure. Renata was tired, but her mind wouldn't rest. She had heard the whole story for the first time and yet what she found was that she knew it already. Inside, she'd known it all along.

The clock struck midnight. Marguerite snapped to attention; Renata realized that for a second or two she'd drifted off to sleep.

"We should go to bed," Renata said. She stood up and collected the dessert dishes.

"Leave them in the sink," Marguerite said. "I'll do them in the morning." Marguerite blew the candles out and inhaled the smell of them, extinguished. *Dinner over,* she thought. But before Marguerite could feel anything resembling relief or sadness or peace, there was a knock at the door. This time there was no mistaking it for something else; there was no wondering if it was a figment of her imagination. The knock was strong, authoritative. Renata heard it, too. Her eyes grew round; the dishes wobbled in her hands.

"We should hardly be surprised," Marguerite whispered, ushering Renata into the kitchen. "We knew someone would come looking for you."

Right, Renata thought. Still, she felt hunted down. "What should we do?" she said.

"What would you like to do?" Marguerite asked. "We can answer, or we can pretend to be asleep and hope whoever it is gives up and comes back in the morning."

"Pretend to be asleep," Renata said.

"All right." Marguerite flipped off the kitchen light. There was no way anyone could see in the kitchen windows unless he scaled a solid eight-foot fence onto the garden patio. Marguerite reached out for Renata's hand. "Let's wait for a minute. Then we'll sneak you upstairs."

Renata could barely nod. She squeezed Marguerite's bony fingers. There was a second barrage of knocks.

"Is there any way we could check . . . ?" Renata said.

"And see who it is?" Marguerite said. "Certainly. I'll go." Marguerite crept into the dark hallway, telling herself she was not afraid. This was her house; Renata was her guest. She tiptoed down the hall and into the sitting room. She peered out the window, terrified that when she did so another face would be staring back at hers. But what she saw was Daniel Knox, sitting on the top step, his head in his hands. He had a small travel suitcase on the step next to him.

Marguerite hurried back to the kitchen. "It's your father."

"He's alone?"

"He's alone. He's brought a suitcase. Perhaps you should come take a look."

Renata followed Marguerite to the window. They pulled the curtain back, and both gazed upon Daniel sitting there. Marguerite's heart lurched. She tried to forget that the last time he stood on the step it was to take his daughter away; it was to pass his terrible judgment. *She pitied you, Margo.* The words she would never forget. He had meant them—and worse still, they were true. But Marguerite found it hard to conjure the old pain. So much time had passed. So much time.

Renata bit her bottom lip. She tried to erase the sight of her father on a different front step, crying because someone in the world had been cruel or thoughtless enough to steal his little girl's bicycle. All he'd ever wanted to do was protect her. He'd come to Nantucket tonight because of her phone call. He had heard it as a cry for help—and now Renata could see that's exactly what it was.

"Shall we let him in?" Renata said. "Would it be okay with you?"

"Of course," Marguerite said.

Together, they opened the door.

August 20, 2006 • 12:22 A.M.

Cade Driscoll pulled up in front of the house on Quince Street in his family's Range Rover. Once he was parked and settled, however, he just sat in his car like a spy, Renata's engagement ring clenched in his hand. On the first floor, the shutters had been pulled, though Cade could see thin strips of light around the edges of the windows. A light went on upstairs. Through the curtains, Cade discerned shadowy figures. Renata? Daniel? The godmother? He waited, watching, hoping that Renata would peer out and see him. *Come down,* he thought. *Come down and talk to me.* But eventually the light upstairs went off. A light came on downstairs, on the right side of the house, and Cade watched with renewed interest, but then that light went out and Cade sensed that was it for the night. They were all going to sleep. He would be well advised to do the same.

Cade opened his palm and studied the engagement ring. He hadn't told Renata this, but he had bought the ring at an estate sale at Christie's; the ring, initially, had belonged to someone else. What kind of woman, Cade had no idea; what kind of marriage it represented, he couldn't begin to guess. He placed the ring in the car's ashtray. Monday, when he was back in Manhattan, he would sell it on consignment.

He resumed his stakeout of the dark house. Like the ring, Number

Five Quince Street contained a story, a secret history. The same could be said, no doubt, for every house on Quince Street and for every bright apartment window in Manhattan, for every igloo, Quonset hut, cottage, split-level, bungalow, and grass shack across the world. They all held stories and secrets, just as the Driscoll house on Hulbert Avenue held the story of today. Or part of the story.

The rest, Cade feared, he would never know.

1:05 A.M.

Marguerite lay in bed, used up, spent, as tired as she'd ever been in her life, and yet she couldn't sleep. There was excitement and, yes, anxiety, about not one but two of her upstairs guest rooms occupied, about Renata and Daniel asleep above her head. In a hundred years she never could have predicted that she would have them both in her house again. To have them show up unannounced and know they would be welcome to stay the night, like they were family.

Marguerite had expected Daniel to be officious, gruff, angry, annoyed, impatient, disgruntled, demanding—but if she and Porter were playing their old game and she had only one word to describe Daniel, it would be "contrite." He was as contrite as a little boy who had put a baseball through her window.

"I'm sorry," he said when Marguerite and Renata opened the door. "I'm sorry. I'm so sorry." The apologies came in a stream and Marguerite couldn't tell if he was sorry for showing up on her doorstep at midnight with his overnight bag, or sorry for coming to Nantucket to meddle in his daughter's affairs, or sorry for keeping Marguerite and

Renata away from each other for fourteen years, or sorry for his punishing words so long ago or sorry for feeling threatened by Marguerite since the day he showed up at Les Parapluies without a reservation, when he pulled out a chair and took a seat in their lives, uninvited. Possibly all of those things. Marguerite allowed Dan to embrace her and kiss her cheek, and then she stood aside and watched as father and daughter confronted each other. Renata crossed her arms over her chest and gave Daniel a withering look.

"Oh, Daddy!" she said. Then she grimaced. "Don't tell me what happened over there. Please don't tell me. I really don't want to know."

"I'd rather not think about it myself," Daniel said. He sighed. "I'm not trying to control your life, honey."

Renata hugged him; Marguerite saw her tug on his earlobe. "Yes, you are," she said. "Of course you are."

"Would you like a drink, Daniel?" Marguerite asked. "I have scotch."

"No, thanks, Margo," he said. "I've had plenty to drink already tonight." He sniffed the air. "Smells like I missed quite a meal."

"You did," Renata said. She shifted her feet. "Can we talk about everything in the morning? I'm too tired to do it now. I'm just too tired."

"Yes," Daniel said. Marguerite noticed him peer into the sitting room. In the morning he would want to see the house; he would want to see what was the same, what was different. He would look for signs of Candace. It was fruitless to hope he might bestow a kind of forgiveness, but she would hope anyway.

"Yes," Marguerite agreed. "You, my dear, have had quite a day. Let me show you upstairs."

Marguerite led the way with Renata at her heels. Daniel, who had been left to carry the bags, loitered at the bottom of the stairs. He was snooping around already, reading something that he found on one of the bottom steps, something Marguerite hadn't even realized she'd left there—her columns from the Calgary newspaper.

"Dad?" Renata said impatiently.

He raised his face and sought out Marguerite's eyes. "Do you enjoy working with Joanie?" he said.

Marguerite raised one eyebrow, a trick she hadn't used in years and years. "You know Joanie Sparks?" she said. "You know the food editor of *The Calgary Daily Press*?"

"Do you remember my best man, Gregory?"

Marguerite nodded. How would she ever explain that she'd been thinking of Gregory just today, and the relentless way he'd pursued poor Francesca?

"Joanie is his sister," Dan said. "I dated her a million years ago. In high school."

"*You* gave her my name then?" Marguerite said. "You suggested I write the column?"

He shrugged, returned his attention to the clippings for a second, then set them down. He picked up his overnight case and Renata's lumpy bag and ascended the stairs with a benign, noncommittal smile on his face. "I did," he said. "And not only that but I read the column every week. Online."

"You do?" Marguerite said.

"You *do*?" Renata said.

"It's a wonderful column," Daniel said.

Forgiveness, Marguerite thought. It had been there all along.

"Well," she said, trying not to smile. "Thank you."

The grandfather clock eked out another hour. The announcement was mercifully short: two o'clock.

Sleep! Marguerite commanded herself. *Now!*

She closed her eyes. In the morning, she would make a second meal, breakfast. She and Daniel and Renata would drink coffee on the patio, read the Sunday *New York Times,* which Marguerite had had delivered every week since the year she met Porter. They would say things and leave many things unsaid. And then—either together or separately—Renata and Daniel would leave to go back to New York. They would resume their lives, and Marguerite would resume hers.

She was not optimistic enough to believe that, from this day on, she would see them often, or soon, though she hoped her status improved from a mere name on the Christmas card list. She hoped Renata would write—or e-mail! She hoped both Renata and Daniel would think of Nantucket on a bright, hot summer day and know they were welcome there anytime, without warning. For them, her door was open.

If nothing else, Marguerite told herself, she would be left with the memory of this day. It would be a comfort and a blessing to think back on it.

There was, after all, nothing like living in the past.

THE LOVE SEASON

By Elin Hilderbrand

In Her Own Words

- A Conversation with Elin Hilderbrand

Food for Thought

- "The Dinner Party"
  © 2006 *Cape Cod Times*

Keep on Reading

- Reading Group Questions

A Reading Group Gold Selection

For more reading group suggestions
visit www.readinggroupgold.com

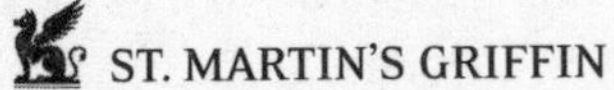

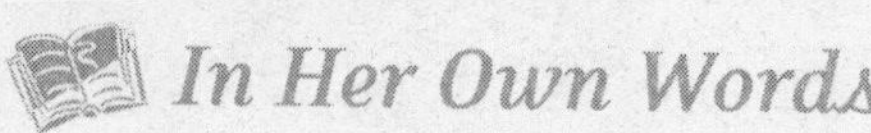

In Her Own Words

A Conversation with Elin Hilderbrand

Your novels—*The Blue Bistro, Summer People, Nantucket Nights,* and *The Beach Club*—are all set in Nantucket. Could you take a moment to talk about this small Massachusetts island as literary inspiration?

"There is no other place in the world like [Nantucket]."

I have lived on Nantucket for thirteen years now, and to paraphrase John Denver, when I arrived in the summer of 1993, I felt I was "coming home to a place I'd never been before." I immediately understood that I belonged on the island, that it was my home. There are so many aspects of the island that inspire me—the beaches, the open moors dotted with ponds, and the historic downtown. What I like best about Nantucket, however, is the fact that it is an authentic place. There is no other place in the world like it. There are no stoplights, no chains of any kind, no strip malls or fast food restaurants. It is original, singular, unique.

In writing *The Love Season,* how did you draw from your own personal and professional experience—as a "foodie," an avid traveler, a mother?

This novel started out as a short story called "Cooking with Herbs" that I wrote while I was in graduate school at Iowa. I wanted to write a story about cooking, which is an avocation of mine. I love to make everything from scratch—my own baguettes, soups, salad dressings, pasta sauces, my own mayonnaise even.

The wonderful thing about transforming this short story about cooking into a novel about cooking, love, death, and family was that I got to enhance every aspect of the novel with the things I had learned since leaving graduate school. I traveled extensively with my husband, and I had three children. Having children expanded my world and my understanding of human nature.

Are you a list maker, like Marguerite? What's on your to-do list at this very moment?

The list is never ending! With three kids, it is a litany of pickups and drop-offs and doctor's appointments and basketball games and play-dates. I also sit on the board of three island non-profits and I am chairing one benefit, editing a major publication, and heading a PR committee. Only a part of my day is spent writing—the rest is dedicated to my kids and to my attempts to make Nantucket a better island for all who live here.

Could you please list, for your readers, some of your favorite books?

Must start with *The Riders,* by Tim Winton. He's an Australian writer and the most brilliant mind I've ever encountered. I wish he was better known in America. Move on to anything by Richard Russo, especially *The Risk Pool,* and anything by Jane Smiley, especially *The Age of Grief.* Other favorites are *Family Happiness* by Laurie Colwin and *Crooked Little Heart* by Anne Lamott.

"I like surprises and developments to unfold as I write."

And what books appear on your To-Be-Read list?

I just started *The Inheritance of Loss* by Kiran Desai, which won the Man Booker this year, and I'm trying to hunt down *The Emperor's Children* by Claire Messud because the readers I trust have been raving about it. Because there are so many demands on my time, I'm pretty picky when it comes to what I'll read. I do read constantly, though, because reading really good writing inspires me to do better work, to concentrate on my language and the flow of my sentences.

Is writing like cooking for you? Do you have a recipe in your head before you approach a writing project?

Never the whole thing. I tend to start out with characters and a general idea of where I want the novel to go. But I like surprises and developments to unfold as I write. I discover the characters and a lot of times they will dictate what happens next. For example, in *The Love Season,* it wasn't clear to me that Renata would escape the dinner party until I actually saw her having cocktails with Cade and his former girlfriend. And I thought, "The poor girl. I have to get her out of there."

What, if any, special ingredients do you bring to the (writing) table?

You asked earlier about my travels. My husband and I have been all over the world—through southeast Asia and Nepal, Thailand, Singapore, Bali; across South America and in Costa Rica and Belize; and to Africa twice—Morocco and South Africa. We also spent three winters living in western Australia. I don't write about my travels as often as I would like to, but having been across the globe has given me a better understanding of people in general, and a sense of adventure and story. I find the older I get, the more deeply I feel things... and this (hopefully) is reflected in my writing.

And what are you working on now?

I just finished writing a novel called *Barefoot,* about a mother of two who is diagnosed with lung cancer, and who goes—along with her sister and her best friend—to Nantucket for the summer. I have started a new, new book called *Cocktails, Dinner and Dancing,* which is about a mother of four children who takes on the task of chairing a huge charity benefit. It looks at the whole world of do-gooding with a new eye. It is very fun to write, which I can only hope means it will be fun to read!

Author photo © Amanda Congdon

ELIN HILDERBRAND grew up in Collegeville, Pennsylvania, and is a graduate of the Johns Hopkins University and the University of Iowa Writers' Workshop, where she was a teaching/writing fellow. Her short fiction has appeared in *Seventeen, The Massachusetts Review,* and *The Colorado Review.* She lives with her husband and three children in Nantucket, Massachusetts. This is her fifth novel.

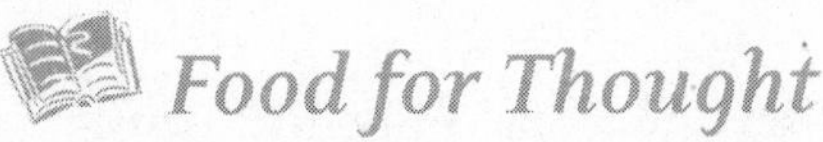

Food for Thought

THE DINNER PARTY

She pulled out her blender and added the ingredients for the pots de crème: eggs, sugar, half a cup of her morning coffee, heavy cream, and eight ounces of melted Scharffen Berger chocolate. What could be easier?
—Marguerite Beale,
self-exiled chef in *The Love Season*

Nantucket author Elin Hilderbrand is making dinner. This is not the Black Angus steak cheeseburgers and Bartlett corn she would normally serve her husband and three children on a steamy summer day. This is a very special dinner—the same dinner her protagonist, Marguerite Beale, makes in Hilderbrand's fifth novel, *The Love Season.*

A fictitious chef who has given up cooking to punish herself after her best friend's death, Beale crafts the dinner only because her godchild is coming for the first time—to learn more about her dead mother.

Hilderbrand is making the dinner for twelve people who helped inspire the novel, which she originally titled "The Dinner Party." The group is gathering at 5 Quince St., in the circa 1730s home where the novel is set.

At 11:30 a.m., Hilderbrand darts into the fish market to pick up smoked mussels, which she will serve with a homemade aioli. "In the book, Marguerite smokes the oysters herself, but that's beyond me," Hilderbrand says, driving toward Bartlett's Farm to pick up fresh dill, basil, and thyme, along with island-grown tomatoes and zucchini. In the novel, Hilderbrand specifically notes that Marguerite does not go to Bartlett's Farm, but says the farm she does visit is modeled on the local landmark.

"There's a little bit of me in Marguerite, in how I cook."

MAKING A NOVEL DINNER

Then, it's back to the house Hilderbrand and her family are renting while their own home—just down the street—is being remodeled. Although some of her equipment—like her tart pan—has disappeared into a box marked "assorted kitchen stuff," Hilderbrand is unfazed.

The biggest challenge to making dinner for twelve, she says, is the refrigerator—finding ingredients in it and then finding space for things like the chocolate pots de crème, which need refrigerating until the 7 p.m. dinner. She plops down in front of the open refrigerator, to start rearranging from the bottom shelf up.

Reading *The Love Season* and then watching Hilderbrand make this meal is a little odd—like playing with a set of nesting dolls or strolling through a house of mirrors.

One can see Hilderbrand in Marguerite, in the list each makes to plan the dinner; in the way the author expertly cracks eggs into the blender for pots de crème and uses her own morning coffee;

and the fact that she actually says, "What could be easier?"—unaware she is echoing the words she put in Marguerite's mouth when writing the book sitting on the beach a year ago.

"There's a little bit of me in Marguerite, in how I cook," Hilderbrand says.

And, yes, that's her jogging in Morocco, unaware —like her character, Candace Harris Knox—that her blonde hair, baseball cap, and running shorts would draw so much attention in the Muslim country.

"*The Love Season*'s scene in Morocco was a conscious effort on my part to get one of our travels into a book," says Hilderbrand, who traveled extensively with her husband, Cliffside Beach Club manager Chip Cunningham, in Southeast Asia before they started a family.

CAPTURING THE ISLAND

But *The Love Season* and Hilderbrand's other novels are also a reflection—and usually a composite—of the people, places, and experiences she encounters living on Nantucket.

Cunningham (a character in his wife's first Nantucket book) says many repeat customers at the hotel he manages look forward to his wife publishing a new novel each season.

"It's part of what they associate with Nantucket," he says. "I'll have Elin come down and sign it for them."

Hilderbrand sees her books as souvenirs—little pieces of the island visitors can take home with them to evoke the feeling of Nantucket long after they've left.

The Love Season earned a four-star critic's choice rating in June from *People* magazine reviewer Sue Corbett, who wrote, "Hilderbrand, who wrote 2002's *Nantucket Nights*, serves up a mouth-watering menu, keeps the Veuve Clicquot flowing and tops it all with a dollop of mystery that will have even drowsy sunbathers turning pages until the very satisfying end."

"Hilderbrand sees her books as souvenirs—little pieces of [Nantucket] visitors can take home with them."

Hilderbrand honed her writing skills at Johns Hopkins University and the University of Iowa's Writers' Workshop. Her cooking got its polish from taking lessons with cookbook author and former Que Sera Sarah owner, Sarah Leah Chase, one of the guests she has invited to this dinner. Hilderbrand explains how she decided to write a couple of novels (*The Love Season* and *The Blue Bistro*) based specifically on Nantucket's food scene: "I did the hotel books, and a restaurant owner came up and said to me, 'You could never write about a restaurant. It would be too scandalous.' I thought, 'Aha, then I have to write it.' "

She prepped by reading copiously, from Anthony Bourdain's *Kitchen Confidential* to Ruth Reichl's *Garlic and Sapphires.* She redoubled her usual food magazine reading of publications like *Gourmet, Bon Appetit,* and *Food & Wine.*

"Rarely do I come across something on a menu that I don't know what it is," says Hilderbrand, who eats out frequently with her husband.

FOODIE STORIES

To further give her books a sense of behind-the-scenes restaurant work, Hilderbrand volunteered to work at Nantucket's well-known 21 Federal restaurant during Christmas Stroll one year. They told her she could pour water, then demoted her to the coat room, saying they were afraid she would spill the water. But she interviewed chefs, bartenders, and waiters, soaking in details—like the banter among kitchen workers—which she re-creates in the conversation between brothers who work in the kitchen of *The Blue Bistro.*

Jane Silva, former owner of the Galley at Cliffside Beach Club (the model for *The Blue Bistro*), is one of several muses Hilderbrand invited to this re-creation of *The Love Season* dinner. Silva spent hours telling Hilderbrand stories about The Opera House, a now-closed, glamorous restaurant where the island's artists gathered and Silva once saw Judy Garland sitting on the piano to sing. Silva says that The Opera House chef, the late Lucien Van Vyve, was her mentor and friend, who often hosted elaborate dinner parties, with hand-painted menus, at his home in the off-season.

Now a T-shirt and souvenir shop, The Opera House is the model for Marguerite's restaurant, Les Parapluies, which, in the book, drew ardent fans willing to eat whatever chef Marguerite felt like having on the prix fixe menu that night.

"It wasn't so much a reflection of The Opera House as it was that she captured the mood of those grand old restaurants," Silva says, sitting on the terrace at 5 Quince St.

DINING WITH FRIENDS

On the night of the dinner party, it is quickly apparent that the dining room of the 275-year-old house was not built to accommodate a dozen. Since her book focuses strongly on female friendship, Hilderbrand asks the guys if they would mind sitting in the kitchen. After some good-natured ribbing about being relegated to the kids' table, they cordially agree.

But first, Hilderbrand says raising her glass: "All of you were important to me while I was writing this book, and that's why we're here. A toast to all of you!"

Dusk is falling hard outside the dining room's bay window as the women sit down to feast on dinner and conversation. Someone asks Wendy Hudson how things are going at the bookstore she owns downtown; someone else asks about when a neighbor will be back on island. As wineglasses are refilled, there's talk about how local produce compares to hothouse; and about the stifling hot weather, which has caused Hilderbrand's homemade baguettes to rise beyond the edges of the pan and form tasty globs of bread.

But quickly, conversations around the table shift to more personal topics: how couples met, children, grandchildren, and friendships. In the wash of words, in the candlelit dining room, it is easy to see these island ties; to imagine Marguerite Beale and her godchild, Renata Harris, in this place, resurrecting secrets of past and present.

By Gwenn Friss, Food Editor

Keep on Reading

Don't Miss Elin Hilderbrand's Other Nantucket Novels

The Blue Bistro

"A wonderful, wonderful love story, the kind that you read, then recommend to many many friends...."—James Patterson, bestselling author of *Suzanne's Diary for Nicholas*

Summer People

"Striking not only for the ingenuity of its riveting plot, but also for the acute sense of character and the finely tuned craftsmanship with which Elin Hilderbrand brings it's every nuance to life."—Madison Smart Bell, author of *Anything Goes*

Nantucket Nights

"Things get more twisted at every turn, with enough lies and betrayals to fuel a whole season of soap operas...readers will be hooked."
—*Publishers Weekly*

The Beach Club

"Elin Hilderbrand's first novel...holds up as a surprisingly touching work...a work of fiction you're likely to think about weeks after you put it down."—*People* magazine

Available from St. Martin's Paperbacks

Reading Group Questions

1. What *is* the love season? Is it a place in time? An environment? A feeling? Take a moment to discuss the meaning of the title.

2. A show of hands: Who has been to the island of Nantucket? How is it similar or different than portrayed in *The Love Season*? Others: Does this book make you want to go there for a visit?

3. The action in *The Love Season* centers around two elaborate meals: the one Marguerite prepares for Renata, and the dinner party at the Driscoll's. What is the significance of food—how it's prepared, served, and appreciated—in *The Love Season*? Discuss the dynamics, and politics, of the dining table.

4. In what ways is reading a good novel like eating a good meal? Are readers ever truly satisfied at "The End"? Or are they always left hungry for more?

5. What are the themes of hunger and nourishment that resonate throughout Marguerite's life? And in this novel?

6. Renata believed that Marguerite was like a shipwreck—*she had, somewhere within her hull, a treasure trove of information about Candace.* Do you think, in the end, that Renata found the answers she was looking for?

Can one individual ever reveal the "truth" about another's life? How is it possible to discover someone's essence after death?

7. Talk about the characters' lives off the island of Nantucket—in Paris, Morocco, and New York City. What did these outside locations reveal about the inner lives of Marguerite, Candace, and Renata respectively?

8. During a moment of romantic desperation, the younger Marguerite had asked herself: *Did love fall into categories, or was it a continuum? Were there right ways to love and wrong ways, or was there just love and its object?* How might the more "modern" Renata answer these questions? How would you?

9. Discuss the symbolism of Renoir's *Les Parapluies* painting as it's represented and referenced in the book. (You may wish to have a reproduction of it on hand during your meeting as well.)

10. Marguerite, during her early visits with Porter, played a game called "One Word." What word would each member of your group use to describe *The Love Season*?

Adrienne did not like being confronted by Caren in her new capacity as Duncan's girlfriend.

"They said they were friends of Cat's."

"Everyone on the island is friends with Cat," Caren said. "If that bar gets any heavier, it's going to sink into the sand. But more importantly, if you let any more people in, you're going to ruin it for the people who are already here."

"I understand that," Adrienne said tersely. "Thatcher just *left* me here to bounce."

Caren shrugged and reached for her hair. With the release of one pin, it all came tumbling down.

"Are you going home?" Adrienne asked.

"And miss first night of bar?" Caren said. "No way."

"Do you want to help me keep the masses at bay?"

"No," Caren said, "I'm going to change."

As she left, more headlights materialized. Adrienne tightened the muscles in her face. Nobody else was getting past.

The next people to approach were another couple on a date. The girl wore a cute sequined dress that Adrienne had seen at Gypsy but couldn't afford. "Sorry," Adrienne told them, and she did, to her own ears, sound genuinely sorry. "You'll have to wait." Like magic, they obeyed, staying right in front of the podium. Turned out, the couple was used to standing in line here. And once this couple formed a willing start to the line, everyone who came after had no choice but to follow suit. In ten minutes, Adrienne had a line a dozen people long. She felt a brand-new emotion: the surge of pure power. She was the gatekeeper.

At one point, a man with wet-looking black hair and a chain with a gold marijuana leaf dangling from it swaggered toward her, nudging aside the couple on a date.

"I'm a friend of Duncan's," he said.

"Everyone's a friend of Duncan's," she said, and she sent him to the end of the line.

Finally, Thatcher came sauntering up with the cash box under his arm and a wad of paper-clipped receipts.

"How's everything going?" he asked.

"Fine," Adrienne said.

Adrienne rubbed her forehead—really, could the man irritate her more?—and headed back by the bar.

"Adrienne!"

It was Duncan, holding aloft a glass of Laurent-Perrier. Only two days earlier, good French champagne had been her favorite indulgence, but now it held all the appeal of a glass of hemlock. Still, the guests at the bar parted for her like she was someone important, thus she felt compelled to take the glass and shout, "Thank you!" over the strains of an old Yaz tune.

Duncan smiled and gave her the "cutthroat" sign.

She carried her champagne to the podium just as two women stepped through the door. They were wearing black dresses and high heels, one woman was blond, the other brunette. They looked to be in their forties. Divorced, Adrienne guessed. Out on the prowl.

"I'm sorry?" Adrienne said.

The brunette flicked her eyes at Adrienne but didn't acknowledge her. The women kept walking.

"Excuse me!" Adrienne called. She put her glass down and took a few strides toward the women until she was able to reach out and touch the middle of the brunette's bare back. That did it—the brunette spun around.

"What?"

How predictable was this? *I was kidding about the bouncer.* What Thatcher meant was, *You, Adrienne, are the bouncer.*

"The bar's full," Adrienne said. "You'll have to wait by the door until someone leaves."

The brunette might have been beautiful at one time but it looked like she'd gotten in a lot of afternoons at the beach over the years without sunscreen—that and something else. When her brow creased at Adrienne's words, she looked like a witch. It was probably the face she used to scare her children.

"We're friends of Cat," she said.

Friends of Cat, the electrician. Cat, who was the most important VIP in the unlikely event of a blackout.

"Okay," Adrienne said, but she didn't smile because she wasn't that much of a pushover.

A minute later, Caren appeared. "Duncan's pissed."

Adrienne blinked. Duncan had every right to be pissed—he'd given her the "cutthroat" sign and not thirty seconds later she let in more people—but